Domme Experience

Experiences: Book 8

Power Exchange and the Making of a Dominatrix

Simone Freier

OTK Publications
www.OTKPublications.com

Domme Experience

EXPERIENCES: BOOK 8

By Simone Freier

Published by OTK Publications
http://otkpublications.com

ISBN: 978-1-942054-21-4
v1.5

Manufactured in the United States of America

COVER DESIGN BY OTK PUBLICATIONS

Caution: This work contains mature content, including graphic sexual descriptions and scenes, and is provided for adults only. Neither the author nor the publisher intend to encourage or promote any of the activities depicted in this work. Many of the specific activities and scenarios described in this work can potentially be dangerous, and should not be attempted without special knowledge or training and, as appropriate, use of sterile single-use supplies. No information contained herein is intended to constitute advice or serve as instructional material, and this work should not be relied upon to ensure safe practices in real life.

Table of Contents

CHAPTER 1: ENGAGING DISCUSSION

A shiver rippled across my skin as I gazed out to the backyard, now white after one of our infrequent January snowstorms. But as my mind returned to the present, I realized that the shiver may have been – at least partially – caused by the reality of my new life.

Sam hadn't thought that I would graduate before the holidays, but my dissertation was accepted and oral defense evidently good enough. I smiled as I mouthed, 'Doctor Kelly Walsh', then flashed on something I'd briefly wondered previously: What name would I use when Sam and I were married?

I shivered again – this time definitely from the cold seeping into my body as I leaned against the sliding glass door of the pool room. Now I visualized my friend, Kathy, with her new beau, Christian, on horseback, looking out over the ocean, and feeling the moist, warm, tropical breeze on the garden isle.

Sam had taken my friends and I on a truly epic trip to Kauai – it had already been six months since then – during which Kathy had met Christian, and Sam had surprised me with a proposal of marriage. I let my mind drift, as I remembered Sam on his knee at the entrance to the sea cave, with the vines hanging down, dripping, and the hot-tub-like pool of crystal clear water, protected from the surf by boulders and the reef.

Then, other images of our island adventure flashed through my mind's eye: The beautiful beach below the Princeville cliffs, where we snorkeled – during the day and at night; the Zodiac ride down the Na Pali coast into sea caves, and the bumpy ride back; the helicopter tour, flying into the extinct crater of Mount Wai'ale'ale – the wettest spot on earth, over Waimea Canyon, and along the incredible Na Pali coastline; and our hike to Kalalau and swim to Honopu Beach, with its rock arch and waterfall.

Sam had been very generous, not only taking my friends on the trip in style, but buying all of us packs, snorkeling gear, waterproof cameras, bathing suits, and dresses. My friends had been very 'generous', as well, playing Sam's little games and each spending a night with him. Of course, we had all become intimate with each other over the past 18 months; we were nearly a family.

I walked back to my desk and sat down, but could not focus on the papers in front of me; they were a draft of the agreement that Sam had negotiated with the university, allowing me continued access to the lab, and giving our company, KS Biotech, rights to future inventions.

But we would need to pay for the patent work, which Sam had said would get quite expensive, when the patents were granted and entered the 'national phase' – each country requiring regular maintenance payments to keep the patents alive.

Instead, my thoughts returned to my future – deciding what I *wanted* for my future. Completing the development of the technology I had invented as part of my Ph.D. project would be most urgent, so that we could raise money for KS Biotech. The alternative would be to give up the project, and find a job with a 'regular' company; but that would probably mean moving, less flexible working conditions, and taking a regular paycheck instead of making a high risk and potentially high reward bet on my own technology.

But I really believed in the technology – a novel approach to new drug development, which could potentially result in important pharmaceuticals targeted to treating worldwide diseases – some of which had reached epidemic proportions.

Tropical illnesses, such as malaria, and sexually transmitted diseases, such as herpes and human papilloma virus (HPV) were just a couple of the areas in which I could hope to make a big impact.

While I looked forward to traveling more with Sam, I knew that I would have to dedicate myself to the project – to the company – regardless of what we would need to give up in the near-term. My breath caught, as I realized what this really meant; in fact, where my entire train of thought was leading me: Sam and I should not rush to get married.

Of course, we loved each other, and wanted to be together always ... but it wasn't clear that marriage would change our lives much; we were already living together, had made a commitment to each other.

I chuckled as I thought again of our Kauai trip, and how we had 'played' with my friends, even after Sam had proposed. It was clear to both Sam and I that marriage wouldn't change our openness, our sensuality ... or our interest in being close with our friends; which sometimes included sexual experiences.

But, although we had developed a polyamorous relationship with my friends, neither Sam nor I had an interest in actually living with them. Julie and Linda had their own lives, and Kathy was now out of consideration, as she had fallen for Christian and was spending most of her time on Kauai.

I laughed inwardly as I remembered Julie speculating about who would be married first; it still seemed likely that Kathy would get married before Sam and I, assuming her relationship with Christian continued to progress as it had over the past several months.

My next thoughts were of the very 'different' wedding we'd attended in Toronto six months ago. Fiona and Justin had put on a double ceremony – the first with family, and the second with their friends at the sex club where Justin worked as a manager.

I wondered whether that wedding had played on Sam's subconscious, perhaps being partial motivation for his proposing to me in Kauai. It was interesting that the wedding trip had included Niagra Falls, often thought-of as a honeymoon destination.

But, I knew that Sam was very emotional about Kauai from the experiences he'd had there with Sarah, and the sea cave had been an incredibly romantic place to propose. We were ready to commit to each other, and we both knew we had done so ... irrespective of when the actual wedding might take place.

Now, I was realizing that perhaps it would be better to delay the wedding for a while; but it wasn't clear to me how long that would be. Just the thought of a wedding led to multiple challenges we would need to face. Not the least of which was informing my parents of our intentions.

Sam, always considerate and 'proper', despite his openness regarding nudity and sex, still wanted to formally request my hand from my father. It seemed oddly the romantic thing to do ... but I couldn't imagine the response it would elicit. After all, Sam was double my age.

I chuckled again, as I *could* readily imagine my father's response: Not good.

Sam was quite handsome and incredibly fit for his age. I chuckled, thinking how Sam had powered the Kalalau Trail, with Kathy, Linda, and especially Julie, struggling to keep up on the rugged 12-mile route. And, Sam was more adventurous, more open, and more sexual than any other man I had ever met.

Although our families had been friends, Sam had never been able to relate to my macho, sports-oriented father. It was almost as if they came from different generations. Sam had a youthful outlook, had high aspirations, and appreciated fine things, while my father acted like an 'old man', and was uninterested in travel, gourmet food or, I had thought, sex.

But things had subtly changed over the past month or so, since Thanksgiving dinner with my parents. We'd had a quiet and cordial get-together, until my mother blurted out that my father was sexually involved with a younger woman.

Now, that was something that I previously *couldn't* have imagined, although I guess no female should be shocked by a man's sexual proclivities – especially one of my father's generation, and someone who sees himself as a 'macho' alpha male. He undoubtedly pictured himself without his beer belly and gray hair.

Sam had said that perhaps this strange turn of events would bode well for my father accepting his former friend and contemporary as a 'son-in-law'. I wasn't so sure: My father was full of double-standards, and probably wouldn't be able to equate his dalliances to his daughter's future life.

I was now getting upset, thinking about my father and, especially, seeing my mother in tears at Thanksgiving.

She had said it was 'OK', that she wasn't interested in sex ... but she was still quite upset. I knew it had very little to do with sex but, rather, basic respect.

Of course, I knew that men were wont to looking for – and often finding – sex outside their marriage; in some cultures, it was not only accepted, but admired. However, in 21st century America, this attitude had to be considered just *wrong*.

I slammed the papers down on the desk and closed my eyes. I wasn't sure exactly why I was so upset, but this had really affected me. I felt my eyes becoming wet. As I shook my head slowly, I was startled by Sam's lilting voice, "What's wrong, Kelly?"

I had come up from my office in the playroom, both to answer any questions Kelly might have about the draft Cooperation Agreement with the university, and to ask what she wanted to do for dinner. It was late afternoon, but already getting dark, the view through the sliding glass doors to the patio and pool gloomy, but at least it had stopped snowing.

I sighed inwardly, as I thought how nice it would be to leave the cold and visit Kauai again; it was whale-watching season, and perhaps Kelly could become a certified SCUBA diver? The water was crystal clear in the winter, with more than 100-foot visibility around Kauai, and up to double that around Lehua Rock, just north of the tiny 'forbidden' island of Ni'ihau.

The thought of Kauai ushered forth deep feelings; a slew of images flitted through my brain – of Sarah, of Kelly, and of Julie, Linda and Kathy – coalescing and focusing into a single image: My proposal to Kelly under the arch of the sea cave.

As I walked into the pool room – now the worldwide 'headquarters' of our new company, KS Biotech – the sound of papers being thrown onto the desk drew my attention immediately to Kelly, who was sitting stiffly in the executive chair, her eyes closed. A pang of pain went through my body as I realized that Kelly was very unhappy about something.

But what could it be? Perhaps she didn't like the draft agreement ... but that wouldn't get her so upset. I then became morose for an instant as I wondered whether Kelly was rethinking our plans for the future – to get married, to build our company, and to continue our open and sensual lifestyle.

Or, maybe it was because I hadn't given her an engagement ring, yet. I had planned to surprise her during our New Year's Eve dinner at the French restaurant, but finally decided that she should help pick it out, at an appropriate time when we could announce our intentions to everyone; 'everyone' primarily meaning her parents.

Kelly jumped slightly, as I asked her, "What's wrong, Kelly?" That was surprising; Kelly was usually a very relaxed person, and we had been living together now for more than a year. I wondered what I could have done to make her so upset.

Looking up at me with wet eyes, Kelly wailed, "Oh, Sam. I don't know what to do ... I'm confused ... and I'm *really* upset."

I stepped over to her, bent down, and kissed her lightly on the lips, as I ran my hand softly through her hair. "I can see that." I followed-up with, "What did I do, this time?"

I immediately regretted saying that, as it seemed too flippant for Kelly's obviously serious mood.

Kelly looked down at the desk and shook her head. Then, she looked into my eyes, and said, softly, "It's not *you*, Sam." After a moment, she looked down again, and said, even more faintly, "It's a bunch of things."

I reached down, and she took my hands as I helped her up; then we hugged, Kelly sniffling a few times. I ran my thumbs across her eyelids to the corners, and wiped away a few tears. Then, I rubbed noses with her, and offered, "Would you like to talk about it?"

Kelly sank into my arms, putting her head in the crook of my neck and shoulder, but I could feel her nodding. I led her downstairs, and we sat together on the couch. "Would you like something to drink? Water, Diet Coke, wine?" Kelly shook her head, and wiped her eyes. I sat sideways on the couch, facing Kelly, one leg under me, and waited ... until she was ready to talk.

Kelly looked up at me, then down to her lap, and shrugged, "I don't know ..." I waited, trying to maintain a neutral expression – interested but not insistent, serious but not sad.

Even when she was upset, Kelly was a beautiful woman. She was only 26 years old, but had maturity and poise beyond her years. Even in jeans and a sweater, her muscular body, full breasts, and fine facial features were evident. Thick auburn hair fell to the couch, and her hazel eyes sparkled iridescently when she finally lifted her head and, leaning forward, gently kissed my lips.

"Sam ... it's nothing ... and everything." She gave me a pained expression, and continued, "Our future, the company, my parents ..." Wow! She had said it wasn't *me*, but this sounded really serious. I slumped into the couch.

As Kelly gathered her thoughts, I realized this was probably about informing her parents that we would be getting married. Other than me, there wasn't anyone else who could have made Kelly so upset.

I offered, "Can we take this one thing at a time?" Kelly nodded slowly, and I asked about the 'thing' that was most important to me, "What *about* our future?"

Kelly began, "I love you, Sam." Uh oh ... this could be worse than I had imagined. I awaited Kelly's further explanation, and realized that I was holding my breath.

"It's just that I don't think we should be in a rush to get married." That was a little surprising, as I didn't think either of us was trying to 'rush' the event. But I hoped that we both still wanted to tie the knot.

I shook my head, "There's no reason why we should be in a rush. I haven't even bought you a ring, yet. And I know it will be difficult for you to tell your parents ..."

Kelly shook her head, "No, Sam, it's not that. I don't care about a ring, and I've been thinking that we should let my parents know sooner, rather than later." Now, *that* was a surprise!

When Kelly had mentioned 'our future' and 'her parents' I had thought that breaking the news to them might be the most concerning factor. After all, they had been social friends of Sarah and I, and Kelly was younger than my sons ... and Dave's sons. I wondered again whether Dave's 'playing around with a younger woman' might have softened him up to receive our message.

Kelly continued, "But I'm starting the year with a new life – I'm out of school, newly engaged, and trying to work out what I want from my life. Getting married just confuses the situation more; I'd like to have a little time getting used to my new life ... and we have a lot of decisions to make, before we get married." She smiled wanly, and I gave her a quizzical look.

"For example, what will my name be? What about kids? How will we travel together, if I'm working ... and would you respect me, if I *don't* work? What about the domme course I've been invited to take with Mistress Elena this spring?" Kelly took a deep breath, "And I don't want to put my energy into planning a wedding right now."

Of course, I understood. Kelly had entered a new phase of her life, and was unsure of her future. I knew that most of her questions were rhetorical, but felt she might be more comfortable, if I tried to address some of them.

"Your name is your choice. Dr. Kelly Walsh would be fine, or Dr. Kelly Johnson; it doesn't matter to me." I wasn't as excited about a hyphenated 'Dr. Kelly Walsh-Johnson', but that would also be fine, if that's what she wanted. I would be calling her 'dear', anyway.

I continued, "As far as kids, I would be OK having them or not having them. As my vasectomy will prevent me from being the biological father, we could adopt, or use a surrogate."

Before Kelly could comment, I continued, "I think you'll be surprised at how much traveling we do for the company ... and we can take extra time off to have fun during each trip."

And, now, the most critical thing. I took Kelly's shoulders in my arms, and said, sincerely, "And, *of course*, I'll respect you, regardless of what you decide to do. I love you, Kelly, and will be supportive of any decision you make."

My brain froze for a moment, and I fleetingly wondered whether that comment would get me into trouble later.

What else had Kelly listed? Oh! "And I *want* to see you take the domme course; I know it's something that you've been looking forward to."

Kelly leaned into me, and we kissed again. This time it seemed more sensual. "Thank you, Sam. I know most of those were minor concerns, but all together, it was just too much to think about." Kelly smiled, and my heart melted.

I nodded, and then gave Kelly a serious look, "And what *about* the company? We're making good progress, and once we get the agreement signed with the university, you'll be able to work in the lab, have access to all the equipment, and perhaps even get a couple of graduate students involved." Kelly nodded.

I smiled at her, "The most difficult thing will be raising initial funding for the company, but that's my job. In fact, I think we should talk with some of the VCs in silicon valley – as early as next month.

"We have our patents filed, the technology developed, and a relationship with the university; we'll need to work on the Business Plan, presentation, and 'elevator pitch', but should be ready to make the rounds in a month or so."

Kelly scrunched her nose, "VCs, elevator pitch?"

I chuckled and nodded, "Yes. The VCs are venture capitalists who invest in small companies with the hope of making a killing on the stock. It's one possible way for us to raise the money we need."

I closed my eyes, not sure how much I wanted to explain right now, then opened them and looked at Kelly, "Actually, VCs are probably *not* the best way to raise money, but they will give us some good feedback.

"And, the 'elevator pitch' is how you get someone interested in putting money into the company in 30 seconds or less – in other words, the time you might be in an elevator with them. It's an overview of the investment opportunity in just a few words – hopefully words that will get someone excited about the possibilities."

I took a breath, "So what are *your* concerns about the company?"

Kelly shook her head, "I believe in the technology, but I'm not sure exactly what our product will be. Should we be a pharmaceutical development company, or sell the machines I've invented? Developing an actual drug will be a very expensive and long process."

I was nodding vigorously. Of course I knew precisely what drug development required, as I'd spent my career in that field. It was beyond something that we could do on our own; we would need one or more strategic partners. And, we would still need a boatload of funding, just to get through the basic toxicity and animal studies required before starting a human clinical trial.

"That's a very good point, Kelly. Let's strategize the 'business model' of KS Biotech later. I can think of a lot of different ways we could position the company."

Kelly broke in, "But what I'm most concerned about is our life together. If I'm working ten or twelve hours a day in the company – ANY company – then how can we do the things we want to do together?

"I want to develop my career, but I also want to spend time with you ... and since you're retired, all of your time is available. Maybe it's selfish of me to want to work, when we could be exploring the world together."

I was shaking my head, and said softly, "No, Kelly. We'll be together, working on the company. And, I'm sure we'll be able to take time to travel and do other things." I chuckled, "Look at it this way: If the company fails, we'll have all the time we want together," Kelly frowned, "but if the company is successful, and we can take it public or sell it, you will have had a successful career, and we'll *still* have time to be together, with a little extra money to boot."

I could see the gears in Kelly's brain turning, but I didn't think she was convinced. I had omitted the third possibility – that the company was successful, and that we could be running the business for the next decade or more.

I really didn't know *how* it would turn out; it was possible, of course, that we would spend years developing a product, and that the company might never get acquired. But these weren't things that should be worrying Kelly.

"So is that it?" I asked Kelly. "We'll figure out a good way to tell your parents, and I'll get you a nice ring; then we can delay the ceremony until you're ready – even if it's a year or more." Chuckling, I added, "I'll wait for you."

Kelly smiled, then frowned. "I'm not worried – too much – about *telling* my parents." She looked me in the eye, and blurted, "I'm worried about my *parents*." I wasn't sure where she was going with this, so just shrugged.

Kelly continued, "I can't believe that my father has been having an affair. And I can't believe that my mother implicitly accepted it. You saw how upset she was at Thanksgiving." Kelly's voice broke, and she was shaking her head again.

Was *that* it? It didn't seem like a big deal, and it certainly didn't seem that Kelly or I could be judgmental about her parents' sex life, given our open sexual lifestyle. But our activities had been a joint decision, while Dave had evidently been having an affair that he was hiding from Darlene ...

"Kelly ..." What could I say? I thought a moment, and said quietly, "We don't really know what was happening ... or what kind of relationship your parents have had. If your mother hates sex, then maybe your father *should* be able to find sex elsewhere, without repercussions?"

I realized that it was really a matter of openness, honesty, trust, respect, and communication ... exactly the things that I valued the most, and the basis of my relationship with Kelly ... when Kelly cried, "It's a matter of respect. I don't think my mother cares about the sex, it's the cheating and lying ... and now he's bringing women to the house!"

Well, I guess Kelly's old apartment over the garage, that Dave had remodeled into his man cave, could be considered 'the house'. I still didn't see why – or how – we would get involved; this wasn't our problem.

"There's not much we can do, except maybe suggest a marriage counselor ... and I doubt your father would agree to that."

Kelly was shaking her head, again. "But how could he have been upset with me 'seeing' you for the past year, if he's doing the same thing? And why now? ..."

Kelly looked up at me, her mouth hanging open, "It was *my* fault – moving out, so my dad could build his man cave. And implying that an older man - younger woman relationship is OK."

I had to chuckle, "Kelly! Now, you're just being silly; you had nothing to do with your father's inclinations. Your mother told us that this wasn't the first time."

I added, "And, from your father's perspective, his 'playing around' doesn't relate to his daughter *marrying* an older guy." I resisted making a joke about 'older guys'.

Kelly was beginning to calm, but still obviously upset. "Yeah, my father is all about 'double standards'. Maybe we should reverse the roles, and I should punish him?" There was a glint in Kelly's eyes, and I couldn't tell whether she was making a joke, or hatching an evil plan.

She continued, "Actually, my *mother* should punish him." I wasn't sure what Kelly was envisioning, but it was clear that Darlene was already 'punishing' Dave, by withholding sex. In fact, that might have been what drove Dave to look for other women. There was always a 'chicken and egg' aspect to relationships.

"Kelly ..." Now, I was shaking my head; I knew that Kelly was upset with her father, but nothing she did would affect what he'd done, and – most likely – wouldn't affect his actions in the future. And nothing that Darlene did now would change anything.

I tried starting over, "I don't think we should get involved. If you really want, we could invite them over for a chat, but I don't know what we could say that could possibly help." I didn't have to point out how awkward it would be, having Kelly's parents talk about their sex life (or lack thereof) with her – and me – sitting there.

Kelly shrugged, "I don't know, Sam. I would like to hear what they have to say ... but I just want to see my father take some responsibility and understand how upset he made my mother. And, hopefully not continue fucking around."

It was unusual for Kelly to use that kind of language, which again informed me of how seriously upset she really was.

Sam was undoubtedly correct – I hadn't *caused* my father to have an affair. But I was still upset with him, for not showing my mother the respect that she deserved.

As I considered it further, however, the thought clarified in my mind that my *mother* may have been partially at fault, for not communicating her feelings to my dad. At Thanksgiving, she'd made it sound as though his finding sex outside marriage was 'OK'; but she had still been crying, clearly upset with the situation.

I decided that I would talk with my mother, just the two of us.

Sam suggested that we go out for dinner, and I went up to the master bath to get cleaned up. As I was brushing my hair, my mind's eye saw my dad, bent over and bound into position, my mother and I taking turns caning him. I had no doubt that I could make that macho man cry, even without my having taken the 'domme' course.

As the fantasy evolved, I pictured both my father and 'the other woman' bound next to each other, both being paddled and strapped and caned. Perhaps Sam was right, that it would change nothing ... but just the thought of my father admitting that he'd done something wrong and submitting to a punishment was making me feel better.

Over dinner, Sam tried again to convince me that we shouldn't get involved in my parents' situation. I understood his points: My dad was being intimate with other partners, just as Sam and I had done; perhaps my mother *had* explicitly 'allowed' him to have an affair? But that didn't jive with my mother being so upset. I resolved to have the discussion with my mother in the next week.

Between bites of sushi, Sam asked, "So what else about our marriage has you concerned?"

I visualized one of the many 'Wedding Planner' lists that I had seen on the Internet. It had been organized in sections – '12 months or sooner', '9 months or sooner', '6 months or sooner'. Beside details of the wedding itself, there were dozens of items that I would never have considered.

"I'm not really 'concerned', there's just a lot to do. What kind of engagement announcement will we send out? Will we have an engagement party? Where will we have the wedding? Will it be a religious ceremony? Who will we invite? Where will we have the reception?" I smiled at Sam and shrugged, "There are dozens of things we'll have to think about."

After stuffing a rather large piece of sushi into his mouth, Sam nodded and chewed, then said, "It sounds like you've already done some research. But those are all easy things to decide – I'll support any decisions you make."

Sam shook his head, while deftly picking up another piece of sushi with his chopsticks, "I thought you might have some *serious* issues to discuss." Then, he popped the sushi into his mouth, and smiled at me, cheeks puffed out.

I remembered the list of financial things, like a budget and wedding checking account, then brought up the only subject that I thought might require discussion.

"Well, what about a pre-nup? Is that something that you will want?" I assumed that Sam would want to protect his retirement, and not lose half if he married and then divorced ... not that I thought that would happen.

Sam shook his head, "No. That's totally unnecessary. I love you, and want to share everything I have with you." Then, Sam glanced at me and raised his brows, "And, even if you take half my wealth, I'll still have enough to be retired."

I still didn't know exactly how much money Sam had, but had to guess it was in the 'several million dollar' range. Still, I was a little surprised that Sam – as business-oriented as he was – would not want to have a pre-nuptial agreement in place, just in case.

Sam put down his chopsticks and smiled, "And I'm expecting us to both make a lot of money with our business. I have confidence that your technology will be successful, and we will be hounded by pharmaceutical companies wanting to cut their drug development costs."

I hoped that would be true, but it seemed that we were a long way from that point. Regardless of how KS Biotech turned out, Sam and I loved each other, and we really didn't need more money; Sam was living comfortably, and we were taking nice trips. If the company could eventually be sold and provide a few million dollars more, that would be great; but I wasn't counting on it.

We went home and watched a movie on Sam's huge screen in the playroom, and then climbed the stairs to the master bedroom, where we undressed silently and crawled under the covers. It was quite cold outside, but the shared warmth of our bodies felt wonderful ... as did Sam's fingers – and then his tongue – as he helped get me ready.

Sam entered me, the feeling exquisite as I thrust up to meet him. My eyes flickered open, and I saw Sam's butt in the air – a normal lovemaking position, but somehow I visualized him in a knee-chest position, awaiting a spanking. My loins contracted, and my eyes closed again, as a ripple of excitement passed through my body.

As we came together, our bodies shuddering, I realized to my dismay – and slight embarrassment – that I had been visualizing *my father* in a knee-chest position, awaiting his punishment. My orgasm erupted as the first stroke of a heavy cane sliced into his bare bottom.

CHAPTER 2: PARENTAL GUIDANCE

I couldn't get the image out of my head: My dad and 'the other woman' strapped down to a double spanking bench, watching each other take their punishment from my mother. I doubted that my mother could provide enough force to wake up my dad so, of course, I would deliver the additional ass-reddening that would be needed.

Sam was still upset with me, saying that my parents' life was none of our business, and reminding me that *we* had intimacies outside our relationship, also. But it wasn't the same! Sam and I communicated our feelings to each other, and jointly decided how far we would go with others.

My father had been *cheating* on my mother – having sexual relationships that he hid, and even bringing his latest slut to the house – to *my* former apartment! And my mother wasn't standing up for herself – at the least, letting my dad know how she felt.

During our Thanksgiving dinner, it sounded like my father hadn't even known that my mother knew that he was having an affair. It was typical that men thought they could get away with something, and not have it recognized by the spouse they'd lived with for decades.

And it was typical that my mother just didn't want to face it, to even *try* to change things. It was sad to think they might continue this lifestyle until one of them died.

It occurred to me that they could possibly get divorced, but it didn't seem realistic, given my parents' personalities and situations. I had to believe that there was still love between my parents, forming the basis of a relationship that could be resurrected.

Maybe Sam was right? Was I acting childish, or sophomoric, to think that I could have any effect on my parents' relationship? I realized that, at heart, my concept was to punish my father, embarrass him as he did my mother, and perhaps make him see how childish *he'd* been, sacrificing a lifelong relationship for a few minutes of sex.

At that moment, I knew that I had to see my parents, talk with them, try to understand their perspective ... and try to get them to understand mine.

Kelly was bent on somehow 'punishing' her father for having an affair. It was ludicrous! I knew that she was trying to protect her mother, but she was meddling in their life, and suggesting something that Dave would see as disrespectful. It couldn't possibly help our relationship with her parents.

And there was no way it would ever change her parents' relationship with each other, something that had been built over three decades. Dave and Darlene were of an older generation; perhaps they were only slightly older than Sarah and I, but they lived a life more reminiscent of my parents' than ours.

I could only imagine a few decent things that could come out of Kelly's plan. Her parents would see how upset she was, and perhaps that would allow Dave to put himself in a position of submission with his daughter. And, Dave would certainly learn how strong his daughter really was – both emotionally and physically.

But there was no way that Dave could be 'spanked' by Kelly without he and Darlene learning about our interest in

BDSM. And *that* might end any chance of them accepting me as a 'son-in-law' – someone not only double their daughter's age, but who also beat her.

Chuckling to myself, I realized they would be more likely to find out that Kelly beat me! Well, they would not only learn their daughter was strong (which they undoubtedly already knew), but that I was willing to submit to *her*, satisfy *her* needs.

I refocused my eyes on the computer screen, which displayed a page of a sex shop catalog featuring a spanking bench. It was black powder-coated steel, very heavy-duty, with thick black pads for the arms, chest, and legs. Everything could be adjusted and locked into position with large black knobs.

It was already huge, and they sold connecting pieces that could be used to make a double bench, just as Kelly had envisioned. With all my Internet purchases of BDSM supplies and equipment, I'd never spent much time looking at 'dungeon furniture'. What you could buy these days, right from your executive chair, was amazing!

Bookmarking the page with the spanking bench I had selected, I tapped the right arrow on my keyboard, flipping through the pages of the huge catalog. There were hooks for the ceiling and all manner of devices for immobilizing a submissive, including the St. Andrews cross, benches and tables, beds, and even stocks and cages.

I perused the catalog, and my other hand went down my shorts, as I envisioned girls in position. On many of the pages, I didn't have to 'envision' anything, as there were images of nude women, strapped down to benches, arms and legs in stocks, a large opening providing access to their privates, and women inside cages, wearing pet play 'tails'.

Eventually, I snapped out of my daydream fantasies, and returned to the spanking bench. The double bench would take up most of the pool room, and I would have to make room in the garage to store it. Fortunately, it broke down into small pieces that would fit in a reasonably-sized cardboard box. Unfortunately, I would have to assemble the thing, once it arrived.

I clicked on 'BUY', and completed the order; the shipping alone was outrageous. Although my 'playroom' was pretty well set-up, I realized that some people must spend many thousands of dollars outfitting their 'dungeon'.

It would be interesting – something different – having a real spanking bench. But the idea of Dave on one of those was crazy. And who was the other woman? Darlene had said she was younger, but I had no idea if that meant 'under 50', or college age. I could picture Dave at a strip joint, but not alone with another woman.

Kelly would have to work this out herself; or just stay out of it, altogether. I wasn't going to get involved. I'd ordered the spanking bench, and Kelly would have to do whatever else she wanted. I thought about flying to the northwest, to see my new grandson again ...

My mother answered the door, looking not too well, and we walked into the family room, where my dad was on his recliner, drinking a beer, and watching the game.

"Kelly wants to talk with us, dear," my mother said as we passed my father and continued into the breakfast room, where we sat around the small table.

"I'm really disturbed by something ..." Now that I was actually going to communicate my feelings to my parents, I wasn't sure exactly how I was going to explain it. My parents waited patiently for me to continue.

"I'm bothered by the relationship you guys evidently have." My father's eyes narrowed, and my mother looked down at the table. I continued, "It's not about sex," now both of them were staring at me, "but about trust, and respect, and communication." Now, my father looked down at the table.

"I don't care if you guys want to play around with other people," I looked at my mother, "or let daddy do that; but you were in tears at Thanksgiving, and I don't think it was because of what dad was doing, but that he was hiding it – *cheating* on you."

My mother swallowed, and nodded slowly. She emitted a partial chuckle, "Well, I don't actually feel 'cheated' out of anything ... but it has hurt."

My mother glanced at my father, then looked into my eyes, "You're right, Kelly, I feel disrespected. And it's been going on for a long time ... years."

My father started to shake his head, then looked down, and just sat there. He knew that arguing was futile. There was no excuse for treating my mother this way.

I looked at my mother, "Are you *interested* at all in sex?" I chuckled, and then clarified, "I mean, with dad."

My mother shrugged, "I don't know. I *used* to be interested," she glanced at my father and actually gave him a smile, "when your father was more romantic. And not seeing other women." My father looked up sharply at her, then looked back down at the table.

The discussion had been going pretty well, so far; my mother was responding to my questions, and my father wasn't trying to deny what he'd done.

"Have you guys ever considered seeing a marriage counselor?" My father looked up at the ceiling, and shook his head, then got up and took another beer from the fridge. When he sat down again, I continued.

"None of this should be any of my business. Sam is upset that I'm even talking to you about this. But seeing mother cry really hurt me."

I turned to my father, "I'm sure it was embarrassing for her, and – now that you know that she's known about your secret trysts – I'm sure you can understand how this has hurt her ... for years."

My father finally lifted his head, looking from my mother to me, as he spoke, "I'm sorry Kelly. And, I'm sorry honey. You know that I still love you ..."

He shook his head, whining, "But men are weak, they need to be sexually satisfied once in a while. You haven't wanted sex, and I didn't think you would want to know if I flirted a little with other women."

Now, I was really getting upset, "Dad! You're a strong, macho, man. Most men are able to control their urges. And – again – I couldn't care less if you had sex with a different woman every night ... as long as you respect mom, which means letting her know, if not getting her agreement."

As I thought about what I'd just said, I realized that it wasn't that easy: My mom really didn't want to know about it, and my dad knew that. And, if she did know, she probably wouldn't be agreeable to it.

I looked at my father, "And who is 'the other woman', the home-breaking slut?" That might have been a tad harsh ...

My father was shaking his head slowly, "She's a nice girl, one of the receptionists at the club. Her name is Jacqueline; 'Jackie'."

My mother broke in, "Do you *care* about her?"

My father quickly shook his head, "No." Then he looked down again, "She was being friendly to me, and –

frankly – it made me feel good that I could attract a woman like that."

My mother was quick to say, "A younger woman." My father just shrugged.

"Dad, Sam is probably right that I shouldn't get involved in your affairs," that didn't come out quite right, but I continued, "but it really affected me, seeing mom in tears. And, knowing that I've enabled your sexual escapades by moving out of the apartment over the garage."

My father was shaking his head again, and gave me a fatherly look – perhaps the first I'd seen in a long time. "No, Kelly. That's not true. I didn't remodel the apartment thinking about bringing women there." He looked down and, under his breath, said, "It just happened."

My mother put her arm on my shoulder, "No dear, none of this is your fault. As I told you, it's been going on for years." Then, she took her arm back, looked me in the eye, and smiled, "You don't think *all* those Saturdays your father was away were spent playing golf, do you?"

That was shocking! Actually, I had never thought about it. And I certainly had not pictured my father having afternoon sex with some other woman. In any case, I still felt hurt, and I knew my mother did, also. I hoped it was a good thing that everything was now all out on the table.

Still, I thought there should be some repercussions; that my father should 'pay' for his misdeeds, at least symbolically. I knew that Sam was against this, but I felt the need; I loved my parents, and wanted to see this resolved, somehow. I hoped it was resolvable.

"Dad ... you've admitted that you cheated on mom, had relationships with other women, even brought them back here. And I'm sure you've been married to her long enough to know – in your heart – how much you hurt mother."

This was the point at which I had to make a decision; but I knew I had already made it.

"I think you should be punished, dad." Then, I quickly added, "And, the other woman, too."

My parents were staring at me, incredulous, both their mouths now hanging open; they were stunned, speechless.

Chuckling, my father said, "You *know*, Kelly, that your mother is going to 'punish' me for the rest of my life, because of this."

"I know that's how it usually goes," I glanced at my mom, "but *my* concept would be that you both take a concentrated punishment – on one day – and then forgive each other, and move on."

I smiled at my father, "Maybe, if you treat her nicely, mother would offer to satisfy your needs more often?" I glanced at my mother, but she seemed to have a confused look, not nodding ... perhaps more in shock than anything.

Finally, my mother opened her mouth, "Does 'both' mean Dave and the other woman?"

A good point; I would need to clarify. "Well, yes – I think dad and the other woman should both be punished," now I looked at my mother seriously, "but I think you should take a small punishment, also."

Before she could ask, I explained, "For *allowing* this to go on for years, not facing it and talking about it with dad." My mother didn't argue, just looked down and wrung her hands. At least, they were both taking it seriously.

My father looked at me, "So ... what? My little girl wants to give us a spanking?"

I hadn't mentioned any specific kind of punishment, but my father had made it easier, "Yes. I think you should endure some pain and embarrassment, just as mother had to. Since everything is 'physical' to you, I think a corporal punishment would be perfect; something you would understand and respect."

The breakfast room was quiet, and I realized I was holding my breath. Would my parents actually agree to this? I thought of Sam, and had to ask myself why I was doing this; was my experience with my parents going to be a turn on? I didn't think so; but I wasn't sure.

I now realized that I *did* have an ulterior motive for punishing my dad: As a show of female strength, that I knew would impress him and, as I had told him, it would be something that he would respect. My father had never really respected me, seeing me as the 'baby girl' of the family, the weakling, and not interested in sports, as he and my older brothers were.

My parents were both looking down into their laps, my mother looking pale. Something had been rattling around in my head, and it now crystalized: My parents would learn about the spanking and BDSM interests of Sam and I. I chuckled to myself – *especially*, if we used the spanking bench that Sam had bought.

Focusing on my mother again, I could well imagine that she might enjoy 'punishing' my father, having control for perhaps the first time in their relationship.

As thoughts percolated through my brain, I recognized that there was something else that had been bothering me: I didn't want Sam and I to announce our engagement – a happy thing – while my parents were brooding about my father's infidelity with a younger woman.

I could not predict where this chain of events might lead, but had convinced myself that the possible outcomes were mostly positive. Somehow, I felt strongly about this. The worst outcomes might be that my parents would divorce, or that my father would disown me as his daughter.

But I really didn't think either of my parents wanted divorce; or, if they did, perhaps it wouldn't be a bad thing? And, although I looked forward to having a close relationship with my parents, I now had my life with Sam. We had wondered previously whether our marriage might cause a rift with my family.

I took a deep breath, and said, "OK. Then I want all three of you to come over to Sam's house, next Saturday at noon. We'll have a little discussion, and then we'll have the punishment session."

My parents seemed a little surprised that I'd pronounced this sentence, but didn't argue. They were too stunned to even ask any questions. Now I started to think of questions ... a *lot* of questions, about what we would actually do.

My stomach did a flip-flop, and I got up and drank a glass of water before sitting back down and staring at my parents. They were very quiet.

"Daddy, there is one important condition, if you accept being punished: You, and Jackie (and mom), will do *exactly* as I say, and submit to your punishment without discussion or argument. And *I* will decide what will happen, and how much you will get before I stop."

I looked into his eyes, "Do you understand?" My father glanced at my mother, and gave a curt nod, then looked down. I hadn't asked him if he would agree; we would see about that if and when he showed up at Sam's house.

It was perhaps optimistic to think that Jackie would actually agree to be punished, but I thought my dad should be forced to think about the repercussions for all of us.

I still envisioned my mother swinging the strap or cane, as my dad and Jackie faced each other on the double spanking bench. But now I realized that I was not turned on in the least. I was just sad.

I couldn't believe that Kelly had actually invited her parents over to be spanked. Even had the situation been different, I don't think it would have been a turn-on to see Dave and Darlene punished. And now, I wasn't sure whether I would even be able to look them in the eyes again.

It was a crazy reversal – a mix-up – of roles, thinking that Kelly would spank her parents, and they could become *my* future parents-in-law. This was the first time that Kelly and I had had a fundamental disagreement: I thought that what Kelly had done, and would be doing, was ethically wrong.

She had meddled in her parents' affairs, and 'spanking' her father was morally highly questionable, especially since she got excited by submission and BDSM. I really couldn't see anything beneficial for her parents coming from the experience.

The only somewhat positive – and very negative – thing that could result would be that our relationship with Dave and Darlene could be severed to the point where they would not be a factor in our getting married. But I didn't want to see that happen; I looked forward to *good* relationships with both my family and hers.

The double spanking-bench was now set-up in the pool room, taking virtually all the space left, with the large desk in front, and file cabinets down the side wall. The massage table was pushed into the corner, near the desk, and Kelly had selected a variety of spanking implements that she had stashed on it, under the folded massage sheet.

The spanking bench had wrist and ankle straps, in soft-lined Velcro, and also a waist strap for the unlucky spankees. I still couldn't imagine Dave agreeing to get into position and take a severe spanking. And I couldn't imagine Darlene wielding the cane, as I knew Kelly was envisioning.

Now, Kelly had spent an inordinate amount of time in the exam room, preparing ... I didn't know what. And I didn't *want* to know. Again, it seemed totally inappropriate to 'share' these things with her parents, and just plain wrong to *force* them to submit.

I smiled, realizing that didn't make any sense. They were coming over 'voluntarily'.

As I had thought more about it, I'd realized that we should have a short legal agreement in place, so Dave and Darlene, and especially Jackie, didn't press charges or sue us. Now, it was prepared, but I couldn't believe it would actually be executed. I shook my head; this whole situation was ridiculous!

A few minutes past noon, the doorbell rang. Kelly slammed closed one of the desk drawers in which she had stored some stuff for today's 'event', and glanced at me. She was looking nervous, and I could see her Adam's apple rise and fall, as she swallowed. My stomach felt hollow.

Kelly opened the door and greeted her parents, as I stood in the doorway to the dining room. She ushered them in, and they sat on the couch. Dave wore a golf outfit, and Darlene was in a knee-length dress, a print of fall leaves on a black background.

Kelly looked around, her eyes finally connecting with mine. I stepped into the living room, and up to the front door, saying jauntily, "I'm going to play a round of golf. I should be back in four or five hours."

"No you don't! Get over here, mister!" She was glaring at me, obviously upset that I was already spoiling her plans ... whatever they were.

I walked slowly over and sat down on one of the armchairs, barely able to look at Dave and Darlene. Shaking my head, I said quietly, "I don't agree with Kelly; this is none of our business." Well, it *certainly* wasn't any of *my* business. Whether it was Kelly's depended on the relationship she had with her parents.

Dave gave me a commiserating look, and Darlene looked down into her lap. Both of them looked weary and not in the least happy.

In the moment that Kelly waited to see if I would follow-up my comment, I flashed on several things. It occurred to me that the values I had impressed upon Kelly were undoubtedly influencing both her judgment of her parents, and her response to them.

Also, I realized that they would be seeing the spanking bench, and experiencing a range of implements not normally found in the average middle-America home. I wasn't going to discuss BDSM with Dave and Darlene, but felt *some* explanation might be required.

I glanced at Kelly and looked seriously at her parents, "Actually, I may be partially responsible for what's going to happen, today." Dave's eyebrows raised, and Darlene looked up at me.

Out of the corner of my eye, I saw Kelly's mouth fall open, but I continued, "Over the past six months that Kelly and I have been together, I have tried to share my values with her – my morals, ethics, beliefs ... and 'way of living'.

"And, I think some of that has rubbed-off on her, for better or worse." Kelly was shaking her head, slowly, but at least her mouth had closed again.

Chuckling, I said, "I think you guys know that I'm a very 'liberal' person ..." Dave and Darlene looked at me; they knew that Sarah and I had frequented nude beaches on our travels, but I didn't think they were aware of our early-marriage 'spouse-swapping' experiences.

"I think people's bodies are their own, to do with as they see fit, whether that's having sex with a person of the opposite sex ... or the same sex (Dave frowned) ... or 'sell' their bodies; and I think a woman has the total right to have sex with whomever she pleases – whether it's for procreation or fun – and take whatever birth control measures she wants, and have an abortion, if she thinks that best."

I knew that Dave and Darlene were of a slightly older generation, much more conservative than me, but I persisted. "The only problems with 'free sex' are STDs, getting pregnant, and the potential for hurting a relationship ..." I looked at Dave, "as you seem to have done.

"But sex with other people doesn't *have* to hurt a relationship, if there is good communication, and if both partners are OK with it."

Dave raised his head, and was about to say something forcefully, but I put my hand up and continued, "Yes, Dave, I realize that most husbands wouldn't dare ask their wives for 'permission'." I chuckled, "And I doubt that most wives would *give* their permission." Dave was nodding.

"That means it probably isn't a good idea for your relationship." I looked at Darlene, "But if you actually could talk to each other about your needs and desires, perhaps you would both learn something.

"Maybe," I glanced at Dave, then back to Darlene, "Darlene would *let* you have sexual relationships," Dave looked to the ceiling, and Darlene gave me a confused look, "or – maybe – she would be interested in satisfying your needs herself." Darlene was noncommittal.

Looking at Dave, I said, simply (and, hopefully, not accusingly), "But by hiding it, you haven't been respectful of your spouse; her feelings. And you betrayed her trust."

Now, I looked into Darlene's eyes, "And by allowing it, you certainly couldn't have expected your relationship with Dave to improve." At least, I didn't think she believed that.

Kelly had let me continue on, and when I turned to her, she shrugged, cautiously. I wasn't sure how to bring up the next subject, and now thought it might wait until *after* Dave and Darlene had seen the spanking bench. It would be obvious, soon enough, that we were into some kinky things – at least, I was.

As open as I tried to be, this situation was making me very uncomfortable; I didn't *want* to discuss BDSM with Dave and Darlene.

And, what would they think of their daughter dating (and marrying!) a 'sadist'? Of course, I wasn't sadistic, but they could hardly be expected to differentiate between our mutually-satisfying play, and something more serious.

I sat back in the comfortable chair, letting Kelly know that I had finished my discourse, for now. Kelly put her hand on my shoulder, and said softly, "I've already discussed all this with my parents." As far as I knew, she *hadn't* discussed BDSM ... and the fact that she 'got off' on spanking as sex play.

Again, I thought how ridiculous this situation was, and how inappropriate – *especially* because of Kelly's turn-ons. Kelly asked me to get the papers, and I walked downstairs to my desk to retrieve them, and was not in any hurry to get back upstairs.

I had been surprised by Sam's little speech, as I knew he hadn't wanted to be here – or get involved – at all. But I couldn't disagree with anything he had said. It didn't matter: We had discussed it, and my father would be subjected to embarrassment and pain; I'm sure beyond what he was expecting.

Although I would have liked to let my dad know what to expect – that his pants would be coming down (and, of course, much more), and that he would be strapped to a bench, I decided it was better to get him into position before he could back out of the punishment.

It was time to bring up the last topic, before we went into the 'dungeon'. Where was Sam?

"There is going to be one more requirement today: That you sign a release. Sam is worried that you could have some legal claim against us. And, I want it to be very clear that you are agreeing to be punished, as *I* see fit, with full cooperation and without complaint."

My father's head snapped up, and he gave me a contorted look; my mom also looked up at me, questioningly.

"This isn't the punishment of a little kid; you are adults, and responsible for your actions ... and their consequences. The punishment is mostly symbolic – of your admission that you've done something wrong, and that you're willing to take a punishment, one that you might think about, the next time a pretty girl winks at you.

"And, by the way, where is Jackie? I thought I told you to bring her today." I had been so focused on my parents that I had forgotten 'the other woman'.

My dad coughed, then looked at me pleadingly, "I spoke with her, and she's very upset." I wasn't sure if this was because my father had suggested that she be punished, or what. He swallowed heavily, "I had kind-of told her that Darlene and I were separated, me living in the apartment."

Now, my mother's head swung around to him, and I realized my own mouth was hanging open, again. He continued, "She *wants* to come here and meet you. And she said she *deserves* to be punished. She said she never wanted to be a 'home-breaker', and that she would be OK being spanked by my daughter."

I gave my father a 'So?' look, and he coughed again, "But she had to work today at the club – couldn't get off – and said she would let me bring her here sometime next week, if you still want to punish her."

Well, it *sounded* like a valid excuse. It would be interesting to meet Jackie, and hear her thoughts about playing around with an older man ... *if* she actually came over.

Sam finally walked back into the living room and handed me the papers. I handed one to each of my parents, along with a pen.

The agreements were only one page each, and basically said that they understood that they had done something wrong, and were willing to take any punishment that I deemed appropriate, fully cooperating, and not complaining.

It was unrealistic to think that my dad would actually cooperate, once he felt the strap ... or experienced the first 'corner time'. But I hoped that we could pull off the next few minutes, after which it would be a relatively easy afternoon. At least, that was my optimistic expectation.

As I had anticipated, my dad only took a cursory look at the agreement, and scrawled his signature at the bottom of the page. Once he was signing it, my mom signed her copy. Sam took the agreements and pens, and disappeared again. If he dawdled this time, I would punish him, as an example to my parents.

Entirely unexpectedly, this last thought got me a little hot. I wasn't going to get turned on by punishing my parents – who really deserved it; but the idea of Sam going over my knee, pulling down his pants, and giving him a good licking *in front of my parents* was a definite turn on.

Fortunately (for him) Sam returned quickly, and I decided it was time to get this done. Although I had thought about it several times, I still wasn't sure of the best approach. I didn't want my father to rebel at the sight of the spanking bench, and considered blindfolding him. And, I wondered whether he would cooperate and take his clothes off, or whether we would need to cut them off ... and give my father a robe to wear home.

"Mom, please wait here for a couple of minutes, while we get dad settled; then, I'll come back and get you." My father squinted at me, while my mother smiled thinly, and nodded her head slowly. She probably couldn't believe this was really happening; I couldn't, either.

"Dad," I glanced at Sam, "and Sam, come with me." I headed through the dining room into the kitchen, and stopped between the breakfast table and the door to the pool room. When the men had caught-up, I looked at my father, and said, simply, "Please undress down to your boxers."

My father looked sharply at me, and I shrugged, "You didn't think I was going to spank you with your pants on, did you?" I chuckled, "That wouldn't be much of a spanking!" Of course, I didn't mention that most of his spanking would be given on the bare.

As he reluctantly pulled his golf shirt over his head, and undid his pants, my father was shaking his head and already grumbling. Of course, I had seen my dad in his boxers, before; but I would be seeing much more of him, today.

That was of no interest to me; if I had thought my mother could spank him hard enough, I would have been happy to let her do the 'honors', while I observed. But I wasn't sure that my mom would be willing, not to mention strong enough, to use the tawse or cane on my dad.

I decided to forego putting the blindfold on him, as I led my dad through the pool room door, and over to the spanking bench, Sam following closely behind. Sam knew what to do: We had to get the padded Velcro restraining straps on my dad as quickly as possible.

As expected, my father took one look at the 'contraption' in front of him, and stopped in his tracks. I chuckled, "Dad, you're too heavy to go over my lap ... and this will be much more comfortable for you."

Of course, my dad was not that much heavier than Sam (maybe 30-40 pounds?), but he had no idea that Sam went over my lap regularly. Well, at least, occasionally.

My father shook his head again, and looked at me; I nodded and pointed to the padded leg rests. I realized I was holding my breath, as I didn't know whether my father would actually cooperate. But – surprisingly – he did, putting his knees onto the pads.

I helped him lean forward, so that his chest was on the angled padding, while Sam quickly slipped the Velcro straps around his ankles, and I got the wrist straps into place. My father hadn't resisted, but I said, "Dad, we don't want you to get hurt, reaching back ... as I swing the paddle ... or the cane."

His head swung 90 degrees towards me, and his mouth dropped open. He was beginning to understand what this punishment was going to entail, and starting to get nervous, if not upset. I knew that his concept was that his 'little girl' couldn't do much by 'spanking' him. But he would find out both how strong his daughter was, and how a strong corporal punishment feels.

Sam and I stepped back to the desk, both of us amazed that my father was now strapped-in to the spanking bench, wearing only his boxers.

I looked at Sam and he smiled, then frowned, "I forgot one of the straps." He stepped over to the spanking bench, and pulled the middle strap around my dad's waist, attaching it to the other side of the bench, and pulling it tight enough that my father would not be able to move.

We then went back to the living room for my mother. Sam turned to me, "May I *please* at least go to the driving range, now? I don't want to be here, while you're punishing your parents."

I glared at Sam. He *knew* that he was going to have to help with a few things; we had discussed this already. He gave me a faux-sheepish look, but it wasn't funny. Under my breath, loud enough for Sam, and probably loud enough for my mother to hear, I said, "I may have to punish *you* today.

"Come along, mother." We walked back through the dining room and kitchen, and entered the pool room, the rump of my dad's plaid boxers greeting us. My mother froze and looked at me. "We'll do the warm-up with his shorts on, but the rest of the spanking will be on the bare."

My father turned his head back toward us, and bellowed, "What? You can't do that, Kelly. A daughter shouldn't see her father that way."

Laughing, I replied, "Well, a daughter shouldn't see her father having an affair. And I did warn you that your punishment would entail some pain *and* embarrassment."

My dad's head had already dropped, and I finished with, "And, you have agreed to cooperate and not complain; it will be *my* choice of how to punish you." I turned to my mother, "And mom's."

My mother looked weak, and I grabbed the first implement from the desk drawer, and stood behind my dad. I held out the paddle for my mother, but she was still frozen in place next to the desk.

I had decided on a rubber paddle, about four inches by a foot, with a wooden handle. It would be easy for my mom to hold, and provide a nice stinging sensation without much force; of course it would be even more 'stinging' on my dad's bare butt.

If my mother helped punish my dad, as I hoped, this would be the first time in her life that she'd had 'control' over him. But she didn't look very eager.

"OK, we'll start easy. I'll give dad the first 100 strokes of his warm-up, and then you can give him the next 100. I'll first get him used to some light swats, and then make it harder as I finish."

Again my father turned back, "You're going to give me two *hundred* swats? Kelly ..."

And once again I laughed, "Dad, this is just the warm-up; to prepare your bottom for the more severe spanking implements, like the tawse or heavy strap, the school paddle, and the cane." He was already whining. "And, you'll receive *additional* punishment, if you don't cooperate."

I laughed, but it came out almost like Julie's 'cackle'. I said, "This is supposed to be a punishment for something that you've done for years, hurting mother ... your *wife*. Suck it up, Dad."

Then, I realized that, perhaps, I should be coming at this from a more 'professional' perspective? "Since you're so concerned that I'm your daughter, I'll make it easier on you, and call you Dave. And mother, Darlene."

I had my mother move to the other side of the desk, near Dave's right side, and I took my position on his left. I would give Dave 'medium' swats, which I had told him would be light; this would increase the tension, and prepare him to expect the harder implements.

Swinging the paddle at only moderate force, it impacted my dad's butt with a loud 'CRACK!!!' He recoiled – as much as the restraining straps would allow – and then screamed, "Kelly!" But I was not stopping, and the next stroke landed, just as forcefully. I glanced at my mother, and it looked like she might faint.

"Mom, can I get you some water? Do you want to sit on the desk? It won't take long for me to finish my part of the warm-up and then it will be *your* turn." My mother stiffened, and shook her head.

I turned back to my father, and continued his warm-up, the rubber paddle against his shorts sounding like a very loud clap. At 20 strokes, I increased the intensity, and began spanking faster, the paddle covering much of his butt, and having only to move a little side-to-side to cover all of it.

After only three strokes at the slightly higher intensity, my dad was bellowing again. "Dave, I don't want to hear any complaining from you. You seem to think I'm spanking you hard, but this is the easy part; we haven't even removed your shorts, yet."

I continued, increasing the force dramatically again at 50 strokes; I was now swinging the paddle about as hard as I could, at this fast speed. My father was already whimpering; I had never heard him do that before. A minute later, I had finished the 100 strokes.

My father cried, "Please, Kelly ..."

Shaking my head, I went around the desk, and pulled a ball gag from a drawer. I wasn't sure how easy this would be, but managed to get it into my dad's mouth, and fasten the strap, before he knew what was happening.

I turned to my mother, and said, "That will make it much easier. He may cry, but at least we don't have to listen to his complaining." My mother gave me the strangest look I had ever seen on her: A crooked smile, not unlike what Sam did sometimes, but it was also a very nervous, weak, and frightened look.

I handed my mother the paddle, and she took it, and looked down at the thick black rubber that swung back and forth, as she moved the paddle. "OK, Darlene, it's your turn to give Dave a little warm-up."

It wasn't clear that she was really going to do it, but cautiously stepped behind my father, and put the paddle on his rear. She glanced up at me, and I nodded. She swung the paddle about as hard as she stirred a stew with a spoon. "You're going to have to do much better than that, Darlene. Or, I'll have to give Dave a really *hard* paddling."

Dave was making sounds through the ball gag. My mother tried again, the swat not much harder than the first. "OK, Darlene, let me demonstrate." I took the paddle from her, positioned myself, and gave Dave ten searing and incredibly fast swats – I'm sure taking less than 10 seconds. There was more screaming through the ball gag.

I held the paddle out, but my mother made no effort to take it. I shrugged, "You *know* that I'm going to spank harder than you would." Now, my mom shrugged. I made an executive decision. "OK, Darlene, I guess you're ready to begin *your* punishment."

My mom looked at me with a shocked expression, but didn't argue. As I walked her to the other side of the spanking bench, I realized that Sam was still in the doorway to the kitchen. "You can stand here, Sam." I pointed next to the middle file cabinet.

Sam reluctantly came into the room, and leaned back against the file cabinet, centered on the spanking bench. I helped my mother onto the bench, and could see that she was in a daze. I fastened the retaining straps, then flipped her dress onto her back.

"Kelly!" Darlene screamed, glancing up at Sam. I lowered her pantyhose, until they were at mid-thigh. We would have to do something about those, later.

Darlene gave me a pleading look, but all I could do was shrug and look away; but that meant facing Dave, which I also didn't want to do. I thought about turning toward the file cabinets, but knew that Kelly would require that I watch. At least, I was in front of Darlene, so couldn't see anything; but I knew she had to be humiliated.

Linda had often called me 'perverted' ... but what Kelly was doing now was something that *I* considered pretty perverted. These were her *parents*! Remarkably, they seemed to be relatively docile and cooperative.

Kelly announced, "I think dad's about 90% of the problem, but you're probably 10% responsible. And I think you'll respect him more – for his agreeing to take a painful and embarrassing punishment – if you get a taste of what he's feeling." Darlene was shaking her head.

"Since he's getting a 200 stroke warm-up with this paddle, you'll only get 20 strokes." I could see that Darlene was becoming frantic.

Our makeshift 'agreements' would mean nothing, if Kelly really abused her parents, and they decided to press charges. Hopefully, it wouldn't come to that. I had to trust Kelly. Of course, I *did*.

Now, Kelly smiled at me, glancing at her father, who looked like a suckling pig with an apple in its mouth, "I need to tend to Dave ... so I think you should paddle Darlene." Darlene's mouth dropped open – and I know *mine* did, as we both shook our heads.

This was too much – beyond the limit. It was unfair to use me to embarrass her mother, who was also my friend. "No, Kelly. That's just wrong. I guess I'm OK watching from here, since I can't see anything, but ..."

Kelly was getting upset, "I don't think my mother will be very embarrassed by *me* seeing her butt. And we're all adults, here." She chuckled, "Didn't you guys ever go skinny-dipping together, in our pool?" I think she knew that we'd never done that, as Dave and Darlene were always too conservative and modest.

Then, Kelly reasoned, "Anyway, *Jackie* is supposed to be where you are – Dave and her being punished ... by *you*. I thought that might let out a little of your passive aggression."

I saw a light go on in Kelly's head, and she exclaimed, "And when Jackie comes over, Dave can be the model, and get 10% of *her* punishment."

Kelly seemed pleased with herself, but she was the only one in the room who was 'pleased'.

I said, "OK. But I'll only do it, if Darlene agrees. I won't force it on her." I hoped that Kelly wouldn't force it on both of us.

I turned to Darlene, "I *told* you that I believe each person should have the right to do what they want with their bodies, including exposing them, or not. It's my opinion that we shouldn't be hung-up about people seeing our bodies; they can usually tell enough about our bodies while we're wearing clothes."

Darlene was giving me a blank stare, but I continued, "I always wanted to invite you guys over for some skinny-dipping, after we put in the pool, but Sarah wouldn't let me."

Then, I looked into Darlene's eyes, and said, "I can't believe that you would really be that embarrassed by casual nudity." She closed her eyes tightly.

Then, I concluded, "But I'll leave it to you, and respect your decision." Glancing at Kelly, I added, "And I hope Kelly does, also." Kelly was glaring at me, again.

Darlene let her head drop, and she shook it, slowly. Finally, she looked up, "Sam, I know you didn't want to be here." I nodded. "And, I don't think you're going to get too excited by seeing an old woman's bottom." We chuckled. "But I'm just not used to other people seeing my body. I'm not a Playboy model, you know."

As I was nodding, we heard muffled speech through Dave's ball gag that sounded like, 'You never were'. That was funny.

There was silence, and Kelly finally asked, "Mom?" Then, she smiled, and rephrased it, "Darlene? What's your decision?" I was amazed that Kelly would actually leave it to her mother, who I was sure would say 'No' to me spanking her.

Darlene looked back at Kelly, "I'm going to be mortified, dear. But if that's what you want, I guess I can let Sam do it." Then, she actually chuckled, "It will probably be lighter from him than from you."

Kelly and I were both nodding, and Kelly said, "Yes. That will undoubtedly be true." Then, she looked at me, "But if he doesn't give you a serious spanking, I may have to spank *his* bottom." That was my warning; but Darlene was only getting 10% of Dave's punishment, so it wouldn't be a big deal, if I gave her a few hard spanks.

Kelly handed me the paddle, as I walked behind her mother, her pantyhose down, and her dress up. I glanced at Dave, and he was squinting at me, I'm sure not too happy that I would be spanking his wife on her underwear.

I positioned myself behind and to the left of Darlene, and placed the rubber paddle on her high-cut panties. "I'll give you two sets of ten, the first lighter, and the second harder." I hoped that Kelly would 'accept' the lighter spanks.

The first time the rubber slapped against her undies, Darlene gave a yelp. I waited a few seconds, and gave her a second swat. She let out a breath. Then, I gave her the remaining eight, waiting a few seconds between each one. I saw Kelly standing with her hands on her hips, about to chide me (or worse) for being easy on her mother.

But I held up my hand, and said, "Let's do the harder ones, now, Darlene. Just try to relax your bottom." I knew that advice was of minimal use, as I placed the paddle on her nude-color panties, and slid it back and forth a few times. I could hear Darlene breathing heavily.

Then, I administered ten reasonably hard swats, about two seconds between each one. Darlene couldn't move, fortunately, but she yelped after each stroke.

Kelly gave me a forced smile, and announced, "Now, Dave will get his second hundred swats. He's probably not even warmed-up anymore, so I'll have to do a good job on these." Then, she chuckled, "Hold your position, Dave." Nobody laughed.

Before we knew it, Kelly was paddling Dave's rear, giving him quite hard swats, about one every second. The evolution was interesting: Dave first bellowed through the ball gag, then groaned, then whimpered, then whined. He was not quite to the 'crying' stage by the time Kelly had finished the warm-up.

I was standing next to Darlene, and saw her flinch several times during Dave's paddling. I wasn't sure what was next, but I hoped it wasn't what I was thinking ...

As Kelly skipped to the corner, and took something from a drawer, she said, cheerily, "That wasn't so bad, was it?" The reply was a couple of grunts. Kelly walked back to Dave, standing where he could see them, and snapped a large pair of scissors closed and open.

Dave's eyes grew large, as Kelly explained, "You'll be getting the rest of your punishment on the bare, and we also have a corner-time to do ... so I guess we'll just have to get you down to basics."

Kelly walked behind Dave, and snipped his boxers on the left side, and on the right, then pulled them through his legs, Dave bellowing again, but now completely nude, being seen from behind by his daughter. It had dramatic flair, but I thought it was being a little rough on Dave.

Then, Kelly walked to me, holding out the scissors. Darlene looked up, a shocked expression on her face again, and – I'm sure – not much less of a shocked expression on *my* face. "Can't I just lower them?" Kelly's response was to snap the scissors at me.

I took them, and leaned over so that my head was next to Darlene's. "I'm sorry, Darlene." Her eyes were closed, and her head shaking slowly from side-to-side. I went behind Darlene, and copied Kelly's moves, snipping the sides of the panties, and pulling them out between Darlene's legs.

It sounded like Darlene was weeping, or at least sniffling. I stood at her side, so she knew I wasn't staring at her privates. This was embarrassing for me, too.

Kelly walked back to her father, and pirouetted around to me, "Maybe we'll just have a 'little' corner-time ... the thermometer?"

Now, *my* eyes closed, and I was shaking my head. I could now see where this was going .. and I wasn't too happy about it. Kelly laughed, "No? OK. Then, we'll do the tawse, and *then* we'll have a 'bigger' corner-time."

Kelly showed her parents the tawse. "This is real leather, a Scottish 'tawse', used in boarding schools until recently. I think you'll find forty strokes a good start to your spanking." That would be harsh, based on the intensity that I was sure Kelly would use.

The first stroke sounded much louder than had the rubber paddle, making a firm 'WHAP!!'. Dave cried out, a slurred 'Ow!' through the gag. The next stroke landed with an even louder 'THWAP!!!'.

Dave howled like a dog, as Kelly kept raining strokes of the tawse down on Dave's butt, giving him only a few seconds between each stroke. Dave let out some gagged screams; and Kelly had only given him ten strokes of the tawse, so far.

Kelly stopped, walked around to face her father, and put her hands on her hips. "Is this how you're going to act, Dave? Like a baby? We're just getting started." She glanced up at me, and I could see the wisp of a smile – one that I didn't like.

"OK, Sam. I knew you'd come in useful, today. Over here ... Now!"

I walked quickly from behind Darlene to near Kelly, and took the standing position. I knew what was going to happen, and *really* didn't want to do it. It was only my love for Kelly – and respect for her dealings with her parents – that encouraged me to submit.

"Yes, Miss?" Kelly smiled, and I could see her body relax, a little. She now knew that I would submit to her. I don't think either of us had any idea how this might affect her relationship with her parents ... or my relationship with my friends.

Softly, Kelly instructed, "Get the chair from behind the desk, and move it here, next to the sliding door, centered on the spanking bench." When it was in place, I assumed the standing position again. Kelly nodded, "Please undress now, Sam."

I just stared at her for a moment, and slowly shook my head. Then, I pulled my tank over my head and – glancing at Darlene – pushed my running shorts down. When I was in the standing position again, Dave's head was turned away, and Darlene's was lifted, her eyes glued to my midsection.

"OK, Sam, please get in the chair position, and I'll demonstrate some of the implements – and corner-times – to my parents."

Corner-times, too?!?! That was really not fair to me – I hadn't done anything wrong. It was bad enough that I had to stand in front of Dave and Darlene nude, submitting to Kelly ... but to give them a view from behind, while Kelly inserted a butt plug was beyond even my limits.

Of course, I had done that for Kelly's friends; but I was also expecting to do that to *them*. Now, I realized that I *would* be doing that ... to Darlene, and Kelly would be doing that to her father.

I had always said, 'fair is fair', but this didn't seem fair to me.

I gave Kelly a disgusted look, and turned to get into the executive chair. Then, I turned back around, and looked back-and-forth to Dave and Darlene. Kelly may punish me more, but I wasn't 'going down' without letting them know my feelings.

"I'm going to do as Kelly has asked ... ONLY because I love her. It isn't fair that I'm going to have to suffer embarrassment and pain: I would rather you not see me in a very compromising position, and I would rather not take part in punishing you. I don't *want* to see Darlene's privates, and I don't want to be the cause of her being embarrassed."

Under my breath, I added, "And it was supposed to be that other woman – Jackie – on the spanking bench with Dave." I shook my head, turned around, and quickly got into position, my legs separated, and my rump in the air. I could feel the breeze through my crotch, tickling my anus. Now *I* was the one to close my eyes and drop my head.

I hadn't appreciated Sam's little diatribe, but as he would be cooperating I had let him go on. Now, he was in position, and my mother was staring at him; his rear was only five or six feet from my parents' faces. I realized that my dad had his head turned the other direction, studiously not looking at Sam.

"Dave! Look at Sam! You will watch carefully, as I demonstrate some of the punishments you'll be receiving." I glanced back at Sam, in perfect position, motionless, his head in his arms on the back of the chair.

I felt a twinge of guilt, and pity for him, as it really *wasn't* fair. Perhaps I was just getting back at Sam for not fully supporting my plan to punish my parents? But I knew that my father would be a little more stoic, if he saw that Sam could take the punishment without complaint.

Picking up the tawse, I positioned myself to the side of Sam; I checked, but wasn't blocking my mother's view of Sam's butt. "OK, Sam. Let's demonstrate each of the implements. You can give me the count for each implement, and thank me. Then, we'll do some corner-times." Sam's bum swayed a little, then he stilled.

I glanced back at my mother, and then to my father, both of them watching intently. The tawse swung, and landed on the lower portion of Sam's bottom in a medium-hard stroke resulting in a 'WHAP!' that reverberated around the room.

Sam sniffed, and – a moment later – said, "One, thank you, miss." As he was cooperating so well, I decided not to give him many strokes; perhaps just four; the same as my mother was going to get."

I let the tawse swing again, this time landing on the crease between Sam's butt and his upper thighs. There was a quiet 'Oooowww!' and then Sam provided the count and thanked me. Sam stayed in position remarkably well for the last two strokes, which I made sure were impressively hard. I rubbed his bottom, and gave each of my parents a proud look.

"You can see from the redness that Sam's bottom took a good tawsing." I glanced at my mother, "The same number of strokes as Darlene will get." My mom's face showed terror; but she gave me a resigned look, squeezed her eyes closed, and let her head drop.

Sam already knew what spanking implements I had selected, and I now asked him, "How many strokes do you suggest I give you for each implement, Sam?" I hoped he realized that I was actually asking how many my dad would be taking, which was ten times whatever Sam – and my mom – would get.

Looking back at me, Sam said, unsteadily, "Ten of the smooth, two of the thin cane, and one of the school paddle?"

I had planned to use a thicker cane on my dad – and probably still would – and give him two dozen hard strokes. Ten with the school paddle seemed too little, but we would have to see ... what it took to really punish my dad, to make him cry.

"OK, Sam. I'll agree to your figures. Prepare yourself." As an afterthought, I added, "You don't have to count or thank me for these. Let's just show my Dad what he can expect."

With my parents silently staring, I gave Sam ten hard swats with the smooth Ping Pong paddle, coming up from under him and impacting his bum with a loud 'SMACK!' Sam waggled his butt a little after the last swat, but was silent.

I was impressed: Sam was not whining, or even whimpering, like he usually did; I guess he was trying to be strong and show my dad that he could take it. Or, maybe Sam was trying to be macho, and show my mother that *he* could take it. In any case, it provided the perfect demonstration for my parents. I rubbed his bum again.

Taking the thin cane from several stored on the massage table, I approached Sam; as he looked up at me, I gave him a sweet smile. I would have to reward him, later. *If* he continued to cooperate.

Sliding the cane across Sam's bottom, I glanced at my parents, then focused on my task, administering the hardest cane stroke I had ever given Sam. Although I realized that, due to the smaller diameter cane, it would not be as severe as the caning I gave him when we visited Mistress Elena.

Sam yelped, but I'm sure he realized that I had selected the thinnest cane we had. The second stroke was no lighter, and Sam was now whimpering. Again, I rubbed his bum, softly saying, "That was a good boy."

Making one more trip to the massage table in the corner, I put the cane back, and picked up the school paddle. Sometimes called a 'sorority' or 'fraternity' paddle, the mean thing was 18 inches long and 4 inches wide. But it was its thickness that could cause the bruising. This was the one without the holes; but I'd be using the one *with* the holes, allowing a faster impact, on my father.

"Finally, this is the school paddle. Sam and Darlene will only be getting one good swat; but I don't know how many you're going to get, Dave, until we get to that point." My dad was now squirming (as much as the restraints would allow), and trying to say something through the gag.

But I wasn't going to let him comment, until I was done with the demonstration. After Sam's swat, I retrieved two small plastic baskets with various rectal insertion devices – actually the same ones that Sam had used when we played that Spank Poker game with my friends on the turntable during my birthday party.

I lubed the thermometer, and announced, "After a spanking with each implement, you're going to have a 'corner-time'. It will be only five minutes, showing off your red butt, AND we'll increase the embarrassment a little with a rectal insertion." My father was continuously pleading through the gag.

I turned to Sam's rear, and pulled his left buttock aside, as I placed the tip of the thermometer on his anus. Then, I slid it into him. I stepped back, leaning over Sam, and pulling his buttocks fully apart, as I slid the thermometer in and out of him. My father was squinting, now silent, while my mother was making gurgling sounds, as she watched the show.

Pulling the thermometer fully out, I placed it on a paper towel, and lubed two of the butt plugs. I held the first up, so my parents could see: It was the large glass plug, with purple glass 'bumps' all down the sides. Now, my father coughed, and was shaking his head.

Sam knew what to expect, and relaxed his anal muscles, as I inserted the plug, moving it in and out nearly six inches, as Sam's sphincter adapted to the increased size of the bumps.

Finally, I showed my parents the short, thick butt plug that had a thin neck and a jewel on the end. Without ceremony, I inserted it into Sam's rear, only the last half inch taking a minute, as Sam's anus dilated.

I pointed to Sam's rear, my parents clearly seeing 'everything'. Sam had done well, so far, so I decided to remove the plug.

I told Sam that he could get up and, after he had donned his running shorts and tank, I handed him one of the baskets. "The thermometer will be a good ice-breaker for Darlene, while I'm tawsing Dave."

Kelly was a monster; but I had made her that way. I turned to Darlene, and she looked at me with wet eyes. I whispered, "I will refuse, if you ask me to."

Darlene shook her head slowly, then let it drop. She was sniffling, so I went into the half-bath, and brought back some tissues. I put some into one of her restrained hands, and used another to wipe her nose.

Darlene looked at me, "I know that Dave is embarrassed with Kelly seeing his private bits ... and I know you were embarrassed to let us see you. I was embarrassed for you, Sam; I'm sure you know that I didn't want to see you that way." I nodded.

She sniveled, "I guess I'll try to take whatever punishment Kelly thinks I deserve." I looked at her, waiting for something else. Darlene turned her head, and looked up at me; she gave me a grimace, and one nod of her head. Then, she looked across to Dave, who was watching our exchange.

As I stood next to Darlene, Kelly was walking behind Dave, with the tawse. She placed it across Dave's butt, and he started talking again through the gag, which made his words unintelligible. Kelly walked around to face Dave, then took off the gag. I wondered whether she would ever get it back on him.

"OK, Dave, what is it? This better be good."

Dave was swallowing hard, and running his tongue around his lips. Then, he looked up at Kelly weakly, and informed her, "I have to pee."

This would be interesting! I really doubted that Dave would get back on the spanking bench if Kelly let him get up to use the bathroom.

Kelly stood with her hands on her hips, shaking her head. Then she looked up at me, and said, "I think we're going to have to catheterize him."

I hoped that Kelly was kidding; we did have a couple of sterile Foley catheter sets, and Kelly had observed the procedure when Mistress Elena had cath'ed me. Although she hadn't really been trained, yet, I could probably walk her through the steps. But it was dangerous. If not done with a completely sterile technique, Dave could get a urinary tract infection – a 'UTI'.

Trying to be helpful, I offered, "You could have him pee into a bottle ..." I thought Kelly might be angry at me, but she smiled, and nodded.

She stood in front of Dave and gave him the choice. "OK, Dave, I can insert a catheter into your bladder; it will take some preparation, and might be a little uncomfortable," That was an understatement! "but you won't have to worry about peeing the rest of the day."

Then, she smiled at her father, "Or, you can do as Sam suggested. I will hold the bottle for you."

Dave was squinting again, "Kelly ..."

She just gave him a dirty look and shook her head. "I guess *I'll* have to decide."

Now, Dave looked at his daughter, and agreed, "I'll pee into a bottle." Kelly laughed, and asked me to find one. I went into the garage and found an old milk bottle – the top big enough for Dave to 'fit'. It was dusty, but I wiped it off, and brought it back to the pool room.

I couldn't believe that Kelly was going to do this to her dad. Actually, I *could* believe it; I had created a monster. And, now, her parents were finding out how their daughter had changed over the past couple of years. Again I wondered how this might affect all of our relationships.

Kelly took the bottle and held it up in front of Dave. "Are you ready?"

Dave looked at the bottle, and whined, "Kelly, *please!*"

Kelly looked at me, and said, "Please get the catheter supplies, Sam."

Before I had even registered what Kelly had said, Dave said, "OK, Kelly. I'm ready. I guess." Dave was staring across to Darlene, who was giving him a sheepish grin.

Kelly got on her knees, her hands reaching under the spanking bench. She looked up at me, and said, "It's time for Darlene's thermometer. Why don't you do that while I relieve Dave?"

I shook my head, as I walked behind Darlene, whispering, "Just try to relax." As many times as I'd said it, I now realized that was a ridiculous thing to say.

Her legs weren't that far apart on the spanking bench, and her hips and butt were big, so there wasn't much actually visible, looking at her from behind.

Using my left hand to separate her buttocks, I inserted the thermometer into Darlene. She gasped, and then made a high-pitched sound that could have been a laugh or a cry. This was obviously very embarrassing for her; and for me.

I moved the thermometer around in her, and pulled it out a few times, plunging it again deep into her. Finally, I left it in, only an inch or so sticking out between Darlene's plump buttocks. About that time, we heard a 'tinkling' into the glass bottle.

I didn't like holding the bottle for my dad, but we were all doing things today that we didn't like. He fit through the top of the milk bottle, and I told him he could begin. It was interesting that this was something that even Sam and I hadn't done.

The catheterization would have been a much more intense experience, but I hadn't been trained for that, and Sam undoubtedly would have balked, had I asked him to 'do the honors'.

My dad finished, and I wiggle the bottle a couple of times to release the last drops. Then, I held up the bottle, "Will that hold you for a while, Dave?" I chuckled, as my father nodded, humiliated, and put the bottle on the desk.

"We still have another thirty strokes of the tawse!" I smiled, "And a lot more, after that." I positioned myself, and placed the tawse across my dad's bum; predictably, he flinched. "I'll leave the gag out, if you behave yourself. You may whine and cry, but I don't want to hear any words."

With that, I began the most severe tawsing that I had ever given. It had been over an hour, and my dad hadn't really been spanked, yet. In fact, his butt was barely red. The strokes were as hard as I could muster, about five seconds between each, and covering my dad's entire rear, as well as his upper thighs.

My father was groaning after the first strokes, whining after the next few, then whimpering, and crying before I had delivered half the strokes. To his credit, he did not yell or scream, or ask me to stop, or call me names. By the time I had completed the last ten strokes, he was blubbering. I had never seen him like this.

I rubbed his bottom, and suggested, "Sam, why don't you tawse my mother, and then we can insert the small butt plugs together?" I walked over and handed him the tawse.

Sam removed the thermometer and – without any warning – let the tawse fly. It was a hard stroke, the sound nearly as loud as when I had been tawsing my dad. My mother screeched.

Sam rubbed her bottom and gave her the next stroke; my mother wailed, 'Ooowwwww!!'

Taking his time, Sam rubbed my mom's butt again, and administered the last two strokes. Now, my mother was crying. It had only been four strokes, but I was surprised that Sam hadn't gone easier on her.

I smiled and nodded, "Now it's time for your first butt plugs." Both my parents groaned; my mother was trying to wipe her eyes with the tissue she held in one hand. Sam was still rubbing her bum.

I held up the small black rubber butt plug; it was only about ¾" in diameter and six or seven inches long. I lubed it, and went behind my father to insert it.

My dad was holding his anus closed, and I gave him a hard slap on his right butt cheek. "Relax your anus, Dave. Or, we'll have to do something more extreme."

Sam had a number of rectal dilators and rectal specula in his exam room, and I was sure that one of those would make my dad a little more docile. But he wasn't doing that badly; the punishment was proceeding more-or-less as I had planned ... so far.

My father finally relaxed, and I slipped the butt plug into him, moving it around for a while. I could not see Sam, as he was behind my mother, inserting the butt plug into *her* rear. When she scrunched-up her face and closed her eyes, I knew the plug had gone in.

After five minutes or so, I asked, "Are you ready for your next spanking, now, Dave? One hundred swats with the Ping Pong paddle." He was shaking his head and didn't answer; and I didn't wait for his answer. I removed the butt plug, and picked up the smooth Ping Pong paddle.

My dad's rear was perfectly situated for giving him a tawsing or a caning, but was a little high to receive a properly swung paddle. Regardless, I did my best, giving him twenty slow and hard swats, alternating sides; then another twenty with two per side each time; and finally six sets of ten swats at a time on each side.

There was a lot of groaning and whimpering, but Dave took the paddling pretty well. Now, it was Sam's turn. I gave him the paddle as I walked behind my mother with him. Her butt was barely pink. But I think the psychological aspect of this punishment would be the most important for her.

Sam gave my mother ten medium-hard swats with the Ping Pong paddle, alternating sides, the whole thing taking less than a minute. Then, he rubbed her, as I gave an approving nod.

"I think they're ready for the next butt plug now – the large bumpy one." Sam nodded, and lubed the one in his basket, and I lubed the one for my father.

I began inserting the plug into my dad, and he groaned. I wondered whether he would feel anything from the prostate stimulation this plug would provide. As it slid into him, I heard Sam ask my mom, "Are you ready?"

There was a moment of quiet, and then my mother asked, "May I please use the bathroom, first?" Sam looked at me and shrugged.

I didn't think there would be a problem getting my mother back on the spanking bench, but decided to give her a choice. "Yes – you may go to the bathroom; Sam will accompany you."

I waited for the predictable 'What!?!' from each of them, and finished, "Or, Sam can get a bucket, and help you pee, right where you are."

Sam's mouth dropped open, and he was shaking his head. I knew that I was pushing him; and so far, he was responding. My mother let her head drop, then looked up and said, "OK. Sam can take me."

Now, Sam was bent behind my mother, struggling with something. A minute later, he stood, holding my mother's pantyhose up, "She couldn't get up until I removed them." I nodded. Perhaps I should have my mother undress, now?

I unstrapped Darlene's wrists and ankles, flipped her dress down, and helped her off the spanking bench. "Come on, Darlene." I was sure that both Kelly and Darlene could tell that I was not at all excited about this.

Darlene and I went into the small half-bath adjoining the pool room, and I closed the door. Darlene gathered her dress, and turned to sit on the toilet, and I turned away from her, and faced the wall. Darlene finished and flushed, and we both washed our hands in the sink.

As I reached for the doorknob, Darlene said quietly, "Thank you, Sam."

We walked back to the spanking bench, and Darlene climbed onto it, her knees on the lower pads, and her chest on the slanted pad. I re-attached the straps, and held up the large butt plug for her to see. She nodded, and let her head drop again.

Kelly now had the cane in her hand; it was a medium-size school cane, a harsh instrument. She asked, "Darlene, would you like to come over here and watch, as I cane Dave?" She chuckled, "Or maybe *you* would like to cane him?" Darlene shook her head to both questions.

Dave's caning was difficult to watch – even from the front. Kelly was unforgiving, as she demonstrated her skill, using all of her considerable strength. Dave cried out after each stroke, and Darlene jumped each time we heard the 'CRACK!!' of the cane against Dave's rear.

Once again, Dave was blubbering by the end, but I was surprised that Kelly hadn't needed to gag him. He really was being incredibly cooperative.

Kelly handed me the thin, whippy cane, and I slid it across Darlene's bottom. Then, I swung it very hard, just through the air, and we all heard the 'swoosh' of the rattan. Darlene jumped as far as the restraints would allow, and she yelped, even though the cane hadn't touched her.

Then, I gave her two medium strokes, each leaving a thin, white line across her reddened butt. She screamed after each stroke, and continued whimpering after it was over. But she didn't complain, or plead with me; she took her punishment with as much dignity as the situation would allow.

We were getting close to the end of the punishment, and I couldn't wait for it to be over; but probably not as much as Dave and Darlene wished it to end. I was rubbing Darlene's bottom, trying to 'erase' the thin white lines.

Kelly looked at me, "Instead of the butt plug, I think the next corner-time should be a nice big enema. For both Dave and Darlene!" She cackled, and I thought of Julie.

Dave bellowed, and I knew that Kelly would be putting the ball gag back in place. Darlene cried, "Haven't we gone through enough, dear?"

Kelly remarked, "Dad hasn't." She thought a moment, and said, "OK, Darlene. If you don't want Sam to give you an enema, you may ask him to bathe you. While he's doing that, I'll be finishing Dave's punishment – it might take a while." Darlene's mouth dropped open, and I was as surprised as she was.

Continuing, Kelly explained, "There will be no corner-time now, but both of you will get the last butt plug when I'm done with dad." She chuckled, "And you can leave them in until you're home. Then take them out of each other." Both Dave and Darlene were groaning.

Impatient, now, Kelly asked, "So what's your decision, Darlene?"

I was going to put up an argument, but couldn't get the words out; I was stunned that Kelly was asking for this. I half expected Dave to object, but he was silent.

Darlene grumbled, "I don't want an enema." It was an interesting answer; getting an enema wouldn't have been much different than me inserting a butt plug, which we'd already done. I looked at Kelly, and she gave me a shrug.

I released Darlene's restraining straps, and helped her up. Kelly commanded, "Stand at attention, Darlene, and let Sam undress you."

Kelly was really going for it; embarrassing her mother every chance she got this afternoon. While Darlene may have passively allowed Dave to fool around, I didn't think she deserved this harsh of a punishment. Although her spanking hadn't been that severe, the day had been incredibly embarrassing for her.

Darlene stood there, while I unbuttoned and unzipped her dress, and lifted it over her head. Then, I unhooked her bra, and she put her arms down, so I could remove it.

Now, Darlene was standing in our pool room stark naked. Dave was staring at her, shaking his head, but didn't say anything.

Darlene did not appear to be upset; she had a resigned look on her face. When I asked if she was ready, she turned her head and actually smiled at me, then gave me a nod. I looked at Kelly, and she nodded. Taking Darlene by the hand, I escorted her to the downstairs bathroom, and into the shower room.

As I held the school paddle, I looked at my dad's rear; it was a dark, dull red, and I could see the blanched white lines of the cane strokes crossing the lower portion of his bum. I walked around in front of him, and he looked up at me beseechingly.

"Dad, you have no idea how upset I've been about all this." He nodded. "And, I'm *sure* you have no idea how upset you've made mother ... over the past several years." I wasn't sure how to continue.

"What we're doing today means nothing; I just hope it is memorable enough that you will *think* next time a girl flirts with you." I'd already said this.

There was nothing more I could do, except finish his punishment. Either he would 'get it', or not. But I was certain we were making an impression on him.

Before he realized what was happening, I put the ball gag back into his mouth, and tightened the strap around his head. Then, I took the school paddle – the one with the holes in it – and stepped behind him. I was going to draw out this last punishment. My dad's little girl would be making him cry, once more.

Darlene and I walked into the shower room, and I held her shoulders. "I'm sorry for all of this, Darlene. As I said, I never wanted to be involved. But I'm 'involved' with Kelly, and she felt strongly that something had to be done. She was very upset seeing you cry at Thanksgiving."

Darlene nodded, then surprised me by giving me a hug. "I know, Sam. I'm not blaming you for anything. Or, Kelly. She's right – Dave was wrong to cheat on me, and I was wrong to let him continue doing it."

Then, she smiled, "Dave and I have had a couple of good talks since Kelly came over; in fact, some of the best talks we've had in years. I don't know if today will change anything, but we were both willing to 'submit' to Kelly, as you would say."

I took off my tank and running shorts, and started the shower. As it was warming up, I turned to Darlene, and told her, "I consider 'bathing' someone to be a *nice* thing, not a punishment. I think Kelly just wanted to put you through one more embarrassment, letting me see you nude." Darlene nodded.

Chuckling, I said, "But now that we've all seen each other, perhaps you and Dave would go skinny-dipping in the pool with us sometime ... or go in the sauna." I pointed to the smoked glass door.

Darlene chuckled, a good sign. "I'm not sure if I'll ever be able to face you again, Sam. This has been very uncomfortable for me." Then, she looked at me with a lopsided smile, "*Especially* you sticking things up my rear end." We laughed, and stepped under the shower.

I bathed Darlene cursorily, covering her entire body. Although I did let my hands graze over her pubic area, and down her butt crack, I kept them superficial.

Darlene's body was out of shape, but I had to remind myself that I'd been seeing twenties-something females for the past two years. Her breasts were large, probably a D-cup originally, but now they hung low, her muscles having lost the battle with gravity.

Her middle was flabby, and she was overweight, but even losing twenty pounds wouldn't take off the roll of fat that encircled her. She had an untrimmed 'bush', but the hair was sparse, as it had been on Sarah in her 'older' age.

I finished Darlene's shower, and realized neither of us had said a word. She washed her own face, and I offered to give her a nice shampoo, but she declined. We got out of the shower, and dried ourselves, and then I put back on my running outfit.

Before we went upstairs, I hugged Darlene again. "Thank you for cooperating today, Darlene. I know that Kelly was impressed, and I was, too."

I chuckled, "If you *hadn't* cooperated, I think it might have been worse: Kelly certainly would have made you and Dave take an enema, and probably do some other things that you wouldn't like."

Now it occurred to me that Kelly had not suggested any medical experiences – like needles or shots – for her parents. That was just as well, as it would have exposed our *other* interest, in addition to spanking.

As we walked upstairs, Darlene still nude but unfazed, we heard gunshot-like sounds coming from the pool room, along with screams – evidently through the gag – after each swat. Kelly was still paddling her father. Before we walked into the pool room, I poured a glass of water for Darlene, which she drank in one continuous gulp.

My dad's rear was really raw, as the thick paddle landed repeatedly.   Sam walked into the pool room, my naked mother in tow. She seemed fully recovered from her spanking. I put the paddle on the desk, and stepped aside, so they could see my dad's bum. My mother gasped.

"We're doing pretty well – about halfway done. Now that you guys are back, I'll give him *hard* ones." My father was screaming through the gag again. I turned to him, "If you don't quiet down, I'll continue until dinner." Dave slowly calmed, and was now sobbing.

Kelly smiled at her mother, who had a contorted expression, "I guess my big, strong, macho dad can't take a spanking from his little girl." She was cackling again.

Darlene and I were staring at Dave's bruised butt. Kelly said, "Well, get into position, and we'll insert the last butt plugs." Then she smiled, and instructed, "You will take them out of each other, after you get home."

Both Darlene and I were shaking our heads as we walked to the other end of the spanking bench, and Darlene got into position without any prompting.

I lubed the butt plug, and pressed it against Darlene's anus. It took some time, but we finally got it in, Darlene yelping as the thickest part passed through her sphincter.

Kelly told her mother that she could get up and get dressed. Darlene put on her bra, and then her dress, letting it drop. Only her underwear was missing, and she didn't bother with the pantyhose.

Leaving Dave strapped down, but taking out his gag, Kelly called her mother over, and gave her a bottle of lotion. Dave now had the jewel of the butt plug showing between his buttocks, matching the one that was in Darlene. Pointing to the lotion, Kelly said, "That will make it feel a little better."

Then, she smiled, "He took his punishment very well, mom. I think you should give him another chance. Let him prove to you that he loves and respects you."

We went into the kitchen, and closed the door, leaving Dave and Darlene in the pool room. Kelly and I were both dehydrated, and each finished a can of diet lemonade, as Kelly smiled at me, and I shook my head. Had all this really happened?

I actually felt pretty comfortable that Darlene would accept the events and move on. By the end of our shower, she had seemed quite comfortable with me.

I wasn't so sure about Dave; whether he could face his 'little girl', after she'd tanned his hide. I thought to myself, 'now, who's the macho one?'.

Kelly unstrapped Dave and let him get dressed, sans underwear, and we walked them to their car. I still had no idea how this would play out, but Kelly had gone through with her plan to punish her parents.

When they had driven off, into the sunset (yes, the event had taken the entire afternoon), we walked back inside, and into the pool room. Kelly smiled, and said, "That didn't go too badly." That was easy for *her* to say.

She told me that her father had promised to return, *with* Jackie, so that she could be punished. I wouldn't need to be the 'demonstrator', which I was relieved to hear.

Although the demonstration spanking had been no big deal, I had been very embarrassed today, getting into the chair position while Kelly's parents watched.

I had no idea what Jackie was like, or whether she would actually come over to be punished. We would see ...

CHAPTER 3: THE OTHER WOMAN

It had been a week since my parents had come over for their punishment. They had been amazingly 'docile' (as Sam called it), and my father contrite, accepting his spanking without much complaint. It felt like he really was embarrassed – not necessarily by getting spanked on the bare by his 'little girl', but by having his extra-marital affairs come out.

I really hoped that my parents would give each other another chance: My dad showing my mom love and respect, and my mom providing a sexual outlet for my dad. If each of them could do these things and forgive each other for the past, there would be hope for their future. Of course, I realized it wasn't that easy to forgive.

My father had promised to bring Jackie over for *her* punishment, and had actually called me to say they would be over tomorrow morning. I planned to go easy on my dad, as he really had cooperated well ... but the more I thought about the situation, the more upset I was that Jackie would go after a married man – even a supposedly separated one.

It really wasn't fair to my mother ... even if she didn't want sex all the time. I chuckled, realizing I had no idea how often my parents had had sex, recently, or in the past.

But if Jackie had wanted to pick up some guy, it was easy – she was at the club, and there were plenty of younger and older men, who *weren't* married.

My father wore a wedding ring, so I assumed that Jackie had known he was married. Flirting would be one thing, but going to bed with him? At his *home*?

Then again, I really didn't know who had initiated the affair; maybe my dad had 'picked up' Jackie? But they both would have responsibility. It seemed like there would be fewer cheating husbands, if women wouldn't go after married men. But that wasn't fair; everyone probably either hid it or had an excuse, like dad had.

Now, I wondered whether I might have 'fallen' for Sam – or even just played with him – had he still been married to Sarah. But I had never been looking for an older man, and had not been seeing *anyone* as a potential partner. No, I wouldn't have been a home-breaker.

There had been no repercussions, so far, from Dave and Darlene, but it had only been a week. They were probably still in shock over the experience they'd had. Kelly had been successful in embarrassing her parents, but I had no idea how that could be of benefit to any of us.

And, *now*, unbelievably, Dave was going to bring Jackie over for *her* punishment. I couldn't picture Dave coming back here, and *really* couldn't understand why this Jackie lady would consent to being 'punished' by strangers.

Kelly had gotten herself very upset over Jackie going after her father, and now saw Jackie as some kind of evil, satanic person.

I smiled, thinking that we didn't even know what she looked like: She could be plus-size or skinny, tall or short; but we knew she was 'younger', whatever that meant. Could she be as young as Kelly? Dave had to be close to 60, so Jackie could theoretically be *my* age! We had no idea what to expect.

The doorbell rang, startling me, and I realized I had been deep in thought. Kelly and I got up from the breakfast table, and walked through the dining room. As we entered the living room, Kelly took my arm, and turned to me. "Sam, will you submit to me, today?"

I closed my eyes. I really didn't feel like getting in a knee-chest position, allowing this Jackie gal to see my privates, and then being tawsed or caned ... to supposedly 'demonstrate' the spanking. Although I knew that it helped for people to see someone else take the same punishment, so they knew they can do it.

Kelly put her hand on my cheek, and said, quietly, "Sam, I won't ask you to take any spankings." Then, she smirked, "I have other plans."

I had no idea what she was talking about, but decided that I would trust Kelly – again – and submit to her desires. Kelly had known this morning that I hoped to 'go out' while Dave and Jackie were here, and she had warned me that I should be here to 'support' her – whatever *that* meant.

"Yes, Kelly. We're now engaged, and I will trust you to not be too hard on me, today." Kelly leaned over and gave me a peck on the lips, then took a few steps to the door, and opened it widely.

"Hi, dad." She sounded serious. "I guess this is Jackie?"

The woman stepped up and took Kelly's hands in hers. "Yes, Kelly. I'm Jacqueline Moret ... 'Jackie'." Then, before Kelly could get a word in, "I'm *really* sorry, Kelly. I had no idea that spending time with Dave would harm his wife or family. He told me they were separated."

They were still standing at the door. Kelly replied, acidly, "Well, if my parents *had* separated, I would hope they could reconcile ... but that wouldn't be helped by some hussy going after my dad."

Dave looked queerly at Kelly, and Jackie took a deep breath. Jackie asked, "May we please come in?"

Now, Kelly looked embarrassed and flustered, and quickly ushered them into the living room. We all sat around the coffee table; this was a true *déjà vu* moment. I glanced at Kelly, and she gave me a thin smile.

Jackie pleaded, "Kelly, I'm *truly* sorry. And I'm willing to show it by allowing you to punish me. Dave gave me a little idea of what to expect – being paddled and strapped."

She looked down, "Of course, I'm afraid." Then she glanced at Dave, "But at least Dave's here with me, and I do trust his daughter."

Jackie was close to tears, "Dave is really a nice guy. And not that much happened." Dave's head swung toward Jackie, and she shrugged.

Smartly, Kelly didn't fill the short gap in the discussion, and Jackie continued. Looking at Dave, she said, "I gave you a 'lap dance' in the coatroom of the club." Dave's eyes closed, and his head went down.

Jackie then looked at Kelly, and said, "And I only went home with him once ... because I was getting off my shift, and Dave was a little inebriated."

Kelly gave her a 'Sure!' look, and Jackie said, "Yes, I would have had sex with him. And I undressed for him ... and then undressed him."

Now, Jackie was laughing – something I wouldn't have imagined possible, under the circumstances. "Then, I put him to bed." Kelly's mouth dropped open, but Jackie finished, "By the time I got him undressed, he was snoring, so I pulled up the covers, kissed his cheek, and drove home."

Kelly looked angry, then confused, then looked at Dave. He shrugged, "I don't remember much, after we left the club."

There was a moment of suspended animation – time stopped. Kelly looked from Dave to Jackie, and back. Her expression was continuously morphing, but I detected a smile on her face, and *she* now started to laugh.

She stifled her laugh long enough to look at Jackie and ask seriously, "So there was no transfer of body fluids?"

Another moment of silence, as Jackie assimilated the question. She answered, softly, "Yes. We kissed a few times." Kelly looked at me with sparkling eyes, and I could only imagine what she was now planning. Actually, I *couldn't* imagine ...

I wasn't sure *what* to think: Jackie and my dad *hadn't* had sex ... at least by our definition, excluding oral contact. But he had still strayed, and she had still responded to a man who wore a wedding ring. As I considered – re-considered – the situation, I no longer thought of Jackie as the devil.

If I could believe what I'd just heard, Jackie should not have to be punished ... much. But I thought I would put some fear into her – just to set the tone, and let her know that I was serious. Then I chuckled, as I thought of one more way to set the stage.

Looking at Jackie, I smiled, and asked, "Did my dad show you his butt?" Now, I looked at my dad, who was cringing, "Have the cane marks faded, yet?" He just looked at me.

Jackie gasped, and repeated questioningly, "*Cane* marks?" Nobody answered her.

"Please come over here dad, so I can see how you're doing. It might make me moderate my strokes with Jackie." Hearing what had happened – if that was ALL that had happened – had lifted a weight from me; I realized that I was now having fun.

My dad sat on the couch, staring at me. I gave him the signal to come with my forefinger, and the sweetest smile that I could muster. I was not planning on spanking him today – even as a demonstration. He had cooperated with his punishment, and was now acting repentant.

My dad slowly walked to me, and I turned him around. "Undo your pants, please." He slowly unhooked the belt, and unzipped his pants. I quickly pulled them – and his boxers – down to his ankles. He began to swing around to me, but stopped, and let his head drop.

Lifting his polo shirt, I examined his rear, and made sure that Jackie could see, also. Sam was sitting in the chair on the other side of the coffee table, studiously looking everywhere but at Dave.

My dad's butt looked OK, but we could still see faint white lines, where the cane had landed. "OK, dad. Please sit back down."

I organized my thoughts about what I would say, then began, "Dad, I don't plan to punish you today. I won't even make you demonstrate each implement ... like Sam did." My dad looked at me with a confused but relieved expression.

"But I do want to talk with you for a while. Then, you can observe Jackie's spanking. You'll see what trouble you've caused for an apparently nice young lady." Jackie appeared to be in her early 40s.

I decided it was time for a little demonstration – that Jackie would give, herself. "Jackie, please stand up."

When she was standing, I said, "Spread your legs apart, and put your hands on your head. That will be your 'normal' position, if we haven't asked you to get in another position." Jackie swallowed hard and nodded.

Jackie was a good looking woman, about my height, and quite slim. She had an oval face, and brown hair that was in bangs and came down to just above her shoulders. She wore jeans, a dress shirt, and comfortable, low shoes. From what I could discern, she was quite small on top, and I was sure that Sam would judge her rear a bit small for spanking.

I turned my chair to face Jackie, which would give a side-view to Dave and Sam; it was the armless wooden spanking chair that we had brought up from the playroom.

"I'm going to give you a demonstration spanking; just a warm-up. I'm doing this mainly to see how well you will cooperate."

I glanced at Sam and back to Jackie, "And, then, I'm going to give you a choice. Finally, I will give you a good hard spanking so that your bottom will be reminding you of this lesson for a while." Jackie looked more frightened, and swallowed again, before looking down at the carpet.

"You will do as I say, hold your position, and keep your hands in front of you. Do you understand?" I had said this a little loudly and harshly, and Jackie's head snapped up nodding vigorously.

"Come over here, please." Jackie took a few steps, until she was standing in front of me. "Lower your jeans, please." Jackie looked down, unbuttoning and unzipping her pants, and pushing them down below her knees. She wore gray cotton bikinis.

I helped Jackie get over my knee, and maneuvered her into position. Her bum *was* small, and I realized this would be a different spanking experience – much different than spanking Linda, in her heavier days. So far, this was going easily and smoothly.

Putting my hand on her right butt cheek, I said softly, "You *must* stay in position, and stay as quiet as you can."

When my hand landed on her bum the first few times, Jackie yelped. Now, as I was picking up the speed and increasing the intensity of the spanking, she was quiet – just breathing heavily – but her legs were kicking, and she was bouncing off my leg.

I decided that I would continue until I thought Jackie had felt enough to put the fear of the heavier implements into her.

Sam and my dad were staring at Jackie's butt – of course. But neither of them was smiling.

Jackie was sobbing now, and I stopped; the bouncing stopped a few seconds later. I quickly lowered Jackie's panties, but she evidently had expected it, and there was no reaction. Then, I put my right leg over her legs, to minimize the kicking.

Looking up at Sam, and smiling, I said, "Please set a timer for ten minutes." He frowned at me, but dutifully lifted his arm, and set the timer on his Apple watch.

I sighed, "I guess I'm going to get my exercise, today!" With that, I began spanking Jackie again, not skimping on my efforts. She was almost immediately in tears.

I glanced up, and saw that my father was looking down into his lap. Sam appeared to be focusing on his watch.

The spanking continued for several minutes, and Jackie was now sobbing continuously. I increased the force again, and the spanks echoed in the small living room. Jackie yelped, and brought her right hand behind her. She had done very well up to this point.

I held her wrist, and brought her arm behind her, up enough to keep above her butt, but not so high as to hurt her. Then, I continued the spanking, giving her another forty very hard spanks.

Jackie wept, her head hanging down, and her body racking, as she took large gulps of air.

Rubbing Jackie's butt, I said brightly, "Well, *that* wasn't much of a warm-up; your bottom is just a medium-rare shade of pink. This won't do at all."

I *was* having fun, now. And I wouldn't be putting Jackie through that much more; spanking, at least. Except for one more demonstration ... and, of course, her finale.

"Sam, can you please bring me the wooden hairbrush?" Sam, of course, had several hairbrushes designated for spankings.

Jackie groaned, "Oooohh, Kelly. Do you *have* to use the hairbrush? My rear is pretty sore, already." She let her head drop again.

I didn't answer. Sam returned quickly, and handed me a beautiful dark wood hairbrush, which had a large, slightly-convex back to it, highly polished, nearly black.

I laid the hairbrush on Jackie's bottom, and chuckled, "I'll just give you a taste of the hairbrush; just so you'll know what to expect later."

Before Jackie knew what was happening, I gave her a very hard swat on each side of her butt with the hairbrush. She screamed, and her lower legs came off the ground, nearly vertical, although my leg was trying to hold them down.

I laughed loudly (trying out my 'Cruela de Ville' impersonation), and said, dejectedly, "OK. I'll only give you two dozen with the hairbrush." Jackie groaned, and was now whimpering. "And *then* I'll give you a choice for the next phase of your punishment."

The hairbrushing I gave her was 'respectable' – hard enough to be challenging, but certainly not using my entire strength. It was enough to cover Jackie's small butt several times, and she was howling by the end.

I rubbed her bottom, and actually felt a little sorry for her. She had voluntarily come over to receive a spanking, and she was cooperating as well as could be expected.

I helped Jackie get up, and she pulled up her underwear and pants, not bothering to button them. Then, she got into the standing position. Impressive.

"Jackie, I would like to speak with my dad for a while, so I'm going to have Sam administer your punishment for the next phase."

Sam instantly sat up, and gave me a 'look'; it was somewhere between surprise and confusion, but I detected no delight.

I nodded and turned back to Jackie. "I will give you a choice: For the next hour or so, you can let Sam give you pain with a little embarrassment, or embarrassment with a little pain."

Jackie just looked at me. I realized that I was now emulating some of the silly things that Sam used to do. I hoped that she would take the embarrassment, and save herself some real 'pain in the butt'.

"I guess I'll take the embarrassment with a little pain." I nodded, glancing at Sam, who was now beside himself. I had *told* him that his submission wouldn't involve him being punished. This should be a treat for him ... and not that bad for Jackie.

"Sam, can you please take Jackie to the exam room, and give her 'the works'?" Sam cocked his head, and I explained a bit more, "A full X, a couple of Es, and a few Ss and Ns."

I hoped that he understood, but knew he had, when he smiled and nodded. Now, *he* was going to have some fun.

Sam led Jackie through the dining room and kitchen, then downstairs, and my father looked up at me painfully. "Kelly, I have to go." What!??!?

"Dad, I just want to talk with you for a while. You're not going to get any more punishment."

He shook his head, "No, Kelly. I'll talk with you another time ... but I don't want to stay here." He looked pleadingly into my eyes.

Then, he said, softly, "I won't be seeing Jackie anymore. Your mother and I have been having some good talks — something we haven't done in a long time." He shrugged, "Maybe Sam can drive her home?"

This was a little surprising, but it sounded like improvement on the home front might be in progress, so I decided to let him go. We stood, and I hugged him. "I love you, Dad."

He squeezed me, tears in his eyes. "I love you too, Kelly." He sniffled, "I've only wanted the best for you ... and your mother. Somewhere, we got off course. But I'm hoping that things will get better."

My dad walked to the door and let himself out. As the door swung closed, I said, "I hope so, too, dad."

Jackie and I walked down the stairs, and I swung open the door. As she stepped into the doorway and was able to see the exam room, she stopped, and looked back at me. Then, she took another step, and gazed around the room.

To the left was the sink and exam table, above which — on the wall — was the sphygmomanometer, otoscope, sharps container, and monitor for my USB microscope. The exam table was covered with a roll of waxy paper, and had a small pillow at the other end.

To the right was a counter, with drawers beneath and cabinets above. On the counter were jars of ancient glass syringes, gleaming instruments – including a few specula, and the supplies for intramuscular injections. To the immediate right, was a small chair.

I said, softly, "Kelly and I play 'doctor', sometimes. Please undress down to your bra and underwear. You can put your clothes on the chair."

Jackie chuckled, as she unbuttoned her blouse, only bare skin beneath. She was incredibly small on top – one of the most flat-chested women I had ever seen ... although I had seen all types on nude beaches and at European saunas. She took off her pants, folded them, and put them on the chair, her blouse over the back of the chair.

I weighed her, and took her measurements, and then had her hop up onto the table. She looked around the exam room, and swung her feet; she didn't look nervous or embarrassed, at all, just curious and, perhaps, amused.

Kelly, I'm sure, thought that this would be a turn-on for me, to 'challenge' Jackie; but I was not turned-on, at all. I wasn't really looking forward to doing this. It might have been fun, if Jackie came over sometime to 'play' with us ... but to intentionally try to embarrass her as a punishment felt inappropriate.

And Jackie seemed like a very nice person; she had actually agreed to come over and be punished by her beau's daughter, and had cooperated fully, so far. She certainly wasn't the 'devil' that Kelly had imagined. And she wasn't the buxom blonde that I had imagined.

"Jackie, I'm sure that Kelly would like me to be a little harsh with you ... and I know what she wants me to put you through." Jackie stopped swinging her legs, and looked up at me, as I continued, "We do these things to each other as part of our sensual play ... not as a punishment. Well, not usually as a punishment."

Laughing, I added, "Of course, everything we do in here will be easier than taking a hard spanking from Kelly!"

Jackie nodded, "That so-called 'warm-up' was pretty hard, and I can't imagine what a caning would feel like." She smiled, "And I don't want to find out."

Then she bit her lips, and said, softly, "But I came over here to take a punishment for 'going after' Dave." She looked into my eyes, "And, I admit, I *did* flirt with him. He had always been a gentleman, until I showed interest." It seemed that Dave hadn't been quite the gallivanting husband that Darlene and Kelly had assumed.

Jackie said, "But he did tell me that he was separated from his wife, living over the garage. Still, I know it wasn't right." She looked into my eyes again, "I don't think I'll have a problem with what you're going to do in here ... as long as it's safe."

I smiled, "Yes – everything will be safe. I used to be in the medical field, and all of our supplies are sterile. And I won't intentionally make things harder on you." I would be giving Jackie 'the works' from her perspective, but really doing only the basic stuff that Kelly and I had done.

"Shall we get started?" I guess I would be examining her small breasts, then giving her a cursory pelvic.

"May I use the bathroom, first, please?"

I nodded, and grabbed a sample cup from a drawer under the counter. "OK. Then let's do a quick urinalysis."

Jackie gave me a 'look', then her face turned serious and she nodded and hopped down from the exam table. She took off her underwear, placing them on her jeans, and I led her across the hall to the bathroom. She glanced at me and shrugged, then sat on the toilet.

I wasn't going to make her do a 'clean catch', nor observe her up close. She looked up, and I handed her the cup. She gave me a small sample, and I tested it, then walked back into the exam room, where I got a few things ready, while she finished. A few minutes later, Jackie came back and hopped up on the table, again.

With little discussion, I conducted her breast exam and had her turn onto her stomach so that I could take her rectal temperature. As far as I could tell, Jackie behaved the way she would have in a regular doctor's office.

When the thermometer was in, I announced, "I guess it's time for you to get a couple of shots ... in your rear." Jackie lifted her head, and her mouth dropped open as she saw me holding the syringe, the needle cap already off. But she silently nodded, and put her head back on the pillow.

I gave her a 3cc shot on each side – about equivalent to getting a couple of penicillin shots. They were given 'quickly', but still took about 30 seconds, each. Jackie lay there accepting her fate with no comment; she didn't make a sound during either shot.

After taking out the thermometer, I had Jackie turn back over, and raised the stirrups. Jackie scooted down, and got her legs up, no instructions necessary. I inserted a gloved finger into her vagina, and then did a rectal. Jackie had her hands clasped over her stomach, and she was staring at the ceiling.

I inserted the speculum, and she let out an 'Aaahhh' when I over-expanded it. "Sorry. Would you like to see your cervix on this monitor?" She lifted her head, and I pointed to the new wall-mounted display that hooked up to my USB microscope.

"Not especially." She let her head drop back onto the pillow. I removed the speculum, and made preparations for the next 'experience'.

Mixing warm water with a few tablespoons of salt in a two gallon pail, I decided to use the metal enema nozzle, rather than the more difficult Bardex system. As I was lubing the nozzle, I explained, "You're going to get a couple of enemas, now. The first will be with this nozzle," Jackie stared at it with wide eyes.

I stepped between her legs and slowly inserted the device. It wasn't until the water was flowing into her that Jackie emitted a few groans.

I stepped alongside Jackie, and put my left hand on her abdomen, which hadn't yet started expanding. "How are you doing?"

Jackie looked at me, and shrugged, "I guess I'm OK. It's just a little uncomfortable." I assumed she was referring to the enema, and not the entire exam room experience.

"You don't seem too bothered or embarrassed by anything we've done, so far," I commented.

Chuckling, Jackie responded, "Women are used to this. None of it is a big deal." Then, she smiled, "But I probably would have been creeped-out, if you hadn't been acting so professionally." I nodded.

"And I'm a pretty open person; I don't get embarrassed by much. I'm not ashamed of my body ... and you're not the first person to see it." We laughed.

For the next few minutes, we discussed nude beaches; Jackie had also frequented them in her younger years. She had never married, and I found that she did real estate on the side, as well as her job at the club. She was a good-looking woman, although I wouldn't call her a knockout.

I wondered why she hadn't settled down with a man ... or a woman.

The enema bag was empty, and I shut off the valve, and removed the nozzle from Jackie's rear. I helped her get off the table, and we went back into the bathroom. By this time, Jackie knew that I would be observing her. I stood in the doorway, as she sat on the toilet and released the first 'flood'.

I decided to learn more about this woman, who was beginning to intrigue me. "What are your sexual preferences?" That was about as direct as I could get.

Jackie looked up at me and smiled, "With the man on top?" I laughed.

"I meant whether you consider yourself heterosexual, or bi. And are you interested in any kinks or fetishes."

"Fetishes?" she replied cautiously. "I do have a pretty big shoe collection." We were laughing again. Then, came the next flood.

Jackie groaned, and then replied, "I'm a pretty simple girl. Just interested in men ... and nothing weird."

I was getting bored, so decided to give Jackie her space, and surf the web for a while. I found Jackie's Facebook page, but didn't learn much more about her.

Then, I checked out a few of my favorite websites, where I got updated on interesting technologies. Finally, I started watching one of the recent TED talks.

As I walked down the stairs, I heard a 'flood' coming out of Jackie. I stepped into the doorway, and expected to see Sam in there with her. Jackie looked up and winced.

"Is Sam getting you all cleaned out?" She chuckled and nodded her head.

I continued into the playroom, and saw Sam sitting at his desk, apparently watching a movie. "Are you having fun, yet?"

Sam turned off the sound, and looked up, "Not really." That was a little surprising. I waited for further explanation. Finally, Sam said, "Jackie is a nice woman. She is very open and has cooperated fully; and I don't think she has been embarrassed."

Before I could reply, Sam added, "I think she's had plenty of punishment. She came over here voluntarily, and appears to be very sorry about involving your dad."

Sam described to me what he'd done already with Jackie, and I finalized my plan for her punishment. I still thought she deserved to be spanked, but was convinced – without Sam's comments – that I should go easy on her.

We heard the toilet flush, and a minute later, Jackie was standing in the hallway, nude. "I guess I'm finished," she said, as she continued into the exam room. When Sam and I got there, she was sitting on the exam table, swinging her legs.

Now for the bombshell that I hadn't gotten the chance to tell Sam. "Jackie, my dad decided to leave." She gave me a questioning look, and I explained, "I had told him that he would not be punished anymore, but he said he couldn't stay, and just walked out the door."

Jackie looked down, and said meekly, "I thought he was going to be supportive, today." Then, she looked up, "But I'm not surprised." After a few moments, she added, "I hope one of you can take me home ... or call a cab ..."

I nodded, "Yes, Sam will drive you home." Sam looked at me surprisedly, but didn't argue. I turned to Sam, "OK, why don't you dilate her for the large butt plug, and I'll get a couple of big shots ready." Sam nodded grimly; he really wasn't into punishing Jackie.

Sam had Jackie get into a knee chest position, and he used a gloved finger to lubricate her, then the large vibrator to begin dilating her anal sphincter. By the time I had finished assembling the shots, Sam was moving the bumpy glass butt plug in and out of Jackie. She seemed to be taking it well.

When the glass butt plug was finally in her, we had her lie on her stomach, and Sam and I swabbed her hips – me on the counter side, and Sam on the opposite side of the exam table, squeezed next to the wall. I told Jackie, "Just count down, now; '3, 2, 1'.

Jackie did the countdown, and Sam and I inserted the needles at 'zero'. We took our time, slowly injecting the saline. Again, Jackie was taking it well. When she was fully injected, we left the needles in her, the syringes wobbling slightly as they stood on her hips.

"Maybe, we should have Jackie squirt a few pints, like we had my friends do?"

Sam said, "It's too cold outside."

I laughed, "Then we can have her on a chaise, and squirt into the shower."

Sam was shaking his head, smiling, "No, I don't think so. I could wash everything down with bleach, but I really think Jackie's had enough 'embarrassment'." Actually, it didn't appear to me that Jackie had been embarrassed, much.

"OK, then we'll take her up to the pool room for the rest of her spanking." Jackie had her head turned toward the wall, but groaned.

We pulled the needles out and dropped the syringes in the sharps container. Leaving the butt plug in Jackie, we helped her off the exam table, and walked her up to the pool room.

She gasped, as she entered the room and saw the spanking bench. It *was* an impressive – and intimidating – piece of equipment. Sam said he would probably have to completely disassemble it, in order to store it in the garage.

We helped Jackie kneel onto the padded support, and put the Velcro straps over her wrists and ankles, and the wide strap around her back. I suggested that Sam play with the butt plug, while I spoke with Jackie.

Standing in front of her, I leaned against the spanking bench, bringing my head down to her level. "I had planned to punish you as I did my dad – using the Ping Pong paddle, then the heavy strap, then the cane, and finally the school paddle."

Jackie's head dropped, and she sniveled. Sam raised up from behind her, where he was moving the butt plug in and out of her rear, and gave me a concerned look. I shook my head, and smiled, then said, "But since you came here voluntarily and have been cooperative, I'll let Sam pick just one of the punishments for you."

Jackie turned her head back as much as possible, and told Sam, "I really don't want to be caned." She turned her head back, and let it drop.

Sam pulled out the butt plug, and wrapped it in tissue, then walked in front of Jackie on the other side of the spanking bench from me. "I think three hard swats with the school paddle should be sufficient." Jackie whimpered.

I shook my head, and put my hands on my hips, "No, Sam. She'll get six hard swats," I looked at him, "unless you would rather her take 12 strokes of the cane, or 24 strokes of the tawse." Sam glanced at Jackie and nodded. It really wasn't his decision.

Taking the school paddle from its hook next to the blackboard behind the desk, I showed it to Jackie, and swung it through the air a few times. If this was all she was going to get, I planned to draw out the experience.

Positioning myself and placing the paddle on Jackie's small rear, I said, "After each swat, Sam will re-insert the bumpy butt plug, until you say 'Ready!' – and then he'll remove the plug, and I'll give you the next swat. Let me know when you're ready to begin."

Jackie looked up at Sam, shook her head, took a couple of big breaths, then faced ahead and dejectedly said, "Ready!" I swung the paddle, and it impacted Jackie's butt with a huge 'CRAAACK!!' There was a half-second of quiet, and then she screamed. She took gulps of air, and her body shuddered.

Sam inserted the plug, and played with it, while Jackie calmed. She sniffled, and then said, "Ready!" Sam pulled out the plug, and I swung the paddle – again resulting in a loud clap, tissue rippling outward, and – a moment later – a scream from Jackie.

After the second swat, she was whimpering, and after the third she was sobbing. By the fourth, she was wailing; I hoped the neighbors couldn't hear.

It took nearly 15 minutes to administer Jackie's paddling, and she was balling by the end. *Now* she had certainly taken enough punishment.

"Sam, please insert one of the jeweled butt plugs. She can wear that home. You can apply some lotion, and then get her dressed and drive her home."

I looked at Jackie, "Although I know it wasn't all your fault, I still resent you for going after my dad. But thank you for coming over, and thank you for cooperating during your punishment. You're probably a nice person, as Sam has said, and I hope you find a nice, *UN-married* man to keep you occupied."

Kelly had made a brief, but bizarre comment to Jackie, and walked out of the room. I undid the restraining straps, but asked Jackie to remain in place, as I smeared soothing lotion on her bottom, and then inserted the bullet-shaped plug.

We collected Jackie's undies, pants, and blouse from the exam room, and I helped her dress. I belatedly brought her a bottle of water from the fridge in the kitchen, then we went into the garage, to my car.

There was little said during the drive. Jackie subconsciously rubbed her bottom a few times, but mostly looked out the window.

When we got to her house, she turned to me, "Thank you, Sam, for being supportive today. Kelly seems like a nice girl, but I know she's upset. You can assure her that I won't be seeing her father any longer."

DOMME EXPERIENCE

CHAPTER 4: PINS-AND-NEEDLES

The patents had been filed, an agreement with the university in place, the corporation formed, and a prototype tested. In order to move forward, we needed capital – as in hard, cold, cash. As a startup, there were several potential sources of funds, and various kinds of investors – from angels to venture capitalists to investment bankers.

I knew that going to venture capitalists (VCs) may not be the optimum approach, as they would undoubtedly take most of the company, in return for a 'seed' investment. It would be far preferable if we could self-fund the company to the next stage, and then sell it. But just the patent work was going to cost tens of thousands of dollars.

Or, we could get a development contract from one of the large pharmaceutical companies, which would fund product development. They would then have rights to use the system to develop next-generation drugs. Or, possibly, we could partner with a company that wanted to develop and market the system itself, as a life-sciences tool.

I had worked with several private investors and VC firms, but they were interested in market-ready drugs. What Kelly had developed was a system that would enable better *design* of drugs. So, it would be of most value to the large biotech or pharma competitors.

We were ready to bring additional people on-board, to assist in the design and testing of the final system, but I didn't want to commit to those expenses, until I had at least approached the VCs – who would give us a good idea of how valuable the technology would be, even if they declined to invest, themselves.

As far as venture capital, there were firms worldwide. In the U.S., the biggest centers of medical and healthcare investment were in the Boston area, the Minneapolis area, and a few smaller locales – Austin, Seattle, Raleigh, San Diego – but by far the most active VC firms were in the San Francisco area; more specifically, 'Sand Hill Road' in the Stanford University town of Palo Alto.

I was once again the 'travel agent', as I began planning two trips: San Francisco in February – a few weeks from now, and Europe – for Kelly's dominatrix course – the first half of April. And, of course, I couldn't go to London and not hop over to Amsterdam to visit Henk and Zöe.

So we would be traveling four of the next six weeks. The plan was to hire a small staff, and work on KS Biotech's first product from May through August, hopefully completing a final prototype that we could demonstrate.

Kelly's advisor, Raj, had suggested that Kelly present a paper at an upcoming biotech meeting in September – in Barcelona. If we were far enough along with the technology, I could set up meetings with all the big pharma companies. This would give us a great opportunity to secure investment funding.

Sam was in a 'business' mode; I had never seen him so focused, before. He had done the market research and written a business plan for our company, KS Biotech, and was now intent on raising the money that we would need to develop our first product.

I had finally convinced him – since all the VC meetings were in the same area, and could be finished in a couple of days, and since I had never been to San Francisco – to take a week, so that we could see the area. Sam was still grumbling about taking so long, but was working on the itinerary, and we would discuss it tomorrow.

My focus was now split between our company and the domme class, which was only 9 weeks from now. Elena had decided to make it a 2-week course, and I would be allowed to spend Saturday afternoon to Sunday night with Sam during the intervening weekend.

I had no idea how many other 'students' there would be, or the split of genders. It didn't really matter: The course would require that we be comfortable topping and being topped by either (or any?) gender.

Now, I thought back on the experiences we'd had with my parents and with Jackie – the 'other woman'. Sam had been very concerned that we were meddling in their affairs (in a manner of speaking, as he would say), and had no 'right' to expect that my parents would submit to an embarrassing and painful punishment.

But they had agreed, and cooperated – although they'd *had* to 'cooperate' with most of their punishment, as they had been strapped down to the spanking bench. Still, my dad was more penitent than angry. Strength meant something to him, and I think he respected the hard spanking by his 'little girl'.

My mother had *not* cooperated, as I had hoped; it was *she* who should have been punishing my dad. I had also hoped that Jackie would be there, being punished along with my father. At that point, I had impulsively decided that my mother should 'share' the experience with my dad.

Sam had not expected to be called into action – either demonstrating the positions and implements, or actually spanking my mother. They had both cooperated well and done their parts.

I knew that Sam was embarrassed by letting my parents see him in an 'exposed' position. And, I knew that he was not comfortable having an 'intimate' experience with my mother. But he had submitted to my desires, and respected my views – even though he had strongly disagreed.

Yesterday, I had visited my parents, and we'd had a good conversation. My father was very apologetic, saying that he realized now that he wasn't interested in any other women, and just wanted to make my mother happy. And I really believed that he was sincere.

My mom seemed to act softer toward my dad, and I'm sure she appreciated both his honest admission of guilt, and agreement to be punished. When my dad had left to use the bathroom, my mother told me that he had been extremely embarrassed by what I'd done to him.

But she'd also told me that his respect in me had grown. My mother admitted that *her* respect had grown, also. She whined that although she may have had some culpability, and had been willing for me to spank her on her undies, having Sam punish her had been mortifying.

I smiled inwardly, as I remembered: Sam had lowered her underwear, spanked her, stuck things up her butt, and taken her to the bathroom. And, as a finale, Sam had bathed my mother. Although I had been the one to suggest it, the thought of my mother standing nude in front of Sam was mind-boggling.

As I thought about it, I guess I now respected my parents more, also. It seemed like they had both matured, over the past couple of weeks. There was certainly still hope for their relationship, provided they continued on the path that I saw when I visited them yesterday.

And, then there was Jackie. I didn't know what to make of her, or how to feel about her, now that I knew that not much had actually happened, and she may not have been the one to instigate the relationship. Now that I was calm, Jackie seemed like a nice woman; it really had been amazing that she'd agreed to come over to be punished. Obviously, she had been racked with guilt.

I also thought that she had wanted to please my dad. But his leaving her with us had surprised all of us, and Jackie realized that he would no longer be 'with' her. I had thought that was very rude of my dad, at the time, but now realized that he'd decided to change directions – for the better – and no longer wanted to be involved.

Overall, I still felt that something good might come of my parents' punishment. I didn't think it would affect the relationship that I – or Sam and I – had with them. I assumed that they would put it out of their minds, and revert to the prior relationships we'd all had. Except the relationship between the two of them – which was already improving, with communication channels opening.

Now, I had to get back to work on the figures and charts that I was preparing for the Business Plan and the presentation we would be making to the VCs ...

Having organized the San Francisco trip, and a rough itinerary for our Europe trip, I wanted to discuss the specifics with Kelly in a casual setting. The jacuzzi would have been nice but, after a week of unseasonably warm weather, we were having a cold snap. We would have to 'meet' in the sauna, instead. Maybe, once we were warmed up sufficiently, a quick dip in the jacuzzi might be possible.

It was Friday, and Kelly would be coming back from the lab early. I printed the itineraries, and some notes for our presentation to the VCs, and put them in plastic jackets – hopefully preventing them from becoming mush in the heat and humidity of the sauna.

Kelly returned, tired from the week, but excited that we would be spending time together – which seemed to have eluded us over the past week or two. After she dumped her briefcase on the pool room desk, and guzzled an entire Diet Coke, we went downstairs, undressed in the shower room, and took a nice long, loving shower together.

Then, I grabbed my water-resistant notes, and we stepped into the sauna. I thought that I might need a flashlight to read the notes, but after a few minutes, my eyes had adjusted to the dim red illumination.

I looked at Kelly: She sat cross-legged, a smile on her face, and dots of sweat popping out all over her body. Kelly was as trim and athletic as ever, even after the excessive holiday food we'd eaten. We were now running only sporadically, as it was just too cold for it to be comfortable.

Kelly's auburn hair looked nearly black in the faint light, but somehow her hazel eyes still sparkled. My left brain knew that it was reflecting the red bulb behind me, but my right brain saw the sparkling as a window into her conscious, the mysterious universe of thoughts and feelings she harbored.

Smiling at me, Kelly quipped, "Do you like what you see, Mister?" We chuckled, but Kelly suddenly frowned, "Sam, why were you so aloof with Jackie? You were going through the motions, but seemed totally disinterested."

It seemed obvious, to me, but Kelly wanted me to spell it out. "First of all, you know that I disagreed with your concept of punishing your parents, and Jackie ... and I didn't think it fair that you dragged me into it. This was *your* thing." Kelly just stared at me.

"Second, I'm not sure that Jackie deserved to be punished, or even treated harshly. And, even after you *knew* that she was only partially responsible – and that nothing really happened – you *still* insisted on punishing her." I was getting hot under the collar ... except that I had no collar.

"And speaking of deserving to be punished, I thought you were very hard on your mother who, after all, was the one 'hurt' by your father's playing around. And *again*, you dragged me into it. I'm not sure your mother and I will be able to look each other in the eyes, after what happened."

Kelly was shaking her head, forcefully enough for droplets of sweat to fly off her nose. But I wanted to finish my thoughts. "Finally, there was no way I was going to get turned on or excited by it, because it was a real punishment, not sexual or sensual."

I took a deep breath, "I saw Jackie not as the hussy you thought she was, but a nice person who was sad that this situation had arisen." Although, evidently, Dave's 'situation' hadn't arisen.

I thought a few moments, and Kelly wisely let me finish, "I think the most likely explanation for her actually coming over to be punished is that she's masochistic."

Kelly shrugged. Now, I let her organize *her* thoughts. We were both dripping with sweat, and would be able to stay in the sauna for only a couple more minutes.

Kelly opened her mouth to speak, then closed it and let her head drop. When she raised it again, she was crying, tears mixing with the sweat streaming down her cheeks. I got up and moved over to her, then pulled her to me. Kelly put her legs around my waist, and our slithery bodies glided over each other.

"What's wrong, Kelly? I *did* try to respect your plan, even though I didn't agree with it." Kelly was silent for a few moments, holding me tightly. Then, she broke down, her body shaking, as she gulped breaths, and let the tears flow.

I continued to hold her, as we stepped down the benches to the floor, and exited the sauna. I got the showers going, and we did a quick rinse; then, Kelly put her towel around herself and plopped down on one of the chaises. I turned off the water, and sat on the opposing chaise.

"I'm sorry, Sam." She was still crying, but I wasn't sure why. "Maybe you were right that we shouldn't have done any more than talk to my parents. And, you're probably right that Jackie is a nice woman. But, this whole thing has made me really upset." I nodded.

"This has been building since I saw my mom cry at Thanksgiving. I took my father's dalliances as a personal affront. How *could* he?"

Kelly gave me the hint of a smile, which was a good omen, and continued, "And my mom allowed this to happen. She knew about his other 'affairs'." I wondered how much 'sex' those had entailed.

"And Jackie didn't show up to be punished with my dad ... so I thought my mother should be shamed." Kelly looked into her lap, tears continuing to fall.

Finally, she looked up at me, "I'm just starting to calm down enough to see that I might have blown everything out of proportion ... and based my decisions on the perspective that you and I have shared."

She chuckled, "You once reminded me that we were not in the 'real' world, that our lifestyle and values would not be accepted by most other people. And, now, my parents have seen something that I never wanted to share with them." Well, they had certainly seen something that *I* never wanted to share with them!

Looking into my eyes, Kelly said, seriously, "Maybe it's *me*, who should be punished?"

I stepped over to her, and pulled her up, hugging her lovingly. "No, Kelly. You were doing what you thought best, and were trying to help your parents. And, from what you've told me, maybe they're responding."

Chuckling, I added, "But I'm not so sure how they're going to respond to us, in the future."

Kelly brightened, for the first time, "I don't think that will be a problem. They will bury it in their subconscious, and I doubt they'll ever say anything about it. And, I do think that my parents respect me – perhaps more than before – and that might bode well for announcing our engagement."

Kelly might have a point. So I offered, "Then, maybe we should go out over the weekend and I'll buy you an engagement ring?"

There was an instant smile on her face, but before she could answer, I asked, "But will I have to re-propose to you ... for the third time, now that we'll have a ring?"

Kelly took the towel out from between us and kissed me. "No, silly." Then, she batted her eyes at me, "But I'll take as many proposals as you want to make. And tell you 'Yes!' every time." We hugged, and went back into the sauna.

When we were settled, I asked, "So can we discuss our travel plans, now?" Kelly laughed and nodded.

"You were right." Kelly gave me a quizzical look. "The San Francisco trip will take a week ... if we want to do some touring, in addition to our VC meetings." Kelly nodded, and smiled.

"Usually, it's virtually impossible to get a meeting with one of the big VC firms – they have to know you already from some prior deals; and it really helps if you've taken a few companies public, and made the investors tons of money."

I wasn't going to explain to Kelly at this moment that most VCs have a portfolio of companies, and only a few of those companies 'make it'. Nine of ten may fail completely, while one is taken public or sold for hundreds of millions of dollars. It all averages out – usually in the VC's favor, if they're doing their job.

"Fortunately, between my personal contacts, and the pharma-oriented VC firms my company dealt with, I was able to get two meetings over two days ... the third week of February – less than a month from now."

I smiled, hoping the surprise would be a good one, "And, if we fly the prior Saturday, we can celebrate Valentine's Day in San Francisco." Kelly was ecstatic. She leaned over, took my face in her hands, and kissed me.

"We can discuss it later, but I thought we might drive up to Muir Woods, where some of the tallest redwood trees in the world are located, north of San Francisco, and have a romantic dinner in Sausalito. I've already made a couple of reservations, as everything is nearly booked already.

"That Monday is President's Day, so we can tour San Francisco without the weekday crowds. Then, our meetings in Palo Alto will be on Tuesday and Wednesday. We'll have time to see the Stanford Campus, one of those days."

I consulted my notes, "Then, I thought it would be nice to drive over the hill to the ocean, and spend a night in Half Moon Bay. And, on Friday, we could drive down to Santa Cruz, and fly out of San Jose on Saturday morning."

"Sam! That sounds terrific!"

I cautioned, "But, keep in mind that we'll have to be ready for the VC presentations, so will need to put in some working time on Sunday and Monday."

Kelly nodded, "Of course. I sure hope we can get the money we'll need to get going!"

I nodded, but warned, "Don't get your hopes too far up. We have to keep a positive attitude, but VCs often dabble with companies for months, and then don't invest in them. Even if they do invest, it could take up to six months for them to do their due diligence, to close the deal, and actually disburse the first 'tranche' of money."

It was appropriate, now, to also let Kelly know some of the disadvantages of going to a VC firm for financing. "The VCs are in this as a business, and they have done this many times, so they're experts at negotiating. Also, *they're* the ones who have the money. 'He who has the gold, makes the rules!' as they say."

I chuckled, but it wasn't really funny – especially when you were trying to raise money. "*And*, they are experts at drawing it out, until the company has nearly run out of cash, and is desperate. Then they toughen the deal."

Kelly shook her head; she had probably never thought about these things. Hopefully, we could develop other strategies for financing, or 'bootstrapping' ourselves, so VC funding wasn't our only option.

"We could potentially get a government grant – from the NSF or NIH, but that would take months of proposal writing and waiting ... mostly waiting. I was prepared to put in more 'founder's capital', but I'd hoped that our shares would be mainly 'sweat equity' – providing our ideas and skills for little or no pay, but getting a percentage of the company, in return."

It was getting hot again, and Kelly suggested that we get out for a while. But I had other ideas. "Kelly, do you think that if we stay in here a bit longer, get really hot, that we could go out to the jacuzzi for a while?"

Her mouth fell open, "But it's *freezing* outside, actually, below freezing. And there's piles of snow!" She was shaking her head, "And is the jacuzzi even warmed up? I don't think I'm ready for another 'cold pool' experience."

I laughed and nodded, "Yes, the jacuzzi is at a moderate temperature, probably 95 degrees, or so. I put the cover on it so not as much energy is lost. And, it may be below freezing outside, but I once swam in Lake Zurich with the water only a couple of degrees above freezing." I now remembered that I had told her that, when we visited the sauna in Zurich.

And, I was *hoping* that there were still a few piles of snow left, in the grass area. After all we'd done, there would be a new experience for Kelly.

We stayed in the sauna another four minutes, until we could take it no longer. Then, we wrapped our towels around us, and walked upstairs, and out to the patio. "Just be careful, in case the deck is icy. I don't want you to have to bring crutches on the trip."

I pulled the cover off the jacuzzi, and we got in. It felt OK, but the air really was cold. At least, it wasn't windy. I hopped out, and went to the wall where the heater control was, and turned up the temperature to 102. "It might take a while to get there, but we could come out a second time."

Actually, the spa was perfect: A very mild and comfortable temperature now, and heating up, as we cooled down in the outside air. The sky was crystal blue, and most of the backyard was white, the dark trunks and branches of the barren trees a stark contrast.

"So, are you happy with the San Francisco itinerary I've put together, so far?"

Kelly smiled, "Yes, it sounds great. But, what do you mean by 'so far'?"

I laughed, "Well, I was thinking about just 'one more thing' ..." I saw Kelly mutter 'Oh no!' under her breath. She knew me pretty well, by now.

"Yes. I thought we might visit one of the iconic sex clubs of San Francisco." Kelly shook her head slowly, but was smiling.

I would need to do more research, before deciding on this; but we had a couple of weeks ...

Sam was in an interesting mood; he almost seemed to be laughing, but I didn't know what the joke was. The San Francisco trip sounded wonderful, and I'd had no doubt that Sam would come up with something like the sex club.

The backyard was beautiful, the sky incredibly blue, and the snow glistening. Of course, the beauty today was totally different than in the spring and summer, when the trees and grass were green, and the flowers blooming. The snow reminded me of our ski experience in Europe.

"Sam, would there be any possibility of us skiing in northern California? Maybe at one of the Tahoe resorts?" I could remember seeing posters of people schussing down the slopes with the blue lake in the background.

Sam looked up at the sky, then scratched his chin. "That's a really good idea ... but we just don't have time. I guess we could skip the Half Moon Bay and Santa Cruz excursions." Then, he laughed, "And, if we'd had more time, I would have loved to show you Monterrey and Carmel ... and San Simeon and Big Sur."

Just as with Europe – and everywhere else in the world – there were too many great places to visit, and never enough time.

I wondered again whether I would be 'stuck' in my career for the next decade or more, then 'stuck' with a family for another decade or two. I chuckled, as I pictured myself *finally* able to ski, as a shriveled-up old grandma. I hoped that wouldn't be my future.

Sam was still thinking, as he lay back, his head against the deck, looking out 'there', somewhere, his eyes glazed over. "It's also going to be President's week, and the ski resorts will be packed. I'm not that excited about lift lines."

The jacuzzi was getting hot, now, and I stood with my back to the wall, over which water flowed into the rock waterfall, and down to the pool. The top half of my body was steaming!

Sam jumped up and smiled broadly at me; now, I *knew* that he'd planned something. "Kelly, would you submit to me?" He held my hips, leaned forward, and kissed my nose, then leaned back again, and looked into my eyes. There was energy and passion in Sam's eyes.

I sighed, not having the slightest idea what Sam wanted to do, but trusting him implicitly. He had trusted me, in my perhaps misguided dealings with my parents, even though I knew he hadn't agreed with my plan.

As I thought about it again, it was astounding that I'd made him get into the chair position in front of my parents, and take some rectal insertions and strokes of some harsh implements. And he had complied, more-or-less willingly.

Spanking my father had not 'excited' me, but seeing Sam's compliance – especially thinking about it now – was a turn-on. My mind now swung to 'maybe we should announce our engagement, soon'; but whether it stayed on that wavelength might depend on what Sam and I were going to do in the next few minutes.

Spreading my feet, and putting my hands on my head, I looked into Sam's eyes, and said, simply, "Yes, Sam. I will submit to you."

We had played together long enough for me to know that those words would start the cogs turning for another adventure; something that I might or might not like, but that I could usually count on to be interesting.

Sam smiled, then hugged me and gave me a big kiss. Before I knew what was happening, he took my hand, and said, mock-sternly, "Come with me!"

We stepped out of the jacuzzi, and held hands as we walked along with winding path of the deck; it *was* frozen. We passed the bench, now covered in snow, and stepped gingerly through the few inches of snow on what I knew was the lawn.

There was a small snow bank built up against the boulders. These were the boulders that had been the scene of a photo shoot with Fiona and I; where Julie and Linda had competed in the spanking contest; and where all of us – including Sam – had squirted milk out our rears.

We stopped, and Sam gave me a crooked smile, "At least, I'm going to do this *with* you; no wimping out, or being a 'baby', this time!" With that, he took a few steps, and let himself fall into one of the snow banks.

Nearly buried in snow, Sam bellowed, and then hopped up, shaking the snow off himself. He was still *covered* in snow. Then, he pointed. I guess it was my turn.

I followed his example, and let myself fall into another mound of snow, which piled up against the next boulder. It was *freezing*!

I hopped up about as fast as Sam had, and stepped to him. There was snow on my head, on my shoulders, and on the tip of my nose. And I felt a coldness 'down there', where some snow must have insinuated its way between my legs. Sam and I held each other and hugged.

This experience couldn't have been more different than hugging while sweated-up in the sauna. It was cold, but it hadn't felt that bad. Not much of a submission challenge.

Sam pulled away from me, and took me by the hand again, as we walked cautiously back to the jacuzzi. It was really steaming, now. Sam turned to me, and said "Pins and needles!" Then, we jumped into the jacuzzi together.

For a moment, the warm water felt great, starting to thaw us. But the next moment ... "AIYEEEEE!!" As Sam had said, there was a 'pins and needles' feeling all over my body. It really *hurt*!

Sam belly-laughed, "Yes, it feels like a thousand pins sticking us – more intense than anything we've done with hypodermic needles."

Sam slid his hands over his arms; we were both feeling the same thing. "Just one more new 'experience' for us to have together." Sam continued to laugh, as the pins-and-needles feeling gradually subsided.

We decided to go back inside, and Sam turned off and covered the jacuzzi. After a quick rinse-off under the rain shower, we re-entered the sauna.

"So, shall we discuss the Europe trip?" Sam raised his eyebrows at me, and I raised them back at him. He held up some plastic-covered sheets, evidently his notes.

"You said that the domme class was the first two weeks of April? Do you know the exact dates?"

I nodded, having just gotten a follow-up e-mail from Elena, "Yes. It starts on April 1, and the 'graduation' – which you may attend, is on April 15. Then, I spend most of the next day with my 'benefactor'."

Sam squinted at me, "April 1 is a Friday. It's strange they would start the course then."

Elena had explained, "Actually, it starts at 2PM on Friday, as some of the 'students' probably have full-time jobs, and they'll only have to take off a half-day."

Chuckling, and shaking his head, Sam, said, "Yeah, and another *two weeks*! That would be a long vacation for any employee."

Now, I was laughing, "I don't think it's going to be much of a 'vacation'." Elena had said there would be a small group, but I had no specifics on the other students. But she *was* specific on why the course would be starting on Friday.

I explained to Sam, "The first 24 hours is supposed to be a pretty 'tough' indoctrination. Elena said we would all have the weekend off – from Saturday afternoon through Sunday afternoon – and then report back on Sunday evening by 9PM."

Sam was nodding, but he didn't understand, yet. "And, we'll be 'off' from Saturday afternoon through Sunday evening the following weekend."

I pulled the corner of my towel up and wiped the sweat from my face, then gave Sam a serious look. "The reason we have a break after the first 24 hours ... is so that we can decide whether we want to continue, to take the entire course."

Sam gave me a surprised expression, and I explained, "Elena says that there are always one or two people who decide they can't handle it." I smiled seductively at Sam, and added, "And she also said that there are usually one or two people who drop out, after they've started the course."

"It sounds pretty serious. Are you *sure* that you want to put yourself through that?"

Nice try, Sam. You *know* that I'm a strong woman. And, you *know* that I will not only go through with it, but not quit, regardless of how tough it is.

I stood and grabbed my towel, then stepped down to the tiled floor of the sauna. Before I pulled open the door, I turned back to Sam, and replied, "I'm sure."

We rinsed under the rain shower, put our towels around our waists, and sat on the chaises. As Sam ran to the playroom bar to get us each a Diet Coke, I told myself, 'Yes, I am sure'.

Sam returned, and we drank our sodas, then Sam let out a loud burp. "As with our Toronto trip, I think we're going to have to reverse the itinerary that I'd been imagining. Instead of going to Amsterdam first, you should take the course first." Sam took another slug of his drink.

"We could leave around the 30th of March, getting you to the course after one acclimatization day in London. Then, we could spend a day or two in London after your course, and fly to Amsterdam. If we stay there a week, we'll be able to celebrate 'Koningsdag' with Henk and Zöe. Then, we could fly back about April 30. So it would be a month trip."

That sounded like a long time to be away from home, and from our company. "What is 'Cone-ings-dock'? Maybe you should visit Amsterdam, while I'm with Elena?"

His head shaking, Sam said, "I don't want to leave you in London." Then, he gave me a silly look, and added, "You might be asked to bring a sub in for one of your lessons." Was he volunteering? If so, that was only his fantasy.

"No, Sam. We're going to be topping each other. Part of the course is 'sub training'. So you're free to go anywhere or do anything you want, while I'm in class." It still sounded funny.

Sam shrugged, "I'm hoping to get appointments with a couple of pharma or biotech companies that are based in London. So I'll be working." I nodded, glad that at least one of us would be 'working'.

Sam continued, "And Koningsdag, or 'King's Day' is a big celebration in The Netherlands. It was called 'Queen's

Day', while Beatrix was Queen, until she stepped-down in 2013 and was succeeded by her son, Willem-Alexander. It used to be celebrated on her mother's birthday, April 30, but now it's on the King's birthday, April 27."

Once again, Sam was a fount of knowledge. "It's also called 'Orange Day', in honor of the Dutch royal House of Orange-Nassau. So everyone wears orange. It's a national holiday, and the King makes surprise visits to different towns and villages. There's also a country-wide flea market."

I smiled, "Sounds like fun! And I'm sure we can count on Henk and Zöe to make it even more fun." Sam was nodding. I could only imagine!

We went back into the sauna, both Sam and I thinking about our upcoming travels. I still hoped that we could do a little Sierra skiing before we left for Europe.

DOMME EXPERIENCE

CHAPTER 5: FRISCO FUN(DS)

We flew to San Francisco on Friday and checked into a small boutique hotel. It had nicely-renovated rooms that included a balcony overlooking the bay, with the Golden Gate to our left, and Alcatraz directly in front of us.

The sky was clear, and there were whitecaps on the water. The handful of sailboats that we could see were heeled over, and a large ship was moving slowly Eastward, probably heading for the container facility in Oakland.

Kelly stepped out onto the patio, "Wow! What a beautiful view!" It was. I put my arms around Kelly and hugged her.

Not only was the San Francisco Bay view picturesque, Kelly was a sight, too: She wore her faux-fox collar ski jacket, that we'd bought in Koblenz, and her hair fell to her waist, the tips and a few strands from her head blowing in the wind.

Blowin' in the Wind: Where the answer is, according to Bob Dylan. I had gone down many roads, some of them small, and relatively unexplored. Now, I was traveling a road with Kelly; we were finding our way together.

Peter, Paul, and Mary ... which led me to '*Puff the Magic Dragon*', and the 'dragon tail' surrounding Hanalei Bay, on the north shore of Kauai; where I'd taken Kelly and her friends, on an epic trip.

What a trip! I wasn't even stoned, but my mind was drifting – perhaps with the wind. As I smiled into Kelly's beautiful face, her hair blowing across it, now, I keyed in again on the faux fur collar. I wondered whether even *faux* fur was inappropriate in this liberal city.

While we weren't going to take advantage of the drug scene, I *was* curious about the BDSM community. So I had made a reservation at one of San Francisco's well-known sex clubs, for our Friday-night entertainment.

We left the hotel in the late afternoon, already dusk and a bit chilly, but perfect for some walking. Kelly and I walked down the hill, passing a multitude of small restaurants, from Japanese, Chinese, and Thai, to Middle Eastern, to seafood restaurants and steakhouses. And that was just on the few blocks we had walked, already!

Kelly wasn't as excited as I was to stop and read every menu, pulling me along, as we walked arm in arm. She also wasn't excited about my suggestion of an Irish pub, so we finally decided on a *tapas* restaurant.

We enjoyed the variety of dishes, and I was happy we had come early enough to avoid the Flamenco dancers. It might have been a fun evening at the restaurant, but we already had a 'fun' evening planned. Actually, it was a bit of an unknown, potentially ranging from watching others do their thing, to participating ourselves.

As I was thinking this, Kelly took a sip of her Rioja wine, and asked, "So what kind of place are we visiting, tonight?" She raised her eyebrows, and smiled, "Do you think it will be like the club we went to in Amsterdam?"

We were both wearing black – black jeans, and black sweaters, with my black 'bomber' jacket, and Kelly's dark gray ski jacket with the faux silver fox fur trim. From what I could tell on their website, the place wasn't as organized as the Amsterdam club, with singles being allowed, and no set time for everyone to arrive.

"It doesn't sound like it, although they did advertise that they have special 'rooms' for various activities, like they had in Amsterdam. And the calendar shows two 'events' tonight: Suspension and Trans. I guess the first is like *shibari*, where they tie the person up and suspend them from a frame or the ceiling."

I looked at Kelly, looking radiant – again – sitting in this small Spanish bistro in San Francisco, candles flickering, and her eyes sparkling.

"And, I assume that the second will be like the club that Henk took us to, with cross-dressers and transgender people. Maybe they'll be singing or performing?" I really didn't know what to expect.

After dinner, we walked around, the place bustling, as was every big city ... but San Francisco seemed especially 'alive'. We walked through part of Chinatown, and walked into a few of the shops. I couldn't tell whether some of this stuff was real or just tourist junk.

I explained to Kelly, "San Francisco Chinatown is reputed to be the largest Chinese community outside Asia," I laughed, "but I'll bet that Vancouver has nearly as many Chinese, not to mention New York and Los Angeles.

"Interestingly, the Asian population in San Francisco continues to grow; I think it's nearly 50%, now, and close to a quarter of all the people in the Bay Area." I thought of how many Chinese, Japanese, Korean, Vietnamese and Thai researchers I had worked with over the past two decades.

We made our way to the club, and paid the stiff 'membership' fee. I wondered whether I would be 'stiff' tonight – in public, for the first time.

A young woman – also wearing all black, including a short leather dress, and black lipstick with a small red 'droplet' at a corner of her mouth – took us on a brief tour, and explained the rules. Mainly, no harassing or pressuring anyone, and no talking in the dungeon area.

There was a small bar on the main level, a lounge with comfortable-looking couches, and two changing rooms. The place seemed OK. There were a fair number of people here, already, and quite a few were watching the scene below.

Peering over a railing to the floor below, we saw part of the dungeon; one guy was flogging three women who's hands were tied, and chained above them. The women were wearing long pants with nothing on top, and being flogged on their backs.

We walked downstairs, and entered one of the smaller rooms. A handful of people were sitting on a mat, watching an older woman (probably my age) humiliating a younger man.

He was on his hands and knees, licking her boots, until she yelled, and he stood at attention; then she proceeded to repeatedly slap him across the face. Kelly looked up at me with a worried expression.

Before I could whisper anything to her, the scene was over, and people were applauding. Then, another younger man (perhaps in his mid-thirties) stepped up and bowed to the mistress. He stood 'at ease', his legs apart, and hands behind his back. Suddenly, the woman kneed him in the groin, and he doubled-over in pain.

The man stood up again, and the mistress kicked him in the balls again. He was wearing a Speedo-type bathing suit or underwear, and had tears running down his cheeks as he stood the third time. I shook my head, and walked out of the room, Kelly following closely behind.

I turned to her, "Kelly ... *PLEASE* don't ever do that to me. I know you're going to be trained, and will probably want to do some extreme things to me ... but that just doesn't look fun, at all. It's painful just to think about it."

Kelly laughed, and took my hand, as we walked around the perimeter, peeking into a few of the rooms.

There wasn't much activity, but it was still early. The crowd looked normal, although black was the predominate clothing color, and there was a lot of leather. There were probably three times as many males as females, and the women who were there were ordinary-looking.

Quite a few of the women had strange hair styles or colors, and more than usual body jewelry and tatts, but probably nothing that was unusual in San Francisco. And, of course, most were from their late twenties to late thirties, with only a few 'older' women and men.

A gong sounded, and people began taking seats on mats surrounding the central open area. As we were already circling the area, we got 'ringside' seats, although we weren't sure what the performance would be.

The space was filling rapidly, and when I looked up, I saw that the railing was packed with people. I also noticed a couple of guys un-cleating ropes that dropped from pulleys on the ceiling down to the floor in front of us.

A young man came out, and the crowd silenced. "My name is 'Z'. My partners and I are with one of the largest piercing and tattoo parlors in the city, and we're going to demonstrate something you may not have seen before – suspension. In particular, we're going to show you – and let some of you try – 'flesh hook suspension'."

Kelly glanced up at me, and I shrugged. I had seen a few pictures on the Internet, but wasn't sure what to expect. The young guy had on very tight black leather pants, and a leather vest over his bare chest. He had long, jet black hair, and a scraggly growth of facial hair.

Walking around the small center area, he continued his schpiel, "What we're doing tonight is considered by some people to be pretty extreme – 'edgy'. And, it could be dangerous, if not done safely. We'll demonstrate suspension from hooks placed through the skin, and also from large-gauge rings that are already in place."

He took off his vest and turned around slowly, letting everyone see his back. There were gasps and, when he turned his back to us, we could see four huge rings through the skin of his upper back. "Since I'm kind-of into this, I have four 6-gauge rings; those will hold my entire body weight."

He turned to face us, and smiled, "It's a very intense experience ... I would say mind-blowing, the first time." He signaled a partner who came out with two short pieces of rope, an S-hook on each end. The hooks went through the rings, and the connecting ropes placed over hooks on the ropes coming down from the ceiling.

As he pulled slowly, the Z was lifted, finally coming completely off his feet, and hanging in the air. He was pulled higher, his feet probably six feet off the ground. Then, the assistant pulled his feet, and let go, the 'suspendee' swinging back-and-forth across the room.

What was most amazing to me, was that he actually had a smile on his face! I realized that I was breathing heavily, and beginning to sweat. Suddenly, it had gotten a lot warmer in here.

It was incredible: The guy was swinging from those rings in his back, and he was now talking to us. "This is called a 'suicide' suspension. I'm hanging by four rings, but most people have six hooks put through their skin."

Then, he actually *laughed*, "But this is not nearly as difficult as the 'Oh-Kee-Pah' suspension, which is also a vertical suspension, but with only two hooks ... in the chest."

I glanced at Sam, and he was shaking his head. I thought I could see beads of sweat on his forehead. I reached over and held his hand. He was still shaking his head, and hadn't taken his eyes off the guy now swinging in a circular pattern, his feet nearly touching the people sitting in the front row.

He was gradually lowered, and there was applause, and a lot of whispering. Next, a cart was rolled out, with a young lady in a bikini sitting on it. Much of her body was covered by colorful tattoos. She waved to the audience, and we waved back. Then, she lay face-down, and the two guys began putting hooks through her skin.

"This is Lucy's first time, and she'll be trying a 'Superman' suspension. We'll use about a dozen hooks, only 12-gauge each. The number and size of hooks is based on the weight of the person, and their level of pain tolerance." As he said this, Lucy whimpered as a hook pierced her upper back.

The two guys worked quickly, placing the hooks in Lucy's upper back, hips, and legs. After that first whimper, she was amazingly quiet. It was eye-opening to see the huge hooks put through the skin – something far, far more extreme than the tiny hypodermic needles Sam liked to stick in people's butts.

And the hooks would have to carry the entire weight of the person. Even as small as Lucy was, each hook would probably have ten pounds of force pulling on it. I shivered.

Sam leaned over and whispered, "The rings in that guy are ten times bigger than the 25-gauge needles we play with; and the hooks in her are five times bigger." He looked at me, "Those *have* to hurt!" I was sure they did.

Six different ropes were used to connect the hooks to four ropes coming down from pulleys on the ceiling.

Slowly, Lucy was levitated. When she was a couple of feet above the cart, it was rolled out of the way.

There was some groaning, but after Lucy quieted, the two guys pulled her aside, and let go – letting her swing across the room in a graceful arc. It was beautiful.

We heard some gasping from Lucy, but then she was quiet again ... as was the entire place – only a few moans coming out of one of the peripheral rooms, and some spanking sounds coming out of another.

As she swung, Z explained, "There are many other suspension positions – the Coma, Lotus, Crucifixion – and they all offer the rush of adrenaline and endorphins, and a feeling of empowerment. Lucy is getting used to the pain ... *Aren't you, Lucy?*"

As Z pulled her back and let her swing again, Lucy hesitantly said, "I think so ..."

Lucy was still swinging, not making a sound. Z looked around at all of us, "Flesh hook suspension is the ultimate experience of conquering fear and pain." He chuckled, "So who would like to try it?"

Sam glanced at me, as I had expected, and I smiled sweetly at him, "I'll try it, if you will."

That was all it took. Sam shook his head, and said, "Can we go upstairs, and get a drink, now?" I laughed, as I stood and offered my hand to Sam. He took it and let me help pull him up, still shaking his head and looking a little peaked. Lucy was now pushing off of the walls, swinging entirely across the room.

When we were in the lounge upstairs, and Sam had his beer, I said, "It's just like what happened with Mistress Elena in London." Sam cocked his head, and I explained, "Exactly your concept – conquering fear and pain – but at an increased level of intensity." I smiled at Sam, "I thought you might really get turned on by it."

Sam raised the bottle and took a swig of beer, then shook his head, "It's too real. Too much pain. Too extreme."

Now, I shook my head. Sam was full of contradictions. He wanted us to experience new things, and was quick to challenge someone to get a needle insertion or small shot ... but we'd all had those experiences. Here was something truly different, something that we probably wouldn't try, without expert instruction.

I could certainly expect Sam to be nervous and fearful of having the experience himself. But he'd had a difficult time even watching Lucy swing, suspended by a dozen large hooks through her skin. Sam wasn't sadistic; as we had learned long ago, he didn't want to really hurt anyone.

Empathy. That's what it was: Sam had too much empathy for other people to inflict something so extreme on them. He didn't want to see people in pain, just enough discomfort to make it challenging for an average person in a home setting. Sam was not cut-out to be a dom.

While Sam finished his beer, I visited the ladies room, which was connected to a small locker room. It was similar to the set-up in Europe, but didn't seem very clean; everything felt a little seedy. This wasn't a place where I would feel comfortable having sex at all, let alone in public.

This triggered the image of Sam and I having sex on those boulders at the edge of the Niagra River, with tourists walking on the trail behind us. That was a nice memory. But having sex in front of a bunch of horny guys wasn't at all enticing. Maybe Julie would appreciate the wildness and outrageousness of the experience ...

Sam seemed to have calmed down – he wasn't sweating any longer. We heard some yelps, and walked to the railing in time to see hooks being placed in a woman's back and chest, as she stood on a small step-stool. Her blouse was off, and she was not wearing a bra, despite being rather large on top. Sam was shaking his head again.

One of the club hosts was circulating through the crowd, saying that the 'Trans' discussion would be starting soon, in an upstairs room.

We went to the room, and took a seat on one of the plush couches. There were three armchairs facing the couches, above which was a large flag with five stripes – the outer ones light blue, the next ones light pink, and the center one white.

The room was about half-filled when two women and a man entered, all wearing robes, and sat on the chairs. The woman on the far left introduced herself, "Hi, everyone. I'm Patty ... formerly 'Patrick' ... and I'm a *trans* woman." She was beautiful, and even had a high-pitched, woman's voice.

"We're going to talk about transgender issues and gender reassignment surgery tonight. But to clear up one thing first – I'm a real woman; and Don," pointing to the guy on the other side, "is a real man." She chuckled, "And Bobby, next to me, is currently in-between."

It was unbelievable: Patty *was* a real woman – obviously, not merely a cross-dresser, like Henk.

Patty looked around the room, "First, let's define some terms. 'Transgender' means a mismatch between one's gender identity and their assigned sex." There was already a guy raising his hand. Patty put a finger up as she answered his presumed question, "'Assigned sex' is the gender that you were given by the doctor when you were born, based on your apparent reproductive organs."

Laughing, Patty said, "I wasn't going to go into this ... but some people are born with ambiguous sex organs – either the clitoris is overly large for a female, or the penis is very small, hidden, or non-existent for a male. I don't know how many of those people have a gender identity issue. I think most of us had normal genitals, but we just didn't 'feel' like that gender.

"But the term 'transgender' embodies many different situations, including trans men, trans women, bi-gender, pan-gender, a-gender, or genderqueer. And these are contrasted with *cis*-gender, which is what I assume most of you guys are – where your image of yourself matches your biological anatomy."

People were looking around at each other, probably none of us realizing that the transgender topic was so complex. Patty explained, "Just to be clear, I'm a trans woman, and Bobby is a trans man."

She added, "And two more important things to remember: Transgender doesn't necessarily mean 'trans-sexual', who are people who have had gender reassignment. Most transgender people probably change esthetic things – like clothes and makeup – and may use hormone replacement therapy, 'HRT', to change their body hair, breasts, and voice."

Patty chuckled, "But that's a long way from being a transsexual. The three of us have undergone various procedures through our transition, and Bobby," pointing to the guy next to her, "is midway through the process."

Now she became serious. "My own journey has been pretty long. I knew that I wasn't a male by the time I was in grade school. But, of course, I couldn't do anything about it until I was out of college. All that time, I had what they call 'dysphoria' – a feeling that I was in the wrong body."

Patty swallowed, and looked down, then back up at everyone. "You have to realize that transgender people were considered mentally ill until recently – just in the last few years. Now, there's a worldwide association for transgender health, 'WPATH', that regulates how gender reassignment is done.

"First, you have to get a diagnosis from a mental health professional, and then go through psychoanalysis." There were a few gasps in the audience, and some whispering. Patty nodded, "For me, it took six months."

She cleared her throat and drank some water from a bottle sitting on the end table next to her. "The second phase is called 'real life experience', or 'RLE'. This is where the person lives on a full-time basis as the opposite gender – adopting the clothing, perhaps getting rid of body hair (trans women), and beginning the name-changing process. This phase can take another six months.

"In the third phase, you usually begin hormone therapy. Trans women take anti-androgens, plus estrogen and progesterone; and trans men take testosterone. It can take two years or more for HRT to produce the effect you're seeking." She looked at the guy next to her, "I think Bobby is about at that stage." He nodded.

Taking a large breath, Patty continued, "And *finally*, if you've gone through at least two years of hormone therapy and have doctor's letters, you can consider the surgical options." She looked around at us, and smiled, "And there are a lot of options – both 'therapeutic' and esthetic."

Laughing her beautiful feminine laugh again, Patty said, "I'll show you guys in a few minutes ... but I've gone 'all the way'." She paused, allowing all of us to try to imagine what that meant.

"After HRT, I had breast augmentation. Then, the serious stuff: Orchiectomy (removal of the testicles), penile inversion vaginoplasty (creating a vagina from a penis), clitoroplasty (creating a clit from the glans), and labiaplasty (creation of labia from scrotal skin)." She looked around at everyone and smiled. Some people looked faint, but nobody left.

"Those were done in several stages, over about a year. Then, I began with the esthetic procedures. There was a tracheal shave and voice modification, chin reduction, rhinoplasty, lip augmentation, contouring around my eyes, forehead lift, hairline lowering, and facial feminization. I also got a mini-liposuction procedure to get rid of Patrick's belly fat."

Sam glanced at me and shook his head. I leaned over to him, and he whispered, "That's a lot of surgeries. And they're all risky."

He smiled, "And you can be assured that I will *NEVER* change my body to a woman's." I certainly hoped that was true … although I could probably love Sam as a woman, too. I chuckled, thinking that he could become 'Samantha'.

Patty asked, "Does anybody want to see how it all came out?" There were murmurs, clapping, and a few cheers. Patty stood, opened the robe, pulled the shoulders down, and let it fall to the floor. Now, there were gasps, and a lot of 'Oooh's' and 'Aaah's'. Then, spontaneously, there was a thunderous round of applause.

Patty did some modeling turns, even spreading her legs and bending over, so we could get the rear view. It was truly amazing. She invited people to come up for a closer look, and one guy asked if he could feel her breasts. Despite the relatively classy behavior of most people here, there were still a few creeps.

After everyone had seen what they wanted to, Patty put on her robe, and sat down. Then, she pointed to Bobby, who smiled and nodded.

"As Patty said, I'm part-way through the transition. But I'm still not sure how far I'm going to go. I've done nearly two years of hormone therapy … but you're never 'finished'; and those drugs have some serious side-effects, like heart disease. The hormones reduced my body hair, then I had laser hair removal on my face, arms, chest, back, and legs."

Sam leaned over, "That's supposed to feel like a rubber band snapping you, every time the laser fires. Getting it over that much area must have taken a long time, and must have been painful." Sam was finding out that a lot of people endured pain far more intense than his little games with spanking, needles and shots.

Bobby stood, and removed his robe. At first, it was fairly shocking – as most of us hadn't imagined what we would see. What we *did* see was a trim, hairless body, with good-size breasts ... and a rather large penis. Bobby danced around, his boobs wobbling, and dick swinging.

As Patty had done, Bobby invited people to take a closer look. This time, nobody asked to touch her breasts.

The last person, a trans man, introduced himself. "Hi everybody. My name's Don – formerly Donna – and I'm nearly done transitioning my body to match my male identity." He glanced at Patty, "I haven't done as much as Patty. After HRT, I started with a mastectomy. Then I had to make some decisions about my sex organs."

I wondered what he meant, but soon found out. "I decided to leave my uterus and ovaries in place. You may have seen the news articles about the trans guy who got artificially inseminated and had a baby; he's now pregnant for the second time. I don't know if I would do that, but wanted to keep my options open."

He smiled proudly, "However, I finally did get a phalloplasty – creation of a penis and testicles, both of which use implants. I've had good luck so far, but there are still problems with a female-to-male transition." He rose and let his robe fall. There were more gasps.

Don had a definite male physique – large muscles in his upper arms, a hairy chest, and thick thighs. He was slightly balding, but had a scraggly beard. From where we sat, he certainly looked like a man; a well-endowed one.

After doing a few turns in a mock-feminine style, Don chuckled, "Would anybody like to see me get an erection?" At any other time and place, that would have been a ridiculous question ... but here in the sex club, after an hour learning about transgender people, it seemed the natural thing to do. A demonstration of his 'technology'.

"If I want to have sex, I just reach under here," putting his hand under his balls, "and pump." He squeezed between his balls, and with half a dozen pumps, his penis had risen into an erection. It looked almost normal, but I could see that he was 'straighter' than most men, when they were fully turned-on.

Don began laughing, until he was choking, then calmed, "And now, Patty and I are going to demonstrate intercourse between a trans woman and trans man." The crowd started to go wild, until Patty gave Don a sharp look.

"Sorry folks, Don's just joking. That's not going to happen tonight." There were a few groans in the audience, and Don dropped his head. Then, under her breath – but loud enough for all of us to hear – Patty added, "I have a headache, anyway."

Don stepped over to Patty and hugged her. Then, everyone was up, and talking with our new trans friends, and with each other.

I had offered to 'play' with Kelly at the sex club, but she wasn't interested. We walked back up the hill to our hotel, the nighttime view spectacular with the lights of the

Golden Gate crossing the bay to our left, and ships still moving slowly through the black water.

As we undressed, I told Kelly, "You know, for having gone to a sex club, I never even started to get turned on. In fact, I found both of the demonstrations a little scary." I shivered, thinking about the 'meat hooks' put through the backs of the people being suspended.

Kelly chuckled, "Me, neither." She dropped the satin nightgown over her head, then pulled her hair out and shook it. Smiling at me, she exclaimed, "But we sure did *learn* a few things, tonight." I had to agree, although those things were nothing that I would ever try.

On Saturday morning, we slept late, and took our time satisfying each other's needs; slowly, tenderly, lovingly. This was our Valentine's Day weekend – not that we supported commercial holidays (we had agreed to not even give each other a card). But we still wanted to make it romantic – especially, in this romantic city.

After we had dressed for the chilly weather – both of us donning long silk ski underwear before putting on jeans, shirts, and sweaters – we sat in the chairs facing the small round coffee table, the drapes open, and expansive windows opening onto the San Francisco Bay view.

"Kelly, I know we're here mainly on business, but I thought we could have a special Valentine's weekend." Kelly raised her brows at me, as I continued, "Passing those Chinese restaurants last night gave me the idea for having a 'Dim Sum' brunch, today."

She smiled, "Those are those little balls, filled with stuff?" I wasn't so sure of her culinary linguistic abilities.

Nodding, I explained, "Yes – they are the Cantonese steamed buns, dumplings, and noodle rolls that are usually served from rolling carts in Chinese restaurants. I think they were originally eaten for breakfast, but in American

Chinese restaurants, they have been a favorite for family brunch or lunch on Sundays and, more recently, on Saturdays, as well.

"Anyway, if that's OK with you, it might be fun to try the different 'stuff' they are stuffed with." Kelly nodded, her face radiant and teeth sparkling, while her eyes were bright, and her hair iridescent, in the light streaming from the windows.

It was my turn to smile, "And, just one more thing ..." Kelly cocked her head, then smiled, and started shaking it slowly, questioning in her eyes.

"We've talked about this lately, but haven't done anything about it: I would like to buy you an engagement ring, today. I've already called one of the top jewelry stores in the city and made an appointment to speak with them."

Kelly's smile grew, and she jumped up and over to me, her arms around my neck, as we kissed fervently. I pulled back enough to add, "I assume we're ready to tell your parents, now? And everyone else." Kelly nodded, and we continued kissing.

We walked down the hill, to the Dim Sum restaurant that I'd seen, climbed the stairs, and were seated in a huge dining room. The walls were bright red, with black trim, and decorative gold accents; there were 'lantern' lights hanging from the ceiling. It seemed too formal for the way we were dressed, but – except for a few Chinese families – most people were dressed just as casually.

We took our time, and sampled a variety of dishes, including some with pork, beef, prawns, chicken, and vegetables. I thought I had heard the waiter describe one as 'chicken feet'. We were stuffed, but I convinced Kelly to split a couple of dessert dim sum, including the egg tart and the mango pudding.

Window-shopping along the way, we walked to the jewelry store, but were early for our 1PM appointment. We were near Union Square, so walked around the area. Seeing the Apple Store, Kelly glanced at me, but I shook my head and, instead, we walked into the square and sat on one of the only available benches.

"I love you, Kelly." I leaned over and kissed her on the nose. She moved to kiss more seriously, but I sat back, and said, "I have some ideas for your engagement ring ... but if you have anything specific in mind, please tell me."

Kelly shook her head, "I really haven't thought about it, Sam." She smiled, "I assumed there would be a diamond. And, I guess I've pictured a gold band; my mother has platinum, but that seems so ancient."

I nodded, "That's great – it fits with some of my ideas. For example, I looked up your birthstone and it's 'peridot'." Kelly nodded, obviously knowing this, already.

"It's supposed to have magical properties that bring power, influence, and a great year. Hopefully, we'll be married in a year, and the next twelve months will be crucial to getting the business going." Kelly smiled, and I added, "Although I know we don't need magic – you're magical enough, by yourself."

Now, Kelly scooted next to me, and gave me a slobbery kiss, oblivious of all the people walking by us through the square. I didn't care, either; we were in love.

Continuing to explain my ideas about the ring, I said, "I pictured a large diamond flanked by peridot stones. But I thought we could leave the design to the jewelry store. Assuming we don't find one already made." It was time for our appointment, so we headed for the store.

Amazingly, once we described what we were thinking, the salesman showed us a half-dozen rings that matched our description. One was white gold, with a small central diamond, and alternating diamond and peridot stones. There was a matching wedding band, with alternating diamond and peridot stones around the circumference. Kelly thought it a bit gaudy.

We then saw one in gold, with a larger diamond, flanked by two peridot stones, and a bunch of smaller diamonds on each side. Kelly nodded, and shrugged. Still another one had a small central diamond and alternating peridots and diamonds inset into the gold. Kelly smiled, "I like this one. But it makes my fingers look big."

Then, the patient jeweler finally brought one that excited Kelly: It was similar to the last, but with a wider band, inset princess-cut peridot and diamond stones, and a larger round diamond in the center. But it still seemed too small of a stone. "Could you put a larger diamond on it?"

Smiling broadly, the jeweler said, "Of course! Let me show you some nice diamonds that would look good."

We sat down, and he proceeded to show us a dozen or so diamonds. He suggested something around one carat, or slightly larger. Kelly's eyes widened when she saw a pear-shaped diamond, one of the more spectacular in the group. The jeweler smiled, "Yes. That's the best stone of this bunch – it's an F-color, ideal cut, VVS1, 1.25 carats."

Kelly asked about the classification, and over the next ten minutes, the jeweler explained the 'four Cs' – color, cut, clarity, and carat. The pear-shaped diamond he was showing us was fairly rare.

Kelly was ecstatic. "You can put that diamond on this ring? Will it look OK?"

The jeweler was now in his element, "Of course, it's no problem at all. And it will look great. I'll have to change the setting, but could have it ready for you tomorrow; we open at 10AM."

Kelly looked at me and smiled expectantly. "Is this what you want?" I asked. Kelly nodded enthusiastically, and I said, "We'll take it. We'll be back first thing tomorrow morning." As the jeweler walked us out, he said, "There's a matching wedding band, but I'll see if I can design one that will fit better with the pear-shaped stone."

We stepped out to the sidewalk, and Kelly turned to me, taking me into her arms, and lavishing me with a great kiss. I chuckled, "Gee, we should do this more often!"

We took the Powell-Hyde cable car down to the bay and I pointed out winding Lombard Street, although we didn't stop. We watched the 'gripman', as he operated the lever that connected the car to the cable, and listened to his schpiel. The cable for this line ran under the street, and was 16,000 feet long – more than 3 miles!

At the end of the line, we watched the cable car turn around on its turntable, and then took a stroll on the small beach of the Maritime National Historical Park. Kelly exclaimed, "Look! There are actually people swimming in this water, and they're not even wearing wetsuits!"

It *was* amazing – like the old men who swim in the freezing lake in Zurich during the winter. I noted, "The water temperature in the bay has to be in the low 50s. I don't think it gets much above 60 degrees, even in the summer."

We watched the swimmers for a few minutes; they were taking long, slow strokes, as they swam across the small cove. We did a quick tour of the Maritime Museum, then walked around Ghirardelli Square.

We both decided that we were ready for a mid-afternoon snack. I started to walk towards a pub, but Kelly pulled me the other direction – to the ice cream and chocolate shop. We split a hot fudge sundae which, I had to admit, was great.

Continuing our tour, we walked past dozens of shops with nothing but tourist junk ... and t-shirts. Kelly suggested that we bring each of her friends a special tee, as we had done from our Europe trip.

As Kelly made her selections, my mind's eye saw me asking her friends to undress to their underwear, then surprising them with a tee – one long enough to be used as a cover-up. How many times had we done that? There was Kelly's birthday party, then our Europe show, the Kauai red dirt t-shirts, and the Kalalau Trail tees, ...

"Sam! Hello ... come in, Sam." I had been looking across the way at the boats, but turned to see Kelly staring at me, and holding a bunch of t-shirts.

"What?"

Kelly shook her head, "You were somewhere else." I guess I had been ... back on the beaches of Kauai. The warm, tropical beaches, with Kelly and her friends ...

"How do you like these?" She held up several shirts that would be perfect for her friends. "And, I found a couple I might wear, and this one for you." Now, she held up a tee that had block letters on the front, 'MY PEN IS HUGE'. The spacing of the letters made it look like 'penis'. I shook my head.

"OK, here are a couple that I thought might be cute." One said, 'It's a Biotech thing ... you wouldn't understand'. I guess it was the proximity to Silicon Valley and all of the biotech companies; I looked at the tees on the walls and saw that quite a few had computer nerd jokes.

"Here's another one." Kelly held it up in front of herself; it said, 'Biotechnology is in my Genes', and showed a colorful, but technical, image of DNA replication. "And this one ..." This last one said, 'Life is Just a Game ... but Biotech is Serious Business'.

I smiled, "I love them all, especially the last one. But I don't think I'll wear the 'pen is' shirt." I looked at the tee-covered walls again. "Maybe *that* one?" It said, 'Biotechnologist by Day … Porn Star by Night'.

Kelly gave me a 'look', and pointed to two other shirts. One had a the elements germanium, nickel, uranium, and sulfur – 'GeNiUS'. The other said 'Biotech Wizard', and had a Fantasia-like wizard with his magic wand. We bought the shirts, and walked along the edge of the water lined up with fishing boats.

We walked around Fisherman's Wharf, and I suggested that we come back here for dinner; I had my favorite of the restaurants on the water, and called them to make a reservation for a window table.

This whole area was crowded with tourists, most of them carrying bags of their purchases, as we were. We walked to Pier 39, and looked at the board listing the vendors. The pier was crowded, but Kelly pointed out some of the boat rides offered, including a wine-tasting cruise, and whale-watching.

"The whale-watching would be great – and I think we're in the middle of the season – but I think we would need a full day." The way Kelly was looking at me, I knew this was something she wanted to do.

"OK. It's already too late today, and we're going on a drive tomorrow … but how about Monday? I had left it open for touring the city; but maybe we could do a whale watching expedition, instead?"

Kelly jumped up and down and clapped, the bag of shirts swinging wildly, and nearly hitting a person who was walking by. We walked onto the pier, and found the tour operator, then made reservations.

The guy laughed, "On most winter Mondays, you would have the boat to yourself, but Monday is President's Day, so we're filling up quickly."

We continued walking on the Embarcadero, the next pier advertising tours of Alcatraz. "This would be interesting; I've actually never done it."

Kelly laughed, "First it's the Sewer Museum in Paris, then the torture museum, and now a tour of Alcatraz Prison." I gave her a sour expression, but she smiled and quickly added, "It *does* sound interesting, Sam. I'd love to visit Alcatraz."

The weather was beautiful, and at least we would get out on the water – and have a different view of San Francisco. It was too late for the 5-hour tour, so we settled for the 2-hour version. The next boat was leaving in twenty minutes, and turned out to be the last one of the day.

We boarded the large ferry-like boat, and went up to the top deck. As the boat pulled out from the dock, we realized that nobody else was up here with us. There was a stiff breeze, and we put on our jackets.

I kissed Kelly, and put my arm around her. "Well, it looks like the perfect set-up for a repeat of our Paris boat cruise. Do you want to sit on my lap, again, or should we use a different position?"

Kelly whined, "Sam, it's only a fifteen-minute cruise; and there probably *will* be people coming up here."

Having just thought of another possibility, I nodded, "OK. Then we'll find somewhere on Alcatraz where we can make love." I smiled, thinking about Niagra Falls, "Our *second* public sex experience." Kelly just shook her head.

The tour was OK – an audio description of the main cell house by some of the guards and prisoners. But the views were spectacular! We spent some time walking around, as I took photos of the Golden Gate and the San Francisco skyline.

We walked around the south end of Alcatraz, and I was excited to see a trail that went down to a small beach below the cliff; we could only see bits of the beach, which might be the perfect 'private' setting for Kelly and I. When we got to the trail head, however, it was marked 'Closed for Season: Sea Birds Nesting'.

My plans were foiled, but only temporarily. We walked down a driveway, behind the main cell house and towards the old laundry. There were very few tourists walking around, and nobody else coming down the trail. At the bottom, there was another beach trail, except it was marked 'No Access'.

The path narrowed, and we sat on a grassy area under a scraggly, wind-blown tree. I raised my eyebrows at Kelly, and she raised hers at me. There was absolutely nobody around.

"Sam, I'm really not interested in having sex here. It's too cold to take my pants off, and a park ranger could show up at any minute."

I hugged her, "You know that I will keep you warm. And the chance of someone seeing us would make it more exciting."

Kelly harrumphed, "Maybe for you. I get excited enough just making love in a nice soft bed." I certainly wasn't going to pressure Kelly, but gave her a longing look.

She said, resignedly, "Well, if you 'need' some pressure relief, I guess I could have my appetizer. Then we could catch the boat back and go to dinner." That wasn't a bad offer. Kelly pushed my chest, and I lay back on the grass, as she unzipped my jeans, and found my hardening shaft.

As I lay there, gazing through twisted branches and dark green leaves to the brilliant blue sky, Kelly did her thing. Or, actually, she did *my* thing. It felt wonderful.

My eyes closed and my back arched, as I came, spewing my cum into her mouth. Kelly continued sucking and licking, as my body convulsed several more times. Then, she crawled up my body and we kissed – a full, open-mouth kiss, somewhat marred by the sticky, salty remnants of my orgasm.

Even as I was becoming more open to sharing body fluids, the idea of tasting my own semen still bothered me. I appreciated even more Kelly's openness, and her willingness to try new things.

I had always appreciated Kelly's beauty. She smiled at me, teeth gleaming and eyes sparkling, her hair blowing around us in the wind. "I love you, Sam."

We kissed again, any thought of cum now gone. "I love you, too, Kelly." I lifted my head to look around; apparently nobody had come down the trail. "Shall we take our boat to dinner?"

Kelly laughed and got off me, and I laughed as I realized that I was 'letting it all hang out'. I put myself away, and we walked, hand-in-hand back up the trail.

We glided across the dark water of the bay, sea birds circling behind us. The lights of San Francisco were coming on, and we could see the Golden Gate on our right, and Bay Bridge on our left.

The restaurant was able to seat us at a corner window table with only a few minute wait, as we were quite early for our reservation. As I poured a Chateau St. Jean chardonnay, and Kelly tasted the sourdough bread, I suggested that we take our time, and have a leisurely fine-dining experience.

For starters, I tried the Littleneck clams on the half shell, while Kelly ordered the Dungeness crab cocktail. It was getting darker outside, but the view was still fabulous. When the appetizers came, Kelly's eyes widened. I laughed, "I hope you enjoy your *second* appetizer of the evening."

We toasted, and I apologized, "I'm sorry that you couldn't be wearing your new ring tonight."

Kelly shook her head, "Don't worry, Sam. We've waited nearly half a year since you first proposed, and we might be waiting much longer before the wedding."

It was true: I'd proposed on Kauai in mid-September, and it was now mid-February. "I hope that we can tell your parents and set a date sooner, rather than later. Maybe have a September wedding?"

Kelly took a sip of wine, and looked at me seductively over the glass. "We'll see, Sam." Then, she became serious, "As far as letting my parents know, I hope we can do that before we leave for Europe. But as far as the wedding, I still can't even think about it now."

Our appetizer dishes were taken away, and I suggested to Kelly that we split one of the pastas, and then order our fish main courses. "That's too much – I can't eat all that; unless you want us to go on a long run tomorrow." I had other plans for the day, which might include running.

We finally decided to split the seafood salad, and then order main courses. I ended-up getting Cioppino as my main course, and Kelly tried the Pacific Rock Cod from the daily fresh fish menu.

The restaurant was now full, and several tables had come and gone while we were having our slow dinner. I ordered a half-bottle of a German *Spätlese* to go with our desserts – the Tiramisu for me, and blackberry cabernet sorbet for Kelly.

After dinner, we walked a few blocks, then took the Powell-Mason cable car back up the hill.

When we got back to the hotel, Sam opened the sliding door and stepped out onto the balcony. The view was amazing, but a cold wind was blowing through the door. I was ready to slide the door closed, when Sam came back in. "I guess it's a bit chilly out there, tonight."

"Don't worry, Sam, I'll keep you warm." I thought it was a good offer. I looked forward to snuggling with Sam.

Sam chuckled, and replied, "Well, you had two appetizers, and now it's time for me to have my second dessert." It took a moment before I realized what he meant. I smiled; that was an even better offer.

We got undressed and under the covers, holding each other until the chill had dissipated from our bodies. We kissed and snuggled. Sam ducked under the covers and kissed my breasts, then 'headed' lower ... and lower (in a manner of speaking).

I closed my eyes, images of the day flitting by as in a time-lapse movie. The Chinese restaurant with its silver cart of dim sum; the beautiful engagement ring that Sam had bought me; the cable car ride; seeing old men swimming in the freezing water; buying tees for my friends – and us; the trip to Alcatraz, and our 'public' oral sex experience.

Finally, there was our romantic dinner, sitting at a corner window table, the candlelight flickering, fishing boats lit up all around us. Sam's efforts were now achieving their intended result, and my body writhed, as the images faded, leaving only my pure love for Sam.

As Sam nibbled my clit, and my orgasm exploded, I realized that our love wasn't 'pure' in that way .. but it was real. And now I was really feeling the effects of the long day, and the big dinner, and the wine ...

I relaxed into the mattress, my eyes still closed, as Sam gave me a peck on the lips, pulled the covers over us, and turned off the light.

"Happy Valentine's Day!" Sam kissed me lightly on my lips, and my eyes fluttered open; it was already morning. Lying on his side, smiling at me, he asked, "Will you be my Valentine?"

I pulled him to me, and we kissed ravenously. Then, we made love – slowly, passionately. Sam *was* my Valentine: His Cupid's arrow had pierced my heart.

As we were getting dressed, Sam pulled open the drapes, and we looked out on the spectacular view, the bay reflecting the blue of the perfectly clear sky. Sam chuckled, "Well, we've been lucky so far. I'd like to take you to the beach and the mountains today; we could still get some fog ... but it sure looks nice out there now."

We packed our backpacks, and went out into the bright San Francisco day. Our first stop was at a Starbucks, for a quick breakfast. Sam had asked if I wanted to go to a fancy Valentine's Day brunch, but I much preferred getting out and exploring in the fresh air.

Next, we walked a few blocks to the jewelry store. My ring was ready, and it looked *gorgeous*! It fit perfectly, and was sized well for my fingers. The jeweler then showed us the matching wedding band, which also had peridot down each side, the top curving in under the large central diamond of the engagement ring.

"Sam, this is beautiful!" I hugged him, and couldn't help but get teary-eyed. Somehow, the ring made our engagement more real. It would become a lot more real, soon, when we announced it to my parents.

Using his Apple Watch, Sam navigated us to the nearest car rental office. Twenty minutes later, we were pulling in to a small parking lot near the ocean. Sam turned off the car. "Let's take a look at Baker Beach. I've heard a lot about it, but never been here before."

We locked the car, and walked down a trail to a beautiful beach below the cliffs. Sam exclaimed, "It really is amazing it's so clear on a February day! I think this part of the coastline gets a lot of fog." It was still cool, but the warmth of the sun felt wonderful.

It was spectacular: The blue Pacific lapping up onto a wide, fine sand beach, backed by cliffs, and to the North, an incredible view of the Golden Gate bridge. There were a few dozen people on the beach, mainly walking – with each other, or with dogs. I could imagine this beach getting packed on a hot summer day.

We took off our shoes and socks, and walked on the damp sand, holding hands. Sam and I had been to several beaches together, all very different. Most similar to this was our run on the beach near Amsterdam. But we'd also been to a small beach on the Isar River in Munich, and run along the path bordering Lake Ontario in Toronto.

And, of course, we'd gone to many beaches on Kauai, including the small beach where we'd snorkeled in Princeville, the beach at Hanalei Bay, Lumahai Beach next to the river, Kee Beach at the 'end of the road', and – especially – Kalalau and Honopu beaches at the end of the Na Pali trail.

Sam pointed – there were dolphins surfing through the small waves just offshore. Gulls flew above us and waddled on the beach. As we walked northward, the crowd thinned out. Then, we started seeing a few nude people. It was a very mellow atmosphere, the only sounds being the breaking of waves, and the gulls squawking above us.

There were some trails up the cliffs, and Sam explained, "Around the turn of the century – the *last* century, around 1900 – they built huge artillery guns up there, called 'battery Chamberlain'. They were huge, disappearing guns, ready to protect the entry to San Francisco Bay."

As we approached the end of the beach, the Golden Gate loomed above us. There were about a dozen people on the sand, and a few more climbing on the rocks, all of them nude. We put down our packs, and pulled out the hotel towels we'd stashed in them.

Sam took his camera, and climbed on the rocks for some great shots of the bridge. I stripped down, and lay on my towel, the sun baking me, despite the cool breeze. This was the first time I'd done this since our trip to Hawaii.

When Sam returned, he gazed at me with a big smile, then proceeded to remove his own clothes. This was very nice and unexpected – being the middle of winter.

"Shall we try the water?" Sam smirked at me. I was game, but doubted Sam would go in, after we'd let our feet test the cold water during our walk. I was feeling warmed up, now, and decided to call Sam's bluff ... or, maybe, call his buff.

"We're going to get all salty," I complained, giving Sam another excuse. I didn't know if there were any showers in the parking lot, but assumed we'd be able to get cleaned off at some point in the day.

I got up, gave Sam a smile, then turned to the sea, and ran the short width of the beach down to the water. The cold wasn't that apparent until I was up to my knees. But I had made my decision. Taking a few more steps, I dove into the oncoming wave.

It certainly *was* refreshing and invigorating ... if not downright freezing. I swam a sort distance out, and treaded water, as I watched Sam walk slowly into the water. I really thought he would wimp out, but eventually, he lowered himself fully, then stood and roared.

I waved to him, "Come on in. The water's great!" Sam shook his head, then dove in and swam out to me. We kissed, then I swam further out, Sam following.

We turned in the water, looking around us: This was an even better view of the bridge. From here, we saw the rocks, beach, and cliffs, topped with a green ground cover; there was no evidence that a huge city was just a few miles from here.

Pointing to the rocks, I yelled, "Seals!"

Sam shook his head, "No, they're California sea lions. See – they have big flippers, and you can see their ears. Seals have small flippers and no ear flaps. Also, you can hear them 'barking', which only sea lions do."

Nearly numb with the cold, we headed back to the beach. We had brought running shorts and tanks, and I suggested that we run the half mile back to the car. We were already salty, so a little sweat wouldn't matter.

As we settled in to the run, I realized how perfect the weather was – it didn't feel cold at all, but there was a gentle breeze that kept us from overheating.

When we got back to the car, Sam looked at his iPhone, and nodded. "Let's visit one more beach." We had to drive only a few blocks, then parked and walked down the steps to China Beach. This was another beautiful spot – a small cove which – the sign said – had been where Chinese laborers had camped in the 19th century.

We walked on the beach, and Sam took a few more snapshots. There *were* showers, but they only had cold water; *very* cold. We showered in our running shorts and my running bra, then went back to the car, where we changed into jeans.

Sam drove us through part of the Presidio. "This was a former military base, first built by the Spanish in 1776, until the mid-90s, when it was turned over to the National Park Service. If we weren't going to drive out of the city today, I would have brought you to Golden Gate Park, where there are museums, the zoo, and nice paths to walk."

After stopping at the small visitor center, we drove across the Golden Gate, and Sam became the tour guide again. "This is probably the most-recognized bridge in the world. It spans the mile-wide opening to San Francisco Bay, and connects the city with Marin County."

Chuckling, Sam said, "I didn't read all the details in the museum, but it's over seven hundred feet high, and over two hundred feet off the water – making it the second most popular bridge for suicides." Just what I wanted to know, for our Valentine expedition.

Sam continued, "It was built during the Depression, and was an incredible engineering job. They used something like 80,000 miles of wire to make the 3-foot diameter main cables; each one has more than 27,000 wires twisted together. And there are more than a million rivets." We drove across the bridge, which handled six lanes of traffic.

Sam exited on the other side of the bridge, and we stopped at the Vista Point for another incredible view of the bridge and the city across the bay. There was a statue, and I read the plaque: It was the Lone Sailor Memorial, representing the last view of the West Coast, as ships head out to sea.

Back on the highway, we continued north, finally turning off onto a winding road, and now climbing into a forested area. We pulled into the parking lot of another visitor center – for the Muir Woods National Monument, which is part of the Mount Tamalpais State Park.

We learned that Muir Woods is an 'old-growth' forest, with some of the tallest redwood trees in the world. The tallest tree in the park is more than 250 feet, and some of these trees are close to 400 feet tall, nearly the height of the Statue of Liberty. That brought back memories of our Paris boat ride, passing the quarter-scale model of the statue.

And these trees were old – typically 600-800 years, although the oldest was said to have lived 1200 years. They could live twice that long ... if the forest survived wildfires and adapted to the changing environment.

We walked several of the trails, along with quite a few other people. I wondered whether Sam would suggest some off-trail 'excitement', but he didn't, and I didn't make him an offer.

Back at the car, Sam looked at his watch and frowned, "I thought we would be able to hike some trails on Mt. Tamalpais – maybe down to Stinson Beach ... but we're just not going to have the time." Sam looked at me with a pained expression, "I guess we'll just have to come back here, too."

There were a lot of places to visit, and never enough time to see everything. I looked forward to traveling more with Sam, but still couldn't envision my career – and perhaps future family – allowing time for the kind of travel we wanted to do.

"I made an early dinner reservation, so we'll have a little time to explore Sausalito."

We drove into Sausalito, and Sam continued south to Sausalito Point, where we would have a view of San Francisco. We found a nice pub, on the water, and were able to get a great window table with a view of Angel Island, Alcatraz, and the city, with its landmark Transamerica tower.

We were only going to order beers, but Sam felt guilty sitting at the table without food, so he also selected the smoked trout dip and a bowl of special French olives.

We still had more than an hour until our dinner reservation, and it was nice to sit in one place for a while. I realized that we hadn't eaten anything since our scones at Starbucks, so a little snack sounded good.

Leaving the car near the pub, we walked around the yacht harbor. Sam pointed out some incredible boats, many big enough to sail around the world in style. "It must be nice to be rich," Sam exclaimed, as we examined a huge two-masted sailboat from the dock.

"You *are* rich, Sam." He held my hand and nodded; we both appreciated the richness of our life together. I still had no idea how much money Sam actually had ... and it didn't matter.

We sat on a bench at the top of the dock, looking over a sea of masts. Sam turned to me, "Kelly, as we're getting married," he chuckled loudly, "and we both like fine things," he smiled at me, "I should 'calibrate' you."

I nodded and shrugged, and Sam continued, "My net worth is around twelve million. I did pretty well in the stock market, and now have a diversified portfolio." I was impressed. Sam explained, "That enabled me to retire, and I could maybe buy a vacation house, or a small boat, and be able to travel internationally."

Then, Sam gave me a serious look, "But something like *this*," he pointed to the yacht we'd been looking at, "is probably several million, just for the boat. A slip in a nice marina like this would probably cost $15 per foot, or around $1200 per month for that boat. And then there's maintenance, and equipment upgrades ..."

Sam was breathing heavily, and I could tell he was getting excited just thinking about this. "Of course, if I sold the house, and *lived* on the boat, that might be different. But I don't think you and I could handle a boat that large, so we would probably need a crew ..."

I nodded, and held his hand. We would just have to suffer with the assets he had. "Sam, I think you have plenty of money for anything we would ever want to do." Now I laughed, "And you probably could find things to spend money on, no matter how much wealth you had."

Sam was shaking his head, "I don't want that much." His smile turned into an 'evil' grin, "But, let's see ..." I wasn't sure what we would be seeing, but Sam began calculating. "Five million for a house in Hawaii, and another five million for a house in Europe, five mil for that yacht, and forty mil for a jet ..."

Now, Sam was going crazy. "Staff for each of the houses, a crew for the yacht, and double crews for the plane would mean about 15 people on the payroll. That would be about a couple million a year – so we would need $40 million invested to pay for that. And if we bought some 'toys' – maybe a smaller boat to cruise the Mediterranean," Sam's eyes went wide, "and a small submarine ... maybe another five million ..."

"OK, Sam, now you're just being silly."

Sam shook his head, "No, I'm just trying to show you ... even with all that stuff, plus another $20 million to give us a million a year spending money, we're still only up to about $100 million. I know people who have sold companies and made twice that much."

He looked at me, "So, if we had *two* hundred million dollars, what would you spend the other $100 million on? Other than buying an island, or setting up an investment company, it's hard to spend that much money."

Like Sam said, it must be nice to have to think about things like that.

We drove the short distance to the restaurant, which was a Victorian house across the highway from the water. I had envisioned a water view – like we'd just had at the pub – but it was getting dark, anyway.

The dining room was quite formal, with chandeliers, velvet drapes, nice table cloths, crystal and silver. We split the roasted artichoke appetizer, and I had the seared scallops, while Sam ordered the smoked duck. It was another incredible dinner.

Once again, I had memories of some of our great meals, including at the sauna in Valkenburg, the *schlosshotel* in Germany, and the Shard in London. At least here people were dressed very casually, despite the fancy surroundings. California style.

I looked into Kelly's eyes, once again glittering, as they refracted the flickering light of the candles. "I love you." Perhaps it was the chardonnay we'd had, or the atmosphere ... or the day of touring, but it just *felt* romantic.

I had to offer at least once more ... or just do it. "Should I re-propose again? The third time's the charm, you know."

Kelly smiled and took my hand. Then, she leaned forward and pointed to her finger, "No, Sam. I already have my 'charm'. And I love it; thank you." We kissed briefly, and I held Kelly's hand up and examined the ring again. It really was nice, and looked great on her.

I gave Kelly the evil eye, and – under her breath – she said 'Oh no'. I laughed, "No, Kelly, nothing like that. Although I did consider an 'outdoor' spanking experience in the forest. But it's Valentine's Day, so I didn't think that was appropriate.

"You didn't even want me telling you about the suicides from the bridge. And after Hawaii, I learned not to tell you about the sharks, until we're out of the water."

Kelly's eyes grew wide, "Are you teasing me?"

Shaking my head, "No, Kelly. The ocean off San Francisco has lots of sharks. I'm sure we'll see some from the boat tomorrow." I smiled at her, "But, as far as I know, there's only been one shark attack at Baker Beach. And that was a long time ago." Now, Kelly was shaking her head.

The waiter came, and I decided to 'dominate'. "We'll have the S'mores pie." After the waiter had retreated, Kelly gave me a 'look'. "What? It's one of their specialties." We would have to continue our running – at least until we left for Europe.

The whale-watching experience on Monday turned out to be fantastic. Not only did we see gray whales, but also dolphin and sharks. It was cold on the boat, but we had bundled up, and wore wind-breakers over our sweaters.

We ate at a Greek restaurant Monday night, and focused on our presentations for the VCs tomorrow. Kelly summarized the technical aspects, and I summarized the business issues, and we asked each other questions. We were as ready as we were going to be.

Early Tuesday morning, we drove south on the 280, taking the Sand Hill Road exit towards Stanford, and turning into a parking lot. There had to be more than thirty buildings here, and I searched for the right one for our morning meeting.

Kelly wore a grey pantsuit with a white blouse, and I had done her hair in French braids. She looked very mature and professional. I leaned over to kiss her, but she shook her head; I guess it would have looked strange had I gone in with lipstick on my lips.

We took our briefcases, and found the venture capital firm, entering through wide double doors to a reception area. Within minutes we were seated in a conference room, with a huge boardroom table, and a wall of glass looking out to scrub brush and trees.

Two rather young guys – probably in their mid-30s – entered and introduced themselves. One was a managing partner in the firm, having taken his company public, and now sitting on the Board of several new startups.

The receptionist came in with a tray of drinks – bottled waters and soft drinks, and pointed to the pot of coffee in the coffeemaker. I connected my computer to the projector, and we began our presentation.

After I gave a five-minute introduction and overview, Kelly took over, describing her invention, and the various diseases that could be targeted for new drug development. The two guys were very astute and asked some difficult questions, but Kelly responded beautifully.

Then, I presented the business plan, including our business model, funding needs, and partnering strategy. I noted that various levels of funding would bring us to certain 'inflection points' in the business, where we could either sell the company to a big pharma or biotech firm, or take it public through an IPO.

There was interest but, as I had suspected, VCs may not be the best route for our business. As we walked back to the car, I told Kelly, "You did a great job! I think they were convinced that your technology will work, and of the value to big pharma."

I sighed, "But I hadn't really nailed down the business model – should we begin development of a drug ourselves, which would require much more funding ... or partner with pharma companies, in which case we might just be a contract R&D vendor. Or, sell the equipment ... but there would be a limited number of customers. Or, license the patents, which would minimize our workload, but also limit our upside."

We drove into Palo Alto, and parked on the main drag, then found a small bistro where we could have lunch and discuss how we would modify our second presentation. Somehow, I had managed to get both appointments on the same day – something so improbable that I felt like I had won the lottery.

The second venture capital presentation went well, but we were advised to come back when we had a definitive drug target, and had some results. Kelly was preparing to test the system for Lyme disease, but we had no data yet to show. It had probably been too early to meet with the VCs, but they had provided several interesting suggestions, which we would follow-up.

In the late afternoon, we checked into our B&B, then went back out and walked around the Stanford campus. It was really quite beautiful. I could see myself being a professor here ... but I was happily retired.

Still, I wondered whether a move to California would provide a better environment for the company, not to mention better weather for an active lifestyle. There was so much biotech talent here, staffing would be easy. And, if we were funded by one of the Sand Hill Road VCs, they would undoubtedly *require* that we relocate the business.

But the cost-of-living was much higher here than back home. I could probably get $800K for my house, but would need to pay a couple million – or more – to equal it in northern California. And it would be an even harder hit on Kelly's parents for us to leave the area; it would be difficult enough telling them we were going to get married.

Kelly and I talked about all of this, and more, as we walked around the area, and ate at a small Thai restaurant.

The inn where we were staying had plush rooms with a balcony and fireplace that burned real logs. We started the fire, and enjoyed another romantic night of lovemaking.

On Wednesday, we drove over the hill to Half Moon Bay, and checked into a luxury resort hotel. It seemed a bit over-the-top, and apparently catered mostly to golfers. Kelly and I would have to start going to the driving range, and playing once in a while – it would be good 'grooming' for her to become an executive.

After exploring the hotel and its beach, we drove north along the coast, as far as Moss beach. I had driven the Big Sur coast – up to Carmel and Monterrey – several times, but had never done this part of the coast. It was foggier here, a thick bank off the coast, and the atmosphere along the beaches cold and wet.

I had thought we would stop at several beaches – we had the full day available. But the weather wasn't cooperating, so I decided that we should see at least one beach ... probably the most famous along this coast: 'Mavericks'. This was the 'big surfing' beach of California.

The beach was beautiful, and Kelly was happy being outdoors, traveling together. But, although it was the right season, the waves were tiny, and there were no surfers.

Walking down the beach, we could see the dome of the Air Force Station over the hill behind us, and a rickety jetty ahead of us; there was a multitude of small boats and masts in a marina far to the south.

We drove to the harbor, and walked into an open-sided warehouse, where huge tanks held live lobsters and crabs, and fresh fish was being unloaded directly from one of the boats. "Maybe the hotel would let me use their kitchen to fix us some fresh crabs?"

Kelly pulled me away from the tank, "I'm sure they have fresh crab, and a lot of other good stuff on their menu."

She was right ... as usual. We drove back to the hotel, and cleaned up for dinner; but not before another lovemaking session, looking out at the beach and the twisted, wind-blown trees.

When I woke early on Thursday morning, I decided to call the airlines. As I was finishing the call, Kelly stood next to me, in her sexy satin negligée. I pulled her down into my lap, and asked, "Kelly, would you mind if we cut the trip short by a day?"

This was a business trip, after all, and we'd completed our business ... and done a lot of nice personal things, also. "Originally, as you may remember, our VC meetings were going to take two days, but we were able to get back-to-back meetings. Now, I'm thinking that it isn't worth spending a day in Santa Cruz ... or even Monterrey."

I smiled at her, "I'd rather bring you back to cover the area in more detail." I knew that Kelly was wondering whether we would *ever* return, but I knew that we would. This area was important for biotech, and we would certainly be coming back many times.

Kelly put her arms around my neck, "Sure, Sam. I'm ready to get back and keep working on the system. I don't think anyone will invest, until we can show some results." Once again, Kelly was undoubtedly correct.

I pushed her off my lap, and let her know, "I got us First Class seats late this afternoon. We'll land late – and not get home until midnight – but we can spend most of the day finishing our Bay Area tour."

We packed for the flight, and drove down the coast to Santa Cruz. I had to see at least one beach, so we stopped at Natural Bridges State Beach. The sky was blue – no fog today – but there was still a chilly breeze.

Next, we stopped at Seal Rock and the Surfing Museum. The museum was OK, and the water coming into the inlets of the rocks was interesting, but now that we were going home, we just wanted to get there.

We ate at a fish restaurant on the Santa Cruz Wharf, which turned out to be better than we had expected, for such a touristy location. We had a window table, and the view was spectacular.

Kelly was staring at her ring. Now that we were going back to our 'reality', I asked, "So how do you want to announce our engagement to your parents? Maybe we should have a small party?"

Nodding, Kelly replied, "Yeah, we can do that. But it should be just the four of us. Let's have them over on Friday. Maybe you can cook something?"

I was delighted to do that. Chuckling, I thought, 'why not *coq au vin*?'. It was my version of the stew that Darlene had made. I could make a nice salad with my Green Goddess dressing, and maybe a cherry cobbler for dessert, with fresh whipped cream infused with a bit of *Kirschwasser*, and garnished with fresh mint sprigs.

Sam had made dinner, and was well-prepared with vodka for my mother and bourbon for my dad. I didn't think there would be a problem, but there were still butterflies in my stomach.

When my parents arrived, we greeted them and brought them down to the playroom. After drinks were served, we told my parents about our San Francisco trip, and Sam projected some of our selfies, and photos he had taken with his DSLR.

My parents were more than cordial – they showed interest in our trip and the fundraising for our business. But, of course, they still didn't understand my invention or what our product would be. Sam refilled the drinks, and glanced at me; I gave him a nod, and turned to my parents.

"Something else happened during our San Francisco trip ... Actually, it happened when we were in Kauai, but it was 'finalized' in San Francisco ..." I held out my left hand, showing them the ring. "Sam and I are engaged to get married." I held my breath, awaiting the explosion from my dad.

But it never came. My mother took my hand, and examined the ring, "Oh, Kelly, this is beautiful." She looked into my eyes with tears in hers, "Congratulations." She leaned forward and hugged me, then got up and hugged Sam.

My father shook Sam's hand, then got up and hugged me. This was a real surprise. He looked into my eyes, and said, sincerely, "We love you, Kelly, and we just want you to be happy. If this is really what you want, we're happy for you." He sat back down and finished his second drink.

Sam turned to my dad, and said, "Thank you, Dave. I wanted to ask your permission to marry your daughter ... but Kelly wasn't sure you would give it."

My mother chuckled, "I've been suspecting this would happen since you got back from Europe, and started living together." That had been more than a year.

She continued, "And, after our 'punishment' – seeing how you two worked together, and how much Sam cares for you – I knew that your relationship was serious." She looked at my dad, "I've been preparing your father for this." Another surprise.

Then, she turned to Sam, "I meant what I said, when I told you to take good care of my baby." She chuckled and finished *her* second drink, then added, "Not that she's a 'baby' any longer."

Sam immediately replied, "And *I* meant it, when I said that I would take care of her. We love each other very much. Kelly is the most important thing in my life." We hugged and kissed – perhaps the first time we'd kissed in front of my parents.

We went up to the dining room and ate dinner, and I described Sam's first proposal, in the sea cave on the north shore of Kauai. And how he'd re-proposed at the French restaurant, and wanted to propose a third time during our Valentine's Day dinner. I told them I'd finally gotten worn down and accepted his proposal.

I also made sure that they knew we wouldn't be rushing the wedding, which my dad seemed glad to hear, although disappointing my mother. While it was possible that we would set a date in the fall, it was more likely that we would 'tie the knot' next spring.

We also told them that we would be going back to Europe, on a 'business trip' during most of April. Of course, I couldn't mention my domme training with Elena. Sam said he wanted to visit friends again in The Netherlands, and that we would be there on 'Orange Day'.

My mother commented several times on Sam's cooking, and my parents both took second helpings of the *coq au vin*. Sam had served a nice red wine, my parents barely finishing their glasses, while Sam and I polished off the rest of the bottle.

I had assumed that my parents would leave after dinner, but as my dad and Sam ate their second helpings of cobbler, Sam looked up and smiled at me, "Shall we share a sauna experience with them?" I gave Sam a dirty look.

Then, I thought more about it: My parents had both been nude during their spanking, and Sam had even bathed my mother. I shook my head, still not able to picture it. Maybe the idea wasn't so far-fetched?

Finishing the last swallow of wine, I put my glass down and looked at my parents. "Sam would like to show his usual hospitality ... but I'm not sure you guys are up for what he has in mind ... and we don't want to push you." Although that's exactly what Sam was doing.

My parents looked at Sam, then me, and I explained, "We often invite our guests to go in the pool in the summer, or jacuzzi in the winter ... and we especially like to go in the sauna when it's cold outside," I glanced at Sam, then back to my parents, "but you can't wear clothes in the sauna. We would all be nude together."

I couldn't believe I had offered that. Now that my parents were accepting our relationship, I didn't want Sam to screw it up by pushing my parents into another embarrassing situation.

We were all surprised when my mom spoke up, "Well, dear, Sam has bathed me, and you've seen your father's intimate parts." She turned to my dad and smiled, "I would go in the sauna with them, if you will." Out of the corner of my eye, I saw Sam's mouth drop open.

My dad shrugged, "I still don't think my little girl ..." He looked sharply at me, "I'm sorry ... that *Kelly* should see her dad that way."

I shook my head, "Dad, a lot of families go to nude beaches together. Just look at Kathy's family."

He grumbled, "But they're hippies." Then, he shook his head, "You're going to embarrass me again ... but if your mother wants to do it, I guess I won't put up a fight."

Sam ran downstairs and brought up the robes, and I took my parents up to one of the guest bedrooms. Then, Sam and I went into the master bedroom and got undressed, donning the 'superman' (and 'superwoman') robes I'd bought for Sam's birthday.

We were getting rinsed off under the rain shower, when my parents entered the shower room. My dad's eyes were glued on me, and I realized that we'd all seen each other nude ... except for my dad seeing me. I was pretty sure he would never call me his 'little girl' again!

We handed towels to my parents and went into the sauna. A minute later, they entered the dark space unsurely, their towels wrapped around them. Sam showed them how to arrange the towels, and they sat on the top bench with us – the men in the corners, and me next to my mom in the center.

The furnace crackled, and Sam stepped down to ladle some water over the hot rocks. A 'whoosh' of steam rose, and the sauna suddenly felt hotter. Sam turned the hourglass timer and sat back on his towel.

My mother lifted my hand but, remembering Fiona's experience, I had taken off the ring. I looked at my parents, "I want to thank you both for making this so easy for us."

Realizing that they may be thinking about the sauna, I clarified, "I mean about us getting engaged. Sam and I really do love each other, and we've been good for each other – we've both grown a lot over the past year." Sam was nodding, but I hoped that my parents didn't ask for examples of how Sam had grown.

My mother smiled, "Yes, dear, we've seen that. You seem to have matured greatly over the past year or so. We are both impressed with your strength, especially your father." I knew that at least his *bottom* had been impressed by my strength.

Then, *she* clarified, chuckling, "I didn't mean your physical strength – that too – but your fortitude. How quickly you finished your doctorate, and how serious you are about your new business."

She turned to my dad, who was listening to the conversation while still staring at my body, then she turned back to me, "We don't really understand what it is you're doing, but we know it's important to you, and we hope you're successful."

I held my mom's hands, "Thank you, mom." I didn't think it was worth trying to explain the technology again.

We were all getting hot, sweat streaming down our bodies. I suggested, "Why don't you guys get rinsed off, and put your robes on, then we'll get our showers. We can cool off on the chaises."

My mother looked at my dad, her eyes glancing down, and my eyes following hers. It looked to me like he might be a little hard ... although it was hard to tell.

He put his hands in his lap, and my mother turned to me, "Dear, why don't you and Sam take your showers, and then give us a little privacy for ours?"

Before I had turned to Sam, he was already stepping down to the lower bench, and then down to the tile floor of the sauna. Sam opened the door for us, and quickly closed it again. We took a quick shower, just a rinse, then put on our robes, and went to the playroom, closing the door behind us.

Sam raised his eyebrows at me, "Well, that was interesting. I don't think your dad has had much experience seeing nude young women."

"Sam! I'm his *daughter*!"

Shaking his head, Sam said, "Yeah, but you're still a beautiful young woman." Then, he laughed, "When was the last time your dad saw you naked?"

That stopped me: Other than possibly seeing me in the pool when he'd found my friends and I skinny-dipping, I don't think he'd *ever* seen me nude.

I chuckled as I remembered: That time, he'd been totally focused on Julie, who had gotten out of the pool to taunt him. Sam poured Diet Cokes for us, and we sat on the couch.

A few minutes later, my parents emerged, in their robes, and sat on the loveseat. Sam offered them drinks, and my dad asked for a 'real' Coke; fortunately Sam had one or two in the bar fridge. Surprisingly, my mom asked for water.

When we were all sitting around the coffee table in our robes, my dad turned to me, "Your mother is getting more frisky in her old age." My mother frowned, and he offered, "She's still sexy ... to me." He winked at Sam.

"That's really great. I'm happy for both of you!" Sam smiled and nodded. I wondered whether my little 'punishment' made a difference, or if something else had happened. I think that had been the first time my mom had seen my dad contrite, apologetic, ... and submissive.

My dad looked into his lap, and said, softly, "When Sam took your mother down, nude, to bathe her ... I know nothing happened; she's told me all about it. But I still couldn't really visualize it, so it's become ... sort-of a fantasy for me."

Sam leaned forward and put his coke on the tray, "Well, I'd be happy to bathe Darlene again ... and let you watch, if you want." My dad shook his head, and started to say something, but got flustered.

I put my glass down, "Shall we go back into the sauna?" My parents looked at each other and smiled.

My father seemed more comfortable the second time, holding my mother's hand, as they sat on the lower bench (out of direct view of my body). My mom couldn't help but ask me about the wedding plans. There weren't any.

"I guess Julie, Linda, and Kathy will be my bridesmaids, plus Fiona, our friend from Toronto, the niece of one of Sam's neighbors. And," looking at Sam, "I expect that Sam's sons will be bridegrooms, plus maybe Justin – that's Fiona's husband – and ... I don't know ... Raj, my advisor?"

Sam nodded and smiled. These were all things we would have to discuss. At the proper time. As I thought more, I added, "We could have the wedding in Sam's backyard – it's really beautiful in the spring and summer."

Then, I raised my eyebrows at Sam, "Or, maybe, we could fly everyone to Hawaii, and have the wedding there?" Sam shrugged, noncommittally.

I could imagine taking my parents to Hawaii, staying in a condo like we'd done with my friends. They hadn't really traveled anywhere, and I knew my dad would love the golfing there. Sam had suggested that we should start going to the driving range, but there were a lot of higher priorities for us.

When we were ready to get out, Sam said, "Now, we'll shower together." My father grumbled, but my mother didn't say a word.

Sam began bathing me, starting with my front, as we smiled at each other. My mom started soaping up my dad's chest, and he – reluctantly, it seemed – washed my mother's breasts.

Then, we switched, with me washing my dad's backside – from neck to feet – and Sam doing the same with my mother. We were both doing a cursory wash only, not getting overly intimate. It was intimate enough that Sam and I were showering with my parents; something that none of us could have imagined happening, just a couple of months ago.

We put on our robes, and walked upstairs. Sam asked, "Dave, can I interest you in 'just one more' helping of cherry cobbler?" Under his breath, he said, "Kelly and I don't need it." We were running every day again, to get a few pounds off from our San Francisco trip.

When my parents came down to the living room, dressed again, Sam handed my mother a 'doggie bag' with the leftover cobbler and a container of the leftover whipped cream. He hugged my mother, and I hugged my dad, then we switched, Sam and my dad shaking hands firmly, as I kissed my mother.

After they had driven off, Sam and I climbed the stairs, nearly in a daze. Sam chuckled, "Well, I guess your parents are turning over a new leaf ... a new fig leaf!"

It was funny, but Sam had told me that one before. I didn't know what to say; the situation hadn't been as weird as I'd expected.

When we were in bed, Sam stroked my hair, "It seems that punishing your parents may actually have done something." He chuckled, "And now your dad gets turned on by imagining his wife with another man."

I wasn't sure that was it, but it didn't matter: My parents had shown more love for each other tonight than I remembered seeing ... ever. I just hoped that my dad wouldn't stray again; but I thought he had learned his lesson. And my mother seemed to be a new person.

I relaxed, letting out stress that I hadn't known I'd had this evening. Suddenly I was very tired. "Sam, can we please just go to sleep, and make love in the morning?"

Sam chuckled and spooned me, letting his arm hang around my waist. "Sure, Kelly. I love you. Goodnight."

CHAPTER 6: CLASSY DOMME

We had finalized our Europe plans, and I'd made all the reservations. Unfortunately, Henk would be traveling, but was supposed to get back in time to join us on Orange Day. Zöe *was* available, and looked forward to seeing us, although we would be staying in Amsterdam.

I was only able to get an appointment with one pharmaceutical firm in London, but was still working on possible meetings in Geneva and Dublin. Kelly was making progress on her technology, developing the user interface software, and already programming the system for the Lyme disease application.

Mistress Elena had requested a deposit of $1000 and sent some paperwork for Kelly to fill out. The contract called for a final payment of another $9K by the first day of class, but said it would be waived if Kelly completed the class and her 'graduation exercises' with the wealthy benefactor who would be paying her scholarship.

The idea of Kelly taking the domme class didn't bother me as much, anymore. It had been more than a year since we'd met the dominatrix, Elena, and our own relationship had progressed significantly. Still, it irked me that Elena hadn't selected me for additional training.

Looking at the calendar on my computer, I shook my head: Time had slipped by quickly since we'd returned from California, and we would be departing for Europe in a little under two weeks.

After Kelly had suggested skiing, I had hoped that we could fly back to northern California and ski at one of the Sierra resorts; we could have flown out on a Thursday night, and returned Sunday night, getting three full days on the slopes, and only missing one work day.

But we had both been very busy, the company taking virtually all of our time, except for our runs in the morning, and dinner together every night; and – in the past week – Kelly studying materials for her domme class. I had offered the ski trip, but we both had decided to keep our noses to the grindstone – especially as we would be in Europe for a full month.

Kelly had again voiced her concern that we might never get to do all the things we wanted – including traveling. Between getting the business started, and then – possibly – starting a family, Kelly figured that it could be a couple of *decades* before we would be able to 'live' again.

But I was more optimistic. Kelly was under no pressure to work this hard – except the pressure she created for herself. And we couldn't envision where the KS Biotech would be a year from now. Perhaps we would have sold the technology by then or, if it wasn't successful, closed down the business. And we really hadn't discussed the question of 'kids', yet.

As far as travel, I was certain that there would be plenty of trips that we would be taking together – whether business or pleasure or, as with our San Francisco trip, a little of each. Raj had already invited Kelly to present her research at a biotech meeting in Barcelona this coming September.

This would be our last 'free' weekend, as next weekend we would be packing for the trip. Kelly came downstairs with a bunch of books and papers under her arm. She handed me a single sheet, smiling as I read it:

	Course Syllabus
FRI	Orientation The psychology of BDSM Understanding Fetishes
SAT AM	DEMONSTRATIONS
MON	The Domme & the Sub Femdom & the Goddess Developing the Scene
TUE	Verbal Domination Humiliation Foot and Shoe Fetish
WED	Dungeon Equipment & Toys Corporal Punishment – Basic
THU	Bondage Corporal Punishment – Advanced
FRI	Anal Play C&B Torture
SAT AM	DEMONSTRATIONS
MON	Medical Play
TUE	Slave Training Advanced Dommecraft
WED	Financial Domination Boundaries and Ethics Legal Considerations
THU	The Business of Domination
FRI	GRADUATION
SAT	BENEFACTOR SESSION

"It looks like a pretty thorough course. Although Mistress Elena cautioned us that each of the topics is usually expanded into a 3-day class, so we'll just be getting an introduction." Kelly chuckled, "And out of the 20 topics, I'm only familiar with five of them."

Handing the page back to Kelly, I mused, "I wonder what 'Advanced Dommecraft' is?"

Kelly held up a bunch of other materials, "Mistress sent us a lot of materials." She put the books on the desk, and flipped through the papers. Then she nodded, "She listed needle play, fire play, electro-play, mummification, breath play, and scarification."

We'd done some of these things but, remembering our half-day session with Mistress Elena, I was certain they would be more serious than what we'd already done. I shook my head; maybe I shouldn't have been so upset about not being selected?

"And she asked us to fill-in these," Kelly said, as she handed me a sheaf of pages, stapled together. There were several lists – bondage, corporal, fetish, humiliation, and bodily functions. I laughed, as I turned the pages and saw the section on 'definition of sex'.

Kelly was to check off things that she'd done, which ones she had enjoyed, and which she would be willing to 'demonstrate' during the class. From what I could see, this meant volunteering to be on the receiving end.

Reading through the lists in more detail, I was shocked: We had only done two or three of more than 40 bondage items, two or three of more than 40 fetishes, and two or three of more than 20 types of humiliation. But we had done about half of the 'punishment' and 'impact & intense play' activities.

Kelly handed me a stack of books, including 'The Sexually Dominant Woman', 'The Art of Domination', 'Whip Your Life into Shape', 'Anal Pleasure & Health', 'The Mistress Manual', and 'Dominating for Dummies'. She smiled, "I also got a bunch of e-books, so I can read them on the plane."

Then, she looked at me seriously, "And we won't have access to our phones, except on the weekends." I had hoped that we could talk every night. I would miss saying good night to her ... and I would also miss daily updates on what was happening and how she was doing.

Once again, I wondered whether this class was something that I would have enjoyed. I felt lucky that I would at least be able to live it vicariously, through Kelly. But I was still concerned about our relationship after the class; especially, what Kelly would want to 'do' to me, using her new skills.

We flew to London in Business Class again, Sam unnecessarily apologetic about not being able to get First Class upgrades. But the flight was great, and I spent most of the time reading the e-books, and re-reading the materials that Mistress Elena had sent.

Despite a year and a half looking forward to this experience, my stomach was in knots; I doubted whether I could have enjoyed the First Class food on this flight, even if we had been upgraded. I was confident that I could take anything that Mistress would throw at us, but it was the fear of the unknown that had gotten to me.

I reclined the seat and looked out the window at the darkening sky. There wouldn't be a 'mile high' experience on this flight, as I was having my period; hopefully it would be over by Sunday. And, fortunately, that meant that I wouldn't need to worry about it for the rest of the trip.

After seeing a beautiful sunrise ahead of us out the plane's window, we circled London in a racetrack pattern, awaiting our turn to land. I could see the Tower of London, The Shard, The London Eye Ferris wheel, and the Houses of Parliament – all places we had visited on our last trip here.

We took a taxi to a hotel Sam had selected in Chelsea Harbor. He explained, "Chelsea Harbor is a renovated area on the Thames, on the west side of London. It is only a 20-minute taxi ride to Kew Gardens. I managed to get a great rate for a marina-view room; I had to negotiate it with the manager, for the two-week stay."

Of course, I realized a 'great rate' in London was still expensive, especially for such a nice area. I guess I was giving Sam a questioning look, as he said, "The best rate I could get for an 'apartment' was about $1200 per week ... and this luxury hotel was only about $1600 a week, so not that bad."

Sam had shared with me some of the costs of the trip, which would total more than $10,000 – even with my discounted domme class (otherwise, it would have been close to $20,000!). Although Sam always tried to wangle a 'deal', he was also used to comfortable living, and now *I* was getting used to a comfortable lifestyle.

After we had decided that I would be taking the class, Sam had not complained once – about the expense, or the time it would take. I chuckled, thinking that he was probably more excited about the second half of the trip, going back to Amsterdam.

We went out onto the balcony of our upper-floor room, and looked down at the small harbor below, sleek power boats ready for a cruise, and a few beautiful sailboats, their masts rocking slightly.

And, above a few other hotel or condo buildings, we could see the Thames. There were high clouds, in streaks, in a pale blue sky; a beautiful day for London. I hadn't yet seen the famous London fog.

Sam opened a map, and spread it on the bed. "Chelsea Harbor is a bit out of the way, but only a five-minute walk to the Imperial Wharf 'Overground' train, and less than a 20 minute walk to the District tube line." Then he smiled, "Taking the Overground line across the river, then the

Southwest Trains, we should be able to get to Kew Gardens in about 20 minutes."

Of course, we would then have the ubiquitous '10-minute walk' to get to Mistress Elena's house. I certainly wouldn't want to get there late, so we would probably have to plan for an hour commute. Now that we were here, I was feeling less nervous about the class, and actually looking forward to getting started.

"So what would you like to do for your day in London?" I shrugged, not having any goals for the day, except relaxing. Sam said, "We haven't seen the Natural History Museum or the Science Museum, yet. Or, if you prefer, we can make reservations for the matinee performance of a play."

I shook my head, "I don't know if I could concentrate on a play, right now. Just walking around museums sounds OK." I realized that I'd been reading through most of the flight, so had been awake for nearly 24 hours, already. And we were just starting our day in London.

We took a taxi to the Natural History Museum, which was uncrowded on this weekday. It was a huge and ornate building, with some great exhibits – especially the skeletons of whales hanging from the ceiling, and the collection of dinosaurs.

Wandering through the museum, we entered the mineral gallery, and found the 'Vault', where some famous gems and stones were on display. We saw a huge emerald, a meteorite collection – including one from Mars, and the infamous 'cursed amethyst', which I'd never heard of, before.

Sam wanted to stop at a pub, but I suggested that we only have beer, and make a reservation for dinner. Browsing on his phone, Sam grinned, "Here's a restaurant that has some real exotic dishes – crocodile, kangaroo, python Carpaccio, and pan-fried crickets."

I shook my head, "I already have butterflies in my stomach ... I don't need crickets."

It took a second beer, but Sam finally found a restaurant he thought would be interesting and made an early reservation for us.

We walked to the Victoria and Albert Museum and looked at the upcoming exhibits. Just after my class would end there was a 'history of underwear' exhibit. We turned north, and walked several blocks to the Royal Albert Hall. There were no concerts tonight, but Sam saw that there was a Vivaldi concert we could attend on Saturday night.

"Sam, let's wait and see how I'm feeling at that point." My stomach did a backflip with a double twist; I guess I *was* still nervous.

We took the tour of Royal Albert Hall, which had been the venue for an unbelievable number of famous musicians over the past 150 years. Then, we walked into Hyde Park and through Kensington Gardens, past the Kensington Palace. We were still early, so we sat on a park bench, while Sam looked at the map of the surrounding area on his phone.

He looked at his watch, and said, "We have time for a movie before dinner. There's an art film theater near the restaurant, and they're playing a film I've wanted to see: '*Jeune et Jolie*' – 'Young and Beautiful', a François Ozon film." I wasn't sure I wanted subtitles, but sitting sounded good, right now.

The theater was incredible – a classic building, but with leather armchairs and footstools. And the film was interesting – about a high school girl that becomes a call girl ... until events overtake her. I yawned, as we exited the theater, and I realized I was starving.

We were in Notting Hill, and the restaurant was outrageous, with columns and arches, as in a medieval dungeon, but ornately decorated. There were several menus, and we started with a sampling of canapés, ranging from cauliflower-truffle risotto balls, to goat's cheese tart with onion marmalade, and seared *foie gras* with a reduced Madeira sauce.

There were no pan-fried crickets, but the food was exotic enough for my taste. I ordered the tuna steak with mango salsa for my main course, and Sam selected the filet with *Béarnaise* sauce. Of course, Sam insisted on sharing the dessert sampler.

My first thought was that we would need to go on a diet again. But then, I realized, I had no idea what food we would be served at Elena's. My stomach was now too full to do any acrobatics; but I wouldn't have to wait long to find out whether my nervousness was warranted.

On Friday morning, after a nice breakfast in the hotel, we walked along the docks. I wanted to get to Kew Gardens, so I packed, and we took the Overground to Clapham Junction, then the Southwest Trains line to North Sheen station, and then walked to the gardens. Fortunately, all my things were in a backpack; there wasn't much to bring.

We hadn't expected much, but the gardens were gorgeous, flowers blooming and the trees a rich green. The Palm House and Waterlily House were hot and humid tropical environments, and there was an abundance of orchids, and other rare flora.

Sam asked me if I wanted a snack, before reporting to Mistress, but my breakfast was just settling ... and I wanted to be well 'settled' before starting the class. It was just after 1PM, and we headed into a small residential area and found 'the house with the dungeon'.

I chucked, realizing that there were dozens (if not hundreds) of dommes in London, and some of these other houses may well have their own dungeons. Dungeons that were hidden from sight, as mothers and their small children walked on the sidewalk outside.

Mildred greeted us, and told Sam that he could stay for the first hour, if he wanted, and if I would allow him. He was delighted to hear this, and was grinning as we were escorted to a large room on the main floor – probably originally a study, but now set-up with a dozen chairs facing a podium.

Over the next twenty minutes, several other women arrived – most, I estimated, were in their thirties, but there was also an older one, perhaps in her 50s ... Sam's age. They spanned the gamut of body types and looks. We nervously introduced ourselves, and took seats. Only a couple of the women had a 'partner' with them.

The room silenced as Elena entered; *Mistress* Elena. She fully looked like a dominatrix, wearing the kind of outfit that Sam had expected the first time we were here: Black leather pants and a black, ruffled corset top, with high heels, and a riding crop in her hand.

"Welcome to my class on skills for a dominatrix. I've met all of you before, and selected each of you to take this course. Three of you are planning to be pro-dommes, and will be apprenticing with me for a year ... and I'll be taking 30% of what you bring in.

"And the other two of you are getting a scholarship to take this course, and will have a session with your benefactor two weeks from tomorrow."

Elena smiled, "I did consider inviting one or two men to attend the class, but the vast majority of the market is for female 'dommes', rather than male 'doms', and having a single gender will make it easier, organizationally.

"You will be practicing on each other, and also on several 'subs' who I will bring in – mostly male, as males will be your primary customers. As you know, providing a safe dominance and submission scene requires knowledge of the implements and techniques, as well as familiarity in feeling these implements yourself."

She continued, "Therefore, over the next 24 hours, you will get to experience submission, in several forms, as a prelude to learning how to dominate."

Elena chuckled, "This is also the time to find out whether you really have the fortitude for D/s ... although I've already seen what you can take and how you can control your bodies."

Elena paced the width of the room, then stopped and looked at each of us. "I will work with you individually to determine your goals. For example, those of you with partners may be interested in a BDSM lifestyle, while others may want to set up your own dungeon business, or work part-time in someone else's dungeon."

Pacing again, Elena explained, "The most important aspect of being a dominatrix is providing our clients a safe and enriching experience." She laughed, "Of course, it is very important to market yourselves, so you *have* clients.

"Dungeon culture, which you will represent as a domme, stresses the acceptance of all people, along with their fantasies and fetishes. You will soon learn that there's a lot of weird shit going on out there, and your clients will undoubtedly ask for some strange things. But it is important not to judge.

"The art of dominance and submission embodies female power, technical skill, sensitivity to people, beauty, and pleasure. These are the elements to which you will be exposed in this class.

"You will not be experts when you graduate, as an entire course could be devoted to each topic; and there are dozens of topics. But you will learn the basics," shaking her head, "and that is more education than a lot of so-called pro-dommes out there have."

Elena smiled, then announced that there would be a little demonstration. She walked out of the room for a minute, and we looked around the room: There was dark wood paneling, and parquet flooring, with bookshelves along the left wall, and high windows on the right wall.

Mistress Elena came striding into the room again, and stood next to the podium. "As you've seen from the materials I provided, your clients may desire any number of things, from bondage, to punishment, to role play, to humiliation, to various fetishes.

"This demonstration will be a short session with a slave-in-training. In this situation, you must have absolute control over the client, keep him unbalanced, not knowing what will come next, and seldom able to please you."

Now, Elena reached over to the podium, and 'dinged' a bell. An older man came scurrying into the room, and up to the front, where he kneeled in front of Mistress. He was overweight and balding, hair only on the sides of his head. He had a round face, and I could picture him as a bank president or politician, had he been wearing a suit and tie.

But he was in a gown – similar to a hospital gown – plain, light beige in color. He was also wearing a slave collar. He looked down at the floor as he said, crisply, "Yes, Mistress."

Mistress looked at us and smiled, "Jerome is a submissive who is into humiliation and, when needed, punishment. As a slave, his function is to please me." She looked down at Jerome, "Isn't that right, Slave?"

Jerome kept looking down, but was nodding vigorously, "Oh, yes, Mistress." Then he asked, unsurely, "May I please clean Mistress' shoes?"

Elena nodded, "That would be nice, Slave." Jerome was instantly on his hands and knees, licking Elena's shoes. After only a minute, Elena yelled, "Have you cleaned the soles, yet, Slave?"

Jerome replied, "Not yet, Mistress. I'm sorry, Mistress."

Elena snarled, "Stand up, Slave!" Jerome was on his feet, hands to his sides, only a couple of feet in front of Elena. Suddenly, she slapped him hard, on the right cheek, then followed-up with a hard slap to his left cheek.

Jerome's head snapped back and forth, then he looked down and said, "Thank you, Mistress. I deserved that."

Elena cackled, "You deserve more, don't you, Slave?"

Jerome choked, then nodded and hoarsely voiced, "Yes, Mistress."

Elena slapped him a few more times, Jerome not making a sound. She glanced at us and smiled, then turned to Jerome and kneed him in the groin. Jerome doubled over and we heard a stifled grunt, then he stood tall ... and Elena kicked him in the balls again.

I could see Sam shaking his head out the corner of my eye. The women sitting on the other side of me were watching intently, their mouths having fallen open.

"Drop that gown!" Elena bellowed, and Jerome's gown fell to the floor. He was wearing jockey shorts. Elena grabbed something from behind the podium, and turned to Jerome, "Open!" Jerome opened his mouth wide, and Elena stuffed a pair of panties into it.

Elena handed Jerome some wrist cuffs, and he put them on, as Elena went to the wall and uncleated a small rope that I hadn't noticed. A hook dropped from the ceiling, and Elena hooked it to the rings on the cuffs. Then, she pulled the rope taut and re-cleated it.

Reaching down, Elena quickly pulled Jerome's undershorts down to his knees, his hardening cock on display for all of us. Then, she turned him around, and took a heavy strap from the podium. Without warning, she let the strap fly, impacting Jerome's butt with a 'CRAAACK!' that sounded like a gunshot.

But it became a machine-gun sound, as the strap continued to rain down on Jerome's bum, and I counted 60 strokes that I estimated took less than 30 seconds. Jerome was twisting, and his feet were stamping, but he let out cries only on the last few strokes. His butt was beet red.

Now, Elena pulled something else from behind the podium, and showed it to Jerome, who had twisted toward us, tears already streaming down his cheeks. She walked nearly halfway across the room, then spun the bullwhip around and put all her force into a stroke that lashed across Jerome's bottom.

He screamed. And he continued to scream, as Elena mercilessly continued to whip him, thin red stripes now covering his rear. When she finally stopped, Jerome was taking long, racking breaths, his nose sniffling, as he said, loudly, "Thank you, Mistress."

Elena selected one of the women in the first row, and instructed, "Please take him to the bathroom, and come back with half a cup of his pee." She turned to Jerome and removed his jockeys, then uncleated the rope, and released Jerome's wrists. Then, she commanded, "Crawl!"

Jerome crawled out of the room, followed by one of my classmates. Elena turned to us, "Of course, every client is different, and you must determine what they want – or what is best for them."

She looked around, "Are there any questions?"

The girl next to me raised her hand, "And does the slave get to have an orgasm, at the end of the session?"

Elena laughed, "Again, it depends on what has been agreed on. In this case, I'm going to allow Jerome to masturbate, but only once he's back in his cage." There were a few gasps, and Elena continued, "I was going to have him masturbate in front of all of you, then lick up his cum from the floor, so I'm giving him a break."

Jerome crawled back into the room, followed by the woman, who carried a plastic cup with a yellow liquid, that we assumed was Jerome's pee. Elena took the cup, and had the woman take her seat, then turned to Jerome, who was kneeling again, this time nude.

She pulled the panties out of his mouth, and asked, "You'll drink this for me, won't you, Slave?"

Jerome didn't hesitate, "Yes, Mistress."

Elena turned to us, "He hasn't tried this, yet." Then, handing Jerome the cup, she commanded, "Drink, Slave!" And Jerome, his eyes squeezed tightly closed, drank his own urine.

Looking at her watch, she announced, "Well, I guess that's as much demonstration as we have time for. Slave will now go downstairs and get back into his cage. He will take my shoes," she took them off and handed them to Jerome, "and lick them clean. Then, he will be allowed to masturbate into this cup."

Jerome, from his kneeling position, looked halfway up to Elena, and said, "Thank you, Mistress." Then, he crawled back out of the room, awkwardly carrying the two shoes and cup, using his mouth.

Elena smiled, "The guests can leave now, and our students will get a break in 24 hours. They must be back here by 9PM Sunday evening."

Everyone stood, and Sam hugged me, and said he would come back tomorrow. I told him not to bother, that I would meet him back at the hotel, but Sam insisted on meeting me here. We kissed, and he left. Now, there were only the five student dommes and Mistress Elena.

As I walked back to the train station, I couldn't help but shake my head ... trying to get some of the images out of it, unbelieving how Mistress Elena had treated her slave. As she had said, it was a session of humiliation. Not my 'cup of tea' ... and neither was the urine.

She had also reminded everyone that a domme must not judge, must be ready to support her client's fantasies, no matter how bizarre they seem. It was a service business, like any other – needing to provide what the customers wanted.

And, like any other business, it required work. A full day of Kelly's class would be spent on ethical and legal issues, and another on marketing the business.

Of course, I didn't think Kelly was doing this to further her career or business prospects. But, as she had once mentioned, being a part-time domme would give her other submissives to play with, rather than topping me.

I would need to get some work done, while Kelly learned the art of domination. I had e-mailed a number of potential strategic partners to KS Biotech, and had calls in to a few investment offices. It was a process that had to be followed-up and slogged through, for any hope of success.

But it was dusk already by the time I got back to Imperial Wharf, so I walked around the area and found an interesting-looking Lebanese restaurant.

It was the start of the weekend, and I already looked forward to seeing Kelly tomorrow afternoon and Sunday.

Mistress Elena welcomed us individually, and Mildred brought out refreshments – I guess it was 'tea and crumpet' time in merry old England. Then, we were shown to our rooms – which were in the basement, through a door in the 'dungeon' that Sam and I hadn't noticed the last time we were here.

There were six rooms, 3 on each side of a hallway, and a communal bathroom at the end of the hall. The rooms were Spartan – not quite 'slave quarters', but not very comfortable, either.

There was a sink in the room, a single bed (at least, it wasn't a cot), a dresser, and small desk and chair, as well as a second chair – a well-cushioned wing-back. The floors were wood, and the only things on the walls were a small mirror over the dresser, and a couple of black-and-white images – a man on a spanking bench, lines showing across his bottom, and another man with his wrists held above him, as a whip lashed his back.

We had been told to undress completely, and put on the garment in the top drawer of the dresser, which would be our 'uniform' for the class. It was a sack dress – not burlap, but still a heavy material (almost like canvas), sleeveless, with a straight knee-length hem.

There were no buttons or other fasteners on the 'dress', so the only way on and off was over my head. It was the color of a brown paper bag, and didn't look much better than one, on me. There had been a pair of slippers in the dresser, but we'd been told to remain barefoot.

I used the bathroom, and headed back upstairs. When we were all in the study, Mistress Elena reviewed the course syllabus, and expectations for the class – both ours and hers. Then, we were each given five minutes to introduce ourselves, describe our past experiences with BDSM, and list our goals for the class and our future.

We all had different motivations. One of the younger women said she hoped to make money by being a pro-domme. Another, a butch-looking lesbian, told us she looked forward to dominating men. The older woman explained that she'd been married and had a family, but was now divorced, and interested in teasing men, and having relationships that she could control, bringing in a bit of extra income.

I explained my relationship with Sam, and what we'd done – mainly spanking, anal play, and medical play. My stated motivations were to learn more about power exchange and domination, both for my personal relationship, and possible exploration with others.

Of course, I didn't mention the company Sam and I had started, that I had a Ph.D., or the fact that Sam had proposed to me. I missed wearing my engagement ring, as we'd been told to not bring any jewelry to the class.

Only one of the women was currently married, her husband evidently having no problem with her desire to dominate other men, as a money-making hobby. I was the youngest of the group; only Susan was within a decade of my age. She was a bit overweight, but in all the right places: Buxom and curvy.

At 4PM sharp, Mistress Elena began her lectures – on the psychology of BDSM and understanding fetishes. She gave plenty of examples from her own 'practice'. Some of the statistics she quoted were probably based on U.K. research, but I imagined that things wouldn't be much different in the U.S.

We learned that roughly half of all men and women fantasize about dominating or being dominated sexually, although only a small number actually participate in some form of BDSM. The research showed that practitioners of BDSM have less depression, anxiety and paranoia, although a higher incidence of dissociation and narcissism.

The psychologists had also studied what happens to people during a BDSM scene. They found that both tops and bottoms go into an altered state of consciousness, the bottom feeling reduced pain, a sensation of floating, and peacefulness – just as I had experienced that first long day with Sam. The top can feel reduced self-consciousness, and a strong focus on the scene.

Elena explained different forms of power play, and the strange reversal of roles being played out. As Sam had educated me, the bottom – the submissive – is the one in control, both by virtue of the agreement with the top, and by their ability to use a safeword. And, the top – the dominant – must be caring and nurturing to provide a safe experience for the bottom.

After a short bathroom break, Elena began the second lecture, on kinks and perversions, describing an unbelievable array of fetishes – from wearing latex, rubber, or leather; to tickling or scratching; to vampires and blood; to lactation or menstruation; to stuffed animals, balloons, bugs, or smoking.

Even a single category, such as foot fetish, had a lot of variations. For example, there could be specific fetishes for shoes, boots, high heels, stockings, socks, or stinky feet.

We shared some of the kinks and fetishes we or our partners had, and several were similar to things Sam and I had done – enemas, hot wax, strap-ons, and pet play, for example. And, of course, most of us had played with spanking implements, such as the paddle, strap, crop, switch or cane.

But there were a few more extreme examples, as well. Pat, the lesbian, said she loved fisting – on someone else, of course. Amanda, the married one, said her husband was turned-on by humiliation – which they'd both only discovered when their kids were grown and had left home.

Susan said she wanted to learn more about financial domination, or 'fin-dom', saying she thought she would be a natural at it. We all laughed, and Mistress said we would get to that in a week or so, and that it wasn't as easy as Susan was imagining.

Elena looked at her watch, then decided to cover one more topic – bondage. She showed images on a large display that was built into the bookshelves on the side of the room. They were pictures of men bound with rope in fancy designs, men shackled to a brick wall, men in stocks, and men suspended on huge hooks – as we had seen in San Francisco.

Then she showed several cock & ball cages, various types of gags, straightjackets, and even mummification (the man's nose and penis the only two parts of him not wrapped in electrical tape). Elena explained that she had first wrapped him in an entire roll of Saran, before finishing with black electrical tape.

When the display went black, Elena chortled, "Well, we want to make sure you guys get your exercise today ... at least your arms." She looked at the large riding crop, then snapped it against the side of the podium, "And I have to get your butts warmed up so I can try out my new crop!"

None of us made a sound, and Elena continued, "Let's see how you do on each other with a simple spanking." She cackled, and announced, "Dinner will be served at 8PM, and I want your butts well-reddened before you sit down at the dining room table."

She pulled two of the chairs to the front, facing into the room. "This is going to take about an hour." She put a sheet of paper on each chair, laughing, "Mildred did these for me. On each line, the first name is the top, and the second name is the bottom. When the spanking is done, cross off that line, and move to the next one."

Susan sat in the left chair, and I lifted the hem of my dress to my waist, and got over her knee, while Amanda lifted her dress and got over Pat's knee in the other chair. Elena set an egg timer for 5 minutes, and sat in the front row, observing. Susan gave me a hard spanking, similar to the hardest spanking I'd received from Sam.

When the timer rang, I sat on the chair, and Pat went over my knee, and Amanda spanked Cynthia, the older woman, in the other chair. Elena set the timer again, and called out, "Begin!"

It *was* exercise: Each of us spanked each of the other women, and took a spanking from each of them. After the second or third spanking, our bottoms were red, and by the time it was over, they were feeling pretty sore. We all performed about the same, taking most of our spankings with little fuss, but kicking and squealing a little during the last one.

We had barely enough time to clean up and get to the dining room by 8PM. There was a table for twelve, covered by a finely embroidered linen tablecloth. The chairs were heavy and – fortunately – well-padded. There were bowls of fresh vegetables in ice on the table – carrots, celery, olives, pickles, and I wasn't sure what else.

Mildred served soups, and put out a basket of freshly-baked rolls. There wasn't much discussion at the table, so Elena told a few of the stories she'd collected from more than a decade of being a dominatrix. I would have to remember some of these to tell Sam.

We were halfway through the main course – a roast with scalloped potatoes – when Elena apologized. "Sorry that we're not having wine tonight, but we can't have you getting tired for your submission experience."

That was the first we'd heard about anything more happening tonight. I was already tired – I realized it was due to jet lag beginning to hit me.

Mildred brought in a huge glass bowl filled to the top with an English 'trifle'. It had several layers of fruit, separated by sherry-soaked sponge cake and custard, with whipped cream on top. I doubted that we would be eating this way every night!

Strong coffee was served, and it would hopefully keep us all awake for our 'session' tonight. We had some free time until 10PM, when we were told to report to the dungeon. I looked into the 'commons' room, where a few of the girls were watching television; but I couldn't get interested, so went back to my room to study my notes.

I couldn't concentrate on those, either, so I took a leisurely shower and put in a fresh tampon. There would be no makeup, and dressing was easy: Just slip the 'bag dress' over my head. After brushing my hair, I spent the last few minutes before the appointed time sitting cross-legged on my bed, trying to meditate.

Promptly at 10PM, we assembled in the dungeon, all of us looking around at the array of specialized furniture and equipment ... plus the implements hanging on the walls, between black-and-white photographs of dungeon scenes. Although the room was bright, the indirect lighting lent a soft feeling to the venue.

Mildred came into the room, carrying a box which she placed on one of the rolling tables, instructing us to put the cuffs on our wrists and ankles. Then, we were told to line up and stand on the black parquet tiles. They were spaced about four feet apart, and ran the width of the room. I hadn't noticed those, before.

We had all read the 'rules', but Mildred asked if we had any questions. When nobody asked any, Mildred explained that this was to be a submission session where we would experience BDSM from the sub's perspective. It was also designed to provide some surprises, and test our openness.

I chuckled, thinking how this already sounded like one of Sam's submission challenges. Mildred told us to lift our dresses to our waists, keep our eyes forward, and be silent. Then, she left the room.

Several minutes later, Elena entered the dungeon, still wearing black, and carrying her crop. "Good evening, ladies." She paced back and forth in front of us. "As Mildred told you, this session is designed to give you a small idea of how the sub feels during a session.

"Each of you will have a slightly different experience, based on what you said you would be willing to try, on the forms you filled-out." Now, I was trying to remember everything I had checked-off. There had been a lot of new things, things I'd never done, many of which I had marked as 'willing to try'.

Elena swished the crop through the air a few times, and cackled, "Now, let's see what this little thing can do." She walked behind us, and I heard a loud 'SNAP!' and a surprised 'Ow!' from Amanda. Then a few more 'snaps' of the crop against bare skin, as Elena moved down the line.

Ow!!! Elena had cropped the back of each of my thighs, and there were two burning rectangles. Most of us were able to remain silent, as we felt the crop on our bums, and the fronts of our thighs. But Amanda squealed again, and Elena shook her head. "Would someone like to demonstrate how to take a cropping, for Amanda?"

I didn't think, just took a step forward, still facing ahead. "I would be honored to please Mistress, if she would like to use my body for a demonstration." In my peripheral vision, I actually saw two of my classmates snap their heads towards me.

Elena smiled, "That would be very nice, Kelly. Please come here and stand facing the class."

"Yes, Mistress," I said, as I took my position, facing forward but trying not to look anyone in the eye. I heard Elena stepping behind me, and I took a breath, "I'm ready now, Mistress." I held the dress a bit higher, to make sure it was well above my waist.

There was a sting and then a white-hot burning on my left buttock, and then another on my right. I held my position, and forced a smile – now defocusing my eyes, and feeling them start to tear-up. Elena stepped in front of me, and cropped my thighs.

"Hold the dress up to your neck, now," Elena said, and I lifted the minimal dress. A moment later, the leather slapper of the crop landed on my belly. My body jerked, and I let out a grunt, but was otherwise still and quiet.

"The top must always be careful with sensitive tissues of the sub, but must also maintain the tension level, and provide a few surprises." Ow!! Ow!!!! The crop landed on the underside of my right breast, then my left. *That* really hurt!

Elena cropped me lightly on the insides of my thighs, moving from my crotch to just above my knees on both sides. It didn't hurt at first, but after several passes with the crop – harder, each time – I knew that my inner thighs were bright red.

"Turn around!" Mistress Elena commanded. I spun around. Elena explained to the class, "We need to re-warm-up your butts, so I'm going to give each of you ten strokes. When I call your name, please come up here, and get into the position Kelly is in, now." She whispered to me, "And then you can go back into the line."

"Yes, Mistress. I understand." I took a deep breath, and said, softly, "I'm ready for my cropping, now, Mistress."

"Good girl," Elena whispered to me. Then, she began applying the crop – on the top of my bum on each side, then a bit lower on each side, and repeating, until the crop was again landing on my upper thigh. I started to whimper, but caught myself, and limited my response to a few sniffles. My entire butt was burning.

Each of the other girls was called, stepped to the front, turned their butt towards us, and lifted their dress, receiving a good cropping from Mistress Elena. There were a few squeals, and Amanda was in tears by the end, but we all cooperated well.

Mildred entered the room again and, one-by-one, slid five ottomans across the floor from the side wall in front of each of us. They were rectangular, about two feet wide; only when one was placed in front of me did I notice that the tufted leather top came off, so that things could be stored inside.

"OK. Get into a knee-chest position on those, with your butts facing me, and your hands on the floor." She was standing near the entrance to the room, where the stairs came down. As we got into position, we heard Elena and Mildred talking quietly.

Now, Mistress Elena spoke forcefully, "You *will* keep your eyes forward! If any of you turns your head to look back, I will be giving an early caning demonstration."

She chuckled, "You may close your eyes, if you don't want to be tempted to look back." That was a good idea. I closed my eyes, and tried to relax.

My chin was on the edge of the ottoman, my butt high in the air, a slight breeze tickling my anus. I waited, and was surprised when music began playing at low volume. It was Bach ... I thought maybe one of the Brandenburg concertos.

My body jumped slightly, when I felt the caress of a flogger being pulled across my back, and down my bottom. There were several more 'caresses', and then the flogger began stroking me, to the right and to the left, back and forth, until my already-sore bottom was burning again.

The flogger left me, and I heard the music again. I jumped a second time, when I felt a cold object against my anus. Realizing that it was probably a butt plug, I relaxed, allowing the device to advance. Whoever was doing this – probably Mildred – was being gentle, and the plug was finally pushed into position inside me.

Then, the flogging started again, harder now, covering my hips and backs of my thighs, in addition to my bum. Just as I thought I could take no more, the flogger began an up-down motion, coming up from under me, lashing my privates, faster and faster.

Suddenly, the music ended, as did the flogging. The room was silent, except for a lot of heavy breathing. "Please look at me, now." I opened my eyes, and looked up, Mistress Elena standing in front of us, next to one of the spanking horses.

I now realized that my dress was gathered around my neck, and I wouldn't have been able to look back, had I tried. All the others were to my right, and I tried glancing, but the dress prevented me from even seeing Amanda, who was only a few feet away.

Elena smiled, and said, "And, now, I will introduce you to your tops – for the evening." She laughed, "Actually, the *morning*. You may have noticed that the 'demonstrations' were to be on Saturday morning ... but it will be Saturday in just a few minutes."

She looked up and nodded, then continued, "Kelly will sub to Master James." I was shocked to see a man step in front of me and bow. The other women must have been watching, as there were a few gasps and at least one groan coming from my right.

Master James bent down and held out his hand, and I shook it ... knowing full well that my body was exposed, bum in the air ... and *he* had been the one inserting the butt plug and flogging me. I smiled at James, looking into his clear blue eyes, and he nodded and smiled at me, then stood next to Elena. He had a beard, and wore a black tee and jeans; he looked fortyish.

"Amanda will sub to Master William." I pushed down the pouf of dress to my right, so that I could see him. Another handsome man, probably also in his forties. "Pat will sub to Mistress Anne." A much older woman walked around in front of her, and shook her hand. "Susan will sub to Master Henry." He was much older, certainly older than Sam.

Finally, Elena introduced Mistress Priscilla, who would be topping Cynthia. Interestingly, Priscilla was the youngest of the domina – probably in her mid-thirties – while Cynthia was the oldest of the students. I didn't know how we'd been matched up, and it didn't really matter.

But, interestingly, James was the youngest – and I thought the most handsome – of the doms. He smiled at me, catching me appraise him. Yes, I had been looking unabashedly at my Master ... but he had been looking at my exposed body for the past fifteen minutes ... or more.

"Please kneel on the ottomans, now, and put your hands behind your back," Elena commanded. The Masters and Mistresses stepped up to their subs, as we took our position, and let our dresses drop. James fastened a collar around my neck, then attached a short leash. I kept my eyes turned downward.

Elena laughed, "Before you take them away, I'd like to try my new crop one more time. Masters and Mistresses, please hug your subs. And you subs, please hug your tops."

James hugged me, and I put my hands around his waist, and buried my head in his chest. Now, Elena was walking back and forth behind us, snapping the crop against our bare feet. That hurt almost as much as cropping our breasts. We each got several strokes on the bottom of each foot.

Then, she and Mildred left the dungeon. I looked up at James, and he asked, "Is there anything you would like to say?" His voice was deep and mellow, as he spoke softly. But there was an intensity to his words, and his eyes looked into mine with incredible force – not looking through me, but looking deeply into me.

I put my hands behind my back again, and nodded, "Yes, Sir. Thank you for the warm-up flogging and the butt plug. I'm here to learn and to please you ... so I will submit to your desires ... up to my limit."

James gave me a curious expression, and asked, "Your 'limit'?"

I nodded, "Yes – transfer of body fluids. Other than that you may do anything with me that you like."

James frowned and nodded, "Come with me!"

Standing, I walked out of the dungeon behind James. I had seen a couple of the other girls crawling out, but James hadn't asked me to do that; maybe he felt that walking would accentuate the pain in my feet from the crop? We went to my room, and James closed the door. I knelt on the floor, my hands in a praying position.

We had a nice discussion, although James let me stay on my knees, while he sat in the wingback chair. He explained that Mistress Elena had trained him several years ago, and that he specialized in topping women. He evidently had a number of regular clientele who – he said – depended on him much as they depended on their hairdresser.

I couldn't help but ask, "Is there ever any 'sex' involved?" Elena had already told us that sex was seldom a part of dungeon play, at least with pro-dommes and, I supposed, pro-doms.

James chuckled, "No. Actually, I prefer men." When I cocked my head, he clarified, "I guess I'm bi, but I haven't had sex with a woman for years." Then, he smiled, "Of course, I have some clients who enjoy a 'happy ending', after a challenging submission scene. But, for legal reasons, I can't officially offer that."

Then, James leaned forward and looked into my eyes seriously, "Mistress Elena has asked me to see that you experience a few specific things, respecting your limits, that will extend the experiences you've already had. And, I'll introduce a few new things.

"You will also be experiencing many new things during the class." He chuckled, "I assume you already know that you'll be practicing on each other, and on a few subs that Mistress will bring in." I nodded.

James instructed, "Please clasp your hands behind your back. I would like to see how far you will submit without being bound. But you will be punished if you get out of position. If you request, I will bind you in position. Later, I'll tie you up for your finale."

Still on my knees, I put my hands behind my back, and replied, "Yes, Master." I had no idea how long the session would be or what the 'finale' might include.

James warned, "You are to be ready at all times, as I may surprise you. Like this." In an instant, James' hand flew across my vision, slapping my face and searing my left cheek. My head jerked to the right, but – as soon as I recovered from the shock – faced James again.

Another slap, this time on my right cheek, snapped my head to the left. These were very hard slaps ... something I'd never experienced (and never really wanted to experience) before.

There were tears in my eyes, as James slapped me half a dozen more times. He sat back and smiled at me. I sniffed, and said, proudly, "Thank you, Master."

"OK. Let's warm up your bottom." Mistress had already warmed it plenty, but I would need more desensitizing, if James was going to use heavy implements ... which I knew he would.

James sat on the straight-backed desk chair, and – without being told – I put myself over his lap. He didn't put a leg over mine, so I would need to concentrate on keeping my legs down.

I hadn't quite finished this thought, when James began spanking me, with a stunning intensity. I bounced a little, but forced my legs straight and toes touching the wood floor. The spanks were coming hard and fast, and I wondered whether I would be able to achieve this kind of spanking power, after we'd been trained.

The impact of James' hand on my bare bottom echoed throughout the small room, and tears welled in my eyes again, and fell onto the parquet tile. I settled myself, trying to relax my body, and ignore the pain.

James continued to spank me, not letting up on either the speed or the force of the blows. It seemed like a very long time, and my bum was getting incredibly sore. I heard myself whimpering – something I rarely did, even when Sam was topping me.

As the spanking continued, on and on, I zoned out. The pain was no longer a focus, my mind drifting; perhaps it was the endorphins? But so far, James had only used his hand. I had only felt this a few times previously. And it was amazing. I was in 'subspace'.

My whimpering stopped, and my body fully relaxed over James' lap. He was now covering my upper thighs with hard spanks, and my entire backside burned.

Suddenly, the echoes faded, and I realized that the spanking was over. Tears were still falling onto the floor, but I had the coherency to again say, "Thank you Master. That was a good 'warm up'." Of course, it had been much more than that.

James patted my butt, and said, softly, "Good girl. Now, please fetch the hairbrush in the bottom dresser drawer." My head fell, and more tears fell, before I could get off James' lap and retrieve the large, polished wood-backed brush.

I hadn't opened this drawer, earlier, and now saw that there was a narrow leather strap next to the hairbrush, spanning the length of the drawer. I turned to James, "Shall I bring the strap, also, Master?"

James laughed a deep laugh, and replied, "Yes, Kelly. That would be nice."

As I took the few steps back to James, and knelt in front of him, I scanned his body, then looked up to his eyes. He was very fit, if perhaps a bit thin, and had a small goatee, and an earing in his left ear. He was quite handsome.

I held the strap and hairbrush in my hands in front of me, and James took them. James raised an eyebrow, and chuckled, "Yes. That's not a bad idea. You'll get a break before we return to your ass."

He turned and put the hairbrush on the desk, and coiled the handle-end of the strap around his hand. I was about to put my hands down, when I realized what he was going to do; so I left my hands out, palms up, and fingers flexed back so my palms were flat.

I looked into his eyes, and he nodded and smiled. Then, the strap landed on my right palm, and – entirely reflexively – my hand flew down and I put it between my knees. Almost immediately, I realized what I'd done, so I quickly raised it and held it out again.

"Sorry, Sir. I'll try to keep them up."

James' only reaction was to swing the strap harder, landing again on my right hand. Then, a moment later, it fell on my left hand. Then, again. Tears were rolling down my cheeks, but I was managing to put my hands back into position after each stroke.

The strapping stopped, and James nodded again, "I can understand why Mistress Elena was so excited about you taking her class. You're a natural sub, and I'm sure you'll make a great top."

James stood, and pointed to the bed. "Now, please lie down on your back, with your feet in the air." I got into position, and James explained, "This is done a lot in the Middle East as a punishment – and sometimes as a turn-on. It's called 'bastinado' or 'falaka'."

As I held my legs vertical, James strapped the bottoms of my feet. They were stinging. Incredibly, after all the things Sam and I had done, this was something new for me. Ow! Ow! Ow! ...

James coiled the strap and put it on the dresser, then sat in the straight-backed chair. I stood on my sore soles and, when he picked up the hairbrush and gave me the 'come here' signal, I got back over his thigh and forced my legs down, toes touching the floor.

"I'm ready for my hairbrushing, Master. I am here to please you." James chuckled and lightly patted my bottom a few times with the hairbrush.

Then, without warning, there was a 'WHAP!' and a burning area on my left butt cheek. Then, on my right. And, now, randomly, all over my bum, the brush coming down incredibly hard.

I grabbed the leg of the chair with both hands, and squeezed my eyes shut. My heart was racing, and my body bouncing, as I tried to maintain my position.

Mercifully, James limited the hairbrushing to a minute, or so – probably fifty or more strokes. James softly told me I could get off his lap. I knew my bottom had to be dark red now, and I wanted to feel it, to soothe it ... but, instead, I got back onto my knees on the floor, and clasped my hands behind me.

"Thank you, Master. That was very enlightening ..." I had to chuckle, "Or maybe 'enreddening'. I've never had a hairbrushing that hard, before."

James laughed, and stood, then signaled me to stand, which I did, my legs apart and hands clasped on my head – the 'standing position' Sam had taught me.

"Come along, Kelly, let's do another kind of scene. Mistress Elena told me you have some experience in this area."

I followed James into the dungeon, where two or three of my classmates were being caned, paddled, or strapped, as they were immobilized on one of the spanking benches, or 'horses'. We walked to the medical corner, where the rolling exam table was located; where Elena had injected Sam's balls. A shiver went down my spine.

James pointed to the table, and I hopped up onto it. "On my front or back, Master?"

"On your back. We're going to do a little labial infusion." I involuntarily jerked my head up, then let it fall back to the table. James was preparing some supplies on one of the rolling metal tables, and I clasped my hands across my stomach, and stared at the ceiling. This would be *something else* new!

James said, "You're doing so well – it's impressive that I haven't had to bind you ... yet. So, instead of using the stirrups, and strapping you down, I suggest we do this casually." He bent my right leg, and let the knee fall outward – the 'half butterfly' position in which Barbara, the esthetician, had waxed me.

James pulled a high intensity floor lamp over, and made a show of filling a 10cc syringe with saline. Of course, we had done that ... but James was using an incredibly thick needle. Fortunately, I didn't comment; when the syringe was full of saline, he took off the huge needle, and put on the thinnest needle I'd ever seen.

He explained, "I filled the syringe with an 18 gauge needle, and we'll start with a 30 gauge for your first injections. Then, we may go up to a 27 or 25 gauge needle." He was pulling my right outer labium with gloved fingers, and staring at my privates.

Then, he said, "You're going to feel a little prick." It was not as bad as a bee sting, but hurt more than the needles we used, being in such a sensitive location. I could feel James injecting the saline. Then, he stuck me a few more times, going up my labium. Each time, he injected more saline, and the area was starting to hurt a little.

He repeated the process on my left side, then suggested I put my head up and take a look. He held a mirror for me, and I adjusted it, until I could see myself: My labia were much thicker than normal.

James put a 25 gauge needle on the syringe, and announced, "Just one more pass. You'll probably be feeling 'fat' down there for a few hours." I hoped to be in bed before 'a few hours'.

"Ow!!!" I couldn't help it – the larger needle hurt, even though it was the size we used for butt injections, and normally we barely felt it. James inserted the needle three times on each side, injecting more saline each time. When he was done, I took another look: My labia were as thick as my fingers!

It felt strange, and I had no idea why someone would want to do this ... other than a medical fetishist like Sam, looking for another medical 'procedure' to give to someone.

James helped me off the table, and we walked to another corner of the room, where there were some coiled ropes, and a swing set-up. It felt really weird walking, with those fat things between my legs.

"I would like to make you cry, now. You've already demonstrated that you're a strong woman, and willing to obey me. For the rest, you'll be able to relax, not hold yourself in position, just 'enjoy' the intensity of the pain."

I figured that I would be crying at some point. And it wasn't that I was afraid to let my emotions out, or even show fear; I just wanted to show my strength and ability to control my own body, against its normal instincts.

James handed me a pair of wrist cuffs, and I put them on, while he lowered a rope from the ceiling. He attached the hook on the end of the rope to the rings on the cuffs, but left the rope slack enough for me to put my hands on my head.

"I'm going to give you one more opportunity to demonstrate your strength and hold yourself in position, while I switch you."

Chuckling, I asked, "You're a switch? And I get to spank *you*, now?" James was laughing, and hugged me, before he took a long switch from a rack on the side wall, and swished it through the air in front of me. It was really intimidating. I took a deep breath ...

"This will just be the warm-up for your caning. Then, I think Mistress Elena will participate in your 'finale'."

The feeling was shocking, as the switch landed repeatedly, my bottom feeling like it was being cut with a sword, over and over, the cuts coming fast and covering most of my butt.

I was mostly able to keep my hands on my head, fighting the need for my hands to go to my bum – which, of course, would have been limited by the rope above me.

I wasn't quite as good at keeping my feet still, as I now realized that I was stamping my feet as the switch continued to land in an almost continuous volley of white-hot slashes. But I managed to keep facing the wall, not twisting or turning, but giving James a stable target.

The switching continued, and I didn't bother trying to count the strokes. Tears were rolling down my cheeks, and eventually (whether it was two minutes or ten minutes, I couldn't tell), I let out a primal scream. Then, I began sobbing.

There were at least another dozen strokes of the switch before James ended the torturous experience. I was still sobbing, my breath racking, and the tears flowing freely. James hugged me again and, releasing the rope, my hands fell over his shoulders.

When I could control my breathing again, I looked into James' blue eyes, and said, hoarsely, "Thank you, Master. That was a switching I won't soon forget." My bum was in throbbing pain, but I didn't dare reach back to rub it.

James nodded and replied, "You're welcome, Kelly." Then, his grin widened, and he pointed to the swing, which was hanging from chains and faced against the side wall. I sat in the leather contraption – which wasn't that different from a swing in the children's park near my parents' house.

"You'll notice that your hips, and top of your bottom, are protected by the back of the swing, and your lower thighs are protected by the seat of the swing. In between is the ideal zone for a caning."

It was obvious, now that he'd pointed it out. The back of my bum stuck through the space between the bottom and back of the swing, making a perfect target. James spent some time swishing some of the canes through the air, and finally selected one from a bunch that stuck up from a circular bin.

"I've never done this before, so thought it might be interesting ... for both of us. I'm going to start you swinging, then have you push off the wall. Each time you get to the top of the arc near me, I'll swing the cane. It's almost like connecting a bat with a pitched baseball."

It would be interesting: I wasn't fastened into the swing, but it cradled me so there wasn't much 'wiggle' room, unless I came entirely out of it. I had no idea how many strokes I would be receiving. But what scared me was the fact that this evidently wasn't my finale.

James pulled the swing back, and let it go. I swung toward the wall, and pushed off with my feet, swinging backwards higher than before. After the third push-off, I was swinging about as high as I thought safe, and the cane landed with a 'CRACK!', the swing now arcing back down.

The pain of the cane was so distracting that I nearly forgot to push off the wall. Each time I swung back, the cane crashed into my bum, the pain searing after I'd already been switched raw.

I was crying again, but didn't care. This was far beyond anything that Sam and I had done. After the eighth stroke – or maybe it was the tenth – James stopped the swing.

"I would like to see if you can take three more hard strokes, holding yourself in position." He helped me out of the swing, and bent me over. "Try to hold your ankles, please."

Sniffling, I croaked, "Yes, Master." Of course, I would *try*, but didn't know if I could do it. I faced into the corner and bent over. James had said I would be able to relax ...

My hands holding my ankles, knees flexed, butt in the air, I felt James slide the cane back-and-forth several times, slightly adjusting it's position. It didn't matter: My entire butt was inflamed, and I wondered whether the next stroke would draw blood.

'CRAAACK!!' I screamed, and my vision temporarily went black. A moment later, realizing that I'd raised up – my hands now at knee level – I bent over and held my ankles again. I felt a hand rubbing my bottom, and briefly flashed on it being too small to be James'.

Then, the next stroke landed. 'CRAAAAAACK!!!'. I heard a shriek involuntarily issue from my throat. The pain was intense, and my knees felt weak.

Just as I was grabbing my ankles again, the third stroke seared into my sore seat. Another scream, and I tried to reach my ankles again, but my body was now shaking. "You may stand, now," James said softly. Then there was applause, coming from behind me.

I stood slowly, put my hands on my head, and turned around. Mistress Elena and a few of the other women – and their Masters – were standing around James, evidently having watched the spectacle on my bottom.

Looking directly at James, I said, "Thank you again, Master. I hope you enjoyed caning me. I'm here for your pleasure."

Mistress Elena was smiling, as were the Masters. The other classmates had serious expressions, and were rubbing their own bottoms. James stepped to me and hugged me again, "Oh, yes, Kelly. I enjoyed it very much."

I put my arms around James and buried my head in his chest. I was still sniveling, and my nose was running. James put his finger under my chin, and lifted my head, looking into my eyes, "And now, I'm going to let Mistress Elena have some fun. It will be your finale."

James turned to Mistress Elena, "Kelly has been a wonderful sub. I couldn't have asked for more." I hoped that was code for 'go easy on her' ...

James walked me across the room to the St. Andrews cross – a huge 'X' of black wood with wrist and ankle straps. I took off the cuffs, and positioned myself against the structure, my legs widely separated, and my arms in a 'V' above my head. James strapped me in, and I realized that there was not the slightest 'play' between my wrists or ankles, and the wooden frame.

I glanced behind me, and was surprised to see all of my fellow classmates and their Masters standing in a semi-circle, watching. Mistress Elena stepped beside me, and grabbed my hair roughly, turning my head toward her. Then, she raised her hand, and I saw a braided handle ... then the 'tail' of the bullwhip. Tears formed in my eyes.

"Yes, Kelly. I'm going to give you one last 'pain' to remember." She cackled, "I haven't had much practice with this, lately."

She released my hair, and I mumbled, "Yes, Mistress." I felt like crying again, even though pain in my bum was actually starting to subside – it wasn't throbbing anymore.

I faced forward, trying to hold my head high. There was some shuffling, and whispering. Then the room was silent. Simultaneously, I felt a knife slice into my bottom and I heard the incredibly loud 'SNAP!' of the whip.

There was no scream, as I couldn't even catch my breath. Tears flew from my eyes, and it was a good thing that I was strapped to the cross, or I probably would have collapsed. As it was, my body was now totally limp.

A second 'SNAP!!' and slice, and this time I screamed. I was full-on crying, now, uncaring what people thought, or what would happen to me next.

There was a third stroke of the bullwhip, but it didn't completely register and, for a moment, I thought I might have fainted. James was unfastening the straps, and he helped me walk back to the exam table, where I lay on my stomach.

I closed my eyes, trying to squeeze out the tears, as I heard several people talking quietly on each side of me, and I felt them putting on bandages. Then, James helped me off the table, and held me, as we headed to my room.

As we entered the hallway, I told him I had to pee, and he let go of me, and gave me a little push toward the bathroom. But I turned around, and asked, "Please, Master, will you help me?"

James took me by the shoulders, and we walked into the bathroom, where he helped me sit on the toilet. It was very painful, and I tried to adjust my position, but gave up and let the pee flow. James stood by me, not saying a word, but helped me get up and walk back to my room.

Closing the door behind him, James turned me around and hugged me; but I was still limp, not capable of responding. James helped me onto the bed – on my stomach, of course, and he stroked my back. I was suddenly incredibly tired.

"Thank you, Kelly, for the experience. You're quite a woman. I don't think Mistress Elena has seen anyone as strong as you, and I *know* I haven't." He gathered my hair and laid it along my side, continuing to stroke my back.

"Mistress Elena instructed us to continue, until our subs were truly about to break." James chuckled, "But your tolerance is much higher than most of the other girls, so we had to give you an extra challenge."

I rubbed the tears from my eyes with the pillowcase, and said, "Thank you, Master ... James, for providing a unique experience for my training. I was happy to please you." I turned my head to him, and smiled; at least I tried to smile.

James knelt at the side of the bed, his face inches from mine. "I would get in trouble, if Elena finds out, but could I offer you a 'happy ending'? It would be *my* pleasure."

I wasn't sure if I could get turned on right now, as sore and tired as I was; but I didn't want to disappoint James. I turned my head into the pillow and nodded.

The hands under me were warm and gentle. I drifted in a state of half-consciousness, until I saw my father on the spanking bench. And saw that I was wielding a huge bullwhip. Now, James was hitting the spot, and my hips gyrated slowly, as my fantasy evolved.

My body spasmed, as I came, James expertly easing off the stimulation, as I drifted again. I felt a sheet lightly falling onto my backside, and I saw James' face in my mind's eye; his smile, his beard, and – especially – his clear blue eyes.

Then, I was asleep.

DOMME EXPERIENCE

CHAPTER 7: DUNGEON DARLINGS

The train clacked along and I gazed out the window, as it headed toward Kew Gardens. I hadn't done much since dropping Kelly off at Mistress Elena's house – other than surf the Internet while I sat out on the patio, and indulged in some beer, which I'd stocked in the room fridge. And I really couldn't imagine what Kelly had done over the past 22 hours.

According to the course syllabus, not much would be covered – just the psychology of BDSM and overview of fetishes. I wondered what the 'demonstration' was, this morning; we had seen a pretty good demonstration yesterday with that poor guy, Jerome.

But, I guess that was what he desired, what he was into. I shook my head, and a shiver ran up my spine, as I remembered how Elena had treated him – slapping his face, kicking him in the balls, making him drink his own urine! Maybe *my* version of BDSM, that included respect, wasn't what some people wanted?

I rang the bell, and was greeted by Mildred, who accompanied me into the study. Kelly and her classmates were standing in the front, wearing simple, tan tunics, and chatting quietly. I recognized a couple of people that had accompanied the students, and the husband of one of them who hadn't been at the introduction yesterday.

Kelly saw me, and her eyes lit up, a wide grin forming on her beautiful face. I was about to run over to her and give her a big kiss; I had really missed her! But Elena came out and asked us all to sit ... except the students; they stood in a line up front, facing the few of us who had come to meet them.

"Welcome, again." Elena said, brightly, "Our students have gone through a lot, since you last saw them. Not only several hours in class, learning the basic principles of BDSM, but also several hours learning what it means to be a 'sub' ... to submit to a Master or Mistress."

I looked at Kelly, and she glanced at me, her eyes twinkling; then she looked straight ahead, letting her eyes defocus. I was proud of Kelly, and knew that she could take anything that a Master would throw at her.

Elena continued, "You may take the students until tomorrow night at 9PM, and I would ask you to be supportive with them. They have experienced both physical and emotional stress, and need comforting."

That would be no problem – I was always happy to 'comfort' Kelly. And she looked none the worse for wear.

"I'm sure you'll get filled-in on what happened here. But in order to give you an glimpse of what they have gone through – *all* gone through – together, my dommes-in-training have agreed to share the result of their experience this morning." Elena chuckled, "Actually, it ended around 3AM this morning."

Elena called out the first woman's name. She smiled meekly, then turned around, and lifted her tunic. Her bare bottom was dark red, with a multitude of white cane marks running across it. There were a few gasps.

Then, Elena called the next name, and the woman turned and lifted *her* tunic, showing a splotchy purple bottom, with thin stripes down her hips and thighs – evidently from a switch or thin cane.

The process was repeated with the next two women, all of the bottoms obviously well-spanked. But 'spanked' didn't quite describe what I was seeing: These women had serious bruises. It was far more serious than anything Kelly and I had done together.

Mistress Elena explained, "Each of these women has had a different Master, who required different things of them. But, as you can see, they all received a good flogging. And some of them have been punished in places you *cannot* see.

"Kelly, you may turn around and lift your dress, now."

Without a word, Kelly turned toward the wall, and lifted her tunic. I was *shocked*! Her bottom had thick white stripes across it, and was bandaged in several places.

"We've allowed each of the women to demonstrate their capabilities to please their Masters. And, in Kelly's case, to please me." Chuckling, she smirked, "And, I'm quite difficult to please." I wanted to chuckle, also, but the room was silent.

"So I used a bullwhip on her. It only took three strokes to realize that she would submit, regardless of the pain." Elena looked at Kelly; more specifically, at her bottom. "She is a very determined woman." Of course, I knew *that*.

It was a little disturbing: I knew that she would take pain *for me*. Now, she was taking pain ... for what? The distinction of graduating from Mistress Elena as a Domme? Kelly had too many other great qualities and abilities for this to be meaningful.

Then, I had to question, 'meaningful for whom'? Once again, I was in Mistress Elena's house, totally confused.

The students were excused, and paraded down to their rooms to change for their 24-hour leave. Elena chatted with us, finally focusing on me, and putting her arm on my shoulder. "Sam, you have a very talented woman on your hands." She laughed, "Or, maybe, under *her* hands."

Now, she looked serious, "She was willing to demonstrate her strength to the rest of the class, and we had to dress some breaks in her skin. But she'll heal in a few days." Elena looked me in the eye, "She's an incredibly brave woman." Again, I could only think, 'I knew that'.

Kelly finally came up, and gave me a kiss. We hugged long and hard ... but I knew not to put my hand on her rear. I looked forward to questioning her about this extreme damage to her body. But before I could say anything, Kelly picked up her backpack, and pulled me toward the foyer.

When we were outside, walking through the upper-middle class neighborhood, Kelly smiled at me. "Well, it was quite an experience ... and that was only the first day."

She looked up at the sky – blue, with high stratus clouds – and quipped, "It's great to be outside, again. I don't know if I can take being in there for nearly a week before seeing you and the outside world again."

We walked to the entrance to the gardens and found a taxi mercifully quickly. "Shall we go back to the hotel, first?" I had no idea what we would be doing today; although I would make some suggestions, it would be Kelly's choice.

Kelly was quiet as we rode back to Chelsea Harbor. We held hands, but she didn't seem anxious to share her dungeon experience; and I wasn't going to push. When we entered our room, Kelly dropped her backpack and flopped down on the bed.

"Are you tired? Shall we have a relaxing day, today?"

Kelly gave me a 'look', "We were up pretty late last night ... this morning. Mildred had to wake me; then, she re-dressed the cuts from the bullwhip. And, we were served a nice breakfast."

I lay next to Kelly, and put my arm across her waist. "It hurts me that you were treated so harshly. I almost cried, when you lifted your dress and I saw the damage."

Kelly was shaking her head, "No, Sam. Nobody treated me 'harshly'. Each of us sub'ed to a Master, and mine – James – was actually very nice to me. But he wanted to see, and I wanted to see, what I could take, how far I could submit."

This was news: I'd had no idea that there would be males involved in the course, at least until the end when Kelly would need to dominate her 'benefactor'. Kelly chuckled, "I guess I didn't have to go quite that far. But it was Mistress Elena who did the damage on my rear, with that horrible bullwhip."

Kelly closed her eyes. When she opened them, they were moist. "Did you know that the tail of a bullwhip breaks the sound barrier? It's supersonic! The crack of the whip is the 'sonic boom'."

I had read in *Scientific American* that this long-held belief had been recently debunked ... but I wasn't going to debate the issue with Kelly; whatever made the sound, it was intimidating.

Now, I was shaking my head. It seemed too extreme, in fact sadistic. But, of course, this was a class on BDSM, which included sadism. I had no doubt that Elena enjoyed hurting people. I rubbed noses with Kelly, then kissed her, as we lay side-by-side on the bed.

We took our time eating a small lunch in the hotel restaurant, sitting on a deck overlooking the yachts in the tiny harbor. Kelly wanted to walk, so we headed out, along the Chelsea embankment and across the Albert Bridge, to Battersea Park.

There were a lot of families on this nice Saturday afternoon, but we found a bench in the Old English Garden where we sat for a while. I had offered to take Kelly to a play, or anything else in London, but she was happy just relaxing outdoors. We did decide on plans for tomorrow, and I made some reservations.

We continued walking, taking nearly an hour before passing under the Wellington Arch, near the corner of Hyde Park, and coming out in an area of huge hotels and restaurants. I took out my phone to search for pubs and restaurants, but Kelly pointed ... to the Hard Rock Café.

It wouldn't have been my first choice, with so many fine dining places nearby. If it wasn't going to be a pub, I would have suggested Chinese, or maybe Indian; but Kelly was gravitating to something a little more 'American'. It was still early, and we had no trouble getting a nice table.

We started with the appetizer combination, then Kelly had a burger and I tried the barbecue, and we finished with their hot fudge brownie. I had to admit it was comforting. And, they had a nice selection of beers.

Now was our chance for a big Saturday night in London, but Kelly was wasted, so we took the tube and overland train back to Chelsea Harbor, and had our own 'party'. Actually, it was quite vanilla lovemaking, Kelly on top to give her butt a break. We re-bandaged her wounds and fell asleep just how we both enjoyed – in each other's arms.

Sam let me sleep late and then ordered a room service breakfast, which we ate out on our deck. The weather was still beautiful, and Sam continued to tell me that this wasn't normal for London. But we weren't complaining.

We took the train and then the tube to Westminster, following what seemed like a circuitous route and taking nearly 45 minutes. Then we walked onto the Westminster pier, and boarded our Thames cruise.

As we had done in Paris, we sat on the top deck, seeing the sights all around us as we motored along the Thames towards the sea. We passed the dome of St. Paul's Cathedral and the Tower of London, passing under the Tower Bridge, and continuing past the Canary Wharf area, known for its skyscrapers and as one of London's financial centers.

But when we arrived at Greenwich, Sam was disappointed in the short boat ride, saying that he had thought Greenwich was much farther from London. Our 'cruise' had not been much more than half an hour!

We took our time touring the area, including the *Cutty Sark*, one of the last of the great clipper ships that plied the tea trade from China and, later the wool trade from Australia. And, of course, we visited the Royal Observatory, which is where the 'prime meridian' marks zero degrees of longitude.

Then, we toured the National Maritime Museum, which had some interesting exhibits. It was when I led Sam into the Greenwich Market, an area of local arts and crafts vendors, that Sam's eyes lit up: There had to be at least two dozen pubs listed on the sign. Sam picked one, and we enjoyed the daily 'pie' and room-temperature draft beer.

Sam had bought a ticket that allowed us to get on and off the tour boat, so we headed back and got off at the Bankside Pier. We took a tour of Shakespeare's Globe Theater ... although it was only a replica, and then visited the Tate Museum, one of Sam's favorite modern art galleries.

I was getting tired, but Sam was looking at his phone again, and suggested that we visit the Clink Prison Museum – which I thought was about as romantic as the Paris Sewer Museum, or Alcatraz. Knowing what would get us going back in the right direction again, I suggested, "Why don't we go back to the hotel and play around a little, before dinner?"

"Play around?" Sam raised his eyebrows at me, and I raised mine at him. But I knew that he would not hold out for the prison museum over some good sex. So we headed back to the hotel, and had some *great* sex.

As I had to be back to Elena's before 9PM, we decided to try a Chinese restaurant in Kew Gardens. I carried my backpack, and we took a taxi, arriving at the restaurant a little after seven, with plenty of time for a nice dinner within easy walking distance of Elena's house.

Kelly didn't want me to go in with her, so I kissed her goodbye from the porch of Elena's house. She seemed upbeat, but I was sad that we wouldn't be seeing each other for nearly a week –the longest time that we'd been apart in more than a year.

I was still nervous about the 'Kelly' that would emerge from the domme class, *especially* having seen her bruised bottom after the first 24 hours there. I trusted Kelly, and was willing to submit to her ... to a point.

That bothered me. If my love were true, then I should be willing to submit to *anything* that she wanted to do. But I realized that I had my own limits ... which were most likely at a lower tolerance for discomfort compared to Kelly's limits.

But if I *trusted* Kelly fully, I would not have to fear submitting to her, as she should take the responsibility to keep the experience within my limits. As I had explained to her, the bottom – or 'sub' – has the real control over how far things go. Still, I was anxious about what Kelly would want to try, when we got back home.

There was nothing to do but accept whatever fate had in store for us. Before the train got back to Clapham Junction, I had decided to put these thoughts out of my mind, and focus on my meeting this coming week. And, hopefully, confirming meetings for next week.

At least, one of us would be working on KS Biotech, while we were here.

We reconvened in the television room Sunday night, Mildred serving milk and cookies. The only shock was finding out that Susan – the woman I'd met when I first arrived – had dropped out. Evidently, she hadn't realized that the giving and receiving of pain would be so serious.

I got to bed fairly early, looking forward to beginning class again in the morning.

Monday was spent in a series of lectures by Elena, and a few role-play experiences. The emphasis was on setting the mood and establishing the roles – the dominatrix and the submissive – before a session began. Expectations of the sub were outlined, and we learned some 'telltale' signs to look for in our sub that would guide us in providing a successful experience.

We also learned about various aspects of 'femdom' – female domination, whether over males or females. And, Elena gave a great tutorial on how to be the 'goddess', ensuring devotion and respect from the sub. The afternoon was spent discussing a multitude of possible 'scenes', and how to set the mood for each scene.

The subject on Tuesday morning was verbal domination and humiliation. It was interesting – I didn't have a problem putting myself into the role, but two of the other women had a difficult time role-playing a humiliation scene without actually being mad at the person.

We learned that verbal humiliation comes in many forms: Belittling, name-calling, degradation, insults and slurs, small body part humiliation, mockery, forced flattery, and scolding. And physical humiliation includes cuckolding, servitude, forced cross-dressing, and using various body fluids.

Mildred handed out sheets that included lists of insults, dirty words, and humiliating phrases. We took a short break, and I studied the lists. A few of the words stuck in my brain, but I couldn't imagine ever using them.

I hadn't realized that humiliation stimulates the brain in a similar way to pain. And that it is especially important that the 'humiliatrix' differentiate between humiliation that is a turn-on to the sub, versus humiliation that truly hurts the sub psychologically.

Elena moderated a brainstorming session where we all suggested alternative forms of humiliation, including online humiliation and public humiliation. It was amazing what we came up with; and Elena assured us that our ideas were nothing, compared to what would be included in our clients' fantasies.

We were surprised when Elena brought in three men on whom she said we would be practicing some humiliation techniques. "Throughout this course, you will have the opportunity to meet some of my 'dungeon darlings'."

She laughed, "These are men who enjoy some of the specific things we'll be learning – and practicing – and they volunteer for a 'free' session with my students."

She looked at the mostly elderly men standing along the side wall. "It's a good deal for them, and a good deal for you." She hesitated, then added, "Of course, you'll also be practicing on each other. We won't have this many men for each of the subjects. But, fortunately, these men don't mind being humiliated any way you like."

According to the clock above the men, it was almost lunchtime; I had no idea whether we would be practicing on them after lunch, or what. My question was answered when Mistress Elena called on me – awakening me from my reverie. "Kelly! Come up front, select one of the men, and see how well you can humiliate him."

As I stepped to the front of the room, Elena turned to the three other classmates, "And my darlings are going to rate each of you on your performances." I had no plan for what I was going to do.

I faced the class, then turned to the men. Selecting, more-or-less at random, the guy in the middle, who was heavier than the other two, with a beer belly that hung over his waist, I said, forcefully, "Hey, fatty! Get over here. Now!" The guy pointed at himself, and I put my hands on my hips, "Yes, you, fuckmuffin. Get over here!"

The guy hurried to me, taking very small steps, his head bowed, and making some kind of sniffing sound. "What's your name, little boy?"

He stood in front of me, head still bowed, "Alfred, Miss." He glanced up at me, and dropped his head again. Alfred was overweight, balding, and had a red face, a network of tiny veins showing on his cheeks and nose.

I said – quietly but sternly, "OK, Al. Drop your pants, and put your hands on your head." He looked up briefly, giving me a curious look, then undid his trousers and let them drop to his ankles. He was wearing boxers with blue polka dots!

"Are you a sissy-boy, Al? Did your mommy pick out those undies for you?" Al looked like he was going to answer, but just made a gurgling sound. Looking at the floor, he shook his head.

"Hold that shirt up, Al. Let's see that belly." It really was huge; kind of disgusting. I wondered whether I could really be a pro-domme, and accept all kinds of clients.

I reached down and quickly pulled his shorts down. Al inhaled deeply, and tried to turn away from the class. Looking at his small penis, just barely visible below his belly, I knew this was going to be easy.

I laughed, trying to cackle loudly like Elena had ... like Julie always did; but it sounded a little forced.

"Ha! Look at that tiny dick!" I turned to the class – noticing the smile on Elena's face as she stood at the side wall observing me – and teased, "Have you guys *ever* seen a dick this small? It's the size of a cocktail wiener! A wiener cock!" The other women laughed nervously.

Then I commanded, "Hold that belly up! Let me get a good look at that tiny dick." Al reluctantly lifted his belly, and I bent over 'sizing up' my sub.

I laughed – for real, this time – holding up the fifth finger of my right hand, "Why it's not even as big as my pinky!" I'd probably over-done it already; this guy obviously knew he had a small penis.

"Are you a pussy-licker, Al?" I wondered what turned him on. It would be pretty humiliating for him to get an erection, standing in front of the women.

I turned my back to the class, and started seductively swaying and slowly lifting my dress (if you could call the brown sack that). Reaching over, I took Al by the hair on the side of his head – which only took a pinch of my fingers, and yanked his head up. Looking deeply into his eyes, I said, softly, "Look at me, Al."

His eyes met mine, and his red face reddened even more, as he lowered his eyes, and I continued to raise the dress. Of course, I was wearing nothing underneath. "Do you want to lick my pussy, Al?"

He didn't respond. So I slapped his cheek. It wasn't as hard as I'd intended, having pulled back at the end, but it was enough. Al's eyes snapped up to mine. "Do you lick your mommy's cunt? Is my clit-bitch going to lick *me*?"

Al shrugged, and I raised the dress further – both in front and back, so the 'audience' would know that I had exposed myself to Al. I reached down and spread my labia, arching my back, offering my privates so that Al could pleasure me.

Not that I thought *for a moment* that he would actually lick me. And, if he tried, I would have dropped my dress and teased him. Now, I stepped next to Al, and pinched his ear - like a grandmother might do, but much harder. Al grimaced, but continued to hold up his belly.

"OK, Al. If you're not going to 'do' me, then lets see how this tiny dick responds to some touching." Again, Al glanced quickly at me, looking into my eyes – first, with an angry look, then with a pleading look. "Hold that belly higher!" Al gave a small nod, and lifted his stomach as far as it would go.

It wasn't far enough. I had to get on my knees – perhaps not the best position for a humiliatrix – and stroked Al, using all of my experience.

I first put my thumb on his frenum and rubbed in a circular motion, while circling my fingers around his shaft. There was an immediate spasm of tissue, and I could feel

Al growing, already. I lengthened my thumb strokes, pressing as I moved from glans to halfway down his shaft.

It didn't take long. I used my 'OK' stroke, and – within two or three minutes – Al had hardened into a respectfully-sized man. "I knew you weren't queer." Twisting my head to the class, I exclaimed, "See, girls, Al is useful, after all."

I turned to Al, "Now, let's see you masturbate, in front of all of us. You can cum into your other hand." Al's mouth dropped open, and he turned to Elena.

"That's enough, Kelly. It was a great performance!" There was applause, and I noticed that the person laughing the hardest was Mildred, standing by the door in the back.

I whispered to Al, "Put your hands on your head, please." For a third time – or was it the fourth? – he gave me a sharp look, then clasped his hands on his bald head. I stepped behind him and pulled up his shorts – his semi-erect penis tenting them noticeably once they were up.

Then, I raised his trousers, reached around and zipped them, and fastened his belt. I hugged him from behind, and kissed his ear. "Thank you, Al. You were terrific, too."

Al started to turn to me, but I walked back to my seat, not looking back until I was settled. Elena was staring at me with a big smile, then she winked.

The other women had their chances, picking the other two men, and not finding them quite as easy to humiliate. The men left, and Elena stepped to the front of the room, "I was going to invite those dungeon darlings to lunch ... to act as our tables, or our slaves ... but I think they've done enough, today."

We filed into the dining room, and Mildred served the soup. I was learning that the noontime 'dinners' were huge, and the evening 'suppers' smaller and healthier.

In the afternoon, Elena taught us a little about foot worship, or '*podophilia*', one of the most common fetishes, along with shoe, boot, sock, stocking, or pantyhose interest.

"It has been proposed by neurologists that the prevalence of foot fetishists may be due to the proximity of the sensory receptors of the feet and the genitals, in the brain.

"As with many other fetishes, interest usually begins in childhood. Some of these men are shy, and can be in their own sexual world without facing you or dealing with emotions. They will rub your feet, kiss them, lick them, view them from different angles, and sometimes even give you a pedicure!

"It's actually a pretty pleasant experience, and there are a lot of dommes who specialize in foot worship. The key requirements are to keep your feet in good shape, and to have a good supply of different-style shoes."

Mistress Elena signaled Mildred, who left the room. "This afternoon, we have two gentlemen who's sexual interest is exclusive to foot fetishes. One of them loves legs in pantyhose, and the other loves licking your feet and sucking your toes."

Mildred re-entered the room with two men in tow. One was elderly – certainly older than Sam, and the other looked like he might be in his 30s.

There were four of us and two of them, so we switched off. Charles, the older gentleman, was into stroking legs through pantyhose; and Jack, the younger guy, was totally into licking and sucking.

Elena explained that many foot fetishists enjoy the smell or taste of feet, or even dirty socks. And pantyhose allows sweat to build up, for an even more distinct odor.

But, from what I could see, Charles was mainly interested in the feel of his hands running along the pantyhose. And it was clear that he was not that excited by seeing under our dresses or running his hand up to our crotches.

I found the pedal attention by Jack very sensual, and I found myself drifting off. My eyes opened to see him concentrating on my left big toe, and I had to ask him. "Jack, would you be turned on or turned off if I were to respond to your erotic treatment of my feet? Would it please you to help me have an orgasm?"

Jack took my toe out of his mouth, holding it gently, as he answered, "I think it would be great, if you could come. It means we would be very compatible." He looked into my eyes, for the first time, "You have the most beautiful feet I've ever seen ... or tasted."

I smiled, and sat back in the chair, closing my eyes, and letting my hand venture down to my clit; over my dress, of course. But as I was wearing nothing underneath, it was easy to develop my arousal as an accompaniment to Jack's sucking and licking.

We had not yet gone through the ethics portion of the class, and I assumed that Elena would stop me, if masturbating would be inappropriate. My own rationale was that I was enjoying the sensual experience, and it would help turn-on Jack, who was my 'client'.

The running of Jack's tongue over my foot, delving between my toes, and then sucking them, as he stroked my lower leg, was creating a wave of sensations that propagated up my body. My eyes still closed, my fingers making minimal motion over my clit, the feelings washed over me in one huge orgasmic tidal wave.

A high-pitched wail began to escape my throat before I realized where I was and who was around me. My eyes snapped open, and Jack smiled, his eyes raised to mine, and his mouth enveloping my right heel.

I looked around the room, and a few pairs of eyes met mine, then lowered. Elena was at the side of the room, talking quietly with Mildred.

With Jack still 'working' on my right foot, I extended my left foot and ground it against Jack's groin. Jack's breath caught, and his head turned slowly to me. I smiled at him, and stroked his hardening dick between my big toe and second toe. Jack was now licking the bottom of my right foot, curling my toes.

Then, *my* breath caught: Was this ethical? Was it legal? Getting myself off, when I was the domme, was one thing. But here, I was having 'sex' with my client. I chuckled, as I remembered the never-ending stream of definitions of sex that Sam and I had used to rationalize our actions since I'd met him.

I retracted my foot. "I don't think I'm supposed to do that. Sorry."

Jack was nodding, "I understand. But I could play with your feet forever. And I appreciate the thought ..."

Leaning over and giving Jack a quick kiss on the forehead, I smiled, "I would have enjoyed it ... if we weren't in a class, learning about the ethics and legality of providing various services to our clients."

As I stood up, Jack winked at me, "Give me a call, when you become a domme." I didn't have the heart to tell him that I lived six thousand miles away.

It was already Wednesday, and we spent the morning in the dungeon. Mistress Elena gave us a tour, explaining all of the equipment, and most of the 'toys'. We would be using many of them over the next week or so.

The dungeon – which was probably thirty by fifty feet in size – was organized in several sections, each one catering to specific kinks and fetishes. There were counters and cabinets on the wall in the medical section, and several cabinets of implements and 'accessories'.

There were multiple drawers of cuffs and chastity devices, C&B cages and butt plugs, Wartenburg wheels and other sensory devices. In several places on the walls hung Tawses and straps of all sizes; leather, rubber, wood and plastic paddles; and canes. There were 'buckets' with more canes, and some with bundles of birch branches.

After lunch, Mistress Elena demonstrated many spanking positions, and the use of the various equipment. There were spanking benches, very similar to what Sam had bought for my parents' punishment. There were 'horses', with curved, padded surfaces over which a sub can be placed.

The safe locations for use of various implements were demonstrated on a couple of my classmates. I was a little surprised that some of the implements were used on parts of the body other than the butt. For example, strapping on the front of the thighs, or lightly switching the stomach.

Of course, Sam had used the flogger on my back and genitals, but Elena demonstrated a cropping of the labia, perineum, and breasts. Even though Mistress Elena was going easy on the intensity of the demonstrations, most of us were squirming by the end.

Elena had avoided my bottom, which was still bruised, although the bandages were now off. But I felt several slaps of the crop on each of my breasts and some hard strokes on my thighs.

Over afternoon tea, Elena discussed the timing of corporal punishments, how to draw out the tension, and the ideal cadence of the strokes for each implement.

We had one more session before dinner, giving each of us an opportunity to fasten each other onto the spanking benches and horses, and apply a minute or two of one implement or another.

Elena was more interested in our 'form' – for example our distance from the bottom when strapping or caning the sub – than the force of our strokes.

On Wednesday evening, we students decided to take a night off, and walked to a local Indian restaurant. I knew that Sam had wanted to take me to Indian in London; hopefully, he was eating as he wanted, while I was here in Kew Gardens.

It was a fun group, and I got to know the other three women – all of whom were intelligent and funny. We drank large bottles of Taj and Kingfisher beers, and had plenty of food to bring back to Mildred, if she wanted a late-night snack.

In the morning, we were back in the dungeon, learning about different forms of bondage. The first hour was spent learning about gags and hoods, cuffs and leashes, straightjackets, dungeon irons, and a wide variety of restraints.

Even just the gags included open mouth and closed mouth, medical oral spreaders, and penis gags – some with the phallus inside the mouth, and others with the cock ready to insert into a partner. It was mind-boggling.

Elena pulled out a drawer full of chastity devices, in an amazing variety of styles. She said she would demonstrate some of those in the afternoon when her next 'dungeon darlings' would present themselves for our BDSM education and pleasure.

In the late morning, after a short break, Elena introduced us to 'Shibari Shirley', a mid-40s woman who was an expert at tying people up with ropes and fancy knots. A man came in with her, carrying two boxes of ropes – perhaps her husband.

"Shibari is a Japanese word that means 'to tie', or 'to bind'. It evolved from '*hojo-jutsu*', which was restraint of captives by Samurai in the 15th to 18th centuries.

"In the early 20th century, 'kinbaku' evolved as an erotic form of hojo-jutsu. Literally, kinbaku means 'tight binding', and it was meant to be a BDSM restraint and torture technique.

"But over the past half-century, a softer, more-artistic form of ropework was developed – shibari – which has now become an art; an art of sensuality and erotic spirituality."

I remembered some of the images in the book that Kathy had bought Sam for his birthday. It really was more of an art than a technique to create pain or restraint for sadistic purposes.

Shirley continued, "The bottom is the model, and he assists the top – or 'rigger' – in creating unique designs that incorporate the knots and curves of rope that enhance the body's natural curves.

"As with other BDSM play, the bottom can get into a 'subspace', a psychological feeling of relaxation and euphoria – like after a great massage ... or after great sex.

"In fact, some of the knots can be placed on pressure points, as in acupuncture, and there is a release of endorphins, as with some other BDSM techniques, such as impact play."

She chuckled, "Sometimes we say the bottom is 'rope drunk', after a session. And, as the rigger, I often get into 'top-space'."

Shirley closed her eyes, for a moment, then looked at each of us, and spoke softly, "It's the smell of the rope and anticipation of the model. It's the two of us cooperating to make an artistic statement. For me, it's the ultimate power exchange."

Turning to the guy, she said, "This is my partner, Nigel. I will demonstrate some techniques on him – especially, as most of your clients will be male ... and there are a few 'special' areas that need tying up." There were some chuckles, and the guy smiled.

Then, he quickly removed all his clothes, and knelt on a mat that had been placed on the floor under a section of ceiling that had several pulleys, with ropes and hooks.

Shirley began uncoiling one of the ropes, saying, "Usually, a shibari or kinbaku session is done with very few words. But, to save time, I'll fill you guys in on some of the technical details, while I bind my model."

As she brought Nigel's hands behind his back, and began binding them with half-hitches and fancier knots, Shirley explained, "There are many types of ropes – materials and diameters. For example, I mainly use linen hemp. It starts out somewhat stiff, but with a few uses softens nicely – no preparation needed ... unless you want to dye it in various colors.

"And, I'm using a 6mm diameter rope, with double-twisted yarns, for our demonstration, today. But there are many other types of rope you can consider. Please take a look at some of the YouTube videos I've made."

Nigel was now on his stomach, and Shirley was tying his ankles to his wrists in a classic 'hog-tie' position. "The main thing I want to convey to you is how to tie someone up safely. As with most other BDSM activities, trust and communication are paramount.

"Observe your partner – look at his face, his breathing, and his skin temperature. The model, or bottom, must have a safeword, but as this is a team effort, I usually ask if a model is OK by squeezing his hand; if he gives me a squeeze back, I know he's comfortable. Just the repositioning of one knot could make the difference between enjoyment and frustration."

Shirley was now making what looked like a cradle, ropes around Nigel's body in several wraps, then coming together in a weave. Lowering one of the ropes from the ceiling, she put the hook around her weave, and began pulling.

Slowly, Nigel's body rose from the floor; he was amazingly-well balanced – something that was a tribute to the hours Shirley had obviously spent perfecting this art. When Nigel was about four feet off the floor, Shirley cleated the rope and turned to us.

"One of the most important safety accessories is a pair of EMT shears, that can quickly cut the ropes off a person in distress. And, the single most important safety measure is to *never* leave the bottom alone. Accidents can happen, and you don't want the bottom to fall and hurt themselves, possibly due to fainting.

"There are the famous cases where soldiers standing at attention faint, due to lack of blood flow to the brain. There is also the potential for 'postural asphyxiation' in Shibari, if the bottom isn't placed in a proper position and able to get sufficient oxygen.

"Placing the bottom in a face-down position, like I've done with Nigel, is even more dangerous. But you see I haven't tied ropes around his chest, I'm not taking my eye off him, and we'll only be doing this for a short time."

Shirley looked at Nigel, then back at us, "This is serious stuff: Your model can *die*, if you don't take care in tying him up, and making sure he can breathe." Shirley lowered Nigel to the ground, and – somehow – quickly released the knots tying his wrists and ankles.

Nigel stood, his legs now apart, and hands still tied behind his back. Shirley laughed, "And now, for some of those 'special' knots."

She showed us how to tie a penis – either for stimulation or to prevent stimulation. And she discussed tying smaller strings to various body jewelry – but only for mild tension, never to support a body structure.

Nigel whispered to Shirley, and she smiled, "Of course, in any long session, your bottom may need to pee. I usually hold a bottle for him, but you could also use a catheter."

She looked at Elena, "Shall I demonstrate, or may I untie him, and let him use the bathroom?"

Elena said, "I think we've all seen enough. What do you think, ladies?" We applauded and headed up to the dining room for lunch.

In the afternoon, we went back down to the dungeon, and were introduced to four of Elena's 'dungeon darlings', who were already standing, nude, awaiting our commands. Elena assigned one of the darlings to each of us, and each of us got to use our creativity in providing a hard corporal punishment to the men.

My 'darling', Roger – who asked to be called 'Rog' – informed me that he was here for 'the works'; then, he nervously gave me his safeword ("pickles"). Elena stopped by to give both of us encouragement.

She turned to Rog, "Kelly, here, is one of the best students I've ever taught. I've matched her to you, since you can take some extreme pain. We have four hours this afternoon for her to show you her stuff."

That seemed to shock Rog, and I had no doubt that 'normal' pro-domme sessions were much shorter. I had no idea whether we really had that much time, or Mistress Elena was just putting fear into Rog before we started.

I spoke to Rog quietly, after Elena left, deciding that Rog could 'calibrate' me – as Sam would say – on the intensity of my punishment. I instructed him to give me a 'rating' after I had thrashed his butt with each implement.

It didn't occur to me until a bit later that I could have flogged his chest, cropped his legs, or strapped his back ... but I was focusing on his bottom – which was unmarked, and a nice light shade of pink.

Rog first went over my knee for the hardest hand spanking I could muster, lasting nearly ten minutes. He wiggled a little, and was breathing hard, but stayed in position perfectly.

When I was finished, and while he was still in position, he told me he would rate the spanking as a '10'; when I questioned him, he clarified, "About a ten out of a hundred." Then, he shrugged, "It was *only* your hand."

That may have been, but Kathy had used her safeword after only eight minutes of a far less intense spanking. I decided to insert a butt plug before the next implement, so selected one from a drawer, and prepared it.

With Rog bending over and holding his buttocks apart, I inserted the plug. He seemed a little surprised at this, but didn't comment or complain.

With the plug in place, and the spanking benches and horse in use, I began by using the flogger – one with exceptionally long 'tails'.

Moving back and forth, I reddened hips, butt, and upper thighs. Then, I let the flogger fly vertically, rotating it so that it first came down on Rog's upper bum, then up from underneath, so that the tails tickled his balls. Some yelps indicated that the thin deer leather was doing more than 'tickling'.

I practiced my aim, keeping my arms always repeating the same stroke, and aiming by moving my feet. Of course,

I avoided the tails landing higher than the top of Rog's butt crack, so as not to damage his kidneys.

Elena walked up and handed me a different implement. "This is the 'cat' – or 'cat-o-nine tails'. It was used in the Royal navy for judicial punishments. You see that it is longer, and much thinner tails come off the end."

I had to adjust my position, but ultimately found that the cat could be accelerated – almost like the bullwhip – creating a small area of intense effect. Rog rocked on his feet, and finally whimpered, twisted, and brought his hands behind him, facing outward to ward off the blows.

I let the cat fly a few more times, searing his palms.

Rog reported that he would 'rate' the flogging at around a 15, until the end, when it might have been a 20.

Then, I had him lie over a tufted leather ottoman. "Will I have to bind you in position, or will you behave, for me?" Rog sputtered that he would try to behave. But after only a few strokes of the Tawse, it was clear that he would need to be restrained.

I found some Velcro strips, and bound his hands to the small feet of the ottoman, and bound his ankles together. Then, I gave him a serious tawsing. It only took a dozen or so hard strokes before Rog was sniffling, and another two dozen before he was crying.

In order to give him his 'money's worth' (had he been a real client), I continued the tawsing to 50 strokes. Rog was bawling by the end, and his butt was beet red. I rubbed him for a while, and spoke to him soothingly. Rog rated the tawsing at only a '50', and I wondered whether I should continue to a hundred strokes.

But one of the spanking benches became available, so I released the Velcro straps, and walked Rog over to it, and bound him in position. Then, I found one of the larger butt plugs, in soft silicone, and replaced the smaller one. Rog was slightly hard, and I stroked him a few times, his penis bobbing with each stroke.

As I fitted a ball gag to him, I said quietly, "Let's see how close to a '100' I can come with the cane." Rog squeezed his eyes closed and nodded. I would be using a medium-weight cane, but a long one; and I would be wielding it as hard as I could. I fully expected to hear 'ickles' through the gag.

Rog was almost immediately shrieking, as I applied the cane with great force. After the first dozen strokes, Rog was letting out nearly-continuous screams ... but he hadn't used his safeword.

I continued the caning, and it hurt; both physically, as my shoulder was getting tired, and emotionally, as I wasn't sure how much more of his pain *I* could take. Stopping at 24 strokes, I lifted the gag off him. "Rating, please."

Rog shook his head slowly, "I guess it's about a '70', Miss." There were thick white stripes crossing his butt, touching and crossing over each other. But it wasn't enough. I sighed, and replaced the gag, seeing – for the first time – terror in Rog's eyes.

As I positioned myself to continue the caning, Elena stood on the other side of Rog, observing. Despite the loud wail after the first stroke, I administered another dozen strokes to Rog's poor bum. He was howling and, when I had finished, blubbering and trying to catch his breath.

Elena nodded and smiled. Without a word, I extracted the butt plug, then rubbed his bottom. Rog was still weeping as I removed the gag. I grabbed his hair and lifted his head so he could look into my eyes. "And what do you tell your Mistress, after a nice spanking?"

Rog nodded, but was still coughing, nearly choking. But his eyes met mine, and he stammered, "Thank you, Miss."

I let Rog's head fall, then took a look underneath: He was still semi-erect, and there was pre-cum on the tip of his dick. Elena was looking over from the spanking horse, and I mouthed, 'May I?'. Elena shrugged her shoulders and nodded. I guess since this was something I was doing on my own – not negotiated with Rog – it would be OK.

I ran to the bathroom and got a hand towel, and returned to the spanking bench, Rog – of course – still in position, and now groaning softly. But those quickly became moans, as I stroked him – first with my hand, and then with the towel wrapped around his shaft.

He shot his load into the towel, and I unstrapped him from the bench. I helped Rog stand and then, surprisingly, he knelt, and put his hands into a praying position, looked up at me, and said, "Thank you so much, Mistress. You may punish me any time."

Then he looked up at me, "And I would rate the entire thrashing very close to a '100'." That was rewarding.

It was Friday, already, and I would be seeing Sam in a little more than 24 hours. The week had gone by quickly – never a dull moment!

We convened in the dungeon, and Mistress Elena took nearly two hours to discuss anal play with a huge variety of devices; not only various-shaped butt plugs, but glass and steel dildos, vibrators, inflatables, beads and balls, animal tails (as we had used during Sam's birthday), and prostate stimulators.

Elena demonstrated on each of us, and I 'got to try' both an anal hook and one of the inflatable penises. I put on a collar with a small ring, and Elena fastened the ring on the anal hook to the collar, my head having to be bent back as far as possible to avoid 'pulling' the anal hook.

The inflatable dildo was inserted into my butt, and pumped – giving a feeling similar to the Bardex enema system, with its rectal balloon. It didn't feel too bad, but I knew that in a male it would be very stimulating to the prostate, or the 'P-spot'. I decided to buy one of these for Sam, when we got to Amsterdam.

Two of the 'darlings' came in after lunch, and Elena showed us how to use the cock-and-ball torture devices and chastity cages. Then she demonstrated techniques for administering an enema, and we divided into two teams, each working on one of the men.

When they had returned from the bathroom, we began inserting larger and larger butt plugs into the men's rears. The insertions weren't as gentle as the ones that Sam and I did, and the diameter of the plugs got much bigger than anything that we had at home.

When both men had huge butt plugs inserted, Elena informed us of the next steps – which would be different for each of them.

She first squirted KY into a dish, and mixed it with several drops of bright-red hot sauce. Then, she coated one of the large butt plugs with it. She invited two of my classmates to don exam gloves and roll their middle finger in the spicy lubricant, and a third to remove the huge plug from one of the men.

When the first woman inserted her finger – immediately sliding it in all the way, since the guy's butt hole was wide open, he screamed. Fortunately, he was strapped down. The two women alternated doing a 'hot lube' of the poor guy's rectum, taking more of the KY each time. He was weeping, and his anus was pulsing.

The other two of us removed the butt plug from the other guy, and Mistress Elena handed a rectal speculum to my classmate, which further dilated the guy's anus. Then, under Elena's direction, we took turns – first inserting two gloved fingers, then three.

After a few minutes, Elena handed me a long rubber glove, of the type used for cleaning around the house. I put it on, then inserted three fingers, then a fourth. The guy was groaning, but it took only another few minutes for me – curling my thumb into my palm and squeezing my fingers together – to get them all into his anus.

I glanced at Elena, and she nodded, "Just take your time. He's doing fine." The guy was emitting a continuous low groan as I pushed my fingers slowly into him. I moved them back-and-forth a little and – after only another ten minutes or so – finally advanced my entire hand into his rectum.

It felt really strange, his tissues squeezing my hand, his anus now around my wrist. I'm sure it felt even more strange for him. As he was in a knee-chest position, and my palm was facing down, I pushed my middle finger downward into his prostate, as the groans became moans, and finally a series of 'Aaaaahh's.

Fisting took patience, but it was an amazing experience to see my hand disappear inside this man. I wondered if I would ever be able to do this with Sam. It was a fairly extreme experience that I'm sure came with plenty of discomfort, if not pain.

After we all cleaned up and went upstairs, Elena surprised us, saying that we would be going to dinner at a very nice French restaurant, here in Kew Gardens. We all grumbled: None of us had anything fancy to wear. I just had my jeans and tee ... in addition to the brown sack dress.

Elena said, "I know the owner very well," she smiled as if to imply that he may be one of her clients, but she kept us guessing, "and they have a special room for parties which he's holding for us. We'll enter the back of the restaurant and go directly to the 'BDSM room'." She cackled, and we guessed that this wouldn't be the first time the restaurant had served one of her classes.

It was a very nice dinner, something really special. Elena was treating us more as equals, now, and she regaled us with many experiences from her dungeon. It certainly *would* be an interesting profession! But I doubted whether I would ever become a pro-domme.

Saturday morning, we were each given a project: A sub would be arriving later, and we were to put on a BDSM demonstration with a ten minute time limit. Elena handed a single typed page to each of us, outlining the interests of the sub, and what was expected – intensity, limits, and – in some cases – specific implements.

All of the scenarios involved corporal punishment, but many also included bondage, anal play, or humiliation. We were to prepare the implements and supplies we would need, and stash them in a section of the dungeon.

Surprisingly, she also told us that we could wear our street clothes, or select from a large wardrobe of dominatrix and fetish outfits. I looked through them, and thought about picking the nurse outfit or one of the bustier tops, but finally decided to wing it, and wear my black jeans and just the black bra that I had worn here.

Mildred set-up half a dozen chairs in the dungeon, and we were given an hour break. I asked Mistress Elena if I could include some medical play, even though it hadn't yet been covered in class.

She said that my sub would probably be shocked, but that I could use needles and give injections, if I wanted. If we were going to give an enema, it would have to be when the subs first arrived, around 11AM. I went to my room, dressed, and strategized the scene.

When my sub arrived, and we were introduced, I brought him into the dungeon and had him undress, then put on an exam gown. His name was Archie, and he was probably in his late 40s, just a bit overweight, but with a great personality.

As he was changing, he was already joking about what might happen in our session. His interest was mainly in being treated as a 'bad boy', spanked and he told me, "You can make up the scene, and explain it to me."

He looked around the dungeon, "And, maybe you can think of something more creative than just spanking me."

He turned to me, "Mistress ... I'm more turned on by the scenario than by really intense pain. Another mistress caned me one time, and I didn't like it, at all. I was bruised for a week."

He looked down at the floor, and said meekly, "But I'll cooperate with whatever you want to do to me."

The 'guests' were supposed to arrive in twenty minutes, and I would have to work fast. "OK, Archie. Here's what we're going to do." It was almost like my doctoral defense, where I had to come up with answers on the spur of a moment.

"You're going to need to be cleaned out, and we'll have to get that done before everyone arrives. Come with me." I led him to the medical section, and told him to get on the exam table on his back. I walked around behind him, and quickly prepared the enema solution, then filled the bag and selected a metallic bullet-shaped nozzle.

Walking to his side, I held up the nozzle. "I'm going to administer a three-quart enema, and when I return, I'll take you to the bathroom." Archie's eyes went wide as he stared at the large nozzle, and he inhaled deeply.

"I need to leave for a few minutes to get ready. I'm going to insert this nozzle, then let the water drain into you. Here is the valve – you can slow or stop the flow, but I want this bag empty by the time I return. I'll give you ten minutes. Then, I'll take you to the bathroom."

I walked to the foot of the table, and had Archie hold his knees to his chest. I donned an exam glove, and inserted my lubricated finger into his ass. He tensed initially, but relaxed quickly as my finger slid deeply into him, and I turned it and pressed upward against his prostate.

"There's not going to be any sex during or after the scene – and you want to act like a little boy, so you shouldn't get turned-on, either. So I'm going to get you started, and I want you to masturbate while I'm gone. If I don't see cum going up your stomach and chest, you'll get a much harder spanking ... young man."

I massaged his prostate with my right hand, while I stroked him with my left. I hoped that nobody would come in to find me helping my sub have an orgasm *before* we started the scene. His manhood responded, and I pulsed my finger against his prostate, as I stroked his growing and hardening length.

"OK. You better get started. Now!" I extracted my finger and wiggled the enema nozzle against his anus, until it entered an inch or so; but it would clearly take some dilation, and we had to do it quickly.

Archie groaned each time I advanced the nozzle further, but in just a couple of minutes, I was able to thrust it into him, his anus sealed around the neck, and the tubing routed between his legs, and up to where he could hold the roller valve. I started the flow – faster than I would have done with Sam.

"You're old enough to know better, but you forged a note saying that you were ill, and couldn't come to school for the past three days. We'll worry about where you've been, later; but today, I'm going to see if you're really ill, and – if you're faking it – I'm going to spank you."

Archie nodded, and I smiled and helped him lower his legs to the table. He closed his eyes, and continued stroking himself, as I turned and walked out of the dungeon.

I found Elena, and described the scene I would be doing with Archie. I hadn't seen anything in the dungeon wardrobe that would be useful, but Elena and I were about the same size, so I imposed on her for some help with a new outfit for the scene.

Now, it was only ten minutes before the guests would arrive. Elena had assured me that she wouldn't bring them down to the dungeon until we were all ready. I dropped the clothes on my bed, and ran into the dungeon, grabbing a few paper towels and moistening them.

The enema bag was empty, and there was a small puddle of cum on Archie's stomach. He was entirely flaccid now, as I had hoped. I cleaned him up, then led him to the bathroom. A couple of my classmates were in there, Cynthia in a stall, and Pat half-dressed.

But I walked Archie – still in his exam gown – into a stall, and closed the door behind us. Archie gave me a pained look, but I just shrugged and pointed to the toilet. It was only a moment after he sat down that the sound of a flood coming out of Archie's rear echoed throughout the bathroom.

I nodded, then left the stall, closing the door, and giving a shrug to Pat. I went to my room and got dressed, then went upstairs. Mildred would have the subs line up in the dungeon.

My heart soared when I saw Sam standing in the study. I hadn't realized how much I'd missed him. His eyes glittered as he saw me, and I ran into his arms. I gave him a small kiss, and he put his arms around me, 'dipped' me, and returned a movie-worthy, lingering, and romantic kiss, ignoring the others around us.

When we finally came up for air, he took my shoulders and held me at arm's length. "This dress is *much* nicer than that brown thing."

I laughed, "Yeah, but it's only a 'costume' for my scene." Sam cocked his head, smiled, and raised his eyebrows. Shit! He hadn't known that we were going to 'perform', today. Well, he would find out soon.

Elena had everyone sit, and explained, "We've finished the first week of the course – more than half of the 'practical' material. So the demonstration today will be given by my students. They've each been assigned a submissive and told to design and show us a scene based on the sub's interests. They're going to only have ten minutes ... so it should be interesting."

Mildred entered the room and nodded to Elena.

Elena smiled sweetly, then – with strength in her voice, she exclaimed, "Well! Let's go down to the dungeon, and have some fun!" Mildred led the small group down the stairs, and into the dungeon, where the subs were lined up against the back wall, each wearing – or not wearing – whatever his domme had selected.

The guests and students sat in the chairs, and Mistress Elena sat on the lower platform of a spanking bench, in front of us. She called on each of the students – me coming last, this time.

My three classmates took very different approaches.

Cynthia, the older, divorced woman – who's sub was a man in his early 40s – called him over to the section just to the left of us.

He was only wearing a 'loincloth', which may have been one of the costumes in the dungeon wardrobe. He had a nice chest of hair, and jet black hair combed back, above a rugged face with a strong – in fact, jagged – chin.

Cynthia turned him to face the audience, then slipped a black leather hood over his head. It appeared to have eye holes, but they were black. Cynthia laced the hood onto her sub, then handcuffed his arms behind him.

She picked up something from the bench behind her. It was a pair of nipple clamps, connected by a chain. She tightened one of the clamps until the sub whimpered, then did the same with the other one. Then, she smiled and tightened both clamps further, and the guy yelped.

Cynthia put a thick leather collar on the sub, which had metal rings front and back. She also put wrist and ankle cuffs on the sub.

Pulling on a tie at the side of the loincloth, Cynthia whipped it off him, throwing it onto the bench. Next, she put a cock cage on him. Finally, she fastened bungee cords from wrists to ankles, so the sub was bent over.

Cynthia turned her sub so that his rear was facing us. She picked up a long, metallic device, and I recognized it as the anal hook. After lubing the ball at the curved end of the hook, she inserted it into her sub's rear. He grunted.

Then, she took a small cord and tied it to the eye in the other end of the anal hook, ran the cord through the back ring on the collar, and back through the eye on the hook. She pulled gently, and the sub made a silent scream, as his head was pulled back.

Cynthia tied the cord, which now made it impossible for the sub to let his head move forward, without pulling on his anus. A most uncomfortable position, as I well knew, having had it done to me, as part of our practical instruction earlier in the week.

Rummaging around on the bench, Cynthia turned to us, and held up what looked like earrings with a long chain, and a metal pyramid at the bottom. There were alligator clips at the other end of the chain, and she proceeded to clip one to the skin of each of the sub's balls.

The sub was now whining. Cynthia picked up an oval-shaped rubber paddle with a wooden handle, and gave the sub a dozen good swats on each side. He was emitting strange sounds – a combination of crying, yelps and occasional wails, as he squirmed from the spanking.

But, much more than the spanking, was the pulling on his anus, as his neck involuntarily jerked, and the pulling on his balls, as the weights swung between his legs. It was actually a pretty funny scene.

I glanced at Sam, and he was entranced by the scene ... but when he turned to me, he looked concerned. Of course I knew that his thoughts would be mostly about what I might do to him, when we got home, after all my training.

There were few other people in the audience – Amanda's husband, Pat's female partner, Sam – of course, and a couple of others, who I didn't recognize.

Now, Cynthia was clipping clothespins to various parts of her sub's body – hips, backs of thighs, and upper arms. Her sub was weeping softly.

Cynthia turned to us, "And, now for the finale ..." She picked up something from the bench and held it up to us: It was the 4-wheeled Wartenberg device. Cynthia rolled it several times down her sub's back, from his shoulders, down his butt and backs of thighs, and all the way down to his lower legs on each side.

The sub was howling like a wolf. Cynthia bent down and unlaced the hood, then pulled it from her sub's head. His hair was matted with sweat, and he took several deep breaths, which quieted him.

Cynthia stood, and asked Elena loudly, "Shall we leave him like this, until the end of the show?" Mistress Elena loved it: Everyone was laughing except Cynthia's sub.

Elena called on Pat, and Cynthia began taking off cuffs, clamps and clips – incredibly leaving the anal hook in place until the very end. Sam reached over and held my hand.

Pat called her sub, and he shuffled over, in what looked like striped pajamas. But his legs were in irons and chained, and his wrists were chained in front of him. I guess it was supposed to be a prison suit.

Pat put a small stool next to the horse, and her sub climbed up, and lay over the horse. Pat knotted a rope to the leg chain, and ran it under the horse to the wrist chains, pulling it and forcing her sub to conform his body to the horse.

Then, Pat pulled the pajama pants down to the leg chains, exposing a big, fleshy, white bottom. Pat roughly jiggled it a few times, and smiled at us. Then, I realized that I could see the sub's upside-down face under the horse. This really could be a fun profession!

Over the next eight minutes, Pat displayed her spanking skills, starting with a warm-up with the flogger – covering the sub's bottom, and all the way down his legs. The sub didn't make a sound, and Pat hadn't used a gag, so I assumed the sub was used to getting spanked.

The series of implements included a huge rubber paddle, then a switch, then a bath brush (by this time, the sub was whimpering), then the tawse, and finally the cane.

By the end, the sub was crying in earnest; but he had never screamed or even yelped. The back of his legs were red, and his butt was a shade of purple, with a large number of white stripes crossing it, and thinner white stripes on his hips, and upper thighs.

Amanda was next. She made her sub stand with his feet on tape marks she had put on the floor, and with his hands above his head, palms pressed together.

Then, she stripped him, ripping his shirt off hard enough that buttons flew around the room. I looked to the back, and saw Mildred frowning.

Amanda, who I thought was fairly sedate and conservative, unleashed the most incredible string of expletives I'd ever heard. She pulled her sub's hair, until his head was touching his back, then slapped his face repeatedly, sometimes slapping the same side two or three times in a row to keep him off-guard.

Then, Amanda began ripping strips of tape – it looked like duct tape – and pressing them onto her sub's chest, taking eight or nine strips to cover him.

She walked the sub over to the St. Andrew's cross, and fastened him to it, facing outward, toward us. Amanda was wearing a skirt and, facing her sub, reached underneath, and lowered her panties, then shoved them into her sub's mouth.

Next, she fitted a C&B device onto him, and stroked him until he was hard. His eyes were now closed, and his erection was gaining altitude. The cock ring would prevent blood from flowing out of his penis, ensuring that his erection would be maintained, through whatever pain Amanda might decide to apply.

I glanced a few chairs to my right, and saw her husband staring at the scene with a bemused expression. I wondered whether he was fantasizing about the treatment he would get, when they got back home.

Amanda took a crop with a large slapper (perhaps the one Mistress Elena had used on us), and began cropping her sub's sides, from under his arms, down the sides of his stomach and hips, and down the outsides of each leg. The sub was wincing and whimpering, a piece of the panty now hanging a couple inches down from the corner of his mouth.

Then, Amanda cropped the insides of his legs, starting at his ankles, and working her way up each side, until she was at his crotch, and let loose a few strokes vertically, the slapper impacting the sub's balls. Amanda chuckled, and stepped back, placing the slapper of the crop on the sub's hardened shaft, gauging the distance.

Suddenly, she pulled the crop back, and let it fly against the sub's dick; he let out a shriek that was muffled by the panties. Amanda applied another two strokes, covering the length of her sub's manhood, which was now visibly throbbing.

Elena pointed to her watch, and Amanda nodded. She turned and slapped her sub's face several times – obviously surprising him. Then, she grabbed the top of one of the duct tape strips, and pulled down quickly.

The sub shrieked, as the tape – and most of his chest hair – came off him. Amanda hadn't waited for his response, ripping each strip of tape off, one, after the other, as the sub wailed. By the end, his chest was mostly hairless with patches of bright red skin.

Amanda turned to the audience and bowed, and her husband clapped - motivating everyone to applaud.

Now, it was my turn. Rather than calling my sub, I walked over to him, took him by the ear, and marched him back in front of the guests. He was shocked when I pinched his ear, letting out a yelp.

"I hope you're beginning to understand, young man: I will not tolerate you skipping school; and, especially, forging a note from me, saying that you were ill." I chuckled as I thought back to Linda's schoolgirl spanking experience, when we'd surprised her with a trip to the exam room.

"I've only given you a first punishment enema, so far, but we're going to have to make sure that you get a good spanking ... and that we treat your 'illness'." I sat on a stool facing the guests, and gathered the dress in my lap, making sure my underwear was on display for the sub. Then, I pulled him across my lap. "We'll just start with a little warm-up."

Before he had even gotten settled over my knee, I'd flipped his exam gown aside, and begun giving him a very hard OTK hand spanking. In less than two minutes, I had applied more than 200 full-strength spanks. Then, I took a hairbrush to his behind. I didn't skimp, and my sub was howling before I'd delivered a dozen strokes ... but I continued to three dozen, before pushing him off my lap.

I had him spread his legs, bend over, and put his hands on the stool. Then, I took a rectal thermometer – waving it to show the guests, and asked my sub to hold his buttocks apart. I inserted the glass tube and roughly moved it around and in and out of him. Then, I had him let his buttocks go, and put his hand back on the stool.

"First, I'm going to give you a couple of shots – just to make sure you're cured, in case you're *really* ill." My sub snapped his head toward me, giving me a pained look (and he'd just begun feeling a little pain).

I swabbed both of his hips, and held up two large shots; they were 10cc syringes with 2" needles, and loaded more than halfway with sterile saline. My sub let his head drop and groaned. I swabbed his hips with alcohol, and removed the needle guard from one of the shots.

Then, I walked up to the guests, making sure they could see the syringe as I squirted saline from the long needle. I heard a couple of guests draw in a big breath.

Stepping back to my sub, I showed him the needle, then jabbed it into his left hip. A moment later, I jabbed the needle of the other shot into his right hip. Once again, my sub groaned. The two syringes were standing up from his butt, and I turned to the guests and smiled. Then, I began injecting my sub, alternating sides until the full 6cc had been injected on each side.

Leaving the needles in, I separated his butt cheeks and moved the thermometer in and out, then finally out of him. I pretended to read it, then put it on the counter, and picked up a large butt plug.

As I manipulated the thick cylindrical form into him, he groaned. "OK, young man. I'll take the shots out ... but you're going to get a lot more needles in a minute." He groaned again.

I removed the shots, and advanced the butt plug into him. Then, I picked up the small bowl with needles that I'd already unpackaged, and showed it to my sub, whispering, "We'll start with fifty needles. But you'll probably be getting the full one hundred by the time we're done." His eyes went wide.

As I began inserting needles into his rear, my sub whimpered. We didn't have much time, so I quickly inserted one after another, until both his buttocks were dotted with blue needle hubs. I glanced at the guests, and saw that a couple of them had closed their eyes.

"Stand up, young man." My sub slowly stood, wincing and groaning as the needles shifted position. "OK. Now walk in front of our guests, and let them see your bottom. You can consider this your first 'corner time'."

I picked up a sharps container from the bench behind us, and led the guy over to the guests – specifically, just in front of Sam – and I turned him around, so everyone could see the multitude of blue hubs. I pulled many of the needles part-way out, various distances, showing the forest of needles that pierced his bum.

"Would you like the needles to come out, now, young man?" The sub whimpered, "Oh yes, Miss."

I pointed to his butt, "I think we're ready for some audience participation. Each of you can pull a few of the needles out, and drop them in here." Sam smiled, and pulled out two needles on each side, dropping them into the sharps container.

Pat, Amanda and Cynthia took their turns ... but Amanda's husband refused; the only other guest to remove needles was Pat's lesbian partner. There were several dots of blood, and I walked my sub over to the bench and swabbed them with alcohol, then with a '2x2' gauze pad. I also had him bend over and quickly removed the butt plug.

With the sub facing the bench, I lifted the front of the exam gown and stroked him. He was already semi-hard, facing down at a 45-degree angle. In well under a minute, he was rising admirably. So much for the pretense of him being a 'little boy'!

I grabbed one more device and one implement, walked the sub in front of the guests, and had him bend over – his butt facing the 'audience'. I held the anal beads by the loop in the string; they were the same as we'd played with on Kauai with my friends.

Again I had the sub hold his buttocks apart, and inserted each of the metallic balls. He yelped on the last (and largest) one, but I didn't have much more time to finish the scene. Having him stand, and turning him around, I was tempted to remove his gown but chuckled, realizing that leaving it on might be more entertaining.

I commanded loudly, "You missed gym class for several days. You will do 25 jumping jacks, NOW!" The sub hesitated, and I swung the switch against the fronts of his thighs. He was immediately jumping up and down ... the front of his gown – tented by his stiff member – also going up and down, and the metallic balls inside him clicking.

When he was done, Mistress Elena was pointing to her watch; I nodded. I had my sub get onto the spanking bench, and quickly strapped his wrists and ankles. Then, I took the thin switch to him. "You've been very bad, little boy. I hope this punishment will teach you to *never* skip school again!"

I applied the switch hard and fast, more than 60 strokes landing before Mistress Elena announced that my time was up. I released my sub, and we both bowed; then, he leaned over and kissed me on the cheek. The guests applauded, and I sat back down next to Sam.

Elena thanked her students and the subs, and Kelly was released for the next 30 hours. She brought me to her room and changed back into her own clothes, then took the clothes she'd borrowed from Elena upstairs to her.

As we walked down the steps of Elena's house and along the small path to the sidewalk, I asked, "Kelly, would it be OK if we just went back to the hotel for a little while? I really miss you ... and I really miss loving you."

She laughed – an easy laugh that I knew indicated that she was already relaxing. "Of course, Sam. I'm looking forward to a little 'loving', too."

CHAPTER 8: SPOUSAL AROUSAL

Kelly was very quiet on the train back to the hotel. When we entered the room, she flopped onto the bed and kicked off her shoes. I climbed onto the bed, next to her, and lay on my side, just watching her. "Are you OK? Had a hard week?" I immediately regretted saying it that way.

Kelly turned onto her side and put her hands around the pillow, "I'm OK, Sam. Just tired, I guess." She smiled and put her hand on my arm, "I learned how to find my 'inner goddess'. It was an interesting week; as I'm sure you could see from our little demonstrations."

Now, I was smiling, "Yes ... they were impressive. You guys fit in a lot of different techniques in a short time. Although they're all seeming pretty tame, these days."

Nodding, Kelly put her head on her propped-up hand, "Yeah. As Elena had told us before, it's mostly a matter of intensity. And, a lot of the scenes are meant to be humiliating or disrespectful – not you're concept of 'nice' BDSM."

That seemed like a strange term, but I knew what Kelly meant. Suddenly, a vision of that guy being kicked in the balls ... repeatedly ... flickered in my mind's eye. I nodded as I sat up, getting into a cross-legged position, then letting my head drop forward, and kissing Kelly lightly on the lips.

Sitting back up, I finally said, "You're right: I do like 'nice' BDSM – especially, if it's going to be done on me."

Giving Kelly a not-so-mock stern look, I pleaded, "Please don't kick me in the balls."

Kelly got off the bed and undid her pants, then pushed them down, along with her cotton bikini panties. I got the message, and quickly undressed at the foot of the bed, then crawled back onto the mattress and lay on my back.

Kelly climbed on top of me, and took me in her hands. She was still wearing her black lace bra which, at the moment, seemed very sexy. I closed my eyes, as Kelly did her magic. As I thought about getting *her* motor going, my eyes popped open, "Let's do a '69' position, today."

No words were needed: Kelly smiled, and turned around, then backed up on her knees, as I took her hips in my hands, and guided her into position. Her mouth was already around me, and my tongue was now lashing her sensitive tissues. Flicking, licking, lapping, ...

We both came, our bodies trembling in spasmodic waves, our attention to each other not diminishing. Kelly sucked me and licked me like a lollipop, and I took a couple of final 'laps' around the 'clit course'. She turned around, and we held each other tightly and kissed ravenously.

Kelly put her legs around me, and we rocked until our combined momentum brought us to a sitting position, with her in my lap. I looked into her hazel eyes and kissed her slowly, sumptuously. "I've missed you."

We took a hot shower together and – although I hadn't planned it – we made love again, this time from behind, with Kelly's hands on the tile bench, and mine around her, providing some 'manual assistance'.

As we were dressing, Kelly laughed, "Well, Sam, I *do* want to try a few things with you, when we get home. I promise that I won't kick you in the balls ... but we've learned some interesting things that I can share with you." She pulled a sweater over her head and smiled, "And we haven't even gotten to the 'slave training' part of the class, yet." I had thought I'd want to hear all the details of Kelly's domme class ... but now I wasn't so sure.

Sam was such an easy tease; although I really would want to try a few things on him when we got back home. But I wouldn't kick him in the balls ... nor would I ask him to lick the soles of my shoes. I probably also wouldn't use a bullwhip on him ... although my pelvic muscles contracted, just thinking about his reaction.

We headed out, taking the tube to Baker Street, then walking across the entire length of Regent's Park, to the London Zoo. The zoo was fun, but I would have been happy doing anything that was outside. It was overcast and cooler, now, but the fresh air felt great after a week in the dungeon.

Sam was especially excited to visit the new 'Land of the Lions' exhibit, which had just opened a few weeks ago. Fortunately, the crowds were thinning, as there was only another hour until closing time. As we walked through the faux-Indian setting, Sam told me about his progress on the KS Biotech front.

"I had a meeting with a 'big pharma' company here in London, and started the process. They seemed interested in the possibilities, and looked forward to meeting us at the Barcelona show. I told them that we would probably have the first prototype working, by then."

That was quite optimistic – especially as that was only four months away, and here we were in Europe, taking a domme class and visiting friends in Holland. I wondered what other trips we might take between now and then, none being planned, currently.

As the evening darkened, we walked around the Camden Town area, stopping at a pub, of course, to quench Sam's thirst. Sam also had an insatiable thirst for sex and, it had seemed, new 'fantasy' experiences. But, amazingly, he hadn't pushed me to tell him some of the experiences I'd had over the past week.

We finally settled on a Thai restaurant for dinner, and a small jazz café for entertainment afterward. But the 'jazz' turned out to be soul music, not one of Sam's favorites. So we headed back to the hotel for some entertainment of our own making.

On Sunday morning, we slept late and ate brunch in the hotel. As we looked out onto the small marina, mostly cloudy skies above, Sam smiled, "I hope the weather holds today; I have a little surprise for you that will require nice weather." I could just imagine one of Sam's 'surprises' ...

We took the Overland from Imperial Wharf to Clapham Junction, and Southwest Trains to Hampton Court. We walked across the bridge to the palace, and bought tickets for the tour and gardens.

Guided through the Great Hall, the Royal Chapel, and the kitchens, we learned about King Henry VIII and other colorful British figures. King William III was actually born as the 'Prince of Orange', Orange being the now-ruling royal family of The Netherlands. We would be celebrating 'Orange Day' with Henk and Zöe in a couple of weeks.

We walked around the gardens, including playing 'Marco Polo' in the famous maze ... until kids all over were yelling 'Polo' back to Sam, as I slipped out the other side. When Sam finally emerged, he was looking at his watch, frowning.

But when he walked up to me he had a lopsided smile, "I have a surprise planned for this afternoon ... and we'll need to get going." I had no idea what Sam was planning.

It didn't matter; I followed him back across the bridge and we had ice cream before catching a taxi.

After a fifteen-minute ride through countryside and small villages, we turned onto a small road, a blue and white sign reading 'Shepperton Marina'. Sam went into the office, and came out with a big smile, and held up a tag from which a key was dangling. I followed him down the gangplank, and we walked down a couple of rows of slips, turning onto the last dock.

Sam pointed: It was a cute little power boat. He helped me onto it, and we checked out the small cabin. Then, he held my shoulders and kissed me; but it was a quick kiss and he was frowning. "It's not going to work." I stared at him, and finally shrugged my shoulders.

"I wanted us to be on the water today ... to give you some relaxation. I found places where we could rent boats, kayaks, or canoes. Like the kayak place next to the office here. And I thought about kayaking giving us some exercise ... but we just couldn't get very far."

I shrugged again. I wasn't interested in going very far, except in my relationship with Sam.

"So I found this place, where we could rent a small boat," he gave me the evil smile, "with a cabin, so we can have a little fun. And I had it all worked out: It's only about twelve miles by river from here to Windsor; I thought we could motor up there, have a tour of the castle, and then cruise back.

"But there's a speed limit on the Thames, and two locks that we would have to go through; so it would take us at least three hours to get there." That wasn't going to work – it was already after two.

Sam continued, "So if we had been here early this morning, we could have done the round-trip, and still gotten you back by 9PM. But now, we'll just be able to putter around for a while, no real destination in mind. It *will* be more relaxing ..."

I hugged Sam, *my* Sam; the one who always strove for the best, but was willing to accept compromise. "Puttering around sounds fine, Sam. We can put Windsor Castle on the 'to do' list for next time."

Sam got the engine going, we cast off the lines, and motored out through the marina channel to the River Thames. The boat's engine *did* make a 'puttering' sound. We made a right turn, and motored past tree-lined banks, a few boats tied up, and rows of Victorian apartments.

Passing under a bridge, we saw a boat ramp with London-area weekenders launching and pulling out their small boats. We continued up the river, wind blowing through my hair as I stood in the cockpit next to Sam. It was quite overcast, now, low clouds darkening the pastoral river scene.

We passed some very nice houses, most with a boat dock and small boat in their 'backyard'. The river bent and twisted, our boat following its tortuous course. When we saw the river forking, Sam idled the engine, and we drifted. "That's the Shepperton Lock – how we get to the higher part of the river, and continue our cruise."

But Sam headed to a small dock on the right, tied the boat, and spoke to some men who were about to cast off on a much larger boat. He came back, smiled, and pointed across the river. We headed down the left fork of the river, and kept to the left, the river forking again into at least three more waterways.

We pulled up at a dock, and Sam tied the mooring lines. It was only a few steps up to the street, and half a block to our right: The Minnow Pub. We were happily surprised to see outside tables; at least they had umbrellas, in case it started to rain.

Sam still wanted to take me to dinner, so he decided to order the English cheese board, artisan bread and olives; along with his beer, of course. I had beer, too, and it was nice and cold. We took our time, enjoying the food and the local surroundings. I was glad that we hadn't tried to squeeze in the long trip to Windsor.

I was getting full, already, but Sam ordered another beer. Then, he gave me the evil eye again, and asked the waiter for a menu. Five minutes later, a large plate was set between us – it looked like a dessert platter.

I looked at Sam, "Which one should we order?"

He laughed, "This is the 'House Sharer' dessert. It has a chocolate brownie, New York style cheesecake, a lemon tart, strawberries, and house-made Bourbon vanilla ice cream cookie sandwich." All I could do was shake my head. There would obviously be some more dieting and exercise when we got back home.

After our lengthy meal, we took the boat through the lock – which was an interesting experience. Several small boats were going through with us, as we all went up several feet, then motored out to the next upstream segment of the Thames. The river was beautiful, but mostly the same – tree-lined banks, some houses, and a few boat docks.

We went through another lock, near the town of Chertsey, and motored a short distance, under another bridge, and alongside a park and campground. We tied up and walked around a few minutes, then took the boat across the river, a little downstream, and tied up to some trees along the bank.

Although we were only about 25 miles from central London – and Sam said we were due south of Heathrow Airport – we were in a totally secluded, forested area, only a few other small boats occasionally passing us as they went up- or down-stream. It was a truly idyllic setting.

I knew what Sam wanted; fortunately, it was what I wanted, too. As Sam set a GPS app on his phone to alarm us if the boat moved, I stepped down into the tiny cabin, and undressed. There was only a small V-berth in the bow, but it would have to do.

As I lay back, my head on the tiny pillow, my legs apart and ready for Sam, I saw him smile as he stepped down into the cabin. I had expected him to undress, but he came immediately to me, holding my hips, and lowering his head to my already-sensitive tissues.

My eyes closed as Sam masterfully manipulated my arousal, bringing me to the brink several times, before he sucked me into his mouth, trilling his tongue against my clit. We were both moaning, and I couldn't help taking Sam's hair in my fists as I arched my back, in the throes of a massive orgasm.

Sam was still modulating his stimulation, as I came several times, finally having to pull him by the hair up to me – and away from my throbbing lower parts. We kissed passionately – perhaps the most longingly ever; we'd never been apart for as long before, either.

"Are *you* getting a little excited, mister?" I laughed, as I reached down, and held his manhood, then stroked him. Soon enough, he was undressed, and my legs were apart again for him.

I *was* excited. But it was more than that: Every time I saw Kelly – saw her poise, her maturity, her stamina, her sensuality, her abilities – I was ... I didn't know how to describe it. 'Re-stoked', re-energized, turned-on again, almost as if for the first time.

And now, we had been apart for nearly a week; which, I had to admit, I had found unbearable. I had been delighted to satisfy Kelly first, but now some of her best 'abilities' (from my perspective at that moment) were being put to good use.

Closing my eyes, my left hand reached under her, caressing her bottom, my head on her shoulder, strands of her hair caressing my face. I entered her, and moved slowly, intently, meaningfully.

I had become more emotional in my older age, and had to stop myself from crying. I loved this woman. Kelly's hips were gyrating, her vaginal muscles squeezing me, a shiver of anticipation running through my body, just before I came.

My entire body was shuddering, almost as if in a seizure; but this was a rhapsody of happiness, as wave after wave of feelings swept over me.

Kelly held me tightly, and we felt the boat rock, as the wake of another boat reached us. Then, just the sound of lapping of water against our hull. I dreamed of the money I'd described to Kelly, and thought briefly of the boat we would have together. Dreams were important, necessary.

We cruised back to Shepperton, and returned the boat, then had the marina call for a taxi, which took us to Kew Gardens. I had already done some Internet research on the restaurants there. "How about Indian food tonight? There's a restaurant near Mistress Elena's house."

Kelly looked at me strangely, then smiled, "I've already been there. But we can go there, if you like. I thought it was pretty good." She hadn't told me about that. I wondered what else she hadn't shared with me ...

I was back in my room at Elena's well before 9PM. Wearing the brown sack-dress, I went upstairs, and joined a couple of others in the TV room. It had been great to see

Sam again – I'd really missed him; but now I was ready to get back to the class, and finish-up; graduate as a domme.

I wasn't worried about the rest of the course – the training on medical fetishes, grooming slaves, financial domination, and legal and marketing aspects. But the session with the benefactor ... someone who'd paid $10,000 to have a day with me, was another story. I had no idea what to imagine, what it would be like.

I pictured a young (40ish), stunningly handsome, single guy, perhaps a billionaire, who might try to 'own' me, pull me away from Sam. Of course, that would never happen.

Or, it could be a much older man. I envisioned a distinguished gray-haired guy in a shiny, paisley evening jacket. Probably a very safe gentleman. Still, it was unnerving to imagine what it would be like ... just a few days from now.

On Monday morning, I was surprised when Elena introduced 'Hilda, the nurse'; she was an actual registered nurse, and took our training very seriously.

She taught us about aseptic and sterile technique, and how to splint and bandage a patient. Immobilizing a sub this way gives the domme full control. And fully bandaging the sub is a form of mummification.

Then, we learned how to start an IV – each of us having to place – and get – a needle in the vein of our upper arm. Some of us did better than others; it took me two tries before getting it in. But Pat, who started my IV took five tries. It was worse than the intramuscular needle insertions that Sam and I did.

We learned the basics of taking temperatures, quickly determining a pulse, using a stethoscope, and measuring blood pressure. And we did finger sticks on ourselves –

which was the most painful part of our morning medical experience. But it wasn't over, yet.

I didn't know if Hilda had planned to teach us how to give shots, but when one of my classmates mentioned my giving shots to my sub during the demonstration, she smiled and brought us to the exam table.

She taught us the basics, and had us all fill syringes – but with only 2cc of saline. When someone asked how big an intramuscular injection can be, Hilda suggested 4cc being the maximum. I didn't tell her than Sam and I regularly gave each other 5cc and 6cc shots.

"Who would like to help me demonstrate?" Of course, I volunteered. As I lay on the table, Hilda showed everyone how to find the various injection sites, then swabbed my left hip and inserted the needle. She demonstrated how to check for blood, then quickly injected me and removed the needle. It was almost as fast as at the doctor's office.

We gave each other a shot – me being the only one that got two. But it was minor; I was used to them. And we all did pretty well doing the needle insertions.

Hilda had lunch with us – another one of Mildred's heavy meals. And she talked the whole time. We heard about ventilating patients, using a mask to deliver nitrous oxide – 'laughing gas', administering enemas – which we'd already done during the anal session, shaving the patient, applying dressings, and even using scalpels to make shallow incisions. It was scary.

For our afternoon session, a couple of Elena's 'dungeon darlings' came in. We strapped them onto two exam tables, side-by-side. Hilda demonstrated use of urethral 'sounds' – metal rods that are inserted a short distance through the urethra. She offered to use an anesthetic jell, but the sub preferred to get the full sensation. Again, it was scary.

Next, Hilda taught us about urinary catheters, and demonstrated catheterizing one of the subs. Then, she removed the catheter, and we worked in pairs on each of the subs, catheterizing them ourselves.

She taught us the structure of the penis, and where we could safely insert needles – although she didn't provide a demonstration.

As a finale, we each 'had a ball', as we learned the technique of scrotal infusion. This was evidently a 'bonus' for the subs – to have two women working on them at the same time. We each called out every 50cc, One of the subs elected to stop at 200cc, and the other at 500cc.

Hilda laughed, "Of course, it would be up to you to decide how much your sub should get."

None of us could believe it: These guys' balls were *huge*. The smaller ones were the size of oranges, and the larger ones the size of grapefruits! Well, not quite. Hilda told us that we could infuse up to twice that amount!

As neither of the men was ready to get up, yet, Hilda demonstrated placing ECG leads on one of the men. On the other man, she used a short needle to inject 1cc into the chest muscles on each side. She told us that some drug abusers inject Ketamine – a very toxic drug.

Two of us removed the urinary catheters, and we helped one of the men off the table. Hilda had the other sub get into a knee chest position and demonstrated the use of the anal retractor. This was a three-pronged device used to dilate the anal sphincter.

The sub took it well ... to a point. Hilda stopped dilating only after the sub's groans became continuous. That was interesting, but I couldn't take my eyes off the gigantic balls that filled the space between his legs. My pelvic muscles contracted, as I realized that this was something I would need to share with Sam.

The rest of the week went quickly. Tuesday morning, we learned the basics of how to train a slave, the use of chains and other bindings, and some more extreme – 'edgy' – things that could be done to a slave, like branding.

We segued into the afternoon with electro-play, very similar to what Sam and I had done on that first long weekend together – nearly two years ago. Then fire-play, breath-play, and scarification. They were all scary, and required serious attention, lest the sub be hurt, or worse.

Tuesday night we all walked to the Chinese restaurant and had a feast, Elena ordering a dozen different dishes for the six of us. We were now a 'family', having lived together for nearly two weeks.

Wednesday was a long day in the study, although the morning started promisingly. Elena outlined some of the techniques of financial domination, and then one of her friends – a *real* financial domme – used a speakerphone to give us a great demonstration, having three sessions with her clients.

In less than an hour, she convinced one sub to send her $2000, another to buy her a Tanzanite ring (of at least two carats) at a swanky jewelry store, and the third to send her a credit card that she would use each time they spoke. It was amazing; but *she* was amazing, talking to the subs so sexily, yet firmly demanding 'gifts' from them.

Wednesday afternoon was not as much fun, hearing lectures on ethics and legal considerations of being a domme. But the 'boundaries' discussion was interesting. How far should a domme go in pleasing her sub; in many different respects, including helping them get off. It really came down to trust between the domme and sub.

Thursday was interesting. Elena decided to take us for a walk in the park – through Kew Gardens, as she told us that being a domme is no 'walk in the park', with the sessions being the least of the worries. There were relationships to develop – with other dommes, with dungeons that can be rented; and there was still a lot of equipment and supplies to buy.

But most of the discussion was on how to market yourself as a domme, and how to protect yourself from unscrupulous – or downright dangerous – clients.

We ate at a park concession, and it was nice being outside for most of the day. I guess this was Elena's way of bringing us back into the 'real' world.

When we returned to the house, and Elena went off to her office, Mildred cornered us, more excited than I'd seen her in a while, and having a huge grin on her round face. "We have a tradition here. Of course, Elena knows about it; it's something of a gift to her students, and it reminds her what it's like to be on the receiving end."

Now, we were all smiling as we realized what Mildred was saying: Mistress Elena would be 'sub Elena' for an evening. And we would be the dommes! Quite a turn of events, and a nice way for Elena to show us that a domme must occasionally take the submissive role; to remain sensitized to the sub experience.

Mildred told us that we would have two hours topping Elena, beginning at 8PM. We would take turns, giving her increasingly intense experiences, and Mildred suggested that we talk together and plan out the session.

Pat, Amanda, Cynthia, and I went into the TV room, and found a pad and pen. We developed a plan of pot pouri, a sampling of experiences. The only two limits that Mildred said Elena had specified were no face slaps, and no more than twelve strokes of the cane. That didn't seem too limiting.

It turned out to be an extraordinary two hours, with Elena demonstrating how a good sub should act. We all got our chances. It was memorable, and I would have no trouble remembering the details, so that I could tell a bedtime story to Sam.

Elena had gone up to bed immediately after her session, Mildred following close behind. I wondered what their true relationship might be. I had taken the last turn, and went down on Elena, making her come as I pinched her nipples, and stuck my fingernails into her hips. Mildred had seemed a little surprised, but not upset.

We were all tired. Maybe it was the fresh air we'd had all day ... or, maybe it was the energy we'd expended on Elena over the past couple of hours. It had been exhilarating to be in control.

Maybe that was part of the excitement? The role reversal – as Sam and I had done, which had been a big turn-on to me during our 'first experience'. Here, Elena – usually completely in control – was giving herself to us, allowing us to play with her body, taking pain ... *submitting*. 'Power exchange'.

I undressed and got into bed. Elena had said that we should sleep late. The graduation wasn't until noon. But I'd helped Elena have her release, and now it was my turn to have mine.

I closed my eyes and let the scenes slide by: Starting with the butt plugs and her enema. Then, we each gave her a shot in the butt. I asked Elena if she had experienced needle play and, surprisingly, she said she hadn't. So I proceeded to make a pattern on the back of her legs, hips, and bum, pinching the skin and slipping needles through.

Then, two of us injected her labia, while the other two inserted needles through her nipples. At this point, Elena threatened to never offer this to one of her classes again.

The rest was a build-up of spankings, switchings, and tawsings. I especially enjoyed using her new crop on her, including her breasts. I have to admit that Elena controlled herself beautifully, despite some intense pain.

As the finale, of course, we took turns caning her, using a medium thickness school cane. Elena squealed and screeched, letting out a few screams by the end. Her bum had been purple after the last strapping, and there were now a dozen thick white stripes covering her bottom and backs of her thighs.

My mind returned to the present, and I realized that I was slapping my clit, harder and harder. Then I came explosively.

That had only been the second orgasm I'd had here in two weeks. The other time, of course, had been in this same bed with the assistance of Dom James.

I did sleep late, and felt rested and fresh after a hot shower. Mildred had put out an entire brunch buffet, including eggs (scrambled and Benedict), sausages, kippers, a few other things I didn't feel like trying, a huge fruit display, cheese board, fresh warm breads and jams.

It was nearly eleven when Elena came to me. "Kelly, there might be a small change in plans." This obviously had to do with my 'benefactor session'.

Elena continued, "Your benefactor would prefer to have the session tonight ... *and* into tomorrow morning; rather than during the day on Saturday. I'd like to confirm a 7:30PM arrival and 8PM start time with them, if that's OK with you." I nodded, glad that I'd gotten a good sleep.

I asked Elena if I could use a phone to call Sam; there was no point in him coming out here for a little ceremony, when I might as well stay here until the session tonight. I called him. But Sam insisted on coming, and being with me until I had to get back to prepare for the session.

When I returned to the study, Elena asked to speak with me. We went into her office – the first time I'd been in there since our first visit here. "Kelly, I'd like to give you the information you'll need for your session tonight." I nodded and listened.

Elena opened a folder that was on her desk, then gave me a smile. "First, your benefactor is a woman ..." *That* was a shock! Most of our training had been targeted to topping men.

"But the session will be with a man – her husband." That made more sense: A domme session as a present for hubby. Elena smiled, "She likes to watch." So *that* was it!

It seemed to complicate the situation. "So she doesn't want to participate?"

Elena thought for a moment, "I don't know. She usually just watches her husband get thrashed. And she's told me that she doesn't like hitting other people or being hit by other people."

Looking at me, she said, "But you can try to be creative with them. What you do during the session is entirely up to you and them." Then, sternly, "But remember: *You* are the one in control. You don't have to do anything you don't want to do."

Elena laughed, "I'm sure they'll be pleased with you. You're certainly worth the ten thousand she paid."

"Ten *thousand* dollars?" How could anyone pay that much for a few hours of getting 'thrashed'?

"Yes. But don't worry, they can afford it. He's well-to-do, with an executive job in an investment company. And she's a billionaire, with some connections to royalty; she founded one of the largest private banks in Britain. This is just a little night out for them."

I could only shake my head. What would it be like to have that much money? Sam had talked about multiple houses, and boats and planes, and a staff ... and that only added-up to $100 million. That was only a tenth or less of what the client had.

My brain quickly calculated: If she had $1.2 Billion, that would be about a hundred times more than Sam. So spending $10,000 on a night's entertainment for them would be like spending $100 for us.

Elena read her notes, "She mainly likes to see him spanked or flogged, but he'll probably submit to anything you want to do. It's mainly about turning her on. She'll expect a session of two or three hours, but ultimately it will be your decision when to end the session.

"You will have exclusive access to the entire downstairs – dungeon, bedrooms, bathroom; and Mildred will be available at any time to assist you; just press any of the call buttons on the dungeon walls."

I was just starting to think of questions. "Will he, or *she*, have the safeword?"

"That's a good question." Elena smiled, "For safety reasons, he should have the safeword, but perhaps that doesn't end the entire session, just that scene. Then, let her decide on doing the next scene." That made sense.

Elena was finished briefing me, but I knew I'd have more questions by tonight. I looked at the clock on Elena's desk: It was nearly noon.

I looked at my watch as I rang the bell: It was nearly noon. Kelly had wanted to save me the trip, but we'd been apart too long already ... again. I was glad that the course was over, and only the session for a dirty old man remaining tomorrow.

As I entered, I saw Kelly in the hall, and my heart leapt. Kelly was radiant. We hugged and kissed, and I congratulated her on graduating as a domme.

We were ushered into the study, and Elena explained what had been covered in the past week and raved about her students. She handed out diplomas – actually, 'Certificates of Completion'.

Along with those, she handed each woman a long cardboard tube. "These are just a few things to get you started." Then, she cackled, "In case you want to demonstrate your new skills to your partner."

I cringed, just imagining the contents of those tubes, and how Kelly would use them on me.

We left Elena's house, and Kelly surprised me with an announcement that her benefactor session would be *tonight* ... and maybe into tomorrow morning.

She suggested we spend the afternoon at the park, and then have an early dinner at a French restaurant – the one where Elena had taken the class. That sounded good to me: I'd only eaten pub food for the past five days.

Except for the day I'd spent in Geneva visiting one of the large pharma companies ... and eaten in a brasserie; which, I guess, was just another type of pub.

I was excited to share the news with Kelly that the Swiss company was also interested in seeing us at the Barcelona meeting where we – hopefully – could show proof of concept with our prototype.

Then, as we lay together under a beautiful, old tree, Kelly shared some of the things *she'd* done over the past week. I closed my eyes when she told me about starting IVs, and had to shake my head when she described slave training.

The gardens were relatively empty, but Kelly was too nervous about her upcoming session with the benefactor to indulge in any 'excitement'. Then, she shared with me the latest information she'd received.

"Sam, you don't have anything to worry about with the 'benefactor'. It's a 'she'." *That* was surprising! "But there's a 'he', also." Kelly explained, and it sounded like something we could do – hire a domme as a threesome; until Kelly told me how much they were paying.

When I stopped coughing, I said, "Well, if the company doesn't work out, maybe you *do* have a new profession." Kelly was shaking her head.

Then, she smiled, "It would be fun. But I'm not sure how many billionaires I could find who would pay for my services."

We had a nice dinner – the restaurant was excellent, and much more creative than the only French restaurant back home. Of course, there were probably a thousand other French restaurants within twenty miles of here. Fortunately, it had opened by 5PM, so we were back at Elena's well before seven.

I was sad to leave Kelly again, but at least she would be done tonight, and we would be back together tomorrow morning. She insisted on returning to the hotel, rather than me coming for her. I gave Kelly one last kiss goodnight, and told her I hoped her session went well. Then I headed for the Richmond station.

Several days ago, we had looked at an online catalog of domme clothing, and all weighed in on our preferences. Now, Mildred surprised me with a full dominatrix outfit, complete with bustier, short leather skirt (both in black, of course), and high heel shoes. I hoped I wouldn't stumble in them.

I prepared a few things in the dungeon, but still wasn't sure of the plan for the entire session. I decided that some good up-front communication would be required.

At 7:45PM, Mildred escorted me up to the study, where I was introduced to the clients: Charlotte and Brian. They were fortyish and very good looking; both of them. Alex would be in her element with this couple. I had expected to be nervous, but they seemed very nice, and greeted me warmly.

Now was the time. "May I take Brian downstairs and prepare him for about ten minutes?"

Elena smiled and nodded, "Yes, Mistress Kelly. I would love to visit with Charlotte for a few minutes."

"Come along, Brian." I led him down the stairs to the dungeon.

"Yes, Mistress." He stopped and looked around the dungeon before following me to the area with the ropes coming down from the ceiling. A wave of emotion passed through me as I remembered being whipped by James.

"Please undress quickly; fold and stack your clothes. I would like to ask you some questions." In a minute, Brian had taken off his dress shirt and slacks, and stood in some very nice boxers, with a black and white modern art print.

I put my hands on my hips, and looked at him. "Everything! Now!"

Brian jumped and took off his boxers and socks, then stood in front of me, his hands in front of him, and rocking from one foot to another. His expression was mostly curious, not particularly embarrassed or afraid. I would have to change that.

"Feet apart, hands on your head! Now!" Brian complied. I organized the questions in my head, while I stepped over to the counter and took the crop, then circled Brian, looking at his body. It was a great body.

"First, I would like to confirm that you're here for a punishment session with a domme."

Brian nodded, and made an 'uh huh' sound, then looked up, "Yes, Mistress."

"Is this mainly for your wife's benefit? Is this something you're doing for her ... or do you enjoy it, also?"

Brian was still nodding, "Yes, Mistress. I don't think I would be seeing a domme, if not brought here by my wife." Then he chuckled, "I couldn't afford it, anyway." Now, more serious, "But I do get turned on thinking about it, afterward."

"Does your wife ever get punished? Is that something that you would like to watch?"

"Sure. I'd love to see *her* submit, for a change. But she's totally against being hit – by anybody. And she doesn't want to hit anyone."

Then he smiled, "But she likes to see *me* punished. Actually, it's real – for several things I've done recently that Lottie didn't appreciate. I'm OK with her methods – it turns her on, isn't that bad for me, and is over quickly. Then we move on."

We had learned about 'femdom' in the class – women in control, punishing their men when they misbehave. It sounded like Charlotte wanted to always be in control.

I discussed limits with Brian, although he told me that Charlotte – 'Lottie' – would set the limits. He said that he might have to be restrained, as his self-control wasn't that good. He selected a safeword only after I insisted; evidently he'd never had one previously.

Brian put on wrist and ankle cuffs, and I hooked the rings in the wrist cuffs to the overhead rope, and pulled until the rope was taut when Brian's hands were on his head. Then I clipped a spreader bar to the ankle cuffs.

I looked at his handsome body. This should be a fun evening. But Charlotte was quite a stunner, herself; she acted like a more sensual and self-confident version of Alex. Not that Alex wasn't confident.

I wondered whether I would be able to break Charlotte down to her essence, then reward her. If she would allow me to do that.

The thought of financial domination flitted through my head and I laughed inwardly. "Will you be OK here for a few minutes, Brian?" He nodded, then looked up: Elena was bringing Charlotte into the dungeon. Let the show begin!

As Charlotte approached, she saw that her hubby was ready for his punishment. And I noticed that Mildred was following behind, carrying a tray with Champagne and a couple of glasses. As she saw Brian trussed up, Mildred didn't miss a beat – pulling a chair over for Charlotte, as well as a side table where she put the tray of Champagne.

"You don't waste any time, do you?" Charlotte was already sitting in the chair, amazed at my efficiency. Or something. I smiled, and Elena winked at me. Then Elena and Mildred left, and I was alone with the billionaire and her husband.

Charlotte reached for the Champagne bottle and frowned when she saw that the cork was still in it. "May I assist you?" I said, taking the bottle, and making a show of twisting the 'key' on the wire cage. "Did you know that it always takes exactly six half-twists to take off the muselet?"

I turned it six times and – fortunately – the wire cage came off. I pulled out the cork with a loud 'pop'.

I poured the wine for Charlotte, waiting for her approval before putting the bottle back on the tray. Then, I walked to the counter, picked up a flogger, and stood before Brian.

"As you can see, I'm prepared to begin Brian's punishment. This will just be a warm-up, a 'teaser'." I looked at Charlotte, "Then, I would like to have a discussion with you on how the evening should proceed." Charlotte nodded, and sipped her bubbly.

"Prepare yourself, young man." It was hard not to laugh; I was much younger than this 'young man', and there was nothing he could to do prepare. "We'll start with a light warm-up."

With that, I began flogging him, lightly at first, covering his hips and buttocks with left and right strokes, then moving to his back with up and down strokes. When his entire backside – including the backs of his legs – were nice and pink, I turned him around, facing his wife, and continued flogging his front.

By the time I was finished, Brian's body was a uniform light red color; he had started nearly pure white, and I wondered if Brian ever got out in the sun.

Now, I took the crop, and told Charlotte, "He didn't undress as quickly as he should have, so I'm just going to give him a little reminder than he must obey me. Quickly, and completely." I turned to Brian, "Do you understand, young man?"

He gulped and nodded, croaking out a 'Yes, Mistress'.

I let the crop fly, and the large rectangular strip of folded leather contacted his bum – first on the upper left, then upper right, and now on the lower left and lower right. Brian was sniffling. I walked in front of him and quickly swung the crop two more times, leaving bright red, rectangular marks on his chest.

Casually walking to the counter and picking up the tawse, I asked Charlotte, "Do you have any favorite implements that I should use to punish Brian?"

She tossed back the last of the Champagne in her glass and laughed, "He's receptive to anything. But I hope to see him caned before the evening is over."

I smiled, "That can easily be arranged." I turned and let the tawse fly, impacting Brian's rear with several loud slaps, and causing him to yelp and twist around. I tightened the rope so that his arms were fully raised.

The next part would be dangerous. I didn't want to sour the evening and my relationship with Charlotte before it started, but we had to establish the pecking order.

"Charlotte, do you love your husband?" I held my breath.

She was shocked by the question, "Of course." She looked up at me, "But there are many types of love."

I nodded, "And would you like to make your husband happy, this evening?"

That stumped Charlotte. Finally, she said, seriously, "You *know* that I am paying to see my husband punished."

I continued to nod. "Yes. But I thought you might like a shared experience. And I know that you don't want to be spanked in any way." I gave Charlotte my most seductive smile, "You're a hot lady ... and I would love to see if I could get you a little more hot ... in a manner of speaking."

Charlotte looked at me curiously, "And what would you want to do to me?" That was a good question. But I had a few ideas ...

"I would like you to submit to me. I might ask you to get your husband off while I spank him. Or, maybe I could fuck him in the ass with a strap-on while he goes down on you. And I would probably ask you to suffer a little pain or embarrassment to please your husband."

"Pain?" She was shaking her head.

"And ecstasy. But you would have to let yourself go. Let me be in control. Trust me." I smiled sweetly, then walked to the counter, and picked up a few supplies. I walked up to Charlotte and uncapped one of the 1.5" needles, and held it in front of her. Her eyes got wide.

"It's very thin. Just a little uncomfortable." I stepped to Brian and showed him the needle; his white face turned even whiter. I turned him around, swabbed his hips, and inserted a needle on each side. He took it well, only groaning once.

As I unhooked the spreader bar and the rope holding Brian's wrists, I glanced at Charlotte; her mouth had fallen open.

"Brian, I would like you to walk across the room, and fetch the thin switch that's in one of those buckets." I pointed. Brian dutifully waddled across the room, the needles in his ass, as Charlotte poured another glass of Champagne.

"Or, maybe *you* would like to fuck your husband in the ass, while I make some nice needle art on his backside?"

Charlotte smiled, "It *does* sound intriguing."

Now for the close: "And I'll only charge you another 50%. $5000." I tried to look serious and not smile, but there was no faking the fact that I couldn't believe I'd asked for that.

Swilling down another half-glass of Champagne, and laughing easily, Charlotte said, "You've got a lot of spunk! And self-confidence."

I nodded, "You don't have to pay me unless you're satisfied with the experience. I guarantee my work."

Charlotte was laughing, and I fully expected her to say 'good joke!' and ask for her husband's punishment to begin. Instead, she put her glass down, leaned forward, and asked, seriously, "What else do you do, when you're not dominating someone, Mistress Kelly?"

This was an area of ethics that we hadn't discussed, but I assumed that a domme could release information if she pleased.

"Well, at the end of last year, I graduated with my doctorate in biotechnology; specifically, the use of DNA and 3D protein folding analytics to determine biochemical pathways that can be blocked to prevent certain diseases."

Charlotte's mouth hung open, and – in my peripheral vision, Brian's mouth also hung open. He was standing there, holding several thin canes and switches. I realized that I had recited the abbreviated 'elevator pitch', for people not in the industry.

"Sorry. My partner, Sam, and I founded a company to develop the technology from my PhD dissertation. It will help big pharmaceutical companies to develop their drugs more economically. And, to develop drugs for important diseases that aren't well-treated today – like malaria."

Charlotte's mouth still hung open, but there was the hint of a smile at its upturned corners. "That's very interesting, Mistress Kelly."

I smiled, "You may call me 'Kelly'." I turned to Brian, "But *you* must use 'Mistress'." Brian gulped and nodded.

"OK, Kelly. And you may call me Lottie." Charlotte put her Champagne glass down and rose, then stepped over to Brian. She grabbed his hair and pulled and he yelped. "Do you really want me to do this? You *know* how I like to be in control."

Charlotte glanced at me seriously, then back to Brian, "I'll do it. Because I'm intrigued with Kelly." Brian looked up, almost beseechingly, at Charlotte, and began to smile. Charlotte yanked his hair, "But it's going to cost you." I had no idea what that meant, but Brian looked down to the floor and nodded.

Turning to me, Charlotte smiled, "OK, *Mistress* Kelly. Let's see if you can 'dominate' me. Make my husband happy. But the only spankings tonight will be on his bum ... not mine."

I nodded, "Yes, Charlotte, I understand." Was she really going to pay me $5000? Of course, I knew that Elena would take 1/3 of the fee. But I was amazed that I could convince this powerful woman to submit – at least, within the limits she had specified.

Giving her a seductive smile, I added, "But – you know – you will have to obey me ... submit to me. And you will receive extra punishment, if you don't cooperate."

Charlotte looked at her husband – who was watching expectantly – and he gave a wisp of a smile and nodded. Then, she turned to me, "OK ... I guess I'm ready." This was the first time that I'd heard nervousness in her voice. She looked at me beseechingly, "May I please drink a little more Champagne?"

I laughed, "Lift your dress above your waist. Now!" A look of darkness and confusion crossed Charlotte's face, then, she slowly reached down, and pulled her short skirt up. She was wearing a beautiful pair of nearly-transparent, lacy thongs, in pale pink.

I turned to her, knelt down, and pulled the thongs down to her knees. I heard a loud exhalation of breath. Then, I filled Charlotte's Champagne glass and tipped the glass to her lips. She sipped the bubbly liquid and smiled. I set the glass down, and turned back to Charlotte, held her, then kissed her on each cheek.

"May I please kiss you?" It was something Sam would ask. It sounded silly, but I didn't want to force body fluid contact with this woman, if she wasn't comfortable with it.

But Charlotte nodded, closed her eyes, and I kissed her – on the lips, at first, but evolving into a full-on, open-mouth, intimate exchange. When we came up for air, I smiled at Charlotte, "I think Brian should get the next part of his punishment ..."

Charlotte was nodding and smiling; then, I continued, "But let's show him that you're really cooperating, and willing to share some of the feelings he's having tonight." A frown came over Charlotte's face, then a look of resignation.

I had Brian bend over and hold his knees, then turned Charlotte around, and had her stand, hands on head, so her butt was a couple of feet in front of Brian. I tore open an alcohol swab, and Charlotte glanced sideways, then her head fell and she groaned.

I stepped to her right side, and swabbed her upper right hip, then uncapped the needle, and – glancing at Brian, who's eyes widened – jabbed the needle into Charlotte's rear. There was a quiet 'Mmmm', but no other reaction.

Then, I swabbed the other side, and inserted a second needle. I let go, only the two blue hubs visible. Charlotte had wide hips, but a fairly small butt – not much extra fat. As Brian watched, not two feet away, I wiggled the needles, then pulled Lottie's skirt down over them.

"Then, I turned, so my butt faced Brian, I reached under my skirt and pulled down my pantyhose, then pulled up my skirt. As Charlotte and Brian watched, I swabbed myself and inserted needles on each side. Then, I pulled my skirt down over them.

Turning to Charlotte, I took her head in my hands, and pulled her to me, ravenously kissing her – on the eyes, the nose, the cheeks, the neck, and – finally – her lips. I reached down and fingered her under her skirt. She was moaning.

I chuckled, "That's enough pain and ecstasy for a while." I lifted my skirt, and grabbed the sharps container, then had Brian pull out each needle, and drop it into the safe storage device. I pulled up my pantyhose and lowered my skirt. When I glanced at Brian, he was staring hungrily at me.

Reaching under Brian, I stroked his masculinity. He was already getting hard. I kissed him on the cheek. The look he gave me was something I cannot describe, but will never forget – a combination of surprise, wonder, thanks, and amazement.

I lifted her skirt and pulled the needles out of Charlotte, then hugged her. Kissing her lightly on the lips, I whispered, "That wasn't so bad, was it?" Charlotte shook her head and gave me an inscrutable smile.

I took her by the hand, and we walked alongside Brian, then I stroked him a few times, and pointed. Lottie was impressed. I had a feeling that Brian didn't get turned on by her that easily.

It was almost too late, but I slipped a C&B device over Brian's length, and fiddled until his balls were in the proper loops. Now, he wouldn't be able to get more – or less – turned on.

"Would you like me to take the needles out, now, young man?"

Brian didn't delay, "Oh yes, Mistress." I pulled each of the needles from Brian's butt.

Charlotte was still holding her dress up, her thong now fallen down around her ankles. I helped her out of them, then reached down and fingered her again – just a tease. Then, I let her drop her dress, and helped her sit down. I poured her another glass of Champagne.

"Let's first see how he does keeping himself in position." Charlotte shrugged and nodded. I set a large darkroom-type timer for 6 minutes; Charlotte could easily see the large clock face.

I pulled a chair over, and took Brian over my knee. The C&B device was uncomfortable, and I had Brian shift position so that it was between my legs. I instructed Brian to straighten his legs and keep his toes on the floor.

Looking up into Charlotte's smiling eyes, I said, "Could you please help me?" Charlotte nodded, uncertainly. "Please count how many times Brian's feet or hands come off the floor. He's going to receive a severe punishment, if he can't hold himself in position for a simple over-the-knee spanking."

Charlotte smiled and nodded, tossing back still another glass of Champagne. Brian dropped his head. I glanced at the timer: It now read exactly 5 minutes. I began spanking Brian, fast and hard. This evening was going to take a lot of energy, and I was glad that I'd had a good night's sleep.

As I spanked Brian – about as hard as I could – I thought of Sam, and wondered what he was doing, now. He was probably sitting on the balcony of our hotel room, looking out at Chelsea Harbor. I focused on Brian's rear, and spanked even harder. He was bouncing around, and I knew that he'd lifted his feet several times.

My thoughts drifted. By the time the timer 'dinged', Brian was whimpering, and his bum was nicely reddened all over. I rubbed it, then looked up at Charlotte.

She smiled, "Seventeen times ... I think." Brian's head snapped up, facing her, then he let it drop again.

"OK. So how shall we punish him?" I wondered what Charlotte would decide.

"He lifted his hands and feet, so I guess you should punish them." That was a great idea!

I had Brian get off my lap and stand facing Charlotte – 'Lottie'. Then, I picked up the tawse. "Hold your left hand out, flat palm, with your right hand supporting it underneath."

He did as I said, and I let the tawse fly, landing on his palm with a loud slap. Brian's hands went down, then he slowly put them back up. As soon as his hand was in position, I gave him a second hard stroke. He let his palm begin to fall, then lifted it again, and I applied a third hard stroke.

Now, Brian put his hand between his legs, and was murmuring a continuous 'Oooooooww!'.

I turned to Charlotte, "Should we only count the ones where he stays in position?" Lottie smiled, and Brian groaned. To Brian, "OK, young man. I'm going to give you one more chance. Three strokes on the right palm, and they will only count if you stay in position."

Brian nodded, a couple of lines of tears dripping down his cheeks. He put his right hand up, left hand underneath to support it. The tawse came down with a loud 'Whap!', and Brian howled; but he more-or-less kept his hands in position.

I gave him ten seconds, then let the tawse fly again. And again Brian cried out. It was clear that he had a low pain threshold; which would make it more difficult to impress Lottie without exceeding Brian's real limit. Perhaps there really was no limit, Lottie being the final arbiter of whether his punishment was sufficient?

After the third stroke, Brian's hands were both red, and he was rubbing them together, as if trying to warm them up; but I was sure they were plenty warm.

Next, I pushed one of the ottomans with the black tufted seat into position, and had Brian kneel on it, his butt facing Lottie, and his feet nicely exposed, facing upward. I gave him a quick stroke on each sole with the tawse.

Then, I switched to the crop; it really was a very versatile implement. I cropped Brian's feet, from toes to heel, alternating sides, then giving several strokes on each side. His soles were bright red, and he was sobbing quietly.

I turned to Lottie, and she smiled and nodded. Then, she poured Champagne into the second glass and held it up to me. Here was another ethical issue: I knew that I should not be under the influence of alcohol while I was topping someone – responsible for their welfare. But a little wine shouldn't hurt.

"Lottie, I need to maintain control. So I'll have a sip ... just to be sociable. But let's save the rest for Brian."

Charlotte laughed, "I brought another bottle that Mildred is keeping cold for us. Have as much as you like."

I nodded, and swallowed a sip of the bubbly: It was incredible! Much better than the sparkling wines we'd had on the Moselle River. I looked at the bottle: 'Pol Roger, Winston Churchill' Champagne. It sounded British, but the label said France. I'd never heard of it.

"Shall I continue Brian's warm-up, now?"

Lottie smiled and nodded, and I heard a stunted 'Warm-up?!?' behind me.

I stood in front of Brian, "Would you like to go over my knee, again, young man?" I took the switch from him, "Or get 100 strokes of this switch." I swished it through the air, and Brian jumped involuntarily.

He evidently thought I'd meant another hand spanking. "Over your knee, Mistress." I picked up the hairbrush, and pulled Brian over to the piano bench by his ear. I sat down, and he immediately got across my lap; the only problem being that I had to adjust him again to avoid the C&B device pressing into my leg.

I rubbed Brian's bottom; it was only a little red – probably less than his palms and soles. It was time that I corrected this. I looked up at Lottie and she smiled and nodded. Then, I proceeded to give Brian the hairbrushing of his life. At least, I knew that it was the hairbrushing of *my* life.

It didn't take long for Brian to start bucking, and I had to grab his wrist to prevent him from reaching back. I stopped, and put my right leg over his legs, warned him about staying in position, then continued. I concentrated on covering his entire butt, and the backs of his thighs ... and he was crying, again.

If this had been Sam, I probably would have stopped; I hadn't counted the strokes, but it must have been more than forty. But Lottie was paying a lot of money to give Brian a memorable punishment, and I didn't want to disappoint either of them.

I really laid it on, giving Brian another sixty of the hardest hairbrush strokes I could muster. By the end, he was howling, and his bum was a dark red color. He slipped off my lap, and stood uneasily.

Turning to Lottie, but looking back at Brian, I said, "I believe in giving spankings in phases, with a 'corner time' between each phase. And the usual corner time is a rectal insertion." Lottie's eyes snapped up, and – in my peripheral vision – I could see Brian's mouth drop open.

"But we'll need to do a little preparation, first." I had Brian get on one of the spanking benches, and strapped him down. Then, I donned a pair of baby blue nitrile gloves, and invited Lottie over to observe.

I lubed my middle finger, and inserted it deeply into Brian's rear. Turning to Lottie, "Why don't you put on a glove, and help?" I don't know if Lottie figured that was a command or what, but she put a glove on her right hand, and I squeezed KY along the length of her middle finger.

Brian's buttocks were well separated in this position, and I instructed Lottie, "Just be gentle. Go ahead and insert your finger. Farther. Now, twist it around, so the pad of your finger is facing down." She did as I asked.

"Now, push your finger in all the way and press down hard. You'll feel his prostate."

Apparently, Lottie hadn't done this, before. I reached around and stroked Brian. "Does that feel good?" There was a long, low, 'Ummm hmmm', as his penis bobbed.

"OK, Lottie. Enough lubrication. Now, let's insert this vibrator." It was about six inches long, and ¾ inch in diameter. I handed it to Lottie, and she slowly inserted it.

When it was fully in, I took over, and pulled it out, then thrust it back in roughly, moving it around in circles. Then, I took it out, and inserted a much larger butt plug. Lottie couldn't help but stare at Brian's rear.

"OK, Lottie, let's get you in position, too." Lottie snapped her head up at me, and opened her mouth, then slowly closed it and nodded. I rolled the other spanking bench alongside Brian's, and strapped Lottie into position.

It was incredible that I now had total control over a billionaire ... and her spouse. Of course, I would honor Lottie's wishes and not spank her; there were many other ways that I could challenge her.

Stepping over to Brian, I lowered my head and whispered, "Would you like to do the honors on your wife?" I got an amazing smile, in return; almost the smile of someone being saved after crossing a desert.

I unstrapped Brian, and helped him stand, the butt plug still in him. He put on a glove, and didn't delay in inserting his finger into his wife's butt. Then, I had him insert a small vibrator and move it around inside her. Finally, we inserted a larger butt plug, and Brian climbed back onto his bench, and I strapped him down, again.

Moving the IV stands into position, I removed the butt plugs, and inserted enema nozzles into each of my subs.

Mildred had made a batch of coffee enema solution, that would help keep them awake. I started the flow, then stepped in front of them.

"This will be the first of two enemas you'll be getting, tonight." Both heads turned to look at me.

Lottie sputtered, "What!?!"

I looked at her sadly, and shook my head. "I knew this was going to happen." Lottie looked questioningly at me, so I continued, "What to do, if you misbehave, don't follow my instructions quickly and quietly, or cooperate ... even though you have agreed to submit to me."

Walking back and forth in front of Brian and Lottie, I explained, "Usually, I would take the crop to you, for questioning what I've told you." I chuckled, "For only one word, I probably would have only given you one stroke of the crop – or, maybe one on each side."

Lottie closed her eyes, and I continued to build the tension. I thought again about financial domination. "So, if I can't spank you, how can I punish you for not submitting?"

It was theatrical, and Lottie didn't believe my act for one moment, but I exaggerated, "Hey, I know! Instead of each punishment stroke, I'll charge you an extra $100."

That was *nothing* to Lottie: For my ten thousand dollars in the bank, compared to Lottie's *billion*, her paying $100 would be like me paying ten cents! Insignificant. But even Brian's *faux pas*, during his hairbrushing, would have yielded another $1700.

Lottie laughed, "OK, Kelly. You can make me pay, financially, rather than spanking me." I hadn't offered a third alternative – getting shots or needles. But I'd be doing that, anyway. I wondered how much money this could add up to, over the evening; which I knew would be very long.

Brian was groaning, as the warm saline filled his bowels. Lottie let her head drop. I rolled a blackboard (actually a 'green' board) over, and wrote 'Lottie's punishments', then one mark.

The enemas were nearly done, but I decided this was getting too boring for Lottie. I rolled her and the IV stand behind Brian, and suggested, "Why don't we have a little more fun, before Brian sits on the toilet?" I pointed around Brian's bottom with my hands. "What do you think? Around here?" I knew that Lottie had no idea what I was talking about.

I took the crop, and circled Brian's bottom, the rectangular marks radiating out – presumably where he would have to sit to expel his enema. Maybe Sam was right? Maybe I *was* becoming a 'monster'?

Closing the valves, I removed the nozzles. I decided to leave on Brian's C&B device; he would probably not be able to pee, which would set us up for the next phase of his ordeal. I looked sternly at Brian, "Don't even think about taking that device off!"

I walked the couple to the bathroom, and put them in adjacent stalls.

While I was there, I sat in another stall and peed. Then, I washed my hands, and – standing between the two stalls (and waiting until Lottie's first flood ended), I said, cheerily, "Stay here, until I come back. Shouldn't be more than ten or fifteen minutes."

Then, I left the loving couple, and walked out of the dungeon and up the stairs.

Elena was surprised, when I knocked on her open office door. "Is anything wrong?" She was about to stand, but I waved her down, and sat in the chair across from her. "No." I chuckled, "They're just in the bathroom together, expelling their enemas." Elena gave me a real 'look'.

"Oh! You didn't know. Elena has agreed to submit to me ... for only another $5000. Of course, you will get your 33% share." Elena's mouth hung open. She pushed a button at the side of her desk, and stared at me, until Mildred appeared.

"Could you please bring us some tea, Mildred?"

When we were alone again, I explained, "Charlotte doesn't like to hit or be hit ... but she was willing to try a submission experience. Kind of a 'two-fer'." I wasn't sure how well that translated into British English.

Elena was still staring at me. Finally, she cleared her throat, and said, "No, Kelly. I've received my fee for this evening's session. Anything extra you can 'sell' them, the money will be yours."

I nodded, and realized I was gulping for air; this was really a surrealistic experience. "Actually, Elena, Charlotte – 'Lottie' – is also going to pay every time she misbehaves. It will probably add up to several thousand dollars more."

It was at that point that I realized that Charlotte didn't have a safeword. I would have to fix that.

Now, Elena was staring again, not saying a word. Mildred came in, and put on the desk a tray of two teas, a small bowl of sugar, and a plate of lemons. She looked at Elena with concern, but Elena waved her off. The tea began to quench my suddenly-parched throat.

"You're amazing, Kelly. This was going to be difficult enough – a real 'graduation exercise' – just topping Brian; but to have Charlotte subbing to you is a real achievement." She looked over her teacup, across the desk, to me: "But make sure she's happy! She's an important client."

I must have given her a quizzical look, because she followed-up, "Charlotte sends men to us, from time to time. I don't always know the relationship – sometimes it's a favor, other times a punishment – and I don't press for information."

We drank the tea, and she smiled, "Good luck." Then, she shook her head, "I can't believe that Charlotte is submitting to you." Elena spun around in her executive chair, and pushed a button; a monitor on the credenza behind her turned on, with half a dozen camera angles of the dungeon.

I smiled at her, and she nodded. She would be watching the proceedings, including Lottie strapped down to the spanking bench. In just a few minutes.

Entering the bathroom, I heard quiet conversation, then flushing of toilets. "Are we having fun, yet?" Both Brian and Lottie gave me a dirty look ... but both of them had the hint of a smile.

Leading them back into the dungeon, I laughed inside: Brian was totally nude, while Lottie – with her skirt back down – looked dressed for a party.

Brian stopped, and asked quietly, "Can you please take this thing off me, and let me pee?"

Just as I'd planned. "No, Brian. Please come with me." I pointed to the medical exam table, and he got up on it; I had him lie back, and I quickly tightened straps across his chest and legs. Lottie refilled her champagne glass, and stood next to the table watching me with curiosity.

"I thought we could give Brian a little break, before continuing his punishment. He's almost ready for the heavy implements." Brian groaned, and Lottie nodded uncertainly.

As I swabbed the tip of Brian's penis with Betadine, and inserted the sterile catheter, I explained, "Let's not have to worry about him needing to pee." The catheter entered his bladder, and urine flowed through the tubing into a closed bag, which I strapped to his lower leg.

Now, I decided – while he was already on the table ... and since I was a monster – to demonstrate to Lottie a scrotal infusion on Brian. I filled two 60cc syringes with sterile saline, and showed them to Brian. He shook his head, then closed his eyes.

I pulled the skin of his scrotum aside, and inserted the needle, causing Brian to yelp. Then, as Lottie's eyes got wider, I injected the full 60cc into his ball sac. Then, I did the same on Brian's other side. It wasn't as impressive as during our class: Brian's testicles were only about the size of billiard balls.

Unstrapping Brian partially, I helped him turn over. I looked at Lottie, "Have you ever given shots, before?" She shook her head. I picked up one of the 5cc shots I'd prepared earlier, and demonstrated the technique to Lottie, letting the needle bobble while I explained injection sites and checking for blood.

Then, it was her turn. She initially didn't want to do it, so I calmly walked to the blackboard, and asked, "Two swats with the ping pong paddle, or two hundred dollars?" I put another two marks on the blackboard, as Charlotte looked at the syringe in her hand.

She finally jabbed the needle in – pushing it the rest of the way, and she did well injecting the saline. She smiled at me, and pulled out the needle.

Then, she looked at me with realization – horror – and I nodded, "Yes, Charlotte, you're going to get a couple of shots now, too. Let's let Brian have a little more fun, before his big punishment."

Lottie started to object again, and I put another mark on the board. I unstrapped Brian, and we helped him off the table, urine bag and all. Then, Lottie reluctantly got onto the table, face-down. There was no need for straps.

I whispered to her, "I'm not going to catheterize you, Lottie. I'm not a *monster*, you know." This really was fun. I'm sure Sam would have loved to have seen this. He was probably asleep by now ... hopefully.

Taking another two shots and supplies from the counter, I demonstrated the technique to Brian, giving Lottie a shot on her left side. When Brian attempted to insert the needle, it went in halfway, and he pulled it out again. "Calm down, and do it slowly."

I hadn't meant a slow insertion, just to take his time. But Brian took me literally, and pushed the needle slowly into Charlotte's right hip. There was a loud 'Ow!', then she was quiet, as Brian injected the saline.

Charlotte got off the table, and pushed her skirt down. Then, she had another glass of Champagne. I asked, "May Brian have a glass, now? He's going to be receiving a severe punishment in the next few minutes."

Smiling, Charlotte filled the second glass, and handed it to Brian, who mumbled, "Thank you, Lottie."

When Brian was finished, I walked him to the short spanking horse, and had him bend over it. He was still wearing the wrist- and ankle-cuffs, so I connected them to the legs of the horse. Lottie turned her chair slightly, so she could see better.

"Now let's see what this switch can do." I swished it through the air again, and Brian appeared to jump, even though he was held in position. "I'll start slowly, to give you an idea; then, you'll get a full-speed switching."

We had never been told anything about a 'full-speed switching', but it sounded good. I glanced at Lottie, and she smiled. Then, I adjusted my position, and placed the switch across Brian's butt.

The first stroke left a thin white line across Brian's buttocks, and there was a shrill 'Ow!' from the other side of the horse. I continued switching him, maybe one stroke every two or three seconds, until I'd counted twenty strokes. Brian's body was contorting slightly when the switch landed each time, and he was whimpering.

I stopped, and turned to Lottie, "We can't have this sniveling! You're husband's a bit of a baby." I wasn't sure if I'd gone too far, but Lottie nodded, laughing and nearly choking on her Champagne. She'd had enough, and I hoped that she wasn't going to call Mildred for more.

Taking a ball gag from the counter, I put it into Brian's mouth, and strapped it around his head. Then, I stepped around Brian, and positioned myself for his switching.

I knew my arm would feel it tomorrow – later today – but I took a couple of deep breaths, and let the switch fly, landing over and over on Brain's poor rear, the strokes now coming at maybe three per second. Brian made keening sounds, as I continued, counting one hundred strokes.

Then, I turned to Lottie, "I don't think that's quite enough, do you?" She just smiled ... but now her hand was under he skirt, fingering herself.

Brian was gurgling through the gag, so I removed it, and asked him if he had a problem. He panted, and whispered hoarsely, "My bottom's on fire."

I laughed and put the gag back on. "Don't worry, I'm not damaging you. But let's see if we can turn the fire up, a little." With that, I re-started his switching, counting out another hundred strokes – and probably taking less than a minute.

Turning to Lottie, I asked again, "What do you think? Another hundred?" Brian screeched. I turned to him, "OK. Maybe we'll do something different."

I walked in front of him, and pulled his head up by his hair, as Lottie had done. "Something a little *more* intense." Brian wailed. It was now that I had to be strong. Lottie wanted me to punish Brian, and Brian wanted to please his wife; and he had a safeword.

Taking the huge wooden school paddle from the counter, I showed it to Brian, and his eyes went wide. I walked around to Lottie, and instructed, "I'll give him five swats, then look at you; if you nod, I'll give him another five, but if you shake your head, I'll stop."

Lottie nodded, and I added, "Just remember, he has his caning ahead of him. We don't want to wear him out prematurely."

He wouldn't be *coming* prematurely, because he had both the catheter in him, and the C&B device around his shaft and his balls. The balls that were now engorged with saline. I wondered whether I'd be able to get the C&B device off him, when it was time.

But maybe it was time for *Charlotte* to come, now? I was willing to get her off, myself, but wanted to support them as a couple, as much as possible. "Lottie, does your husband give good head?"

She laughed, "He's not bad." Then, she looked at me curiously.

I unhooked Brian, and we all walked over to the bed in the corner. I had Brian bend over the corner of the bed, putting a folded pillow under him. Then, I took several ropes, and tied his arms, then his legs, first hooking them into a spreader bar.

Then, I had Lottie lift her skirt, and I helped her position herself on the bed, legs spread, to allow her mate to give her his oral attention.

"Brian, you *will* continue to give Lottie head, until you get her off, even though I'm spanking you. I'll give you a little rest between each set of five swats ... and you'd better do your best. Otherwise, Lottie will authorize another five swats."

Under my breath, but loud enough to hear, I sighed, "This could be a long evening."

Brian was already whimpering. With the gag out of his mouth, this could be a loud session. I gave Brian a few very light swats with the board, and said, "You'd better get started, young man!"

I let Brian have a few minutes, and Lottie seemed to be responding. Then, I put the paddle across his rear. "Prepare yourself: Here is the first set of five."

I was getting pretty good with the paddle, and the first swat was a gunshot that echoed throughout the dungeon, followed quickly by Brian's scream, that reverberated throughout the room. I rubbed his bottom, and gave him ten or fifteen seconds to recover, then the second swat. Brian howled.

It continued like this through the first set, and then the second set. When I asked Charlotte about the next set, she nodded, "Then let him have ten minutes to work on me."

I nodded. Then, I gave him another five hard swats. He was sobbing, as he attempted to get Lottie off, but I could see that she was now getting turned off.

"This won't do, at all!" I exclaimed. I helped Lottie off the bed, then held her and kissed her. She sat down on the edge of the bed, while I walked across the dungeon and brought back the saline-filled bucket, KY, and huge 200cc syringe. Lottie's eyes went wide.

I filled the syringe, lubed the plastic tip, and inserted it into Brian. As I held it there, I turned to Lottie, "Let's give him something to do, while we get it on." Lottie looked a little stunned, but I wasn't sure whether it was the syringe enema or the 'getting it on' that surprised her.

After injecting several syringes into Brian, I gave Lottie the 'honors'. Once again she forgot, and shook her head. But when I got back from making another mark on the blackboard, she took the syringe and began injecting warm saltwater into her hubby's ass.

We only did a dozen or so squirts, but that would keep Brian out of commission long enough. I untied him and removed the catheter, then escorted him to the bathroom, telling him to stay until I came back for him. Then, I returned to the bed, where Lottie was still sitting.

I smiled, and pulled her up to me. Then, as we kissed, I let my hand drop down and under her skirt. Lottie was wet, already. As I was about to push her down to the bed and work on her, she surprised me.

"You have such beautiful long hair, Kelly. And a beautiful face." She hesitated, then, "May I please see your body?"

I wondered what Elena would do in this situation. Probably punish the sub for overstepping her bounds. But Lottie was the one paying tonight, and I was both her top, and putting on the show she was watching while I topped her husband. It was complicated.

In any case, I certainly had no qualms about anyone seeing my body. I removed the skirt, my thong, and then – with Lottie's help – the bustier. Standing before her, nude but not naked, I felt confident. I did a few turns, and bent over to allow her to see me from every angle.

Lottie gazed at me for a few moments, and shook her head. Then, she quietly took off her own dress and bra, and pulled me onto the bed with her. We held each other and kissed, coupling wordlessly, our legs wrapping around each other.

Lottie was small on top, and her hands were attracted to my breasts, cupping, massaging, squeezing gently. I turned her onto her back, and straddled her, lowering my head to give a small kiss. Then, I looked into Lottie's eyes, and saw her signal; maybe she had nodded slightly, but it seemed as though her eyes communicated everything.

I went down on her, using all of my skills – and some acquired from Julie, when we'd had the slumber party at my birthday and, more recently, when we were on Kauai.

Arching her back, Lottie issued a shrill shriek, as she came … multiple times. I lay on her, our bodies intimately touching, as we kissed again.

Sitting up, I made several suggestions to Lottie, the first being that Brian be given a reward before his final punishment, the caning. I offered Lottie the chance to 'peg' Brian, using the strap-on dildo … but she wasn't interested, and I wasn't going to push her on it.

She did agree, however, to allow Brian to have sex with her while I pegged him. Of course, I would give him a little more stimulation, á la Sam. Then, he would get his caning.

I showed Lottie several canes, suggesting that I show Brian a thick one, but actually use a much thinner rattan. I really felt, looking at his bottom, that Brian had suffered enough. Gamely – despite lots of yelling and crying – he hadn't used his safeword.

Then, I had a brilliant thought – the perfect 'gift' for the billionaire who has everything. "Lottie, after Brian's caning, we could do just one more thing …" She looked at me expectantly, already smiling – knowing that I would come up with something good.

"Elena did this to my partner, when we first visited here. It seems a little extreme … but it's only an act. Just to intimidate Brian, and to see how far he'll go to please you."

Now Lottie was looking at me with impatience. So I spit it out: "We could brand him." Lottie gasped, and I laughed, "Actually, I'm talking about a 'mock' branding; for a few seconds, he will believe he's being branded. It should bring out even more endorphins than his caning."

Lottie was initially shocked, but laughed when I explained what we were going to do.

I also suggested to Lottie that we remain nude for the rest of the session, to give Brian a little more 'excitement'. She agreed. I let her finish the Champagne, while I went to the bathroom to fetch Brian.

When I entered his stall, Brian had his elbows on his knees – reminiscent of Rodin's 'The Thinker'. "Are you ready to come out, now?"

Brian looked up at me with sad eyes; then, as he realized that I was nude, he smiled and sat up. He shook his head, "Not really."

I asked, "How much more time do you need?"

He pretended to look at his watch, "Oh, maybe a day or two?" I laughed, and Brian got up from the toilet.

Whispering, I told Brian that we would be 'treating' him, and then he would be caned. He couldn't take his eyes off me; I doubt if any other domme had been nude during one of his sessions.

As we walked into the hallway, I told him, "I expect you to cooperate. Remember: Pain and pleasure." Brian grumbled something that I did not understand.

When Brian saw Lottie standing by the bed nude, his mouth dropped open. Then he looked back at me. I nodded, "I convinced Lottie that – as you've been such a good boy, taking your punishment well – and, as you will be taking a very severe caning in a few minutes, we should reward you."

I looked at Lottie, and then back to Brian, "Would you like to make love to your wife?" As Brian nodded, I laughed, "OK. But there is good news and bad news." He turned to me, all ears.

"The 'good' news is that I will be pegging you – fucking you in the ass – with a strap-on. Brian gave me an incredulous look. "It's the good news, because I think you'll find it very pleasurable."

I started walking toward the bed, and Brian croaked, "And the 'bad' news?"

Turning back to him, I said, "Well, in order to prepare you for the caning, I need to keep your endorphin level high." Brian gave me an even stranger look. "So, I'll be 'tenderizing' your butt with a couple of needles." Brian winced.

"OK. If you prefer, I can use the small strap. I can see the sides of your hips need more reddening. And I could even-out the marks from the paddling ..." Brian shook his head, and I went to the counter for the strap-on, and a few supplies.

With Brian over the corner of the bed, I slowly inserted the dildo into him. The other end was inside me, so I would be stimulated, also.

When it was in, and I was easily moving it back and forth inside Brian, I had him stand up, and suggested that Lottie get over the corner of the bed, so he could enter her from behind.

But Lottie wanted to look into Brian's face, so she lay on her back, her legs up, and over Brian's shoulders. As Brian got into her, I took two alcohol swabs and cleansed Brian's entire butt. He whined, as the alcohol burned his raw skin.

Then, I took a needle in each hand, and told Brian he could get started.

It actually looked like a good position, and Brian was down low enough that I could move the dildo in his rear. As Brian was getting turned on, his thrusts more urgent, I began sticking him on both sides with the needles.

Although there was a little pain (even more, since he'd been paddled), it wouldn't be enough to turn him off. What probably *would* turn him off, if he thought about it, was his upcoming caning.

I looked over Brian's shoulder and held the needle up. Lottie nodded, and I thrust it into Brian's hip, where she could see it. Then, I did the same on the other side. I let Brian get to his climax, and then gave him a flurry of sticks – probably more than ten on each side – as he orgasmed.

It hadn't been a turn-on for me; I'd been focusing too much on Brian and Lottie. I pulled the dildo out of Brian, and took off the strap-on. Lottie excused herself and went to the bathroom, giving me a chance to prepare Brian.

I walked him over to the St. Andrew's cross, and fastened him onto it, with straps around his wrists, upper arms, waist, upper legs, and lower legs. He was entirely immobile, and I was in full control.

"How many strokes of the cane have you had, before, Brian?" I hoped he could calibrate me a little, even though Lottie would be governing the number of strokes. I walked around the large 'X' and showed Brian one of the thickest canes, then swished it through the air a few times.

"Six?"

I laughed, "Are you telling me, or asking me? I'm sure you've had at least twelve strokes of the cane, if Lottie had her way."

At that moment, Lottie was walking, still nude, back into the dungeon. "What 'way' did I have?"

"How many strokes of the cane has Brian had before? I want to make this a 'special' punishment that he'll remember."

Before Lottie could say anything, Brian blurted out, "I'll remember *this* experience for a *long* time, Mistress Kelly. Even without the caning."

I walked around the cross again and put a ball gag into his mouth.   Then, I blindfolded him.   Laughing, I explained, "It will be easier this way."

Lottie finally responded, "He's received twelve strokes before." She looked at the mean implement in my hand, "But not with *that* big of a cane!" Then, she looked at the small table with the empty bottle of Champagne. "Maybe, I should call Mildred for the second bottle?"

I shook my head, and – fortunately – Lottie complied. She pulled her chair over to near the cross, and I quietly exchanged the thick cane for a thinner one; it was still a formidable instrument of pain.

I swished the cane and Brian's body rippled; he was too tightly bound to actually 'jump'. Loudly, I announced, "OK. Then I guess I'll have to give Brian 24 of the best." I put the cane across Brian's rump and slid it back and forth, as he whimpered.

Lottie said, "I would be satisfied with twelve strokes, if they're hard. And then, we can do the other thing you suggested. I think that will give Brian enough for one evening." It was certainly morning by now.

I nodded, and Lottie smiled, "Of course, Kelly, *you're* the domme. If you think Brian should get 24 strokes, or even 36 strokes, I won't stop you." Brian was groaning through the ball gag.

"We'll see. I'll certainly give him extra strokes, if he gets out of position." Of course, there was no possibility of that. Even Brian had to laugh a little at that one.

"OK, Brian. Here we go." I was getting pretty good at the cane, also. I let it fly, and it struck the middle of his butt. That would probably be the highest stroke that I would do. Brian screamed, and it didn't sound like the gag was doing it's job.

The second stroke landed even harder, about an inch below the first; I had been aiming for a half inch, hoping that the twelve strokes would uniformly cover the lower half of Brian's bum. Brian shrieked.

I walked over to the cabinet and rummaged through the gags, selecting one that had a short 'dildo' that would fill Brian's mouth. I would have stuffed Lottie's undies into his mouth, but that could be dangerous. Elena's lecture resonated in my brain.

When the gag was in, I continued the caning. Brian tried to scream when every stroke landed, but this gag kept him a little quieter.

The caning wasn't difficult, but it took energy. When I glanced at Lottie, I couldn't tell whether she was looking at Brian's rear, or my breasts wobbling, and long hair swaying back and forth behind me.

Brian was emitting a continuous, loud cry by the time I was done, and his bottom was striped from halfway down to the top of his thighs. The stripes were quite parallel, but not spaced precisely equally. I would need to practice more. By now, I had decided that Sam would be my slave, at least for a month.

I rubbed Brian's butt, then gave Lottie some soothing cream to smear on him, as I got the 'branding' supplies ready. Of *course*, I wasn't going to brand him for real. It would be orchestrated to seem like a branding, at least for a few seconds.

When I returned, I silently showed Lottie what to do, and she nodded. I rolled over a metal table on which I had set-up the Bunsen burner, a ring stand and a clamp. I took off Brian's blindfold, and he blinked in the bright light of the dungeon.

Then, I clamped the brand – I think it was a real branding iron – to the ring stand, the end in the flame. It quickly turned red, then orange, and finally a bright yellow. Brian was trying to yell through the gag, but it wasn't working.

I stood in front of him, adjusting the angle of the branding iron in the flame. Behind him, Lottie held the block of wood with animal skin stapled to it. I twirled the iron, and Brian shook his head, and tried to move … but he was fixed in position.

Turning to Lottie, I asked, "Shall we let him watch?" Then, I shook my head, "No. It will be more humane, if he's blindfolded." As Brian stared at the white-hot branding iron, I replaced the blindfold. He was making all kinds of noises through the gag.

I said, strictly, "Brian, if you have an emergency, nod your head, and I'll take off the gag so you can tell me about it. But if you don't really have an emergency, I'll double your caning to 24 strokes." I glanced at Lottie, and she seemed transfixed.

"Now, Brian, do you *really* have an emergency?" He was silent and still. Then, slowly, he shook his head.

Facing Lottie, I said, "Just as I thought. Trying to get out of it." Then, I walked around the cross and kissed Brian on each cheek. I whispered, "Your wife owns you and you will obey her. Show her how much she means to you by taking your branding like a man."

I picked up the hot iron, and handed it to Lottie, who held it under Brian's nose. I went to the fridge, and took an ice cube from the freezer. Then, I walked back to Brian, and held the cube above his hip. "Ready, Brian?"

He was screaming into the gag, again; but the message was for Lottie, and she smiled and nodded. I counted down, "Three, two, one, …"

As I contacted Brian's skin with the ice cube, Lottie held the branding iron against the skin, making a sizzling sound, and creating putrid smoke that rose into Brian's nose.

He screamed like a banshee – even through the gag – and then went silent. I rolled the table away, and took off Brian's blindfold. His eyes were closed and his head lolled sideways. I quickly grabbed the smelling salts, and held it under his nose. Fortunately, he woke up quickly.

My heart was in my throat, and I'd had a good lesson on why a domme must be careful with her sub. I took the gag out of Brian's mouth, and unstrapped him from the cross. Lottie and I helped him sit down in the chair, and I called for Mildred.

It seemed to take a long time, but Mildred finally arrived, and we requested the second bottle of Champagne. Mildred was in her bathrobe, but left without a word, bringing an ice bucket on a stand, with the Champagne and some fresh glasses.

I popped the cork, and poured a glass for Brian, then for Lottie, and finally for me. After explaining to Brian that the 'branding' had been fake, I toasted to the couple who had been my first official clients.

Turning to Lottie, "I don't mean to imply that the session has to be over ... if there's something else you would like me to do. I'm yours as long as you like."

Lottie laughed, "OK. Then come home with me. We can punish Brian every day, and then you can 'satisfy' me."

We laughed, and headed for our clothes. Before either of us had put anything on, I asked Lottie, "May I please kiss your husband?" She shrugged and nodded.

Stepping up to Brian, I leaned into him, and pressed against his broad chest. "Thank you for cooperating, Brian. You did very well. I'm sorry if I was a little harsh on you." I kissed him on the lips, then we consummated an open-mouth kiss, and Brian held me tightly to him.

"Mistress Kelly," I nodded, and Brian looked down, "That was the best punishment session I've ever had." Then he looked me in the eye, "You may punish me any time. Whenever my wife requests it." Then he hugged me, and kissed me on the cheek, "Thank you."

We got dressed and went upstairs. The house was quiet. Before they left, Lottie wrote me a check. There had only been eight marks on the blackboard, but Lottie paid me an even $6,000. Not a bad night's work!

Even better, she told me to contact her via e-mail with our KS Biotech prospectus. She promised to present the opportunity to her bank's Board of Directors for a possible investment.

I hugged Brian again, then kissed Lottie. She thanked me again, and they left into the fog that now enveloped the neighborhood.

My mind was in a fog now, and when I looked at the clock in the study, it was 3:30AM. I went down to my bedroom and crashed: It had been a stressful session, but I think everyone was satisfied in the end.

CHAPTER 9: DUTCH HOMEBODIES

I stared out the window into fog, as the train clacked along, headed back to Clapham Junction. Exhausted after the marathon session with Charlotte and Brian, I had slept six hours, and wouldn't get back to Sam until nearly noon.

It was chilly, as I walked from Imperial Wharf to the hotel, thinking about Elena's class, and my session with the billionaire and her husband. It had been quite an experience, one that I'd been well-prepared for after the course and my time with Sam, but one that went way beyond the things he found 'comfortable'.

Sam would not have enjoyed being thrashed as I'd done to Brian; and Sam was quite limited in his repertoire of BDSM activities ... although that was probably due to his focus on specific turn-ons.

There was an amazing world of things to do, and people who enjoyed doing them. I shivered, as I walked up the steps to the hotel entrance.

I heard a knock on the door; Kelly was finally back. I had expected her to return around midnight, and hadn't gone to sleep until 1AM.

This morning it was foggy and cold, so I'd sat in the hotel room, updating the KS Biotech business plan (again), and waiting for my love to arrive: Dr. Kelly Walsh – biotech researcher, fiancé, and trained dominatrix.

Kelly looked tired as we kissed briefly, and she trudged into the room. I took her backpack and put it on the small sofa, then held her tight, and we kissed again – this time, seriously.

"Welcome back." I smiled at Kelly, still holding her. "It must have been a long session."

Kelly laughed, "Yeah, you could say that." I waited for more details, and she finally yielded, "We started just before 8PM, and ended around 3:30 this morning. Elena and Mildred were asleep, and there were no trains running, so I decided to get a little shut-eye. Very little."

I wasn't going to pry, but hoped Kelly would share some of her experiences with me. Now, she was undressing, and I looked at her hopefully.

"Later, Sam. I need to get a shower." I watched her undress; even after all this time, I marveled at the perfection of her body.

My manhood stirred below, and I would have to take care of myself while Kelly was in the shower. The shower was small for the two of us, and Kelly obviously needed her own space, right now.

By the time we headed out, it was mid-afternoon, and Kelly was starving; I was, too. I had done my homework, and had some places in mind for our last meals in England. Taking the District Line to Embankment, we climbed out into real 'London fog'. The bridges disappeared into the mist less than halfway across the Thames.

It was a brisk walk to the restaurant, 'Rules', which was reputed to be the oldest restaurant in London, founded in 1798 by Thomas Rule. It served traditional English food, along with various fish and game dishes.

We got a nice, warm, cozy booth of dark wood and red tufted leather. Pictures hung everywhere on the walls in the Eduardian-decorated room.

We ordered drinks – a Guinness for me, and the 'Kate Middleton' for Kelly. Then, we perused the menu. It was a difficult choice, but I started with the pickled herring with dill and watercress, and Kelly selected the caramelized onion tart with endive and stilton.

When we were settled, I toasted 'Domme Kelly'. Kelly's hair shone, and her eyes sparkled. "Was the course all you expected, and hoped for?"

Kelly chuckled, "Well, I didn't know exactly what to expect ... but it was certainly interesting. Mainly, I have a lot more confidence now, having 'practiced' on quite a few subs." I raised my eyebrows, and she raised hers, then she laughed and took a sip of her drink.

I lifted my beer glass, "Good. Then, you won't have to practice on me."

Kelly nearly choked, she was laughing so hard. "You're right. I don't have to practice on you. I'm ready to give you the full professional treatment, no practicing required." I put down my beer, and the waiter delivered our appetizers.

After trying a taste of the herring, I said, "Well, I have some good news. I flew to Dublin and visited another pharma company a couple of days ago. They are very interested in your technology, and we're going to set-up a meeting in Barcelona."

Kelly smiled and nodded, "That's great, Sam." She took a bite of stilton and walnuts, then put her fork down. "I may have some good news, too." She laughed, "Actually a couple of pieces of news." I was all ears.

"First," she dug into her purse and pulled out a folded paper, then gave it to me; it was a check for $6,000! She continued, "I managed to 'upsell' the billionaire lady on submitting along with her husband."

My groin suddenly spasmed.

"And, she didn't want to be spanked, so each time she required 'corrective punishment', I fined her $100." That was Kelly, the businesswoman. "So I think it should pay for most of the trip; at least getting to London and staying for the two weeks."

We drank our drinks in silence. Then, Kelly surprised me again. "The second piece of news is that Charlotte – that's her name – is Director of a bank, and she's going to present KS Biotech as a potential investment for the bank."

That was amazing. "But how did KS Biotech come up in a submission session?"

Kelly nodded, "It was strange. First, Lottie was the client, observing the session and paying the bill. Then, she was the submissive, part of the scene. I didn't do that much to her; but I made her come, so I think she was happy." Kelly still hadn't answered my question.

"But before she was willing to submit to me, and *pay* me for the session, she wanted to know more about me. I don't think I mentioned the company name, but told her that you and I were developing the technology from my Ph.D. work to help pharmaceutical companies develop new drugs. She seemed very intrigued."

"That's fantastic, Kelly. They could be the ideal funding source."

The waiter came, and we ordered our main courses: The seared diver scallops with hazelnut butter for Kelly, and the roast loin of venison for me. The menu warned about 'shot' in the wild game, but hopefully there wouldn't be any lead in my loin. I chuckled, as I knew I had gained weight, and would have to diet again ... or run more.

I looked at the wine menu and decided to get two 'jugs', each a half liter. For Kelly, I ordered a chardonnay from Burgundy, and for me, a pinot noir, also from Burgundy.

"So how was the experience of dominating a billionaire? I can't imagine that too many people have ever done that." I drained the remainder of my Guinness.

Kelly laughed, "It was fun. Next time, I'll charge her $1000 for each misbehavior."

Kelly finished her drink and smiled, "But mostly, she wanted to see her husband punished. He said it was 'for real'. I never heard what he did that was so bad." Now she looked at me seriously, "But his bottom was pretty well thrashed, by the time I got done with him."

I was going to comment, but she cracked up again. "I even 'branded' him. Lottie was pretty excited about that."

"Lottie?" Was Kelly now on a nickname basis with a billionaire?

Kelly nodded, "That's what her husband calls her, and she let me call her that, too. She's a nice woman."

My head was spinning. Kelly and I had spent nearly two years developing a multitude of shared experiences. But in the past two weeks, it sounded like she had grown and matured through even more experiences; ones that had not been shared with me.

I was happy for Kelly, but realized that our relationship would continue evolving, as we both grew.

Change was inevitable. I felt a bit like I had when Robert had come home from college the first time; he was still my son, and I still loved him ... but he'd changed. I would never see him as a little boy again.

Kelly put her hand on my arm, "What's wrong, Sam? What are you thinking?"

I shook my head, "It's nothing. Just about the inevitability of change."

Our food came, and we both enjoyed the meal. And, of course, we had to try the desserts (OK, *I* had to try them; but Kelly didn't put up a fight). I ordered the sticky toffee pudding, and Kelly tried the Champagne-Elderberry cheesecake.

We finished the evening with a cappuccino for me, and Earl Grey tea for Kelly, along with a couple of chocolate truffles.

Kelly was shaking her head, "I hope you're going to be up for a lot of running, when we get home." I furtively reached down and let my belt out a notch.

Sunday morning was our last day in London. We ate brunch at the hotel, and Sam was excited to see that the Cirque du Soleil show that he thought had run through the end of March was extended through the end of April. It was at the Royal Albert Hall, which we'd visited before; evidently the posters had already been taken down.

The show was great. It was a mostly-female cast of performers, with a totally-female rock band.

Afterward, we found a small pub in Kensington, which had good beers and great food. Sam got the 'bangers and mash', and I splurged with the Sunday Roast – which included goose fat potatoes, mushy peas, and Yorkshire pudding. We would definitely be running, if not going on a diet, when we got back home!

We flew to Amsterdam on Monday morning, and stayed in the same hotel as before – and nearly the same room, only a floor lower. I felt very comfortable here.

Sam had the '*chipkaarte*' transport cards from the last time, and he loaded ten Euros of credit on each of them when we got on the tram. Of course, Sam had to make his usual first stop at his favorite 'coffee shop'.

We drank guava juice while smoking a tiny bit of *hashish* in the wooden pipe that Sam had brought. But it continued burning, and we continued smoking, until I realized that I was totally stoned. I think the last time – for both Sam and I – was in Hawaii, on the beach in Hanalei.

As Sam finished up the last of the hash, he looked at the map app on his phone. "Oh! The torture museum is just a block away!"

Here we go, again. We'd already visited one torture museum in Germany; but we'd skipped the prison museum in London and the sewer museum in Paris.

This time, I let Sam have his way ... and it turned out to be pretty interesting. It was also quite gruesome, seeing the instruments of torture, such as the 'skullcracker', the inquisition chair, and the rack.

We walked along the Singel Canal, enjoying the day; it was overcast, but the temperature seemed warmer than in London. Sam gravitated into a bakery which had dozens of delicious-looking items, as well as an entire chocolate truffle case. It looked good, but I dragged Sam back to the sidewalk.

"Oh!" Sam was pointed: The sign said '*d'Vijff Vlieghen*'. "It's the famous 'Five Flies' restaurant." Sam walked in, and made a reservation for dinner. They didn't open for another couple of hours.

We walked down *Kalverstraat*, the walking street with tons of shops – mostly clothing and junk. But there was method to Sam's madness, and we ended up at the Belgian beer bar that he and Henk had taken me to on our last visit here. We sat at a small table in the window, watching people – mostly tourists – pass by.

When he was on his second beer, Sam pulled out his phone. He smiled and pushed one of the numbers on his contact list. "Hello? May I please speak to Sofie?" Then, Sam sat back in his chair and closed his eyes, "Sofie, this is Sam. You met Kelly and I at the Sauna in Den Ilp, about 18 months ago. We talked with you and Greetje about BDSM and sex clubs."

Now, he was nodding, "Yes. Yes. I was just wondering if we could get together, as a group; perhaps visit one of the clubs that you recommended. Uh huh. OK, that would be great! Thanks. Bye bye."

He hung up and took a large swig of his malty beer, and looked at me. "We have a date with Sofie and Greetje on Friday evening. I think they're going to take us to a club." Then, he put his beer down and mumbled, "And I think *I'm* going to be the bottom, this time."

I remembered that Greetje tied men up, and Sofie beat them. This would be fun! A lot had changed in the past year and a half: We'd gotten engaged, and – just in the past two weeks – I'd become a pro-domme.

The dinner at the Five Flies was good. The food was excellent, but not particularly Dutch (which I didn't mind), but the restaurant itself was incredible – built into several houses from the 1600's.

The walls were brick, and the ceiling wooden with rectangular beams that were held up by huge logs. The lighting was dim, picture lights highlighting some of the gilt-framed paintings and lithographs, at least one of which was supposedly an original Rembrandt.

Sam suggested going back to one of the sex shops, where he could peruse the toys, but we had the rest of the week free, and we had just flown in this morning. I was still tired from the class and session with Brian and Lottie.

It was a fun week, walking around the town, shopping for sex toys, eating some great meals, and going to saunas. And, making several short excursions.

Tuesday, we went for a run in the morning, spent time at the Rijksmuseum, ate at a stand, then spent the rest of the afternoon and evening at the sauna in Den Ilp.

I was finally starting to relax, and 'come down' from the domme experience. I enjoyed playing some of Sam's games and satisfying him, without the responsibility of satisfying a paying client.

On Wednesday, we took a 20-minute train ride to a very picturesque, village called 'Zaanse Schans'. It was the site of a historic battle between the Dutch and Spanish, the Dutch winning in part by building earthen defenses on the Zaan river, called 'Schansen'. It was quite touristy, but we were nearly the only ones there on this Spring weekday.

There were many waterways, and lots of windmills actually turning in the breeze. The little village was recreated from old Dutch houses, and there were demonstrations of cheese-making and shoemaking. It was cute, and very different from being in Amsterdam.

Yesterday, we'd gone to several sex shops, where Sam bought some toys. And I had found a more upscale store where I could buy a couple of outfits for clubs. I was considering wearing my domme outfit when we met Sofie and Greetje tonight at the sex club.

Now, we were on another train – this one to Alkmaar, where we would see the famous (but also touristy) cheese market, held every Friday at 10AM. Alkmaar was in North Holland, the same direction but farther than Zaanse Schans, taking about 45 minutes by train from Amsterdam.

The 'market' was mostly a tourist show, with presentations and ringing of carillons. We learned that this town had been the official weighing site since 1365, and the cheese market had been taking place since 1600.

We ended-up spending most of our day in Alkmaar, shopping, and eating typical Dutch snacks like 'poffertjes', light, fluffy buckwheat pancakes sprinkled with powdered sugar. Of course, Sam went overboard, and got a dozen of them, which we ate with tiny wooden forks, sitting on a bench in the square.

Then, we took a boat excursion around the town, which was literally encircled by water. Ancient houses came down to the water. As the boat glided under low bridges, it felt almost like Disneyland. The town was beautiful, with tree-lined canals, skiffs tied up against a low brick embankment, on top of which cars and bicycles drove past busy shops.

We returned to Amsterdam, and took the tram to our hotel in the 'Old South' section of town, on the Amstel Canal. We dressed and packed a duffel bag for the club, but not before we tried a few of Sam's toys (including a very strange-looking prostate stimulator), and made love.

As we didn't have to be at the club until 8PM, Sam wanted to try another typical Dutch restaurant, '*Haesje Claes*', which was very similar to the Five Flies inside – having many small rooms with traditional old Dutch architecture, and decorated with mirrors, Delft tiles, paintings, and many knick-knacks that I couldn't identify.

We split the appetizer tasting, and Sam ordered a nice bottle of red wine. He suggested the '*Stamppot*', a mixture of mashed potatoes and vegetables, topped with meatball, sausage and bacon. But I'd already had the 'Hotchpot' on the last trip, and knew how filling it would be.

Instead, I decided on the mussels in a wine sauce, while Sam went for the duck leg candied in goose fat, with sauerkraut and port sauce. We were stuffed, and agreed to skip dessert, as we'd had plenty of sweets in Alkmaar.

At eight o'clock sharp, we walked into the club, which was in a renovated building in the *Jordaan* neighborhood. Sofie and Greetje were in the foyer, talking with another, older, woman – probably in her mid-40s. Greetje smiled when she saw us, and waved us over.

We hugged each other, and gave the traditional three kisses on the cheek (left – right – left). Sofie introduced us to Anouk, who was the owner of the club.

Anouk was dressed severely in all black. Both Sam and I had worn jeans and black sweaters or jackets, and would change into the 'dungeon' clothes from our duffel. But Greetje and Sofie looked a little frumpy in housedresses that might be worn going to the market.

We were led into a very modern-looking bar – dim lighting, stainless steel and glass, with blue and pink neon accents. The four of us sat a small table, while Anouk greeted other guests. A waiter came over and took our drink order.

Sofie smiled, "So what's new with you guys, in the past 18 months since we met at the sauna?" She looked at Greetje and laughed, "For us, it's about the same – our kids are now in elementary and middle schools, and we're still doing the 'housewife' thing."

Sam laughed, nearly falling out of his chair. "Well, there have been a few developments with us ..." Sam glanced at me, and I nodded. "For example, Kelly and I are now engaged to be married!"

Sofie and Greetje smiled and clapped, then leaned over the table to hug us. "That's wonderful," Greetje said. "When's the wedding?"

Sam and I looked at each other, and I took over, "We're not rushing it; it might not be until next year." I took a sip of my drink, "That's partly because Sam and I have started a company together." Sofie's and Greetje's eyes were wide; they were nodding slowly.

Sam jumped in, "Actually, the company is based on the work Kelly did for her Ph.D. dissertation. She's now '*Doctor Kelly Walsh*', soon to become Doctor Kelly

Johnson." Or something; I still hadn't spent a minute worrying about my marital name.

Sofie looked at me with respect and admiration, "Congratulations, Kelly. Doctor Walsh. That's incredible." She glanced at Greetje, "We didn't even know that you were going to school."

Now, Sam was laughing again, "And ..." He glanced at me, but I didn't know what he was going to say. "Kelly just finished a course in London, and is now a professional dominatrix!"

Sofie's mouth hung open, and Greetje was shaking her head slowly, "*That's* even *more* incredible! How did you find the time to do all these things? You must be working 24 hours a day!"

I shrugged, "I guess we're pretty energetic. Sam has also taken me to Toronto and to Hawaii, since we saw you guys." I didn't volunteer how much fun we'd had with my friends ... although I had no doubt that Sofie and Greetje would take it in stride.

Sofie turned to Sam, "Last time we met, you said that you wouldn't mind me spanking you, sometime." Smiling, she asked, "Is tonight the night?"

"And I would love to make an artwork of you ... with some rope," Greetje chimed in.

I looked at Greetje, "I would love to watch you show off your Shibari skills. Maybe you could teach me the ropes?" That hadn't come out quite right, but Greetje knew what I meant. She smiled and nodded excitedly at me.

Then, I added, "And I'm sure that Sam wouldn't mind being the model and bottom for us, tonight." Sam gave me a sour look, but he'd asked for it, and I knew that he was expecting to sub for our Dutch homebodies.

As Sam finished his drink, I asked, "Shall we get changed?"

Greetje shook her head, "We can do that in the 'dungeon'." As we followed her through a back door of the bar, she explained, "Anouk owns both the bar and the club, but they're separate; a lot of people come to the bar not aware of what goes on behind these walls."

We climbed up some stairs, and then up more stairs. Sofie said, "Anouk's family owned the building, a bunch of old apartments. When her parents died, and left her some money, she renovated the building, making each of the ensuite apartments into a room that can be used for a variety of things."

As we walked down a long hall, passing other rooms, I wondered whether these chambers were used for more than just BDSM. We entered a good size room. It was larger than the one at the other Amsterdam club we'd visited, but had a similar wall of BDSM restraints and implements, and a door to a small bathroom in the corner.

Before the door had even swung closed, Greetje pulled her dress over her head. She wore black lace bikini panties and bra. I guess we had all seen each other at the sauna, so there was no need for privacy here. I took off my jeans and sweater, and put on the domme outfit – black bustier with short black leather skirt, and high heels.

Sofie went into the bathroom, and came out in a skimpy thong, and no bra; she was small on top, and had brown hair that came down to her shoulders. She had a sweet face – big eyes, small nose, and luscious lips. I realized that I hadn't informed Greetje or Sofie about my interest in women.

As Sofie pulled on a pair of long, tan-colored pants – which had me wondering – she looked at Sam, "Are you going to stand there watching us, or would you like to participate, too?" I tried not to smile. Sam started undoing his belt.

Now, I could see that Sofie's pants were 'Safari' pants, held up by a wide leather belt. She pulled a hat out of her bag, and put it on. It looked like an Australian outback hat ... but maybe it could have been African. I was momentarily dumbfounded.

Sam was also entranced by Sofie's topless outfit, until she pulled a whip out of her bag, uncoiled it, and let it fly – halfway across the room – making a loud snap at the end. "I won't ask, anymore, Sam. If you're not undressed in less than a minute, I'm going to try this whip on you."

Suddenly, Sam had his pants and underwear off, then his sweater. He fumbled undoing the buttons of his shirt, and looked silly standing in his socks. But they were soon off, also – the floors being wood, so hopefully warm. Now, Sam stood at attention, fully nude, while Greetje and I finished dressing.

Greetje had put on a black leotard – it had long sleeves, and came down to her ankles. She was barefoot, and I decided to kick off my heels; they were overkill for this situation ... unless I decided to do a 'trampling' demonstration on Sam.

Sofie lowered one of the ropes that went through pulleys on the ceiling, and attached them to wrist cuffs that she'd put on Sam. Now, she blindfolded him, and cleated the rope so that his hands were above his head. I had visions of my recent experiences in Elena's dungeon.

And I wondered whether Sofie would actually use the bullwhip on him. I hoped not; that was too severe for Sam, and the marks might show when we were at saunas over the next week. I watched, as Greetje selected several coils of rope, and Sofie began working on Sam.

First, she put on fur mitts, and lightly stroked Sam's back and butt, then his chest and downward. Sam was responding with an 'Mmmmm' that kept going up in pitch.

She reached into her duffle, as she knelt to stroke Sam's lower legs, and replaced one mitt, then the other, with mitts that had the texture of rough sandpaper. As Sam, unaware, was basking in the feeling of the fur, Sofie roughly pulled the new mitts down Sam's back and chest at the same time.

There as a predictable 'Arrrrggh!', as Sofie continued to exfoliate Sam using the mitt. Sofie treated Sam to several additional textures, getting more and more extreme, until she put on gloves with tiny spikes all over them.

I felt the tips of the spikes, and Sofie smiled; then she lifted the back of my skirt, and gently slapped me on the butt with the mitt. Owww! That hurt! I wondered if I had tiny spots of blood on my bum.

Sofie gave Sam some light slaps, on the hips and the butt, and he yelped ... but there were no marks. I would have to get some of these!

"Now, we'll start with the whip," Sofie said, chuckling. She held the whip at nearly its end, and waved her hand back and forth, giving Sam some good licks with the thin end of the whip.

Sam was whimpering, and on his toes, doing a little dance to try to avoid the whip. But he was blindfolded, and Sofie moved around him silently, swinging the implement like a flogger.

I looked over the implements on the wall, and selected a heart-shaped crop; I was starting to enjoy using the crop, which gave a severe sting, but required very little energy.

Sofie stepped away from Sam, as I swung the crop, the slapper impacting Sam's chest – a small heart now overlying his larger heart. And, Sam did have a big heart.

Next, I gave Sam a flurry of crops on his hips and bum. He yelped some more, but I don't think he had any idea who was cropping him.

Greetje said, in a stronger voice than I'd heard her use before, "Enough playing around. He's mine, now." Greetje lowered the rope, and removed the wrist cuffs, but left Sam blindfolded.

She whispered to Sam, "Relax your body, and let me put it into position. Please tell me, if the ropes are uncomfortable; we need to work together to make this an enjoyable experience."

Greetje really was a wizardess with the ropes. She quickly bound Sam's arms together behind his back with intricate knots, the rope passing over his shoulders, and crisscrossing his upper back. Several bands of ropes kept his upper arms against his body, more loops keeping his wrists together, and his lower arms parallel to his waist.

"Do you need to pee, Sam? This will be your last chance for a while ... unless you want me to hold a bucket for you, while you're trussed-up."

Sam didn't think he had to go, but let me take him into the bathroom to assist – as his arms and hands were now bound. I thought it considerate of Greetje to let him take care of this now.

When we came out, Sofie wanted to see how far Sam would submit to some bottom-warming. She had him stand, feet apart and bending forward, as she flogged him for several minutes, the strokes becoming harder, the deer leather tails swiping his hips from side to side, and reddening his butt.

I knew it had to hurt, and Sam whimpered a few times, and was groaning by the end, but he had done very well. He had stayed in position, only moving his feet and lifting his head a few times.

Now, we helped Sam get onto a small padded table, on his back. Greetje continued to bind him, his knees to his chest, and multiple wraps of rope tying his ankles to his hips. Finally, she bound his feet together, again with some intricate knots, and one strand of the rope weaving through Sam's toes.

Sofie smiled, "This will be a nice position!" She turned to Greetje, "Maybe, you could lift his feet a bit?" Greetje nodded and connected one of the ropes from the ceiling to the rope binding Sam's feet ... then pulled. Sam's butt was now off the table, and his anus exposed and relaxed.

As Sofie selected a strap, I picked one of the jeweled butt plugs – the same ones we had at home – and inserted it into Sam's rear. He hardly made a sound. I was very proud of him, cooperating this well, still blindfolded, three women 'working' on him.

Sofie took a one-inch wide, two-foot long leather strap to Sam's bottom, starting easy and working up to some hard strokes that caused Sam to yelp.

She turned to me, "He's doing pretty well. Do you want to take advantage of him in this position, before we let Greetje continue binding him?"

I didn't say anything, but took the largest crop from the wall and nodded to Sofie; she stood out of the way. Sam had taken a good spanking, but I thought he needed just a couple of surprise strokes. He was still blindfolded, and I gauged the distance and stepped into position quietly.

Then, I gave Sam a very hard stroke of the crop on each side of his butt. He screamed when the first stroke landed, and the second was already over before he could react again. There were now two large dark-red rectangles on Sam's bum, and he was sniffling.

Hanging up the crop, I smiled at Greetje and she continued her human macramé project. She wrapped a short length of rope around the base of Sam's cock, under his balls, and then continued winding the rope around his member.

"We can give him another sensation later by turning him on; his erection will be constrained by the rope. It should be a frustrating tease for him." Greetje was clearly in her element, now, working quickly, and checking with Sam occasionally, as she positioned the ropes.

She tied the end of his penis to the ropes binding his feet. As I stood at the end of the table, Sam's balls just below his heels, I thought how interesting it might be to give him a scrotal infusion; but we didn't have the supplies, fortunately for Sam.

We helped Greetje turn Sam over, his knees and head against the padded table, his butt in the air. Greetje lowered three of the ropes from the ceiling, using what she called a 'trucker's hitch' so that she could adjust the lengths. We each took a rope and pulled, and Sam was raised a few inches off the table.

It took Greetje several minutes to adjust the ropes the way she wanted them, Sam's head facing nearly down, and his butt the highest part of him. She pointed, and I removed the butt plug, Sam yelping again as the thickest part passed through his sphincter.

Then, she rummaged through her duffel, and pulled out a large candle – probably an inch in diameter and a foot long; it was red, and would have looked nice on a Christmas dining table. She handed it to me, and I lubed it and inserted it into Sam.

Greetje did more adjusting of the ropes, until the candle was vertical (although it bobbed from side to side, as Sam's muscles contracted and relaxed). Then, she lit it.

It was an amazing work of art: Sam hung in mid air – the table now pushed back into a corner – his body apparently relaxed; at least, he wasn't complaining about any pressure points from the rope.

But it was the lit candle sticking up from his rear, the ropes from the ceiling, and all of the knot-work on Sam's body that combined to make this an incredible sight.

I took pictures with my phone, and Greetje took a long series of photos with her DSLR – which, she said, would become part of her portfolio.

Sam had been very quiet for a while, and I asked, "How are you doing, Sam?" He replied with a loud snore. I was surprised. "Are you bored, Sam? Maybe we can find some large skin hooks, and I can demonstrate 'suspension' to Sofie and Greetje … if you need a little more stimulation?"

Chuckling, Sam said, "Actually, I'm very relaxed. It's not that uncomfortable. But … could you please take the blindfold off? It's getting a little claustrophobic."

I looked at Sofie and Greetje, and they nodded. I removed the blindfold, and we showed Sam some of the pictures. He was surprised to see a lit candle rising from his rear – he'd thought it was a vibrator or a butt plug.

Then, as Sam watched, Greetje began undressing – taking off her leotard, as well as her bra and underwear. Then, Sofie undressed, also. They walked around Sam, stroking him with fur and feathers, letting him suck their breasts, as I stimulated his frenum between my fingers.

Sam moaned, but that turned into a groan, as his manhood expanded against the coils of rope. This was a different kind of C&B torture. Even after taking Elena's class, I was learning new techniques from Greetje and Sofie. And, I was sure I'd only scratched the surface of the BDSM world, even as my own repertoire was expanding.

Greetje said, "Maybe he would like to satisfy you?" She pulled the padded table back under Sam, and pointed. I took off my skirt and thong, and lay back on the table, my legs apart and feet together.

Greetje and Sofie carefully lowered Sam until his mouth was touching me, then I adjusted my position until it was over my clit. Sam gave a very respectable demonstration of his oral skills, getting me off after just a few minutes.

But my turn-on was at least half from looking up at Sam, hanging from the three ropes, his arms bound behind him, and the red candle still burning down. The other half was from thinking about 'Slave Sam', and some of the things I would do with him, when we returned home.

I extricated myself, and we lowered Sam onto the table; then I extracted the candle from his butt.

While he was still face-down, Greetje quickly untied the knots and freed his hands and arms. Then, we turned him over, and she undid his feet, unwrapped his legs, and – finally – unwrapped the coil of rope around his dick.

Sam sat up, then got off the table and stood, as we inspected the patterns that the rope left on his skin. We took a few more photos.

Then, we all hugged each other – all of us nude, except me, as I was still wearing my bustier. I had thought it was a great experience – something *else* new; and Sam had also enjoyed the experience, even with the spanking that Sofie had given him.

As we had learned in the class, Sam was now experiencing an endorphin high, and he said he felt as if he were floating.

We all got dressed and had another drink in the bar, before Sofie and Greetje said they had to get home to their husbands and children.

It had been quite an experience. Getting spanked by Sofie had been minor; but getting tied up by Greetje had been *major*. I was still on a high from the experience.

Being suspended, blindfolded, and under the control of someone I barely knew, was different than I had expected. I'd relaxed and let Greetje do her thing, and had felt a real rapport with her. It had been an intimate experience, cooperating to achieve something beautiful.

My only frustration had been getting turned on and not being able to have my release. But that was remedied when we got back to the hotel, Kelly being delighted to satisfy me, after my performance at the club.

On Saturday we slept late, then went for a run; but it turned out to be a 'walk in the park' as families were crowding the pathways, the day being gorgeous, and flowers blooming everywhere.

Back at the hotel, Sam rented one of the small rowboats, and took me on a tour along the Amstel Canal through the 'old south' neighborhood of Amsterdam.

In the evening, we went to a concert, and had a late dinner at one of the Indonesian restaurants. It had been a nearly perfect day.

On Sunday morning, we took the train to Utrecht, and were picked up by Zöe at the station. We would be visiting Zöe today and tomorrow, then returning to the hotel, where we'd left most of our stuff, taking only small backpacks for the couple-day excursion.

Getting on the highway, Zöe drove us to Rotterdam, where we visited a sauna on the outskirts of the city. It was small, but ornately decorated – gold faucets, beautiful tile work, and nice gardens with all the flowers in bloom

We spent the day relaxing in the saunas, steam bath, swimming pools and jacuzzis, eating salads in the sauna restaurant, and visiting with Zöe.

"You're a *what*?!?!" We had already told Zöe about my Ph.D. and the company, but were just now getting around to telling her about the London portion of our trip.

As I smiled and nodded, Zöe looked at Sam and chuckled, "This time, Kelly and I will have to get *you* on the coffee table in a knee-chest position for our pleasure!"

Of course, Zöe – all of us – were remembering the evening we'd had, when Sam had wanted to show off my submission skills ... and then we'd had a group experience.

Then, she looked at me, "You know, I never got to try that cane on you; maybe, now, we can try it on Sam?"

That was an interesting idea ... but now I realized that we hadn't given Zöe the biggest news. I hadn't been wearing my ring – at Elena's, or in the saunas – and I wondered whether Sam had told her. But, if he had, she would have said something.

I glanced at Sam and turned to Zöe, "And .... Sam took me – and three of my friends – to Hawaii last fall ..." Zöe smiled and nodded pleasantly. Then, I added, "... where he proposed to me."

Now, Zöe's eyes glittered, "Kelly! Sam! That's great! I'm so happy for you guys." She kissed both of us on the lips. We toasted with our iced teas.

Sam shrugged, and meekly admitted, "I guess I never let you or Henk know ..."

As we finished our salads, we told Zöe about the Hawaii trip, and how Sam had proposed. And that we'd bought a ring in San Francisco that I would have to show her when we got back to the house. Zöe was amazed that so many things had happened with us, while she and Henk were in the same jobs and relationship with each other.

The rest of the afternoon alternated between taking quiet saunas, and going in the pool or jacuzzi where we could talk more. When Zöe asked about my friends (and exactly *why* Sam had taken them to Hawaii with us), we told her a few stories of our experiences.

Sam and I alternated giving quick snippets of our experiences with my friends – starting with Sam giving two of them OTK spankings. Then, I mentioned the threesome that we'd had with Julie. Then, Sam described the school-girl spanking scene we'd had with Linda.

Finally, we both told Zöe about the submission challenge that Sam had given my friends; or, more accurately, put them through. As she was into some kinky things herself, Zöe took all our stories in stride.

In the late afternoon, we showered together – with a couple of dozen other people – at the sauna, then Zöe drove us back to the townhouse in Driebergen, and we unpacked the car and dressed for dinner.

Although we'd gone through the train station, I'd never seen Utrecht. Zöe gave us a tour, walking along canals and past dozens of restaurants. She'd already picked one and made a reservation. It was an African restaurant, with dishes from all over Africa – very exotic, and *another* new experience for both Sam and I.

Back in the townhouse, all of us in robes or night clothes, Sam mixed up a batch of Margaritas, and we sat on the couch talking. We let Sam off the hook – this time – with most of the conversation being me regaling both Sam and Zöe with stories from the past two weeks at Elena's.

On Monday, Zöe drove us to Amsterdam, and spent most of the day taking us to her favorite shops and art galleries, and showing us a couple of the apartments that she had for rent. If we needed to stay in Amsterdam for an extended period, Zöe would definitely have a place for us.

We checked back into our hotel, had a snack in their bar, then sat on the balcony of our room, looking out over the rooftops of Amsterdam, and smoking the last of the hash that Sam had bought.

Sam decided that we still had some room in our backpacks, so we shopped again at several of the sex shops in the city. But, as Sam had so many toys, already, he didn't find many new things to buy.

On the other hand, I had now been introduced to a much wider range of BDSM activities, so I found quite a few playthings to add to our collection. Unfortunately, most of these shops dealt in cheap tourist junk, not the kinds of robust products that would be needed in a dungeon and used by a pro-domme.

Wednesday morning, Henk and Zöe drove into Amsterdam and parked at our hotel. Then, we took off walking around the city. It was one of the most interesting days of the year: 'Köningsdag', the celebration of the King's birthday.

As Sam had explained, it was also called Orange Day, as the royal family descended from the House of Orange. So we all wore orange, as did most of the population of the country.

There were flea markets set-up everywhere – on nearly every major street. Everyone was jubilant – although some were obviously getting a too-early start on the alcohol.

But with Sam and Henk leading the way, we got an early start, also. It was a fun way to end our trip; not that the rest hadn't been fun. We partied with Henk and Zöe until late in the night, and bid them farewell until our next trip to Europe – which would be in a few months.

CHAPTER 10: SLAVE SAM

Only a week home, and we were already back into our routine, the Europe trip now part of our memories. Sam and I were running every morning, and I spent most of my days in the lab. It would be a miracle to complete the prototype and conduct the 'proof-of-principle' testing before the Barcelona trip.

We had decided that it was time to add some limited staff to KS Biotech, and hired three of my acquaintances from graduate school to work part-time for the company.

One woman was a masters candidate who could use the work on our technology for her thesis project. Another was a software engineer. And we hired a young guy who was supposed to be a 'crack' electrical engineer.

We would be using the lab for only a short time, as Sam had completed the licensing agreement, and we planned to move the system into our pool room (aka the 'headquarters' of KS Biotech) by July for further testing.

I wanted to share the potential upside success with my friends and family. So I transferred stock totaling 0.5% of the company to each of my friends – Julie, Linda, and Kathy, and my two brothers, and 2.5% to my parents. If we could sell the company for $100 million, my friends would each get half a million dollars!

That left me with 75% of the company which – of course – would be diluted when we brought in new investors. But either the company was going to be worth something or not; and having 75% versus 80% was of no consequence to me. Sam had transferred 1% of KS Biotech stock to each of his sons, and still held 8% of the company for his initial investment. And Raj had 10% for his consulting services.

Sam and I were finally going to spend some time together over the weekend. He had been prodding me to tell him more about the domme course, to share my knowledge, and I had finally decided that he should get a taste of real submission.

Kelly had done well this time, suffering almost no jet lag. We'd started running last weekend, and I'd barely seen her during the week. I grabbed an IPA from the fridge and went down to the playroom, first turning on the heat in the sauna, then sitting at my computer, sorting the photos we'd taken on the trip.

I had spent most of the week preparing and forwarding information and thank-you letters to each of the pharma companies I'd visited, as well as several others with whom I'd had e-mail communication. Now, success of the Barcelona trip – and our fund-raising efforts – would depend on Kelly and her team completing and testing the prototype system.

As a photo popped onto the screen of Kelly's sore bottom after the first 24 hours of her domme class, I sat back in my executive chair and re-imagined the stories that Kelly had shared. There was that first weekend, submitting to James; humiliating Alfred; teasing Jack, the pantyhose fetishist; spanking Roger; fisting another male sub; and performing with Archie in front of an audience.

Of course, I wanted to hear more details about her benefactor session with Charlotte and Brian. And, she'd mentioned that she and the other classmates had topped Elena – something that must have been interesting ... and something I would have loved to observe.

My hand went down, into my pants, and I adjusted my growing length. I was getting turned on thinking about her experiences; but I knew that Kelly would want to try some of her new skills on me. I trusted her – both to respect my limits, and to give me some experiences that would be challenging.

I heard the front door slam closed, and shut down my computer before going upstairs to greet Kelly.

We kissed, and Kelly gave me a strange look, "You're drinking beer, already? I thought we might open a bottle of wine."

I took a last swig from the bottle, and dumped it into the recycling bin under the sink. "Sure, that would be great. What kind of wine did you have in mind?"

Kelly laughed, "I don't care. Something red. I've had a hard week, too." She went upstairs to get changed, and I went downstairs to the wine cellar and selected a nice Chilean cabernet.

As I got out of my 'lab' jeans, and into a spring dress, I considered the situation. What I really wanted to do was to make Sam my slave for a month. But I would probably settle for a week. And we would have to order a few more things, before it could happen.

I sat on the bed and searched the 'net on my laptop, finding several items that would be needed. One was quite expensive – nearly $1000, including shipping. I was going to ask Sam for a 'graduation present', and then decided that I would pop for the item myself, as I had earned

$6000 during the trip. It was a splurge, but could be fun, as long as I was the dominant.

We wouldn't receive the stuff for a week, so I could begin preparing Sam now. When I looked at the calendar, I had to laugh: We could begin Sam's experience a week from now, on Friday ... the 13th.

I typed a quick schedule for the week, then closed my laptop and went downstairs. My pelvic muscles were already clinching when I visualized some of the scenes I would have with Slave Sam.

Kelly came bounding down the stairs, and I handed her a glass of wine. She seemed particularly ebullient. "It looks like you've recovered quickly from your hard week."

Smiling, and taking a sip of the wine, Kelly replied, "Not exactly. Just thinking about the future, rather than the past." I was wondering whether she'd re-thought the timing of our wedding, or just thinking about plans for the weekend.

Then, she clarified, "Do we have any plans for the week after next? And, maybe, the next couple of weeks after that?" This sounded serious. Maybe Kelly was thinking about a late-season ski trip; but it wouldn't need to be that long. I gave her a quizzical look, and she shrugged, "We can talk about it later."

I wasn't going to push her; she would let me know what she was thinking when she was ready. But I checked the calendar on my Apple watch, and saw that there was nothing scheduled for the next few weeks. Of course, I had KS Biotech work to do, every day.

We went out for sushi, and had a great meal. We'd gone out for hamburgers twice in the past week, and salads another two times – having missed our local eats during the month in Europe. I'd also cooked Italian one night, and steaks another.

It was finally warm enough to enjoy the backyard and the barbeque, and the gardeners had kept the yard in pretty good shape while we were gone. I turned on the pool heater, so that it would be warmed up over the weekend. Kelly hoped to have her friends over for a quick visit, as they clamored to hear about the Europe trip and her domme class.

Tonight, we would be using the sauna for the first time in nearly six weeks – the longest it hadn't been used since I'd met Kelly. We undressed in the master bedroom closet and put on our 'Superperson' robes. I hugged Kelly and held her tight; then we went down to the sauna.

When we were settled on the top bench, Kelly smiled, "There are two things I'd like to ask you: One is very minor, and the other is very major."

Uh oh. I couldn't imagine what could be 'major' that Kelly would need to ask me. I nodded, uncertainly.

"First, may I have my friends over on Sunday? They've been asking me about the domme class, but I want to tell them about it in-person."

Well, that was certainly minor. "Of course, Kelly, you know that's always OK. I love your friends, and we haven't seen them for quite a while."

Kelly nodded, "Thanks, Sam. We've been waiting all week to spend the weekend with each other, and I didn't want to intrude on anything you had planned. But it would be fun to see them, again."

Now, Kelly sat on her towel quietly, looking down, beads of sweat forming all over her body, reflecting glints from the red bulb that illuminated the sauna. She was obviously trying to decide how to ask me something ... or *whether* to ask it.

But that was silly – we had an open and honest relationship, and she knew she could ask me anything. So, perhaps she didn't know if she wanted to hear the answer I would give?

She finally lifted her head, wiping a drop of sweat from the tip of her nose, and smiling. "Sam ..." I waited in anticipation, as her smiled faded, and she became serious. "Would you be my slave for a month?"

At first, it didn't register. We'd talked about one of us being a slave; but, of course, I'd always assumed that *Kelly* would be *my* slave.

And now, as I realized that Kelly was a full pro-domme ... and remembering the stories she'd told (mostly only a teaser, as I hadn't heard any of the complete stories) about her experiences in the class ... she wanted *me* to submit.

I was now sweating profusely, and wasn't sure that it would have been much less, if we hadn't been in a sauna.

But I'd had to expect it: There was never any doubt that Kelly would want to try things on me, 'show off' her skills, and see how I would react to some of the harsh things that she had learned.

I *knew* that she would introduce me to new experiences – as I had for her, nearly two years ago. And I knew that I would agree to submit to her; because I loved her, and respected her. And, because *I* was curious, also. What would she do? How would I react? How *painful* would it be?

Sam's eyes were closed, and his face looked a little pale. I had little doubt that Sam would submit to me – at least for some defined period of time, whether a weekend, a week, or a month. But it was clear that he was already intimated by the prospect. That was a good start.

I really hadn't been sure that I wanted to do this – subject Sam to pain, and even embarrassment. He loved me, and would submit to me, *had* submitted to me. But what I wanted was for Sam to really experience submission as he would with a domme.

He'd had a taste when we had visited Elena on the first trip; but now, he should have the full experience – the fear, uncertainty, feeling of helplessness; willing your mind to accept pain that your body wants to end.

It wasn't that I was sadistic, wanting to hurt Sam. But this shared experience could help him understand what I'd gone through, and what 'real' BDSM entailed – something that I was certain that Sam didn't *really* want.

And it might free him of his curiosity – near obsession – with my becoming a domme. He had been great about supporting me in my taking the class, and now he was scared of what I might 'do' to him, the unknown of what I had learned and experienced.

Perhaps one slightly harsh experience would rid him of his fears, and satisfy his desire to participate. It had been clear for a long time: Sam was an 's-type', a good submissive, bottom, pet, or slave. I was more a 'D-type' – dominant, top, owner, or master ... although we were really both 'switches', being able to take either role.

It was getting hot in here, but I had to communicate with Sam. I stepped down to the lower bench, and Sam followed me. We re-adjusted our towels, and then Sam just looked at me, not sure what to say.

"Sam, I know that you'll submit to me, if I ask ... even if you don't want to. That's not a question, and this isn't a test." I took a deep breath, "But I think you're curious about some of the things I've learned, and I'd like to share them with you."

Now I had to think through the details. "Not everything. I'm not interested in humiliating you, or financially dominating you." I waited for his retort, 'You're *already* dominating me!' ... but it never came. Sam was listening; and we were getting hot again.

I led Sam out of the sauna and under the shower. Then, we sat on our towels on the chaises, facing each other. "Sam, why did you want me to submit to you during our first weekend together? After I'd already spent that first day proving that I could and would submit to you."

Sam shrugged, "Because it turned me on?" Then, he said, sheepishly, "And, because I wanted to share some new things with you. I hoped that it would turn you on, too." And, it had; at least some of it.

"So, that's why I'm asking you for this: To share some experiences with you, give you some perspective on what I learned, and see if it will be a turn-on for either of us."

I looked at him seriously, and a bit sadly, "Look, Sam, I'm certainly not going to 'force' you to submit to me, ever. But if you're not going to let me give you a taste of what I learned at Elena's, please don't keep asking questions about the class or my experiences there."

In a way, it would be a win-win for me, either way; but I truly hoped that Sam would submit voluntarily. Then, we could move on from the 'domme' experience to new ones.

Sam was nodding slowly, glanced at me, then looked down, "But would it have to be for a full month?" I had anticipated that. I could tell him that half a month or three-quarters of a month would be fine, but decided to give him a break.

"The reason for a month was so that you would get into a routine – a repeating weekly schedule, your new 'lifestyle'. But we can start with a week." I smiled, thinking about it, "Then, you'll have a daily repeating schedule."

Sam got off the chaise, and knelt at my feet, then took my hands in his, "Kelly, I love you. And I respect you, and your ideas. But I'm afraid ... you *know* that I'm kind of a wimp." I nodded; yes, I knew that.

Finally, Sam pulled my head down and kissed me. I didn't put up a fight. "OK, Kelly. I'll do it." He looked into my eyes, "I'll be your 'slave' for a week."

Then, he swallowed, "I'm trusting you not to torture me, to make it unbearable, or to really hurt me."

I shook my head, "There's no negotiating, Sam. You'll get exactly what I want to do to you – or with you, or what I want you to do to me. You *know* that you'll have a sore bottom, and will have to put up with some discomfort, and maybe even embarrassment."

Now, Sam looked up at me questioningly, but I did not provide details. I chuckled, "It's just as you told me – warned me – that first day, when you made me sign the contract."

"No, I didn't *make* you sign it. You wanted the experience, and I needed assurances that you wouldn't hold it against me. And, anyway, most points of the so-called 'contract' were instructions for your day of submission, and what you could expect."

Nodding, I laughed, "And, I just informed you of what *you* can expect, as my slave." The subject was over, and we went back into the sauna once more, before going upstairs to dress for dinner.

Julie and Linda arrived about noon on Sunday. We all hugged, as we hadn't seen each other since Christmas; well, *I* hadn't seen them, but Kelly had gone out to lunch with them back in March.

Kelly asked, "Will Kathy be coming, today?"

Julie laughed, "I'm *sure* she's 'coming'. But, no, she won't be here." Julie glanced at Linda, and back to us, "She's been on Kauai for the past few months, living with Christian."

Kelly raised her eyebrows at Julie, and she continued, "But we've been communicating by e-mail, and she said she would call us this afternoon, so she can tell all of us hello."

We took sodas from the fridge, and went out to the backyard. We hadn't sat out here for a long time. But it was a beautiful day – ultra-blue skies with puffy clouds floating by. We'd evidently missed the rains when we were in 'sunny' London.

Linda was radiant, today – she'd kept the weight off, done something with her hair, and seemed very upbeat. I had to say something. "Linda, you look particularly ravishing today ... almost like there's an aura around you. I love to see you smiling, like that."

Julie swung her head to Linda, who glanced at Julie and gave her a slight nod. Then, Linda exclaimed, "I have a new boyfriend ... a steady one."

Kelly and I hugged her and congratulated her. "So tell us about him," Kelly said as we all sat down at the glass-topped table.

Linda shrugged, "He's tall, not so dark, but very handsome. He's in his mid-30s, and in great shape – he runs marathons, and exercises every day before he comes home from work."

Kelly stared at Linda, willing her to tell us what he did. Linda smiled, "He's an attorney and a CPA; he works with corporations to optimize their investments and financial strategies, internationally."

I glanced at Kelly, and she had a blank expression. In fact, it was nearly the same expression that I'd seen on

Linda and Julie's faces, when Kelly tried to tell them about KS Biotech and the technology she'd developed.

Linda chuckled, "Like how much of their profits to keep offshore, or when to buy back their stock." She took a swig of her Diet Coke, "Anyway, he's a hunk ... and very good in bed!"

Now, we were all staring at her. She just shrugged. Turning to Kelly, she said, "So tell us about your domme class." Julie laughed, and nodded.

Kelly thought a moment, and said, simply, "It was very intense."

I couldn't resist, "Yeah. After the first 24 hours, her bottom was raw. And then, the Mistress used a bullwhip on her, and sliced her open – they had to dress the wounds."

I was starting to get worked-up, thinking about all the intense experiences that Kelly had endured ... and now wanted to put me through. At least she didn't own a bullwhip, yet, as far as I knew.

But she had just told me she'd ordered quite a few 'toys' on the Internet, and would repay me for what she charged on my card. According to the bills I saw on my Apple watch, it totaled more than $1000.

I cringed, thinking about what she could have ordered that was so expensive; and what she intended to do to me with it. But I loved Kelly, and had to trust her: If she wanted me to have this experience, I would submit to her.

"Those were the only two really painful experiences ... except for Elena cropping me on the breasts." My friends' mouths hung open. "But it was interesting – there are really a lot of different areas within BDSM, and we got a smattering of many of them."

I continued, "Like 'fin-dom', financial domination. We had a lady come in to demonstrate dominating a few guys on the phone, and she ended up with several thousand dollars in cash and presents."

Now, Linda's mouth was open wider, and Julie leaned forward, "How do I get into that?" We all laughed. But, actually, Julie might be a great financial dominatrix, with her self-confidence and assertive personality.

Linda said, "So it wasn't all about spanking?"

"No. In fact there was less than a day of the two weeks learning how to wield the cane, and other implements." My friends were staring at me questioningly.

"For example, I learned how to be a goddess, and have men treat me that way." Sam squinted at me and shook his head slowly; I hadn't mentioned the details to him.

I added, "Some women enjoy being a 'humiliatrix' – and we got a chance to humiliate some older men. They looked like bankers. And, how to do 'cock-and-ball torture'." Linda's eyes went wide.

"And, of course, there was instruction on medical play, fire play, and very edgy things like 'scarification'." I glanced at Sam; he had slunk down in his chair, and looked a little pale.

This was fun! "And we learned the ins-and-outs of slave training." Now, *Julie's* eyes were wide, and *Linda's* mouth was hanging open. Now, for the kill, "I've asked Sam to become my slave. And he's agreed."

Sam's eyes closed, and now his face was flushed. Then, he nodded, and said – without mirth – "But only for a week."

I smiled, "Yes. Then, we'll see if he's willing to live a slave lifestyle, full-time." We hadn't talked about this, and I had no intention of really suggesting that.

But Sam's response was predictable: He groaned, got up, and went into the kitchen, coming out a minute later drinking beer from a bottle. I was starting to build tension already, and Sam's 'experience' wouldn't begin for another five days.

Linda asked, "But, would you ever consider doing it professionally? Could you make money?"

Laughing, I replied, "I'm *already* a 'pro-domme'. Not only did Elena get paid $10,000 by the benefactor for a few hours of my time," my friends gasped, "but I managed to sell the benefactor on some additional services ... and she paid me $6,000."

Julie asked, skeptically, "Some extra services?" It didn't sound so good, when she put it that way. But, of course, I hadn't been paid for *those* services ... that was something I'd wanted to do for myself.

"Actually, the 'benefactor' was a woman." My friends continued to be more and more shocked, with each new revelation I made. "And she's a billionaire." Now they were beside themselves.

"Sam, maybe you could open a bottle of wine for us? A nice light red would be good," Linda said. That was a good idea. I had a lot more things to share.

While Sam was downstairs in the wine cellar, I explained, "The woman (Charlotte) was paying Elena to watch her husband (Brian) be punished by one of the domme class graduates.

"But I convinced Charlotte – Lottie – to pay 50% more for her to share some experiences with her husband. But she didn't want to be spanked ... so I had to use other techniques on her. I think she was pleased with the results.

"In fact, she – or the bank she runs – might invest in our company, KS Biotech." My friends were shaking their heads slowly; it was a lot to take in.

As Sam returned with the bottle, an opener, and glasses, I decided to change the subject. "We haven't told you about the Netherlands portion of our trip."

Sam spoke up, "I'll show you some pictures and a few videos when we go downstairs."

I smiled at Sam, "But we don't have pictures or videos of our sauna experiences ... *or*, you being tied up and flogged by Sofie and Greetje in the dungeon."

My friends were shaking their heads again, and both Sam and I were about to explain, when Julie's cell phone rang. She smiled, tapped a button, and set it on the table.

"Hi, Kathy! How's Kauai? And Christian?" Julie chuckled, "You're on speakerphone with Linda, Kelly, and Sam." We all shouted 'Hi, Kathy!'.

Kathy was ebullient, "Hi, everybody! And to answer your question, Julie, Kauai is dreamy; and so is Christian." She still sounded very much in love.

"So I've decided to stay here," Kathy said, then followed-up quickly, "and I'd like all of you to visit me in June ... and be in my wedding." Now, we were all screaming.

When we had calmed down, Kathy explained, "Christian was very busy with his company through the end of March; they had a very good fiscal year. Then, he took me to Tahiti in April, and I met some of his relatives who are still there."

We were all shaking our heads in wonder, but didn't want to interrupt. Kathy continued, "We were staying in Bora Bora for a week, and that's where he proposed to me – in the Tahitian moonlight, under a palm tree. Christian is really romantic."

Over the next ten minutes, we all got our questions in, and learned that the wedding was set for June 25. Kathy wanted us to be bridesmaids, and Sam to be a groomsman.

When the call was over, we were all in shock: We had certainly known that Kathy and Christian were serious ... but the wedding was a surprise, especially how soon it was – just over a month from now!

In the meantime, Linda may have found her mate. It was still possible that all my friends would be married before me. Well, at least, we would have some good 'wedding practice' by then.

We finished the bottle of wine, but not our conversation. Sam took us to the Chinese restaurant, where we told a few stories from the rest of our Europe trip, learned a little more about Linda's new partner, and marveled again that Kathy was getting married.

On Thursday, we received a huge box, and several smaller boxes – things Kelly had ordered. I called Kelly, and she requested that I not open the small boxes, but that I should assemble whatever was in the large box.

I had to use a dolly to get it from the front door to the pool room, as it weighed a ton. I didn't recognize the name of the Internet store on the shipping label, so I opened it ... and found a bunch of heavy metal parts, and a multi-page instruction booklet.

When I saw the title, I began to sweat. It said, 'Deluxe Bondage Cage, Black'. I turned the page, and read the 'features': solid steel construction, wheels for mobility, lift hooks, feeding slot, padded vinyl floor, and a 'head trap' for restraining the captive's head above the cage.

This was serious dungeon equipment. Between this and the double spanking bench, it wouldn't take much more equipment or 'furniture' to fill an entire dungeon. Maybe that was the next evolution of my playroom? I just wasn't too crazy about being the sub in the dungeon.

By the time Kelly came home, I had it assembled. It looked like one of the cages in a circus, where they keep the lions and tigers. It was only about two by two and a half by four feet in size; too small to comfortably fit anyone large, or who has old joints. I groaned.

Kelly came into the pool room and kissed me, then examined her new 'toy'. Without missing a beat, she asked, "Sam, can you please put a couple of hooks in the ceiling beams? And you can bring in those pulleys that you used for the pirate ship."

I was going to be in the cage, suspended in our pool room? I groaned again.

Kelly laughed, "If I hear a groan after midnight, when you become a slave, you'll be severely punished. A slave must be totally cooperative, and not complain about anything." I had to make a conscious effort not to groan again right now, just hearing this.

It was going to be a challenging experience. But, Kelly would be quick to remind me that I'd challenged her, *and* her friends ... multiple times.

In less than an hour, I had put in the hooks, found the *blocks*, and strung the rope. I'd had to use two more blocks on the back wall, in order to get enough leverage for Kelly to be able to raise the cage with me inside. Not that I actually got inside – I just sat on the cage, while Kelly struggled with the ropes.

We went out for pizza and salads, something I usually make at home; but it was late, already, and I was nervous about tomorrow. Kelly laughed, as she informed me that I would not have to purge my digestive tract, as I'd made her friends do for their 'challenge'.

She also said she wouldn't starve me; in fact, as the slave, I would be expected to make whatever meals Kelly requested. I decided I could survive a week as a slave.

I worked on the computer, as Sam watched a movie – enjoying the last of his freedom for the next week. I printed out the schedule for Sam, and posted it on the fridge with one of our BDSM logo magnets. Each day had the same basic structure, with periods left open for 'new experiences'.

I'd had to decide what I wanted from my slave, and made sure there was both some pain for him, and plenty of pleasure for me. I went into the backyard and called Linda, explaining what I intended to do, and asking her a favor.

She was only too happy to oblige, and still laughing when we hung up. The image in my mind's eye *was* pretty funny. I just hoped that Sam would cooperate.

I went downstairs and sat on the couch next to Sam, as he finished the movie. It was only 10:30PM. Sam turned to me, "You don't *really* want to start my slave experience tonight, do you? It's been a long week, and I'm tired, already."

I shook my head, "No, Sam, we're not starting tonight. We're starting tomorrow morning," I could see Sam relaxing, until I finished the sentence, "at 12:01AM. You won't need much energy." Sam rolled his eyes and shook his head; something that I would punish him for, if he did that during his tenure as a slave.

Then, I made him an offer. "How about if we begin at 11PM? I'm not going to torture you – make you stay awake all night, or sleep in that cage ... at least, not tonight. We can try to be done for the evening by midnight."

Sam reluctantly nodded, stood, and saluted, "Your slave, reporting for duty, Miss."

I laughed, "OK. You may call me 'Goddess' for the next week. And I'll call you 'Slave'."

Sam chuckled, then stood straighter, "Yes, Goddess." I was enjoying this, already!

"OK, Slave. Go upstairs, and run me a hot bath. Then get undressed and stand in front of the bed." Sam was nodding.

"Yes, Goddess." He ran across the playroom and up the stairs.

I went up to the pool room to retrieve several packages that had arrived in the last couple of days. I also took a 70% chocolate bar from the desk drawer where I'd stashed it. Finally, I collected the implements I would need for this evening's fun.

When I got to the top of the stairs, I heard the bath still running, so I used the guest bathroom, and looked through a few of the boxes of my stuff we'd stored in one of the guest bedroom closets.

After the water was turned off, I waited another five minutes before entering the master bedroom where, as he'd been told, Slave was standing, feet apart, and hands on his head. He was trying to see what I was carrying, so I commanded, "Eyes forward!"

I put everything on the bed, and took out what we would need. First, was the penis cage, a metal wire chastity device. Slave would be pleasuring *me* tonight. I could give Slave a chance to masturbate for me, before we put on the cage, but that would be too generous, for his first night.

Walking around Sam, I knelt and began fitting the cage onto him. As with C&B rings, there was a closing ring around the base of his penis, and another to hold his balls. Then, the cage spiraled around his length, with a small opening at the tip for him to pee.

We had learned in the class that it would be difficult, and very uncomfortable for Sam to have an erection, and the cage prevented him from stimulating himself. I caught

Sam glancing down again, as I put a small padlock on the ring around the base of his dick.

"I said, eyes forward! You're not a very well-trained slave. I guess I'll have to train you, myself."

I picked up my new crop, with the heart-shaped slapper, and showed it to Sam. "I was *going* to just use this, to make little hearts all over your bottom. But now, you've earned a punishment, and I don't want to spoil the heart pattern."

Walking behind Sam, and swapping the crop for a small strap and very thin switch, I said, "Turn around, Slave! And remain in the standing position." As Sam turned around, facing the bed, I walked around him, carrying the small implements.

Without warning, I strapped the back of his thighs, just under his butt, making half a dozen horizontal stripes down the backs of each leg. Sam let out several 'Ow!'s, and stomped his feet several times.

"Now, I'll have to give you corrective punishment: You *know* that you should have been silent, and still." Fortunately, Sam didn't dare to groan.

The switch was very whippy, and made thin white horizontal lines in-between the red stripes from the strap. Sam whimpered a little, but held his position.

"Are you ready for some hearts, now, Slave?"

"Yes, Mis ... Goddess," Sam croaked, a little flustered.

"Then lie over the foot of the bed." As Sam did this, I took a couple of Velcro straps and bound his wrists and his ankles. His upper legs looked almost like a barber pole, the alternating red and white stripes now at a slight diagonal.

Silently, I took the crop and positioned myself. Then I let it fly, impacting Sam's butt with a loud 'Whap!', and leaving a red 'heart' . I had a lot of leverage, and really laid it on, producing about 40 hearts in less than a minute. Sam was whimpering again.

As I undid the Velcro straps, I asked, "Can you please start acting like the slave you are? I'd like to take my bath, now." Sam nodded and stood.

Before he could reply, I said, "Please put this on, then light some candles in the bathroom." I handed him a slave tunic that I'd purchased.

Sam put on the simple garment, then scrambled to find the thick candles, put them around the tub and on the window sills, and light them. Then, he turned off the electric lights, rendering the room into a romantic cave with flickering orange lights.

I got undressed in the closet, selected some bubble bath and sprinkled it into the tub, then stepped into the water; the temperature was perfect!

"You may bathe me, Slave." I handed Sam a washcloth and pointed to the body wash. He smiled, sat on the side of the tub, and began on my shoulders and back. I stood so that he could wash lower, and turned around, so he could wash my front.

Then, I laid back in the tub, and lifted each leg, in turn, so Slave could wash them. It was luxurious, feeling the softness of the bubble bath, and Slave's caresses with the wash cloth.

Finally, I stood, so Slave could wash my bottom and genitals. When he had finished with the wash cloth, he put his hand under me. "May I, Goddess?"

I decided to tease Sam a little; I would be doing a lot of that over the next week. "You may get me started, Slave."

As I faced away from him, Sam let his hand slide up, until his fingers were lifting my hood and gliding alongside my clit. I let myself drift, closing my eyes and envisioning some of the things I had planned for Slave Sam.

"That's enough, Slave. Stand in the corner, hands on hips. You may watch your Goddess rise to the heights of ecstasy."

Laying back in the tub, with only my head sticking out of the bubbles, I closed my eyes, and did myself, making only small movements, and taking the time to savor the bath ... and having my own slave.

I would be letting Slave satisfy me in a while, but I decided to put on a little show. I slowly moved my body, contorting, my legs out of the water, then back in, my hands below the bubbles, presumably working on my sensitive tissues.

But actually, I was pretending, faking it. I wondered whether Sam would be able to tell? Although my motions were exaggerated, and I wasn't touching myself 'there', I really was turned-on.

After several minutes of increasingly erotic movements, I arched my back, let my eyes open and roll back into their sockets, and screamed. Sam knew I normally didn't scream having sex, but I thought I'd given him a pretty convincing performance. I let my body slip below the water, again.

Hearing some soft whimpering, I opened my eyes: Sam was in position, but his eyes were closed. "Is there a problem, Slave?"

Sam's eyes snapped open, and he shook his head. Then, he smiled crookedly, and said, "I was getting a little excited, watching Goddess. And this *thing*," he pointed down, "hurts."

I chuckled, "Suck it up, Slave."

Then, I remembered the chocolate. "Slave! Please go downstairs and open a nice Port, and bring the bottle and one glass up here. You can also bring the chocolate bar that's on the bed." Sam raised his eyebrows and smiled, then hurried off. I thought how nice this treatment would be on my birthday, rather than a spanking.

Sam would be having his birthday in a couple of weeks, then we would be leaving for Kauai. It was amazing that Kathy was getting married. And to such a hunk. And, going to live on an island.

Sam had convinced my friends and I that Kauai was a very special place. My mind's eye saw the sea cave, the blue water, and Sam on his knee, proposing to me.

Slave re-appeared, and poured me a glass of Port. Then, he opened the chocolate, broke off a square, and held it out; I opened my mouth, and he popped it in. I savored the flavor, letting the slightly bitter dryness coat my tongue. Then, I took a sip ... several sips ... of wine.

"You may stand in the corner again, Slave. But face away from me. That way, I can admire your hearts and stripes, and you won't have to suffer with that cage."

I would call him, when I was ready for more chocolate or Port. The candles – in brown and orange and yellow – were flickering, glossy streaks of wax dripping down their sides.

Seeing that, and remembering Sam in position on the bed, gave me an idea for an activity for tomorrow. One that I hadn't originally planned.

Yes, this was going to be an interesting week!

Kelly took her time in the tub, requesting one more piece of chocolate, and two more glasses of Port. It smelled good, but it was clear that she wasn't going to offer me any.

Finally, Kelly stood, and I rinsed her off using the hose attachment, then dried her with a fluffy towel. Then, Kelly asked me to transfer the candles into the bedroom. I was finally going to get some satisfaction, after being painfully contained by that chastity cage.

Kelly came into the bedroom, and handed me a comb and a brush. I sat on the end of the bed, as she stood before me, her hair down below her waist. I brushed her hair, and combed out all of the knots.

She was a beautiful woman, and my manhood still stirred, when I saw her nude; especially, in a bedroom with flickering candles, and her freshly-washed, nice-smelling body inches from me. But that dang cage kept cutting into me, every time the blood flow increased down there.

When her hair was done, Kelly turned around, and took me by the shoulders. "Thank you, Slave." Then, she kissed me on the forehead.

She took the brush from me, and smiled, "Let's just clear those hearts off your bottom. She sat on the bed, and I got across her lap, her leg over mine. Without warning, there was a flurry of stings, as the brush landed over and over; and it continued until I was sobbing. But I had held my position pretty well, considering.

Kelly pushed me off her lap. "Now, please kneel on the floor at the corner of the bed." Kelly pulled a pillow down, and lay back, her crotch just off the corner of the bed, and her legs hanging down on either side of the corner.

"Make me come, Slave!" I knew what to do, and was very good at it. Kelly's body spasmed, as waves of pleasure flowed through her. My trilling tongue did the trick, and Kelly orgasmed repeatedly, crying out, "Make me come, Slave! Make me come!"

Kelly's body relaxed completely, her eyes still closed. Then, she crawled up the bed, pulling the pillow with her, and got under the covers.

"For your good cooperation, I'm not going to make you sleep in the cage. And as I may need your services during the night, I want you near. So you may sleep on the floor, at the foot of the bed."

She threw me a pillow, and added, "You may take a sheet and blanket from the hall closet, if you need them." I was shocked. But Kelly pulled up the covers and rolled over, settling herself into a sleeping position. I brought in a sheet and blanket, and made a small 'bed' for myself.

Then, I extinguished the candles, and curled up on the uncomfortable floor. My bottom hurt. And the chastity device was very uncomfortable. I didn't know if I could even get to sleep without masturbating; and there was no way to do that.

I heard myself groaning before I remembered to be silent, lest I get another punishment from 'the Goddess'. I lifted my head to glance at the digital clock on the nightstand, and saw that it was 12:30AM. Kelly was already snoring.

The alarm on my phone woke me at 5:30AM, and I walked around the bed and kicked Sam lightly a few times. He opened his eyes, and started to groan, then stopped. To his credit, a few seconds later he was standing, and said, "Good morning, Goddess. How may I be of service?"

"I'm going on a run. You may carry my water, and a few other things. We're going to leave at 6AM sharp."

Of course, I didn't need help carrying anything, but I would give Sam another surprise challenge by collecting some stones along the stream, and putting them into his pack. I chuckled, thinking that if Sam were my slave for a few months, I could really whip him into shape.

I told Sam that he should always be behind me, but to keep up with me. Then, I took off on our normal course, running as fast as I could ... and still make it the full four miles. Usually, we both wore fanny packs with water bottles; but today, I was 'free', and Sam wore a hiking-style day pack.

It took Sam several minutes to catch up to me, but was available when I stopped for some water a couple of times; and added some nice, smooth, river rocks to his pack. Slave didn't complain. But, I would be increasing his load each day.

After we crossed the stream, and turned onto the bike trail, I sprinted, feeling energized, as Sam strained to keep up. He was panting when we entered the house; we'd done the run in 33 minutes, our best time, yet.

"OK, Slave. You may bathe me downstairs, and then make breakfast for me. I would like to eat at 7AM."

When we were undressed and ready to get into the shower, Sam asked, "Could you please take this *thing* off me, for a while ... Goddess?" I'd forgotten he'd had to deal with that during the run, and was pleased that he hadn't complained earlier.

"Yes, Slave. I think you've earned the right to take one shower without it ... as long as you don't let yourself get turned on. If you *do*, it's going right back on you, and then you will be punished."

He nodded, and I commanded, "Bring me the key. It's on the desk in the playroom."

When we were finally in the shower, Slave bathed me nicely with the Loufah, and I allowed him to wash me inside, as well. He was only slightly hard by the end, still facing down.

I washed my own hair, as Slave bathed himself. After we'd dried off, I instructed, "Please put on the same slave tunic as last night, wearing nothing underneath. If I see you touching yourself, or get the slightest turned-on, I'll put the chastity device back on."

Slave had breakfast ready by 7AM – or at least enough for me to start, as he continued cooking. He looked cute in that outfit, which only came halfway down his thighs. I smiled, as I thought of still another challenge for Slave, later this morning.

"This is going to be your daily schedule through next Friday." I had just added a day to Sam's slave scene, but he didn't comment, as he was focused on the page before him:

6	Carry things for Goddess on run
7	Make breakfast for Goddess
8	Enema & medical
9	Morning maintenance spanking
10	Open – Goddess choice
11	"
12	Caged
1	"
2	"
3	"
4	Afternoon punishment
5	Cook & clean
6	Bathe & pleasure Goddess
7	Dinner – serve Goddess, or take her out
9	Evening medical experience
10	BDSM surprise
11	Pleasure Goddess as directed
12	Sleep where Goddess decides

His eyes grew large, as he looked through the schedule, and he started to shake his head ... but wisely gave me a single nod. "Yes, Goddess." Now, he had a good idea of what to expect.

I smiled, "So, when you've finished cleaning up, please prepare an enema for yourself; it must be a different way, every day. How about we use the 200cc syringe, today?" Sam looked down, unhappy, and nodded.

"And, you'll need your inoculations, today. So please prepare two 6cc shots." There would be a lot more than that, but I would be doing most of the preparations, to keep him in suspense.

Then, I finished my breakfast and spent some time on the computer. When I entered the exam room, Sam was sitting on the table. "Knee chest position. You may keep the tunic on." Sam complied immediately, and I began injecting the warm saline into his rear.

I decided to count the syringes, but not stop until Sam complained. That came at 22 syringes, but I didn't know if it was because Sam was in pain, or if he had counted, also, and felt that was enough.

I took the bucket from under the exam room sink, and put it on the table. "Squat over this and release the enema." Sam's mouth dropped open, but he obeyed, if rather slowly.

As Elena had done, the first time we were in her dungeon, I challenged Sam with many of the same things we'd done many times before, just making it a bit more intense.

When Sam was done, I told him to clean everything up, and went back to the computer. In five minutes, Slave was standing before me. "I'm ready, Goddess ... for whatever you would like me to do, next."

"OK, Slave. Now put on an exam gown, and lie on your back on the table. I'll be there when I'm ready." Of course, I purposely spent time reading some articles in the biotech journals, leaving Slave on the exam table wondering would come next.

When I went in, I turned to the counter, and took a few things out of the cabinet and drawers that I had bought. I assembled a large needle with sterile tubing that fit onto a syringe. Then, I took an elastic band, and an alcohol swab and turned back to Sam. Slave Sam.

"Squeeze your fist, please." Sam's eyes went wide again, and I knew that this was beyond his normal comfort zone. I tied the elastic band around his arm, and tapped just below the elbow to bring out the veins, just as we'd been shown in London. Then, I swabbed the area, and inserted the needle, bevel up.

Sam was looking the other way. "Watch, Slave!" I commanded. When I had his attention, I pulled back the plunger of the syringe, and drew a few cc's of blood. Then, I removed the needle, and had Slave hold a cotton ball over it. Finally, I taped it, and asked Sam to sit up.

Now, I turned again to the counter, and assembled two 2cc shots, with one-inch needles; shorter than we usually used for the butt, but perfect for the arm. Incredibly, with all the intramuscular – IM – shots we'd given each other, none had been in the deltoid muscle of the arm.

I took Sam's arm, and found the injection site, swabbed him, and gave him the injection. This was a large shot for the arm, and I took my time, as Slave scrunched his eyes. Then, I gave him one on the other side.

Sam had done well; I was proud of him. "Now, Slave, before I put back on the cock cage, would you like to have an orgasm?" I knew that Sam usually had at least two orgasms per day – whether making love, by my hand or mouth, or by his own hand. He had not had release for at least 48 hours, now, something that I knew was not pleasant for him.

Slave smiled – for the first time – and nodded, "Oh, yes, Goddess." I nodded and turned to the counter again. I put on a yellow rubber glove, similar to one worn for washing dishes or cleaning floors.

I sat in the chair next to the door. "Stand in front of me, please. Then you may masturbate into this glove." I couldn't remember ever seeing Sam masturbate standing up. "And, don't you dare get anything else soiled!"

It took several minutes, Sam closing his eyes, and stroking himself, but he eventually made progress. When he was ready, he looked down and nodded at me, and I put my hand out. Sam awkwardly aimed, and continued to stroke, finally coming in several spurts, covering the glove, and oozing down between the fingers.

When he was done, I commanded, "Kneel, Slave!" Sam was surprised, but immediately knelt, and I held the glove a few inches in front of his mouth.

"Now, clean this glove! I want you to lick it up, then suck each of my fingers." Although Sam was getting used to body fluids, this was still difficult for him. I was coming close to his boundaries, and hoped that he would continue to cooperate.

But, without a word, he consumed his own semen, until the glove was clean. Then, he sensuously licked my fingers, as I'd instructed. Again, Sam was making me proud.

If Sam had agreed to be a Slave for six months or a year, I could have tried another technique we'd learned – that I hadn't shared with Sam, yet: Milking.

It was a method of training him to release his built-up semen without a forceful ejaculation. This would cause a dribbling, and no contractions of muscles around his prostate, denying the 'satisfying' feeling of a male orgasm.

The training would take three months, and Sam would be able to control his release – having normal, full-force, orgasms (when allowed), or being forced to release his fluid without gaining the satisfaction of a normal orgasm.

I had Sam stand again, so that I could put the chastity device back on him. But he was not flaccid enough. So I slapped his dick repeatedly, coming up from below it, as it bounced, and eventually shrunk to a manageable size. I fitted the cage onto him, and snapped the padlock closed.

"On the table. I'll give you the other two shots, now." Sam climbed up onto the table, and lay on his stomach, as I swabbed him, and inserted the needles, one after the other. Then, I injected him and left both needles in, the syringes sitting on each of his hips.

Then, I turned off the exam room lights, and said, "I'll be back in a while."

With that, I shut the exam room door, and headed up to the playroom to prepare for Slave's next experience. I knew the exam room was pitch black without the lights on, as I'd found out a long time ago. This would be a new experience for Sam. Again.

When I was ready, I went down to the exam room, turned on the lights, and took out the needles. Sam was very quiet.

"Come with me, Slave. It's time for your maintenance spanking." As we walked up the stairs, I made sure he understood. "We'll be on this schedule every day." I heard Sam start a groan, then stop. I chuckled, "You'll get used to it. Maybe, you'll want this as a permanent lifestyle?"

We entered the playroom, and I pointed to the spanking bench. Sam hung his head, then wordlessly climbed onto it, and I fastened the straps. Slave would be getting a different punishment every day, but this one had to set his expectations – and fears.

I put a ball gag and blindfold onto Sam, then walked around the room, swishing one cane or strap after another. Then, I took my new bullwhip – one that I never intended to use on Sam – and practiced with it, making a very loud 'snap' that caused Sam to jump each time.

Finally, I turned on the sound system that we almost never used in here, and turned up the volume on a heavy metal piece – I think it was from the 60s. I hoped Slave would enjoy it.

I took a tawse, and applied it to Slave's bum, with hard, steady strokes. I got into a cadence of about one stroke every three seconds, and continued, in time with the music. I didn't have to count – I had selected a song that was nearly five minutes. That would be long enough.

Sam was sobbing by the end, but had been very strong. I felt bad, as the ball gag probably hadn't been necessary. Or, the high volume of the music.

Taking a medium-weight cane, much larger than we'd used on each other before, I slid it across Sam's butt. Sam involuntarily emitted a high-pitched groan, and I chuckled, "Don't worry, Slave, this song's much shorter."

The music and Slave's caning started, the yelps seeming to fit in with the music. After 16 strokes, Sam was bawling, and I knew his bottom had experienced enough, for now.

I removed the gag, and Sam continued to weep. It took a couple of minutes, but he finally rasped, "Thank you, Goddess." I rubbed his bum, and he flinched as my hand passed over the welts from the cane.

Leaving Slave blindfolded and still bound to the spanking bench, I went into the kitchen, and followed the recipe that I'd found on the Internet. Wanting to be sure, I called Barbara, and she confirmed the formula.

It only took a few minutes to cook. Back in the pool room, I released Slave, and told him to go down and lay on his back on the exam room table. Then, I took the pot and a trivet, along with some talcum powder, a spray bottle of water, and a few other supplies I'd stashed, and went downstairs.

Sam was looking curiously, as I put the pot down. Goddess' choice became Goddess' surprise, when I announced my intentions: "I like my slaves clean-looking." Then, I elaborated, "Above, and below." It took Sam a minute to process what I was saying.

"I'm going to clean you up. I don't want to see that hairy ass of yours every day that I punish you. And, you'll look much cuter with this hair off your front." I gave his pubic hair a tug, and Sam squealed.

I was stunned, and I realized that my mouth was agape. Was she going to wax my *genitals*?

I cleared my throat, "May Slave comment, M'lady?"

Not waiting for her answer, I said, "Sam will be accompanying her lordship to Hawaii in just a few weeks. And, although Slave must do whatever you command, I don't think Sam will be too happy – going on nude beaches with bare pubes."

Kelly put her hands on her hips. "Sam will have to suck it up." That was a disappointing attitude for my fiancé to be taking. I would do as Kelly wanted, but – as I'd told her – I wouldn't be happy about it.

Continuing, Kelly said, "I could do a complete body wax. You'd be red as a lobster from head to toes. And, although I like your chest hair, it might be nice if you had a hairless back." I realized that I was shaking my head; it hurt, just thinking about it.

Then, Kelly relented, "OK, Slave. I'll only do your pubic area ... and your butt. And, yes, Sam will have 'bare pubes' on the beach in Hawaii." She looked at me derisively, "Now get yourself ready!"

"Kelly ..."

Kelly laughed. Then, she strapped me down to the table, my knees butterflied out, and my feet sole-to-sole. The restraints were unnecessary, as I would have held still;

and it was frustrating for my arms to be bound – I couldn't even scratch my nose!

How much was Kelly expecting me to accept? Or would she continue testing me until I broke? I wasn't happy today – with slurping up my own semen, being given an enema and shots, taking an unbelievable spanking, and now ... Kelly was cutting off my pubic hair.

I wasn't embarrassed going nude around other nude people, or even dressed people. But this wasn't 'natural'; it would look strange, and people would wonder ...

And I *didn't* have a hairy ass! That wasn't nice. I was just glad that I had little back and chest hair.

My head fell back onto the pillow, and I tried to forget about what was happening. Maybe, it would grow back quickly? I thought about plans for Kauai. Although Julie and Linda were paying their own way to the wedding, I had offered to find a rental house, where we could all stay.

Kelly began with scissors, trimming my pubic hair nearly down to the skin. Then, she took one of her razors, and carefully shaved me. Everything went well, until she tried to shave my balls; after two nicks, she agreed to use my electric shaver.

I gave myself over to Kelly, allowing her to groom me as she saw fit. Of course, being strapped down, I had little choice. I knew that if I – as Sam – objected, Kelly would not force me to submit. However, I didn't want to disappoint her, and was willing to suffer a little to make her happy. I hoped this would make her happy.

The first few pulls of the sugaring wax were painful. Kelly improved with practice, but it was still agonizing. I wouldn't want to go through this every month or two, but didn't plan to, as this would be only a *temporary* 'body modification'.

Again, it was when she was trying to hold the skin of my scrotum taut to apply the wax – and then pulling it off – that I got nervous. But Kelly didn't hurt me too badly.

She said, "Well, this part is going to be harder than I thought, especially when I wax them. Maybe, I should do a 100cc infusion? We can do one side, then the other. That will smooth out your skin, so the wax will pull off. *Should* pull off."

I was cringing. Although the small infusion Elena had done hadn't been that bad, I really didn't want Kelly to do that. But – as a good slave, and a good partner – I would allow her to do what she pleased with me. Then I would decide whether I could go to Kauai, or not.

Sam was acting like a baby – screaming with every pull of the sugaring wax. I was starting to get pretty good at this; maybe, I should try waxing myself? Or, maybe let Sam take care of some parts that I couldn't see.

When I'd mentioned the scrotal infusion, I hadn't been planning on doing that; at least, not today. But it really would make things easier; and it was *another* new thing for Sam – at least with this intensity.

I removed the hair on his triangle, and the hair around the base of his penis. Then, I had him get in a knee chest position, so that I could remove the hair between his buttocks. He didn't really have *that* hairy of an ass.

But he could sure scream! I closed the exam room door, and thought about having Sam bite on a towel. Then, I prepared one of the 200cc syringes, with a 22-gauge needle, and filled it with sterile saline, finishing a bottle that usually hung from one of the IV poles.

I held up the huge, and very intimidating, injection, and Sam predictably squeezed his eyes shut. A tear dripped from the corner of one of his eyes. "It's OK, Slave, I won't make you watch. But I could set up a video camera, and put it on this screen?"

Sam shook his head, his eyes still glued to the big needle, and even bigger syringe. Several smaller syringes might have been just as impressive, and easier to handle. But I would make do.

I swabbed his left ball sack, pulled the skin to the side, and carefully inserted the needle a short distance. Then, I began the infusion, slowly pushing the plunger of the giant syringe. Sam groaned a little, but behaved well.

After injecting 100cc on his left side, I repeated the process on the other side. My slave was really 'ballsy', now. He had giant balls, each about the size of a plum. But it really wasn't enough to smooth his scrotal skin.

So, I prepared a second syringe, and infused another 100cc on each side. Now, his balls were closer to the size of oranges, and his skin was starting to smooth. I looked at his scrunched-up face, "Maybe just one more? My Slave would really have big balls, if they were the size of grapefruits!"

Despite the possibility of being punished, Sam groaned. "Please, Goddess, have mercy. I'm just a lowly slave." He closed his eyes and sniffled. I decided to go easy on him.

We finished up Slave's waxing, the screams now dulled by the towel stuffed into Sam's mouth. He turned over for me, so I could finish the areas between his butt cheeks, and underneath him, which elicited a few more shrieks.

My entire groin area was burning, and I was somewhat relieved – but even more nervous – when Kelly unstrapped me, and had asked me to get into a knee chest position.

Kelly asked me to turn over onto my back again, so that she could disinfect and moisturize my enflamed skin. Then, she surprised me – a *welcome* surprise, this time.

"Sam ... Slave, you're going to have to keep this area clean. I think you're going to be too raw to put back on the cock cage, so you're going to have to control yourself: No orgasms, unless I allow it." Well, that was something: At least, she would leave off that horrible device.

Now, she was smiling at me, "But since you've been so cooperative, I'll give you a little reward, before I clean you up." Then, she went down on me.

I helped Sam up, and we went into the bathroom to look at his waxing job in the mirror. He gasped when he saw himself. It *was* pretty shocking.

"But I really think we'll have to finish-up with your back and chest in the next few days; they didn't look noticeable, before, but don't match, now." I chuckled, and added, "And maybe your legs." Sam didn't complain, but there was no 'Yes, Goddess', either.

We cleaned up everything, and went upstairs. I looked at the clock, and it was nearly noon. "Since it's such a beautiful day, let's roll the cage out to the patio."

Sam shook his head, but helped me maneuver the thing over the sliding door track and out to the patio. Fortunately, there were wheel locks, as I wouldn't want Sam to be locked in a metal cage that rolled into the pool.

There really was a lot of responsibility to being a good dominatrix. I shivered, as I thought about some of the possibilities, and I would have to call on Linda to be ready to assist, while I was in the lab.

Sam got into the cage feet first, contorting his body to fit – which it did, just barely. Then, I closed the small door, and put on a cable tie; it wasn't as foolproof as a padlock, but a lot quicker to get off, in an emergency.

I opened a can of tuna, and dumped it onto a paper plate. Then, I brought it to Slave, sliding it through the food slot. He just looked at me – with amazement, bewilderment, curiosity, and not a small amount of fear.

I turned and went back inside, where I made a tuna salad for myself, putting it on a bed of lettuce, and cutting the last of our baguettes to eat with it. We still had to go to the market today.

In order to maximally infuriate Slave, I opened a beer, and brought it, and the large and fancy tuna salad out to the patio table, and proceeded to eat it, and continue reading technical papers on my iPhone.

Then, I realized I hadn't properly documented Sam's slave experience. I surreptitiously snapped a few images of Sam, in the cage, near the side of the pool. And, next, I let Sam see that I was photographing him – actually, videoing him – a hairless, nude, caged man.

He curled up, and then lay on his back, his feet up against the top of the cage, trying to find a position that wasn't too uncomfortable.

I went back to my salad and finished it, then went inside, and sat at my own desk. There was still a good view of Sam, so no danger that he would be getting into trouble. I wrote a list of some of my favorite dishes that Sam made, and brought it, and a pad and pen out to Sam.

"Please write down what you'll need at the market, to make these dishes for me." Then, I told Sam, "We're going to have to alter our schedule for today … and reduce your cage time."

Sam sighed audibly, and I added, "Of course, it will need to be added to another day."

I waited for the predicted groan, but it didn't come. Sam was already being trained to be a good slave ... and this was only the first full day! But I would have to go a little easy, as I didn't want Sam – my partner and fiancé – to resent me.

When Sam had written his list, I cut the cable-tie and opened the cage. Sam clumsily extracted himself, and we rolled the cage back into the pool room.

Then, I led him down to the playroom, where I presented him with his next costume ... 'outfit'. It was a Roman toga, cream color, with the top going over one shoulder, the other bare.

But, first, I fitted the penis cage to him and locked it, then allowed him to put on a thong – it was actually one of his European bathing suits. This was generous, as I could just as well have left him with nothing on underneath the short toga.

Unfortunately, with Sam's balls enlarged, and wearing the cock cage, everything didn't fit into the skimpy suit. So Sam *would* have to go to the market with no undies.

Next, I put a slave collar on him, one I'd recently bought, and hoped it would fit; it did. And, I took a dog leash, and snapped it to the ring on the collar. I tugged, and Sam followed me.

When we got up to the kitchen, I grabbed my bag – Sam having no pockets – and turned to him, "Do you have your shopping list, Slave? You're taking me to the market."

Now, Sam's face turned white, as the blood drained from it. "Kelly ... Goddess ..."

But I'd already turned and walked through the door to the garage, holding it open for Slave. He grumbled, as he reluctantly started the car and backed out of the driveway. Of course I was pushing him; this was the kind of domme experience he'd asked about, and had wanted me to share with him.

I remembered the movie that Sam and I had seen on our first trip to London ... *'Venus in Fur'*, a Roman Polanski version of the Sacher-Masoch story. A man *thinks* he wants to be dominated, until he experiences the reality of it. In many ways, just like the situation with Sam.

We got to the market, and I pulled Sam along by the leash, as he pushed a basket. We passed a few people who stared and smiled at us, and Sam grumbled.

"I could have led you by a leash connected to a genital piercing." I laughed, "Or, I could unsnap this leash, and snap it to your cock cage."

Sam quickly shook his head, "I apologize, Goddess." I nodded uncertainly, and pulled him along. Not a minute later, we passed the beer section, and Sam stopped to take a case. I pulled his chain, and he grumbled again.

I nodded, and made a show of opening my purse, and taking out a short punishment strap – only eight or nine inches long, and an inch wide. I faced Sam toward the beers, lifted the back of his toga, and gave him a couple of hard slaps with the strap.

He squawked at me, looking left and right to see how many people were around that might have seen me strapping his bare bottom. I didn't think there were more than one or two.

"Do you want *more*, Slave? Or will you behave and not complain?" I waved the strap in front of his face, considering whether I should give him a slap on each cheek with it. Sam hung his head, and said, "No thank you, Goddess, I've had enough. I'll behave."

Slave did behave, reasonably well, finishing the marketing, driving me home, and starting dinner.

"It's time for your afternoon punishment, now, Slave." Sam was standing at the stove, and turned to me, his mouth dropping open. I shook my head, "You've *seen* the schedule; you shouldn't be surprised."

Sam turned down the flame, and came with me into the pool room. I pointed to the spanking bench, and he hesitated; then, he got onto the bench, and I strapped him down. He'd done well so far, today, and didn't deserve much punishment.

But I had to get him used to a schedule, keep his fear level going, and establish my own dominance. I picked up the transparent plastic school paddle – the one that Linda had given us. I stood in front of Sam, and slapped my own hand with it; it smarted.

"I could ask you how long a paddling you deserve, but I'll just go with what I think. Maybe five minutes." That would be a very long paddling.

I stepped behind Sam, and placed the smooth plastic paddle across his bottom. He flinched, and then stilled as I pulled the paddle away, and gave him a hard swat, coming up from under him. Then, another hard swat across the middle of his butt.

Linda's paddle wasn't nearly as serious as the thick wooden one that we had, but it had a definite effect on Sam's already-sore bum. He squealed after each of the strokes, and I waited a minute, playing with my watch. Then, I gave him one more hard swat, and he whimpered.

I quietly sat down at my desk, opened my computer, and left Sam to wonder about his punishment. But that would be all he was going to get ... until tomorrow.

When I unstrapped Sam and let him off the spanking bench, he asked, "Shall I finish dinner, bathe you, or pleasure you now, Goddess?" I decided that he could finish dinner first, while I bathed myself. Then, he would come down to the playroom to pleasure me.

After my shower, I lay back on the playroom bed, my eyes closed, fingering myself. This had been a pretty good 'first day' for my Slave.

A few minutes later, my Slave climbed onto the bed. He started to spread my legs so he could go down on me, but I said 'No', and had him put on a blindfold and lie on his back.

Slave 'pleasured' me with that interesting-feeling cock cage that provided a good stimulus for getting myself off. Slave was surprised, and that was one of my goals – to keep him off-balance, uncertain, *scared* of the unknown and what would come next.

I allowed Slave to have dinner with me ... but he had to sit on the floor, at my feet. Also, he had to eat with his fingers. Then, he cleaned up the dishes while I prepared his 'evening medical experience'.

Sam unenthusiastically came into the exam room, and I pointed to the table. He lay on his back, in his toga, while I fumbled with a small tank and regulator. A large tube connected the regulator to a full-face mask – which actually was a surplus dive mask, used by the military.

I turned the valve on the tank, and heard the hissing of gas flowing through the hose and into the mask. Sam's eyes went really wide, as I placed the mask over his nose and mouth. "Breathe deeply, now."

This was a potentially dangerous activity. I'd picked up the assembled set-up at a dental supply store, claiming that it was going to the college lab for some animal experiments. If I didn't operate this correctly, Sam could suffocate.

There was a small metal tank of nitrous oxide – 'laughing gas' – and another of oxygen. And there were pressure gauges and flow meters used for mixing the gases. I used a 50:50 ratio, which would be safe.

Sam trusted me, and breathed through the mask and, within a few minutes, had noticeably relaxed. I could tell he had a big smile, even though the mask was covering most of his face.

He breathed deeper, and I confirmed, "Yes, it's nitrous. It will help you get through your most extreme BDSM experience of the day, coming up." Sam's eyes closed, and he sniffled.

Then I gave him a 'red herring', "Your bottom is *already* looking pretty sore. I'm not sure how much more it can take. Maybe we'll find out."

But we probably wouldn't, as I wasn't planning to spank him again, until tomorrow. I'd decided to give his butt a break, and try a couple of nipple piercings. It would only be with the thin, 25-gauge needles, but I was certain it would be an intense experience for Sam.

And, again, it would be something new. Sam whined, when I told him what I would be doing, but he held still and let me pierce him, only emitting a quick squeal when each needle went through.

Sam was sniveling, very unbecomingly – and not at all appropriate for a slave. But I'd given him enough to think about for one day.

"This was a good first-day for you, Slave. I think you've got the potential to learn. You'll just need some training every day." I tweaked the needles that were still through Sam's nipples, and he yelped.

"So I will reward you, tonight." Sam's eyes lit up, and this was the first sign of hope I'd seen in him all evening. But it wouldn't be what he was expecting.

"I'm going to go upstairs and work for a while. Maybe thirty minutes. I will allow you to do as you like: You may just lie here, work on your computer, even go upstairs and have a beer, if you like." Now, Sam's eyes really lit up.

"But we'll keep those needles in until I'm ready to go to bed. Then, I'll remove them, and we can sleep together in the playroom bed." Of course, that meant sleeping in the same bed, not a promise of sex.

I'd allowed him to have one orgasm today, and that would have to be enough. Slave took advantage of my offer – I think he had *two* beers. Then, we went downstairs, I pulled out the needles – with more squealing from Slave – and we got into bed.

Before he had even gotten settled, I turned off the lights, and said, "Good night, Slave."

There was no groaning or complaining; just a very dejected, "Good night, Goddess."

We followed nearly the same schedule on Sunday, Kelly going a little easier on me. We ran to the pond with full packs, and set out the sheet. Then, Kelly took me across her lap for a very long hand spanking. It wasn't nearly as bad as the tawse and cane had been. And, fortunately nobody else came down the trail.

Even with my nearly full pack, Kelly still insisted on dropping in a bunch of large rocks. When we returned to the house, Kelly administered my enema, and I bathed her.

It was now Monday morning, and I was sore in several places. The worst part had been four hours in the cage, although I'd found that I could sit with my knees up.

The evening medical experience last night had been insertion of a Foley catheter, to drain my bladder. Kelly had been taught well, and showed off her skills. Still, it was very uncomfortable and, in my opinion, beyond what should be done safely in a BDSM scene.

Then, she'd followed that up with a Shibari session — while the catheter was still in me, a urine bag taped to my leg. She fumbled a bit with the ropes, and we both had greater respect for Greetje's abilities.

On this morning's run, I'd started out with a light pack, but Kelly had filled it with thirty pounds of rocks by the time we had left the stream.

I enjoyed cooking for Kelly, and bathing her ... but still didn't like getting enemas. I had selected the Bardex device to get it over with; it was one of the most uncomfortable sensations, especially when Kelly over-expanded the internal balloon against my rectum.

When Kelly was finished, and I was getting off the exam table, she surprised me: "I need to work in the lab this week, Slave. I'll be leaving around 8AM, and I hope to return by 4PM. So I've asked Linda to assist me.

"She will come over this morning to administer your maintenance spanking." Kelly chuckled, "And I told her that she can play doctor with you in the exam room." Then, she looked at me sharply, "*She* will be the doctor."

That was OK, as Linda would probably go easier on me than Kelly. But then Kelly added, "And, as it's dangerous to leave you in the cage without supervision, I've asked her to keep an eye on you from Noon to 4PM, every day through Thursday."

Over the weekend, Kelly had asked me to install an IP camera that could be panned and zoomed to observe the pool room, and which could be logged-into remotely. I had assumed that she would be the one keeping an eye on me. Now, I was learning that Linda would be watching me, as I contorted myself in the cage. Although I would not be able to see her, there would be a two-way audio connection. At least, Linda and I had been very open with each other, and were beyond embarrassment.

Kelly had left a stack of paper cups in the corner of the cage that she said I could use if I needed to pee. She also left a water bottle next to them, and told me I would need to finish drinking it while I was in the cage.

I finished in the bathroom, took a quick shower, and put on the slave tunic. The slave collar was still tight around my neck, and the penis cage was still annoyingly installed, down below.

Kelly had asked me to clean the house. She said that my afternoon punishment would be based on how much dust and dirt she could find. I did the mopping and vacuuming, then dusting, then ran the dish washer and did a load of laundry. I had been tired after the run, carrying all those rocks, and now I was exhausted.

Linda arrived just after 11AM, and chuckled when she saw me in the slave outfit. I offered her coffee or something else to drink, but she declined.

"Kelly told me to do something with you – I mean, *to* you – in the exam room. Then she said you needed to be spanked. She didn't give any details, except that I should take my time, and make it hard."

Linda batted her eyes at me, "She said you should be crying by the time I lock you in the cage and leave." That didn't surprise me.

As we walked down to the exam room, I explained to Linda, "I'm not crazy about being Kelly's 'slave', especially as she's intent on filling my days with pain or discomfort.

"And my nights. She's made me sleep at the foot of the bed," I shook my head, "after satisfying her ... and then having to wear *this* thing." I lifted the front of the slave tunic, so Linda could see the cock cage.

Linda's eyes went wide, then she broke into a belly laugh, bending over and starting to choke, she was laughing so hard. I patted her back, "Maybe, *you* need some 'medication'?"

Linda chuckled, "The hairless slave! Smooth as a baby." Then, she glanced at me, "Maybe, Goddess will lend me her slave, so I can practice being the mommy, and slave can be my little baby?" I hoped not.

"It doesn't look like there would be much room in there for you to get too turned-on." Linda was looking closely at the chastity device, which included a tiny padlock. Kelly had decided, only a day after my waxing, that I would have to wear the thing.

I shook my head, but realized my other head had a mind of its own, and my caged manhood expanded enough to give Linda her answer. "It's pretty painful, if I get turned on. But Kelly *has* rewarded me a couple of times, taking the cage off, and allowing me to take care of myself."

"Maybe I can convince her that I should have an affair with her slave?" Linda smiled seductively.

I hopped onto the exam room table, and asked, "What will my 'treatment' be today, nurse?"

Shrugging, Linda said, "I don't know. Most of the time I've been in here, you've examined me, given me an enema, and," Linda smiled again, "shots. And I'm not really interested in examining you, Sam."

"I've already had one enema this morning. But Kelly was upset it made her late getting to the lab. She'll probably have you doing it for the next three days." I gave Linda a long look, "At least, I *hope* my slave experience will only be for one week."

Linda ran a finger across her lips, then asked, "We had fun in Hawaii sticking you with needles – what were there, about sixty left from the box you brought?" I cringed, thinking about it, and hoped Linda didn't want a repeat performance.

Then, she asked, "How many shots have you taken, at the same time? I don't mean like at the doctor's office, getting one at a time; but I know you and Kelly play around a lot. And I know you sometimes leave the shots in, for a long time."

"I've gotten two at the same time, one on each side. But I can't remember getting more than that." I felt a chill, as I realized that this would be Linda's selection.

"OK, slave. Get eight shots ready; they can be small ones, only 2cc." Linda laughed, and was heading out of the exam room.

"Eight? That's a lot!"

Linda stopped and shook her head. "Kelly warned me about this. She said that if you complained about anything, I should increase the punishment." I realized that I was shaking my head; but I had no doubt that Kelly had told that to Linda.

"OK, then. Make up ten shots." My bottom hurt, just thinking about it. And this was just the medical part, not even the 'morning punishment', that I knew was also coming.

When Linda got back from the bathroom, I was still assembling the shots. When I had them all lined up on the countertop, I could only hope that Linda would show some mercy and not use them all. Or, maybe use some on *her*? Now, the chastity cage was hurting me again.

But that was wishful thinking. After what I'd put Linda, Julie, and Kathy through, they wouldn't hesitate to give a little back to me.

I got onto the exam table on my stomach, and flipped up the back of my slave tunic. The chastity device was really uncomfortable, as it pressed into me. I put my head on the pillow and closed my eyes.

Linda swabbed my entire butt. Then, she inserted one needle after another, until there were five sharp pain points on each side. I could feel the needles moving around, as she checked for blood – as I had taught her.

Then, I could feel the saline going in, pinching, on one side, then the other, back and forth, until my entire butt was sore. I wondered how long she would leave them in.

"I'm going upstairs for a few minutes. When I get back, I'll inject the other half." What!@?! I groaned, but fortunately Linda was already going up the stairs.

It had to have been at least five minutes, and my bottom was throbbing. Now, Linda came into the exam room, and immediately began injecting more saline – in the ten different places. I controlled myself and didn't groan, but had to ask, "Are you having fun, M'lady?"

Linda wiggled a couple of the shots, "Oh, yes, Slave. We'll have to do this again!" I hoped not.

Now, she sat down in the chair and began flipping through pages in a magazine. After another several minutes, she got up and put her head next to mine. "You're very brave, Sam, to do this for Kelly. But I know you like to give each other challenges."

She chuckled, "My new hookup and I have tried a few things. Maybe I should bring him over here and introduce him to medical play?"

"I'd love to hear some of your stories, Linda, but just not right now; especially, if they might turn me on."

Linda laughed, "Yeah, that would be a good torture: You would have to stand there, as I did sexy things, and try not to get an erection. I'll bet I could make that cage hurt pretty bad." I knew she could; I had to put those thoughts out of my head.

Finally, Linda began pulling the needles out, and shoving the shots into the sharps container. Then, she swabbed me again, and patted me down with a gauze pad.

"Are you ready for your spanking, now?"

I got off the exam table. The clock said it was only 11:30, and I was supposed to be in the cage at noon. So Linda would only have 30 minutes to spank me; but that would be plenty.

We walked up to the pool room, and I saw that Kelly had laid out several implements on the big wooden desk. I took the tunic off and got onto the spanking bench, then asked Linda to fasten the restraining straps around my wrists, ankles, and lower back.

"I won't strap you down if you don't want me to," Linda offered.

Shaking my head, I declined, "Please use the straps. I don't think I'll be able to hold my position, otherwise."

Linda came around, put her head next to mine, then kissed me. "I'm sorry, Sam. We both know what Kelly expects. But give me a safeword, just in case."

"No, Linda. I'm going to try to take whatever you give me. There's a ball gag on the desk, in case I get too loud."

Linda kissed me again, then gave me a wicked smile. Even having lost weight, she was a strong woman. And I knew what to expect.

Well ... Linda didn't disappoint Kelly. After about a ten minute flogging that had my entire backside burning, she selected a large rectangular paddle, made of thick rubber, with a wooden handle.

I was nearly screaming with every stroke. That thing was really a mean implement; my butt was going to be raw. Despite my whimpering and groaning, Linda continued, until my bottom was on fire. It *had* to be noon, already.

"OK, Slave. Let's finish-up with the school paddle. I'll use the transparent plastic one that I gave you." That was something; at least the plastic paddle wouldn't bruise like the thicker wooden one.

Then, Linda announced, "Forty swats." That was way too many with that implement, and especially with my already-sore bottom. Maybe, she was just trying to intimidate me? If so, it was working.

Linda did give me forty swats, although they weren't as hard as they might have been. But my butt was burning. I wondered whether Kelly had been watching via the webcam. She would see the result later, in any case. And I was supposed to get an *afternoon* punishment, also!

I groaned as Linda was undoing the restraining straps. She gave me a questioning look, and I shrugged. "I just don't know if I can take this for many more days."

"Do you want to do anything, before I lock you in that cage?" I nodded, and headed to the half-bath.

Linda watched me pee, and it was embarrassing, as the stream wasn't always straight, and when it hit the metal chastity device, it got messy. I cleaned up as best I could, then walked to the cage.

As much as I would have liked a beer right now, I was hoping that I could make it four hours without peeing … and didn't' want to push my luck. I had already put my laptop and phone inside, which would take my mind off the cramped conditions.

Kelly had agreed to let me use the computer, both for planning the Kauai trip, and for working on the KS Biotech presentation and communicating with pharma companies (little would they know that they were speaking with a nude man who was in a metal cage). I would need to start working on the travel plans for Barcelona, where Kelly would present her research in just a few months.

I kissed Linda once more, and climbed into the cage. She closed the door, and I jumped when I heard it snap. Linda fastened the cable tie, and checked that the EMT shears were on the desk, in case of an emergency.

Kelly got home at four, and let me out of the cage. It took a full five minutes for me to straighten out. When she saw my bottom, she decided not to punish me further. But I cooked her a nice dinner, then bathed and pleasured her.

She decided to combine the evening medical experience and BDSM surprise. After removing the chastity device, inserting a butt plug, and having me lay on my back on the exam table, she proceeded to stroke me.

Unfortunately, that ended way too soon, and Kelly, the monster, skewered the skin under my penis. The sticks burned, and she continued until there were eight or nine closely-spaced needles. Then, she took dental floss, and made a miniature corset on me.

Now, I was wondering whether I should dismantle the exam room, get rid of all of the instruments and supplies, and lead a needle-free life.

The next three days were similar, and I was starting to get used to the routine; not that I liked it. Linda would come in around nine in the morning, and give me an enema. Then, she would have me pleasure *her*, with a massage or foot rub or getting her off using my hands or mouth.

We would usually have an hour or two to visit. I would practice my KS Biotech presentations on her, and talk about some of the strategies for moving the business forward. Linda was quite helpful, and I decided to speak with Kelly about bringing Linda into the business.

Kelly insisted on setting up a scrotal infusion, with a hanging bag of saline, and big needle, and having me show

Linda how to administer it. That necessitated leaving the chastity device off, making it almost worth it.

Linda infused 500cc, making my ball sacs look like grapefruits. It was an uncomfortable feeling, but Linda was impressed with the result. "I always knew you had big balls, Sam, but *this* is something else!"

Then, under her breath, she mumbled, "I'll really have to bring Matt over here."

The last two nights, Kelly allowed me to sleep in bed with her. Although she had me satisfy her before we went to sleep, both nights she woke me in the early morning, and made love to me. Then, we went back to sleep.

Kelly agreed that Thursday would be the last day of slavery. It was similar to the others, until Goddess' evening BDSM surprise ... when she decided to try fisting on me. I nearly revolted at that point, but allowed her one hour if she promised to take it really slowly and back-off, if I told her it hurt.

She did manage to insert the largest butt plug we had, which had never been in my rear before – or, Kelly's. And she finally got three of her fingers into me, plus about half of her thumb. The feeling of her hand inside me, pressing on my prostate would have been intriguing ... but the process hurt too much. I just couldn't relax enough.

Looking back on the week, I had to admit that I'd gotten a lot of exercise – carrying those rocks on our runs; the house was now spotless, as I'd cleaned every day; and I *enjoyed* cooking for Kelly, and bathing her. And I certainly enjoyed pleasuring her.

I hadn't liked getting enemas or getting spanked, but by far the worst part of the experience had been the cage. Being contorted into a small space was uncomfortable, and I'd eventually had to pee in the cups.

On Friday night, I took Kelly out to a nice dinner at one of our favorite Italian restaurants. After we'd ordered, Kelly raised her wine glass in a toast. "Thank you, Sam, for being my slave for the past week. I'm sorry you didn't enjoy it; I thought maybe you would want that as a long-term lifestyle."

Ha! Not the way I'd been treated. I knew that Kelly had compressed a lot of things into one week, but it had been too much. I raised my glass, "You're welcome. It was an interesting one-time experience. But I don't think I would treat you that badly, if you were *my* slave."

Kelly sipped her wine and shook her head. "You mean, you wouldn't have spanked me every day?" I hadn't really thought about how I would treat Kelly; I probably *would* have spanked her. But I wouldn't have put her in a cage, or asked her to sleep on the floor.

Kelly took pains to explain that she'd tried to approach this professionally, coldly, and share some of the things – both physical and mental – that she'd learned in her class. Once again, Kelly had shown that she was a very strong woman. But, of course, I already knew that.

I'd shown her that I was willing to submit to her, and respect her needs and desires; and that I would try to be strong for her. And I'd shown her that I loved her very much. But, of course, she already knew that, as well.

CHAPTER 11: KATHY GETS MARRIED

I was making good progress completing the system. The custom electronics were being built, and the algorithms that formed the heart of the system were ready for testing. There were still plenty of software bugs, and the overall packaging was just now being designed. But I would have the prototype ready for the Barcelona show.

We all flew together to Kauai, although Julie and Linda were paying their own way, and had to sit in the back, while Sam and I had wangled first class upgrades.

Renting a van, like before, Sam drove us to the west side, where he'd rented a house on the ocean in Kekaha that had been arranged by Christian. Sam had said we were getting a special deal, but it still cost more than $5,000 for the week; quite a splurge.

When we walked through the front door, we were mesmerized by the view; and there was even a pool! We picked our rooms and got settled, then went out onto the deck. The backyard was mostly grass, bordering the beach, with a small rectangular pool.

Sam brought out a pitcher of Piña Coladas, and a tray of glasses, and we sat around a table on the expanse of grass. Sam toasted, "Well, here's to our *second* trip to Kauai together. At least, mostly together."

We sat quietly, sipping the pineapple and coconut flavor of the islands, hearing the palm fronds rustle, feeling the gentle warm breeze. We were in paradise, again.

On Friday, we visited Christian and Kathy, and got a tour of the property. It was a magnificent piece of land, tens of acres, on a plateau that rolled-off gently toward the sea, with a panoramic ocean view.

There was the main house, a guest house where Kathy's parents were staying, a separate garage/workshop, and a stable. There were also at least three dogs, some roosters, and a peacock. Kathy looked like she was in heaven, and Christian couldn't keep his hands off her.

He really was a hunk of a guy – jet black hair combed straight back, tanned skin, and a refined look, although he was clearly a rough-and-tough male. His smile sparkled, framing perfect white teeth. He wore a thin leather braided cord around his right wrist, and the engagement ring on the fourth finger of his left hand.

Christian was also fairly wealthy – although Kathy had never gotten into specifics. But his family owned a lot of land in both Hawaii and Tahiti, and Christian had founded and was sole owner of a successful sunglass company, with worldwide operations, and headquarters in Honolulu.

We now learned that Christian's parents had both died in a car crash. Sam was visibly upset, having been reminded of Sarah's untimely death.

We re-met Kathy's parents – whom I hadn't seen in a decade. And Sam had evidently never met them. Andy was now balding, and had a rotund belly and an incredibly long and untrimmed beard that was once red, and now speckled gray. There was a perennial smile on his face, and I had always envisioned him as the 'jolly' one.

Karen was still a beanpole, her long hair now silver, and wrinkles emanating from the corners of her smiling eyes. She was always a down-to-earth, friendly woman. Kathy had always referred to her parents as 'hippies', going nude around the house, smoking joints in front of the children, and growing their own vegetables.

Now, they were semi-retired from jobs in the graphics arts field – but still doing commercial artwork for companies and publications, mostly via the Internet. Andy wore a pair of baggy shorts and a faded Aloha shirt; Karen wore a long, wrap-around skirt in a floral print, with a bandeau top. Like daughter, like mother.

In the late afternoon, a small bus took the wedding party to the venue – on the grounds of beautiful private gardens, with a small stream rushing by, backed by the mountains. The flowers were amazing – plumeria and torch ginger, among many others – as was the aroma.

There was a gazebo laced with vines and tropical flowers, and white chairs lined up on either side of the aisle. We met the other friends and family who would be taking part, and practiced our entries, standing on each side of the gazebo – as the bridesmaids, and groomsmen.

Then, we were bussed down to the town of Ele-ele, where we took over a small brewpub. It was a fun evening, with music and dancing, playing games, and lots of food and drink. Fortunately, the bus driver was sober, and we all made it back to Christian's house.

The others departed for their homes or hotels, leaving Kathy and Christian, Kathy's parents, Sam and I, and Linda and Julie. Both Christian and Sam were feeling the alcohol, but became energetic again, when Kathy suggested that we all go in the hot tub.

It was an old-style, redwood tub, probably eight feet in diameter. It was cozy for the eight of us, but we all fit in. It was already dark, and we were outside, with the spectacular ocean view, still a line of red on the horizon.

Two things were noticed by the women in the group, although it was too dark, and too quick to see much: Sam's pubic area was bare, and Christian was *very* well-endowed. Nobody commented, all of us suddenly tired in the warm water. We were all very relaxed and comfortable.

This was another 'different' group – people in their twenties, thirties, forties, and fifties. Andy climbed awkwardly out of the tub – the rest of us getting an interesting look up at his genitals.

He returned, a few moments later, lit a joint, and passed it around, as he climbed back into the hot tub. I hadn't known whether Christian smoked, but I guess he did. It was a *big* joint, and before long we were all floating ... and not necessarily in the water.

We looked up at the sky, and the stars were incredible, the arc of the Milky Way, familiar constellations, and even a few meteors. Christian turned off the pump motors, and it was silent. Kathy leaned over and kissed Christian. In 48 hours, they would be a married couple.

On Saturday, I had hoped we could drive up to the north shore; I wanted to see Hanalei, again, snorkel at our favorite beach, have lunch by the Princeville Hotel pool.

But we had our own pool, and the girls convinced me to relax, and enjoy the spectacular backyard of the house we were renting.

It wouldn't be great snorkeling here, as the water carried mud from the Waimea River, and nearby small boat harbor. But how could I not enjoy a bevy of beautiful women, getting their all-over tans around the pool?

As I lay on a chaise working on my own all-over tan, my mind wandered. I had taken some good dive trips on boats leaving from the harbor not a mile away from us. But a dive certificate was necessary – something that I'd hoped that Kelly would get sooner or later.

Why not sooner? I called my friend who owned a dive shop in Kapaa, and we talked about what might be possible for next week. It would take a lot of work on Kelly's part, and she would have to give up part of the trip.

Now, I thought, maybe we could *extend* the trip? Get in some good diving, while we were here. Or even go over to the Big Island for some diving; and touring. Kelly had never been there, and it was really the best island to see a wide variety of Hawaiian environments.

When I was off the phone, I sat on the chaise, and turned to Kelly, "Would you please consider doing something for me – and for you – that will change our lives?" That was probably a bit over-the-top.

Kelly looked at me quizzically, and I explained, "There are a lot of places we may travel – like here – that have great SCUBA diving; and there are a lot more places I would like to travel, just to do some great diving. But all of that depends on you getting your dive certificate."

Kelly squinted at me, and nodded, "We've talked about this, before. I'd *love* to dive with you ... *if* we can find the time for me to take the classes, and dive training. I just don't know when we'll ever find the time."

I smiled, "How about next week? Monday, Tuesday, and Wednesday? It will be an intensive private class – just for you – all day for three days." I smiled seductively at her (well, I was *trying* to smile 'seductively'), "And, we could extend our trip, and do some boat dives after the class. I wouldn't mind being here another week."

We probably wouldn't be staying *here*, as I couldn't afford another week's rent. But, maybe in Kapaa, or back on the north shore, again.

My mind started to wander, but Kelly brought me back to reality. "I would do that. Not for you, but for *me*. I've always wanted to SCUBA dive, but it was just a dream."

"That would be great. I'll see if we can extend our trip – maybe through next weekend. And my friend in Kapaa has an instructor who will be your private tutor."

Kelly smiled and nodded. She looked over at her friends, who had been listening to our conversation. "Sam, what if my friends are interested, also?"

I smiled, having anticipated that, "Well, my friend will give me a big discount on two people, and even bigger discount on three. And I would be happy to pay for it – for all of you, if you're interested."

Then, I looked at them seriously, "But it *will* be a lot of work – book-learning, as well as time in the water, probably doing some uncomfortable things."

When Kelly snapped her head to me, her mouth open, I explained, "For example, taking your mask off underwater, then having to find it with your eyes open, and not breathing through your nose. Or, sharing your regulator with another diver, confident that you'll get it back for another breath."

Kelly nodded, and both Linda and Julie were now fully engaged. Linda blurted, "I'd *love* to learn how to SCUBA dive. I've always secretly wanted to do that." Julie was nodding slowly, but didn't seem so sure.

I called my friend back, and told him to book the instructor, starting Monday morning. There would be two, or possibly three people in the class. He said that he would e-mail me the PDF of the book, so the girls could get started studying.

The house had a computer and printer hooked up, so I printed out three copies of the first few chapters of the book. I went out to the pool, and informed the girls, "You guys are scheduled for a three-day, open-water SCUBA course Monday through Wednesday of next week."

They looked me blankly, so I continued, "Here are the first few chapters of the book you'll have to learn. You'll be in the classroom every morning, and in the water every afternoon. If you pass all the tests, you'll be certified by the time you leave on Thursday."

Then, I let them know, "Kelly and I will probably extend our trip a few days, so we can take a couple of boat dives. If you guys want to extend your trip, you're welcome to stay with us and come on the dives."

In less than ten minutes, I had turned their 'island vacation' into an intensive class, with some serious studying required. But I knew Kelly's friends could handle it, if they wanted to; and, they were already very comfortable in the water, so I was optimistic that they could handle the SCUBA skills comfortably.

I went inside and got on the phone with the airline, hoping that I could extend the trip and get a first class upgrade on our flights back. Then, I would have to find a place for us to stay a few extra days.

As I was skimming through the dive book chapters, I heard the sliding doors to the house open. Kathy and Christian, and Kathy's parents, Andy and Karen, walked onto the narrow deck around the pool. We were all nude, of course, something that we considered natural now.

"Wow! This is beautiful," exclaimed Karen, as she walked onto the lawn, and across it to the beach. She turned toward us, "Christian, if you had told us about this house, we would have stayed here, and let Kelly and others stay in the guest house!"

She may have been facetious – although I thought not. But Sam got excited, and turned to Christian, "Could we please stay in your guest house a few days, through next weekend? After Andy and Karen have left. I've enrolled Kelly in a SCUBA class next week, and I'd like us to do a few boat dives when she finishes the course."

Christian nodded, "Andy and Karen are flying back on Thursday, and Kathy and I leave Monday on our honeymoon. But the housekeeper will be there, and you're welcome to stay in the guest house – or in the main house."

Sam looked like the cat who'd just eaten a canary. "Thank you, Christian."

The new guests stripped down, and we all sat around the pool, enjoying the sun and gentle breeze. Christian had done a double-take on Sam's bareness, and I explained that he'd agreed to become my slave for a week, and I'd shaved and waxed him.

Kathy thought it funny, but Christian didn't know what to say. Kathy's parents were laughing hysterically. Sam stood and turned around, reaching back to his butt, and asking if the marks were still there. But any evidence of the tawse, paddle, or cane were long gone.

I'd had to do a double-take when Christian took off his pants: He had the largest shlong I'd ever seen. I wondered if Sam would feel embarrassed or envious; but he seemed mostly self-conscious about his bare pubic area.

Kathy and Christian told us about their upcoming honeymoon, which would be a month trip through Australia and New Zealand, with a stop-over in Tahiti to see family. It sounded terrific.

Linda told everyone about her new boyfriend, who sounded like quite a catch. And Sam explained the business we had formed, KS Biotech.

But most of the afternoon, Christian regaled us with stories from his life in the islands – tales of sailing, hunting, and local politics. Even Sam was enthralled by the breadth and depth of Christian's experiences.

Sam and I went to the market, and brought back things to make dinner. We put the potatoes in the oven, and I made the salad, while Sam got steaks and fresh fish filets ready to go on the outside grill. We dressed for dinner, but ate outside, pulling another table and some chairs from the house.

The sunset was beautiful, even though we had no chance of seeing a green flash from here, as the setting sun passed behind the mountains to the west.

We gave Christian and Kathy our best wishes for the wedding tomorrow. It would be an early-afternoon ceremony, with a big luau afterward. Christian drove Kathy and her parents back to his place, leaving only Sam and I, and Linda and Julie, at the house.

Sam gave us an introductory lecture on the physics of diving, but none of us were excited to begin studying tonight. Nevertheless, we all read the first chapters before retiring to bed.

We kissed each other goodnight, but there were no 'extra-curricular' activities. We were tired, and it would be a big day tomorrow.

Sam made breakfast for everyone on Sunday morning, and gave another impromptu lecture on diving, following the next chapters in the book. We were a bit more into it, and asked some good questions.

Julie still wasn't sure that she wanted to take the dive class. Although she was a great swimmer, she had an aversion to the few principles of dive physics and physiology that she needed to learn.

But Sam and I encouraged her to get through it, as that would open up new possibilities for travels and experiences together.

Around noon, we all got dressed in our wedding attire. The bridesmaids wore island-style dresses in a palm frond pattern. The groomsmen wore long cream-colored slacks and a similar palm frond Aloha shirt. We piled into the van and drove to the wedding venue, the gardens still spectacularly saturated in color.

Kathy had selected me to be the 'maid of honor', the other bridesmaids being Julie, Linda, and Christian's younger sister, Tania, who was beautiful. She had flown in from Honolulu this morning.

One of Christian's friends was the 'best man', the other groomsmen including Sam, Kathy's younger brother, and another of Christian's island friends.

It was a short but beautiful ceremony, tears in all of our eyes by the time Christian kissed Kathy, and they walked up the aisle and out into the gardens. The bridesmaids and groomsmen then walked up the aisle arm-in-arm, me being paired with Sam, and Christian's sister paired with Kathy's brother.

There wasn't a formal reception line, there being only twenty or thirty guests, plus the wedding party. After most of the other guests had given their good wishes to the bride and groom, Sam and I congratulated the couple.

Sam kissed Kathy on the cheek, and I kissed Christian on the cheek. Then, Sam shook Christian's hand, and I gave Kathy a kiss on the other cheek. I winked at her, "I'd give you a better kiss, but don't want to mess up your lipstick." Kathy laughed, and we hugged each other.

Linda and Julie hugged Kathy, and then hugged Christian. Linda had to keep wiping away her tears. I had to wonder how serious her relationship was, and whether she would be the next one of us to tie the knot.

The music started, with a local group playing traditional Hawaiian songs. Champagne cocktails were passed around on a tray, as well as some upscale island-style hors d'oevres – ahi poke bruschetta, mini *laulau*, crispy fried local lobster bites, taro chips with mango moose, and teriyaki beef skewers.

We heard a conch shell horn blow, and were ushered to an area of the gardens where the Kalua pig was being roasted in an *imu* oven. Christian explained that '*Ka lua*' means 'in the hole', or in the ground.

He told us that the pig is actually being steamed, using hot rocks as the heat source, and various leaves and other plant material for the moisture. They had begun early this morning.

A couple of local guys shoveled the soil from the pit area, and then lifted off a large tarp-like piece of material. Under that were banana leaves and *ti* leaves. When those were removed, the entire pig was lifted out of the *imu* on a metal screen.

Christian led us to a small clearing in the garden, where half a dozen tables were set up, as well as a small dance floor, and a stage for the musicians. It was an intimate setting, strings of tiny lights crisscrossing the space, and beautiful tropical flower arrangements on all the tables.

Sam brought a couple of Mai Tai's from the bar, and we found our seat assignments. Surprisingly, we were at the main table with Kathy and Christian, Kathy's parents, and the two siblings. Julie and Linda were at another table with Christian's two friends and their dates.

I sat next to Kathy's brother on one side and Sam on the other. Next to Sam were Karen and Andy. After several toasts, the food was ready and we lined up for the buffet. It was an incredible spread, reminiscent of our luau on the last trip ... but much better, every dish being special.

We ate and drank, and danced, and visited with Kathy's brother and her parents. We all played 'musical chairs', visiting people at the other tables. Kathy looked radiant, and her parents were beaming. I hadn't really ever gotten to know them, but they were interesting people.

Karen and Andy told us about some of their travel adventures and various protests in which they had taken part. And I told them about Sarah's accident, and the status of my two sons. We hadn't known each other during our kids' high school years.

When Kelly got up to visit Julie and Linda at the other table, Karen turned to me, "Thank you, Sam, for everything you've done for Kathy. Bringing her here to Kauai, buying her snorkeling gear, and accepting Kelly's friends into your group." I didn't really have a 'group', and now had to wonder what Kathy had told them.

Karen read my mind. "Kathy told us about your relationship with Kelly, you guys being into BDSM, and being open about sex and nudity." I nodded, and awaited any other revelations, but they didn't come.

I explained to Karen and Andy that I had deep feelings for Kauai – now even more, since I had proposed to Kelly here. And that I had wanted to share some experiences with Kelly and her friends – snorkeling, hiking to Kalalau, taking a helicopter ride over the island.

Karen finished her Mai Tai, and turned to me, "Kathy also told us that, even being with four women, you have always been a gentleman." I shrugged. Then, she added, "And that you're a very good masseur." I guess Kathy was pretty open with her parents.

In talking more, I learned that Karen and Andy had been to Kauai once before, and had driven the north shore, but had never really seen much except the tourist spots. As the girls would be in class the next few days, I offered to show Karen and Andy the north shore.

I had to drive to Kapaa every day, anyway, so we decided to spend two days on the north shore – one touring and one snorkeling, similar to what I'd done with Kelly and her friends on our trip here.

My buddy at the dive store had told me that the class would be in the water Tuesday and Wednesday afternoon at Tunnels Beach, so I reversed the order of the tour days. I would take Andy and Karen snorkeling at my favorite little beach on Monday, and then do the north shore tour on Tuesday.

Kelly returned, and we enjoyed one more dance before collecting Julie and Linda, and driving back to our beach house.

Sam offered to make us drinks, but we were already soused from the wedding, and still had to study the dive materials tonight. Julie, especially, was nervous about the bookwork for the class. And I think we were all a bit anxious about some of the things we would be doing under the water.

I still couldn't believe that Kathy was married! The wedding had been beautiful, and Christian was an amazing guy. They would be taking an extended honeymoon, then living on Kauai. It was hard not to be just a little jealous.

But Sam and I had our own goals, KS Biotech being at the top of the list. Had we not been studying for the class, I would have been putting in some work on the presentation for Barcelona. And had Sam not suggested and organized the dive class, I may not have been certified for years.

Linda seemed the most relaxed and self-confident about taking the dive class, and not only let Sam make a Piña Colada for her, but asked if he would give her a massage.

He looked at me questioningly. "Go ahead, Sam. I'm going to be busy studying. You know I don't mind." I smiled at him, "Why don't you spend the night with Linda? If she'll have you in her bed." I had no idea whether Sam and Linda would want to get it on; and it didn't matter.

Lying on my stomach on the bed, I began going through the text, making notes in the margins, and compiling a list of questions on a small pad. This stuff wasn't difficult; the challenge was just the short time we had to learn everything and pass the test.

Julie was already in her room, studying. I was sure that we could get her through it. And she was the strongest swimmer of us all.

I turned the page to the second chapter: The physics of diving. I flipped through the pages. Hydrostatic pressure, Archimedes' Principle, Boyle's Law, Henry's Law. As with many fields, one had to know the basics, but they probably weren't what I would think of first, when a shark bit my air hose.

Linda and I sat in the lawn chairs looking out at the black ocean and stars above. This was the west side of the island, which got much less rain than the north shore, where we had stayed before.

I turned to Linda, "You're not nervous about the dive class? I think Kelly wants to get a running start ... and Julie is terrified; but I know you guys will do fine."

Linda took a sip of her Piña Colada and nodded, "I'm not going to sweat it." She smiled seductively, and lifted her foot into my crotch, where she manipulated me with her toes. "And I'm sure you'll be happy to tutor us, if we need help tomorrow night."

"Of course – I'll be glad to help." A few scenes from my roleplay with schoolgirl Linda flashed through my head. A year or two ago, I would be fantasizing how I would punish the three girls, if they didn't learn their lessons.

But now, I just wanted them to succeed; and I knew they would. I lifted Linda's foot out of my crotch. and glanced down to the growing bulge in my pants. "What about your 'steady' boyfriend?"

Linda took another sip of her drink and shrugged, "I have strong feelings for you, also, Sam. And they don't threaten my relationship with Matt. I guess I've learned a little from Kelly."

She chuckled, "I could give you head, or we could have sex – as we've done in the past – and that shouldn't affect your relationship with Kelly, or mine with Matt." I fully agreed, *in theory*.

"I assume that Matt doesn't know about me?" Linda shrugged again, "I've told him about Kelly, and that she's engaged to an 'older guy' ... who's pretty interesting."

She laughed, "He doesn't know any of the things we've done. But it would be interesting having him come over for his birthday, and all of us spank him. He'd be pretty shocked." She added, seriously, "But he's open, and very liberal. I don't think he'd have a problem with a little birthday party celebration."

I could see the gears turning in Linda's head. And the gears were turning in my head, too. Despite being slightly inebriated from the wedding – or, perhaps because of it – I suddenly became concerned about further widening our circle of sexual partners. It just seemed dangerous.

Kelly would chide me for my concerns; just as I would chide her for her worry about sharks. I had strong feelings for Linda, also; I just wasn't sure that I wanted effectively to have sex with Matt. This was something I would need to think about. As far as tonight, I would share a bed with Linda, but not have sex with her.

"Do you really want me to give you a massage, tonight?" Linda smiled and nodded. Then, she finished her drink, got out of the chair, leaned over, and kissed me. On the mouth.

It was something we'd done countless times ... but now I had had body fluid transfer with Linda – and, by extension, Matt. And I hadn't even met him, yet! Maybe I was a bit drunk? Things seemed more complicated than they should be.

Linda headed to her bedroom, while I put our glasses in the dishwasher, found a bottle of vegetable oil in the pantry, and grabbed a towel from the hall closet. This really was a nice house, but I still would rather stay on the north shore. I wondered what $5,000 a week would buy up there for a vacation rental.

I gave Linda a very thorough full-body massage, using all the techniques that Liz had taught me so many years ago. The lights were out, only a candle lit on the dresser, and my eyes closed – feeling my way along Linda's body, as my thoughts wandered.

It was nice to be on Kauai again, and going to the north shore for the next couple of days. And I was glad that Kelly and her friends would get their dive certificates. Hopefully, we could take some epic dive trips together.

But Kelly and I had a lot of work to do, to get ready for Barcelona. From my chats with the pharma companies, I felt optimistic that we could cement some kind of deal. The business model was still in flux, something that would need to be solidified, for us to have a chance to raise money. Kelly and I would have to take time for some strategy meetings.

And, the more I thought about it, the more it made sense to ask Linda to join the company. In the near term, she could help with the myriad of things that needed to get done. And, in the longer-term, she could be a valuable member of the management team, as she was able to see the 'big picture' clearly.

"Are you on autopilot?" Linda's voice startled me, and I realized that I was massaging her breasts, chest, and shoulders for the third time. Glancing at my watch, I was shocked to see that more than an hour had elapsed; and that it was now morning.

I pulled Linda up and hugged her, getting oil on my tank. We took a quick shower, and got into her bed. I briefly considered checking in on Kelly, but decided to give her space; she was probably already asleep by now.

"Linda, I would actually be OK with just going to sleep tonight." I smiled at her in the moonlight coming through the skylight, "But I'd be happy to get you off, if you want." Then, I had a better idea. "Or ... why don't you get on top of me and masturbate? You can have me facing down or up, and I'll be your human mattress."

Linda shrugged and crawled on top of me. I did stir below, but hoped that I could have an experience like I'd had with Kelly: Getting into her head, rather than mine, and feeling her emotions, excitement, orgasm.

We already knew that Linda was a very sensual creature, and she didn't disappoint. For a moment, I felt bad that I had made her satisfy herself; but, then, I relaxed, closed my eyes, and began to 'feel' her every movement. It was – again – an incredible experience, feeling a woman satisfy herself on top of me.

It was lucky that I'd set an early alarm, as Sam, Linda and Julie were all still asleep. I first woke Julie, then went into Linda's bedroom, where she and Sam slept soundly – on opposite sides of the bed. I bent over and kissed Sam, and his eyes fluttered open.

He smiled at me, and I pointed to my wrist, indicating that we were already late getting ready for our dive class. We were supposed to pick up Karen and Andy in forty five minutes!

Sam crawled out of bed, and headed toward our bathroom, while I slipped into Linda's bed, and snuggled up to her. It only took a few moments before she turned over, obviously realizing it wasn't Sam against her body.

"Good morning, Linda. We need to get going, or we'll be late for the dive class." Linda nodded, yawned, and threw down the covers. We both climbed out of the bed, and I gave Linda a quick peck on the lips.

Somehow, we all got ready, Sam even packing for hiking and snorkeling. We picked up Kathy's parents, right on time, and headed around the island to Kapaa.

Julie was still a bit terrified of taking the class; and it would have been nice for Kathy to learn to dive with us. But Linda and I were excited to be doing something we'd wanted to try for a long time.

The instructor wasn't much older than us – maybe in his early 30s – and looked like a California surfer, with blond hair and a big smile. He wore surf trunks and a faded t-shirt with a picture of a shark on the back. I think we all relaxed at that point, even Julie. Suddenly, it seemed like this would just be another fun experience.

I completed my 'transaction' with the owner – both of them: Paying for the girls' dive class, and getting some fresh Hawaiian bud. I knew that Andy and Karen would appreciate it.

After checking on the logistics with the instructor, Zach, I kissed Kelly and told the girls goodbye. I would be picking them up at five, and we'd all go to dinner on the East shore.

It would have been great to have rented tanks, regulators, and BCs and take Andy and Karen diving on the north shore. But they didn't have certificates, and – I found – had never even tried an introductory SCUBA experience. They said they had done some snorkeling ... but I would find out their real experience level soon.

We stopped at the market in Princeville, and bought sandwiches and snacks, then drove to the trailhead and hiked down to the little beach, where I'd taken Kelly and her friends. Andy was overweight, and the hike seemed tough to him. But, predictably – and thankfully – the beach was empty.

Stepping from one huge lava boulder to another, I made my way down to the beautiful hundred-yard crescent of sand. The conditions were perfect – calm, clear water, and no one else here. I guess the summer vacation hadn't quite started, yet.

I laid out a king-size sheet on the sand at the far end of the beach, near the cliff that rose to houses in Princeville, and took off my tank and running shorts. Andy and Karen weren't far behind, and we were all nude sunbathing within minutes.

Sitting on the edge of the sheet, I watched Karen, as she explored the beach. While she and Andy were perhaps five years younger than me, Andy was balding, and Karen's hair was mostly gray. She wore it long, and I could easily imagine her as the flowerchild of the '70s.

For my taste, she was too thin and small on top, and had a small butt. Definitely not a very spankable butt ... not that it mattered, as Karen was totally against anything that might be considered violent. Her pubic hair was untrimmed, but at least she had shaved her underarms.

She turned to walk back, and smiled as she saw me lighting up. We passed around a small pipe, and again I wondered whether all my definitions of sex meant anything.

Here, I was sharing a pipe, transferring saliva, with people I had no intention of having sex with; but last night I had been uncomfortable thinking about going down on Linda, or her blowing me, after she'd slept – what? one or two times? – with that guy, Matt.

Andy and Karen took out their snorkeling equipment, and decided to try out the shallow part of the reef. They sat on the large rocks, still nude, and donned their mask, fins, and snorkel. I kept an eye on them, through their ten-minute snorkel tour of the shallows, but they seemed to be comfortable in the water.

As they walked back from the water, Karen gushed, "We really saw a lot! We even saw an eel in one of those holes in the reef." She sat down next to me, the sun rapidly evaporating the drops of water all over her body.

Turning to me, she said, "That was really nice of you to buy the underwater camera for Kathy. She showed us some incredible pictures." I assumed, that the pictures to which Karen was referring were the underwater shots.

"Well, why don't we have a snack, you guys can rest a little, and then I'll take you on a bit longer snorkel tour – like I did with Kathy and her friends."

Andy and Karen smiled and nodded, but I doubt they expected an hour-long tour. As we ate our snacks and drank our sodas, a couple of young women walked onto the other side of the beach. They also shed their clothes, and lay on their stomachs, taking in the sun. They were already bronzed, probably locals.

A half hour later, we were all getting ready for the snorkel tour. I led Andy and Karen through the narrow channels into deeper water, then swam underwater between the outcroppings of rock and coral.

We were all still nude, although I usually wore a suit when doing a long snorkel, and diving through holes in the reef. As we drifted into deeper water, I did a few surface dives, and then swam through a small lava tube, Andy and Karen kicking their fins to catch up as I surfaced at the other end of the tube.

Around the point, we headed toward the waterfall and, as with the girls, we saw a multitude of green sea turtles feeding on the seaweed. I took Andy and Karen into the sea cave, and we stepped onto the small beach and took off our masks, fins, and snorkels in the dark space.

Then, we walked through the 100-foot long lava tube. It was only about eight feet in diameter, and was pitch black in the middle, only the light from the far end illuminating the sand in front of us. We walked out, under the arch of the cave, ferns poking from the rocks on each side, and vines hanging down, dripping, just as it had been when I brought Kelly here.

When we had walked to the water, I turned and pointed, "Here's where I proposed to Kelly. It wasn't exactly a planned part of the trip ... it just happened." I looked down at the sand, a lump in my throat and tears forming in my eyes. Karen hugged me.

"Before that, I brought Kelly, Julie, Linda, and Kathy here. They did a great job snorkeling; I hope they do well in the dive class." I looked at Karen, then Andy, "It's too bad that Kathy couldn't join them. But I suspect that Christian will see that she gets certificated."

Andy nodded, "Yeah, he's already talking about that. Maybe it will happen when they're in the South Seas."

We sat in the shallow, warm pool of crystal clear water, as waves lapped gently onto the rocks that separated the pool from the ocean. I closed my eyes and visualized my trip here with the girls. It really had been an epic trip.

When we were back on the beach, we took a few more tokes, and then ate our sandwiches. Somehow the fresh air always made me hungry. We relaxed on the beach, Karen reading a book and me taking another long snorkel off the reef. Andy seemed content to doze, Karen making sure he was covered with plenty of sunscreen.

As I rubbed sunscreen onto Karen's back, she reminded me, "I'd still love that massage, if you're up for it. Maybe tonight?" I smiled wanly, and nodded unsurely; I didn't really know what we would be doing tonight.

In the late afternoon, we packed up and climbed the trail back to our car. We had brought a change of clothes to wear for dinner, but needed showers before putting them on. I drove to Kapaa, but it was a bit early to pick up the girls.

Fortunately, the beach park had showers, so we cleaned up, dressed for dinner, and then headed back to the dive shop.

We walked in through the back, where they were filling tanks, and into the shop. In the small classroom, Zach was reviewing the various kinds of dive maladies, such as overpressure injuries, nitrogen narcosis, oxygen toxicity, and decompression sickness, or 'the bends'.

I walked into the room, "And, there's shallow water blackout, where you can become unconscious if you hyperventilate, and then get caught underwater with insufficient oxygen in your lungs."

Zach smiled and nodded. "Your second instructor is here, so I guess I'll see you guys tomorrow morning." I was about to apologize, when Zach laughed, and I realized he was joking – at least partially.

We headed down the coast, and arrived at the Japanese restaurant just as they opened. As we'd done before, we got a Teppanyaki table, and made it a long and enjoyable dinner.

Despite the drinks, I didn't feel tired when we exited the restaurant a couple of hours later. I drove back to the west side, intending to drop off Andy and Karen. As we arrived at their condo, Karen asked, "Sam, it's still early. May we drive over to your house, and visit for a while longer?"

I started to nod, but before I could respond, she added, "And I'd love to get a massage, if you're up for it."

I shrugged and looked at Kelly. She shrugged and smiled, "Go for it." I guess I was now the 'masseur of the house'. At least, I'd get a little extra exercise.

The girls decided to go for a nighttime swim in the pool, and Andy offered to 'keep an eye on them'. I set a large towel across the foot of the bed in the master bedroom; it was too bad that there wasn't a proper massage table. I also only had vegetable oil, not a nice coconut oil made for massages.

Karen didn't seem to mind. She undressed and lay face-down on the towel. "Shall I drape you with this sheet? If you're chilled, I can turn off the fan."

Karen shook her head, "No, Sam. I'm fine. The temperature is perfect."

Once again, I applied the skills I'd learned from Liz, taking my time, going mostly by feel, as the only light was the moonshine through the large skylight. Karen had little fat on her, and the 'feel' was much different than when I had massaged Linda – even with Linda's new weight-reduced figure.

By the time I finished her backside, and was massaging the soles of her feet, Linda was snoring softly. I worked my way back up her body, with light strokes, until I reached her head. I massaged her shoulders and neck, as I leaned down and whispered into her ear.

"Would you like to turn over, Karen?"

After a few deep breaths, Karen lifted her head, "I guess I fell asleep."

I continued to massage her shoulders. "I didn't know whether to wake you, or let you sleep. I'm ready for you to turn over, now; if you want to. Or, I can cover you and let you take a nap for a while."

Karen turned over, chuckling, "No. I'd like to get the rest of the massage. Then, I can go back to the condo and sleep."

I massaged her forehead and ears, then her neck and chest, my hands diving between her breasts then around and back up to her chest. Karen had relatively small breasts which had sagged from a lifetime of not wearing a bra. Her gray hair was a little stringy, but still long, and her face was beautiful, despite some creases.

Moving downward, I massaged Karen's stomach, hips, and legs, my hands running up to her crotch, both of us being completely comfortable, despite my proximity to her intimate areas.

It was Karen and Andy who took regular beach vacations to Mexico, where Karen apparently enjoyed pampering massages and spa treatments. I wondered how my massages compared; at least, I'd relaxed her enough to fall asleep, something I considered an accomplishment.

I finished her massage, and gave her a kiss on the forehead. "How are you doing? Would you like a 'happy ending'? Or, if you like, we can get in the shower and I can bathe you – get the oil off. And, maybe, *then* give you a happy ending." I doubted that she would agree to that, but I felt that we were close enough for me to ask.

Karen smiled, then lifted her head and gave me a peck on the lips, "That's a nice offer, Sam, but I'm not really up for that, tonight. But if you'd like to bathe me, *without* the 'happy ending' that would be nice." She batted her eyes at me, "I'm *already* happy."

We took a nice shower together, and I bathed her thoroughly, including her genitals and anal area, including a quick finger in her rear. Karen seemed more amused than anything, and didn't seem at all bothered.

Surprisingly, she then proceeded to bathe me, including all of *my* intimate parts. Neither of us was turned on, but it was still fun – even at my old age – to take an uninhibited shower with a female who I barely knew.

When Karen and I walked out into the yard, everyone was sitting around the small table, the girls wrapped in towels. Karen was dressed again, and I'd put on my running shorts and tank. Andy looked up and smiled, "So how was it? Is Sam now going to be your new masseur?"

Karen laughed, "It was great. And I'd *love* him to massage me regularly. But I haven't asked about his rates, yet." Maybe Kelly would be a pro-domme, and I would be a masseur?"

Andy stood and nodded, then looked at me, "Am I next?" All eyes turned to me, and I stood there dumbly; I was a little stunned. Of course, I could give Andy a massage ... but I had never massaged a man, and was still a bit hung-up about contact with another male – especially as intimate as this would be.

Kelly, immediately understanding my discomfort, and wanting to rub it in, looked up at me brightly, "Go ahead, Sam. We can talk with Karen for a while."

She had called my bluff, although I didn't know if Andy was really serious. But he was standing, and looking at me expectantly, so I guess his request was serious.

I looked at him pleadingly, "It's getting late, and I've probably had enough exercise for one day. Maybe tomorrow night, if you're still interested, Andy?" He smiled and nodded. I couldn't tell if he was testing me, or was truly interested in a massage.

Sam and I walked Andy and Karen to their car, giving them a hug and waving as they drove off. Andy was a really nice guy; Linda, Julie and I had grown to like him, none of us really having gotten to know him previously.

"So are you really going to give Andy a massage, tomorrow night?"

Sam shrugged, sheepishly, "I don't know if he really wanted one, or was just teasing."

Knowing this would irk Sam; I laughed, "I *know* he wanted a massage. He looked disappointed when you suggested tomorrow night. But he'll probably hold you to it." Sam was shaking his head, and I knew he hoped that I was wrong.

Sam and I got into bed, and I told him about the first day of our dive class. It had been pretty intensive, but we'd all asked good questions, and had them answered. Sam was surprised when I told him that Zach had taken us across the highway to a beach in Kapaa, where he had us do a couple of swimming races, the salty waves slapping into our face providing a little challenge.

Julie had done fine with the dive physics, as Zach had made it very simple to understand, and he gave good examples of why we had to learn it. The next two days would be only a couple of hours in class in the store, and then actually using SCUBA equipment out at Tunnels Beach, on the north shore.

Sam and I were both tired, and we made love quickly, then fell asleep in each other's arms.

The second morning of class was even more intensive, finishing most of the book. We would be taking a written test tomorrow morning. Then, we were fitted with equipment – buoyancy compensators, weight belts, and shorty wetsuits – and learned how to assemble the tanks and regulators, and check the pressure.

We squeezed into Zach's truck, all the equipment in the back, and drove up to the north shore. It was beautiful, and I'd forgotten how green this side of the island was, compared to the south shore and west side. There were dark clouds, and on-and-off light rain, but it was still warm, both the air and water temperatures in the low 80s.

Sam was planning to take Karen and Andy on a north shore tour, starting with the Kilauea lighthouse and secret beach, then Hanalei Bay and Lumahai Beach, before going back to the Princeville Hotel for lunch.

Then, they would drive to the end of the road, snorkel Kee Beach, go for a swim in the wet cave and see the 'blue room', and finally meet us on Tunnels Beach. Zach had brought equipment for Sam, so that he could join us on our last dive.

We learned how to breathe through our regulators and clear them underwater; how to clear our masks underwater, and how to clear our ears – something Sam had taught us, and we'd all tried, unsuccessfully. But the dive equipment enabled us to descend slowly, and work on clearing our ears before diving further.

We all struggled, initially, at keeping our depth regulated, using the buoyancy compensator, but were finally able to 'hover' a few feet above the sandy bottom, just swaying back and forth with the current.

Our last exercise of the morning was 'buddy-breathing', where we shared an air supply with one of our dive buddies. It was a little uncomfortable to give up your air, but we trusted each other implicitly, and all did fine with the exercises.

We had a small lunch – Zach had brought sandwich fixings, and some raw vegetables – until the rain started again. Then, we sat in his truck for a while, as he explained the hand signals, and gave us some 'local knowledge' of the reef, channels, lava tubes, and sea life. It helped that we'd learned some of this from Sam during our last trip.

Finally, the rain stopped, and we changed tanks, put on our equipment, and got into the water again. This time, before any lessons or tests, Zach led us into the sea cave that Sam had told us about, under the reef. There were rays of light coming through small holes in the reef above.

Zach faced a corner of the cave, and put his fingers to his eyes, indicating that we should look in that direction. Then, he put his fingers together vertically, his thumb horizontal against his forehead. When Linda realized that he was signaling 'shark', her eyes went wide.

We swam slowly in that direction, and saw two reef sharks lying in a corner of the cave. We hovered, watching them, and responded to Zach's 'OK' signals. Then, he led us through the cave, and I was surprised, checking my gauge, that we were at a 50-foot depth.

Back in a shallower, sandy area, perhaps 30 feet down, we practiced taking off our masks, and putting them on again, clearing them underwater. Then, Zach made us do the same thing, except swimming 50 feet with our eyes open underwater – the salt stinging – and then putting our masks on and clearing them.

We learned how to orient ourselves in the water, breathing through the regulator while on our backs looking up at the surface, and how to maneuver through very narrow caves and holes in the reef.

Julie indicated that her air pressure was low, so we headed back to the beach.

Andy, Karen, and I applauded, as we watched the three girls emerge from the water, carrying their fins, and with their BCs still on, tanks on their backs. They helped each other out of their BCs, and Zach and I carried the spent tanks back to his truck, and fresh tanks down to the beach. I realized how out-of-shape I was by the time we'd finished carrying the thirty-pound tanks, two at a time.

Kelly, Julie, and Linda looked invigorated, and were talking excitedly to Kathy's parents. Zach continued the class, outlining the exercises for the next dive session. He reviewed the dive tables, and had the girls use a small circular device to calculate the allowed bottom time at a forty foot depth after the surface interval they'd just had.

Eventually, we connected the new tanks to the BCs, and carried the equipment down to the water, where we put it on, and swam out to the center of the sandy area, surrounded by the reef.

The first activity was breathing from a free-flowing regulator – sipping the air bubbles, as they explode from the mouthpiece.

Next, we would drop to the bottom, stabilize ourselves, then take off our BC, tank, and weight belt, then slowly ascend to the surface. Then, dive back down, breath through the regulator, then put back on weight belt and BC. Zach had me demonstrate, which I was able to do fairly gracefully, despite not having dived for several years.

The girls did fine, although Linda had to do two surface dives to reach her equipment, and Julie fumbled getting the BC on for several minutes, nearly panicking. But they'd all kept their wits about them – the most important rule of SCUBA diving.

Finally, we did the same thing, except also taking off our mask, snorkel, and fins. It was uncomfortable, even for me. Keeping eyes open despite the stinging saltwater; breathing through the regulator, while getting water up your nose; and putting on the equipment in the right order.

Watching Kelly and the others, it was amazing to think that they'd struggled for minutes to don simple snorkeling equipment at the little beach less than a year ago. Now, they looked competent and confident in SCUBA gear.

We helped Zach pack the truck, and I drove the girls and Andy and Karen into Hanalei for dinner. Julie and Linda were hyper-animated, telling stories of the dives they'd done so far. I teased them that they shouldn't have alcohol, if they were going to dive tomorrow ... and then we all ordered Mai Tai's.

It was incredible that tomorrow was the last day of the short class. The girls wouldn't be really competent, of course, until they'd had much more experience – boat dives, deeper dives, night dives. I hoped to do some of these with Kelly during our extended time on Kauai.

We drove back to the west side, and said goodbye to Andy and Karen, as they would be flying home tomorrow. Kathy and Christian were already in Australia.

When we got back to the house, I offered drinks and suggested going into the pool. But the girls had had enough water, and wanted to study for the exam tomorrow morning. In fact, I couldn't recall ever seeing all three of them so serious.

I retired to the backyard, sitting in the dark, looking up at the stars, and smoking weed. My feelings for Kauai continued to grow; if we weren't trying to build a company, I would almost want to live here. The soft, warm breeze caressed my skin, and a meteor flashed across the dark sky.

As nervous as we'd all been, we passed the test easily – me acing it, Linda missing one question, and Julie missing three; we'd all been well over 80%. Sam had gone to the beach in Kapaa, and now returned, as Zach packed the truck. We followed him in the van, as we again drove up to the north shore.

On our first dive, we learned how to navigate underwater, following our compass on the bearings that Zach wrote on his slate. Then, he led us just into the mouth of the sea cave, and had us wait, while he set-up a course outside the cave.

He gave us each five little metal hoops from the pocket of his BC, and told us to follow the courses on his slate. We had to find a small yellow stake and drop our hoop over the stake, before finding the next one.

Despite the 'exact' course and distance, none of us could find the stake without a lot of searching, including Sam. We realized how difficult it would be to find something underwater, even if we had good directions.

We did a final dive, focusing on relaxing and minimizing our air consumption, while we followed Zach on a tour of the reef, including the deeper water outside the reef. I looked around at my friends, and they smiled through their regulators, and gave me an 'OK' signal. It looked like they were all comfortable, maintaining neutral buoyancy, and having fun.

It was our longest dive, yet, and also our deepest – although we'd stayed at a 60-foot maximum depth for only a few minutes. We saw sea turtles, and lots of fish, as well as reef animals illuminated by Zach's powerful underwater light.

We dove through a small lava tube, just wide enough to accommodate us and our tanks (my tank scraped the rocks a little), and we hovered on our backs near the top of a sea cave, with the silvery surface of the bubble of air trapped underneath.

I was glad that Zach didn't make us breathe from that air, although I could imagine it being a possibility, in an emergency.

Back on the beach, we were all excited – even Sam. We'd seen a lot, and hadn't worried about the mechanics of diving – just relaxed and enjoyed ourselves. Zach said he'd hoped we could last an hour on our tanks, and I came close, at 53 minutes.

We filled-out our logs, and Zach broke out some sparkling wine, which he poured over each of our heads, and then we drank the rest. Zach admonished, "Only *after* the dive!"

We loaded everything back into Zach's truck, and he offered to stay as long as we wanted to answer questions. We had a few, but he'd done a good job, and we'd already been asking questions for three days. He congratulated us, and said we could pick up our 'C-cards' at the shop in the morning.

Then, he drove off, and we sat on the beach, now nearly empty, sun close to the horizon, as we sipped the wine, and marveled that we were now certificated SCUBA divers! Sam was smiling broadly, as were my friends.

We drove back to Hanalei, and parked at the restaurant on the river where Sam had taken us for incredible ahi. Waiting for our seats, we sat on the outside deck, drinking Mai Tai's again. These tasted particularly good; maybe it was the taste of success?

Dinner was incredible, and we were all feeling 'high', without having smoked anything for the past few days. We were still talking about our dive experiences as Sam drove us around the island to the house.

We all had to pack – Julie and Linda flying back home tomorrow, and Sam and I moving to Christian's guest house. When we finally congregated in the kitchen, Sam mixed up the last batch of Piña Coladas, and we all toasted to the trip.

Then, Sam smiled – I *knew* that smile – and he announced, "OK, girls. I want to see you all in your underwear, lined up behind the living room couch, in ten minutes!" He hadn't discussed anything with me, and I wondered whether he would try to 'challenge' us again.

Ten minutes later, we stood behind the couch, feet apart, hands on our heads. We'd decided we might as well humor Sam. We were all wearing bikini underwear and top-free.

Sam came in, dressed as usual in his running shorts and tank, and paced in front of us. He stopped, turned to us, and smiled, "You may be wondering why I asked you all here, tonight."

We were a little tipsy, and Julie exclaimed, "No. We're not. Are we, girls?"

Linda chuckled, "He's going to stick needles in us, again."

I shook my head, "No. He knows that if he brought another box of 100 needles, we'd use the rest of them on him." I certainly *hoped* he hadn't brought any 'supplies'.

Sam stood there looking at each of us. Finally, I couldn't take it any longer. "OK, Sam. Exactly *why* have you asked us here?"

He shrugged, "I *told* you: I wanted to see you in your underwear!" That was funny, but none of us were laughing. I stared at Sam, willing him to let us know what was going to happen.

Finally, he chuckled, took a couple of steps, and opened the coat closet door behind him, pulling out a box. Opening it, he said, "I got a bunch. You guys can pick the one – or two – you want." He held up one t-shirt after another, for us to read them, and then handed them to us.

They were all black, with the white outline of a diver on the back with a red and white dive logo. On the front were various taglines: 'Divers do it deeper', 'Instant diver: Just add water', 'The deeper you go, the better it feels', and 'Welcome to the food chain: You're no longer on top'. this last one had a stylized picture of a shark on the front.

We picked the ones we wanted, then Sam pulled out a last tee. "I thought I would buy one for myself, too." He held it up: It said, 'Dive Naked'. The small print added, 'Everything looks bigger underwater'.

We laughed, and held up our tees. We had a pretty good collection going – my birthday tee, the tees from Europe, the Kauai 'red dirt' tee shirts, and the Kalalau trail tees; and now dive tees.

Sam pulled me aside, and whispered, "May I still kiss Linda, even though she's had sex with Matt?"

I was astounded, "What!???! What are you talking about? I thought we took transfer of saliva away from our definition of 'sex'? You're just being ridiculous, Sam." He shrugged. I couldn't believe it: I thought he'd had sex with Linda when they'd slept together Sunday night.

"Congratulations, Linda! You're a certified SCUBA diver. I'm proud of you," Sam said sincerely. Then, he hugged her and gave her a deep kiss.

"Thank you, Sam," Linda replied, as she pulled on the tee. It came down far enough to be a beach cover-up.

Sam congratulated Julie, then hugged and kissed her. She pressed herself against Sam, and gave him a lingering kiss, then pulled on her tee.

It was my turn, and I didn't skimp on my kisses for Sam. He had again been generous, and we'd again finished our trip with new experiences. Well, Julie and Linda were finishing their trip; Sam and I would be doing some diving for the next few days.

Now that we all had our C-cards, it would be nice if we could take more trips together – to clear, warm waters, and more adventures. But I couldn't imagine when or how that would occur, with Sam and I focused on the business, Linda having her own boyfriend, and Julie having to work.

Sitting on the living room couch and loveseat, we shared pictures and videos taken during the trip. Of course, we hadn't had cameras during our dive class, but Sam had snapped quite a few of us during our underwater exercises at Tunnels Beach.

We visited until late, Sam making a few phone calls to set-up the next few days, and Julie and Linda finishing packing for their flight tomorrow. Then, we sat outside in the lawn chairs, under a canopy of bright stars, smoking the last of Sam's weed.

"Thank you, Sam – and Kelly – for everything. This was another interesting trip, and we're going home as divers. I was really glad we could be together again for a week, and appreciate your sharing the house."

Sam shrugged, "Of course, Linda. We've enjoyed it, too." Then, Sam's voice broke, "We really are a family.

And it was sad – but also happy – that Kathy is married and off on her own life. And, I know it's only a matter of time for you ... and Julie."

We were all silent for several moments, thinking of the experiences we'd shared with each other, over the past couple of years.

Julie said quietly, and very sincerely, "Yes. Thank you. Both of you. I do feel like we're a family." She got up, stood before Sam, bent down, took his face in her hands, and gave him a long and passionate kiss. Then, she stepped in front of me, and held me by clumps of my hair, pulling me toward her and kissing me deeply, savagely.

Looking at Linda, Julie asked, "Shouldn't we *really* thank them?" We all knew what Julie meant. Thinking about it, we hadn't really done any playing around on this trip – except for Sam sleeping with Linda ... and it sounded like that was *all* they did.

Linda smiled, "Yeah. Maybe we should go down on Sam, and prepare him for Kelly? Or, I could go down on Sam, and you could go down on Kelly."

Getting more worked up, Julie replied, "Or, we could all bend over the couch and let Sam take us from behind, like we did the last morning we were here on the last trip."

Sam shook his head, "You guys don't have to 'thank' me that way. You were very welcome to stay with us, and we've enjoyed it, as always. I consider you guys thanking me by taking – and passing – the dive class."

Then, he looked obliquely at Linda, "And what about Matt?" My friends probably didn't realize that Sam was still nervous about expanding our sexual 'contacts'.

"What about him?" Linda asked. "We're not exclusive, yet, and I don't see our playing around in any way interfering with my relationship with Matt."

I wondered if I'd perverted all of the girls; had *I* been Matt, I wouldn't have wanted to learn that my partner was having sex with other men. Or, man.

I would also have to make a decision – *another* decision – about where we would draw the line, regarding our sexual adventures. I looked at Kelly, and she shrugged, knowing my thought patterns.

Finally, *I* shrugged, "I would be happy just snuggling in bed with my favorite three beautiful nude women. But, I'll take whatever you guys want to give me ... as long as Kelly's OK with it."

Of course, I knew she would be OK with just about anything. We really were a polyamorous group. And Kelly knew the risks of increased sexual contact, so could make her own decision.

Linda laughed – almost a cackle – and responded, "Well, you know, Sam, we never gave you a birthday spanking. Wasn't it only a couple of weeks ago?"

She was right: I'd had my birthday a week before the trip. Kelly and I had gone out to the bistro for dinner, and had an intimate evening together – no spanking at all. But, I didn't mind going over Linda's or Julie's knee for a bare bottom spanking.

Then, I realized we had a birthday girl. "Well, you know, Linda, that *your* birthday is coming up in a couple of weeks. And we haven't spanked *you*, yet."

Linda pushed me into the master bedroom, Kelly and Julie following. "I'll let you make dinner for me again, and spank me, *on* my birthday." She sat at the foot of the bed and patted her lap.

As I took off my underwear and pulled off my tank, I said, "I'd love to make dinner for you, and spank you, on your birthday." It was becoming a tradition.

I got over Linda's lap. "This will be a 100-spank warm-up. Julie will give you the same ... and Kelly, if she wants. Then, we'll discuss your *real* birthday spanking." With that, she began spanking me, hard, alternating sides.

It didn't hurt that much, especially compared to the spankings Linda had given Slave Sam. And it was over quickly. Julie took Linda's place, and I got over her knee. She gave me another hundred spanks, and my bottom was definitely getting warmed up.

After Kelly had finished her turn, and I was rubbing my bottom, the girls left the room for a moment. When they returned, Julie chortled, "Lie down on the bed, Sam, and we'll get you ready." I wasn't sure what I was getting ready for, but it sounded good.

I put my head back on the pillow, and Kelly crawled up my body, her legs pinning my arms to my sides, and her hands around my head. As she lowered her head and began kissing me, I felt the first strokes along my manhood, Julie and Linda both working on me.

Then, they licked me and sucked me, and finally one of them took me into her mouth, the feeling glorious. I kissed Kelly deeply and realized my erection was now in another mouth. My eyes fluttered closed.

"OK, Kelly, he's ready." It was a rude intrusion into my fantasies, as I was nearing orgasm.

Kelly laughed, rolled off me to the side, and got off the bed. She smiled sweetly at me, "They want to give your birthday spanking while you're making love to me on the corner of the bed." That didn't sound like a bad plan.

I got off the bed and behind Kelly, pushing her gently over the corner of the bed, so that I could enter her from behind. "No, Sam. I want to see your face." She turned around and laid back on the corner of the bed, scooting down until her butt was off the bed and her legs pulled up to her chest.

I slowly entered her, pulling her to me by her hips. She put her arms around me, and pulled me down to her. We had just started kissing, and I'd made only three or four thrusts, when Julie said, softly, "OK, Sam. Stop moving, now. It's time for your birthday spanking."

Linda became hysterical, as she asked, "This is your 60th birthday?" That wasn't even funny.

Julie piped up, "I think he's only 55." Then, I felt something smooth grazing my bottom. On both sides. "How many is it, Sam?"

I opened my eyes, and Kelly was smiling brightly at me. I answered, "Fifty two." Kelly held her arms around my back tightly, and we kissed again.

'Whap!' 'Whap!!' There was a sting on my left side, then on my right. Then, the spanking continued, alternating sides, and getting more and more intense.

I realized – from both the feel and the sound – that the girls were using an island slipper on me; just as I had on Julie, during her birthday bash the last time we were here.

But Julie had been half my age. I put my arms around Kelly, and tried to relax, but the girls were spanking me 'out of sync', and now the slippers were coming down together on both sides. It really smarted! But, of course, not as much as if it was Kelly spanking me.

Spankings turn me on, usually; even the idea of me getting spanked. But by the time the 52 swats were over, I had shrunk, and was coming out of Kelly. She chuckled, and reached down, putting my flaccidity between our stomachs.

Then, Kelly held me tightly around the back again, and Linda announced, "Now for the three 'special' spanks. Kelly suggested I use your leather belt."

My body actually shuddered, and Kelly held me, as Julie called out, "Good health!" I heard the loud 'Crack!' of the belt before the pain registered; it *really* stung!

But before I could recover, Julie called out "Good wealth!" and a second searing 'Snap!' of the strap smacked sore skin. One of the girls rubbed my butt, but too soon Julie shouted "Long life!", and the third stroke landed. I couldn't help but cry out.

Kelly wanted to kiss me, but I couldn't catch my breath, so she continued to hold me. Finally, we kissed, and she pushed me back, so she could get off the bed. I had thought I would be having an orgasm at the end of the spanking. This wasn't very satisfying.

But Julie and Linda brought me into the bathroom and cleaned me, while Kelly sat on the toilet. I must have given a strange look, as Linda consoled me, "Don't worry, Sam. I'm going to satisfy you. And Julie's going to satisfy Kelly. We should all be very well satisfied, before we go to sleep." Julie and Kelly were nodding, with big smiles.

We went back into the bedroom, got into bed and turned off the lights; moonlight streamed through the skylight illuminating the room – at least, enough for our purposes.

Kelly and Julie got into a '69' position, and Linda pulled me to her. It didn't take long before I was turned-on again, and slipped into Linda's warm wetness.

As Linda had predicted, we all had nice orgasms, and took turns holding and kissing each other, before pulling up the covers.

We dropped off my friends at the Lihue airport, and continued up to the north shore. Sam wanted to give me an intensive dive experience over the next few days, and had organized a different type of dive every day. Today, we would be diving off the beach of the Princeville Hotel, in Hanalei Bay.

We drove through the *porte cochere*, and let the valet take our car, each of us carrying our packs with snorkeling equipment. Our walk through the lobby – with its Italian marble columns and floors, and chandeliers – didn't seem like the hike to a dive spot. It was gorgeous, but I wasn't sure it fit in with the 'island style'.

Taking the elevator down to the beach level, we walked out onto the deck surrounding the infinity pool, beyond which was deep blue ocean and, in the distance, the Bali Hai ridge. A multitude of palm trees and colorful tropical plants made *this* area seem perfect for the island.

Sam rented equipment at the beach-level concession, and we headed out through the narrow channels, much as we'd done when snorkeling the north shore. Fortunately, it was high tide, so we could make it to the outside of the reef.

Sam kept a close eye on me, and we used our BCs to stabilize ourselves at various depths, while we examined the reef. It was interesting, and we saw eels and octopus, and candy cane shrimp, Sam's dive light making things much more colorful, even during the day.

We stayed out nearly an hour, as our maximum depth had only been about thirty feet. Then, we sat under the pavilion of the pool restaurant, and had a leisurely lunch. A second dive in the afternoon was more challenging, as we carried the equipment down the beach, then swam on the surface across to the Hanalei Pier.

Diving around the concrete pilings of the pier, Sam pointed to a strange-looking fish. He pulled out his slate, and wrote, 'flying gurnard!'. I had never heard of such a fish, and started turning in another direction, when Sam pulled my arm and pointed. He swam quickly toward several of the 'gurnards', and they unfolded transparent wings, bright blue colorations on the wingtips, as they swam off into deeper water.

We were tired after the second dive and, rather than stay at the hotel, or on the north shore, for dinner, we headed back to the west side.

Sam had checked us out of the house this morning, and we were packed and ready to get to Christian's house while the housekeeper was still there. We got settled in the guest house, which was quite nice, and headed down to the local brewpub for dinner.

On Friday, we did a two-dive boat trip from the west side, the Kikiaoloa Harbor being easy walking distance from our rental house ... but we were now staying several miles away, up on the plateau.

I really enjoyed these dives. We saw plenty of sea turtles, which were friendly enough to swim up to us. We also saw moray and conger eels, which the divemaster delighted in handling, holding them close to our faces, as they opened and closed their mouths, tiny sharp teeth glistening.

Back on the boat, having refreshments, I logged my deepest dive, yet: 65 feet! Sam and I sat together on the bow, drinking sodas, and enjoying the warm sea breeze and salt air. The rocking of the boat was making me sleepy.

"When we come back here, we can do some dives on the submerged reef off Kalalau. It's really wild; lots of sharks, too. And there's even a good dive outside Na'wili'wili Harbor – loads of eels, octopus, and nudibranchs."

Diving was something Sam really enjoyed. I was glad that I could get my card and share the experience with him.

Our second dive was much shallower, along the coastline, exploring underwater caves, swimming through lava tubes and under arches, and looking for animals. I was getting comfortable with the equipment, and breathing more normally. I had brought the camera down, this time, and took a lot of snapshots.

Back at the dock, we helped carry tanks, wash off the BCs, and grabbed our junk. We were really tired. "Sam, I'm not sure if I can do this four days in a row. That's a lot of diving."

Sam kissed me, "There's only two days left. If you're too tired tomorrow, we can cancel for Sunday. But they'll both be very special days."

Sam was double my age, but had more than double my energy. He offered, "Why don't we stop at a market, buy some steaks, and I can grill them back at the house? I'll make stuffed baked potatoes, and asparagus with brown butter. That should give us energy for tomorrow."

That was a good idea. If Sam had the energy to cook, I would love to crash at the house, and not go out to dinner.

Saturday morning, I was feeling rejuvenated. We had to leave the house early, despite the boat being on the west side. There were three couples, plus the captain, dive master, and cute female assistant.

Heading to the west, the sun behind us, we could barely make out the flat-top island of Niihau, and the conical Lehua Rock to its north. The seas were balmy, which Sam said was very lucky; but the rolling boat was still making my stomach do flip-flops.

It took more than two hours to get there, and we circled Lehua Rock, the boat engine at idle as we rounded the north side, and drifted into a small cove. The dive master pointed, and we saw a pod of more than 40 spinner dolphin, including a lot of babies.

We put on mask, fins, and snorkel, and dropped into the water, watching the graceful performance, the babies sticking by the mothers' sides, as they maneuvered through the water. I took a few snapshots, then climbed back onto the boat. We motored to the south, and anchored between Niihau and Lehua Rock.

The first dive was a 'wall dive', descending up to 100 feet beside a rock and lava wall. As we returned from the dive, I looked behind us, and realized that we were eight – the divemaster, six of us, and a huge monk seal that was tagging along.

The water was crystal clear, being far from the runoff of Kauai and the other populated islands. When we got back to the boat, the divemaster told us that the visibility was more than two hundred feet! Only the Red Sea and a few other isolated spots in the world are better.

While we were eating sandwiches, chips, and fruit, the dive master explained the history of Niihau. It is a private island, owned by the Robinson family, and dedicated to protecting the Hawaiian way of life. Only 100 or so native Hawaiians live on the island, practicing the ancient customs, and speaking the Hawaiian language.

The second dive took us through underwater rock arches, into sea caves, and under a ledge, where we found several sharks. It was tiring, but exhilarating – to be able to fly through the water in three dimensions, visit unexplored places, see animals in a very different habitat. I was getting hooked on SCUBA diving.

The trip back to Kauai was a never-ending pounding into waves – even though it was summer, and the seas were supposedly calm. We were really exhausted when we got back to the house, but showered and dressed, then drove to dinner on the south shore.

As I was sipping the Chardonnay, my fish arrived – it looked fantastic. "Sam, today was a great experience. But maybe we should just relax, tomorrow? How much more can we see?"

Sam laughed, "If we'd seen everything, then we wouldn't have to dive again. But each dive site has its special features. Tomorrow, it will be just the two of us ... with me being the divemaster, and RJ being the captain."

"RJ? That should be fun." There was no way I could forget the character that had taken us on a tour of the Na Pali coast. Sam had met this salty sailor years ago; after our last trip, he had offered his boat to Sam and the nude (or at least, topless) young women with him.

"We'll take it easy – just one deep dive, and one very shallow dive. We'll get an early start tomorrow, and should be finished with our dives and back to Hanalei by early afternoon. And *then* we can rest and recover."

As the wine started to relax me, I decided that if Sam could do it, I could power through the next 18 hours.

RJ really was a character. As soon as he saw us parking by the river at Black Pot park, he strolled over to us, and hugged me tightly, before shaking Sam's hand.

His bare chest was covered with gray hairs, matching the stubble on his face. I'd forgotten how weathered and creased his skin was. And I wondered if that was the scent of alcohol that I was detecting.

The first words out of RJs mouth was 'Where are the other girls?'. Sam laughed, "They're all married off, now. Kelly's the 'old maid' leftover." My flip flops were in my hands, and I took one to Sam's butt, getting in a few good swats before he stepped away.

He grinned at me, and I said, quietly, "And you think you're going to get sex, tonight?" Sam was grinning even more, knowing that I probably wouldn't punish him that way. He evidently had a short memory of his slave experience.

I turned to RJ, then quickly stepped up and kissed him on his stubbled cheek. "Maybe I should give RJ a try? He might be more of a gentleman."

Sam frowned, and told RJ, "Don't touch her. She's my fiancé, now."

RJ raised his eyebrows, and I nodded. "It's true. He proposed in a sea cave at the end of our last trip here." Then, I held his arm, and added, "But Sam and I have an open relationship, so I'm sure he won't mind if we play around a little."

That was too much for both Sam – who began carrying the four tanks and our BCs to the boat, and RJ – who hopped onto the black Zodiac and began stowing things. Within ten minutes, the boat had been backed into the river, and we'd made it over the sand bar and into the bay.

It was a beautiful day, mostly blue sky with some puffy clouds, the water out to sea an incredibly deep blue. I was surprised that RJ made a right turn out of the bay, rather than going down the coast towards Kalalau.

As we cruised by the Princeville Hotel, and the condo we'd stayed at, I undressed and got into the Lycra body suit that Sam had bought for me this morning, when he rented the tanks. He had also bought a shorty wetsuit for himself.

Although I had my suit on under my shorts and top, I took it off and slipped into the Lycra suit nude. RJ hadn't looked back, and I would give him a nice surprise after the first dive.

Sam pointed out Anini Beach, Kalihiwai, and then Secret Beach, as we headed for the Kilauea Lighthouse. The boat slowed, and RJ brought it around, facing North, maybe fifty feet offshore from a small island.

Then, he dropped the anchor, and dived over the side to make sure it was set. The boat rocked on some small waves, but it was pretty calm, no wind, and quickly getting hotter. Especially in the Lycra suit.

Sam pointed, "This is Moku'ae'ae Island, separated from the lighthouse point by a narrow channel. We're anchored in a shallow area, which we'll dive later. But the first dive will be a deep one," Sam smiled, "probably 100 feet. And we should see quite a few neat things."

"A hundred feet? That's almost double the depth I've dived so far."

Sam shrugged, "It's really no different when you're deeper. Except we'll have to keep an eye on the dive computers, and have a dive plan where we do the deep part first, and then slowly explore the shallower depths, as nitrogen comes out of our blood.

"As you learned in the class, what you *don't* want to do is come up quickly, where bubbles can form, giving you the bends. I've only been 'bent' once, but it was scary."

We hooked up the BCs and regulators to the tanks, and Sam helped me on with my rig. I was too hot to stay on the boat, so Sam let me get into the water – sitting on the tube, and leaning back, until I did a backflip. He told me to swim to the anchor line and hold onto it.

I put air into my BC so that I was floating on the surface, and breathed through my snorkel, as I kicked my fins, and headed to the bow of the Zodiac. The leash for my camera was around my wrist, and I took a quick snapshot of the Zodiac, with Sam putting on his BC and tank.

I found the anchor line and held on, looking around with my head just under the water. It was very clear, perhaps eighty foot visibility. Not nearly as good as Niihau, but much better than the south shore.

Sam swam up to me, and he signaled to descend and stabilize my depth. Then, we swam slowly, hand-in-hand, until the ledge dropped off into deeper water. We followed the rocks down, and Sam squeezed my hand excitedly. He pointed out a lion fish, it's poisonous spines just waiting for an unwary fish – or diver.

As we'd learned in the class, I tried to look around, as well as up and down. Glancing to the right, there was a beautiful silhouette of the rocks above us, crystal clear blue water above, the sun's rays emanating from the highest rock. I aimed my camera, moving it a little to the left to balance the shot.

Then, I saw it: A *very* large shark, swimming near the surface, in our direction. I snapped the picture and turned to Sam; but he was twenty feet farther out, and ten feet farther down. I didn't have anything – except my camera – to bang on the tank, and I didn't want to wreck the camera.

So I swam down to Sam, pulling his arm, and pointing above us. My grabbing his arm startled him, and I had to remember to stay calm, myself – the most important thing in diving.

The shark was still swimming toward shore, then veered off to our right, and out of sight. Sam smiled through his regulator and gave me the 'OK' sign. I returned it, glad that the shark hadn't shown interest in us.

Sam led me down, and I kept a good eye on both the depth gauge and dive computer, as we descended below 50 feet, then 60, 70, 80. I shrugged at Sam, and he pointed down. We spiraled down, to our left, along the rock wall that formed the drop-off from the shallow ledge where the boat was anchored.

Pointing again, Sam swam slowly forward ... into a large sea cave. The back of the cave was only about twenty feet from us, and there seemed to be nothing much of interest, except some large, rounded boulders dotting the sandy bottom inside the cave. I shrugged.

Then, Sam hovered next to one of the boulders, and put his hand on it. Oh my! The 'boulder' turned out to be a gigantic sea turtle. It must have weighed several hundred pounds. I realized that all the other boulders were also sea turtles, but Sam led us back out of the cave, so we didn't disturb more of them.

We practiced ascending – slower than our bubbles, and hanging out at various depths along the wall, where we saw an eel, and some nudibranchs. I was getting better at recognizing the sea life that was so well camouflaged. I snapped a few pictures, as Sam held his dive light on some of the interesting creatures.

Finally reaching the shallow ledge, which was about 20 feet down, Sam pointed, and I saw the dark shape of the boat. RJ threw a line over, which we held onto, as we took off our BCs and tanks, handing them up to RJ. Then, we pulled ourselves onto the tubes, and made a not-so-graceful entry into the boat.

Now, I sounded like Julie and Linda, as I told RJ what we had seen. It had certainly been one of the best dives I'd done, so far. And it had only been an easy twenty minute boat ride, not a 2-3 hour slog.

Sam thought the shark was an 'oceanic gray', about ten feet long. But it had looked more like 15 feet, to me.

RJ gave us sodas, and I unzipped the top of my suit … down to my navel. He ogled me, as expected, then chuckled, and got his lure box from inside the console. I remembered that lure box, even before he pulled out a joint and lighter.

"But, Sam, we're going to do another dive. And our instructor was adamant about us not having alcohol or drugs before we dove."

Sam shrugged, "You don't have to turn on, if you don't want to." Then he laughed, "And our second dive won't be much more than a snorkel; our maximum depth will probably be less than twenty feet."

That reminded me to check the dive computer and my depth gauge. Our first dive had a maximum depth of 105 feet! And our 'bottom time' was an incredible 40 minutes.

That's basically impossible, according to the dive tables; but modern dive computers enabled short deep excursions, using all the rest of the dive time to get the nitrogen out of your blood. And all we'd had to do was hang out at a few shallower depths as we ascended.

RJ offered us some cookies, and I took one, and asked if I could do some nude sunbathing. RJ nearly choked on his cookie, he was laughing so hard.

As I unzipped the thin Lycra suit and stepped out of it totally nude, RJ told Sam, "Well, Sammy, if you keep bringing beautiful girls, I'm *happy* to take you out on the boat." I gave RJ a smile, and lay on my back on the black rubber tube of the inflatable.

The sun was scorching, and when I thought I heard my skin sizzling, I turned over onto my stomach. The tube was warm, and the boat was rocking gently. I could stay here all day and relax.

I was startled when Sam rubbed suntan lotion on my shoulders and backside – from neck to ankles. I might have dozed off for a few moments.

"Are you ready for the next dive?" I squinted up at Sam, and said, "You just put suntan on me. Let me lie here a *little* longer." Then, I asked Sam what time it was; I'd slept for half an hour.

When I heard the hiss of air coming from the fresh air tanks Sam was hooking to the regulators, I got up, and put on my bikini, RJ watching intently.

I didn't want to get suntan lotion inside the suit, but Sam suggested I wear it; we could wash it later. We put on our equipment, and got back into the water. It felt really cold, this time, although it was probably still around 80 degrees. We dropped down to fifteen feet, and swam across the ledge toward the island.

Sam led me around the south end of the island – the side that faced the lighthouse. We went under a narrow rock arch, and Sam shined his light on the ceiling. It was encrusted with lobsters! I thought how excited Linda would have been.

We continued a little farther, and there was a small cave – maybe ten feet wide and deep, and five feet high. Sam put his finger to his lips – be quiet? – and pointed to the back corner of the cave. There was a white-tipped reef shark; I would guess this one might have been four or five feet long. I nodded, and gave Sam the 'OK' sign.

Then, he put up his hand – stay here – and he swam to the other end of the cave, hovered a couple of feet over the sand, and swam slowly into the cave, turning around to face me, now nearly parallel with the shark – and only a few feet away from it! I grabbed my camera, and took several shots, and even a short video.

It had been a lot of trouble – renting the tanks, driving here, hauling them to the boat, and now hauling them back to the car. And it had been exhausting.

But it had also been exciting! I felt like I was a diver. And I could see taking trips with Sam, doing boat dives, having more new experiences together in the future.

We went down to Hanalei with RJ and Sam bought a couple of rounds of drinks. After returning the tanks in Kapaa, we continued to the south side, where we ate dinner at a restaurant situated in a quaint plantation house.

When our drinks came, Sam remarked, "So we're finishing another trip. This one was different."

I nodded; they were *all* very different. "Kathy is now married, and my friends and I have our C-cards." I looked seductively at Sam over the rim of my glass, "And I feel like I'm a real diver, after doing ten dives in the past five days."

Sam smiled, "You *are* a 'real' diver. And you did great on all the dives. I just hope you enjoyed it."

"Of course. I've been thinking about all the places you said we should dive. If we ever get the time."

We would be flying home tomorrow, and had to get back into the swing of working. We had a lot of work to do to get ready for the Barcelona show, where we hoped to raise money and generate interest among the pharma companies. I would be presenting a technical paper, the first for me at a major conference.

Back at Christian's guest house, we packed and Sam smoked a joint that RJ had given him. Then we took advantage of the redwood hot tub.

I let my mind drift, as memories from the trip rolled through my head – Sam's bare pubes and Christian's well-endowed manhood; Kathy's beautiful wedding, and her funny parents; our dive class, where we mercilessly teased the instructor; and the incredible dives we'd done in the past few days.

Sam hugged me, and I briefly thought about our own wedding ... then work filled my brain. We had to hire a staff, finish the prototype, test it, and show up in Barcelona with something to sell. I was exhausted, already.

CHAPTER 12: DESIGNING WOMEN

It seemed like a whirlwind – time was flying by too quickly. There had been distractions, such as Linda's birthday and my birthday, and now our trip to Barcelona was only six weeks away.

We just didn't have the manpower – or womanpower – that we needed. Sam had suggested that we hire Linda as an 'office manager', if she was interested in helping us. And I still had Amy, Caitlin, and Jeremy working on the project at the university.

At this stage, it made sense to move the prototype and staff to Sam's house. Raj gave his approval, and we made offers of part-time work, and cleared out the pool room – which mainly entailed Sam disassembling the double spanking bench and storing it in the garage.

Sam bought four used desks and two lab benches, based on a sketch I'd made of the room layout. It would be a tight fit. Hopefully, we could move into real facilities after we returned from Barcelona; if we were successful.

It was the middle of the summer, now, and we decided to leave the pool room's vertical blinds closed, covering the sliding doors to the pool, and keep the air conditioning on.

Sam had wanted the 'employees' to use the sliding door, coming around the garage and through the backyard. But it was easier just letting them come through the living room, dining room, and kitchen. It wasn't an ideal set-up.

I was a little surprised when Linda accepted our offer, enthusiastically. She said she had great faith in my abilities, and would have fun working with us. She also reminded me that I had given her 0.5% of the company, so she was extra-motivated to help us make it a success.

Linda's first assignment was to arrange our travel; but Sam spent so much time with her, guiding her on his preferences, airline and hotel clubs, and other factors, it probably would have been quicker for Sam to do it himself.

It took a full week for Amy, Caitlin, Jeremy and I to move all the equipment to the house. There was a lot more test equipment required, and we had to sign our lives away – to the tune of $85,000 to the university – to borrow the equipment.

I submitted the 'abstract' of the paper I would present in Barcelona, introducing the world to my new technology. And Raj, being the program chairman, put my presentation in one of the plenary sessions, as 'Featured Research'.

Of course, he would have to disclose his financial interest in the company. But it could be a breakthrough technology, and it would be he and his student that had developed it.

We established working hours, Linda set up the books, and we bought a small fridge to put in the pool room, for drinks and lunches. At this point, we were all using our laptops; but Sam was prepared to buy computers, and set-up a more sophisticated network, if it was needed.

It was only a week later, when I walked into the pool room and caught Amy peeking out of the verticals and giggling. She jumped when she heard me step over to her, and I looked outside: Sam was climbing out of the pool, nude, and walking to the jacuzzi.

Caitlin and Jeremy were there, and had certainly seen Amy peeking through the blinds. I had no idea if they had also peeked, and seen Sam nude.

I called the team together. "Amy, I'm sorry if you were offended by seeing Sam nude."

Before I could get another word in, Amy shook her head, "I'm not offended. It was just weird ..."

"Yes. We're a new company. And we don't have funding to move into real facilities, yet. We want to run the business professionally ..." I looked at each of the faces in front of me, "But this is our home. Actually, this is *Sam's* home. I will ask him to be more discrete."

I continued, "We don't think there's anything wrong with nudity. We're not asking to see *your* bodies; but please don't get upset if you see ours." Jeremy was smiling, his hands between his thighs.

I couldn't resist; this could defuse the issue. "Would you guys be interested in coming over here for a company pool party, next weekend? A *nude* pool party?" I held my breath. What I was doing was questionable, and I had no doubt that Sam would be upset.

There was silence in the pool room, only the hum of the air conditioning providing background noise. Amy and Caitlin looked at each other and shrugged.

I looked at Jeremy, but spoke to all of them. "This is certainly *not* a requirement for working here. We won't judge you if you don't want to participate. It just might be a way for us to loosen up, get to know each other."

The girls were nodding, and Jeremy was looking down into his lap. I told him, "We do not equate nudity with sex. All I want is for us to accept each other – our brains and our bodies, with all the flaws of each, and appreciate each other, for our unique characteristics.

"Anyway, please think about it. If you guys don't want to do it, we won't. But please don't ogle Sam, if he's doing *his* thing." I thought about speaking with Jeremy separately, but would give him the benefit of the doubt.

When I informed Sam of the plan, he was quite upset, as I had expected. "You can't do that, Kelly. That's crazy, and probably against all kinds of employment laws. We could get sued for sexual harassment." Sam was getting really worked up. "We need to run the company professionally, separate from our private lives."

I nodded, "Yes, but the company is in our house. And one – or more – of our employees saw you nude in the yard. *That* would probably count as sexual harassment."

That was ridiculous. We'd had the blinds closed, and nobody could see anything, unless they tried ... and if they weren't working, as we were paying them to do.

I realized it was a little more complicated. I shouldn't have gone in the pool. But it was the middle of summer, and I was supposed to be – mostly – retired. And Kelly's team was here, in our house, almost all the time.

We could start looking for an industrial site to move the company; but it would cost several thousand dollars per month, and I was essentially funding the operation out of my own pocket.

The solution was simple: I just wouldn't go nude while they were here. But, now, Kelly had invited them for a nude pool party! "You don't even *know* them! They could have deep religious or moral beliefs ..."

Kelly shook her head, "I *do* know them, Sam. I've worked with them for over a year, now. Except Jeremy; he's younger, and more introverted, kind of shy."

Kelly smiled, lasciviously, "And if he gets turned on, I'll just have to get him turned off again." She quickly added, "Not in *that* way ... but by talking to him." I didn't think 'talking' would change the sexual desires of a red-blooded, college-age American male.

We had to run the company professionally. But we had no employees, only part-time contractors, all three from the university, and Kelly trusted them. Still, Kelly had to differentiate between her friends and her *business associates*. Linda presented the only challenge, as she was both a friend and, now, working for our company.

"Kelly, this is about our future: We have to treat our employees – and consultants – with dignity and respect. And we don't want to make them uncomfortable. KS Biotech should provide a welcoming environment, a trusting environment."

There wasn't much more I could say. "Why don't we cancel the pool party, and tell your staff that I won't be going nude in the pool anymore. That was the genesis of the problem ... and I apologize. I probably shouldn't have gone nude, and will agree that while our staff is here, this is a business establishment."

Kelly hugged me, "Yes, Sam, you triggered the issue. But it *is* your house, and I think the only disrespectful thing was Amy peeking through the blinds." After giving me a peck on the lips, she continued, "These are my friends, as well as my colleagues. Let's have the party, and adjust it so that everyone is comfortable."

I didn't know if that was possible. But KS Biotech was Kelly's company, and all I could do was advise her. I could always go visit my son and new grandson ... and let KS Biotech have the house for the summer.

We'd made a lot of progress during the week, and we would have our little party today. Although Sam disagreed with my approach, he reluctantly got everything ready – washing the patio furniture, marketing, making macaroni salad and coleslaw, and now getting the grill ready for hamburgers and sausages.

We were now fully moved in to the pool room, and the team was working together well. Although the engineering we were doing did not require Raj's help, I felt a little bad for not inviting him, if this was going to be a KS Biotech 'company' party.

But I didn't think he would appreciate the social pressure to go nude, and it might put him in an uncomfortable – or even legally dangerous – position with Amy and Caitlin, who were still his students. And Sam would have probably gone ballistic, if I had asked Raj to join us.

Anyway, I looked at this as a 'team' party; we'd all been working together on the project for a long time. Even Jeremy had been helping us with packaging concepts and electronics design for the past six months. And I didn't think that my college classmates would have a problem with skinny-dipping on a beautiful, hot summer day.

Around 1PM, everyone arrived, and we ushered them to the backyard, where Sam put out some appetizers, and big pitchers of lemonade and iced tea. We did have beers and wines available, and would probably offer those with dinner; but Sam was still nervous about the company sponsoring a party – especially one with alcohol.

We were all in shorts and tees, except Sam and Jeremy, who wore tanks. It was funny seeing Sam in his running shorts, alongside Jeremy in his surf trunks. I would have to work on Sam to bring his 'style' up to date.

When we were all seated around the small, glass patio table, and had taken some food and poured our drinks, Sam stood. I really hoped he wasn't going to embarrass me and get too hyper about the 'PC' issue ... or non-issue.

"Welcome to the first KS Biotech pool party." Under his breath – loud enough for all of us to hear – he added, "And possibly the last." I frowned at him, but he persisted.

"I apologize having started all this by skinny-dipping while you were working. I didn't mean to offend anybody."

"You didn't offend anyone, Sam," Amy said.

Sam continued, "It would be great if we could all be casual, spend some social time together, be friends. And, like Kelly has told you, we don't consider nudity a big deal. You certainly don't *have* to go nude today; and if you object, *we* won't go nude today."

Taking a big breath, Sam continued, "You guys are employees ... or contractors; we can also be friends, but the company must come first. So, we want to treat you right. We don't want any hint of sexual harassment, or forcing our ethics and morals on you.

"We just want to get the product developed, and be able to fund the company, so we can be successful." Sam sighed, and hung his head. I appreciated what he'd said, but there really was no problem. It was something that he'd perceived as a problem, when nobody else had.

That was enough. Sam had had his say. I stood and announced, "I'm hot." It was quite warm, today. I pulled down my shorts, and took off my top, then walked casually to the pool, and climbed down the steps into the water.

I didn't look back – either literally or figuratively. Floating on my back, looking up at the crystal blue sky, I tried to relax. It was a lot of pressure, getting ready for our make-or-break chance in Barcelona. Within a few minutes, I could see others in my peripheral vision.

My little speech had been serious, but now it seemed pedantic, as the girls – and Jeremy – stripped down, and got into the water. I went into the house and grabbed a beer, finishing half of it before leaving it on the counter and joining everyone outside.

It wasn't really a matter of nudity. We all had bodies, and we all knew what the other sex looked like. But we had to run KS Biotech as an ethical business. I guess it might not be considered 'sexual harassment', if nobody felt harassed ...

I took off my tank and running shorts and dove into the pool, then swam over to Kelly, who was floating on her back with her eyes closed.

She opened one eye at me, and said, "Just relax, Sam. Try to have fun. My team has a lot of work to get done in the next few weeks. Let's let them unwind and have a good time at the party."

I tried to relax, and it did seem as though everyone was happy. Linda arrived and joined us in the pool, and helped me get the dinner ready. Everyone wore something when they were out of the pool – even if it was just a towel wrapped around the waist.

Amy was as tall as Kelly, and very trim, with relatively small breasts, and short, dark-brown hair. Caitlin was shorter and more rounded – similar to Linda before she lost weight; her hair was a sandy blonde and came down below her shoulders. She was cute, and had a very nice 'spanking bottom'.

Jeremy was a strapping college kid, tall and slender, with a scraggly light-brown beard, and disheveled hair. He seemed like a nice guy, although we hadn't had the chance to talk about much except the project.

I guess Kelly had been right, and we hadn't had to be too concerned about our skinny-dipping pool party. Everyone got along well, and I think they enjoyed the informal dinner and wine that I served.

Kelly had spent time with each of her staff, and it appeared that she'd built a cohesive team. We still had to bring a couple more people on-board, to finalize the human interface design and complete the validation and verification ('V&V') of the software, but I was impressed with Kelly's management skills ... so far.

It was only a couple of weeks later that I had my doubts, again.

My team was working hard but, with our deadline looming, I was getting nervous. We had hired another two engineers – both women, who had been recommended to Raj by the engineering school of the university. One was a software engineer, and the other was a human interface engineer, both still taking graduate classes.

Although I was pretty strict about working hours, I instituted a 'casual Friday' policy, allowing lounging by the pool – with or without suits. As most of my staff were working nearly full-time, now, this was appreciated. And we actually had some good technical discussions, sitting around the pool.

The problem began when Amy came to me excitedly, and showed me a Facebook page; it was Caitlin's Facebook page. And it showed a picture of Caitlin and Jeremy, both nude, Jeremy facing away from the camera, hugging our prototype system (or 'humping' it), and Caitlin – facing the camera – pulling Jeremy's head toward her and kissing him.

It would have been a cute picture – and I saw a resemblance to some of the sexy European perfume advertisements. But I was not amused: The KS Biotech logo on the system was clearly visible, and Caitlin had posted the photo publicly.

Sam and I were trying to keep our system 'under wraps', until after my talk in Barcelona. We were planning to show it to our invited guests – mainly pharma and biotech companies – in a hotel suite. But even showing the size of the system could potentially hurt us, if a competitor saw the image.

Not only had Caitlin broken her confidentiality agreement, but Caitlin and Jeremy had mocked our company and the system. It would be embarrassing if the post somehow went viral, and was seen by people in the biotech field. I had to take swift action.

Sam had finally decided to visit Robert and Jessica, and his grandson, who was now turning one. I felt a little guilty that I wasn't visiting them with Sam, but we were down to the wire on finishing the prototype in time to ship it to Barcelona for the demos.

Everyone had now arrived, and begun working. Linda would manage things, while I asked Caitlin and Jeremy to come downstairs with me. I led them to the office area, and they took the two seats in front of the desk, while I sat in the executive chair.

I leaned forward, and put my elbows on the desk and chin in my hands. Looking at each of them in turn, Caitlin finally broke. She whispered to Jeremy, "She's seen it." Jeremy looked at the ceiling, and started unconsciously stomping his right foot.

"Do you need to pee, Jeremy?" I asked, realizing that I already had an acidic tone.

"No, Ma'am." The foot-stomping ceased.

Looking at Caitlin, I nodded, "Yes, I've seen it. If you had hidden the KS Biotech logo, it might almost have been OK. But if a competitor wanted, they could search on LinkedIn, or through the university, and probably find that you guys worked for the company.

"This is very embarrassing. Not only have you guys breached your non-disclosure agreements," both Jeremy and Caitlin shrunk down in their chairs, "but you've mocked the company and our new system, and may have embarrassed me at the university, and throughout the field." Now, they were both looking into their laps.

Finally, Caitlin looked up at me and said, pleadingly, "We're sorry, Kelly. We were just playing around, and thought it would be fun. We didn't mean any harm."

"I know you didn't ... but this was a very serious offense." I leaned back in my chair, thinking how this should proceed. Armed with Sam's openness, I decided to go through my reasoning with the two sad figures in front of me.

"Under normal circumstances, I would probably fire both of you. We need honest and reliable people here. And, if you would like to terminate your consulting contract, you may do so. I won't press charges, but I also won't give a recommendation to any future employers."

I looked at them, and shook my head, "You *know*, if a competitor actually used that image against us, we could sue you for thousands of dollars, and would end-up attaching your wages for years."

Trying to calm down, I offered, "But maybe there's another way to punish you guys for this." Now, they were both fidgeting, Jeremy wringing his hands, and Caitlin biting her nails. "We could dock your wages ... maybe $1000?" Both of them looked up at me, and their mouths fell open.

"At $100/week, that would take ten weeks." They were only making $300-400/week, so that would be a big fraction of their income. The problem was that we only had a month before the prototype had to be shipped; I couldn't guarantee ten weeks more of consulting projects.

"But, if we target 4 weeks, when we leave for Barcelona, we would have to deduct $250 per week from your consulting payments."

Caitlin ventured, "Kelly, this is my only job. I'm paying my own way through school, and have to pay for an apartment." Her voice cracked, and her eyes were glassy with tears.

I shrugged, "You should have thought of that when you decided to mock the company ... and then post it *publicly*." My mind reeled as I wondered who in the world had already seen the post. We sat silently for a couple of uncomfortable minutes.

"Please remove that post immediately." Caitlin nodded and sat there. "I mean *now*!" She pulled out her phone, and hit a few keys, then nodded and put her phone away, and clasped her hands in her lap.

"I like you guys, and you've done a good job, so far. But I'm going to have to punish you in some way. And, as the rest of the company is already aware of this, I would like to set an example, so nobody else jeopardizes this company with something so stupid."

Sam would kill me for what I was thinking. But it really was the expedient solution. I closed my eyes, and counted to ten, trying to calm myself. When I opened my eyes, both Caitlin and Jeremy were looking at me.

I asked, "Who came up with this hair-brained idea?"

Jeremy looked at Caitlin, and she timidly raised her hand, then quickly put it into her lap.

"Can you guys think of any other way that I could punish you? And set an example?" I exhaled loudly. Sam would be upset, but the answer seemed simple enough.

When Caitlin and Jeremy shook their heads, I shrugged, "The only other kind of punishment I can think of is not allowed; that's *corporal* punishment."

Caitlin and Jeremy both looked up and, after a few seconds, their mouths were hanging open again.

I nodded, "You would have to request it, and sign a release, admitting to the offense, and indemnifying me and the company against any liabilities." Maybe I shouldn't have been working this out aloud?

I stood and shook my head, "That's ridiculous. I'll let you quit or we'll dock your pay and put you on probation."

Caitlin cried, "Please, Kelly. We'd rather take the corporal punishment, whatever that is." She looked at Jeremy, and he shrugged and nodded.

Sitting back down, I leaned forward and spoke softly, "*If* I agree to this, it would be a hard spanking of some type – probably a strapping, paddling, or caning – on your bare bottoms."

I looked at two neutral expressions in front of me, and continued, "If you want the punishment to be private, I would suggest 100 strokes of the strap (I was thinking of using the tawse) over your jeans ... or 50 strokes on your underwear, or 25 on the bare.

"And, if you will take your punishment in front of the other staff, to set an example, I'll reduce it to 75 strokes over your jeans, or 18 strokes on your bare bottom."

Then, I looked at Caitlin, "And, for *posting* it, I will also give you six hard swats with the school paddle on your jeans, or three on the bare." I couldn't believe I'd offered this. Sam would kill me. But it *was* a practical solution, if not culturally accepted ... and ethically questionable.

"We've all been nude together ... but if you insist, I can give you the punishment over your jeans." I chuckled, "My arm will be sore, afterward."

I shook my head again, "I really can't ask you to take a corporal punishment; I think docking your pay would be the most acceptable solution." I sat back in the executive chair, "What do you think?" I had been recording the entire conversation, but knew that wouldn't be of much use, if Caitlin and/or Jeremy decided to sue us.

Caitlin and Jeremy whispered to each other, then Caitlin sat up straight, and said, "OK, Kelly. We'll take the corporal punishment ... in front of the others ... and on the bare."

It was incredible that it had come to this. I would edit one of Sam's 'agreements' and have Caitlin and Jeremy sign it, admitting to their offense, and accepting the decision to take a corporal punishment.

"OK. Get back to work. I'll come up in a while and call your names. You will come forward, and sign the agreement I prepare, then do as I say. If you cooperate, we can be done in ten minutes, and you guys will have a sore bottom, but we can get back to work ... and hopefully never have something like this happen again."

Caitlin and Jeremy were nodding cautiously. Then, they went back upstairs. I pulled one of the agreements that Sam had written, edited it, and printed two copies. Then, I selected the 24-inch leather tawse, and the school paddle, and went upstairs to the pool room.

I handed Linda, who was sitting at the large desk, an iPad with Caitlin's Facebook page. She glanced at it, then put her hand over her mouth, and looked up at me, her eyebrows raised as high as I'd ever seen them. I nodded.

As I placed a bath towel horizontally at the front edge of the desk, and straightened it, Linda looked at me with large eyes; she had already figured out where this was going.

Then I addressed my staff, "May I have your attention, please?" Everyone looked up from her desk or lab table ... except Caitlin and Jeremy. I knew that they hadn't meant to harm the company, but their actions were inexcusable; hopefully, I could use them to deter any further incidents.

"Most of you have probably seen the picture that Caitlin posted this morning – of she and Jeremy nude, in front of our prototype ... with the KS Biotech logo prominently visible."

I took a deep breath, "As I explained to Caitlin and Jeremy, that was a breach of their confidentiality agreement, and could seriously jeopardize our success. I know they didn't *intend* to harm the business, but they also didn't *think* about it.

"Now that they understand how serious this is, and as a way to set an example for the rest of you, they have agreed to be punished." The room was silent, but I had everyone's full attention.

"We discussed several possibilities: We could terminate their consulting contracts, or sue them for breach of fiduciary duties, or dock their pay. But for expediency, they have agreed to take a corporal punishment." There were several gasps, and a lot of wide eyes were staring at me.

I nodded, "Caitlin and Jeremy, please come to the front of the room." They got up and sheepishly approached me. "Please stand in front of the desk, facing your coworkers, feet apart, hands on head." They did so, the room silently anticipating what would happen next.

"Caitlin, would you please tell us, in your own words, what you did, why it was wrong, and why you would prefer to take a corporal punishment."

She was nearly in tears, as she pleaded to the team, "I'm really sorry. It was just supposed to be a joke. I didn't mean to hurt the company. I understand now that this could result in competitors finding out about our system, and could be embarrassing for Kelly and the company."

Nervously, shifting her weight from foot to foot, she added, "And I would much rather get spanked than be fired or lose pay. Jeremy and I would like to get this over with, so we can be on good terms with Kelly, and get back to work. I need the job and the money."

"Jeremy?" I wanted both of them to make a statement, so there was no confusion or argument later.

He shrugged, "I guess I'd rather take a lickin' than any of the alternatives." He cracked a smile, "I haven't been spanked for a long time, but that was the normal way I was punished at home. Not fun; but it's over quickly."

I turned to the three women still at their desks, "Do you have any questions or comments?"

After a moment of silence, Amy asked, "Does that mean that *we* will get spanked, if we do something wrong?"

Chuckling, I responded, "This doesn't mean anything for the future; it's a special case. I cannot make anyone take a corporal punishment, and was reluctant to suggest it in this case ... but it seemed to be the quickest way to make an impression on Caitlin and Jeremy, while setting an example for the rest of the team.

"And, I certainly *hope* that none of you pull something this stupid. We can play around when we're taking a break out at the pool, but please show respect for the company; I expect you to be serious and working hard when you're here. And *not* doing anything that might harm the system, the company, or other members of the team."

I hadn't meant to give such a long speech. Turning to Caitlin and Jeremy, I instructed, "Please turn around, drop your pants and underwear, and bend over the desk." They slowly complied and I stepped to the side of the desk. I whispered, "Please put your feet apart as far as your jeans will allow."

Then, I put the agreements in front of them, along with a couple of pens. They briefly read the one-page documents, and signed them, and I collected everything, and put it in the second drawer of the desk, from which I pulled out a couple of Velcro straps.

Handing them to Linda, I instructed, "Please lower yourselves onto the desk, your chests flat on the wood, and put your hands together in front of you." They did so, and Linda wrapped the Velcro around their wrists.

There was no intention to torture or torment my charges, only to administer a quick and fair punishment. I lifted the tawse, and held it up, so Caitlin, Jeremy, and the others could see it. "We will begin with 18 strokes of this leather strap for each of them."

I stepped in front of the desk, and positioned myself to the side of Caitlin, who was on the right, facing Linda and the blackboard. Placing the tawse across her rounded butt, I quickly pulled it back, and let it fly, flicking my wrist, as my dad had taught me in various sports.

"Ow!" Caitlin's body jerked, and she whimpered, but stayed in position.

Stepping back, I let the tawse fly again this time impacting Jeremy's lean butt. He grunted, then also whimpered. Aiming a bit lower, I cracked the leather into his butt again, and he howled.

Moving back to Caitlin, I administered three hard strokes. There were shrieks, and 'Ow!'s, and shuddering of her body, but Caitlin took her punishment well.

Now, I moved to Jeremy again, and gave him four hard lashes with the strap. His response was virtually the same as Caitlin's, and he was now crying softly, and taking racking breaths. I rubbed his bottom quickly, then returned to Caitlin.

When I carefully placed the tawse across the middle of her bum, her body shivered. I proceeded to dispense strokes of the two-tailed leather implement, giving her five more, over about half a minute. Now, she was crying; more like wailing. But still not complaining.

I was proud of my engineers; they had shown remorse, and were taking their punishments well. It was now that I realized that the rest of the room was silent. In fact, it felt like no one was breathing.

I rubbed Caitlin's bottom for a few moments, and she sobbed quietly. Then, I moved back to Jeremy, and gave him six even harder strokes – about as hard as I could muster. My arm *was* getting tired!

Jeremy was nearly blubbering. I pointed to the Kleenex box on the side of the desk, and Linda pulled a few tissues, and put them into the hands of the punishees.

As I stepped to Caitlin, she moaned; it wasn't exactly a complaint, but I knew that she was dreading what was to come in a few moments. I unleashed the hardest tawsing that I had ever given, seven strokes on her bare bottom in less than a minute.

Caitlin was wailing so loud, I considered using a ball gag, but we were almost done. I gave Jeremy six stinging strokes, and he wailed. Then, I stepped back to Caitlin, and gave her two searing smacks of the tawse on her rear. She yelped both times, but never moved.

I put the tawse down on the desk, and addressed the room. "I hope Caitlin and Jeremy, and the rest of you, have learned that I won't tolerate anything that could hurt the company."

With that, I leaned over to Jeremy, and said, "Please stand in front of the blackboard." Linda undid the Velcro, and Jeremy shuffled to the blackboard, and put his hands on his head. His butt was a dull red, as was Caitlin's.

But I was not finished with Caitlin. I picked up the school paddle – six inches wide, and 18 inches long, solid wood – and announced, "Now, I will punish Caitlin for coming up with this stupid idea, and actually posting pictures on the Internet."

I stood to the left side of Caitlin, and laid the paddle across her butt. She exhaled, and I said softly, "You will receive three hard swats. And you must stay in position."

This was supposed to set an example, so I decided to not be easy on Caitlin. I swung the paddle, using all my strength, knowledge, and practice. 'CRAACK!' It sounded like a gunshot. A moment later, Caitlin screamed.

Sliding the paddle back and forth across her bum, I took my time; I lowered the paddle slightly, then pulled it back. After holding the paddle in position for a couple of seconds, I guided it in an accelerating arc to the lower part of Caitlin's rear. There was another gunshot sound.

Rubbing her rear, I could feel a raised area, and the heat generated by her reddened bum. I walked back and forth behind her a couple of times, then took my position, placed the paddle across her bottom, then pulled it back, letting it immediately fly through it's upward path, and impacting Caitlin's butt with one more echoing gunshot.

Caitlin was crying now, but I gave her credit for holding her position. Then, I saw that Linda had been holding the Velcro wrist strap, keeping her in place.

I put the paddle on the desk, and asked Caitlin to stand next to Jeremy, facing the blackboard. There were two very sore rears now on display. Caitlin's had some circular white areas, surrounded by much darker tissue;

she would undoubtedly have black-and-blue marks tomorrow.

"Hopefully, Caitlin and Jeremy have learned their lesson – and there won't be anymore funny business – and *certainly* no more posts, involving KS Biotech. I thank them for taking their punishment cooperatively. Let's all move on, and get back to work."

Turning to Caitlin and Jeremy, I said, quietly, "You may pull up your pants, and go back to your desks, now." They returned to their seats, and I suddenly felt very tired. I looked at Linda, and we nodded at each other, neither of us smiling. I went into the kitchen, and poured a tall glass of iced tea, then drank it in a few seconds.

Going down to the playroom, I decided to lay on the couch. My head was splitting, and I felt weak. I closed my eyes, and tried to relax ... but felt like crying. As I wished that Sam were here, I did cry, the emotions of the day, and of the entire summer, finally breaking through to my core.

CHAPTER 13: BARCELONA BEAUTY

The system had passed its operational testing – although whether it actually would enable new drugs to be identified remained to be demonstrated. But all of the elements of the system were in place, the packaging looked nice, and the human interface was novel, practical, and well done.

I hoped the science behind my methodology actually worked, but there appeared nothing now to indicate otherwise. My paper had been submitted, a Powerpoint presentation completed, and our travel arrangements made. We would only be visiting Barcelona on this trip, as it was a make-or-break opportunity for our business.

Linda had arranged for a shipping company to crate the prototype and transport it to Spain. Although Sam had wanted to stay in the old and quaint part of town, we would be hosting a hospitality suite at the hotel adjoining the convention center, so it was most practical for us to stay there.

It would have normally been too late to secure a room at the posh hotel, but there was a block of rooms reserved for invited speakers, and Raj pulled some strings. Sam had gotten us business class seats, traveling through Heathrow, and hoped that we would be upgraded to first class on the transatlantic segments.

I was still working with Amy and Linda on producing the final documentation, including a User's Manual, a spec sheet, and a short White Paper describing the positive results the system had yielded in our research to date. We would have to get these printed and bound – something Linda would take care of, while I packed for the trip.

Sam had been very busy scheduling meetings with most of the big pharma and biotech companies, including some international players I hadn't heard of, before.

We also sent invitations to selected key opinion leaders, so-called 'KOLs', to visit our hospitality suite and view a demonstration of the prototype. Just meeting and briefly talking to these experts, in combination with my presentation at the conference, would elevate me within the field, and generate interest among both academic institutions, and private companies.

Linda was working with the hotel to arrange catering, including breakfast items, drinks, afternoon appetizers, and desserts. She also coordinated with the A/V manager, so that we had a projector (which Sam told us they called a 'beamer' in Europe), and a screen.

By having a working relationship with the hotel, she was able to provide us with a suite large enough to be our hotel room and the hospitality room for our customers. She showed me some photos, and the beach and sea view looked spectacular.

I gave a practice presentation to Raj, and several more to Sam. There was nothing else to do; we were ready.

––––––––––

We had shipped the equipment, but now had an entire suitcase of product literature, the White Paper – which Linda had prepared, and preprints of Kelly's paper. Hopefully, it would all be given out at the conference, so we wouldn't have to schlep it back home.

We both packed, as usual, with only a carry-on rolling case and a backpack each. We had briefcases inside our packs, and new KS Biotech business cards incorporating a logo that Amy had designed.

As the prototype wouldn't be there, most of Kelly's team could take a break, but Amy, Linda, and a senior consultant we had hired would be working on completing the design history file required for regulatory submissions.

The new school year was starting, and Raj had recruited two grad students to continue the research targeting Lyme disease. Kelly had agreed to mentor them when we returned from Barcelona.

And – most importantly – we had just received a first response from the U.S. Patent Office, allowing most of the claims we had written. This was a major coup, occurring just before the international meeting.

We threw a small Labor Day party, and I smoked some chicken and ribs, made my signature potato salad, and even made a batch of sangria – something I hadn't done since our first trip to Kauai a year ago.

Kelly's team was invited to arrive at noon, and enjoyed a skinny-dip before Raj showed up at 3PM, when we requested that everyone wear a suit. It wasn't about openness or modesty; it was just out of respect for Raj, during the 'official' portion of the party.

When I returned from the visit with my son's family, I had been shocked to learn of Kelly's decision to use corporal punishment on her staff – even if they were just consultants, and not employees.

It was certainly an 'expedient' approach, but just not acceptable in 21st century society, and her concern about a single Internet post had opened the company to potential lawsuits, and a reputation for not respecting our employees.

Kelly agreed in principle, and admitted that she'd been emotionally caught-up in the breach of trust her staff had shown. Hopefully, we would manage these kinds of issues better in the future, if they occurred.

Despite the pressures of the business, and a few minor disagreements, Kelly and I were getting along well together. I attributed this mainly to our respect and love for each other. We could disagree on things, then make a decision with no lingering resentment. Regarding the business, it was Kelly's call, as she was the CEO and majority shareholder.

Incredibly, we'd already been engaged for a year. We planned to celebrate – just the two of us – in Barcelona. Kelly had been right about not rushing into marriage, with everything else we'd had to do. If we were successful in raising money for the company, I was hopeful that we could set a wedding date for next spring.

Our flights were very nice – first class to Heathrow, and European 'business class' (which was similar to first class in the U.S.) to Barcelona. Kelly spent half the time on our trans-Atlantic flight reviewing her presentation, and our marketing pitch, and the other half sleeping.

We took a taxi to our hotel, one of the luxury high-rise buildings near the convention center at the end of the *Avinguda Diagonal* boulevard, overlooking the beach and Mediterranean or, more properly, the 'Balearic Sea'.

The weather was spectacular, and we hadn't even seen a haze of smog, when we'd landed. It was Saturday morning here, so we could relax a little before the conference began on Monday.

Had we not been on a business trip, I would probably have selected a hotel in the old part of town, near the 'Gothic Quarter'. But the view from our room was incredible. As it should be, for the price they charged!

Kelly came bouncing into the bedroom of the large suite, as I gazed out at the view. "Well, the prototype arrived, and it's in the receiving area, so the hotel has to deliver it up here. But I don't know how soon that will be."

It was already late morning, and I wanted to get out and do something. "Let's go for a walk around the town. We can test the system this evening; and we have all day tomorrow." Although I hoped we could do a bit more touring tomorrow, also.

We put on shorts and nice t-shirts, and I carried my backpack – unloaded, and then re-packed with the things we'd want, including a couple of towels, bottles of water from the hotel, bathing suits, and flip flops.

I was glad to be outside and get some exercise, after the long flights. It had been 24 hours since our alarm had gone off at home; but as I'd slept on the plane, I felt energetic. It was hard to believe that this was our third trip to Europe. And just two years ago, I'd never traveled outside the U.S.

Sam led me past the convention center, and onto a walk above the beach. The weather was beautiful, and it was warm, but not hot, as it had been at home.

Looking at his map, Sam said, "I think this is the 'Platja de Llevant'." The beach was more crowded than I'd expected. Sections of the beach appeared to be family oriented, but there were also quite a few women going topless.

Walking farther, we passed the 'Platja de Nova Mar Bella', and Sam pointed, "That is Mar Bella beach." We decided to stop for a beer and snack at one of the 'chiringuitos', a small beach bar where we sat a few feet from the sand.

After our break, we took off our shoes and walked down to the water, and continued south. Near the end of the beach, next to a breakwater, was the 'naturist' section – a nude beach, right at the edge of the city. It was even marked on the tourist map, in yellow.

We found a relatively empty spot, and sat on one of the towels Sam had brought. I debated on whether to go in the water, but finally decided to take advantage of our stop when Sam told me we had another 'few hours' of walking ahead of us.

Sam sat on the towel, while I stripped down and took a quick dip – after tying my hair up, so it wouldn't get wet. There were showers, but I'd have to wear a suit, and get it wet. And Sam had forgotten to pack a plastic bag where we could store wet bathing suits.

Continuing our walk, we followed the waterline to the middle of *'Platja del Bogatell'*, and then went back to the walkway, passing one more beach – *'Platja Nova Icaria'*, before arriving at the *'Port Olimpic'*, where there were dozens of restaurants looking out over the small harbor.

"We'll probably eat at one of these, or one of the nicer restaurants on the beach. One of the main specialties here is *'Paella'*, a saffron-flavored rice dish with seafood ... and in Barcelona, there are all kinds of paella."

Sam chuckled, "Actually, paella comes from Valencia, and we're in Catalonia ... but as seafood is one of Barcelona's specialties, I guess it makes sense."

We continued further south, now on a wide walkway lined with palm trees on one side, and the beach on the other. There was a strange sail-shaped building in the distance, which Sam said was a luxury hotel.

"Those buildings to our right are part of the university, and the biomedical research center." I had probably read papers by some of the researchers, but couldn't recall any names.

As we continued along the beach, it seemed that a lot more of the women were topless, despite the crowds that covered the beach as far as we could see.

"This is the famous '*Barceloneta*' beach. This beach and the other beaches we've seen were 'built' for the 1992 Olympics; they had to import tons of sand from Egypt. This all used to be an industrial area, before government money was invested in the Olympics, and the entire city coastline was redeveloped."

We made a sharp right turn, and walked along a tree-lined boulevard, passing another small boat harbor on our left. We stopped at one of the shops for some ice cream, before continuing on. "How much farther do we have to walk?" I was already starting to get tired.

Sam laughed, "We're not quite halfway through our afternoon tour." He looked at his map, and then around us, and said, "OK. We'll come back to see the aquarium, the Maritime Museum, the Catalonian Museum, and '*Las Ramblas*', the boulevard down the center of which are booths for tourist junk, jewelry, art, and small eateries.

"We'll get a transportation pass, so we can take the tram and subway next time." That sounded good.

We walked by a couple of parks, and then entered the 'Gothic quarter', which was a maze of apartments, restaurants, and shops. Entering a small square, next to a large church, Sam consulted his map. "This is the '*Basilica de Santa Maria del Mar*', a church built in the 14th century. I haven't been inside, before."

It was truly impressive, brick and stone construction, a wide nave, and stained glass windows high on the side walls. There was an old wooden organ suspended on one wall, and a rose window above the doors we'd entered.

Amazingly, there was an English tour starting in a few minutes that would take us down to the crypt, and up to the roof. Sam bought tickets, and we had an interesting tour, only three other couples with us – each from a different country in Europe.

After the tour, we continued our exploration of the ancient streets, which Sam said was called the '*Borne*' neighborhood. I had to pull Sam away from some of the restaurants and bars we passed.

Finally, Sam smiled and pointed, "Here's the Picasso Museum, probably the most-visited museum in the city." It was obvious, by the line of people coming out the door, and along the street.

Sam looked at his watch, "Maybe we should just wait in line; it shouldn't be long. We could show up when they open tomorrow morning, but I'd rather we visit '*La Sagrada Familia*', the famous Gaudi church. We won't get in, unless we hit it first thing in the morning."

It didn't even take ten minutes, and we were in the museum. I didn't know much about Picasso, but enjoyed some of his works.

I was glad I had on my running shoes, as we continued walking, finally exiting the old neighborhood, and entering a large park, the '*Parc de la Ciutedella*'. There were plenty of families with small children and strollers walking along the various paths.

"There's also a zoo here – something else to come back to … if we have time." Now, we strolled along a beautiful walking street, lined with palm trees, and ending in a large arch. Sam informed me, "This is Barcelona's 'Arc de Triomf.'" It was red brick, with dual columns on each side, and much smaller than the one in Paris.

We continued walking along a tree-lined boulevard, the blocks filled with small shops, and several stories of apartments above, each with a small balcony with wrought-iron railing. My feet were getting tired. "Sam, do you know where you're going? Are we actually going to see something, or just keep walking?"

Sam turned to me and took me in his arms, "I'm sorry, Kelly. It seems farther than I remembered. Yes – we're heading toward the '*Sagrada Familia*', Gaudi's famous cathedral ... which has been under construction for the past hundred years.

"But I'm getting tired, too. So why don't we stop at one of these tapas bars? It can be a snack, or our dinner. I'm ready for a beer!" That sounded good.

Within the next block, Sam found a corner bar with outdoor seating. Only a few tables were occupied, and we sat at one with a view of the boulevard, and the people walking by. The waiter came, and we ordered our drinks, then Sam perused the menu.

Sam was smiling, his eyes growing larger, as he read through the two-page list of tapas, and he ordered several dishes when the waiter returned with our beers.

I took a sip of my beer, and sat back in the chair, looking up at the blue sky. It was a beautiful day. We'd flown in first class, and had already seen a lot of Barcelona. Tomorrow, I would have to check out the system, and make sure our hospitality suite was set-up.

The food came, and kept coming. Sam chuckled, "Well, I guess this *might* be our dinner."

Then, he pointed at each dish, and rattled off the names: *patatas bravas*, with an aioli and spicy tomato sauce; *anchoas*, white anchovies with vinegar and parsley; *ensaladilla russa*, a rich combination of potatoes, peas, and eggs thick with mayonnaise; *gambas al* ajillo, shrimp in garlic and white wine; a plate piled high with roasted *padron* peppers; and a bowl with several types of olives.

When I thought that was all, the waiter returned, bringing a plate of *pan con tomate*, and another with *butifarra* sausages and Catalan cheese. Sam smiled at me, as he adjusted the plates on the small table, and I knew that wouldn't be all.

"Aaahh!" Sam exclaimed, as the waiter came a third time placing a plate of Catalan cured ham in the only remaining space on the table.

I just stared at him, "I hope you're hungry!" We dug in, and it was delicious, but there was no way we could finish it all. The ham was unbelievable – I'd never tasted anything like it.

As Sam finished his beer, and signaled the waiter, he said, "Maybe we should have a nice bottle of wine with this ... but we might not be able to walk much further."

Shaking my head, I responded, "I'm not sure how much more I can walk, anyway."

I think Sam took that the wrong way, as he ordered a bottle. When it came, he explained, "This is a Catalonian wine, called 'cava'. It's has relatively low alcohol content, and is made using the *method Champagnoise.*"

Of course, we'd learned about sparkling wines on our trip through the Moselle region. After a sip, I smiled at Sam, "It's really good, especially on a warm afternoon."

He nodded, "The waiter had suggested we try a rosé cava, but it sounded too sweet ... for eating with anchovies and sausages." We were making a pretty good dent in the food; at least, Sam was. I was nearly stuffed, already.

I'd been right: Neither of us felt like walking. Sam said that he'd wanted me to see the outside of the *Sagrada Familia* today, but had actually made a reservation for a tour tomorrow morning. We walked a short distance to the tram, bought a multi-day pass, and took the short ride back to the convention center and our hotel.

There were a lot of skyscrapers with interesting architecture, and a huge shopping mall across the street from our hotel. Sam was already reeling off things we should do and see here; but this was a business trip, and I had to focus on my presentation, the pitches to the biotech companies, and demonstrations of the prototype system.

The suite had a nice bathroom – actually two, if you considered the powder room – and Sam and I took a hot shower together. As I washed him, his manhood grew, and I stroked him with my hands. Then, I took him into my mouth, as the water streamed over my head.

I was tired, and it was easier having 'quickie' sex, than getting in bed and making love, then having to get cleaned up again. Standing, I pressed myself against him, his cock now vertical between our stomachs. We kissed, and when I looked into his eyes, he gave me an imperceptible nod.

Sam stooped a little, as I guided him into me. Then, astonishingly, he lifted me, his hands under my buttocks. I put my arms around him, and tried to support myself to lighten his load.

But, as inebriated as he was, Sam had not only gotten it up, but was able to engage in some strenuous sex. Not exactly what I'd had in mind. But it turned out to be very nice. We finished our shower, dried off, and walked back into the bedroom nude. We had a spectacular water view. Although it was getting darker, it was still early.

But it felt late to us. Sam closed the black-out drapes, and we got into bed together and snuggled. It had been a nice introduction to Barcelona, but a long day since we'd left Sam's house. The room was air conditioned, but our bodies were warm, and the bed was ultra-comfortable.

Within minutes, Sam was snoring softly. Random images from the day flew through my head, and I was out.

We were awake really early. When I pulled the drapes open, the sea view was about as dark as it had been when we went to bed. But we'd slept nearly ten hours.

Kelly was already tinkering with the system, after I'd helped her uncrate it. When I went into the main area of the suite – a 'living room', and dining room with large table that could be used for meetings – the system was on, lights blinking, and a soft hum coming from the corner.

I couldn't help but smile, as I saw Kelly – nude – bent over the system, flipping switches, and typing into the keyboard. When I laughed, she turned to me; I pretended to hold a camera and click a picture. "Would you have to spank me, if I took a sexy picture of you with the system?"

She smiled, "Yes. But if you want to be spanked, you can just ask me." She turned back to working on the system, typing in a few more instructions, while referring to the new operating manual they had written.

It wasn't that I wanted to be spanked; I'd just wanted to take a few pictures. Kelly was still the sexiest woman I'd ever known. Somehow, the incongruity of her curvy body and the high-tech system gave me a hard-on. I hoped we could make love, after she was finished checking-out the system hardware and software.

But this was just too good. I grabbed my phone, and took a few surreptitious shots, before turning on the flash and taking a couple of 'real' photos of Kelly and the system. She swung around to me, "Sam! Be nice. I'm trying to work." That last shot had been great – capturing her, facing me, as her hair flew horizontally over the system.

I put the phone down on the coffee table, and lay on the couch, casually stroking myself

Finally, Kelly came over and put her hands on her hips, "OK, buster, let's have the phone." She was a pretty good actress – she actually sounded serious.

I picked it up and held it to me, then shook my head. She stamped her foot. Grinning, I said, "But, Kelly, I haven't posted anything; they're just for us."

She nodded, unsmiling, "Yeah. Jeremy didn't post anything, either. And he got 18 strokes of the tawse. In front of the whole company." She *did* sound serious.

Standing up, and hugging her, I softened, "But you're so beautiful."

"Give me the phone, Sam." I gave it to her, and she actually erased the photos!

"I don't believe it. You don't *trust* me, now?" I had to chuckle, "Do you know how many tens of thousands of other pictures I have of you?" She knew exactly what I had.

Now, Kelly softened – a little. "Sam, I am highly sensitized to this situation; it's not funny. I'm very nervous about the presentation, and meeting all the key opinion leaders ... then making presentations to the huge companies."

Nodding, I apologized, "I understand, Kelly. I'm sorry. And you can strap me, if you want." I hoped she wouldn't. Then, I ventured, sheepishly, "I'd rather make love to you."

She smiled, "OK, Sam. I've decided." Good. That was a close one; and I'd only been *teasing* Kelly. But the pictures really were good.

Then, she continued, "Please bring me your widest belt." Oh, no! Kelly, the domme, rears her head, and is going to shred my rear. It wasn't funny. Of course, I obeyed, and brought her my heavy leather belt – the one I'd brought to wear with jeans.

I handed it to her and shrugged, "I thought you could just bend over the back of the couch, while I satisfied you."

"Oh you did, did you? How about if *you* bend over the back of the couch?" She laughed, "If we had the strap-on, I might consider that. But I was serious. You're going to bend over, and let me strap you." I must have given her a sour face, as she nodded, folding the belt casually.

"Here's the deal, Sam. I'm going to give you 18 hard strokes of the strap." I couldn't believe my ears; my butt was going to hurt for the rest of the trip. Then, Kelly added, "But, I will only give you two now. Then, we can make love." That sounded good.

Then, monster domme-Kelly smiled, "Then, we're going to go on a short run. And we're going to race. If you can keep up with me, or beat me, I'll forgive and forgo the additional strokes." She gave me an evil look, "But if you fall behind ... your behind is going to get 16 of the hardest strokes I can muster with this wimpy belt."

The belt *wasn't* wimpy ... but I hoped we wouldn't have to find out. Then, Kelly pointed to the back of the couch, and I walked around and bent over. I guess I *would* be finding out. Without discussion or warning, Kelly gave me a very hard stroke of the belt, and then another one.

My bottom was burning, but I stayed in place. "Thank you, Miss." Then, silently, we switched positions, Kelly bending over the couch, and me entering her, taking her roughly, and slapping *her* butt a few times. I reached around and fingered her, and we climaxed nearly together.

We cleaned up, and put on our tanks and running shorts. I figured this would be a short run – only about 3 miles, round-trip, so we wouldn't take a pack or water bottle. I looked at my watch, and was surprised to see it wasn't even 8AM, yet. We would still be able to get to the cathedral when they opened.

Leaving the hotel, after we passed the convention center and reached the beach walk, Kelly explained further. "We're going to run down to the far breakwater of the Mar Bella beach. Then, I'm going to take a quick dip. And then, we'll run back to here." She pointed to a sign, "I'll decide whether you're keeping up, or not. And then I'll decide how much more punishment you need."

Kelly had decided, and I would respect that and submit. After all, I had taunted her ... and had to expect that she might call my bluff. It was obvious that Kelly was under stress – we both were. Not only was this our make-or-break chance for the business, but it would be Kelly's first big presentation at a major conference.

We ran along the nearly-deserted walk, making it to the breakwater in well under fifteen minutes. It was still early, the morning mild, and there were only a handful of people nude on the beach – one middle-aged woman, and the rest men. Kelly took off her tank, sports bra, and running shorts, then handed me her Apple watch.

I sat on the beach and watched, as Kelly swam strongly and confidently away from the beach. She looped around, and swam back, probably taking as long as the run. Then, she put on her clothes and, without discussion, said, "Ready, steady, go!"

My heart went from 60 to 160, as I jumped up and ran after her. We were both running well, these days, and probably had about the same stamina, but Kelly was faster, and could beat me any time she wanted. It was a *déjà vu* moment from our run in Toronto, when *I'd* challenged *her*.

When I could see the concrete pavilion of the convention center, Kelly was only a hundred yards ahead, and I gave it everything I had. I had *nearly* caught up with her by the sign, only a few feet behind her; and ready to throw up.

I collapsed to the ground, sitting, rocking, wheezing. Kelly bent over me, "Are you OK, Sam?" I nodded, and took a few minutes to catch my breath. Then, Kelly gave me a hand and pulled me up, and we walked back to the hotel. I was fine; it had just been that last sprint ...

Sam had pushed himself. Well, I guess *I* had pushed him; perhaps too hard. But there would have to be one more little tease, before I'd let him off the hook.

When we got into the room, I commanded, "I want you undressed, in the standing position, holding the belt, ready to present it to me for your punishment." Sam started to give me a 'look', but looked down and nodded.

After I'd taken my soaked clothes off and peed, I went back into the living room, where Sam was dutifully in position. I took the belt, folded it over, then pointed to the back of the couch. Again, Sam *started* to say something, but just exhaled, turned around, and bent over.

I put the belt on his sweaty butt and held it there. Then I quickly pulled it back ... and walked around to the other side; I spoke softly to him.

"I appreciate you trying, Sam. I won't punish you. But please don't take any more pictures like that, or joke around. We need to focus and be serious."

Sam nodded, and looked like he was going to cry. "I'm sorry Kelly. You're absolutely right. I guess I was trying to keep it humorous, relaxed."

Shaking my head, I admitted, "I don't feel very relaxed, right now. Maybe, after my presentation. And maybe not until we're back home." Sam nodded and held me, our sweaty bodies merging.

We took the tram, and then walked to the *Sagrada Familia*, which I'd yet to see (although I'd seen pictures on the maps and tourist brochures). There was *still* a line, even on a Sunday morning. But with our reserved tickets, we could get into a much shorter line, and were met by a tour guide, right on schedule.

It really was an incredible structure – gigantic, organic, imposing. Sam had explained a little about Gaudi, who had taken over the project in the 1880s, and worked on it for more than 40 years, until his death in the mid-'20s. At that time, it was only 20% complete.

The tour guide told us the current architect estimated it was now 70% complete, and it is projected to be completed by 2026 – a century after Gaudi's death. The outside was incredible, with multiple tall, thin towers, flying buttresses in the back, and decorated everywhere with detailed – and sometimes weird – sculptures.

The inside was even more amazing, with brightly-colored stained glass windows, a lot of blues and greens, with abstract modern patterns. A forest of huge columns rose toward the ceiling and split into three or four smaller columns, which split again, like branches of a tree.

We were actually able to take an elevator partway up one tower, continue climbing, then walk across a bridge, coming down another tower via a spiral staircase. It was a surrealistic experience, the columns tilting, and morphing their shapes in a beautifully organic manner.

After the tour, we took the metro L2 line, from the back of the cathedral, to '*Passeig de Gracia*', and Sam – guided by his Apple watch – led me a couple of blocks to one of the famous Gaudi houses, '*Casa Battló*'.

It was amazing; I would have to describe it as 'weird and wonderful' fantasy architecture. The façade was colorful and the structure organic, the columns looking like bones, and the protruding balconies like skulls. There was stained glass on the second floor, and the building looked like it could be an alien construction in some sci-fi movie.

We walked another three blocks, and saw our third Gaudi masterpiece for the day, '*Casa Milà*', also called '*La Pedrera*'. It was another purely organic edifice, horizontal waves of concrete dividing half a dozen floors, with incredibly intricate wrought-iron railings on the balconies.

Walking another couple of blocks, we hopped on the metro again, rattling through the underground tunnels. We got off at the third stop, and Sam smiled, "Now, we're on '*La Rambla*' ... or '*Las Ramblas*'. It's actually five boulevards joined into one."

It was a busy area, a wide central pedestrian walkway, with booths selling flowers, drinks, and art, flanked on each side by a narrow two-lane roadway, then sidewalks, and dozens of shops and restaurants. But Sam had his eye on the map, and something specific.

He took my hand, and we walked along with the rest of the tourists. The walkway was paved nicely with 'wavy' tiles, and – as with the rest of the streets – there were several floors of apartments above the shops on each side.

"Oh! What is that?" Sam pointed to a second-floor window that said 'Jambon Experience'. He quickly checked on the web, and turned to me, "Let's do this, after the museum. I'm getting hungry." He smiled, "And *then*, we can have a long lunch."

"OK, Sam. But I need to get back soon. The system turned on, and there wasn't any smoke ... but I still have to go through the full checklist."

Sam nodded, "Let's eat while we're out, and get back to the hotel before sunset. Then, you can check out the system. And, don't forget that you're giving your talk in the morning."

Of course, I hadn't forgotten about the talk. I was well-prepared, and couldn't worry about that. I would go through the presentation once more tonight, and again in the morning. But the system had to be operable, so that I could demonstrate it to the big pharma companies.

After a few blocks, we got to Sam's destination. I should have guessed: It was the 'Erotic Museum of Barcelona'. Reminiscent of the erotic museum we had visited in Amsterdam, this one had a collection ranging from ancient erotic art, to the Kama Sutra, to oriental erotica, a collection of porn videos from the 1920s made for the King of Spain, pin-ups, and an 'erotic garden', with phallic-shaped plants and sculptures. Pretty lame.

There were a few interesting fetish and BDSM devices, including the 'Chair of Pleasure', on which a woman sat, while a crank moved a dildo in and out of her. More interesting were some erotic Picasso prints, now that we'd seen the evolution of his works in his eponymous museum.

As we walked out, I whispered to Sam that – with a few more purchases – he could make his own fetish and BDSM museum. He chuckled, but now was intent on going to the 'jambon experience' – to learn about Iberian ham.

Actually, it was pretty neat, and we learned a lot. I'd had no idea that there were so many varieties of ham. And these were just from Spain. Sam reminded me that there was great ham in the areas around Valkenburg, where we'd gone to that incredible spa.

I chuckled as I remembered Sam joking about the happy cows of Belgium, who's rich cream made the best sauces in the world. Now I realized that I *was* getting hungry. The ham experience concluded with a tasting – and it was very good; but it only whet our appetites.

Sam led me up one of the major streets of the old town, and we turned onto a square that had several restaurants with tables in the '*plaça*'. We looked at a few menus and picked one. It only took a small meal, and large bottle of wine for us to be fading again.

We made it back to the hotel, and I completed the system check-out. And, after Sam went to bed, I practiced my presentation for tomorrow.

As I lay in bed – the time still early – I focused on a key issue that we *still* had not resolved: What was our business? Would we sell machines to pharma companies, or conduct funded research? Or should we develop our own drugs. One of my slides showed a pipeline of potential blockbuster drug possibilities that the system could target.

Sam had educated me that it was much too expensive to begin drug development without significant funding or, better, a strategic partner who could take on the heavy lifting, such as the clinical studies.

At this point, our main asset was the concept and the intellectual property. But we'd gone far enough with the system to show the feasibility, and our seriousness at disrupting the field. I hoped.

Actually, there were many different fields, if you considered the types of diseases targeted. It would be a huge bet. But we didn't have that much to lose. I would need to show confidence and strength tomorrow, and when we showed the system to the big companies over the next few days.

My brain couldn't stop, and it was midnight before I finally fell asleep. By then, I had a pretty good plan for moving forward, 'monetizing' the company, as Sam would say. The next three or four days would be critical.

We would need a little luck to pull this all together; and I was *assuming* that several of the companies would show interest. But I could now relax a little, having a definite goal for the company in mind.

I glanced at the clock once more: 12:25AM. Our alarms were set for 6AM, as the conference began at 8AM, and we had to get our badges, and submit slides for my presentation, which was scheduled for 10AM.

Kelly's 'featured research' presentation was well-attended, there being more than 2,000 people in the plenary session. And she did fabulously well, even addressing several questions at the end, extemporaneously, confidently, and with full mastery of her subject.

While I knew a lot about drug development, and a little about biotech – regenerative medicine, I could not claim a detailed understanding of Kelly's technology. Her system combined many of the latest technologies that weren't even known when I got *my* advanced degrees.

I hoped that my contacts within the industry, and being able to set up these meetings, would be helpful. If not, we either had a very long road ahead of us, or we could give up the technology – and give it back to the university.

We went to dinner with Raj and one of the conference chairmen, at a seafood restaurant in the complex at Port Olimpic. The paella was the best I'd ever eaten – although I hadn't had real *'Paella Valenciana'* for several years; actually a couple of decades.

Valencia was only a couple of hundred miles down the coast. And just *up* the coast, was the *Costa Brava*, and *Costa del Sol* which, I recently learned, are all built-up with condos, now.

Kelly was holding her own with the top academics in the field, and I could add little to the conversation. I was very proud of her. Looking out to the boats in the small harbor, I thought how we could buy a small boat, sail the south seas, and never have to worry about working again.

But Kelly was self-motivated, very focused, and assertive. I chuckled, but when Raj looked up at me, I turned it into a cough. Kelly was a *dominant*. She would have her way, get what she wanted. And I would help her.

The past three days had been a whirlwind of meetings – at the convention center, and in our hospitality suite. Kelly had made contact with the key researchers in the field – and had at least had coffee with most of them. Most of the researchers were male, and obviously taken by Kelly's beauty and charm. And, of course, her intelligence.

We'd met with all of the big pharma firms and some of the biotech companies, and the meetings had gone well. Amazingly, the prototype worked (as far as needed for the demonstrations), and everyone was impressed. It seemed that Kelly had introduced the next revolution in custom pharmaceutical development.

From the first meeting, Kelly had pushed her new concept of the company – licensing the technology for specific fields, providing the equipment, and then the support to assist in developing next-generation drugs.

There were U.S. companies interested in military targets, such as plague and anthrax; Asian, African, and South American companies interested in tropical diseases; and several others interested in specific targets, such as sexually transmitted diseases.

It was mind-boggling, and I struggled to keep up taking notes, while Kelly kept everything in her head – including the companies, target diseases, and potential advantages of her technology.

We were back in our room after the last dinner meeting, our return flights beginning at 8AM tomorrow morning. We undressed, and I was ready to get into bed, when I saw Kelly putting on her running outfit.

"What are you doing? You can't possibly go for a run, after the dinner and wine ... and full day of meetings."

Kelly smiled, "I need to unwind. Just one more time in the Mediterranean. The water and air temperatures are the same." She looked at me, "Do you want to come?"

What a question! Of *course*, I wanted to 'come' ... in bed, with Kelly. But I wouldn't wimp out on our last night here. If Kelly wanted to swim, I would go with her.

Sam put on his running outfit, and we walked to the beach. There was nobody here, and we only went far enough to be out of sight of the convention center. I undressed, and walked slowly into the water. It was chilly, but I had been overheated all day, expending both physical and nervous energy. Once I was in, the water felt great.

I was surprised that Sam actually joined me. But he had been very supportive during the conference, accepting my new concept of the business model, arranging the meetings, and logistics of the hospitality suite, lunches, and dinners. His contacts had been invaluable; between Sam and Raj, I had been introduced to all of the major players.

And I had introduced them to my novel technology. The reception had been terrific. But it remained to be seen whether the interest would coalesce into contracts. I floated on my back, looking up at the sky, a full moon hopefully portending good luck for the future.

Sam swam up to me, and we held each other. I knew he'd wanted to show me much more of Barcelona – even renting a car, and driving up into the mountains. But we'd had no time for sightseeing since last Sunday.

I had a pretty good feeling for Barcelona, now, but the most important thing was the business. All of our meetings had gone well. We would have to follow-up, and wait for the various companies to come back with their proposal or indication of interest.

We had really learned a lot at this meeting about the important worldwide diseases, and current research targeted at developing drugs to prevent or cure them.

As I had already known, malaria was one of the most important diseases, with half the world population at risk, and more than 200 million cases per year. Dengue fever was another worldwide problem, with 400 million people infected annually, 100 million of them requiring treatment.

Less well known are onchocerciasis, or 'river blindness', which affected 200 million people globally; and lymphatic filariasis, or 'elephantiasis', that threatened a billion people and infected 120 million each year.

Other similar tropical diseases, such as leishmaniasis and chagas, affect millions more people each year. By comparison, Lyme disease, which I had been working on, only has an incidence of 500,000 people per year. And newer threats are always appearing, such as Zika – which already affects more than half a million people per year.

Altogether, there were more than a billion cases per year, and over a million deaths each year, from these diseases. The overall market was huge. Each of the diseases was a target for pharma and biotech companies.

The common factor was that all of these were 'vector-borne' diseases, transmitted by mosquitos, worms, or other creatures, and were typically bacterial or viral – exactly the kinds of diseases that my system was designed to target.

Back at the hotel room, I made love to Sam, and then stayed up late, reviewing the conference papers and collecting further information on vector-borne diseases.

On the flights home, I would write a new Business Plan, incorporating my concept for monetizing our business by working with multiple strategic partners, providing our technology, and licensing each based on the potential market-segment size.

CHAPTER 14: TRICK OR TREAT

Tonight was Halloween, and I planned to dress up in one of my costumes, so that Sam and I could have our own little 'party'.

Over the past six weeks, we'd been working nonstop to respond to the pharma companies who showed interest in my technology – signing nondisclosure agreements, sending our new Business Plan and drug pipeline, providing our patent documentation, and having long Skype calls with business development and R&D people.

The interest generated by my Barcelona presentation had been incredible, and now we were trying to carve up the markets – by geography, disease, and other factors – so that we could begin negotiations. There were companies from South Africa, Israel, Japan, India, Brazil, Switzerland, Ireland, Canada, and – of course – the U.S.

Each pharma developer had its own pipeline, and was interested in targeting one or more specific diseases. The problem was that there was more than one company interested in certain drug targets, such as dengue and Zika.

As we didn't have facilities and ongoing projects (other than Lyme disease), our main asset was the IP, and my ability to assist with detailed knowledge of how the system should work. We had decided on multiple licensing of our technology – assuming that a few of these companies were as serious as they appeared to be.

But one of the implications was that I might be roped in to consulting for the next five years, having to 'commute' between companies in Africa, South America, Europe, and Asia. Sam had said that we would probably be traveling a lot, but years of continuous international travel would be difficult, tiring, and probably inconsistent with starting a family.

As I sat at my desk in the pool room – KS Biotech headquarters – I looked across the empty desks and lab benches to the prototype system, now on a rolling metal cart. It had weathered the round-trip shipping to Barcelona, which was promising, although we would have to conduct more rigorous shock and vibration testing.

The page in front of me listed the companies that were most interested in a licensing deal: There was one from Ireland, one from Switzerland, one from Israel, and a couple from the U.S. Some of the others had dragged their feet, or were not positioned to invest $100 million or more for a license.

However, there was also a Japanese drug development company which asked extremely technical questions, and told us that they would consider acquiring the entire company. But they needed more information, more proof that the system would, in fact, work, and said their acquisition offer would depend on how many other companies showed interest in licensing the technology.

Sam and I had worked out a formula for valuing the various markets, and determining a license fee. He had suggested the typical tactic of taking a royalty – which could eventually yield the biggest return for us.

At just a dollar per patient, these markets would each generate huge royalties. It was mind-boggling to think that we might be paid hundreds of millions of dollars over the next decade or two.

But this approach was mired in complications, like demonstrating that a new drug determined by my technology was actually something that could be manufactured, not be toxic, and successfully pass through years of clinical trials and regulatory approvals.

My concept was to grant unlimited, perpetual rights to our IP, as applied to a specific disease, for a one-time license fee. However, when we calculated what the fee should be, it was in the range of $50M to $250M per disease, depending on the market rights granted.

Sam warned me that the pharma companies would probably not pay such a lump sum up-front, but make 'progress' payments at certain milestones. It would still take a decade of my working with these companies.

But Sam also suggested that some of the companies may not need or want my help – even though I had invented the technology. Sam was also certain that none of the companies would pay *him* for consulting, as they already had big R&D departments with plenty of managers.

A totally different approach would be for the pharma companies to fund the development of their product inside our company, and then to pay us royalties. It might be the best route, if we wanted to grow KS Biotech, and someday sell it or take it public.

But all of these companies were better positioned to do the drug development than we were; our only contribution could be building the machines. Each company would need only one or two, but it would still be a major project for us to develop commercial products.

I put my head on the desk and closed my eyes, trying to visualize another strategy. Sam had already suggested to the two biggest companies (one in the U.S. and one in Switzerland) that they buy 100% of the rights to our IP. In other words, we would be selling the company, as all we had were the IP and equipment assets.

But both pharma companies had specific gaps in their product pipeline, and weren't really interested in all of our potential markets. Both of them had developed drugs for tropical diseases, although that wasn't the main business of either company.

The Japanese company was a medium-size pharma developer which had a few drugs on the market, but they didn't appear to have the funds to acquire us – according to Sam, based on his analysis of the private company information they had supplied us. But they seemed eager to continue the discussions, and there was no harm in that.

I was nearly finished with the simple pasta dinner, the heat turned down and sauce simmering on the stove. And the Caesar salad was ready – I just needed to mix the lettuce, my home-made croutons, Parmesano-Reggiano cheese, anchovies, and the dressing, which I'd made this morning. So I decided it was time to open the wine.

We were staying at home, just in case any trick-or-treaters came by. But this was a neighborhood of mostly older people, whose kids had already left the house.

We would keep the lights on, had a lighted pumpkin on the front porch, and a bowl of various miniature chocolate bars. I expected it to be a quiet night, except for the role play that Kelly and I would be doing. She already had the nurse outfit and accessories laid out.

Pouring the Amarone and swirling the glass, I tested the wine – the complex flavors as wonderful as the nose had been when I opened the bottle. I carried my glass and one for Kelly, and opened the door to the pool room. It looked like Kelly was sleeping.

As I quietly turned to step out of the room, Kelly said, "It's OK, Sam. I was just racking my brain, trying to optimize our strategy with the pharma companies. It's great that we have so much interest, but we're going to have to decide soon what we want, and how we're going to handle the negotiations."

I laughed, "It will mostly depend on the *offers* we get from the various companies. And they're likely to all be different, so not easy to compare."

Kelly rubbed her eyes and got up, and I handed her a glass of wine. We toasted, "Here's to making *some* deal. And, hopefully, soon – before the end of the year." Kelly nodded and we sipped the luscious wine.

We walked into the kitchen, and Kelly sniffed the aroma from the pasta sauce. "Why don't we get 'dressed' for dinner? We can start our role play. Maybe I'm trying to seduce nurse Kelly, and have her over for dinner ... but she hasn't had an exam and her immunizations in quite a while, so Dr. Johnson will see her in his home exam room."

Kelly laughed, "Maybe *Doctor* Walsh will have to treat her male nurse?" That was funny, as she really *was* Dr. Walsh; but, then, I was really Dr. Johnson.

But I quickly came back with an excuse. "I don't think I would fit into the nurses uniform." We laughed as I stirred the sauce, and took a small taste from the spoon.

Kelly seemed to accept that, and went upstairs to put on the costume. All I had to do was go downstairs to get my lab coat, which was hanging on the back of the exam room door.

Maybe I should surprise Kelly by going nude under the coat? Of course, I had to expect that Kelly would inflict some medical procedure on me. But she would probably be doing that, anyway, regardless of the scene's backstory.

I sighed as I undressed in the shower room, then donned the lab coat with my name embroidered in blue script above the left pocket. It wasn't much of a Halloween costume; but it would be just the two of us. And I'd stuffed a few 'supplies' into the pockets to get our play started.

As I walked up the stairs from the playroom, I heard Kelly coming down the stairs from the master bedroom. We smiled at each other, as we inspected each other's costume. We both had stethoscopes around our necks. Kelly's hat was slightly crooked, so I adjusted it.

Then, we heard the doorbell ring. Kelly skipped over to the door, and grabbed the bowl of candy. I was really surprised that we had any kids showing up tonight.

Kelly pulled open the door, and I heard a cheery "Trick or treat!" I saw Kelly staring out the door, and her mouth had dropped open. Someone must have a really good Halloween costume.

I walked over to the door, as Kelly screeched, "Amy? What are *you* doing here?" Then, as we both scanned Amy's costume, Kelly broke into a belly laugh – something I hadn't heard for a long time. But Amy was also laughing, and so was I.

That was because Amy had a bandage around her head, with a red splotch which was supposedly blood. She wore a pale blue hospital gown and slippers, and dragged an IV pole – complete with hanging bottle, valve, and tubing – next to her.

I looked at Kelly, and she looked at me. Then, I said, jauntily, "I think we have our first patient!" Little did Amy know how serious I was, and what kind of experience may have been prompted by her Halloween costume.

Kelly waved Amy in, and asked again, "*Why* are you here?"

Amy nodded, "I was on my way to a party not far from here, and thought I would drop by and trick-or-treat." She lifted the IV pole into the living room, and Kelly closed the door. "But I was just going to say hello, not really come in. I didn't want to bother you guys."

Kelly was shaking her head, "It's no problem, Amy. Why don't you disconnect yourself and let's sit down."

The tubing from the IV bottle was taped to Amy's wrist. She pulled it out, then rolled the valve open, and sucked from the tubing. A dark golden liquid flowed through the transparent tubing, and into her mouth.

I cocked my head, and Amy swallowed, then said, "It's Fireball – the cinnamon brandy." That was pretty clever. But Amy was a clever girl. She was cute, and had a short brown pixie hairstyle. And although she was as tall as Kelly, Amy was a little too thin, for my taste.

We sat in the living room, and Kelly glanced at me, then asked, "Amy, we've been working together quite a while, now, and we trust you. And we would like to share something with you ... but you would have to keep it confidential. Could you do that?"

Amy shrugged and nodded, then said, "Sure." She looked at me and back to Kelly. This could really be a fun roleplay evening, but – again – we were treading on thin ice doing something with our employee ... or consultant.

Kelly looked at me, and I knew she was considering whether we should share something so private with someone we worked with. But we had an unusual situation anyway, as we had gone skinny-dipping together many times. But this was different; it was a fetish. I shrugged and gave a small nod to Kelly.

She began, "Before I met Sam, he got interested in 'playing doctor'." I saw Amy's eyes grow larger, and the hint of a smile form on her face. "And he convinced me to play with him."

Kelly looked up at Amy, "And I found that I like some of the stuff. Sometimes I'm the patient, and sometimes I'm the nurse, and Sam is the patient." Amy was nodding slowly. And we do things that most people would consider painful or embarrassing. That's part of the turn-on."

Amy said, quietly, "Yeah. My partner *hates* going to the doctor. So I go with her. Even for a simple gyn exam."

Kelly was momentarily shocked, finding out that Amy was gay. We'd always assumed that she had a boyfriend, or was unattached. Then, Kelly glanced at me again, the corners of her lips raising into a smile.

"Would you want to play doctor, with us? It looks like we're ready – with the doctor, nurse, and patient." Amy nodded, and was beginning to smile, also. She glanced at me, and I shrugged. It was something I would love, but only if both Kelly and Amy wanted to play.

Then, Kelly warned, "We will treat you like a real patient, and you'll have to accept our judgment and act like a cooperative patient."

Amy frowned, and I added, "But everything will be done safely, all single-use sterile supplies, and proper aseptic procedure. We won't really be diagnosing or treating you, just sharing a few things that we do together."

Of course, we weren't planning to share the rest of our BDSM fantasies and scenes. I turned to Kelly, and asked, "Shall we show her? She should understand what will happen, before she agrees to play with us."

Kelly gave me a questioning look, and I pulled out a syringe from my lab coat pocket, already loaded with 3cc of sterile saline, and fitted with a 1.5-inch 25-gauge needle. Amy gasped, as I held up the shot. Kelly shook her head.

Before Kelly could suggest that she give me the shot, I turned to Amy, "Nurse Kelly needs to get a small 'booster' shot." Kelly sat on the couch, unmoving, as Amy and I sat in chairs on opposite sides of the coffee table, waiting for her response.

She reluctantly said, "OK, Dr. Johnson. I knew I was going to get the shot." She looked up at me, "How do you want me?"

That age-old question: How did I want Kelly? My manhood stirred, as I thought of a few ways. But I snapped myself back into the real world, and said, "You could lie on the couch ... but it might be easier for you to stand next to Amy, and let her see the procedure up close."

Kelly stood and stepped next to the chair in which Amy sat. Then, she pulled up the single-piece nurse outfit, exposing her white stockings, garter belt, and bikini panties. She reached under and pulled the panties down, then put her feet apart and her hands on her head, in the 'standing' position.

I came around, pulling an alcohol swab from my pocket, and tearing it open. I was on her right, and swabbed her right hip. Then, I pulled the needle guard off the syringe, held it up, and pushed the plunger so that a thin stream of saline arced through the air.

I looked at Amy, and she volunteered, "I'm OK. I've seen my partner get shots."

Nodding, I turned back to Kelly and made her skin taut between my fingers. "Here it is." I plunged the needle all the way in, then quickly put some tension on the plunger to make sure I wasn't in a blood vessel. Then, I let go of the syringe, and it bounced a little, and drooped a little, but stood out from Kelly's butt.

Glancing at Amy again, and seeing a nod, I injected the 3cc into Kelly's gluteal muscle. When all the saline had been injected, I again let go of the syringe, then turned to Amy, "Do you have any questions?" She shook her head, her eyes still focused on the syringe.

"OK." I pulled the needle out, and put the syringe on the side table, carefully fitting the needle guard onto it. Then, I took a small round Bandaid from my pocket, and put it on Kelly – where a tiny drop of blood had formed.

Kelly pulled up her underwear and let down the nurse outfit, then sat back down on the couch. She smiled at Amy, "So what do you think?"

Amy shook her head slowly, "I think it looked like it hurt."

Kelly shrugged, "The needle part isn't bad. But the injection is uncomfortable for a few seconds." Then, she said, "Actually, Sam has made 'art' on my backside using needles." Now, Amy was taken aback.

But Kelly persisted, "For example, on my birthday, he made a corset down my back, with pink satin ribbon laced back and forth around the needles." Amy shook her head, slowly.

Then, Kelly added, "But we'll all try to have some fun. If you get shots, I may need to get the doctor caught-up on his vaccinations." I knew that would be coming.

Finally, for the kill, Kelly offered, "Maybe, after your injuries are cured, you can be a student nurse, and we'll get you started with some procedures on a male patient." I visibly cringed, and Amy looked at me and laughed.

Kelly remembered to say something I'd intended to repeat, "But, Amy, you don't have to do this. Only if you think it will be interesting. This will be *completely* separate from work, and entirely up to you."

Amy was nodding, and Kelly suddenly frowned, "But aren't you supposed to be at a party?"

Shrugging, Amy said, "I was invited, but I don't have to go. I won't know most of the people." She smiled, "And playing doctor sounds more interesting."

Looking a bit sad, she said, "It would have been great if my partner could be here, but she's on the East Coast, now, at some business meeting."

Amy looked back and forth to Kelly and I, and asked, "Can I say 'no', if it gets too intense for me?"

"Of course, Amy," I said, "we're not going to force you to do anything. But we hope that you'll be strong, and try some experiences, even if they may be challenging for you."

"OK, I'll 'play' with you guys." She chuckled, "It wasn't exactly the Halloween games I expected ... nor is my quick 'hello visit' turning out as I had expected." Kelly and I were nodding; it wasn't the evening *we* had expected, either.

Kelly stood, "Why don't you take Amy down to the exam room, and get her started with a basic exam and some 'preparation' for later." She smiled at me, "I'll set the dining room table for dinner."

As I stood, Amy giggled, and Kelly glared at me. What? I looked down, and realized that I was turned on by giving Kelly a shot, while Amy watched ... and the imminent experience that Amy and I would have together.

Unfortunately, I was wearing nothing underneath the lab coat, which was now visibly tented. Shrugging, I turned my back to Kelly and Amy, and lifted the lab coat to my waist. Then, I dropped it, and turned around, "I was going to have a surprise experience with Kelly ..."

I put my hands in front of me, and walked past Amy. "Come along, dear, we'll take a look at your condition. And you won't need the IV pole." Amy followed me down the stairs, still giggling.

"Excuse me a moment, so I can put on some underwear." I walked through the bathroom and into the shower room, then pulled on my European black bikini brief. I had no doubt that it would be coming off, later.

I punched in the code for the electronic lock, and swung the door open, letting Amy get the full impact of the brightly-lit exam room. "Wow. You guys are serious!" She took a few steps into the room and looked around.

This was really a déjà vu moment. At least Amy was here to play with us, not to be punished. Amy spun around, now animated, and a smile on her face. "So what do you want me to do?" It sounded like she was going to make an effort to take our medical fetish as a positive, if not 'fun' experience.

"I assume you're wearing something under that gown?" Amy laughed, and undid the gown's tie, taking it off, exposing her jeans and long-sleeve t-shirt.

"OK. Please get undressed and," I opened one of the drawers under the countertop on the right side and pulled out one of our hospital gowns, "put on this one. You can put your clothes on the chair." Amy nodded and began unbuttoning her jeans.

I stepped out of the exam room, swung the door mostly closed, and went back into the shower room, first adjusting the temperature of the sauna, then taking the rest of my clothes across the playroom and stacking them on one of the chairs in front of the desk.

When I returned to the exam room, knocked on the door, and opened it, Amy was ready for me. Another déjà vu moment: She was sitting on the table swinging her legs, exactly as Jackie had.

I weighed her, measured her height and breast-waist-hip dimensions, and even used calipers to measure the fat on her hips and belly, and under her arms, so that I could calculate body fat percentage – which I expected to be low.

Then I went through the usual exam procedure, looking into her ears with an otoscope, having her say 'Aaahh' as I put a depressor on her tongue, and feeling her glands. Using the stethoscope, I listened to her heart and lung sounds.

"Are you ready for a breast exam, now?"

Amy shrugged, "Whatever."

I undid the tie around her neck and lowered the top of the gown. Of course, I had seen Amy's breasts, but did a close examination. Then, I had her lay back, and I conducted the usual manual breast exam, palpating each of her B-cup mammaries.

"Please turn over onto your stomach, now." Amy complied, and I unfastened the tie around her waist, and flipped her gown back on each side, exposing her butt. Then I lubed the rectal thermometer.

Holding it up, and turning to Amy, I said, "Let's get your temperature started." Amy closed her eyes.

I separated her buttocks, and slowly inserted the thin glass tube, moving it around and back-and-forth. Amy didn't make a sound. I left the thermometer sticking out about an inch, and stepped to the sink to wash my hands.

"Let's see how you do with a couple of needles."

Amy whined, "A *couple*?" Her head dropped back onto the small pillow, and she sighed.

I swabbed her right hip and quickly inserted the needle. Amy's bottom quivered. "That isn't so bad, is it?" I asked, optimistically.

"It doesn't hurt too bad ... yet."

Chuckling, I said, "This is just a needle insertion, not an injection. You'll get those later." Amy groaned.

Reaching across her, I swabbed her left hip, and inserted the second needle. There was a quiet 'Mmmm' from Amy. This wasn't the Halloween she'd expected.

I put my head near Amy's, and stroked her hair. "You're doing great. We'll just do a couple more things and then go upstairs for dinner." The needles had been in her for a couple of minutes, and she wasn't complaining.

"Would you like me to take the needles out, now? And the thermometer?" Amy nodded, and I pulled out the needles, dumping them into the sharps container.

After moving the thermometer around a bit more, I removed it, also. Then, I flipped Amy's gown back, and loosely tied the waist. "OK. Please turn over and scoot down, and we'll do a quick pelvic exam." I raised the stirrups, and Amy got herself into position, pulling the gown up to her waist.

I examined her genitals, including lifting her clit hood. Then, I put on a purple Nitrile glove, which I lubed with a small dab of KY. "Are you ready?" Amy nodded, her head on the pillow, and eyes closed. I inserted my middle finger deeply, and felt her cervix.

"To test your vaginal tone, please squeeze my finger a few times." Amy complied. Then, I pulled my finger out pushed it back in, while inserting my fourth finger into her rectum. Finally, I slid my fingers out, inserted my middle finger into her rectum, and did a 'bi-manual' exam.

I took off the glove and washed my hands. Then, I selected a speculum from the counter, and held it up for Amy to see. She groaned again. After running warm water over the blades, I inserted them gently into Amy, twisted the device 90 degrees, and turned the screw that separated the blades. Amy emitted a long 'Aaaaahh'.

Having not used it for a while, I pulled out my USB microscope and turned on the wall monitor. After a bit of finagling with the camera-tipped probe and light source, I finally got a great image on the screen. "This is your cervix." Amy looked at the monitor and shrugged.

"The last thing we're going to do before dinner is give you a couple of enemas, and then a small shot – like you saw Kelly get."

Amy whined again. "Enemas? *Two* of them?"

I nodded, "We'd like you to be cleaned out, for this evening's activities." Actually, we had no specific 'activities' planned. I glanced at my Apple watch and was surprised how late it was, already.

Relenting, I agreed, "OK, I'll only give you one enema. But it will be a big one, and we'll do it two different ways." I lubed a stainless steel, bullet-shaped enema nozzle, and held it up for Amy. She was slowly shaking her head.

As I put the cold metal against her anus, she flinched. "Just try to relax your anal muscles for me." It took a few backs-and-forths before Amy's body took in the nozzle. I connected the tubing, and started the flow of warm saline.

Amy groaned again. I mixed a second batch of enema solution in a large plastic bowl, and took out the 200cc syringe. When the bag was empty, I knew that two quarts had gone into Amy's colon. I closed the valve, and removed the tubing from the nozzle.

"Let's get you turned over and into a knee chest position, now." I lifted Amy's legs from the stirrups, and she slid back on the exam table, turned over, and got into position. She was being incredibly open with me, and very accepting of all the 'procedures' I had done.

"I'm going to pull out the nozzle, now." Amy squealed as the nozzle came out. "And, I'll finish your enema using this." I showed her the huge syringe, with the small, rounded plastic extension that would go into her. It was already filled with about three ounces of warm saline.

Although groaning a few times more, Amy took a dozen squirts of the syringe. As I was doing the last few, Kelly walked into the exam room.

She stood next to the counter, across from Amy's head, and asked, "Are you getting all cleaned out?" She chuckled, "I asked Sam to 'prepare' you ... although I'm not sure what we're preparing for. Let's talk about it over dinner."

Kelly walked out, and I finished Amy's enema and helped her off the table. I walked her into the bathroom, and intended to give her some privacy, but a few seconds after she sat down, a flood of water issued from her rear. She smiled at me, sheepishly.

"Take your time. I'll come back down in ten minutes, and we'll finish up your exam room experience." At least, I doubted that we would be doing anything else after dinner.

When I went back downstairs, I knocked, then pushed the door slightly open and peeked into the bathroom. Amy was still on the toilet. "I'm almost done," she said.

A few minutes later, she came into the exam room, and I asked her to get back onto the exam table in the knee chest position. She gave me a 'look', and asked, "What now?" Then, she got into position.

"I'm going to insert these." I held up the string of three stainless steel anal beads – the ones that we'd all experienced during our visit to Honopu Beach on Kauai. As I lubed them, Amy chuckled, "I think I should have picked a different Halloween costume."

I inserted the heavy metal balls into her rectum, and laughed, "Or maybe you just trick-or-treated at the wrong house." The last ball took a few more moments, and I said, "I guess you can consider the medical experience as a 'trick', but we have a nice dinner waiting for you as a 'treat'."

I had Amy lay down on her stomach, and prepared a 3cc shot. "I think Kelly may want you to try some more intense sensations after dinner ... but we'll start with this small shot." I held it up, needle guard off, the gleaming stainless steel needle intimidating.

Then, I explained, "The needle will feel the same as before. I'll let you get used to it, then inject the saline." I darted the needle in, and Amy sighed.

Then I announced, "And here's the injection."

As 2cc, then 3cc, was injected, Amy said, "Ow. It's starting to hurt, now."

I finished injecting her, and left the syringe bobbling atop her small bottom. "So how would you rate the pain?"

Amy chuckled (a good sign), and answered, "Well, the needle was less than a '10' ... but now it's about a '20'." I pulled out the needle and put some pressure on the injection site with a gauze pad. Then, I put a small Bandaid on her.

She got off the table, and re-tied her gown. Then, we went upstairs.

Sam and Amy came into the kitchen, and I pulled the garlic bread out of the oven, then divided the salad onto three plates. We all went into the dining room, where I had lit candles, and already poured glasses of wine.

Amy said, "Thank you for having me over for dinner, on zero notice." We both nodded, and told her she was welcome. She looked at me, "And the 'doctor play' was interesting ... but not that exciting; too much like going to a real doctor."

She looked at Sam, and back to me, "And those metal balls inside me aren't too exciting, either." I hadn't realized that Sam had inserted the anal beads, and made Amy keep them in during dinner.

Between bites of salad, Sam suggested, "Why don't we go in the sauna, after dinner. I think the patient needs some heat therapy, and her doctor and nurse should observe her." Amy chuckled. We had never been in the sauna with any of my staff; in fact, I didn't think they even knew that we had a sauna in the house.

Sam's pasta was great, as usual, as was the wine. So far, no other trick-or-treaters had rung the bell, and it was getting late, so we extinguished the candle in the pumpkin, and turned off the porch lights.

We brought Amy downstairs and into the playroom. Sam went behind the bar, and handed us water bottles. Amy was looking around, and I realized that she'd never been down here; only Jeremy and Caitlin had come down, when I'd had to talk to them about their stupid prank.

I undressed, stacking everything on one of the chairs. When Sam came over, he took off his lab coat; I had forgotten that he was only wearing skimpy underwear.

Amy asked, "Can you please take these ball-thingies out of me before we go in the sauna?"

We walked to the exam room, and Sam said, "Just lie on your back and pull your knees up to your chest." Amy got up onto the table, and hiked up her gown, then got into position. Sam had her breathe in, give a push, then let her breath out, as he removed each of the metal spheres.

Passing through the bathroom and shower room, we went directly into the sauna, each taking a towel that Sam had stacked on the chaise. The heat felt good.

After the first sauna course, we rinsed off under the shower, Sam gradually turning the temperature from warm to cool ... and the leg jets to cold. We wrapped in our towels and sat on the chaises with our water bottles.

"So do you have a serious partner? Or just someone you live with?" I really didn't know much about Amy's personal life. Even our casual Fridays out by the pool were usually focused on talking about the prototype system, or their classes at school.

Amy was cute, but not petite: She was tall and thin. But her short hair and her personality reminded me of Fiona. My PC muscles contracted involuntarily.

"Well, we've been living together for a year ... and we are lovers; but we give each other the freedom to have other relationships."

She laughed, "But Fran has had only one other 'encounter', and I've been working too hard to be out finding other people." She took a swallow of water and looked at me, "As far as 'serious', we're not planning to get married, or anything."

Sam asked, "What do you think about men?"

Amy shrugged, "I don't know. Men are OK. They just don't turn me on." Sam shrugged and nodded.

We went back into the sauna, Sam lying on the top bench, and Amy and I sitting on the lower one. We were all silent for the next ten minutes, the sweat dripping down us, as the sauna furnace creaked.

When we'd had enough, we exited the sauna, and got under the shower together. Without any discussion, we all bathed each other.

As we were rinsing, I whispered to Sam, "Can you give us a few minutes of privacy, please?" Sam raised his eyebrows, and I nodded. "You can also make up three big shots ... for the 'finale'." I raised my eyebrows at him. He smiled and nodded, then got out of the shower, dried off, and waved, as he walked out.

Amy and I caressed each other, then I hugged her, and moved my mouth close to hers. I looked into her eyes, and her lips turned up into a smile.

We kissed, ravenously, as the water streamed over us. Then, I went down on her. She quickly got into a sensual mode, something I'd never seen, and orgasmed as she held my hair.

I turned down Amy's return offer; perhaps some other time. As we dried off, I gave her a peck on the lips, and said, "Thank you for playing with us. We'll just have our little finale in the exam room."

Amy looked skeptically at me, and shook her head. "I should have known you guys would be serious about this, when you said you 'played doctor'. You guys are serious about everything." That wasn't really true, but Amy had only seen us in a work environment.

We walked across to the exam room, and I saw that Sam had three 6cc shots prepared and lined up on the counter.

Sam looked at Amy, and said, "Well, young lady, we've done most of your exam, and now you'll have to get your injections." He glanced at me, and I saw the wisp of a smile on his face, even though he was trying to talk to Amy seriously.

He reached for the colonoscope that was a decoration on the wall, and took it down. "But, first, we need to do the 'internal' exam." Amy's eyes widened, and she turned to me, her mouth dropping open.

Of course, I knew that Sam was joking, as we'd never used the four-foot long, half-inch diameter black tube. I wasn't sure that Sam even had all the parts for it. So I went along with the Halloween trick.

"I don't think he'll insert more than a foot or two. Then, you can see what your bowels look like, from the inside."

Amy was shaking her head. She said, "I've already seen my cervix. I don't care to see my bowels." Her shoulders dropped, and she said softly, "Please, Sam. You can give me the shots, but *please* don't stick that thing into me." When her voice broke, we realized that we'd taken the scene a little too far.

Sam looked at me, and we both cracked up. Sam put the scope on the counter, and hugged Amy. "No, Amy, we won't do that. At least, not tonight." I playfully slapped Sam's arm, and gave him a dirty look.

He smirked, "But she's all cleaned out, already. We could probably get some good pictures."

Sam had pranked Amy, and now it was my turn. "You know, Sam ... I've gotten a shot, and Amy's going to get her shots ... so it's only fair if you get one, too." Sam scowled, but he must have known I would ask for that, when he made up three shots.

But Sam had had his kicks, and I wasn't finished, yet. "And, as Amy is studying drug development, she should at least learn how to give a simple intramuscular injection." Sam had a look midway between anger and resignation.

Turning to Amy, I said, "I'll get him ready, and then you can insert the needle and inject him." I glanced at Sam, who still had a scowl on his face, and added, "And I'll let you decide if you want to give him a few smaller shots, to get the practice." Now, Amy's mouth was hanging open.

Sam asked hopefully, "Amy, do you really want to do this? We don't want to *force* you to give any shots." Yeah, but he was hoping that *she* would be getting the needle.

Amy hadn't refused, so I put my hands on my hips, and said, "OK, Sam. Get on the table." He reluctantly did so, as I re-wrapped the towel around my waist.

I showed Amy how to find the injection sites, but told her I would teach her more details later. My PC muscle contracted, again. I picked up one of the syringes, uncapped the needle, and squirted some saline in a thin stream. Then, I handed it to Amy.

I swabbed Sam's butt, and showed Amy how to stretch his skin between her fingers. She positioned the needle, and took a deep breath. Then, she inserted it smoothly into Sam. She smiled, and looked at me. There was a half inch of needle still showing, so I pushed it in, then checked for blood.

"You can inject him, now." Amy nodded.

Then, she asked, "Sam, do you want one big shot, or two small ones?"

Sam sighed, "Since you did so well inserting this one, you can give me one on each side." That was nice of him; it would have been easier on him just getting a single shot.

Amy slowly injected half of the saline, then looked up at me. "You can pull the needle straight out." Amy pulled slowly, until the needle was out. "Why don't you go around to the other side of the table for his next shot?" I held the syringe, as Amy squeezed between the exam table and wall.

I handed her the syringe, and swabbed Sam's left hip. Amy did another good insertion, and injected the rest of the saline. Sam had taken it well.

Sam got off the table, and I suggested that he get dressed. When he was out of the exam room, I held Amy and kissed her. "Thank you again. I hope its been interesting for you." Amy nodded, and gave me a small smile. I added, "And please keep this experience private."

Amy got onto the table, and Sam came back into the room, wearing his lab coat; I assumed he now had his regular clothes, underneath. I handed Sam one of the syringes, and he smiled.

"Amy, we're going to give you both shots at the same time. We'll be done quicker, that way." A lame excuse.

I went around to the other side of the table, and we swabbed Amy, then inserted the needles at the same time.

When we had injected about half of the saline, Amy groaned softly. But she had cooperated nicely.

It had been an interesting and surprising Halloween evening! An unexpected 'treat'.

DOMME EXPERIENCE

CHAPTER 15: SAMURAI PRIDE

We had made great progress with several of the potential licensees of our technology, providing data for their due diligence, and beginning negotiations on the structure of a license agreement. Sam was working on a 'Letter of Intent' that captured the agreed-upon terms.

And, in an incredibly positive development, our patent had been granted. Normally, this would have taken many months more, but the university attorney petitioned the United States Patent Office to expedite the issuance and, of course, we paid the required fees.

Sam and I took Raj to the French restaurant, where we celebrated with a bottle of Champagne, and then one of Sam's favorite Bordeaux wines – something we normally wouldn't have popped-for, if not for a special occasion.

Raj was excited about both the success with my paper in Barcelona – leading to intense interest in our technology – and the granting of our first patent, which we hoped would protect KS Biotech from much of the competition. At least, it would give us a head start.

I'd never seen Raj so animated: He was practically bubbling over with excitement. During the dinner, we discussed our model 'Letter of Intent', and the pros and cons of the various strategic partners. Even Raj wasn't sure what to suggest regarding negotiating with multiple companies at the same time. It would be tricky.

When we mentioned the Japanese company that stated they wanted acquire us, Sam noted that they didn't appear to have the money to make a reasonable offer ... but as they were a private company, we didn't have much insight into their details.

Raj hadn't been drinking his wine, but now took a sip. "I can't release any confidential information of companies that I've consulted for ... but maybe I can give you a hint that will be useful." He sat there silently, as Sam and I waited for his nugget of information.

Finally, Raj leaned forward, and whispered, "There is a company ... a mid-size pharma company in an Asian country ... that has developed a Malaria drug."

He swallowed, "It's not the final answer, but can help for a short time. They've been doing clinical studies in several third-world locations, but kept them under wraps – at least from the mainstream pharma companies and researchers." I wondered whether Raj was telling us that the company would be a competitor.

"I heard a rumor – in Barcelona – that the Japanese regulatory agency, PMDA, will be approving the drug soon. Once they do that, third world nations around the world will approve the drug, and the company will suddenly have access to a gigantic market." Sam whistled softly.

"PMDA?" I asked. I was familiar with the FDA in the U.S., but hadn't learned much about regulatory agencies in other countries.

Raj smiled, "It's the 'Pharmaceuticals and Medical Devices Agency' of the Japanese government." He took another sip of wine.

It was a week later, the week before Thanksgiving, when Sam came running up to the pool room and excitedly pointed to a printout. "Our potential acquirer just went public on the Nikkei exchange in Japan."

Sam was trying to catch his breath. "They have a market cap of 4.5 billion dollars, and just raised nearly $3 Billion." He smiled, "That means they have plenty of money for investment." Sam paced back and forth in front of my desk, "I need to call them, but it's still too early." Then, he ran back downstairs.

Being acquired was the ideal solution for KS Biotech. But none of the other companies had entertained that prospect; they only wanted rights to certain applications of our technology – to treat specific diseases.

And the main problem with the Japanese company was that they didn't appear capable of making a high enough offer to interest us, with all of the other companies clamoring to negotiate with us. Now, according to Sam, they would have the ability to make a competitive offer ... if they so decided.

We had a nice Thanksgiving dinner with my parents, my mother cooking the traditional dishes that I had grown up with. They weren't as refined as Sam's version, but I considered them the 'classics'. There hadn't been much discussion, as Sam was whirling in a world of strategies and contracts and negotiations.

Once again, we tried to explain the business to my parents, without dwelling on the technology. My mother's eyes widened, as we rattled off the 'value' of the various market segments, but my father was very skeptical that we could really sell our company, or change the world – which my technology had the capability to do.

I glanced at Sam, and he nodded. I looked across the table to my parents, and announced, "We're going to Japan next week." Already, my parents' eyes were wide. "There's a company that might want to acquire KS Biotech. And we have to meet with them – so that I can explain and answer questions about the technology, and so that Sam can begin negotiations with them."

My father shook his head in disbelief; I don't think he had any idea of how real this was. My mother changed the subject, asking me when we would be having the wedding.

As we drove back home, I stared out the window, not seeing anything. I really believed that we were close to success. But my parents – especially my dad – couldn't accept that, didn't want to believe his little girl could amount to anything.

In my younger days, I would have lashed out at them, done something wild. But now, I was just sad, sorry for my parents' lack of vision, and their lack of confidence in me.

Of course, I realized that we may *not* be acquired, for many different reasons. And the deals with the other companies would only give us a small up-front payment, with royalties not being paid until the drugs were developed, regulatory approvals obtained, and marketing underway. That could be a decade or more.

And Sam had warned me that even a successful business deal would probably take 6 months or more, for the due diligence to be completed, legal agreements to be put in place, and a myriad of other details to get done.

So maybe my father was just being realistic. But I was motivated to show him how successful I could be. Rather than crying, I re-dedicated myself to making KS Biotech a success – whichever way we did it.

We landed at Narita airport in a rainstorm. Kelly had only gotten a few glimpses of Japan's coastline between the clouds, as we descended. I'd been able to get a 'companion' business class seat, again, through one of my credit card companies, and the airlines had been great – giving us first class upgrades a couple of days before the flight.

Kelly and I went through customs, and downstairs to the arrival hall, where I bought tickets for the 'Airport Limousine Bus'.

We had already changed money, so I led Kelly to the sidewalk, where we found the position for our bus, and stood in line – actually between the lines painted on the concrete. Each bus took people into Tokyo, to specific hotels. Ours was in the *Shinjuku* ward, a bustling area of shops and offices in high-rise buildings, and the busiest railway station in the world.

Kelly pointed, as we passed Disneyland Tokyo, on the outskirts of the city. The sun was setting, and lights were coming on as we entered the metropolis.

We had been lucky: Although Narita was only about 50 miles from Shinjuku, the bus ride could take 2-3 hours; but we made it in less than an hour and a half – the shortest time I could remember, in all the trips I'd made to Japan. We were both tired, after the 12-hour flight, and nearly 24-hour day, since we'd gotten up this morning.

Arriving at our hotel at the end of the day, the streets were thronged with people, on the sidewalks and crossing the street, everyone walking quickly, but orderly. Kelly gawked, having never seen such large crowds before. Colorful lights advertised the shops and restaurants in each building, the scene looking almost as garish as Las Vegas.

It was really nippy, about the same temperature as it was at home. The skies were cloudy, but at least it wasn't raining here ... for the moment.

Kelly was impressed with the ornate hotel lobby, but shocked at the small size of our room. I laughed, "And this is a four-star hotel. I've stayed in much smaller rooms."

There was barely enough space to walk around the small bed. But we had a fabulous view over the city.

It seemed like there were a lot more skyscrapers than when I was here the last time. But that was nearly ten years ago. I knew Tokyo pretty well, and would take Kelly on a day of touring tomorrow – Sunday – before we would begin our business meetings. We planned to return on Friday, if we were far enough along with the company.

Walking down the crowded sidewalk, we looked up at small signs on each building, showing the shops and restaurants on each floor. I was surprised to see a 'tapas' restaurant; it was funny, as we'd just come from Barcelona.

But then I saw their beer list on the window, and decided this might be an easy way to break-in Kelly on Japanese culture. There were around 90,000 restaurants in Tokyo, so every type of food was represented. This might be interesting. And I could go for a good beer.

The restaurant was in the basement, wildly decorated, with a large menu of small dishes – some of which were bizarre. We made a selection – again, more than we could eat, but this would be an 'experience'.

We figured out that ordering was via a small jukebox-style device on the table, where we punched in each dish: Salmon-avocado Carpaccio, a Japanese 'pizza', *kara age* – Japanese fried chicken, grilled scallops, and a few other dishes. They had a nice beer selection, more than the usual Sapporo, Kirin, and Asahi.

It turned out to be a fun evening. I offered to order a masseuse through the hotel, but Kelly was too tired, even for a massage. After visiting the top floor bar – with an even more spectacular view of the city – we went to bed.

Tomorrow would be the start of an interesting week. I just hoped that this opportunity was 'real', and not a lot of wasted time and work for nothing. It was a long-shot that we could get the deal done, but Kelly remained positive.

She made love to me, taking the top position. That was fine with me. Kelly would clearly 'dominate', in any area of life that she wanted. And I would support her fully.

Sunday morning, we ate an early breakfast in the top-floor restaurant of the hotel. Then, we set out for the day. I intended to give Kelly a reasonably full tour of Tokyo, by subway and on foot. How much we saw only depended on our stamina.

When we walked out of our hotel, I told Kelly, "You know, this is going to be tough. We can't properly see Tokyo in less than two or three weeks. And, including the short excursions – like Hakone, Nikko, and Mount Fuji – we could easily spend a month.

"And I would have *loved* to take you to Kyoto, and the Osaka area, Nara, and Kobe. Just taking a trip on the bullet train would be fun. And staying in a '*ryokan*', or Japanese inn, with its special baths, gardens, and in-room dining. And going to one of the '*onsen*', spas in the hills that have natural pools and beautiful gardens."

Kelly was shaking her head, "I *know* this is a business trip, Sam, and that we don't have much time for touring. Maybe we can come back some day and explore other areas."

"I hope so. If we sign a deal with the pharma company here, we may be coming back a lot!"

I had worked out a rough itinerary for the day, but felt compelled to show her a sight – just across the street – that would give her an initial 'feeling' for Tokyo.

"Before we start the main tour, let's visit the train station." Kelly looked at me like I was crazy. "Shinjuku Station," I pointed to the '*higashi*', or west, exit of the huge structure, "is the world's busiest train station, with more than 3.6 million people going through it every day."

We walked across the street, and up an escalator. "It's not the trains that are interesting ... although we could go to one of the tracks that has a bullet train; but there are several stories of shops and restaurants – basically a huge mall, which is part of the train station."

We walked by restaurants with realistic plastic models of their food; camera stores, and shops specializing in video games; and a large department store, girls dressed in dark blue skirts and white blouses ready to greet customers, as they entered the store.

After a random walk through the station, and seeing enough to impress Kelly, I now needed to figure out how to get out of here, through the west exit. Fortunately, I knew the Kanji symbol for exit, '*deguchi*', and headed that way.

We walked through back streets and alleys, mostly apartments around us, and navigated to the Yoyogi Park and the Meiji Shrine. Fortunately, I had read-up on some of the sights, so I could act as a tour guide.

"We're going to see the Shinto shrine of Emperor Meiji and Empress Shoken. In 1920, after their deaths, the shrine was dedicated, and people from all over Japan donated trees – 100,000 of them – to make this small 'forest' in the middle of the city."

Before Kelly asked, I explained to her, "Shinto was one of Japan's ancient religions. But it is more spiritual, than religious. It values harmony with nature, and believes that all things are imbued with divine spirits, or '*kami*'. Similar to what was portrayed in the movie, '*Avatar*'."

We walked under the '*Torii*', or temple gate, and through the park toward the main shrine. Kelly pointed at one of the trees, "What are those?" Hanging from hooks on the tree were small wooden tablets, with writing on them.

"Those are called '*ema*'. People write their wish on one, and hang it near the shrine, for good luck."

Inside the main building, they were selling shrine-related materials: Stamps and seals, amulets, and cards with sayings of the Emperor. Kelly bought two of the *ema* tablets, and wrote out her wishes. Then, we hung them on one of the camphor trees.

Wrapping up our visit to the shrine, we walked through the Meiji Jingu '*gyoen*', or gardens. They were nice, but not like I'd seen in the summer, with all the flowers. At least, it hadn't snowed here, yet.

We exited the southeast corner of the park, and crossed the street. "This is the Harajuku district – which is supposed to be the center for youth fashion. I've never walked through this area."

We walked several blocks, but Kelly wasn't excited. Stores like The Gap, and small boutiques were everywhere, but I was glad that Kelly didn't want to browse and shop, as we had a lot more of the city to cover.

After getting on the Metro at the Meiji Jingu Mae station, I explained to Kelly, "There are 23 'wards' in Tokyo, and they are divided into 'districts'. A lot of them are filled with specific types of shops.

"For example, Shinjuku – where we are staying – is famous for camera stores. Jimbocho is filled with book stores and sports stores. Akihabara specializes in electronics. Roppongi and Akasaka are a couple of the good restaurant and night club areas. And, of course, Ginza is famous for its high-end shopping."

At the first stop, we exited the subway car, and climbed the stairs to one of the many levels, then found a station map. "This is Shibuya Station, one of the busiest railway stations in Japan, with over two million passengers per day. And the Shibuya ward is now one of the most upscale and most crowded areas in Tokyo.

"The intersection in front of the station – if we can find that exit – has a 'scramble crossing' – where traffic stops in all directions, and throngs of pedestrians cross in amazing synchronization. But, as you can see on the map, there are over 40 exits."

Finally I recognized 'Hachikō' as the name of one of the six main exits, and we headed that way. It was only about half a mile of walking before we saw the light of day. The area was as crowded as I remembered.

Kelly was astounded. We crossed the street in one direction, and then another, just taking in the energetic atmosphere. There were huge video displays and a multitude of lit signs, similar to Times Square in Manhattan (which, I now realized, Kelly hadn't experienced).

I headed back to the station, and Kelly asked, "We're not going to walk around this area?"

"Well, we can. And I'm almost ready for lunch. We could spend a full day walking around this area, shopping and eating. But I thought we could have lunch in Roppongi, which is mainly a nightclub area, with tons of small restaurants."

Kelly shrugged, and we found our way to the Yamanote Line, an overland train that would take us to the Hibiya subway line. It took a bit longer than I'd planned, but we finally walked out into Roppongi, and along a street filled with restaurants.

We looked at a few menus, and I explained to Kelly, "In the U.S., when we have 'Japanese' food, you can get all types of dishes, from sushi to yakitori to tempura.

"But most restaurants in Japan specialize in a particular type of food. So you can have a 'sushi-ya', or sushi place; or a yakitori-ya, tempura-ya, and many others. One of my favorites is the unagi-ya – or place to get eel."

Then, I found something that I thought would be different, and fun. I pointed, "This is a *'kushi age'* place; I haven't been to one of these in years." Again, it had been a couple of decades.

"I think it translates, roughly, to 'fried sticks'. They put different things on a skewer, batter them with panko, and fry them. And they have different dipping sauces."

We sat at the counter, watching a couple of cooks making the 'sticks', and frying them. One of them came to us, and we ordered beer. There was a conveyor belt in front of us, and we could select whatever sticks came by. Then, we would be charged by the number of sticks.

Although we didn't eat fried foods much, any longer, these were good, and made a fun lunch. There were sticks with shrimp, asparagus, shiitake mushrooms, chicken (although I wasn't sure exactly what parts), yams, lotus root, and pork with scallions.

I had originally planned this as a 'snack', but we ended-up finishing an embarrassing number of sticks. And got a bill to match. I planned for us to be in Asakusa to visit the temple, and eat dinner at one of the restaurants there.

We took the Hibiya Line a short distance, then walked ten minutes to the Tokyo Tower. "This is modeled after the Eiffel Tower, as you can see. It's 1100 feet tall, one of the tallest in Japan.

"But later, we'll also go up to the top of the 'SkyTree' – which, at more than 2,000 feet, is now the tallest tower in the world, and the tallest structure, second only to the Burj Khalifa in Dubai."

Kelly asked, "Two towers in one day?"

It would have been great to space things out, but we only had today to tour. The rest of our week would be spent in business meetings.

The view was nice, the atmosphere clear and the cloud cover starting to break. I had hoped that we could get through the day without rain ... and we'd been lucky, so far.

I looked at the map on my phone, and realized that with only another short walk, we could be at the dock where we could take a boat tour of Tokyo Bay. I would have to forego my visit to Akihabara, and we would be too late to see the museums in Ueno. But we could spend the late afternoon and evening in Asakusa.

"What would you think about a little boat cruise?"

Kelly smiled and nodded, "That sounds good. It would be nice to get off my feet for a while." I didn't mention that we had a 20-minute walk to get to the dock.

The boat ride was OK, but in less than an hour we could only tour the inner harbor. It was a huge boat, mostly used for lunch and dinner cruises. But it gave us a chance to relax. There would be a lot more walking, today.

We took the subway to Asakusa, and walked through an area dense with restaurants before reaching the Hozomon Gate, the main entrance to the temple grounds. It was a huge and ornate structure, mostly in red, with three large passageways, and roofs that swept upwards on each side.

It was already getting dark, but the gate and other main buildings were lit dramatically. I took quite a few pictures, most with Kelly in the foreground.

We learned that the Buddhist temple was dedicated to one of the Buddhas – the 'Bodhisattva of Compassion', a statue of which was found 1400 years ago by two brothers casting nets in the nearby Sumida river. The temple is the oldest in Japan.

After seeing the Asakusa Shrine and 5-story Pagoda, we walked back out the Hozomon Gate, and down a long, narrow corridor, the Nakamise shopping street, usually crowded with people, but relatively calm on this Sunday evening. There were tiny shops on either side, selling tourist junk, t-shirts, candy, and a few local food specialties.

When we got to the Kaminarimon Gate, I led Kelly to the side, and picked up my phone. There was a famous eel restaurant around here somewhere, but I had to look it up.

Fortunately, it came up quickly, including a phone number; so I made the call. They told me the restaurant was completely booked for the evening, but that if we came quickly, they could squeeze us in. According to my phone, we were only five minutes away.

When we entered, I had to hold Kelly back from stepping onto the polished wood floor. "We have to remove our shoes, put them in one of the little boxes on the wall, and put on a pair of those slippers." I pointed. We were greeted by a kimono-clad woman, stunning in the perfection of her makeup.

She seated us at a table facing out windows that looked over the Sumida River and SkyTree tower on the other side. It wasn't the romantic booth that I'd hoped for, but it was amazing we'd gotten in.

This wasn't going to be a cheap dinner, the eel priced about like a fine steak in the U.S. But it wasn't a surprise. We started with a sashimi plate, and our usual beers. Kelly's eyes widened when the beautiful creation was put down in front of us.

The octagonal plate, decorated around the raised edges, contained a tiny portion, by our standards. But it was arranged artfully – the perfect pieces of fish, the ginger and wasabi, and decorative leaves and flowers, integrating the arrangement. I had to take a picture.

It seemed like only a taste, but we savored it, agreeing that it was probably the best sashimi we'd ever eaten.

Then, the eel came – each of us receiving a bento box with beautiful lacquered filets. These were not the limp things over a mound of rice, as usually served at home.

"This is INCREDIBLE!" Kelly looked up at the ceiling, her eyes closed. "Why can't we get this at home?"

Ha! I would *love* to be able to eat fresh eel from Tokyo; würst und brot from Zurich; and patisserie from Paris. But that was another reason for traveling – to taste the flavors of the world, things we couldn't get at home.

It *was* a very special dinner. I leaned over and kissed Kelly. It was getting dark, and we could see the lit SkyTree tower, along with our reflections in the window.

That reminded me to make reservations for the SkyTree. Again, I hoped that being a Sunday evening would allow us to get in. Luckily, I was able to reserve an 8PM visit, to both the 350 meter and 450 meter observation floors. That was 1200-1500 feet up!

I turned to Kelly, "Something else that we could do this evening, that's nearby, is go to a public bath house. I did some research, but couldn't find one with 'mixed' gender bathing. So we would have to be separated. And I would have to tell you the procedure."

Kelly shook her head, "Something to leave for next time."

Nodding, I said, "There are so many things to do. Japan has natural hot-springs and spas – called '*onsen*', and many *do* have mixed bathing." I wondered when we would get the chance to visit Japan again, and have the time to do the things we wanted. An image of Kelly and I skiing Sapporo popped into my head.

We were at the station in five minutes and, after a five-minute train ride, we were at the base of the SkyTree tower. We went up to the 350-meter floor. Kelly dared me to stand on the glass floor – looking down 1200 feet. But it wasn't too bad, as I was completely enclosed. It had been much more scary for me looking over the rail of the Eiffel Tower.

The view was incredible, all of Tokyo now lit, looking like a sparkling jewel.

Then, we continued up to the 'Tenbo Galleria', which had panoramic glass windows. I was fine, my acrophobia not bothering me, even though the windows slanted slightly out.

When the elevator reached the bottom, I yawned, then said, "You know, we still have to visit the Ginza tonight." I didn't know if the big department stores were open, but hoped that Kelly was as tired as me. She was.

It only took two different subway lines to get back to our hotel, not arriving until nearly an hour after we'd exited the tower. It was almost ten o'clock, and our business meetings started at 8AM tomorrow morning.

What a whirlwind the past few days had been! The pharma company had already done a ton of work to understand my technology and how to apply it to their drug development goals. I had actually met a couple of their researchers in Barcelona, and we got along well.

Sam had been in meetings with their business development people, and worked out an approach to valuing KS Biotech. But it would depend on getting 'Letters of Intent' from the other companies with which we were negotiating. And, that wouldn't happen while we were here.

On Monday, we had toured the plant, and been taken out to dinner at a 'soba-ya', a place that specialized in thin buckwheat noodles, artfully arranged on a miniature tatami mat (at least, that's what it looked like), and dipped into a broth.

Sam had taught me that slurping soups was not only acceptable, but expected, as a show of enjoyment. But it was still awkward, when we made slurping sounds at a business dinner.

On Tuesday evening, the business development executives took us to a 'yakitori-ya'. The charcoal grilled skewers of chicken, wrapped with a scallion, were incredible.

But our friendly colleagues also insisted that we try some of the more traditional varieties ... which was a bit of a challenge. There was '*tsukune*', meatballs of chicken cartilage; '*bonjiri*', chicken tail; and '*sunagimo*', chicken gizzards (Sam claimed he put turkey gizzards into the Thanksgiving stuffing, but I had no idea what they were).

Then, they ordered more plates, with '*shiro*', or small intestine of the chicken; and '*reba*' – liver pronounced with an 'r' substituting for the 'l'. I ate a skewer of each, but preferred the '*toriniku*', or plain, old, white-meat chicken skewers.

We also had some delicious non-chicken dishes, including '*ginnan*', a skewer of seeds from the Ginkgo Bilboa tree; '*enoki maki*', enoki mushrooms wrapped with some meat; and '*asuparabekon*', or asparagus-bacon skewers.

We had bowls of rice that the Japanese men lifted to their mouths, shoveling in mouthfuls with their chopsticks. They taught me many different customs, and phrases – including some slang.

Of course, we had needed something to wash it all down, and the VP of business development decided that we should have a sake tasting. By the time we were midway through the meal, there were at least a dozen 'tokkuri' – decorative porcelain flasks – on the table.

Each had a card that indicated the name, type and source of the sake, hanging from a thin gold chain. Each sake was at a different temperature, some slightly warm, and others slightly chilled. It wasn't what I had expected.

I had learned the first day that Japanese custom was to pour each other's drinks. Not only was it polite, but it was nearly impossible to track how much alcohol we'd had, as my cup seemed to be full every time I reached for it.

During the long dinner, we learned that sake is *brewed* in a process more similar to beer, than being fermented like wine. The 'table wine' of sake is called '*Futsū-shu*', while the good stuff is '*Tokutei meishō-shu*'.

There was no chance that I would ever remember the names, or the flavors, but we tasted the eight varieties of 'special designation' sake. From '*Honjōzō-shu*' on the bottom rung, through '*Ginjō-shu*', to the '*Junmai Daiginjō-shu*', which we were told cost more than most fine bottles of wine.

Needless to say, Sam and I were in no shape for lovemaking, after all the alcohol. But we had been tired every night, with no energy for anything more exciting than simple sex.

Sam had explained that over the past several decades, both Japanese men and women had delayed their sexual experiences – many still virginal in their 30's and 40's. There were entire industries providing substitutes, such as realistic dolls, sex toys, and porn videos.

Most executives, like the men we had met with, were on an upward ladder within their organization, working from early morning to late night – having drinks with customers or the boss, and working at least a half-day on

Saturdays. Their wives never saw them during the week; only on Sunday was the man with his family.

I also learned that most of the executives in large companies, if they want to rise to the top, take foreign assignments – wherever the company sends them. These are often for a few years.

As Sam noted, and the pharma guys confirmed, the top Japanese executives would be posted to the U.S. Since this could be for 2-3 years, or more, they would bring their family.

But the wife and kids would be living the American lifestyle, learning that strict obedience to the husband and father is not the norm. And, over time, they would change their values, frustrating the man, and making it difficult for them to return to Japan and fit in with society.

This morning, we had finished discussing specific terms of an agreement. The main – and most important – term not yet resolved was the valuation, which would depend on our agreements with other firms.

The Japanese company wanted to develop certain applications, but would do contract research for the other companies we would license, thus offsetting some of the expense of the acquisition. I was glad that Sam took the lead in our negotiations.

Sam told me that he suspected that the Japanese company would acquire one or more of the licensed companies, instantly increasing its revenues, and making its stock price sky-rocket. It didn't matter to us; in fact, having multiple companies do the development would probably relieve me of having to constantly be available for consulting.

As a final 'commitment' and celebration, Sam and I were taken to dinner Wednesday night by the president of the company, Makoto Yamamoto, along with his VPs of research, marketing, and business development.

Yamamoto-san led us through the neighborhood near the office to a small sushi-ya, one that he'd frequented for more than 30 years. He and the chef – reputed to be one of the best in Tokyo – were close personal friends.

The six of us took up the entire sushi bar, and there were only a handful of other tables in the tiny restaurant. After a few words with the chef-owner, we toasted with '*birru*'. There were a lot of '*kompai's*, and we all poured each other more beer.

Two platters of sashimi and sushi were placed on the bar in front of us. They were spectacular – true works of art, down to the tiniest details. Makoto showed us the proper way to eat sushi, carefully lifting the fish off the rice, dipping it soy, and then replacing it before downing the entire piece in one bite.

And the fish was '*oishii*', really delicious. Despite our visits to Hawaii, the west coast, and Europe, this had to be the very best fish I'd ever eaten. It wasn't a huge amount of food, but it was really special.

As we walked out of the restaurant, I started my thank-you's, making a small bow to Makoto, and saying, '*Domo arigato gozaimashita*'.

The ending, which many '*gaijin*', or foreigners, didn't know, indicated that I was thanking him for what he had already done – in the past. I assumed that Sam and I would be going back to our hotel for the night.

But Makoto had different ideas. We shook hands, then he pulled me along and pointed down the small road to a busy boulevard. When we got there, he hailed a couple of taxis. Now, I realized that he was sending us back to our hotel, and obviously taking another taxi back to the office.

We said our good-bye's to everyone ... but were surprised again when Makoto got into the taxi with Sam and I Perhaps he was personally taking us back to our hotel. The other executives waived to us cheerily, as the white-gloved taxi driver turned into the lane of traffic.

When the taxi pulled over, I had no idea where we were, until all the lights and crowds told me that we were in Shibuya – which we'd only seen from the front of the train station last Sunday.

We walked several blocks, through smaller streets brightly lit with thousands of signs indicating restaurants and shops on each level of every building. There were hordes of people walking on the sidewalk and in the street, barely making room for one direction of car traffic.

Makoto led us up the stairs of a building, to the third floor. Then, we ducked under the '*noren*' – the traditional cloth with the place's name in Kanji characters, and entered a small anti-room that had a trickling of water coming down a rock face on one wall, dark polished floors, and the usual shoe boxes and slippers.

A kimono-clad woman greeted Makoto warmly, and ushered us into an ultra-modern room – with indirect lighting, stainless steel tables, abstract art, and comfortable couches around the edges of the room. The bar looked like a spaceship, all of the bottles back-lit and shining in a gradation from clear, to yellow, to orange, to amber.

Seating us in a corner of the room, the hostess nodded and left us; but not a minute later, a waiter brought a large bottle to the table. Around the neck was a gold chain – like the sake bottles – but the 'card' was solid gold, and engraved with Makoto's name.

When I looked up, two cute, young, Japanese women bowed, and sat on either side of Makoto and Sam, with me in the middle. They immediately started talking – the one next to Makoto speaking in Japanese, and the one next to Sam speaking English.

Both of them had placed a hand on the men's thighs, and neither paid much attention to me, until Sam explained that I was the president of our company.

My mind wandered briefly, and I thought of a 'Kelly sandwich'. But, although it would be fun dominating him, Makoto was not a person I would choose to sleep with.

In any case, he was married and had a grown family. As I saw a hand moving up his thigh, I realized that his family didn't preclude a little nighttime flirting with a hostess in his 'karubbu' ... club.

We toasted several times, but the scotch – Makoto had said it was aged 24 years – was a taste that I would have to acquire. When one of the hostesses began to refill my glass, I waved her off. Makoto turned to me, "Would you like something different?"

I nodded, "It's delicious ... but could I have something a little lighter, please?" Makoto laughed, and spoke quickly to one of the girls, and she brought back a tall glass with clear, bubbly liquid.

Makoto said, "That's a 'chū-hai. It's made with a Japanese liquor called 'shōchū'." He laughed, "It means a shōchū highball. I think this shōchū is made from yams; and since it's winter, it may be flavored with chestnuts. It's half as strong as whiskey."

I sipped it, and smiled. It was similar to a vodka and tonic. "Thank you, Makoto." I raised my glass, "We really look forward to working with you. I would love to come back and visit Japan again."

Sam said, "I would like her to see Kyoto, and Osaka castle during cherry blossom season, and stay in some ryokans, and visit a few onsen."

Makoto laughed, "There's a lot to see in Japan, even if you just stay on Honshu, the main island. But my favorite place is the 'inland sea'. I keep my boat on the island of Shikoku." I realized I would have to learn a lot more about Japan before I came back again.

He sighed, "But I don't have time to enjoy it much." Makoto was a very hard working person, like all the other Japanese men I'd met. The girl next to him asked him something – perhaps to explain our conversation – and they spoke rapidly but softly in rhythmic Japanese.

The girl next to Sam asked us if we had been to a ryokan or onsen, and Sam responded that he had, but it was something I had not yet experienced.

She giggled, and asked if we could bathe nude in a mixed onsen. That gave Sam the opportunity to 'get started' ... but I hoped he didn't go on forever, with our concept of openness.

Sam told her that we liked 'hidaka no kaigan', by which he meant nudist beaches; but there was something lost in translation, until the girl realized what he was trying to say. There were evidently few nude beaches in Japan, although there were public baths and onsen, some of which were 'mixed' gender.

A three-piece jazz group set-up and played softly in a corner of the room. This wasn't the loud karaoke-singing type of bar that I would have pictured; it was very refined, only a few small groups of people chatting softly. All the men wore suits and ties; there were no other female guests at the club.

It was nearly midnight before we left the 'club'. Fortunately, we only had a couple of meetings in the morning – to look at future IP and review existing worldwide patents, which Sam and I had already done. We would have our last afternoon in Japan free, then fly back home on Friday.

We wrapped up our business with the company in the late morning, Kelly satisfying the research team regarding the patent coverage, and me reviewing the final agreement terms with the business development and marketing teams. As we walked to the metro to get back to our hotel, the enormity of what we were doing finally hit me.

Assuming all of our other negotiations resulted in signed LOIs, the Japanese company would pay us ...

I had to stop and shake my head. Kelly looked at me curiously; and I thought it was a curious thing, myself: All this time, we had been negotiating, throwing around big numbers, holding out for certain market valuations ... but everything was theoretical.

Now, I had the chance to think about what this really meant. At the *least*, the Japanese company was committing to a $300 million valuation, and IF all of the other companies signed letters of intent ... we could be paid more than $1.6 billion dollars. My heart was pumping, and I felt sweaty.

Of course, it was unlikely that *all* of the deals would go through. In fact, we were fairly sure that one would not be concluded, as it was in conflict with the Japanese company, both of them targeting the same markets.

"Sam?" Kelly was now looking at me with concern; I guess my thoughts had drifted off, as we stood on a side-street. I hugged Kelly, and held her tight.

"You *know* that this entire deal could fall apart." Kelly frowned and nodded. She had an incredibly positive outlook, and didn't want to hear this. But it was only the prelude to the real message.

"But, if we're able to close the deal, you could be a very wealthy woman." Kelly shrugged and nodded.

"No. I mean *really* wealthy." I held her hand and looked into her clear hazel eyes, "Kelly ... you could be a *billionaire!*" It really hadn't sunk in for either of us.

We boarded the subway, and it was too loud to continue the conversation until we reached the hotel. We undressed and hung our business attire, then put on jeans and long-sleeved t-shirts. We would have to pack tonight.

Sitting on the edge of the bed, I tried again. "It's very unusual for a company to pay up-front for technology. Usually, it has to be proven, products developed, then clinical studies performed, and regulatory approvals obtained. As you know, it's a five to ten year process.

"But in this case, they are confident in your technology, and the licenses with other companies – if they agree to work the Japanese company – enables the Japanese company to instantly increase its revenues, and show their shareholders that they are growing quickly and have a lot of potential.

"And, because they just went public, they have some serious money to throw at our technology." Kelly nodded, already knowing most of this.

"But I think I'm now understanding their strategy. The Japanese think long-term, sometimes a decade or two ahead. And their key markets, enabled by our ... *your* technology, are tropical diseases in third-world countries, where the cost of a drug is paramount.

"So they want to avoid future royalties, as that might increase the price of the drug beyond what the market would accept. By paying up-front, when they have the money, and when the stock market is happy with them, they can prepare for a tough market, and still make a profit for the shareholders."

Kelly said, "That makes sense. And it's only about a third of the money they raised."

Shaking my head, I reminded her, "But they may want to acquire one or more of the companies we're negotiating with. It's probably more complex than we think."

We had lunch in an Italian restaurant near our hotel, then took the metro from Shinjuku station to Ginza.

The Ginza area was even more incredible than Shibuya, in terms of lighted signs, and upscale stores. We walked by all the big European brands, like Dior; some huge Japanese companies, like Sony; and even the ubiquitous Apple Store.

Sam said, "On weekend afternoons, this road is shut down, and made a pedestrian walkway. So even with the people on the sidewalk now, it would be more crowded on the weekend." It was pretty crowded, now.

We went into the Mitsukoshi department store, and took an elevator to the next floor. A young girl – dressed in the 'uniform' of this particular store – held the elevator doors open and then, as they closed, she bowed, her head barely out before the doors closed completely.

There were candy counters, cosmetics, clothing, and even an entire prepared food market. We went up a few more floors, and looked at some of the furniture that went into Japanese homes.

It was interesting, but we weren't going to buy anything. Everything was incredibly expensive. How could all of these people pay for these things? The stores were crowded, and people were busily buying things. I would have to ask Sam how the salaries in Japan compared with those in the U.S.

What Sam had said suddenly stopped me. With the money he had, we could buy anything we wanted in this store. But, as he'd said, if we closed any of the deal, we wouldn't have to worry about money. As I thought for a few seconds, I realized we *would* have to worry.

What would we do with the money? How would we invest it? And how could we help the world? Our contribution to the development of tropical diseases would help in the long-run. But would there be things we could do now? More than a billion people in the world didn't have ready access to water, and more than two and a half billion didn't have proper sanitation.

Sam had led me out of the store, and we stood on the sidewalk while he consulted his phone. I looked around and laughed when I realized he wasn't the only one doing it.

Finally, Sam asked, "What would you like to do, the rest of the afternoon? We can try to get into a Kabuki performance. Or, visit some of the other shopping areas – like Jimbocho, for books and sports equipment."

Before I could answer, Sam smiled, "I'd love to walk around Akihabara for a little while." That was the area of electronics and other high tech shops.

"And you should really see Ueno, where there are some of the best museums, like the Tokyo National Museum, and the museums of art and science. And, they have a zoo. With pandas." Then Sam smiled, and pointed to his phone, "And Akihabara is on the way to Ueno."

Sam had already made up his mind, and I would go along for the ride. It was mind-boggling that we could be on the verge of a major success. But I didn't know if, or how, it might change our lives.

We walked another ten minutes to the Hibiya station, and then a little further, crossing a busy road, and Sam pointed. "Those are the grounds of the Imperial Palace. It's huge." We looked across a moat to a stone wall behind which was a row of trees.

Chuckling, Sam said, "It isn't impressive, until you tour the grounds – which can only be done a couple of days a year ... Or, if you consider the property values in the center of Tokyo. It's astronomical."

Sam tapped the screen of his phone several times and squinted. "The Imperial Palace grounds cover 280 acres; that's about 12 million square feet. And land prices are 3 million to 20 million Yen per square meter. That's about $2,000-15,000 per square foot. So ... the grounds would be worth something like $25-100 *billion*."

That was my Sam, the nerd. When we got off the subway and walked down a street in Akihabara, Sam became even more of a nerd. There were shops for electronic parts, cables, appliances, and the usual consumer products. I let Sam window shop.

We got to an intersection, and Sam pointed to a big building, "BIC camera is one of the biggest camera stores here. We didn't visit the main branch in Shinjuku – or Yodobashi, another big store – so I'd like to pop in for a few minutes, and see what they have."

Sam already knew the latest in tech from the Internet, but I was curious to see how a camera store could be that big. The answer came, as we walked the stairs from floor to floor.

It was more of an electronics store, with whole floors devoted to specific items: cellphones and pocket cameras; DSLR and large-format cameras and lenses; studio photography and darkroom equipment; calculators and PCs; and home appliances.

Sam handled some of the cameras, and then spent time in the drone department. There were hundreds of people in the store, and everyone seemed to be buying something.

We walked back to the metro, and took the same line to Ueno, a huge park with museums, shrines, temples, and the Tokyo Zoo. It was a pretty area, with wide paths leading to all the buildings.

We visited the National Museum of Science and Nature, and then the Tokyo Metropolitan Art Museum. It was actually pretty interesting, with paintings, calligraphy, and sculpture. Sam was fascinated with the collection of swords, and I enjoyed the ceramics, lacquerware, and textiles – which included some beautiful kimonos.

The zoo was fun, also. Of course, we saw the panda exhibit, just inside the gate. The paths were beautiful and we got our walking in for the day. We sat on a bench, under weeping willow trees, and looked out at a large pond. Then, Sam leaned over and we kissed.

"Well, I think you've probably gotten a pretty good feel for Tokyo, in the short time we've been here." We'd actually seen quite a bit. Sam looked at the map on his phone, and scrolled around the area.

"We could still go to a public bath, or 'sento', if you want that experience. Unfortunately, I don't think there are any mixed-gender places in Tokyo. And, you would probably need someone to show you the procedure.

"Basically, you would buy a kit of soap, shampoo, and towel, then go into a changing room and undress. When you come out, there will be a room with faucets, and maybe low showers. You would sit on a stool and bathe yourself, including washing your hair.

"Only then could you go into the public pool and soak in the hot water." Sam smiled, "But if we get to come back and I take you into the countryside, we can visit some real 'onsen' – spas with natural hot-springs. And, if we find a 'konyoku onsen', we would have coed bathing, like in the saunas of Europe."

I declined the public bath house offer. "You've shown me a lot of Tokyo. And I'm ready to go back to the hotel and pack for our flights tomorrow." I gave Sam a loving look, "And then, you can take me to a nice dinner."

We took the Yamanote Line from Ueno back to Shinjuku. As this was an overland train, we were able to see many different parts of Tokyo. Sam had said it would be a dozen stops; not the most direct route, but we only had to take one train, and not have to navigate the stations.

Back in our room, I put on my running shorts and tank. We hadn't gone on a single run during this trip, having had to work from early morning to late evening.

Sam chuckled, "We could still have the hotel send up a masseuse, if you'd like."

I *was* a little tense from all the stresses of the week. "Actually, I wouldn't mind if *you* gave me a massage." As an afterthought, I added, "And we could make love first, so *you're* not so tense." Sam smiled and began undressing.

Chuckling, he said, "This is the first time I'll be giving a 'happy beginning'. It was a great idea."

When I came out of the bathroom, I was surprised that Sam was on the phone. He hung up and turned to me, "We'll need some oil, so I ordered a cup of vegetable oil. They couldn't understand what I was asking for or why, so I just told them I would be using it to massage my wife."

That was close enough, I guess. "You could have used the body lotion they provided." But I realized that those tiny bottles wouldn't cover much of my body for a massage.

We put on the terrycloth hotel robes and slippers, and began packing, as we waited for room service. Fortunately, they came quickly, and they had understood Sam. Now, we had a *lot* of oil.

Sam put two layers of bath towels on the bed, and I sat in Sam's lap, as he drizzled me with oil. I dipped my hand into the oil, and ran my fingers through Sam's chest hairs. When our fronts were slick with oil, we held each other and kissed. We hadn't had much romantic time, this week.

I lay back and Sam straddled me. Then, I massaged *him*; at least one specific part of him. He entered me, and our bodies glided over each other, as I tightened my vaginal muscles around him. Sam knew how to 'hit the spot', and soon my body was on fire.

Wrapping my legs around Sam, I thrusted my pelvis up to meet him. We moved with raw passion, our intensity feral. The orgasm ripped through me, and I continued to thrust until Sam came, moments later. Both our bodies spasmed, over and over, until we were drained, and I relaxed into the bed, Sam's body melting around mine.

After several minutes, Sam gave me a peck on the lips, and climbed off me. "OK, Dr. Walsh, are you ready for your massage, now?" I smiled and nodded. Sam had me turn over and lie on my stomach. Then, I closed my eyes and focused on relaxing each part of my body.

Sam was on the bed with me, sometimes straddling my body, and other times kneeling next to me. As usual, he gave me a great massage, and I was drifting off to sleep by the end. I had lost track of time, and just wanted to keep my body in this relaxed state as long as possible.

Covering me with another towel, Sam kissed my nose, then went into the bathroom and got the shower going. He would probably want me to join him; but I was so tired ...

"Good morning, Kelly." My eyes snapped open, and Sam smiled. He was already dressed in casual business attire. What time was it? I glanced at the alarm clock, and realized I'd slept for more than an hour.

"Why don't you get cleaned up and ready for dinner. I'm doing a little more research. You asked for a 'nice' dinner ... and in Tokyo, the most special thing would be to have a '*Kaiseki*' meal – a gourmet, multicourse, artistic food experience.

"But it might be better experienced with Makoto, who can explain each course. A lot of these restaurants don't have an English menu. And it's a little late to make reservations." It was already nearly 8PM.

Sam chuckled, "And ... a Kaiseki meal for the two of us might run $1000 or more." I shook my head, still wondering how people could afford it. Sam said, "Usually, it's a business expense – like the 'club' last night."

"Sam, we don't have to do anything that fancy tonight."

"Or, we could go to one of the good Kobe steakhouses. They are easier to find, and would probably cost under $300-400, if we got the typical 6-8 ounce portion." I shook my head.

I asked, "Is there any other type of typical Japanese food I haven't tried?"

Now, Sam laughed uproariously. "Kelly, we haven't scratched the surface of Japanese cuisine – '*ryori*'. You haven't even had *fugu*, the poisonous puffer-fish.

"And there are many simple dishes, such as *tonkatsu* – pork cutlet, *okonomiyaki* – pancakes, *onigiri* – rice and seaweed sandwiches, *sukiyaki* – a type of beef 'stew', *yakisoba* – fried noodles, *chankonabe* – a Sumo wrestler dish." Sam took a deep breath.

"OK, I get the idea."

Sam snapped his fingers. "I know what would be fun, and you would like it. While you get dressed, I'll do some Internet searching and look at Yelp reviews; then, we can also check with the concierge for recommendations."

As we walked toward the front doors of the hotel, a young guy dressed in hotel uniform, complete with cap, ran to a bin and brought an umbrella to us. We didn't even know it was raining. Of course, we'd brought our own umbrellas, but this was easier than going back to the room.

Fortunately, the restaurant wasn't a long walk. We were seated right away, and provided rolled-up damp towels to clean our hands. We ordered beers, and Sam perused the menu. It wasn't very big – only two pages – and one entire page showed selections of thinly sliced raw meat on a platter.

Sam selected one, and an appetizer of '*gyoza*', and the waitress took our order. On the table between us was a gleaming, gold, hammered-metal pot on a matching plate. The pot had a top with handles, and a vent through the middle.

Sam had something like this at home that I'd found in one of the cabinets. "Is this a 'Mongolian hot-pot'?" We'd never used the one Sam had.

Taking a swig of his beer, Sam smiled, and said, "We're at a '*shabu shabu*' restaurant. It's very similar to a Mongolian hot-pot, where we cook the vegetables and our own pieces of meat in the boiling broth. High-end restaurants like this one use beautifully marbled meat, shaved so thinly you can almost see through it."

He chuckled, "Do you know what 'onomatopoeias' are?" I shook my head.

Then I laughed, remembering some of the Japanese foods Sam had rattled off – although I knew this wasn't one of them. "Are those the Japanese pancakes? Are we going to have those, too?"

Sam looked at the ceiling, returning the tease, "Those are 'okonomiyaki'." Now, he was laughing, too.

"They're words that sound like the sounds they describe. For example, in English, 'splash' sounds kind of like a splash. And 'beep' sounds like a beep. Or, 'tick-tock', 'flip-flop', 'sizzle'. A lot of bird and animal names and sounds are onomatopoetic.

"You know the film company, Kodak? It was named for the sound their original early 20th-century box cameras made, when the shutter was pressed." Sam really was a fount of knowledge; some of it pretty random.

He smiled, "So, *shabu shabu* is the sound the beef makes when you dip it into the boiling broth, like 'swish swish'." It was a long explanation for a simple answer.

A plate of gyoza was placed on the table. They were half-moon shaped, with scalloped edges and browned top. They reminded me of Italian ravioli. We'd eaten gyoza at home, but these were in a different class – delicate but crispy, the filling tasty but not overpowering.

The waitress returned, and began placing dishes on the table. A large, beautiful bowl contained an artful arrangement of cabbage, enoki mushrooms, some large round mushrooms, scallions, tofu, and rice noodles. There was an egg in a small bowl, and several other bowls with various kinds of sauces.

We watched, as she poured broth from a steaming ceramic pitcher into the golden pot, and carefully placed bunches of the vegetables next to each other in the broth. She adjusted the flame and left, then came back a few moments later with a huge round platter of the beef.

Sam had said 'marbled', but I'd never seen anything like it before. Sam had to take a picture with his phone. Then, he took a few of me, holding chopsticks above the pot of vegetables.

The platter reminded me of the Iberian ham platters we'd had in Barcelona. But, rather than cured ham, this was raw beef. And, instead of having a few large areas of fat, the beef was so finely marbled that it just looked like a paler shade of meat. The edge of each piece was folded, so that it would be easier to pick up with chopsticks.

Our waitress returned with a couple of plates that had country scenes glazed in light and dark greens. She broke the egg over the broth, then served a portion of the cooked vegetables – still artistically arranged, and each separate – onto plates she put in front of us.

Sam refilled my beer from the large Sapporo bottle, and held up his glass, "Here's to completing our trip here, successfully ... I hope." I wasn't 'counting my chickens', yet, but it did seem hopeful. But the thought of valuations like we'd discussed was too unreal to even consider.

We picked up paper-thin slices of meat with our chopsticks and, within a few seconds of being dipped into the pot, we were eating beef that melted in our mouths.

Sam explained that one of the dipping sauces was miso-soy based, and the other – a thicker brownish-orange sauce – was made from sesame seeds. They were both delicious. We also had chopped green onions and ginger, which we could use as a garnish.

We took our time savoring the meal – 'fine dining', as Sam would say. I agreed with him: This really was fun, and special; and the flavors were great.

I jokingly asked, "I guess we're not planning on going to any sex clubs, tonight?" We had already learned quite a bit about the sex lives – or lack thereof – of Japanese men.

Sam slurped some rice noodles into his mouth, and looked up from his plate, "I've never been to anything remotely sexual in Japan. But I understand they have some pretty bizarre 'clubs' – including many with role-play. As far as I know, those are more like a brothel.

"I've read a couple of articles on the 'Happening Bars', which I understand used to be sex clubs where singles could come to have orgies. But they're now considered a scam – nothing we would go to."

He ate a piece of the incredible beef, and smiled, "But I've also heard about 'Couple Kissa' clubs, which are for couples only; basically swinger bars. We would have to swap partners with another couple – hopefully one that spoke English. But I've also heard that many of those clubs may not admit foreigners."

Neither of us was too excited about expanding our circle of sexual relationships, especially on a casual one-time basis. We'd had fun swapping BDSM partners in Amsterdam with Max and Brigitte, but that hadn't included sex.

We finished the second – or was it the third? – large bottle of beer, and Sam suggested a 'light' dessert of green tea ice cream. It was something I enjoyed, and we'd had it many times in our local Japanese or Chinese restaurants.

But after the first taste, I knew this was special. While it was similar to the usual green tea ice cream, it had a very distinctive flavor.

Sam explained, "It's called '*matcha*' ice cream, and uses the special green tea powder that's used in Japanese tea ceremonies ... something *else* you'll have to experience next time."

We walked back to the hotel – this time not having to use the umbrella – and Sam insisted on having a nightcap at the penthouse bar.

It was a dark place, very subdued, with comfortable seating arrangements, and glass windows on two sides, affording an incredible nighttime view of Tokyo. We sat in large chairs across a small table next to the windows on the east side. We could see from Tokyo Tower on our right, to the SkyTree in the far distance to our left.

It had been a good trip. We'd worked hard, and provided all of the information Makoto's company had requested. Now, it depended mainly on having signed letters of intent with one or more of the other companies.

Sam ordered Champagne cocktails, and we toasted again. It was already December, and we'd had an incredible year. My mind spun, as I realized it had only been *this* year that I'd taken the domme course in London, and we'd visited Henk and Zöe in Amsterdam. And then, Kathy's wedding on Kauai. And our trip to Barcelona.

I guess my mind was reeling from the alcohol. But it was still surreal to think that we could end the year by selling KS Biotech. I might be out of a job.

We packed and went to bed. There would be plenty of time tomorrow morning for some lovemaking, before we had to leave for our flight.

CHAPTER 16: HOLIDAY SEASON(ING)

Kelly and I were working hard, trying to satisfy the concerns of the half-dozen companies with whom we were still negotiating. The Japanese business development team had authorized us to let the other developers know that we might be acquired by a large international pharma company, and that they would accept the license terms that we had mostly drafted. It was a complex situation.

After another week of having discussions with each company and re-writing agreements, the possibilities had been narrowed down to one of the U.S. companies, the Swiss company, and the Israeli company. These were smaller pharma developers, and an agreement with a large firm could lead to their own acquisition.

I was fairly certain that Kelly and I would need to visit these companies before entering into an agreement with them. But Kelly had met several of their researchers, and we were only negotiating a letter of intent, not a final agreement.

At least, we didn't have to hop on a plane, and conduct business through Christmas.

We took the KS Biotech team out to a Szechwan Chinese restaurant as a company holiday dinner. Raj excitedly informed me that he'd spoken with his contacts at each of the companies, and it looked like they were ready to sign. What a Christmas present that would be!

Kelly had hoped to throw a small party for her friends, as we had done last year. But Kathy was not coming back to the mainland over the holidays. And Linda was spending a week in Florida, where her boyfriend's parents lived. It seemed her relationship with Matt was getting serious.

We had Dave and Darlene over for a simple Christmas dinner. The relationships between the four of us seemed to be improving, and Dave and Darlene were actually a 'couple' again – something I hadn't seen since well before Sarah died. Kelly and her mother were closer than ever.

They even went into the sauna with us, again ... although we took showers separately. Between sauna courses, all of us in our robes, we showed Kelly's parents some of our pictures from Tokyo. They were happy our business meetings seemed to be successful, but they still had no idea what this could mean, if we closed the deal.

Kelly and I had also avoided the subject of talking about how our lives could be different – not just with other people, but with each other, too. But there were many things that could go wrong, before we closed a deal.

Even if none of the other companies signed a Letter of Intent, the Japanese company would most likely acquire us. And though the valuation would be far less, it still would amount to a lot of money. And if we could close all four companies ...

But even the Japanese company wasn't a sure thing. There were *never* any 'sure things' ... until the money was in the bank. If the stock market fell, or their new drug wasn't as successful as planned, they could delay or walk away from a deal with KS Biotech.

It had been a nice evening with Kelly's parents. They were turning into people that I wouldn't mind having as parents-in-law. But, I guess we were changing, too.

The holidays had been quiet so far, and I was wondering how we might spice-up the last few days of the year. After checking with Sam, I e-mailed Julie, inviting her to join us on New Year's eve. We hadn't seen her for several months. And we'd missed her birthday, as we had been in Barcelona.

Then, I got a call from Alex, Sam's neighbor. She'd wanted to have her niece Fiona, Fiona's husband Justin, and Justin's sister Jasmine come out for Christmas dinner. Fiona had a project with a deadline, and couldn't leave Toronto, but Justin and Jasmine were here, and Alex relayed that they would like to visit us.

Alex had to go to a business meeting out of town for a day, so we set up the visit for that day. It was too bad that Fiona wouldn't be here, but I was sure that we would have fun with Justin and Jasmine.

Sam made a chicken salad that we would serve for lunch, with bread for sandwiches and pitas for a wrap. He also made a batch of coleslaw with a garlicky dressing. For dinner, we planned to barbeque ahi, and Sam would be making his stuffed double-baked potatoes, and a big salad.

We greeted Justin and Jasmine warmly, and brought them down to the playroom, where we sat around the coffee table, and got caught up with each other. We'd only met Jasmine once – at the wedding – and didn't really know much about her.

Jasmine was a 23 year old beauty, with fine facial features, a small nose, and pale blue eyes. Her straight platinum blonde hair fell past her shoulders, and contrasted with the pink sweater she wore over black jeans.

Justin was as handsome as ever, his beard and hair – a bit more red than my darker auburn shade – was neatly trimmed, and he comported himself with an air of confidence. I wondered how much his marriage to Fiona had impacted his outlook. He seemed very happy.

Sam and I updated Justin and his little sister on some of our recent adventures.

It was incredible that since Justin and Fiona's wedding, the only time we'd seen Jasmine, we'd been to Kauai twice; Europe twice – including England, The Netherlands, and Spain; and, recently, Japan. Now, Sam was planning our next trip, which included Israel.

The description of our first Europe trip led to a discussion of the sex club that Greetje and Sofie had taken us to. And, of course, Elena's domme class in London.

That was when Justin admitted one of his motivations for visiting us. "Actually, Kelly, you guys got me interested in needle play – something I'd never heard of, until Fiona told me about her 'experiences' here ... and the pictures she saw of your needle 'artwork'."

I glanced at Sam, and he nodded. A few minutes later, he returned with his laptop, and found two series of photos. One showed the needle 'artwork' that Sam created on my backside during our first long weekend together. The other series was of the corset Sam made on my back during my 25th birthday party, just a few weeks later.

It was amazing to think that was two and a half years ago! Sam and I had shared many BDSM experiences since then, and we'd played with needles ... but never tried making another needle play artwork.

I would be a willing 'canvas' for Sam, but he hadn't been motivated. Perhaps sticking needles in me wasn't as exciting, now that he knew that I would willingly submit because I loved him. And I knew that he wasn't excited about being *my* canvas, although I knew that he would submit to me, if I asked him.

Justin and Jasmine were looking at the images on Sam's screen – Justin with a smile, and Jasmine with wide eyes and her mouth open. "I can show you what it's like, if you want," Sam offered to Jasmine.

She squinted her eyes and shook her head. "I don't think so." She stared at the screen and advanced through the images.

Justin countered, "Well, *I* would like a needle play experience ... if you're up for it." He looked at me seriously, with only a hint of a smile. He explained, "Fiona's 'played' with me a few times, but she's not really interested. And I'm looking for someone through the club, but haven't connected, yet."

I looked at Sam, "Do you think you could entertain Jasmine for an hour or two?" Predictably, Sam smiled.

Then, he asked, "Shall we have lunch, first?"

We sat around the breakfast table, and Sam set out the chicken salad, coleslaw, multi-grain bread, and pitas, along with olives, pickles, and some carrots and celery sticks. He set a pitcher of iced tea on the table, and we all served ourselves.

Turning to Jasmine, Sam asked, "Do you go to Justin's club often?"

Jasmine chewed her sandwich and smiled, "No. I've only been there a few times." She glanced at Justin, "But I was there on Halloween, and it was pretty neat." We'd had a 'pretty neat' Halloween ourselves.

"What was your costume?" If Sam hadn't asked the question, I would have.

Jasmine chuckled, "A Las Vegas showgirl. The top was a bra frame lined with rhinestones, and covered with ostrich feathers. And the bottom was a rhinestone crystal 'belt skirt'. It is basically a fancy jeweled belt, with strings of rhinestones hanging down. It didn't cover much."

She laughed, "And I didn't wear a thong or anything underneath ... but I got myself 'vajazzled'." Sam looked at her questioningly, and she explained, "I had crystals glued on – surrounding my lips, and radiating upward in several lines of jewels."

Sam closed his eyes and shook his head, I'm sure trying to picture Jasmine's privates. I was surprised that he hadn't asked to see any pictures. But the day was just getting going.

When we finished lunch, Sam suggested that he show Jasmine some of our travel pictures on the big screen in the playroom. But I'd decided that it would be easiest to do Justin's needle art on the bed in there, and I wanted to create a bit more 'atmosphere' than having our travel pics flashing on the screen and Sam and Jasmine yapping in the background.

While Sam went downstairs to retrieve his tablet, I went upstairs to change into a running outfit. Justin and I had not yet discussed the plan for his artwork, but I wanted to get comfortable, as I had a feeling he would want an intense – and prolonged – experience.

Kelly took Justin downstairs to the playroom. I was glad that we had recently re-stocked our medical supplies. It was funny that Kelly and I hadn't done much medical play recently; now that I thought about it, the only recent time I could remember was with Amy at Halloween, and when I'd been Kelly's slave.

Jasmine helped me clean up the lunch things, and then we worked together getting the dinner started. She washed and prepared vegetables for the salad, while I made the marinade for the fish. I got the potatoes baking, and made the salad dressing. Everything else could be done at the last moment.

As we washed our hands in the kitchen sink, I asked Jasmine, "So what would you like to do, today? How can I entertain you?" In earlier days, that would have led to a multitude of thoughts on just how I could 'entertain' her.

But, as cute as Jasmine was, I wasn't looking to have an experience with her. She'd already turned down my half-joking (well, not-so-joking) offer to give her a feeling for needle play. And, after having seen me spanked at Fiona and Justin's wedding, she hadn't indicated any interest in learning more about BDSM.

When she shrugged, I offered, "Well, the jacuzzi isn't heated ... but the sauna is, if you're interested."

Jasmine nodded, "That would feel good." Then, I saw a glint from her eyes, and she grinned, "But there *is* one thing that I might ask of you." Uh oh ... I wasn't sure what could be coming next.

"Alex told me that you gave her a great massage. And, when I told her that I'd never actually had a full-body massage, she suggested that I ask you for one ... if you're up for it." What a nice surprise! I was sure Alex knew it would be enjoyable for *both* of us.

When we walked into the pool room, I realized that the massage table had been pushed into the corner – against the sliding glass door, and near Kelly's desk – and not very accessible to give a massage. I pulled it away from the window, and made sure my rolling metal stand had the oils I would need.

"Would you like the massage first, and then the sauna, or the sauna first, and then the massage?" I could think of advantages both ways. "And could I offer you a little wine, so you can get started relaxing?"

"Some wine would be nice. Then the massage." Jasmine frowned, "But I'll need to get showered before the sauna."

I chuckled, "That's part of my 'massage services', bathing you afterward." Again, I was only half-joking.

Jasmine smiled, "Yes. Alex told me about that, also." My reputation had preceded me. And I guess it must have been good, as Alex had recommended that Jasmine try me.

"OK, Jasmine. You can use that bathroom (I pointed to the half-bath at the back of the pool room), and get undressed. You can put this sheet around you. I'm going to change into 'working clothes', and get the wine."

After going upstairs and putting on a running outfit, I went downstairs to the playroom to get the wine. There was quiet discussion between Justin and Kelly. I was tip-toeing across the carpet, when Kelly looked up. I waved to her and pointed to the bar, and she nodded, and turned back to Justin.

I retrieved a nice rosé wine from the bar fridge, and tip-toed back upstairs, stopping to adjust the thermostat upward by two degrees before grabbing two wine glasses and returning to the pool room. This was the *third* déja vù, when I saw Jasmine sitting on the massage table, the sheet pulled up around her, and swinging her legs.

Opening the wine, and pouring glasses for both of us, I toasted, "Here's to your first massage experience." We sipped the cool, fresh wine that had a distinctive floral bouquet. Then, I reverted to the teacher; actually, it was my penchant for honesty and complete disclosure – I think – that drove me.

"There can be many 'purposes' for a massage. But my goal is to help relax your muscles, and relax your entire body. It should be something that you enjoy. And, if done right, you'll have a 'tingling' feeling afterward.

"So, it's very important that you're comfortable. If I do anything that doesn't feel good, please let me know." I had to chuckle, "Actually, a good massage can hurt a little, if your muscles are knotted up ... but I'm not trying to do a 'therapeutic' massage.

"And, you have to know that I'm not a licensed masseur." The wine was tasting better. "So I won't charge you for the massage." Now, Jasmine laughed, easily, as she drank the wine and continued to swing her legs.

She was only four years younger than Kelly, but there was a huge difference in their maturity levels. Jasmine seemed self-confident, upbeat, and relaxed; and she was certainly cute. But Kelly had a more mature bearing, while still being young and playful.

Perhaps Kelly wasn't quite as 'playful' as she'd been when we met, but our shared experiences and trust in each other – *and* willingness to submit, occasionally – had solidified our relationship. I could easily imagine having an 'infatuation' with Jasmine; but I was in love with Kelly.

I offered Jasmine a second glass of wine, letting her know that it would be OK, if she fell asleep during her massage. But she declined; which was good, as I would have probably joined her ... and I had to save my strength for the massage.

Jasmine lay on her stomach, and I explained the face hole in the table, which she thought weird. I draped her with the sheet, then turned it down to her waist. Warming the oil in my hands, I realized that I should have probably put on some 'new age' music, lightly in the background.

I gave Jasmine the usual massage (at least, the way I'd been trained to give one), starting on her shoulders, neck and back, then massaging her butt with my hands under the sheet. Re-draping her, I exposed her right leg and hip and worked down her muscles to her foot, where I spent time massaging her sole.

Re-draping her again, I worked from hip to foot on her left side. I folded the sheet so that it was tucked between Jasmine's legs, and covering just the middle of her butt. Then, I worked up on both sides, from her ankles, calf, thigh, and hip. My hands wrapped around one leg and then the other, giving her long strokes, nearly to her crotch.

Once again, I covered Jasmine fully with the sheet., and ran my hands up her back until they were holding her shoulders. Bending over her, I whispered, "You can turn over, now."

I held the sheet up as Jasmine turned over onto her back, then let the sheet fall, covering her again. Her perky breasts tented the sheet, and her nipples were clearly outlined . "How are you doing?" I hoped she was enjoying the experience.

"It's wonderful. I'm feeling very relaxed." She closed her eyes, and I continued, massaging her ears, forehead, and face. Then, I let my hands dive under the sheet, between her breasts and down as far as I could reach, then coming up the sides of her body.

Jasmine was doing fine, comfortable with me seeing and touching her body. Of course, we'd seen most of each other's bodies during Justin and Fiona's crazy wedding party at the club. And Jasmine and I would be going into the sauna in just a little while. It was nice that this generation seemed much more relaxed about nudity.

Folding the sheet down to the top of her pubic hair, I massaged her middle – hips, stomach, and chest, this time coming up between her breasts and over her shoulders.

Although not a 'usual' part of a massage, I finally glided my oily hands over her breasts; not lingering or massaging her breasts directly, but covering them along with the rest of her upper body.

I re-draped her, and folded the lower portion of the sheet between her legs, exposing her entire lower body, except for a swath of sheet hiding her privates. Taking my time, I massaged each of her legs again, from the hips down, and then focused on a toe massage.

After re-draping her again, I bent down and kissed Jasmine on the tip of her nose. Her eyes blinked open, and she smiled. "I really could have fallen asleep. And my body really *is* tingling."

Now that the 'official' massage had been finished, and well-received, I asked hopefully, "Would you allow me to give you a 'happy ending'?"

"A wha ..." Then, she grinned, "You're sweet, Sam. I don't think so, right now. I'm too relaxed to get 'excited'."

I tucked the sheet in around her body, and kissed her on the nose again. "Why don't you close your eyes and just relax and enjoy the feeling?" Jasmine nodded. "I'll come back in a few minutes and bring a robe for you to wear down to the sauna ... if you're not asleep."

As I turned to head out of the room, Jasmine reached out and grabbed my wrist. "Thank you, Sam. It was a great massage; I really enjoyed it."

Before I could make a joke about Jasmine not having had any massages to compare mine with, she chuckled, "At least, that was definitely the best massage I've ever had."

We laughed, and I said, sincerely, "You're welcome, Jasmine. I'm glad you enjoyed it." It had been good exercise ... and I always enjoyed doing nice things for cute nude women.

I went downstairs and peeked into the playroom, then waved to get Kelly's attention. I gave her the dive sign for 'Are you OK?', and she gave me the same sign, letting me know that everything was OK. Justin was silent, and Kelly returned her focus to his backside.

After undressing in the downstairs bathroom and donning a robe, I selected one for Jasmine, and went back upstairs. I wouldn't bother her if she was sleeping.

But she was awake and sitting on the edge of the massage table again, the sheet pulled up around her. I handed her the robe, and she let the sheet drop and hopped off the table to put on the robe – which was way too long for her.

I poured another glass of wine for each of us, and we toasted to Jasmine's first massage. The price had been right, but she should really try a professional massage, next time. In any case, she seemed content.

"Shall we get a shower and go into the sauna?" I didn't know whether she'd ever been in a sauna before. I led her down the stairs, but she had to lift the robe to avoid tripping. I got the shower started and we hung our robes and got in.

Jasmine was happy to let me bathe her, and she was very nice to return the favor and bathe me. We both covered all of each other's bodies, but didn't dwell on the sensitive areas. Jasmine had a lot of poise and confidence, for her age. But she still seemed a girl, compared to Kelly's rapidly-maturing womanhood.

We stepped into the sauna, and I showed Jasmine how to position her towel to keep her feet off the lower bench. But she decided to sit cross-legged. As the warmth enveloped us, Jasmine closed her eyes.

"If the massage, and wine, and sauna really do put you to sleep, I can tuck you into the bed in our guest bedroom, and let you nap for a while. I have no idea how long Kelly will be working on Justin, but it looked like a pretty big project."

Jasmine shook her head, "I guess Justin likes pain."

"It isn't as painful as you think, and you get used to it. The endorphins produced in your body dull the pain." I wondered whether Jasmine might give me a chance to demonstrate, but from her prior response, I doubted it.

We made it a full ten minutes before we were boiling, then got out and rinsed off together. We put on our robes, and sat on the chaises, and I poured the rest of the wine.

"For full disclosure, it's not really a good idea to drink wine and go in the sauna. So please be sensitive to your own body, and let me know if you're feeling weak." I got up and ran over to the bar fridge and pulled out two bottles of water.

It wasn't until I got back to the shower room that I realized I had forgotten that Kelly and Justin were still playing. Maybe the wine *was* affecting me?

Jasmine said, brightly, "I think we should check on Justin and Kelly." She stood and opened her robe, then re-wrapped it tighter and belted it. She lifted the hem and walked out of the bathroom and into the playroom. I followed her, curious to see what she would find.

I looked up and saw Jasmine and Sam walking toward us. Justin had already told me that he wanted to 'show off' his needle artwork to his sister, so I waved them over.

We still weren't done, but the main pattern of scrolls and swirls now ran from his thighs to his shoulders, arcing across his upper back. Spiral offshoots covered most of his butt, and I was now working on a chevron pattern down each of his legs.

As Jasmine approached the bed, she asked, "So how's my masochistic brother doing?"

When she actually saw Justin's body skewered with more than a hundred needles, she gasped. "You really *do* like pain. That looks horrible!"

Then, she turned to me, "I mean, the 'artwork' is beautiful ... but I can't believe anyone would volunteer for that." I slipped another needle through a pinch of skin on Justin's calf, and Jasmine winced.

Sam chuckled, "I tried to explain that they were thin needles, and the endorphin rush should mitigate some of the pain. I offered her a chance to see what it feels like, but she hasn't made up her mind, yet."

Of course, I expected that Sam would 'offer' something like that, and it appeared that Jasmine would not be interested. I decided to help out, although I doubted that it would change Jasmine's mind.

"The two types of needlework here are straight-in insertions, where the design is based on the hub color. And different colors represent different thickness needles." As Jasmine stood at the foot of the bed and watched, I inserted a needle in the middle of Justin's left butt cheek, and another on the right side.

"So what do *you* think, Justin? Is it as painful as it looks?" Of course, I'd experienced it, so knew exactly how it felt.

Justin turned his head, "It's not that bad, although it's pretty intense when you first start. I barely felt the needles Kelly just inserted."

Then he chuckled – and immediately moaned, as his back muscles had moved. "The other needles that skewer my skin do hurt when they're inserted. But after a while, you don't feel individual needles. Actually, my body feels alive, and I feel almost like I'm stoned."

I decided to give Jasmine a further demonstration, so I took a pinch of Justin's calf and pushed a needle through.

It was only going through the skin, but there was pain when the needle pokes from the inside back out.

"How long will you guys be?" Sam asked.

I shrugged, "At least a half hour, maybe more. Justin wanted me to do his entire body, but we agreed to do just his backside." I looked Sam in the eye, "I'm going to have him stand and walk around a little, when we're done." Of course, that would be painful, but liberating.

Sam turned to Jasmine, "How about one more sauna course?" Jasmine smiled and nodded, and they took their leave. I knew that Sam would come up with *something* to keep Jasmine amused.

Jasmine and I sat on the lower bench of the sauna, and I turned over the hourglass, a fine stream of sand now falling through its waist. Jasmine had her hands in her lap, and – even in the dim red darkness – I was sure she was moving her fingers.

Following my 'openness' policy, I asked, "Were you turned on by seeing Justin skewered with needles? Your brother in pain?" Although he was obviously not in that much pain, now that he was 'in the zone'.

Jasmine shrugged, "Maybe, a little." She thought a few moments and looked up, "It's not really the pain that turned me on – Justin wasn't even crying, and didn't make a sound when Kelly inserted the needles.

"But the casualness of Kelly, sitting there and inserting needles one after another, and Justin being so relaxed as he let Kelly stick him ... was impressive. I'm not sure which part exactly turned me on, but the scene was surreal."

Yes, we'd had a lot of surreal 'scenes' over the past couple of years. As memories flooded my brain, I became sad that Kelly's three closest friends wouldn't be joining us this holiday season. Except Julie, who would be going to New Year's dinner with us.

"Jasmine, you must have gotten shots before ... and maybe even in the rear, like penicillin?"

"Sure. In fact, because I was having long and heavy bleeding during my periods, my ob/gyn switched me from an IUD to birth control shots. I go in every three months, and get a shot in the rear."

She looked up at me quickly, flinging a sweat droplet from her nose, "And it's not a fun experience. But a few minutes of pain is worth it to avoid a month being really uncomfortable."

"The injection part hurts more than the needle, in my opinion. So maybe I could show you what a very thin needle feels like, when nothing is injected." I held my breath, not really expecting Jasmine to respond positively.

"Let me think about it." That was the best I could hope for ... and she was still moving her fingers in her lap. She wiped her face with a corner of the towel. "Can we get out, now? I'm getting hot." According to the timer, we'd made it 8 minutes.

When we were in the shower, I said, "And now for the finish of your massage – a body washing." I began soaping her shoulders, then chest, then her breasts. Jasmine seemed quite content to let me continue.

I moved down her body, quickly passing through her pubic area on the way to her legs. Once she was soaped-up, I took a Loufah and scrubbed her from neck to toes.

Then, I turned her around, and soaped her backside with my hands, and then scrubbed with the Loufah. Squeezing more soap into my hands, I returned to her butt, massaging, and letting my fingers slip down her crack and over her anus.

As she hadn't complained, I inserted a finger into her rear – the soap making it very quick and easy. Jasmine stiffened for a moment, and then relaxed. Rather than take my finger out, I inserted it further. "Is this OK?"

Jasmine slowly nodded. "Sam ..."

I waited for her to complete the sentence, but she was quiet. I pulled my finger out, and stepped in front of Jasmine. "What is it? You should tell me, if I do anything you don't like." I started soaping myself.

Shaking her head, Jasmine lowered her eyes, "Sam ... could I please take you up on that 'happy ending', now?"

I almost laughed; maybe Jasmine really was getting turned on by the idea of needle play. I hugged her, our bodies pressed together as the water streamed over us.

"Of course, Jasmine, I'd love to do that for you." I hoped she wouldn't mind just a 'hand-job', as I didn't plan on going down on her.

I turned her around, and put my arms around her waist, reaching down to her folds with my fingers, and began stroking her clit, a finger on each side, then massaging her hood in a circular pattern.

As she started breathing heavily, I put one arm under her – between her legs, my hand now reaching up, fingers sliding along her clit. I had intended on holding a breast with my other hand, but couldn't reach that far, so I massaged her butt.

She put a hand on mine, and guided me, letting me know when I was in the right spot by her sudden intakes of breath. Jasmine was thrusting, now, her body suddenly spasming as she came. She lifted my hand off her, and I came around and hugged her again.

We finished washing ourselves without discussion. As we were drying off, Jasmine said, "OK." It was so quiet, I wasn't sure it was directed at me. I tilted my head, and she looked at me, her blue eyes sparkling, "I guess you can show me what the needles feel like."

Before I had even processed this, she said, urgently, "But you have to stop, if I don't like it."

"Of course, Jasmine."

As I combed out her hair, I explained that the submissive, or 'sub', was really in control of a scene. And the dominant, or 'dom', had the responsibility of taking the sub to her limit, but not beyond. I emphasized that everything is done with love and respect.

We put on our robes, and walked across the hall, where I punched in the code to open the exam room door. It was still another déjà vu moment, when I pushed the door open, and Jasmine stared, her mouth dropping open.

"We like to play doctor, sometimes."

Jasmine shook her head, unbelieving. "Are you a doctor?"

I laughed, "No. This is all for play – nothing too serious. Actually, I have a doctorate, so you could call me 'Dr. Johnson' ... but then you'd have to call Kelly 'Dr. Walsh'."

Nodding, Jasmine said, "Yeah, I guess I remember Fiona telling us about you examining her piercings."

"She also let us stick her with some needles. Actually, Kelly and I inserted ten in her bottom, and Fiona didn't complain. But I guess it's not something that turns her on, either.

"Why don't you just loosen the sash of the robe and lie down on your stomach." She did as I asked, and I lifted the bottom of the robe up to her waist. Then I lubed the thermometer and held it up, "We'll just take your rectal temperature, to get you into the medical mood."

Jasmine laughed as I inserted the thin glass tube. "I can't remember ever having my temperature taken that way in a doctor's office." Then she surprised me, "And your finger wasn't a big deal, either."

"Have you tried anal sex?" Jasmine shook her head. "Have you had anything larger than a finger inside you?" Again, she shook her head.

I stepped to the counter and opened one of the drawers, taking out three very different possibilities. Then, I pulled out our largest butt plug – something that was too large for comfort, and held it up. "If you want a 'bigger deal', I could give you a different kind of experience."

Jasmine's eyes went wide seeing the huge plug. I laughed and put it back into the drawer. "I was actually thinking about one or two of these." I first held up the bumpy glass plug, which wasn't more than an inch in diameter, but had bumps along all the sides, which would provide an interesting sensation.

"Or this one." I held up the bullet-shaped metal plug with a jewel at the end. "The neck is narrow, so once it's in you, it would be comfortable."

Then, I lifted the anal beads by the string, "And these will pop into you easily, and provide a completely different kind of feeling."

Especially, if she was doing jumping jacks. I saw Kelly and her friends on the sand dune on Honopu Beach, each with one of these inside them, watching *me* doing jumping jacks with the balls clicking – Kelly 'punishing' me for trying to get out of having those balls inside me.

And those had been in all of us during our 'epic' swim to Kalalau. I was ready to go back to Kauai again, especially during these cold winter months. But it looked like our foreseeable future would be filled with travel and business meetings. I wondered when we would ever get back there.

As I was having these thoughts, I opened a couple of packages of needles, and an alcohol swab. "Are you ready for a little 'prick'? It shouldn't feel worse than a mosquito bite." Jasmine looked at me doubtfully, but gave a nod.

I swabbed her and quickly inserted the inch-and-a-half needle up to its blue hub. There was a soft 'Ow', and then she was quiet.

"That's all there is; it's not going to get any worse."

Jasmine chuckled, "Still, I don't like mosquito bites."

I reached over and swabbed her other hip. "Shall we balance it out with one more?" Jasmine put her head in the pillow and I darted the needle into her.

"Now just relax for a minute or two." I spread her buttocks and slid the thermometer back and forth a few times, then took it out of her.

After washing my hands, I put my head near hers, and stroked her hair. "You're being very brave, young lady."

She chuckled again, "How long are you going to leave them in?"

I shrugged, "Until you tell me to take them out."

Smiling, she said, "Well, they're not that bad. But you can take them out, now." I pulled the needles out and dropped them into the sharps container.

"Would you like to try some of the butt plugs, now?" I intended to have her roll over onto her back and pull her knees to her chest.

Jasmine replied, "Not especially. Maybe we could do that some other time?" I chuckled and nodded, but it was doubtful that I would get the chance to play with Jasmine again. I pulled her robe back down, and she sat up on the exam table.

Suddenly, an image popped into my head – Justin standing, facing away from my camera, Kelly's needle art on his back; and Jasmine standing next to him, facing the camera ... with needle art on her front.

Of course, I knew that she wouldn't tolerate hundreds of needles in an intricate pattern, to match Justin's. But perhaps the same effect could be obtained with less than a tenth that many needles, *if* Jasmine were willing ...

I told her about my 'vision', and suggested that she try a few superficial needles. She wasn't crazy about the idea, but could visualize what I was describing, and decided it would be a neat image, and that her brother would be proud of her trying something so extreme. Once again, she relented on the condition that I would stop when she'd had enough.

Jasmine hopped down from the exam table, and went across the hall to pee, while I set out some supplies. When she returned, she took off the robe, dropping it on the chair, and hopped back onto the table.

I had her lay on her back, and then used several alcohol swabs to clean the areas that I would target – her breasts, abdomen, hips, and fronts of her thighs. As a last-minute thought, I had her take a couple of Advil; they would take time to act, but might lessen her discomfort.

Taking a small pinch of skin at the edge of her right areola, I pushed the 25-gauge needle quickly through, eliciting a quiet 'Ouch!' from Jasmine. Then, I did the same on her left side.

Over the next ten minutes, I placed a rosette of six needles radiating out from each nipple, six more – in two rows of three on her abdomen, looking like the buttons of a double-breasted jacket, and finally another dozen that made three downward-facing 'arrows' on the front of each of her thighs.

I was amazed that Jasmine had not only let me insert 30 needles, but hadn't even complained. Her eyes had been closed the entire time. "This is probably good enough for the photos ... unless you would like me to fill in some of the gaps."

Jasmine opened her eyes and smiled. That was a good sign. Then, she shook her head, "I think I've gotten a pretty good feeling for this 'hobby' of yours." She laughed, then immediately groaned due to the movement of the needles. "Actually, I feel like a pincushion, and I'm not sure any more would make a difference."

I laughed, and nodded, but didn't push her any farther. However, I did have one more idea ...

We were basically finished with Justin's backside artwork, and I had no idea how many needles we'd used, but nearly two boxes of the 25-gauge needles, and probably half a box of the 23-gauge and 21-gauge sizes. Altogether, he must have 300 needles in him.

I glided my fingers across the hubs of the spirals of needles on his hips, and the chevrons running down the backs of his legs, potentially releasing more endorphins. Justin appeared to be in a different 'space'.

Sam walked across the playroom to his desk, then walked to the bed with a camera bag over his shoulder. "Are you guys ready for the photo-shoot?"

Justin turned his head, "What photo-shoot?"

"We always like to document our work ... and there will be a special surprise." I looked up at Sam probingly, but he just smiled, keeping me in suspense. He stepped up onto the bed, and snapped some photos of Justin from the side and from above – Justin groaning every time Sam took a step on the bed.

Sam turned on a handheld flash, triggered by the flash on his camera, and took a bunch more shots, varying the position of the lights, and making adjustments on the back of his camera. Then he hopped off the bed, and Justin moaned. "I'll be right back. Then, we can help Justin up, so I can take some really *good* pictures."

Sam put his camera stuff down, and headed toward the hall. I couldn't imagine what the 'surprise' could be. A few moments later, I heard some moaning from the exam room, and then Jasmine and Sam walked toward the bed – Sam still in his robe, and Jasmine totally nude.

It wasn't until she came closer that I realized that she now had some needle art on *her* body ... although it was sparse, compared to Justin's intricate design. She beamed at me, and all I could say was "Wow! You did it!"

Jasmine nodded, "Sam tied me down and forced me to endure this torture." Sam was stammering for a response. But I knew that he hadn't forced Jasmine – at least, not physically; that wasn't Sam's style.

When she was standing at the foot of the bed, at Justin's feet, she whistled and said to Justin, "I feel like a porcupine has showered me with quills, and it's only been a few minutes. And you have ten times the needles and they've been in ten times as long."

Justin couldn't turn his head enough to see Jasmine, so Sam and I helped him slide off the bed and stand up. There were a lot of 'Aaahh's', but we finally got him up.

When he saw Jasmine, he smiled. "Gee, sis, if I'd had any idea you would be into this, I'd have just asked you to play with me. We wouldn't have had to fly all the way out here." He surveyed his sister from top to bottom, and shook his head.

Jasmine laughed, "I'm not really *into* this. But Sam had an idea for a photo that I thought would be interesting. And I wanted to get a feeling for what you were going through ... and *boy*, do I have a 'feeling'."

Sam chuckled, "Then, we're ready to finish your backside ... and Justin's front." I gave him a dirty look, and he backed off. We positioned Justin against the foot of the bed, facing the bed, and Jasmine next to him, facing outward. I had to admit that this made a pretty good image – the needles on Justin's back and Jasmine's front.

As he stepped around in front of them, holding his flash at various angles, he snapped a bunch of shots. Then, he asked me to turn down the lights over the bed, and he repeated the process, taking both natural light and flash photos. Sam even tried some shots with the remote flash facing upward from their feet.

Justin and Jasmine were natural models: They changed their positions slightly between each shot, and looked very relaxed. Justin's head was turned, looking at Jasmine, and she looked at him, her hand on his shoulder, then reaching around his front.

"Hey, Sis!" Jasmine chuckled. I hadn't seen, but could imagine what Jasmine had grabbed. They were obviously very close with each other. Jasmine put her hand around Justin's head, and pulled it toward her, their lips just inches apart, eyes gazing into each other.

Sam continued to take photos, then I turned up the lights, and he took some close-ups; of the needles surrounding Jasmine's nipples, the four legs adorned with arrow patterns, and the spirals on Justin's hips and butt.

Then, Sam headed for the exam room again. Justin gave Jasmine a peck on the lips, and said, "Thank you, sis. That was really courageous, and I appreciate you doing it for me." Then, he grinned, "These pictures should be interesting. I might have to make a poster and put it in my office at the club." Jasmine didn't seem concerned.

When Sam returned, he spoke to Jasmine, "I have one more idea ... if you'd let me do it. We can be completely finished in five minutes." He held up a handful of needles, and Jasmine rolled her eyes.

Turning to me, Jasmine asked, "Does he do this to you all the time?" I had to laugh, since I couldn't remember the last time Sam had stuck me with a needle.

Sam inserted three needles on the sides of each of Jasmine's hips, then pulled them out so the stainless steel was showing. Next, he took a ribbon – it was the pink one from my 'corset' – and looped it across Jasmine's front, back and forth between the needles in her hip. It made a kind of 'skirt' that hid most of Jasmine's privates.

One more round of photos, and Sam was done. "Are you guys sure you don't want us to finish your backs and fronts?" Nobody was laughing, so Sam escorted Jasmine back to the exam room.

I turned to Justin and noticed that he was a little hard. "You've been a great 'canvas' for my artwork. I hope you like it ... and it wasn't too painful."

Justin smiled, "I only saw the small images on the back of Sam's camera ... but it looked beautiful. And it's been an interesting – and just a little painful – experience. I don't think Fiona would enjoy it, but there really is a 'rush'. I feel really buzzed right now."

Chuckling, I reached over and held his cock. "Looks like you're feeling some other things, too. Did seeing your little sister with needles in her turn you on?"

"Maybe a little. I never thought she would give it a try. Sam must be pretty convincing."

My mind swirled, as I hoped that he was convincing with the companies with whom we were negotiating. Now *that* would really get *me* feeling buzzed. I still didn't want to think about the possible money involved.

I took Justin's frenulum between my thumb and forefinger of my left hand, and moved them back and forth like I was calling for the bill in a restaurant. My right hand glided carefully down his growing member, trying not to pull the series of rings adorning the underside.

"Would you allow me to reward you now, for your cooperation in making the needle art? But only if Fiona would allow it."

Justin looked into my eyes, "You don't *have* to ... but I wouldn't refuse. And Fiona and I have already played around with you and Sam."

I nodded, "I would like you to take me from behind ... after I give you some oral attention. But would you mind if we used a condom? I'm a little nervous about your jewelry and piercings."

"Sure. That would be fine. But only if you would enjoy it ... and Sam would allow it." Touché. Sam would probably be a little surprised we were going this far, but I knew he wouldn't resent it.

"Just a moment. You can do yourself and get ready."

I ran across the playroom and into the bathroom, where I took a condom from the medicine cabinet. Then, I stepped to the exam room door. Sam was sitting in the chair with Jasmine standing before him, as he pulled out the needles and dropped them into a sharps container.

When he looked up, I said softly, "Could you guys please give us some privacy for a few minutes." I let Sam see the condom in my hand, and he gave me a lopsided smile, and nodded.

Returning to Justin, I put the condom over his now-hard and upward-pointing cock. Then, I took him into my mouth. The feeling of his rings was interesting, and I swirled my tongue around them.

When Justin's breathing told me he was ready, I took off my running shorts and bent over the corner of the bed. This would be the easiest position for Justin – to avoid undue movement of the needles – as he could remain standing.

As Justin's length slid into me, my body trembled. My hands reached under and took care of my own needs, as my fantasy took over. I held myself on the edge, until Justin came, and then let myself climax. I heard a soft 'Oooww!' as Justin came out of me, and changed position.

I sat on the corner of the bed, and Justin turned around so I could remove the needles from his backside.

Jasmine had yelped when I removed a few of the needles, but she did very well. It had turned out to be quite a 'brother-sister act'. I knew that some of my photos, with perhaps just a little processing, would be epic.

I had been surprised when Kelly stuck her head in the door holding the condom, but not shocked. I had hoped that the needle play experience would be a turn-on for Justin, and for Kelly. So it wasn't surprising that one or both of them would be interested in sex by the end.

After swabbing Jasmine with an antiseptic solution, we went into the shower room and got dressed. "Jasmine, I apologize if I pushed you too hard, today. I know you were afraid of needles. But I was really proud of you." I hugged her as she stood in her panties and bra.

Jasmine grinned, "I wanted to push myself; especially after seeing my brother. And it wasn't as bad as getting shots at the doctor's office." She pulled her sweater over her head, and chuckled, "But I surprised myself, also."

It was New Year's eve, and I couldn't believe another year had flown by. I had barely gotten my degree a year ago, and now I had published a paper, made presentations, and was granted a patent. Now, we were on the verge of selling KS Biotech, and stood to make a lot of money.

Julie came over in the late afternoon, and Sam opened a bottle of French Champagne. We toasted to each other's success in the coming year, and marveled at what had transpired over the past twelve months. Kathy had gotten married. I'd become a pro-domme. And Sam and I had traveled to Europe twice and Japan once.

We told Julie about our upcoming speed-trip to New York, Geneva, and Tel Aviv. Then, Sam blew it by suggesting we toast to KS Biotech which, he told Julie, could net her 'one or two million dollars'.

The problem was that the deal with the Japanese company may never close, in which case KS Biotech could be worth nothing ... until we came up with another strategy. It wasn't fair to get someone excited about something that might not actually occur.

I told Julie that we had a lot of work to do, to make it happen, and that there was a good possibility we would fail, and her stock could be worth nothing. Giving each of my friends and my brothers 0.5% of the stock hadn't seemed like much, but if we could close *all* the deals, each of them would receive as much as $6 million!

We went to the French restaurant, which we hadn't been to in a long time; actually, the only times this year may have been on my birthday, and when we celebrated the patent granting with Raj. There was a special multi-course New Year's menu, with wine-pairing.

George, the waiter, told us that they had only one seating, so we could stay as long as we wanted. And that there would be fireworks in the nearby park. I suspected that Sam, Julie and I would have some 'fireworks' of our own, tonight.

We really hadn't seen much of Julie since Kathy's wedding on Kauai. It wasn't for lack of friendship, or desire, but just a fact of our current existence, putting all of our time and energy into the company.

The dinner was incredible – both the dishes and wines very special, and George 'sneaking' a platter of all the desserts, as well as a nearly-full bottle of the dessert wine, onto the table for our enjoyment. And weight gain. Sam and I were only running sporadically now, but we would have to resolve to keep fit, in the new year.

Sam drove us home in silence, all of us fading rapidly, due to the excessive food and drink. We went downstairs, and Sam stepped behind the bar. I was about to get upset with him – we *certainly* didn't need any more alcohol – until he emerged with three bottles of water in his hands.

"Thank you, Sam," Julie said gratefully.

Taking a swig of his water, Sam asked, jovially, "Anybody up for the sauna?" Both Julie and I groaned.

Julie said, "How about if we just take a quick shower together, and then climb into bed?"

We undressed by the desk, and got into the shower. Sam bathed Julie, while she bathed me, while I bathed Sam. I held his cock and teased him a little, but – as I had suspected – he wouldn't be 'up' for anything tonight.

But the shower had awakened me, at least enough to think about making it with Julie. When we walked into the playroom, Sam groaned, "We missed midnight!"

I kissed Sam, and then Julie kissed Sam, and finally Julie and I had a prolonged deep kiss, our naked bodies pressed together. When we came up for air, I turned to Sam, "I don't think we missed anything, tonight."

We crawled into the big bed in the playroom, and dimmed the lights. I held Sam, and whispered, loud enough for Julie to hear, "You're not going to get it up tonight, so Julie and I are going to make it ... and we'll let you watch. And then, we'll both take good care of you in the morning."

I lifted my head so that I could see Julie, "If all of that is OK with Julie." She smiled and nodded. I kissed Sam again, "Good night, Sam. And happy New Year!"

Julie moved over and kissed Sam, "Good night, Sam. And ditto for me." Then, Julie moved back to the other side of the bed, and I crawled over Sam and on top of Julie.

Sam knew his limits, and hadn't complained. He would get to watch us now, and 'have' us in the morning. I kissed Julie savagely, and we held each other tight. Then, I turned around, and we lay in a sideways '69' position.

My arm hung over Julie's waist, and I held her butt, as I used my nose to massage her hood, then let my tongue swirl around her clit. Julie was doing the same to me, and I could almost imagine that I was alone, doing myself.

We climaxed nearly together, and I turned around and climbed on top of Julie again, kissing her languidly, and holding her hair. As we came down, I realized that I'd completely forgotten that Sam had been watching us.

I lifted my head and looked over to him, ready to thank him and tell him good night again ... but he was gently snoring. Kissing Julie again, I whispered, "Thank you for being our friend, Julie. Happy New Year."

Julie hugged me tightly, and then I crawled back over Sam, and lay next to him. My fiancé, the man I loved. How different my life would have been had I not met him! I couldn't even imagine.

Of course, we would keep our promise: As I drifted off, I already started thinking of how Julie and I could creatively take care of *Sam's* needs, in the morning.

CHAPTER 17: NOUVEAU RICHE

I knew we would have to do it: All of the companies wanted to meet with us in person, and talk with Kelly about technical matters. The Letters of Intent were worked out, in principle, and would be signed when we visited each company. At least, that was the plan.

The itinerary was done, and reservations made, for a 'quick' trip to New York, Geneva, and Tel Aviv. The Business Class fare would allow us to change dates for each leg of the trip, depending on our meetings ... if flights were available. Late January wasn't the ideal time for any of these places, but this wasn't a pleasure trip ... although getting the LOIs signed would definitely be a pleasure.

We began our 2-week junket by flying to New York on Sunday. It would have been nice had we been able to fly in on Friday, or even Saturday – both to get in some sightseeing, and perhaps even try one of the BDSM clubs.

But it had taken every bit of our time to prepare to leave this soon. Kelly and her team had done preliminary work to show feasibility of using her technology to target drugs in the specific areas of interest of each of the companies.

She was still crunching numbers, as we flew over Manhattan, and came in for a landing at La Guardia. We took a taxi into the city, where we were staying at a well-located boutique hotel. Instead of backpacks, we were each carrying a roll-on case and a large briefcase.

Having never been to New York, Kelly was amazed at the skyscrapers towering above us, as the taxi took us across the Queensboro Bridge into midtown.

I was amazed how fast we'd gotten into town: The trip, usually via FDR drive or the midtown tunnel, could easily take more than an hour, but we'd done it in half the time, as it was Sunday.

After checking in, we walked down to Times Square, more a spectacle than ever, with nearly every building lined with flashing lights, scrolling signs, and video displays.

Then, we walked to Rockefeller Center, where people were ice skating in the sunken rink, backed by the huge gold statue of Prometheus and surrounded by flags. "Prometheus was the Greek titan who stole fire from Mount Olympus and gave it to man, beginning the development of civilization," I explained to Kelly.

"Do you want to ice skate?" Unfortunately, the Christmas tree was already gone, but it might be a fun, and unexpected, thing to do on our first day in New York.

Kelly smiled and shook her head. We walked to 5th avenue, and window-shopped some of the top jewelry and clothing stores.

I checked my watch, as we would be meeting my son, Mark, at his apartment in the East Village. I had never been there, and was curious to see how he lived. He kept telling me that it was a very small place that he shared with his partner, Greg.

Mark was an artist, and not particularly interested in material things. But Sarah and I had brought him up with good food, and cultural experiences; I knew that he was struggling – as were most of the artists and musicians in the city. But I respected his courage and fortitude.

Kelly wasn't terribly interested in most of the stores – and the prices of things were outrageous. It was only open another hour, but I suggested we sample MOMA – New York's famous Museum of Modern Art. It was enjoyable, but too rushed of a visit. Walking a block or two, we stopped at an Irish pub, with dark wood paneling, and St. Patrick's day posters already up.

Over beers, I had to apologize to Kelly again. "As with most other big cities, it would take weeks to see New York properly. At the very least, you should see the Empire State building and Freedom Tower, take a cruise, walk through Central Park, see the Museum of Natural History, the Metropolitan Museum of Art, the Guggenheim, ..."

I took another quaff of Guinness. "Then, there's the Statue of Liberty. And seeing plays, and a concert at Carnegie Hall. Just walking around the neighborhoods is fascinating – Chinatown, Little Italy, Wall Street, ..."

Shaking my head, I could only say, "There are a lot of places I'd like to take you back to ... to really experience them."

Kelly put her hand on mine, commiserating, and nodded, "I know, Sam. Maybe, someday, we'll have time to travel, and see everything we want."

We walked along 59th street, overlooking Central Park, and then back down 7th Avenue past Carnegie Hall. Then, we took the F train down to 2nd Avenue and Houston. I tapped my Apple watch, and navigated to Mark's apartment – along a small park, up Avenue A, and then turning on East 3rd Street.

Fortunately, the building had an elevator, as Mark and Greg were on the top floor. Mark greeted us and we all hugged. We toured the 2-bedroom single-bath apartment which, although the rooms were very small, was actually quite nice. It had fresh paint and wood floors, and a brick wall in the living area.

Mark took us out onto the patio, which was just big enough to fit a wooden table and chairs, and a few plants. It had a spectacular view over the city, all the way to the Empire State building. I turned to him, "This apartment has to cost a fortune!"

Mark nodded, "We were able to get it for under $4,000 a month ... but Greg is paying most of the rent, as he uses the extra bedroom as an office."

Our brief tour over, we took the elevator down, and Mark led us a few blocks to a local bar. It didn't look like much outside, but it was packed inside – mostly with men, but there were a few women, also.

Mark turned to us, having to yell to be heard over the din of the music and everyone shouting, "This is a hetero-friendly gay and lesbian bar." He looked up and smiled, then waved to someone across the room.

We followed each other through the crowd, and found Greg at the other side of the bar. Kelly hugged him, and I shook his hand, and he introduced the guy he was with, evidently one of his advertising colleagues. Mark turned to us and shouted, "Beers OK?" Kelly and I nodded.

I leaned my head near Greg, and spoke loudly into his ear, "We just saw the apartment. It's great! Especially the patio overlooking the city."

Greg smiled, "Yeah, we were really lucky. We're halfway through a two-year lease, so we have a year before having to worry." Of course, I couldn't tell Mark, let alone Greg, that he may not have any money worries in a year. At least, if this trip was successful.

Mark brought the beers, and we attempted to have a conversation. Kelly and Greg were talking animatedly, but I couldn't make out a word. The bass of the techno music was booming, and my head was starting to hurt. I was clearly the 'old man', in this environment.

Not soon enough, we finished our beers, said our goodbyes to Greg and his friend, and headed back out into the crisp, cold air. Mark led us to a small Spanish restaurant in the neighborhood, and we had to laugh: We hadn't told Mark about our Barcelona trip. But it turned out to have great food and, even better, it was quiet.

Somehow, we also hadn't told him about our earlier Europe trip, or the Japan trip. Now, I realized why: I hadn't wanted to bring up Kelly's domme training. It was something that I still didn't feel comfortable discussing with my sons.

We did explain why we were taking the trip – to try to negotiate strategic partnerships, and a potential sale of the business. Mark knew that I'd given him 10% of my stock, 1% of the company. But he had no idea that if all our negotiations were successful, he could net $10-12 million.

Kelly and I took the subway back to midtown, and walked to our hotel. We sat in the lobby bar, which was done in an ultra-modern style. As we sipped our drinks, we discussed our strategy and plans for the next two days.

We really had no idea how much time would be required with each of the companies. We would have to remain flexible, and adjust our itinerary, as needed. I just hoped that the hotels I'd selected would be able to accommodate us, if we changed our dates.

Our meetings took the full two days, and Kelly answered the technical questions expertly. We agreed on the Letter of Intent, but we didn't leave with a signed agreement. The company would have to get Board approval, as the transaction would involve the Japanese company, and a potential partnership or acquisition.

I had hoped to take Kelly to one of my favorite Italian restaurants in the city, but we were able to make our original flight, which departed Tuesday evening.

We arrived on Wednesday morning in Geneva, both of us having slept three or four hours on the flight. We took the five-minute train ride into the city, and then a 10-minute taxi ride to the headquarters of the pharma company. We didn't have hotel reservations here, but would have one of the company admins make one for us.

As we took the elevator up, I mentioned to Kelly, "You know, if we had a free day here, we could drive to Chamonix, and ski Mont Blanc." Kelly rolled her eyes; but I was serious. It was only an hour or so south, and was a beautiful place to visit – even if we didn't go skiing.

We sat in a conference room, with a huge boardroom table and comfortable chairs. There was a partial view of the lake, which looked inviting ... except that it was quite cold outside. The company executives came into the room and greeted us warmly.

When the introductions were finished, an assistant came in carrying a platter of sandwiches and fresh vegetables. Another woman brought a tray with bottled waters and several kinds of soft drinks – all in miniature cans – as well as coffee and hot water for tea.

While most of us were eating, Kelly gave an overview presentation on her technology, and the progress we'd made since the Barcelona meeting. The company then presented their commercialization strategy to us.

We had expected a lot of technical questions, but were informed that the due diligence for our project had already been completed by their research staff, some of whom Kelly had met in Barcelona.

However, they deemed it important to convince their consultants at the ETH – the Swiss Federal Institute of Technology, which is located in Zurich. They took care of booking flights for Kelly and I this evening, and booked a hotel that I suggested.

Three of the executives took Kelly and I out to an early dinner at a brasserie that was within walking distance of their offices. It turned out to be a very upscale place, and I was glad they were paying the bill.

We began with a seafood course – the pharma guys had raw oysters, I had the mussels in a wine broth, and Kelly tried the escargots in garlic butter. Then, the main courses, including the entrecote with Béarnaise sauce for Kelly, and the 'choucroute' plate for me – which included sausages and confit of duck.

Of course, wines were ordered for each course, and we were well-sated by the end of the two-hour meal. We were also well-satisfied business-wise, as the Letter of Intent had been signed.

Without ever having stepped foot inside a hotel in Geneva, we were off again, taking the short flight to Zurich. This time, I had selected one of my favorite boutique hotels, on Zeefeldstrasse, a shopping street on the east side of the lake. There was a tram stop less than a block away, and plenty of good restaurants in the area.

Our meeting on Thursday morning was basically a symposium that had been set-up at the ETH. After having a nice breakfast in the hotel, we took a tram to Central, and then the Polybahn funicular up to the university.

I explained to Kelly, "The ETH, usually called the 'polytechnic', is more than 150 years old, and ranks with MIT, Stanford and Cambridge as one of the top universities in the world. There's a sister school near Lausanne, which has a lot of medical technology development, also."

Kelly's presentation was wonderful, and there seemed to be a lot of interest among the faculty and graduate students attending. A couple of the professors took us to lunch at the 'dozentenfoyer', the faculty restaurant, which offered a nice buffet.

Amazingly, we were finished in the early afternoon, and returned to the hotel to change into casual clothes. We both wore silk long underwear, as the weather was nippy, and the cloud cover made it look like it would start snowing, anytime.

As Kelly finished getting dressed, I read a list of current exhibits at some of the museums in town. We decided to visit the main art museum, the '*Kunsthaus*', to see the Giacometti exhibition. I also saw that Mozart's opera, 'The Magic Flute' (it was listed as '*Die Zauberflöte*') would be playing at the '*Opernhaus*' tonight.

We had the hotel procure opera tickets for us, and set out on our afternoon adventure. After the art museum, we walked down the hill to Bellevue, across the bridge and along the '*quai*', passing the few boats that plied the lake in the winter. Then, we walked through the arboretum, and down the gangplank to the sauna.

It was a relaxing experience, as usual, the three saunas relatively uncrowded on a midweek afternoon. Most of the other sauna-goers were most likely housewives; I seemed to be one of only a few males here today.

During our second sauna course, Kelly turned to me, and said softly, "I'm surprised we're not flying to Tel Aviv this afternoon or tomorrow morning."

"I called the airlines, and they could change our routing , so we can leave from Zurich, but they didn't have room in first class until Saturday. And it wouldn't help for us to get there earlier, as Friday and Saturday are the 'weekend' in Israel. I e-mailed the company there, and we've confirmed meetings on Sunday."

Two thirties-something women came into the sauna, nodded to us, and sat on the 'L' portion of the top bench. Through the windows over the door, we could see the lake, and through the small windows behind us, we could see into the park, the trees barren. The women started talking quietly in Swiss-German.

Kelly asked, "So what are we going to do, tomorrow? It would be neat if we could have a day of skiing."

I shrugged, "We'd have to rent a car, drive through the snow, and then rent our equipment. I'm not sure I'm up for that, and then having to fly early the next morning."

One of the women turned to us, and spoke in perfect English, "You might want to look into the 'Snow'n'Rail' pass. That combines the train fare and lift ticket at a discount. It's really a great deal."

The other woman nodded, "Yeah, my husband does that with his buddies – when they want to come back drunk. Which is usually.

"For example, you can get to Flumserberg by taking the tram, then the train, and finally a cable car. You could be skiing two hours after you leave your hotel in Zurich."

I smiled, and turned to Kelly, "I've been there. I mentioned it to you when we drove into Zurich from Munich on our last trip."

Kelly smiled, "That would be fun. We just need to rent skis, boots, and poles." That was a bit simplistic; we would probably also have to buy some shell pants to go over our jeans. And we didn't have goggles or gloves. Still, we could leave early, and had the whole day.

We walked out onto the deck, wearing only slippers we'd taken from a bin, and carrying our towels. Kelly teased, "Are you going to go for a swim?"

Laughing, I answered her, "Not today. The water temperature is about two degrees Centigrade – just above freezing. Quite a bit colder than the last time we were here." Then, I raised my eyebrows, "But if you want to dunk, I'll do it with you."

Kelly raised her eyebrows back at me, "I don't think so. I did it last time." She wrapped the towel around her, "And I'm already getting chilled out here."

We took one more sauna, then caught the tram back to our hotel, changing once at Bellevue. I pointed to the opera house as the tram clacked along. It was within easy walking distance, if we didn't want to take the tram, although it might be a very cold walk back.

Kelly and I made love before taking showers and getting dressed for the opera. I had a suit and tie, and Kelly wore a business-oriented pants outfit, so that she could use her long underwear.

As we walked toward the opera house, we managed to catch a tram the last few blocks. I was already chilled, despite wearing the warmest clothes I had.

The opera house was rather dull on the outside, with block construction and stately columns in tones of gray. But inside, it was ornately detailed, mostly in gold, with frescoes on the ceiling, and a huge chandelier. Three tiers of balconies surrounded the main floor seating.

We found our seats, in the second balcony, off to the side ... but we had a good view of the stage. I hadn't been to many operas, and didn't think Sam was an 'opera person', but we both enjoyed the music, costumes, and dancing. During the intermission, we drank Champagne.

After the performance, we ate at one of the bar-restaurants in the opera house, Sam having their specialty – a flaming tart, and I had a quiche and salad. Then, we took a tram back to the hotel and climbed into bed together, holding each other tightly to share body warmth.

On Friday morning, we headed to the snow. As the women in the sauna had told us, it was amazing that we could take a tram from in front of our hotel, then a train from the main station, following around the west side of the lake, through the countryside, and along another lake, finally arriving at the tiny *Unterteizen* station.

We walked through a short tunnel under the highway which led directly to the cable car. Partway up, we had to switch cars, then continued to the top. Across a parking lot we found the ski rental shops and Flumserberg ski resort.

It was a bigger production than I'd realized, and we ended-up buying quite a few things. Sam suggested that if we couldn't fit it into our roll-aboard cases, we might leave it with the hotel.

I noted, "Well, we certainly won't need ski wear in Israel!"

Sam laughed, "Actually, there *is* skiing in Israel ... on Mount Hermon. But it's in the far northeast of the country, and it won't compare to the skiing here." That was a surprise; I had thought of Israel as one of the warm Mediterranean countries.

Finally outfitted, we took the lift up, and began our ski day. I was again surprised at how good a skier Sam was; neither of us had skied much over the past few years, until our Europe trip, but it was obvious that Sam was an experienced skier.

We stayed mainly off-piste, only once 'getting into trouble' coming down an unknown face, and having to dive straight down between the boulders. It was a fun day.

Having only eaten '*gulaschsuppe*' at the mid-mountain restaurant, we were ready for a nice dinner by the time we returned to Zurich. It was Friday evening, but our hotel concierge was able to get early reservations at the *Kronenhalle*, which Sam told me was one of the most famous restaurants in the city.

We were seated at a window table, and the restaurant was very nice, if a bit austere. Paintings and drawings filled the dark-paneled walls, and the tables looked beautiful, with cream-colored tablecloths and flowers. It was dusk outside, and I could see flurries of snow drifting down into the street.

I almost choked, when I opened the menu and saw the prices; they were in Swiss Francs, which were about the same as the U.S. dollar. Then I heard Sam clear his throat, as he perused the wine menu.

He smiled, and when he saw me looking, he explained, "Well, I found some third-growth Bordeaux wines for under $200, and a few other 'deals' ... but maybe we could just get a carafe, tonight? They have a Margaux that might be nice."

Of course, I would be happy with whatever Sam picked. We were tired from skiing, and had to get up early for our flight to Israel.

I selected the sea bass, and Sam chose the traditional veal with morel sauce and '*rôsti*' potatoes. After we ordered, Sam leaned toward me across the table. "This place got famous in the 1920s and '30s, when all the great scientists and artists came here. For example, Sigmund Freud and Albert Einstein were regulars.

"Legend has it that the owners would provide food to the artists and hang their works on the wall; so it became kind of a museum of great works. Giacometti – who's sculptures we saw yesterday – created the furniture, Chagall designed the stained glass window of the bar, and Picasso donated some of his sketches."

Sam knew a lot, and he'd been here before, but I'd seen him reading up about this restaurant on the Internet. It *was* an impressive place.

The food was great, and the carafe of wine was as good as any bottle Sam could have ordered. It was snowing outside, so we called a taxi to take us back to the hotel.

On Saturday morning, the sky was clear, and there was only a little snow on the sidewalk, so we rolled our cases the few blocks to the Stadelhofen station, and took the bi-hourly train to the airport.

The flight was nice, and in less than four hours we were flying over the beach and a line of hotels, then landing at Ben Gurion airport in Tel Aviv. By the time we got through immigration, and took a taxi into town, it was mid-afternoon.

Sam had stayed at this boutique hotel, which was across the street from the beach, and had requested a specific room. It was on the top of five floors, and had a large balcony with expansive view of the Mediterranean.

Directly below us was the main beach highway and, across the street, a promenade – beautifully swirled in two tones of brown stone, then the beach. Several breakwaters in a line protected the beach from waves.

There were palm trees lining the beach walk, and people were riding bicycles, rollerblading, and walking on the beach, despite the cool weather. I had to laugh as I realized that we were skiing in the alps, yesterday.

We walked along the promenade next to the beach on our right side and a boulevard on our left. The sky was blue and the water an even deeper blue, but there was a chilly wind.

As we walked through a park and back onto the promenade, next to rocks that went into the water, we saw several kite surfers ahead and, in the far distance, the point with the old town of Jaffa, topped by a bell tower.

We climbed ancient stone steps, worn down by millennia of people before us, and wove through narrow passages, until we emerged onto a plaza that overlooked Tel Aviv.

There was a photographer taking pictures of a bride and groom in their wedding clothes. Sam turned to me, "If we get all these contracts signed and behind us, maybe we can start thinking about a date for our wedding."

I nodded. That was a nice thought, but at this point it was difficult to believe that we would actually close deals worth hundreds of millions of dollars. It was still too much to think about.

We walked down to the clock tower, and Sam consulted his phone. "There's a very well-rated wine restaurant somewhere around here." After a few false turns, we found the place, a charming 'cave' restaurant, the entire place built of stone in the shape of a gothic arch.

After a bit more Internet research, Sam ordered the Geshem *'Chateau Golan'* reserve. A plate of bread and terrine of butter was placed on the table, and I realized that I was famished, not having eaten since our flight.

One taste, and I was in heaven: It was the best, crustiest bread and butter I'd ever eaten. Then, the wine came, and it had to rank among the best that we'd had. And that was saying a lot.

The menu was incredible, as was the food when we tasted it. Sam started with the leek and mushroom ravioli in a blue cheese fondue, and I had the hearts of palm salad with endive, roasted tomatoes, figs, and pistachios in a date honey dressing.

For our main courses, Sam had the goose breast with dumplings, and I had the mussels over squid ink pasta. After sharing a dessert – the tahini parfait, and finishing the wine, we were ready for a taxi ride back to our hotel and a good night's sleep.

Dressed in our business attire – but with Sam *not* wearing a tie – we took a cab to the *Herzliya* area, where the pharma company was located. Our meetings here were focused on the business deal, including the potential investment or acquisition by the Japanese firm.

It was strange to be starting the business week on a Sunday, and I felt jet-lagged, even though we'd been traveling for a week. Lunch was brought in, and we worked the full day, and then took a taxi back to our hotel.

We walked up the sidewalk toward the main strip of hotels, and ducked into an 'American' sports bar. As with most of the other large hotels or restaurants we'd seen, there was an armed security guard at the entrance, who checked my purse.

Although this place didn't give us an opportunity to sample Israeli food, I was happy getting a burger and fries. And Sam was happy with the beer selection.

"You know, Kelly, if we can come to an agreement on the Letter of Intent tomorrow, we could possibly fly home on Wednesday. But we might want to consider staying a couple of extra days, so that you can see more of Israel; especially Jerusalem."

It would be nice to tour the country, but I also wouldn't mind getting home a bit sooner. Sam said he would check with the airlines tomorrow around noon, when we had a better idea of our schedule.

As he glanced at the browser on his phone, his eyes went wide. "The restaurant-bar we're at, right now?"

I nodded, as he kept reading. "It was the site of a Palestinian suicide bombing – more than a decade ago. Three people were killed and 50 injured. The security guard in front, who blocked the guy from getting into the restaurant, prevented a lot more people from being killed."

He chuckled, "They were actually from London, came in just like we did, through the airport." That was little consolation. The place was packed, nobody worrying about the occasional suicide bomber. What a strange way to live!

Tuesday turned out to be a short day. We were able to finalize the LOI – although, once again, it would have to be approved by their Board, so we would not be carrying back the signed agreement.

One of the key sticking points to the agreement – as with both the New York and Swiss companies – was whether I would be available to consult for them. I had mixed feelings, being glad to help make the technology a success and develop new drugs, but not wanting to be busy full-time, traveling to each client.

In the LOIs, Sam had negotiated one day per month for each of the companies, at a $10,000 per day rate, plus first class travel. At this point, I was almost hoping that they wouldn't need my services.

But we weren't quite finished, yet. The pharma executives wanted us to visit their main research facilities in the north of Israel, to make a presentation on my technology, and to help develop a work plan for moving forward with their drug development process.

We went back to the hotel in the early afternoon, and Sam made hotel reservations in Haifa, and plane reservations for our return home. He was able to secure first class seats on Friday.

Then, we took advantage of the couple of hours until we would be picked up by the pharma executives and taken to dinner, to celebrate the deal. Sam changed into a bathing suit and tank top, saying that he was going to challenge himself with a swim.

I hadn't brought a suit, and wasn't interested in swimming – the air was chilly, and there was a wind that whipped up whitecaps beyond the breakwaters.

We went out to the balcony, and sat at the small table, looking out at all the action on the beach, promenade, and street below. Sam looked at me, with his lopsided smile ... that could only mean one thing. I slid my chair over, and reached under his suit. He was already getting hard.

He put his finger to his lips, then reached over, and undid my pants. I stood, and he pulled my pants down, and struggled, as I lifted my feet, to get them off of me. My underwear was next. Sam stood, and turned me toward the beach, my arms on the low parapet of our balcony.

As I watched people walking on the sidewalk not fifty feet below me, and people rollerblading on the promenade, and people walking on the beach, Sam entered me. It was almost public sex, but nobody could really see anything ... except *my* lopsided smile.

Strangely, it was a turn-on, having sex while watching people go about their business 'within spitting distance'. My vision blacked out, as my own excitement crescendoed, Sam pounding into me from behind.

Sam did his little swim, around two of the breakwaters, while I got showered and ready for dinner. We were picked up at seven, and driven to a private club somewhere south of Jaffa. The place was swanky, and there seemed to be a lot of business people here, many men wearing suits or sport jackets, but no ties in sight.

There was some quiet discussion with the waiter, and a bottle of white wine was brought to the table and poured. We all toasted to the technology, future products, and the relationship. The executives were regaling us with stories of some of their drug development hits and misses, when the waiter returned and put a huge platter on the table.

It was a seafood 'tower' that was artistically arranged with crab claws reaching out all around and the antennae of several large lobsters gracing the top of the display. There were oysters and mussels on ice, at least two dozen huge shrimp, and a variety of sauces in small bowls, lemon halves, and seaweed, parsley and other decorative greens.

We dug in, but even after a half hour of eating, we had barely made a dent. The conversation was interesting, and we learned about the role of the 'chief scientist' of Israel, and government sponsorship of advanced research.

These guys were senior executives, and had all traveled the world; they were very relaxed and self-confident. Sam told some of his own stories from his experiences in managing pharma R&D, and working with some of the major players.

I asked about the shellfish, which I had thought wasn't allowed, and they laughed, saying that they didn't 'keep Kosher'. We learned that about 75% of the population of Israel was Jewish, nearly 20% Muslim, and the remainder mostly Druze and Christian.

When I asked, they explained that 'Druze' is a separate religion, incorporating elements of Islam, Judaism, Christianity, and even Greek philosophy. The Druze speak Arabic, and have their own foods and customs.

They told us that their R&D staff comprised people of every religion, who got along well, even socially. All Israeli citizens are expected to serve in the IDF, the Israeli Defense Forces, and many Druze are members of the Israeli parliament.

The waiter returned, first pouring a red wine, and then putting plates in front of us. They were beautiful, nearly works of art, but I did not recognize the food. The waiter announced, "This is our chef's special: Seared foie gras with figs and a port wine reduction."

Of course, Sam and I had tried the goose liver paté, and various '*terrines*' in France, but these were whole goose livers with a thick, syrupy wine sauce, sitting on pieces of brioche, complemented with micro-greens.

I glanced at Sam, as he put the first piece in his mouth, his eyes closing and a huge smile on his face. I tried mine, and it really was outstanding ... just a bit rich for my taste.

The 'bad' news was delivered near the end of the meal: The R&D staff would not be ready for our visit until Wednesday; we would have to fend for ourselves tomorrow. I knew that wouldn't be a problem.

Sam nodded, and excitedly described how he could show me some of the beaches and important towns on the way to Haifa, and a few of the sights we would see there.

As this was my first time in Israel, the executives were insistent that I get to see Jerusalem, even if for only a day. They suggested that we spend Thursday seeing the old part of the city before flying out on Friday.

When Sam finally acquiesced, they said they would make reservations for us, and would e-mail the information to us tomorrow. We would be sleeping in five different hotels on this 12-day trip.

A three-tiered tray of small pastries, some with honey and others with pistachios, as well as '*halvah*' made with tahini, was placed on the table. Then, a fine brandy was served. We were stuffed, and well-lubricated with liquor by the time we were driven back to our hotel.

On Tuesday, I rented a car, and we began our drive north. Kelly had suggested that we do a run, as our bodies were feeling the rich food. After checking on the 'net, I drove nearly to Herzliya, but turned off to a parking lot on Tel Baruch Beach.

It was one of the few beaches considered 'clothing optional', but we ran in our shorts and tanks. The cool weather was perfect, and we ran all the way to the Herzliya marina, and back, a course of five miles.

We dried off with a towel 'borrowed' from the hotel, and continued our drive north on Highway 2. About an hour later, we drove into Caesarea, an historic port town built by Herod the Great around 20 BC. We toured the ruins, including the bath houses and Roman theater.

Caesarea had been under the control of the Romans, then the Byzantines, then the Muslims, and was conquered around 1200 AD by the crusaders.

We ate at a small café overlooking the crystal clear water. The weather was beautiful, if a bit cool, and the water looked inviting. As I sipped my Goldstar beer, I quipped, "I'd love to spend a day here snorkeling ... or maybe diving. Just off the breakwater – now submerged – are the ruins of the ancient port."

I realized that I kept telling Kelly that we would have to come back and visit places, but if the contracts were signed, we might be coming here – and to Switzerland, *and* Japan – regularly.

We only had salads, but as with many Israeli and Arabic restaurants, a dozen or so small bowls were placed on the table, containing hummus, eggplant dip, olives, taboulleh, and other delicacies, along with a basket of warm pita bread.

Kelly was floored. "But all I wanted was a salad." She tore a piece of the warm bread and dipped it into the hummus, and smiled. "Wow. I've never had pita or hummus this good before." Despite our best intentions, we finished most of the side dishes, as well as our salads.

Another thirty minutes north, along the coast, we arrived at our hotel – one of the only beach hotels in Haifa.

I could have selected one of the big hotels at the top of the hill, with a view and easy access to numerous restaurants, but this seemed more interesting.

We got a corner room with a large balcony overlooking the sea, and unpacked. Still in our running clothes, we decided to make this a 'beach day', rather than rushing out to tour the sights.

Walking south along the promenade, we passed many beach restaurants, most of them closed on this winter weekday. Continuing onto the beach past the end of the promenade, we walked along the waterline, watching the seabirds as they poked around in the sand.

The beach was nearly empty, and we sat on the sand, looking out over the water. I leaned over and kissed Kelly lightly. "So how are you doing? Not too exhausted from our quick trip?"

Kelly chuckled, "Well, it has been a whirlwind. But it's been good; especially, if we can get the LOIs signed."

I turned to her, "We're going to have to start thinking about some things, as it's getting more real. And we'll need some professional help." When Kelly cocked her head, I explained, "Think if we are paid a billion dollars; we might have to pay hundreds of *millions* of dollars in taxes."

That was a sobering realization, even to me; and I'd thought a little about it. "That's one reason why we're talking about selling the business – the stock – rather than selling the assets."

I smiled, wondering if there might be another way. "If we just sold the patents and the prototype, then KS Biotech would get the money, and have to pay taxes. Then, when KS Biotech pays us – whether in a salary or dividend – we would have to pay taxes. So the money would be double-taxed.

"On the plus side, that would mean KS Biotech might have half a billion dollars in the bank, ready for its next blockbuster product development. You could become a 'serial entrepreneur', and keep developing new products, or starting new companies."

It was much more complex than that. We would need to find someone who could help us structure the deal with the Japanese company; that would be the key.

We walked back to the promenade, and went into the first restaurant, 'The Camel', that was open to the beach air. It was a funky place, decorated wildly, and we sat on a couch, with a low table in front of us, as we looked out at the sunset, perfectly framed in our view.

It turned out to be great: I had a great hamburger, and liter of Murphy's stout, and Kelly was very happy with her Israeli appetizer plate, with falafels, and more hummus. I hoped her stomach would be OK in the morning.

We were up early on Wednesday, and Kelly navigated me past Haifa, through Nesher, and around the mountain to Yokne'am, which was a research and industrial area in the countryside south of Haifa.

The head of R&D and key scientists greeted us and gave us a tour of their modern facilities. Things had really progressed, since I'd been active in the field. Then, we went into a large conference room, and were served coffee, with plates of cookies placed around the table.

As Sam reached for a cookie, several men entered the conference room. I stood and shook their hands warmly, having met them in Barcelona. They were professors in biotechnology from the Technion University, which Sam had said was on the hill above Nesher.

The atmosphere was very casual and congenial – much more so than either New York or Switzerland, but I couldn't ignore that the room was filled with international experts.

I gave an updated talk, summarizing the most recent results of our studies on Lyme disease, and predictions of protein folding for prospective drug formulations.

Although the talk was only 45 minutes, the discussion continued for several hours. Pizza was brought in, and Sam indulged, but I was busy answering questions, and standing at the white board drawing schematics of the system and writing a simplified version of our algorithms.

Everyone seemed pleased, and we were back at the hotel in the late afternoon. Sam went for a swim, taking twenty minutes to go from one beach, around the breakwater, and back in to the other beach.

He had been out of sight for more than ten minutes, but I had great confidence in his abilities, especially in the water. I had dipped my foot in, yesterday and today, but the water was too cold for comfort.

Next to the hotel was a Druze restaurant, which we decided to try, although Sam was really torn. He told me about Italian, and French, and pub-style restaurants 'on the hill', and also complained that he hadn't really shown me much of Haifa.

We could have stayed here tomorrow, but everyone said that I should see Jerusalem ... and I wanted to. Had we not been so focused on getting these deals done, we probably could have taken another week here.

Sam went on and on about places we wouldn't see on this trip – including Rosh Hanikra, at the border of Lebanon, with a cable car that takes you down to sea caves that you can walk through; and the Dead Sea area, with its desert springs, and the Masada hill with its ancient palace.

Sam told me the story of the 960 Jewish inhabitants, who decided on mass suicide, rather than surrender to the 10,000 Roman soldiers, who had built a ramp to the top of the mountain.

The menu of the Druze restaurant was exotic, and the owner hovered over us, making sure that we were happy. A number of bowls and plates were put on the table: Olives, salmon dip, '*baba ganouj*' (eggplant dip), pickles, stuffed grape leaves, hummus, '*shulbata*' – a grain and garbanzo bean dish, tomato and cucumber salad, '*labneh*' – a yogurt cheese, and, of course, warm pitas.

Sam got the '*syfcha*' – pastry with ground veal & lamb, and I ordered the '*masakhan*', which was like a pizza with chicken & onion, flavored with '*baharat*', a pungent and sweet spice mix. It was really a unique experience.

The owner came over and asked how we were doing. Sam was effusive in his praise for the restaurant. Then he asked, "Are there whole Druze towns in Israel?"

The owner sat down with us, and explained, "Yes, there are quite a few – mostly here in the Haifa area and even farther north." He laughed, "Actually, I live in a town that was mentioned in the Bible. It's on a hill, and there are three 'sectors' – one Jewish, one Christian, and one Druze.

"At the top of the hill, we have a small shopping area – and one of the best ice cream shops around – where we all congregate. We live separately, but are still connected."

It was an interesting place – each sect having ancient traditions, and perhaps historically in conflict. But they all seemed to get along well, on a day-to-day basis.

On Thursday, we drove to Jerusalem, and checked into the hotel that had been reserved by the pharma company. Sam had been shocked at first, then happy that we would have a unique experience, then concerned about the price of the room. It was the famous 'American Colony Hotel'.

Our room wouldn't be ready for several hours, so we left our car, and walked to the old walled city of Jerusalem, entering through Herod's Gate.

There were a number of men offering guide services, and Sam decided to let one show us around. He'd been here before, but said he didn't know enough to lead me on a proper tour.

Starting in the Muslim quarter, we wound through narrow lanes, paved with large stones, now shiny from centuries of foot traffic. There were small shops of all types – some touristy and others more local.

One entire shop featured scarves, another dozens of kinds of olives, and still another, spices in decorative pyramids. A tiny 'closet' of a shop had a tailor, working with a foot-powered sewing machine. A butcher shop had animal parts hanging that Sam photographed, but didn't look appetizing at all.

The guide took us down the '*Via Dolorosa*', or 'Way of Sorrow', where Jesus carried the cross, finally ending up at the Church of the Holy Sepulchre, on the site where he was crucified. Outside the church, dozens of shops sold religious items.

We walked through the Armenian quarter, stopping to pick up a few pastries, which we ate along the way.

And in the Jewish quarter, we saw the 'wailing wall', most of it allocated for men to pray, a smaller portion for the women. We went into the archeological site at the left end of the wall, and saw some of the ancient remains of old Jerusalem and the First Temple.

Our guide pointed out the golden 'Dome of the Rock', just visible to the upper left of the western wall. It was part of the '*Al-Aqsa*' mosque, an iconic landmark, and thought to be one of the oldest mosques in the world.

After tipping the guide, we exited through the Zion Gate, and visited the City of David, the site where ancient Jerusalem was founded.

Then, we did one of the most interesting things of the day, so far: Climbed down a shaft and walked through the nearly half-mile long 'Hezekiah's tunnel' where water for the city of Jerusalem was diverted and hidden from the attacking Assyrians.

There was water at the bottom, but fortunately we didn't have to slog through knee-deep water, as described in the guide book.

Walking back up along the outside wall of the old city, lined with tourist busses, the driver of a small van approached Sam, and offered to drive us around to some of the sights. Sam negotiated a deal that included dropping us off at the hotel.

Over the next couple of hours, we visited the Mount of Olives, which had a spectacular view over the old city; we drove by the '*Knesset*' – the parliament of Israel; and we stopped for another view – from the opposite direction, on one of the overlooking hills.

Finally back at the hotel, we were given our room key, and directed to another building, where we climbed a cantilevered outside stairway to the third (top) floor, and entered our room. It was incredible!

The large bedroom included a small seating area in the corner, where the hotel had provided a bottle of wine and bowl of fruit. The huge bed had a modern version of a canopy. We went out onto the small balcony which overlooked a well-manicured garden that was walled off from the rest of the neighborhood.

And the bathroom! It was all done in terrazzo and tile, with a sunken black Jacuzzi tub in the center, sinks on each side, a separate toilet room, ... and a steam room.

Predictably, Sam smiled and pointed. We took a shower together (not feeling particularly clean, after trekking through the 2,000-year old tunnels), and then spent time in the steam room. As we were flying out tomorrow, we opened the wine, and toasted the trip. It had been successful business-wise, and another shared adventure for Sam and I.

We ate dinner in the hotel's courtyard restaurant, which was romantically lit, and nearly a jungle – with palms and other trees, and a multitude of potted plants. Sam had thought they wouldn't be serving out there, as the weather was chilly. But it turned out to be *another* beautiful experience.

It was already Valentine's Day again. A year ago, we had been in the Bay Area trying to raise money ... and now, we were close to concluding a major sale of our company. At least, I hoped we were close.

We had finally received all three signed LOIs from the pharma companies we'd visited, and were now finalizing negotiations with the Japanese company for the acquisition. Kelly was preparing another patent, but had done everything she could do, technically.

There were two issues remaining: The Japanese company wanted to give us stock for a portion of the sale, which would be beneficial to us, tax-wise, but we were haggling on a guaranteed valuation for the stock, or issuance of additional shares, if their stock price dropped.

And the ball was really in our court regarding the second issue, how to best structure the deal to minimize our tax impact. Our corporate attorney didn't do that kind of work, but had suggested several firms, which I was in the process of contacting.

On the positive side, the Japanese company was as enthusiastic as ever, and had proposed a deadline of March 31 for completion of our transaction. That would actually be incredibly quick, for an M&A transaction of this size.

As far as we were concerned, the sooner the better, as so many things could happen that could cause the deal to go off the rails. Of course we understood why the Japanese company wanted us to take stock – both to ease their cash requirements and so that we would have 'skin in the game'.

But there seemed to be an undertone ... something else happening with the Japanese company. I got vibes each time we had a conference call, but they weren't giving us any information. They were now a public company, so had to be cautious about divulging their plans ... but we had a non-disclosure agreement that should protect them.

I finished going through my e-mail and was turning off the computer when Kelly came down to the playroom. We were planning to go out to the French restaurant tonight, and it looked like Kelly was ready: She wore an emerald color sweater that contrasted nicely with her auburn hair.

"We have a slight change in plans," Kelly bounced into the room and plopped down on one of the chairs in front of the desk. I awaited the details.

"I spoke to Linda, and it turns out that she and Matt were also planning on going to the French restaurant, tonight. So we decided to make it a Valentine double date."

That was a surprise, but a nice one. I came around the desk, pulled Kelly up, and kissed her passionately. "Happy Valentine's Day."

She smiled and waved her hand. "We don't have to celebrate every holiday, and certainly not commercial ones.

As far as I'm concerned, every day is Valentine's Day." I nodded, and kissed her again. Then, I went upstairs to get dressed for dinner.

We met Linda at the restaurant, and she introduced us to Matt. He was handsome and stylishly dressed.

After we sat down, Linda went on and on, telling Matt that he really needed to taste my cooking which, she asserted, was better than any restaurant. Then, she turned to me, "If Matt agrees, maybe you could make a special dinner for his birthday – which is coming up in June."

I knew that Linda's between-the-lines intent was to share with Matt our custom of giving birthday spankings.

She smiled coyly, and told us a little about Matt. He had both legal and accounting degrees, and worked for a law firm in town, specializing in tax structuring – exactly what we needed!

Throughout the dinner, I kept thinking of questions to ask, and Kelly kicked me under the table each time I turned the conversation back to business. My shin was starting to hurt. Finally, Linda suggested that they come over for a while tonight. "Kelly and I can go in the sauna, while you and Matt work on business."

It didn't have to be binary – one or the other; I just wanted to give Matt an introduction, and find out whether he would be interested and able to help us. We could easily do that in the sauna.

At the end of the meal, Matt insisted on picking up the tab, despite my protestations. I finally gave in, and told him, "Well, then, I *am* going to have to make dinner for you." I didn't mention 'birthday', but glanced at Linda and she smiled knowingly at me.

Linda and Matt followed us back to the house, and we went down to the playroom, where I offered everyone after dinner drinks. Kelly decided to make coffee, and I took out the bottle of Kahlua, if anyone wanted Mexican coffee.

I handed Linda a couple of robes, and she led Matt to one of the upstairs guest bedrooms. In the meantime, I got undressed and put on the 'Superman' robe, then went back to my desk and pulled up a few things on the computer – Kelly's executive presentation, the signed LOIs from the three pharma companies, and the draft acquisition agreement from the Japanese firm.

Kelly returned with a tray of coffee and stuff, and put it on the coffee table. A minute later, Linda and Matt came down in their robes, and Kelly poured coffees, then left to put on her robe.

We sat around the coffee table, and I couldn't help but remember some of the experiences Kelly, her friends, and I had had here. As Linda's eyes scanned the room, there was the hint of a smile that betrayed her thoughts of our past experiences, also.

Linda turned to Matt, "Sam is quite the techie. He has a huge video screen, computer-controlled lighting, and multi-channel surround sound." Fortunately, she didn't mention the video cameras or the 'gadgets' that I built, including the insertable, remote-controlled vibrator.

"Has Linda told you about our company, KS Biotech?" Of course, Linda worked for the company, so that was a part of her life, which she would have shared with Matt.

Matt nodded, "Basically, although I don't really understand the technology. Are you going to sell the hardware? Or license other companies? Or, develop drugs yourselves?"

I answered, "We've considered all those options, but it turns out that a Japanese company is interested in acquiring us. And we have already negotiated letters of intent with three mid-sized pharma companies to license the technology for their specific markets.

"It's all based on Kelly's technology, which could revolutionize the drug development process, especially targeting diseases which are 'vector-borne' – carried by or caused by other organisms." Matt nodded, thoughtfully.

I got to the key point. "So we're pretty close to getting paid a lot of money, and our main challenge now is minimizing the tax impact."

Matt smiled, "That's *my* specialty."

Now, I smiled, "Yes, I was excited when Linda told me. So maybe we could hire you to help out?"

Matt shrugged, "It would have to be through the law firm that I work for. We'd probably want to have an upside in addition to our basic fee. How much money are we talking about?"

Before I could answer, Matt continued, "If it's a matter of a few tens of millions of dollars, and you're willing to take it over time, or as stock in the acquiring company, we may be able to keep the taxes low. But if you're talking about a hundred million dollars or more, it will be difficult; there could be a pretty high tax obligation."

I shook my head, "As it stands now, if we can close at the valuation the Japanese have offered, it would be roughly one point three billion dollars."

Matt coughed on his coffee and sat forward on the edge of the couch, "Did you say *billion* dollars?" I nodded and smiled.

At that point, Kelly walked in, wearing her 'Superwoman' robe, and sat on the loveseat, her legs folded under her. "Did I miss anything?"

Linda put her coffee down and turned to Kelly. "Are you guys really saying that you might sell the company for more than a *billion* dollars?" Kelly and I nodded slowly.

We could see Linda swallowing, or gulping, trying to catch her breath.

"And I have half a percent of the company?"

Matt snapped his head to Linda, and his mouth opened. "You didn't tell me about that."

Linda shrugged, "I didn't think it was a big deal. I had no idea how valuable it could be. Sam and Kelly never discussed it with me."

She took Matt's hands, "I wouldn't have wanted to be seen as puffing myself, if I told you about stock I owned when we first met. And, after seeing your parents' lifestyle in West Palm Beach, the small amount of my stock wouldn't be impressive enough to even mention."

Matt was nodding, slowly. "So you might be worth six million dollars." He raised his brows, "Less the taxes you'll have to pay. If it's capital gains, you might have to pay more than a million dollars in taxes." Now, Linda was shaking her head in disbelief.

I summarized, "So that's the problem. It will be a sale of all of our stock, in return for cash and stock in the Japanese company. But we need some good advice on how to best structure the deal."

Kelly chimed in, "I can't even *imagine* having to pay two hundred million dollars in taxes!"

Matt smiled, "Let's meet next week. I'll present the opportunity to the partners. I think they'll be very interested in working with you."

Kelly finished her coffee, "Can we please go in the sauna, now? It's Valentine's Day, and this discussion isn't very romantic."

We got up and headed to the sauna, but Linda quipped, "Well, Kelly, I think learning that I may get five million dollars is pretty romantic."

We knew she was kidding, but there was something to it. You couldn't equate money with happiness, but an unexpected windfall is always nice, and can be a turn-on.

Taking off and hanging our robes, we entered the sauna, all sitting on the top bench. Matt seemed relaxed with his own body, and didn't ogle Kelly. I think he was turned-on about handling the KS Biotech transaction.

Kelly told Linda about our most recent trip, including our ski day and tour of Jerusalem. Kelly's travels had progressed far beyond Linda's lifelong dream to visit Paris.

I thought about the possibility of taking Kelly's friends on a trip to Europe, if our deal could be closed. Of course, they would be able to take their own trips, each being a multi-millionaire. It was difficult to believe this was all happening – very surreal.

Kelly offered to let Linda and Matt use the shower first, but Linda insisted that we take our showers together. Then, once we were under the water, Linda preemptively squeezed soap into her hands and began washing me. I gave Kelly a look; she shrugged and began bathing Matt.

Not considered was the fact that we only needed to get rinsed off after this first course of the sauna. Linda was getting a kick out of bathing me in front of her boyfriend; of course, I was getting a 'kick' out of it, also.

Matt didn't seem too shocked or bothered, and I wondered how much Linda had shared with him about our open relationships and semi-sexual activities. Perhaps she was testing him, convinced that she wanted to have as open, trusting, and respectful a relationship as Kelly and I.

We dried off and put on our robes, then returned to the playroom. I took drink orders – bottled water and Diet Coke – and picked up the remote from my desk. I lowered the screen, and projected the title slide of Kelly's short presentation.

"Sam! That's not suitable for a Valentine's Day party."

Linda piped up, "Actually, Kelly, I'd love to see it. We worked on the early versions, but I'd like to hear 'the pitch'."

Kelly shrugged, and stood, walking toward the screen, as I advanced to the first slide. Kelly and I had done this many times, now, and she gave an excellent, enthusiastic, presentation. This version was for non-technical people, so appropriate for Linda and Matt.

When Kelly finished, Matt was very impressed. I flipped through some of the other documents, "We can go over these later, but here's the term sheet with the Japanese company, and here are the signed letters of intent with the three pharma companies."

Matt asked, "Can you come to our firm next Tuesday, and present to our partners? I'll have to confirm it tomorrow."

We agreed, and I was about to turn off the video, when Kelly asked me to show some pictures from our recent travels. Linda suggested that we not go back into the sauna ... and asked me if I had any 'bubbly'. I opened a Schramsberg reserve, and poured the pale liquid into fluted crystal glasses.

Toasting to Valentine's Day – and to selling our company – we sipped the wine, as I cued up some images from the trip. By the time our show was done, and the sparkling wine finished, we were all tired. And we all wanted to spend the last hour or two of the day showing our love for our partner.

We met with Matt's firm, and the partners decided to take on our project. One of the main challenges was to get everything done within the next month. Estimated legal costs would be fifty thousand dollars, plus one percent of the amount of taxes saved over the 20% that we would pay as capital gains, a formula that I had suggested.

Sam was spending nearly every day at the law firm, and he and Matt were becoming close. We hoped that there would be a future between Matt and Linda.

I tried to follow along with all the legal and accounting machinations, but let Sam handle the details. Matt had suggested some form of tax-free corporate reorganization, and they were looking at a 'forward subsidiary merger'.

Sam and Matt communicated with the Japanese and, in early March, Makoto shared something that had been – and still was – very confidential.

They had been working on being listed on the NASDAQ stock exchange. A subsidiary would be formed in the U.S., and KS Biotech merged into it. We would be getting some combination of cash and stock in the publicly-traded company. The only limitation was that we could sell no more than 10% of our stock per calendar quarter.

With this information, Matt and his firm completed the deal structuring and, miraculously, the Japanese agreed. Sam pointed out that we were now a key part of the Japanese company's strategy. The acquisition would be shown in their prospectus and S1 filing.

The last two weeks in March were a blur. My team was finishing up the documentation package that we would deliver, while Sam and Matt completed the negotiations.

Then, we had to fly back to Japan to sign the final contracts, and participate in promotional activities. We were only there a few days, but happened to arrive at the peak of the cherry blossom season.

With everything going on, Makoto insisted on bringing us down to Osaka on our last day, to tour the company's top secret research facilities ... and to take us to Osaka Castle to see the cherry blossoms in their iconic setting.

We took the '*Shinkansen*' – the bullet train – and Makoto entertained us with stories of the various Japanese prefectures. We passed Mount Fuji, and lakes where *unagi*, the endangered freshwater eels, were farmed.

The R&D labs were incredible, and we were told about several of the pipeline drugs in development. We ate *soba* in the company cafeteria, and met many of the senior researchers. Makoto hinted that – despite not being included in our agreement – he might want me to consult for the company. I remained open to the possibilities.

In the evening, Makoto took us to dinner in '*Osaka-kita*', north Osaka, filled with restaurants and clubs. We sat on tatami mats around a table in a small private room, and toasted our transaction with Sapporo beers.

Then, three women, dressed in traditional *kimono*, kneeled next to us. They showed us a large 'pot', but it was made of paper. They poured in broth from a pitcher, and lit the fire underneath. Then, they cooked the vegetables and meat in the broth – similar to our *shabu shabu* experience – and served it, as we ate.

Makoto explained that this was a very special type of cooking in a paper vessel, called '*kami yaki*'. In the taxi back to *Shin-Osaka* station, Makoto apologized that he couldn't bring us to one of the clubs. But we would be taking the last bullet train back to Tokyo, and leaving for the U.S. tomorrow afternoon.

The Japanese company was listed on the stock exchange in early April, Sam and I flying out to New York to attend the celebrations. We didn't get to ring the bell at the market opening, but we were walked through the floor of the exchange.

We dined at the 'Four Seasons' restaurant, Makoto selecting a fine wine that probably cost more than my car. Our deal was due to close in two weeks, but I still couldn't fathom the 'reality' of having an obscene amount of money.

The company would sell for $1.3 billion, but Sam kept cautioning me that more than half our value would be in the new stock; if that plunged, we could be left with only the 40% we would receive in cash ... but that would still amount to $500 million. It was totally unreal.

By the third week of April, money was transferred, stock certificates delivered, and a multitude of additional agreements signed. With Matt's guidance, we created trust accounts, and deposited funds. Although there was still a large tax burden, I would be worth a cool *billion* dollars!

Sam and Raj would walk away with $80 and $100 million ... although I hoped Sam wouldn't walk away. My parents were suddenly worth $25 million – which they couldn't imagine.

Matt helped us – and my parents – select several investment advisors, each managing a portion of the wealth. We divided the stock between several brokers, and set stop loss limits, in case there was a market downturn.

My three friends and two brothers were paid just over $5 million each – which none of them could believe. All of our lives would change; we just didn't know how.

Matt's firm made over a million dollars, and Matt was made a partner. I took Matt, Linda, Sam, Julie, and my parents out to dinner, at a nice Italian restaurant, both to celebrate Matt's promotion, and to thank everyone for their help in making the company a success.

It was the next day – only a week after our deal closed and the press release went out – that I started getting calls.

Our local newspaper sent a reporter and photographer out, resulting in headlines the next day – 'First Billionaire in Our Town'. I had to insist that the photographer include Sam in the picture, and Raj should have also been here, as the project began with his suggestion for my doctoral work.

The following day, we were called by Bloomberg and The Wall Street Journal, and gave telephone interviews.

Two days and many phone calls later (most screened for us by Linda), our story was on CNN, and the other major networks and newspapers.

Sam and I were flown to New York, and then to Los Angeles to do interviews and be on the morning programs. Sam took me shopping both places to buy appropriate outfits for the shows.

The television producers mostly wanted to focus on me – the 27 year old, female, small-town inventor of an important technology, and CEO of a company we'd just sold for more than a billion dollars.

But a couple of the shows made it a love story, between Sam – the senior researcher and businessperson, and me – the young student. They introduced him as my fiancé.

It was amazing how true that story was. Sam and I had been a good team, and I expected that to continue, whatever we did in our lives.

It was the first of May when I was contacted by Time Magazine: They wanted to put me on their cover. Sam and I decided to take my parents with us; they hadn't been to New York in decades. My parents were pretty much in a daze, as we took them on a first class flight, then stayed in a penthouse suite in one of the top Manhattan hotels.

We wouldn't always be splurging like this – our 4-day trip could cost twenty thousand dollars; but we wanted to impress on my parents the reality of the situation. They were definitely impressed, but it was still unreal.

Sam and I were just beginning to consider what we wanted to do with our lives, and with the money. We agreed that we wanted to continue to help humanity, as we hoped the drugs developed by my technology would do.

But our minds were boggled, also; it would take some time to understand what this new wealth meant.

CHAPTER 18: JAKE'S JINX

My parents came over on Sunday, somewhat distraught, and wanting to talk with us seriously. The weather was finally nice, and the temperature warm, so we brought them out to the backyard and sat around the glass table.

"What are we supposed to do?" my dad asked, softly, glancing at Sam and back to me.

I asked, "What do you mean?"

"About the money." I wasn't sure what he was asking. Then, I realized that his question was the same as ours: How would we invest and best use the wealth that we had?

"You don't have to do anything, dad. You have nearly nine million dollars in the bank. Actually, six of that is in tax-free municipal bonds; they are pretty safe, and will give you an income of about $200K per year. And your four brokers are managing half a million each in the stock market.

"You should have something like seven to eight hundred thousand in your bank account." My father was nodding; he knew all this, already, as we'd met with the brokers and discussed the investments.

"Your house is paid off, and you can use the money for anything you like." I chuckled, "For example, if you wanted to buy another house, you could probably pay for it by writing a check." My mother's eyes were large, as she listened to the discussion.

"If you need more than a few hundred thousand dollars for anything, you can sell some of the stocks.

"*And*, don't forget that you also have around fifteen million dollars in the stock of the Japanese company. We've instructed the brokers to sell 10% every quarter – so that would increase your assets by about half a million dollars per month." It really was incredible.

"But you don't have to do anything with the money, unless you want to buy something, or give some to charity. I doubt that you guys will want to buy an airplane or yacht," my mother started choking, "but you could take a really nice month-long cruise a couple of times a year.

"That might cost $100,000, but with only half the money you have now, you could afford 50 years of cruises. And you have plenty of money to fly anywhere in the world you would like to visit, and stay at the nicest hotels."

Both of my parents were shaking their heads slowly. I knew that they really didn't have many aspirations, or desire material things. I decided to let slip an idea that I was toying with.

"You don't have to change the way you're living at all. But you could buy each other things, whenever you want – like a pool table for dad's 'man's cave'."

Still addressing my parents, I looked at Sam, "In fact, I was thinking about taking Sam on his birthday next week to pick out a sports car that I could buy for him."

Sam's eyebrows lifted and he smiled, but shook his head, "I don't need a sports car, Kelly. It's a nice thought, though." I could see the gears turning in Sam's mind – other things that he might want for his birthday.

Sam changed the subject, "Talking about cruises and traveling, Kelly and I were thinking about taking you guys on a trip to Europe. We had a good time with you on our short New York trip, and it would be fun to show you some of the places we've visited."

Of course, that wouldn't include the sex clubs. But, now that my parents had been so open with us, we might well take them to some saunas. It would be fun to see their reaction to being with a few hundred other nude people.

Then, Sam took my hand. "And I was hoping that we could take your parents somewhere else." I couldn't imagine what he was thinking, until he continued, "To Kauai. For our wedding. What do you think about September?"

That was a surprise. But I guess not that much, as we'd discussed setting a date when the business was sold. We hadn't discussed Kauai, but it would be a great choice. "That sounds nice. I had been thinking about a June wedding, but that might be too soon to arrange it."

Sam retorted, "With the money we now have, it shouldn't be any problem getting things done quickly. We could hire a wedding coordinator, and let her do most of the work." It wasn't the work; and Sam was right that money could speed things up.

"I'm OK with either timeframe. September would be fine." My parents listened to our exchange with bated breath, then my mother exclaimed, "That's great! Congratulations!" We all hugged each other.

I had expected the wedding to be in Sam's backyard. But I had to admit that Kauai would be more special. Kathy was already there, and we could fly Julie, Linda and Matt with us – as money was not a limitation.

That got me thinking about who else we would invite: Certainly Alex, Fiona, Justin, and Jasmine; and Raj; and my KS Biotech staff (who'd been paid well, but hadn't had any stock in the company); and, of course, Henk and Zöe.

I laughed inside, as I decided that we should also invite Mistress Elena, and perhaps even Lottie and Brian.

It wouldn't be as interesting of a wedding as Fiona and Justin's, at the sex club, but I could still imagine some fun experiences that we could share with the entire wedding party. We would have to start the planning soon.

I was delighted that Kelly was receptive to my idea of getting married on Kauai. It would be a challenge to make all the preparations – whether in June or September. Linda would be able to help, as she was great at organizing and scheduling.

We were planning a quick trip to see my sons – and grandson – in a couple of weeks. Each of my sons now had nearly ten million dollars, part in a trust, part in cash and stock, and part in the equity of the Japanese company.

We had been concerned about the Japanese company's stock keeping its value. But, incredibly, in the six weeks since its listing, the stock had risen from $25/share to $30/share – a gain of 20%. Kelly's net worth had increased more than $100 million!

Over dinner one night, I suggested to Kelly that she might want a pre-nup agreement. She was shocked, "Why? You didn't want one, when your assets were 1,000 times mine ... and now my assets are only ten times yours. And if you take half, I would still have more than I would ever need in a lifetime."

I let the issue drop. We truly loved each other, and although there was no way to see into the future, we both believed our love would be enduring.

Kelly was still the most beautiful woman I'd ever seen ... and the brightest. Our three years of shared experiences had joined us in a way that decades often didn't, with other couples. We could communicate mentally and knew how each other would respond, in most cases.

The issue of Time Magazine, with Kelly on the cover, came out, and we were sent a box of copies, and another box filled with international newspapers featuring articles on Kelly's success. She had become an international sensation, overnight.

Kelly was now intent on working towards enabling other women in STEM and business careers. Some major women's groups had already enlisted her help. And both universities and businesses were hounding her for speaking engagements.

Linda suggested that we hire an agent, who could manage the public opportunities. Far from having more time, it seemed that we would be busier than ever.

I was very proud of Kelly, the technology she had developed, and her persistence and willingness to work hard. She had been successful beyond her wildest dreams – and *my* wildest dreams, too.

To think this had all begun less than three years ago, with a lunch meeting to provide some career counseling to Kelly! We continued to live in a surreal world, where many of our dreams had come true.

We had also developed some intimate friendships, and a close relationship with Kelly's parents. They seemed to be happy with each other, and accepting of me, as their future son-in-law.

Kelly and I would be getting married soon, and we looked forward to sharing a beautiful life together.

I sat at my desk in the pool room, reviewing a press release that the Japanese company wanted to issue on their intent to acquire the three companies we'd licensed. Their stock, just today, had gone up by 10%, increasing the value of my portfolio by another $75 million.

The day was warm, the pool room open to the backyard, the sliding glass doors pulled back, and a breeze filtering through the screens. Sam had gone marketing, so that he could make his own birthday dinner. We had invited Linda, Matt, and Julie to help us celebrate.

My eyes defocused, as I gazed across the room, the desks and lab benches still in place. We would probably give those to the university. It would be nice to decorate this room, rather than devoting it to the business.

Something caught my peripheral vision, and my head turned toward the pool. My body froze in terror.

There was a man, standing just outside the screen slider, staring at me with wild eyes. He was tall and thin, with a ragged pale red beard that matched his disheveled hair. He wore a faded t-shirt over a pair of work pants that were spattered with paint.

I had never seen him; at least, not for the past two decades. But I instantly knew who he was.

"Hello, Kelly." He slid open the screen and stepped inside. My stomach felt hollow, and I gasped for breath. I had no way to protect myself. My iPhone was sitting on the desk, and I tapped on an app and began recording audio.

Forcing myself to calm, I tried not to grimace. "Hello, Jake." My birth father looked around the room, and back to me. I shivered, despite the warm weather.

"Your aul fella's grand, thank you for askin'." He looked me up and down, although I was still sitting at the desk. "You're a fine thing. I been read'n 'bout you ... and you done a'right."

I muted the phone, then tapped Sam's number, and turned the phone screen-down onto the desk.

"What do you want, Jake?"

"It's been *donkey years*. I jus' wanted to see my litt'l girl." He pulled out a small metal flask and took a swig, then stuck it into his back pocket. He slurred, "An' I thought you might want to share the riches." He glared at me, and a shiver ran up my spine.

"Why were you in jail for the past ten years, Jake?" I knew I had to stall, and that Sam must be on the way. But I wasn't sure what he could do.

Jake shrugged, "They called it 'armed robbery', but I wasn't carryin', and nobody got hurt." He chuckled gruffly, and pulled a small pistol from his right pocket, then looked down at it, turning it over, as if he were examining it for the first time. Then he put it back into his pocket.

"I'm not dangerous, Kelly. I would never hurt my litt'l girl." I'm a bit *langers*, but I jus' wanted to drop by, and ask you for my cut of the dough." A *cut* of the *dough*?

If my birth father had come to me and asked for help, I might have set-up a trust that would give him a good income to live on. But he acted like he *deserved* a portion of my money.

"Did you kill my mother, Jake?" I realized that my voice was thin, and my body slightly shaking. I wasn't sure that I wanted to hear Jake's answer, but I'd had to ask.

Jake took a step toward me, then another. I put up my hand signaling him to stop, and fortunately he did. He shook his head sadly, "Your *aul wan* was a useless bitch."

I glared at him, and he continued, "Silly cow wasn't on the *smarties*. After you came along, all we did was fight. I enlisted in the Army, but ended-up peelin' potatoes in Saudi Arabia for three years. Then, things went *arseways*.

"When I came home, nobody'd give me a job. Dot was a *fecking* bitch. She'd get *flaming*, and start throwing things. There were no *snogs*, and no *feak*. It was *gobshite*!"

I didn't know any Irish slang, but got the gist of what Jake was saying. I let him continue.

"The only time there was some *craic* was when we were with you, or when we got *gee-eyed*. After they took you away from us, your ma got dodgy, and sometimes I had to take the piss out of her. We were on the needle, then."

He stopped talking and shrugged. The room was quiet.

"And that tool of a *mingin* sister was a *fecking shitehawk*. I may have to pay her a visit." I didn't know if that was a threat, or just bluster.

Jake looked around the room again, and took another step toward me. I let my hand drop down and pulled open a desk drawer that happened to store my bullwhip. The one I'd only practiced with a few times. But there was no way that I could protect myself from an armed intruder.

"I'm *skint* right now ... just out of the slammer, you know. So I could use a few *schnozzlewoppers*."

It might be worth giving him some cash, except that we didn't keep any in the house. And, I was sure this wouldn't be the last time Jake would come knocking. Once I gave him something, there would be no end to the nightmare.

But I had to play along for a while, long enough for Sam to get here. Again, I wasn't sure what he could do, and I was now upset with myself that I'd called him. As a gun was involved, and I had been threatened, the police should be called. But I couldn't do anything that would incite Jake.

"How much do you need?" I was envisioning Jake asking for ten thousand dollars – something that was within the realm of possibility, had he approached this in a different way.

Jake fingered his ragged beard, "Well, I guess you don't want me comin' 'round again, an' askin' for more." I nodded.

"So, how about a hundred million *snots*? I just opened an account, so you can wire the *quid*. I'll wait."

I was incredulous. This was insane. I hoped that Sam would get here soon.

"What a dumbass you are! You think I could just wire that much? Everything is invested in stocks. And do you really think I would do anything for you? After what you did to me? And my mother?"

Jake took another step toward me; now, he was less than ten feet away, just past the first row of lab benches. I slowly pulled the bullwhip out of the drawer. My hand was shaking, and my throat dry. This couldn't be happening.

My eye was caught again by a form moving slowly on the patio. I didn't turn my head, but could see that it was Sam. I froze, but a moment later Jake turned to look out the sliding door. He chuckled, and pulled out the gun.

Sam stood there, holding ... what? Was that the sword from his pirate outfit? It was metal, but certainly not sharp enough to do any damage. What was he thinking?

"Step out of the house, Jake." Sam's voice was loud and resonant, full of authority.

Jake shook his head in disbelief. As he stepped to the opening where the screen had been pulled back, he looked back at me, and said, "This fella's a serious neddy."

Without thinking, I stood, and yelled, "Sam, he's got a gun!" But Sam didn't back off.

"What's it going to be? Murder, now? And you've already admitted to one murder. Drop that gun. NOW!"

Sam was amazing. But how could he save me with no real weapon – certainly nothing that could counter a gun.

Jake laughed, and calmly lifted the gun, pointing it at Sam. Unbelievably, Sam lifted the sword and ran at Jake.

"No!!!" I lifted the bullwhip, and let it fly.

In an instant, the gun went off, and the bullwhip struck Jake. It hadn't done what I'd hoped, which was to flick the gun out of his hand.

Jake felt the blood on his cheek and laughed, as Sam staggered backward, and fell into the pool, the water quickly becoming red. "No!" I screamed involuntarily, as I lifted the bullwhip again.

"You BASTARD!" Jake and I both turned, the sound coming from behind me. It was my mother! The room was filled with explosions, flame and smoke coming out of the barrel of my mom's gun, and the room smelling of cordite.

I turned to see Jake raise his hand to his shoulder, blood now reddening his t-shirt. With a glare and the most crazed, inhuman snarl that I'd ever seen, he raised the gun towards my mother. "Jaysus! You Cocktrough!"

The bullwhip was already flashing toward Jake when the gun went off. I thought it was echoing, but realized that *several* guns had gone off, Jake hit multiple times. Half a dozen black-suited guys, obviously a SWAT team, ran into the room and jumped on Jake.

More guys rushed through the door from the kitchen, and I couldn't see what had happened to my mother. Had Jake shot her? Then, my body spun around, looking toward the pool. Several people were huddled over Sam.

Her face was beautiful, bending down and kissing my lips lightly, as I lay in the hospital bed. Tears came to my eyes, "I'm sorry, Kelly."

Kelly frowned, "For what, Sam? You're my hero."

I shook my head, and had to groan, as the pain in my shoulder throbbed. Nevertheless, my brain suddenly decided to play with her. "For not being able to cook my birthday dinner for you and the others." Kelly laughed.

But I had to explain, "I didn't know he had a gun, until you yelled. I was listening the entire time, but he kept saying he wasn't dangerous. So I thought I could do something"

"But what happened? I know you called my mother, and that's why she got involved. But why not just let the police do their thing, without *you* trying to save the day?"

The pain killers were obviously wearing off, and my shoulder was hurting again. It was heavily bandaged, but I'd been lucky that the bullet had gone right through.

The doctors had told me that the small caliber slug could have been very dangerous, had it hit a bone and been deflected into one of my critical organs. I would certainly have been taken to surgery, had I even survived until I got to the hospital.

Of course, now that I'd had time to think a little, I realized it had been a foolhardy scheme. But I had relied on the police getting there, and just wanted to delay Jake long enough. If he had disappeared, we would have always been worried about him coming for Kelly again.

I tried to breathe deeply, but even that hurt. Looking up at Kelly, I smiled, "You were very smart. As soon as I heard, 'What do you want, Jake', I knew. I got the call in my car; I'd only had to make one more stop – at the pastry shop, for the birthday cake. I was just pulling into the parking lot.

"I didn't want to lose the call, so I went in, and asked to use their phone. I called Darlene, and told her Jake had shown up, and that she should call the police. I told her to stay put, as I was on the way to the house.

"When I got home, I realized that I had nothing to protect us with – no weapons. Mark had a great little crossbow when he was a kid, but it's packed away in some box. I had always thought about buying a Taser, but there was really never a need for one.

"So all I could think of was the pirate sword. It has a real metal blade, although it can't actually cut anything. But if Jake had been unarmed, it might have been a little intimidating."

Kelly gave me a look. "OK, I guess it wouldn't have done much. But I really thought I could talk him down; at least, long enough for the police to take him away. I was sure that after being in prison for ten years, he must be on probation, so he would have been back in the slammer for most – or all – of his life.

"Anyway, that's all I knew, until Jake shot me. It was instantaneous, and then everything was in slow motion – me staggering backwards, then tripping and falling into the pool.

"I knew I'd been shot, because it felt like someone took a sledge hammer to my chest. But all I could think of was that you were still in the room with that psycho. That I hadn't saved you." There were tears, again, and I shut my eyes. "I'm sorry, Kelly."

Kelly's voice was soothing, "You were great, Sam." There was a pause, and then, "So you didn't know that my mother was there?"

What!?!@? My eyes snapped open, and I tried to lift my head, momentarily forgetting about my shoulder. But an intense flash of pain nearly blinded me, and my head fell back to the pillow.

Kelly explained, "After you called her, she immediately called the police, as you had instructed. But my parents had been prepared for Jake to appear someday. My dad bought a gun, and both my parents learned how to shoot at a firing range. That was when I was in high school, and not paying much attention to them. I'd forgotten about it.

"My dad was playing golf when you called, so my mom loaded the gun and drove over to the house. What I don't know is how she got in. We never gave her a key."

I could answer that. "Because when I first got home, I quietly unlocked the front door, so that the police would have easy and quiet access. I didn't know where you guys were, in the house, but assumed it was the pool room, as you're usually at your desk, and that's where your phone is, when you're home."

Kelly nodded. "Anyway, just after you were shot, my mother yelled from the kitchen door, and started shooting at Jake. Amazingly, one of the bullets hit – I think it was in his right shoulder, just like you. When Jake raised his gun to shoot my mom, the SWAT team took him down."

I shook my head just enough for Kelly to see, "It's amazing that she didn't hit *you*." I shook my head more, despite the pain. Looking longingly up at Kelly, I said softly, "It could have been a real disaster, many different ways." Yes, we had been *very* lucky.

"Is your mom OK?" I asked.

Kelly nodded, "Jake only got off one shot," now, she grinned broadly at me, "and you're never going to believe where it hit ..." All I could think of was getting plaster and paint guys to the house for repairs.

Chuckling, Kelly finally said, "In the middle of one of the school paddles that we hung next to the blackboard, by the kitchen door – the solid paddle."

That was funny. Now, the solid paddle had one hole in it. I still wondered whether it had gone through and hit the wall. And I briefly wondered where the bullet was that had gone through me. The police had probably found it, already.

Kelly continued, "Jake is dead. The SWAT team wasn't taking any chances. I was standing there, frozen, the whole time bullets were flying." Kelly had been incredibly composed and brave ... as I would have expected of her.

It was unbelievable: We had just made a fortune, literally, and were ready to enjoy our lives ... and Jake could have destroyed everything. There would probably be psychological ramifications from the experience, but we'd all come through it alive.

We had a spanking good birthday celebration for Matt. He was a trouper – just like my three friends had been, all the times Sam had challenged them. This time, I took the role of 'challenger'.

Linda was turned on by the whole experience, and even more turned on by Sam's cooking, and the birthday cake, and the real French Champagne. Matt promised to take her to Paris, as a belated birthday present.

Sam was healing well. The bullet had actually just made a small tunnel at the edge of his right shoulder. He was able to shower, but still used a sling, and it still hurt to use the keyboard for an extended time.

We now planned to go to Kauai next week, as Kathy and Christian had invited us – as well as Linda, Matt, and Julie – back to Kauai for their first anniversary. Kathy was doing research, and had some suggestions for possible venues for our wedding.

I decided that we could splurge on hiring a private jet to take us all – including Kathy's parents, to Kauai.

The doctors said that Sam would recover completely, but shouldn't go back into the ocean quite yet; and, his shoulder wouldn't tolerate putting on a BC for diving.

But we could now go back anytime we wanted; even for just a weekend. We'd decided on a September wedding, on Kauai, when Sam should be completely healed.

Sam and I were spending a lot of time with my parents, as the traumatic events had brought us even closer together. The demise of Jake had lifted a huge weight from my father's head, which – unbeknownst to me – had afflicted him for the past decade.

I was feeling very differently about my parents – especially my dad – now that I understood much more of what they had gone through. And, of course, I was feeling very close to my mother, as she'd risked her own life to save mine. Recently, and twenty years ago.

The Japanese stock went up another 10%, making my 'net worth' around 1.35 billion dollars. Just the quarterly sale of the stock would net $40 million a month! I decided it best not to think about these figures, and keep my focus on looking ahead to the things I wanted to do.

But there were still a lot of questions – not just about my business life, but also in my personal affairs. Should we have children? If so, would it be through adoption or surrogacy? And would we want to continue the level of intimacy we'd had in our relationships?

The overwhelming question for me was how to make a difference in the world, utilizing my wealth to leverage opportunities to help people. I'd already contacted some of the well-known foundations, one important one associated with a guy who'd become a billionaire at 31.

I would be 28 in the next couple of months, and already felt pressured to do something meaningful. But we would also need to ensure that Sam and I took a balanced amount of time for the travel and other things we wanted to do, together.

We'd already had an incredible string of experiences, from sexual exploration, to international travel, as the 'first floor' of our relationship. But the foundation had to be the openness, honesty, and trust that we'd established.

Sam and I loved each other very much. He still loved Sarah, but had been able to move on to new relationships. And we loved my friends, in a special way. Again, shared experiences had been a large part of bringing us together.

I loved my parents more than ever, and I knew that Sam loved them, also. We would actually have fun traveling with them. And being able to introduce them to new things that they would like, despite having been set in their ways all the time I'd known them.

We'd come from very different places, but Sam and I somehow had meshed at the right time in our personal lives. My career had been our original focus, and that had – with a lot of luck – resulted in me becoming a billionaire.

I had the flexibility to work for a major pharma company, start more companies of my own, or invest in promising startups. But I was now planning on doing other things that would be rewarding. There was a lot to decide, and it would be difficult.

Whatever was ahead, whether challenges or successes, I looked forward to sharing more new experiences with Sam, as we continued on life's journey together.

###

Thank you for reading Book 8 of the Experiences series. If you enjoyed it, please take a moment to leave a review at your favorite retailer. And, if you liked this story, you'll LOVE the finale in Book 9: <u>Ultimate Experience</u>!

- Simone Freier

Discover other titles by Simone Freier

Experiences Series Book 1: Origins of a Fetish

Experiences Series Book 2: First Experience

Experiences Series Book 3: Weekend Experience

Experiences Series Book 4: Birthday Experience

Experiences Series Book 5: European Experience

Experiences Series Book 6: Friends' Experience

Experiences Series Book 7: Island Experience

Experiences Series Book 8: Domme Experience

Experiences Series Book 9: Ultimate Experience

Connect with the Author

Follow me on Twitter: http://twitter.com/SimoneFreier

Friend me on Facebook: http://facebook.com/SimoneFreierAuthor

Subscribe to my blog: http://SimoneFreier.com

Favorite me at Smashwords: http://smashwords.com/SimoneFreier